BACKSTAGE MURDER

Carlotta's dressing-room door was still closed when Lindy returned backstage after the show. With any luck, she had gone back to the hotel already. Maybe Jeremy had fired her after all.

The dancers were still onstage. No one seemed eager to leave the comfort of the proscenium.

She walked into the cluster of bodies. "That was pretty good. You all really pulled it together. I have a few notes, though—"

Suddenly the air was rent with a loud wailing.

Lindy gazed sternly at the group. "Now what have you guys done?"

"That's not Carlotta," said Rebo. He rushed off the stage followed by Juan and Eric.

Carlotta's dressingroom door was open. Rebo stopped suddenly, causing a domino effect as dancers piled up behind him. Lindy slipped under his arm and froze.

Carlotta lay on the cement floor, still in her *Carmina* dress. One leg was bent under her, the knee sticking out in a grotesque parody of a ballet step. One arm was flung dramatically out to her side. It was the last theatrical gesture Carlotta Devine would ever make.

Books by Shelley Freydont

BACKSTAGE MURDER
HIGH SEAS MURDER

Published by Kensington Publishing Corporation

BACKSTAGE MURDER

SHELLEY FREYDONT

Kensington Books
http://www.kensingtonbooks.com

KENSINGTON BOOKS are published by

Kensington Publishing Corp.
850 Third Avenue
New York, NY 10022

Copyright © 1999 by Shelley Freydont

Kensington and the K logo Reg. U.S. Pat. & TM Off.

First Printing Kensington Hardcover: October, 1999
First Printing Kensington Paperback: August, 2000
10 9 8 7 6 5 4 3 2 1

Printed in the United States of America

One

Lindy Haggerty downshifted the Volvo up the slope of her driveway and reached toward the radio. The Rolling Stones replaced Offenbach's frenetic cancan music. The Rolling Stones. They must be fifty if they were a day. Hell, the whole world was getting older.

She stopped the car at the kitchen door and leaned across the front seat for her groceries. As she did, the waistband of her jeans cut into her stomach. Older, and fatter, she thought. I shouldn't have had that pizza for lunch. She pulled the bags out of the car and headed toward the kitchen.

As she stuck her key in the lock, balancing a grocery bag on each hip, the telephone rang. Bruno began to bark at the same time. The blue *New York Times* bag lay on the flagstone stoop. She opened the door and kicked the paper across the threshold in one smooth movement. With the grocery bags sliding down her thighs, she hurried across the mudroom and into the kitchen. Sixty pounds of Irish Setter leapt forward. "Down, Bruno." Both bags fell to the floor. A head of lettuce rolled out of a bag and under the table. Bruno buried his head in the bag, and Lindy lunged for the phone.

The message machine had clicked on. She stopped for a

second, hand resting on the receiver. Telemarketing? She picked up anyway.

"Lindy? Lindy, is that you?"

"Yes?" The voice sounded familiar. She sat down at the table, unbuttoned her jeans, and reached for the *Times*.

"It's Biddy." Lindy paused as she opened the paper. "Arabida McFee."

"Good Lord, Biddy. It's really you? I haven't talked to you in . . ."

"In ten years."

Had it been that long? They had been best friends. "That long? Well, you know when you take the Holland Tunnel to New Jersey you end up in Outer Mongolia. Where are you?"

"In New Jersey."

"You retired?" She couldn't believe it.

Biddy laughed. "Of course not. I'll still be on my feet when I'm eighty-five. I'm at the Endicott Playhouse. I'm rehearsal director for the Jeremy Ash Dance Company."

"Jeremy Ash? Didn't he retire?"

"Yes, but he's back. He's got a terrific group of dancers. We're on a Northeast tour and open in New York next month."

"That's great." Lindy was hit by a momentary pang of envy. Where had that come from? She hadn't thought about dancing in years. As good as it had been, she certainly wouldn't want that kind of stress back in her life.

"Anyway, I was really hoping that you'd come to the theater tonight. It's our opening night here, and it would be great to see you."

"Tonight?" She felt a flutter of panic. "Let me check my calendar." She scrolled her finger across the wall calendar above the phone. April 14. Biddy had an opening night at the

Endicott, and she had . . . an emergency meeting of the Jaycee family talent show committee.

"I'd like to, but . . ."

"Please." The word shot out of the phone, obliterating the last ten years and propelling Lindy into the past. She recognized the urgency in Biddy's voice, and in her mind, Lindy could see Biddy scrubbing her hair as she waited for her answer. She always did that when she was upset. The wildness of Biddy's hair was the weather vane of her feelings.

"Biddy, what's wrong?"

"Nothing."

"Biddy," she prompted.

"It's just—I'd just really, really like to see you."

Biddy's voice unleashed a tidal wave of reminiscence. The applause, the fame, the good times they had together hit her with an intoxicating rush. Even the bad times seemed not so bad when you had a friend to support you. Curiosity and loyalty tugged at her. It was obvious that something was wrong, and Biddy needed her, but did she really want to go back? Even for a minute, even as a visitor, even for a friend?

She glanced back at the calendar. Oh, what the hell, it was only one evening, for old times' sake. There'd always be another committee meeting. "Okay, I'll see you tonight."

"Thanks."

She pushed the off button and phoned the Jaycees.

A frump. When had she turned into a frump? Lindy looked down at her jeans and oversize fisherman's sweater. The jeans were designer; the sweater, imported. Casual chic on the outside, but the inside was strictly suburban frump.

"Frump, frump, frump," she yelled into the walk-in closet

in her bedroom. She hadn't seen Biddy in years, and she didn't have a thing to wear. A pile of rejects lay jumbled on the bed next to Bruno. He was whining in his sleep, a paw lying territorially over a navy-blue sequined jacket.

She pulled a teal-blue sheath from a hanger. She wore a lot of blue. It brought out the blue in her eyes. Well, a girl had to work with what she had, or in my case, thought Lindy, what I have left.

Rows of other clothes hung patiently waiting. Lindy pointed an accusing finger at them. "I know what you're thinking. I'm fat. The only thing that hasn't gotten fat is my hair. And it's too short to be fat."

She struggled into the dress, turned to the mirror, and gave her reflection an appraising look. Was this the figure of a once thin and lithesome dancer?

In her image of herself, she was still the eighteen-year-old who astounded the New York critics in her first professional season; as alluring as she had been throughout her full career; just as vital and in demand. Sure, that had been before marriage, children, and a decade in the suburbs, but still . . .

She frowned at the image in the mirror.

"Your gut is sticking out. Pull it in," she ordered. Bruno slunk off the bed and padded down the hall, his tail drooping.

"You're not in trouble, Bruno," she yelled after him. "I am."

She added the sheath to the pile and went back into the closet. She passed the size tens, then the size eights, caressing them distractedly with the tips of her fingers. In the remotest, darkest corner of the closet, shoved together like shimmering sardines, she found the sixes. Expensive, bought years ago on a dancer's salary off the clearance racks of exclusive boutiques. It had been a few years since she had been able to wear them. At the rate she was going, she would never see the inside of a six again. Well, someday she would go on a diet, tomorrow maybe.

She touched a full skirt of peach organza bought in Cannes, a white leather miniskirt from Milan, a gold knit sweater dress, so petite, from ... where? She couldn't remember. Even her brain had the frumps.

She pulled the miniskirt over her head. It wouldn't button. It wouldn't zip. It wouldn't even slip down her thighs to the floor. She pulled it back over her head, returned it to the hanger, and reached for her latest and largest old standby—the black silk pants suit. At least it fit, but why shouldn't it? It was a size ten and had elastic around the waist. She tossed it on the bed.

Six hours, a new dress, and twenty-five sit-ups later, she was speeding down the Garden State Parkway toward the Endicott Playhouse.

"You were meant for me-e-e ... ," she sang along with the radio. She felt good, if a little nervous. So she had retired. She had a successful life in the suburbs. So, maybe, she had gotten a little older, a little fatter. So had everyone else. Right? Biddy would still be glad to see her.

She could still remember the first day Biddy showed up at rehearsal, having aced an open audition over 150 other girls. Open auditions, known in the business as cattle calls, were notorious for never landing anyone a job. But Biddy with a formidable technique and an unparalleled joie de vivre had been the exception that proved the rule. The artistic director adored her; he would greet her each morning with *"Ca va? Poulet?"* and soon the rest of the company began calling the angel-faced Arabida, "Biddy."

They hadn't stayed in touch. When she and Glen had left the city in search of the perfect house, the perfect neighborhood, the perfect school system, Lindy had left her career and her friends behind.

And in the new adventure of life in the suburbs, she had forgotten them: the friends who celebrated when you got a good review, and commiserated with you when you didn't, the flowers backstage, the international tours, the applause as the final curtain lowered on a stellar performance. Hell, she had even forgotten the corner deli and how admiring construction workers whistled at her lean dancer's body as she raced to the subway.

Instead, she had transferred her professional zeal to amateur fund-raisers, tackled car pools like they were international tours, and gladly traded the flowers backstage for Rice Krispie treats at the neighborhood coffee klatches. While Glen rose to heights in the telecommunications industry, commuting daily to the city, and traveling to conferences across the country, she schlepped kids to school with all the enthusiasm of an opening night.

She had approached suburban life just like an extended run on Broadway and it hadn't disappointed her. There was no lack of angst on the playground, and plenty of drama in the PTA meetings. She had even witnessed a few diva attacks outside the principal's office and felt right at home, at first.

Okay, so there wasn't much applause, and the pay wasn't great, but her current audience could be just as fickle as any paying ticket holder. Maybe, the scenery *had* gotten a little dull over the years. Well, to be honest, so had the characters.

It was only seven o'clock when she pulled into the parking lot. Even though Biddy would be too busy to talk before the performance, Lindy had subconsciously arrived in time for hour call.

She hadn't been to the Endicott Playhouse since she had retired from dancing. Now that she was here, she had butter-flies. She got out of the car and smoothed the skirt of her new outfit, a flamboyantly royal-blue dress with matching jacket, and picked her way across the graveled parking lot, wobbling dangerously on four-inch heels. They hurt like hell, but one had to make some concessions to art.

She climbed the stairs to the stage door holding tightly to the rusty handrail. Fighting off a serious attack of déjà vu, she stopped at the security booth. The guard buzzed her in. Biddy, as efficient as she was effervescent, had remem-bered to leave her name at the door.

Inside the theater was dark, like the inside of all theaters. Instinctively, she closed her eyes. It was an old theater trick to adjust the eyes quickly to the absence of light. She breathed in the musty air, years of accumulated dust and sweat assaulting her senses, and opened her eyes. Bright lights illuminated the stage, but the contrast only added to the darkness of the backstage area, reducing the figures there to amorphous shadows. She was jostled by someone carrying a pile of spandex and chiffon draped over one shoulder and holding an overflowing laundry basket with both hands.

She took a tentative step forward. She could see parts of the stage through the wings, the entrance areas to the stage separated by black curtains called legs. Metal pipes holding side lights were positioned at the back of each wing. Dancers, wearing layers of oversize practice clothes, were on stage, warming up to individual music that played from headsets.

A couple practiced a lift that was giving them trouble. The girl took a few preparatory steps toward her partner. He lowered in a deep *plié*, hands forward to catch her hipbones. He lifted her a few feet off the floor and gave up. The girl backed up, rolled her sweatpants down below her hipbones to give him a better grip, and tried again. She got a little higher on the second try.

He's holding her too high, Lindy thought automatically.

"Watch ya back." She jumped aside as a ladder carried by two stagehands careered around the corner. They maneuvered it through the second wing and onto the stage. Lindy followed them, stopping at the edge of the black curtain.

"Heads up!" All motion stopped, frozen midmovement. Every head turned upward as a long metal pipe, a batten, was lowered from the flies above them. It was burdened with lighting instruments. It stopped about six feet from the floor. Abruptly everyone returned to what they had been doing, avoiding the lowered batten and ladder.

One of the stagehands climbed up and began adjusting the lights. He was extremely thin; his sinewy arms stretched taut out of his sleeveless T-shirt as he handled the heavy equipment. He looked vaguely familiar, but Lindy couldn't place him. That wasn't unusual for her. She rarely forgot a face; she just couldn't always attach it to a name. All that visual training, she supposed. And anyway, she hadn't seen these people in years. Of course they had changed.

Biddy was standing at the front of the stage. She was easily recognizable; she hadn't changed at all. But I have, thought Lindy with a surge of panic. The stage lights silhouetted the cinnamon curls that wisped around Biddy's head like finely spun cotton candy. A sweater was tied around her still thin waist and fell straight past her narrow hips. She was leaning on a pair of crutches, surgery maybe? She was in her late thirties. It was probably time to start having everything replaced.

She caught sight of Lindy, waved energetically, and began hauling herself toward the wings. The toe of a plaster cast stuck out from beneath the left leg of her voluminous black stretch pants. She progressed in a syncopated rhythm; first crutches, then cast, crutches, cast, *lub dub*, *lub dub*, until she was standing next to Lindy at the side of the stage.

"Wow! I can't believe you're here." Biddy wrapped her crutches around Lindy and hugged. "You look great! It's just like you never left." She pulled back and looked at Lindy affectionately. "You're taller."

"Thanks, it's just the shoes. I'm still five-five and holding. But still taller than you."

"Heck, everybody's taller than me."

"But remember," Lindy started.

"Height is just a state of mind," Biddy finished.

"But a cast is not a state of mind. Biddy, what happened?"

"You know, graceful old me." She shrugged, lifting both crutches off the floor and bringing them down with a thud.

It was a standard joke: the most graceful dancer on stage could trip over a piece of paper anywhere else. But here, too, Biddy was the exception that proved the rule.

"An accident," she said. "Broken in two places."

"Ouch." Lindy moved aside as the ladder was taken offstage. She watched it pass. "Who is that? The skinny one with the black hair? He looks familiar."

"Lindy, that's Peter Dowd. You know him."

"That's Peter? God, I didn't even recognize him." Peter Dowd was a much sought-after production stage manager in the dance world, organized, intelligent, and patient. A PSM on the dance circuit was responsible for setting up and striking a show, dealing with the stagehands, laying the Marley floor, hanging lights, moving scenery, keeping everyone on schedule, as well as calling lighting and music cues during the performance. But this was not the Peter Dowd she remembered. Always svelte, he was now painfully thin. He was prevented from being truly handsome by acne scars that canyoned his cheeks. Those cheeks had become almost cavernous, and his face seemed etched in a permanent scowl.

"He's, uh . . ." Biddy's green eyes searched the air above her for the right word. "Changed a bit, I guess." She looked sympathetically into the darkness where Peter had disappeared. "But it's so-o-o good to see you."

While Biddy hauled herself from dressing room to dressing room, giving last-minute corrections and words of encouragement, Lindy stood out of the way, letting the ambiance take hold of her. It felt good to be back, even as an observer. The mania of preperformance was soothing.

She was drifting somewhere between the past and the present when Biddy shook her. "I'm done. Let's get out front."

She led Lindy to their seats at the back of the orchestra and sat on the aisle so that she could stick her cast past the row in front of them. Lindy reached across her to grab a program from a passing usherette.

Biddy opened her spiral notebook and turned to a fresh

page. "Remember these?" She pulled a ballpoint pen from her pocket and pressed a button on the side. A small beam of light illuminated the writing tip.

"Do I. Though I always preferred taking performance notes in the dark. It wasn't too bad as long as you didn't keep writing over the same line."

"And remember, you used to always keep a mystery to read during the intermission."

"I've got one in my purse."

Biddy laughed. "Just like old times."

Not exactly, thought Lindy. "So . . . what's on tonight?"

"A new commission. *Carmina Burana*."

Lindy groaned. "Not another new *Carmina*." *Carmina Burana* was composed by Carl Orff in 1937. For orchestra and voices, it was based on the secular texts of thirteenth-century Benedictine monks. Its combination of folk simplicity, ritual and infectious rhythm as it portrayed the joys of eating, drinking, and lovemaking was captivating, and it had been used or misused by scores of professional and student choreographers ever since. "Aren't there enough, already?"

"More than enough. But this was choreographed by David Matthews."

"No kidding. He's the hottest choreographer in town. It must have cost a fortune."

Biddy shrugged. "He wanted to do a *Carmina*, so we got him cheap. Anyway, he's a friend of Jeremy's."

"Lucky you."

"Yeah, you should see the audience perk up when they recognize the music from the car commercial. They feel really cultured. Anyway, it's pretty clever. A story line, which is more than I can say for most of the 'new' ones. It's a long first act, but we end the evening with a lighter piece. If the Orff music doesn't drive you crazy before it's over, I think you'll be impressed. The only thing is . . ."

The houselights began to dim. Before Lindy could open her program, they were sitting in total darkness, and the tape had begun to play.

"Still working with canned music, I see," she whispered to Biddy.

"For the tour and for the New York season. There's no room at the Joyce for an orchestra, much less a full chorus."

"I remember."

"But after that? Keep your fingers crossed."

The front curtain opened revealing a smoky stage. Whiffs of fog rolled out into the first few rows. Several people coughed. Lindy grimaced and slid down in her seat. A painted backdrop of black and gold slashes gradually came into view as the stage lit up with a soft amber wash. Stage right held a metal frame about fifteen feet high that looked like a jungle gym squeezed and twisted by a giant hand.

"I bet I can guess who the set designer is," whispered Lindy.

"None other. David always uses him. He has perfected mixing business with pleasure. If he ever gets a new boyfriend, maybe his work will get lighter, both figuratively and literally. Wait till you see the props."

A woman in the row in front of them turned in her seat and scowled. At least, Lindy guessed she was scowling. It was still too dark to see much more than the stage, itself, and the outline of the woman's perfect hairdo. Lindy pulled a face and settled into her seat, hoping she could sit through another *Carmina*.

Two male dancers, costumed in beige pants and tunics, entered from upstage left carrying a girl curled into a contraction above their heads. They laid her so that she draped over the lower bars of the tower. With long, open strides they circled the metal frame, climbed halfway up the back and hung there.

Lindy slid further down in her seat.

As the music crescendoed, another dancer appeared. She walked slowly across the stage, draped in a smoky-gray cloak that trailed several feet behind her. Her face was covered by a voluminous hood. Abruptly she turned to the audience, the cape swirling around her feet, and threw her arms open, revealing a sparkling gold lamé lining. At the same time, the hood fell back, and she was bathed in a blinding light.

Lindy jolted upright. "My God."

Several faces turned with disapproving looks.

"Biddy, it can't be. Tell me that is not Carlotta."

Biddy gave her a rueful smile. It was easy to see her expression reflected from the light that now radiated from the stage. "I'm afraid so."

"She's older than I am. What the hell is she doing out there?"

The sprayed-in-place perm turned around. "Sh-h-h."

"I'll tell you later," Biddy whispered.

Lindy opened her program and turned the pages until she got to the cast list. She held it up until she caught enough light to read. It was true. Carlotta Devine, ancient and ugly, not to mention mean. Carlotta had never been pretty even as a young woman, but she had always been mean. No, that wasn't fair. Life had made her mean.

With a knotting stomach, Lindy peered at the figure on

stage. Dark eyes, set too close together, eyebrows plucked to a thin, miserly arch that looked painted on, long face and chin that had to be expertly shaded with makeup to keep it from looking sinister even in her prime. Carlotta was no longer in her prime and hadn't been for a decade. And though makeup might do wonders for a less than perfect face, they hadn't invented a cover-up that could conceal Carlotta's vicious personality. She would wreak havoc in this company of young dancers. What had Jeremy Ash been thinking?

Carlotta flung herself about the stage. Lindy gripped the arms of her seat. Seeing the body draped over the railing, Carlotta ran to it and pulled the girl into her arms. The figure poised momentarily in Carlotta's grasp, then slowly moved her hands from her face. She stepped forward onto half point, arms falling gracefully to her sides. The light caught her features and held them for a breathless second. Then she crumpled to the ground, long blond hair cascading around her, blending with the gold of her costume.

Beauty and the Beast, thought Lindy with a shudder.

Carlotta walked forward and into a large circle. When she reached upstage center, two other dancers in robes removed her cloak and carried it offstage.

From downstage right, a male dancer stepped into a pool of amber light and reached longingly toward Carlotta. He was slender and sandy-haired and looked more like a schoolboy than the woman's enamored lover. Carlotta ran toward him, and he pressed her into an overhead lift that should have been beautiful. Carlotta, though thin, was not easy to lift. Her arms stretched out above her like unruly vines. Lindy could see the tendons in her neck straining with the effort of staying aloft. Her young cavalier seemed about to perish beneath his load, and Lindy's whole body tensed as she subconsciously tried to help him.

She could feel Biddy watching her and wondered what on earth could have made Biddy want her to see this. As if reading her thoughts, Biddy shifted her eyes back to the stage.

The *pas de deux* ended with one final lift, which carried Carlotta offstage. The boy barely got her to the edge of the stage, then dumped her unceremoniously into the wings. They were replaced by a quartet of male dancers. Lindy straightened up and breathed deeply as they bound over the floor in athletic jumps, falls, and turns.

By the end of the piece, she had begun to squirm in her seat and wondered what she would say to Biddy. Actually, the choreography wasn't bad, and the music didn't drive her crazy. But it would take a few changes to make this a success. First of all, recasting. Put the pretty girl, what was her name? Lindy looked in her program. Andrea. Put Andrea into Carlotta's part. Get rid of Carlotta completely. Paul (the schoolboy) would be a perfect lover for Andrea. Then . . .

Her attention was brought back to the stage by a sudden dimming of the lights. Two rows of robe-clad figures walked straight across the stage, each holding a three-pronged candelabra of flickering candles. The lights continued to dim until the stage was virtually black except for the twinkling of the artificial flames. Well, really, thought Lindy. David Matthews had turned a celebration of secular life into a morality play. But it was pretty effective.

Gradually light suffused the surface of the metal tower, now a funeral bower? The bodies of Carlotta and Paul lay draped over each other at the apex. At least, he's on top, thought Lindy irreverently. Blackout.

After a suspended interval, the audience began to applaud loudly. Biddy let out a long breath, snapped her notebook closed, and turned to Lindy.

"Thank heavens, they seem to like it. Now, intermission, an upbeat dance to end the evening, and they'll go home happy."

The curtain opened for the bows. The corps came forward, still in their robes, bowed in perfect unison, then backed away. Paul led Carlotta and Andrea forward and then backed them into line. Andrea stepped forward by herself. The applause swelled. A few whistles and cheers. Before she rose from her curtsy, Carlotta stepped forward, regarding the audience with a regal hauteur, and cutting Andrea's applause short. Andrea began to back into line.

The applause rose once again, then stopped suddenly as a gasp rolled through the house. Lindy jerked forward. From above Andrea's head, a batten from the flies plummeted toward the stage, slicing the air between the two women as they exchanged positions. Carlotta froze, arms held slightly outward from her body as the batten bounced on the floor at her feet, then rebounded into Andrea.

It hit her on the calves, and she pitched forward. Her hands shot out before her as she stumbled a few steps, then fell to her knees. The audience watched in suspended horror. Her hands grabbed the edge of the stage as she fought to keep herself from plunging into the seats below. Steel cables snapped in the air behind her.

The corps stood frozen, smiles hardened into a rote expression. The front curtain began lurching closed. Andrea pushed herself backward, struggled to her feet, and managed to limp upstage out of the way of the curtain. She tripped over the batten and fell headlong into Carlotta as the curtain closed, billowed out, and settled in a cloud of dust.

Biddy reached for her crutches. Lindy bolted out of her seat and started to climb over her. She stopped, surprised. What was she thinking? This was not her company; she was just a visitor.

"Come on," said Biddy. She swung her crutches into the aisle. Lindy followed her for a few frustrating steps, then ran ahead clearing the way.

The audience was vibrating with worried exclamations; a voice rose over the loudspeaker announcing the intermission. Lindy closed the stage door behind them.

The dancers stood in a nervous cluster around the prostrate body of the young ingenue. They talked in agitated whispers. Biddy and Lindy pushed through the crowd. Peter Dowd bent over the girl, smoothing her hair out of her face and talking quietly. Jeremy Ash stood just beyond them, staring at the scene. Biddy bent down next to Peter, her cast thrust awkwardly out to the side.

"Is she hurt?"

Peter glanced at her, eyes panicky. "I don't know, I don't think so."

Andrea lifted herself to her elbow. "I'm okay, really." Her stage makeup stood out starkly against her pale skin.

Peter turned back to her and began to lift her carefully to her feet. The company took a step backward. Supporting her with both arms, he led her toward the dressing rooms. Biddy followed.

"Clear the stage, now," ordered Peter over his shoulder.

Everyone moved slowly away from the batten and wandered into the wings. Carlotta took one step toward Jeremy, hesitated, then followed the others offstage.

Lindy and Jeremy were alone on the stage. It must be him, thought Lindy. His back was to her but she recognized his silhouette. He just stood there looking into the wings, where Peter had taken Andrea. Then slowly he walked toward the dressing rooms.

Lindy waited until he was gone, then looked up, careful not to stand under any of the battens or electrics. The one that lay on the floor was empty; no lighting instruments or scenery was attached to it. It wasn't in use for the performance. Why would it suddenly plummet downward?

The Endicott Playhouse was on a counterweight system. She remembered that from years before. The lock must have been triggered by mistake. She had seen that happen once before, years ago on Broadway. A dancer had been knocked out by a piece of flying scenery. She shivered; one batten could have taken out the entire line of dancers. It was too horrible to contemplate.

Peter walked back onto the stage and motioned to a stagehand who was standing by the rail on stage right. Lindy took the opportunity to disappear. This wasn't exactly a good time to renew old acquaintances. She watched from the wings as Peter reached down toward the batten and held it steady as the stagehand raised it into the flies and winched it off at the rail. He watched it stop above his head, then wiped his forehead with the palm of his hand; the stage lights tinged his skin with a yellow pallor. He would never have overlooked an unsecured pipe in the old days. What had happened to him?

He stood staring up into the flies, then smashed his fist into his other hand and walked toward the rail. Lindy's stomach lurched in sympathy for the stagehand who waited for him.

"What a nightmare," said Biddy, clunking up behind her. "She's not hurt, just a few bruises. She's scared out of her wits, but she's going on with the next piece. Jeremy's with her."

They watched Peter stride toward them. Biddy looked at him expectantly. "What happened?"

Peter stopped momentarily in front of them, then looked down at Biddy's cast. His eyebrows furrowed. Without speaking, he walked past them to the door to the dressing rooms. "Five minutes, everybody."

Lindy and Biddy exchanged looks.

They returned to their seats. Biddy sat down and dropped her crutches to the floor.

"The audience is jumpy as all get out," she said as she scanned the seats around them. "Let's just hope Jeremy's piece takes their mind off of falling debris." She opened her notebook. "It's a real gem. Edvard Grieg's *Holberg Suite*." She sighed heavily. "God, what a night."

The audience didn't quiet down until the house was completely dark. The *Holberg Suite* music began abruptly; violins startled the audience into silence. The curtain opened. The stage erupted with a burst of nervous energy.

"Settle down," whispered Biddy.

"Settle down," echoed Lindy.

As the piece progressed, the dancers began to relax. The music seemed to carry them along as it embraced the audience and lulled it into tranquillity. Andrea entered, composed and in full command of the stage. Lindy could feel the audience respond to her as six men lifted her gently, then passed her from one to another like an elegant present. The movement at first enchanted, then wove a seductive web over the theater. The energy diminished so imperceptibly that Lindy jumped when the notes of the last movement began. The stage filled with the entire cast, moving expertly through intricate patterns.

When the curtain closed on the final pose, the audience burst into applause. They jumped to their feet with a roar when Andrea took her bow. They loved her, and the accident had given them a vested interest in her success. Lindy stood and joined in the applause.

The enchantment left with the darkness. Backstage was filled with pedestrian activity. The wardrobe mistress was collecting dirty socks and whatever needed mending. Stagehands hauled pieces of scenery back into the shop for storage until the following night. Dancers packed up practice clothes or lounged in their dressing rooms smoking cigarettes. Just like any other night in the theater. Just like nothing had happened, thought Lindy.

They met Jeremy Ash as he came out of the girls' dressing room. He was tall, solid but thin, and about as gorgeous as a man should be. Wavy blond hair curled over the collar of his black turtleneck. His camel-colored trousers still held an immaculate crease, not even a wrinkle at the hips. He must have been standing backstage during the performance. Lindy hadn't seen him in the house. Maybe he was too nervous to sit still; some directors were. Jeremy Ash didn't look nervous, just incredibly tired.

Biddy enclosed his arm in hers and led him forward. "Lindy, this is Jeremy."

"Hello." She held out her hand and pulled in her stomach. "It's a pleasure. The performance was impressive."

Jeremy's weary expression rearranged itself into one of politeness. "The pleasure is mine. I hope 'impressive' doesn't fall into the category of 'unbelievable' and 'you should have seen yourself up there.'"

Lindy felt a rush of embarrassment. "Of course not. I thought it was stunning."

Jeremy grimaced.

God, her conversational skills were as flabby as the rest of her. "I meant the dancing."

"Thank you." He smiled suddenly. It was dazzling. "You know, we've actually met. And of course, I've seen you on the stage."

"You have a good memory; that was quite awhile ago."

His smile disappeared. "Yes."

Behind him, the door to the first dressing room swung open and banged against the wall. Carlotta stormed out and descended on Jeremy, her Japanese robe flying out behind her, revealing more of her body than anyone cared to see. Black hair, dulled to a matte finish, brittle and broken from years of hair spray and dye, flew out stiffly from her scalp.

He turned around abruptly, then started back with obvious repugnance as she stopped in front of him. The entire backstage area was suddenly quiet, the dancers stopped in the process of leaving, eyes focused away from the outburst. They became a tableau behind Carlotta and Jeremy, exaggerating their every move.

"What is it, Carlotta?" he asked. For a man, known for

having a pet name for everyone, he seemed particularly formal. Lindy could guess why. She couldn't come up with a nickname for Carlotta that was anything but obscene.

"I know what you're trying to do. You think you can frighten me away." Carlotta turned in a dramatic slow-motion pirouette, mesmerizing her prey, forcing all eyes to look at her. She snapped her head back to Jeremy as if spotting a turn. "It won't work. Do you understand? Some-one will pay, but it won't be me."

Jeremy looked at her blandly, except for one momentary bolt of hatred that shot from his eyes. Lindy saw it. He blinked, and it was gone. "What are you talking about, Carlotta? No one is trying to hurt you. It was an accident."

Carlotta raised a long finger to his chest. "If you think you can replace me with that little bitch, think again. I'll finish her, and don't think I won't."

Jeremy flinched. "That batten hit Andrea, not you."

Carlotta smiled, baring cigarette-stained teeth. She ran her finger slowly up his chest and under his chin. "Your aim never was that good." She flicked his chin with her fingernail, then turned spasmodically, her hair lashing across his face, and strode back into her dressing room.

The door slammed closed, and Jeremy turned to Lindy.

"A fitting exit for Medusa," he said. He seemed completely unaffected by her outburst. The dancers continued to stand where they were, faces strained, bodies tense.

Jeremy smiled slightly. "We should get so much drama on the stage."

Lindy smiled as graciously as she could, but she couldn't think of anything to say. No one would ever talk to a director the way Carlotta had. How could she get away with it? Even for Carlotta, her actions seemed extreme.

"Excuse me, Lindy, it's been delightful to see you again."

As soon as he left, the dancers crowded around Biddy.

"Why doesn't he do something?" asked Paul. "She's ruining everything, and he just takes it. I hate her." His lower lip trembled.

"Yeah," said a tall black dancer. "If he'd just cooperate, we could have the bitch out of here." He jabbed the air with an unlit cigarette.

"He's under a lot of pressure. Help him out, okay?" said Biddy.

"We've been trying, but he doesn't pick up on one damn cue. What's the matter with him? I'd kill the bitch if she talked to me that way."

"Look, Rebo, it's been a hectic night. Go back to the hotel and get some rest. Try to forget this. It was a great show; celebrate a little." Then she smiled. "But not too much."

Lindy remembered that smile. It had carried them through some rotten times, as well as some good. It looked like the Jeremy Ash dancers would be needing it now.

The dancers began moving toward the stage door. Only Andrea remained, braced against the wall.

Lindy walked over to her. "Rough night."

Andrea smiled feebly.

"Don't let her get to you. It's all show."

Andrea opened her mouth, and a convulsive sob escaped. Her eyes filled with tears, then she turned and ran down the hall after the others.

Lindy turned to see Biddy staring after Andrea's retreating form. She seemed pretty close to tears herself.

"Come on, old friend, I'll buy you a drink, or better still, why don't you spend the night at my house. That way, I won't have to not drink and drive, and you can see Glen." Lindy dropped her arm across Biddy's shoulders. "And then you can tell me what the hell is going on here."

Lindy could feel Biddy fighting with herself, torn between her need to stay with the dancers and a greater need to talk to Lindy. Just like the old days, when they had been so close that one could tell what the other was thinking just by walking into a room.

"Okay." It was quiet and calm, but Lindy knew Biddy as well as she knew anyone, and she suddenly understood why Biddy had asked her to come.

Two

They drove north on the parkway. Lindy's evening at the theater had piqued her curiosity and unearthed feelings that surprised her. She felt vitalized. First the batten and then that scene with Carlotta. It was awful. She had loved every minute.

"And remember those two Italian silk merchants in Tokyo?" asked Biddy.

Lindy slowed down at the token booth and threw in thirty-five cents. "The night of the earthquake? How could I forget? I thought it was the sushi that made the earth move."

"Well, it certainly wasn't the two Italians. And speaking of Italians . . . ," Biddy paused. "I wonder what ever happened to Gianni?"

"My faithless *amoré?* Who cares? Probably still chasing after young American girls, only he's bound to be older and fatter and bald. At least, I still have hair."

Gianni BonGiovanni, purported count and definite rake, had wined and wooed Lindy from Milan to Venice to Porto-fino. He filled her dressing room with flowers, bought her presents, plied her with Chianti and champagne, and then promptly disappeared, leaving her to deal with the two unsavory gentlemen who wished to know his whereabouts.

"Maybe the Mafia got him." Lindy turned the car into the driveway and stopped at the front door.

"Wow, Lindy, this is gorgeous. I had no idea."

"Biddy, it's pitch black. How can you even tell what the house looks like?"

"There's the porch light and anyway . . ." Biddy inhaled deeply.

"If you sing, I'll break your other leg."

Biddy laughed. "Remember, we used to sing entire conversations."

"It's amazing what depths touring can plunge you to." Lindy opened the car door. "Take me back to Flagstaff," she sang. Biddy joined in and they warbled their way up to the front door, two girls again. Biddy, young and fiercely optimistic; Lindy, a little older and wiser, but immediately drawn to the insouciant charm of the younger woman.

It was Lindy who had convinced Biddy to take night courses in accounting at Pace University. And it was Biddy who had held Lindy's hand when Gianni had dumped her, bullying her into laughter and taking her shopping to forget her woes. It was great therapy, shopping. The habit had stuck with her.

"Don't mind Bruno, just don't let him knock you over," said Lindy as she opened the front door and led Biddy into the entrance hall.

There was no sign of Bruno. Lindy turned on the entry lights and ushered Biddy down the hall. "I'll get you settled in the guest room, and then we'll find Glen. If Bruno didn't greet us at the door, they're both asleep in front of the television."

They found Glen and Bruno in the family room, snoring in tandem. Glen sat in one corner of the couch, his feet propped on a leather ottoman. Bruno was stretched out beside him, his head resting in Glen's lap. The blaring sounds of a chase scene ricocheted around the room.

"Scratch that," yelled Lindy over screeching car wheels, police sirens, and gunshots. She closed the door, shutting out the noise. "Surround Sound," she explained in a quieter voice. "How about a glass of wine?"

Lindy poured out two glasses of white Bordeaux and returned the bottle to the pewter ice bucket. She sat down on the Sheraton sofa, slipped off her shoes, and tucked her feet underneath her. Biddy sat next to her with her cast resting on a pillow on the marble coffee table.

Biddy took a glass as her eyes scanned the room. She clinked Lindy's glass with hers. "It's so posh."

"Medium posh. You should see the other side of town."

"Is that a real Ming vase?" asked Biddy, indicating the object with her wineglass. "I'd have been a nervous wreck raising two kids and a dog with all this breakable stuff around."

"Oh, we lost a few pieces, but I broke most of them. Anyway, I've become an instant empty nester. No sooner did I get Cliff off to college, then Annie wins a music scholarship to spend her junior year abroad. Bern Conservatory. She's only sixteen, but . . ." Lindy shrugged. "I had to let her go. We're an independent lot, we Haggertys. Anyway, I left for New York the day after high school, and I've done okay."

"You've done great."

Biddy's superlatives were beginning to annoy her. She didn't want to talk about herself. She hadn't done much lately, she was just busy. "Glen made all the money. I just did the grunt work."

"I'd hardly call raising two children 'grunt work.' "

"You'd be surprised." Lindy stretched out her feet next to Biddy's on the coffee table and declaimed in a public-television voice: "I've perfected driving a station wagon into a fine art, taken grocery shopping into the next century, and created more amateur ballets in twelve years than all the choreographers in Soho put together. Two thumbs-up."

"Be serious."

"I am," said Lindy. "But in addition to the boring stuff, kids are pretty cool. And the suburbs is the best place to raise them. I mean, poor Cliff spent his first year of life on tour with me, sleeping in the bottom drawer of a hotel dresser. Now, he can communicate with the whole world, electronically, without ever leaving his bedroom."

"I think I'd rather tour."

"Hmm."

"Do you think you'll ever go back to work?"

The question hit her like an ice cube from the wine bucket. Lindy shrugged. "I don't know. I can't see spending the rest of my life doing amateur fund-raisers."

Biddy sipped her wine and looked at Lindy over the rim of the glass.

Lindy returned her look. Biddy's cheeks were mottled with pink. "Biddy, what's going on?"

"I wish I knew." She placed her wineglass on the coffee table and began to scrub her hair. "You saw what a mess things are. I'm so confused. I really wanted to work for

Jeremy. He's incredibly talented. I couldn't believe it when he actually hired me as rehearsal director, that he would trust *me* with overseeing his creations.

"And everything seemed fine until Carlotta showed up. It was about three months ago. No one had heard anything about her being hired. Jeremy just said she was in, and there was no use talking about it. Now, everything is falling apart."

"Odd."

"More than odd. Jeremy can barely look at her. He completely ignores her. You can imagine what kind of rehearsal environment that makes. Before she came, he was always around, shaping things, directing, hands on. Not like other choreographers who turn over their work the minute the last step is finished. He was really so powerful in rehearsals. But now, half the time he doesn't even show up when she's supposed to rehearse, and I have to take the rehearsals alone. And he's turned over everything in the theater to Peter; he's the only person in the company who attempts to control her. Then she insisted on Paul as her partner. They look ridiculous together. He's really talented, but he's so tied up in knots, he can barely move."

"He and Andrea would be the perfect casting for *Carmina*. Surely, David Matthews could have insisted that Jeremy use her."

"He did, but Jeremy refused. There was a big to-do, and we were afraid that David would pull *Carmina*, but for some reason he didn't. Everybody hates Carlotta. They avoid her like the plague and then play all sorts of practical jokes on her. It's a nightmare."

"Tonight was not a joke."

"No. It was just an accident."

Lindy pointed to Biddy's cast. "Like that?"

Biddy's eyes widened. "Yeah," she said slowly.

"How did it happen?"

Biddy picked up her wineglass and took a sip. "I was rehearsing Carlotta in that fast section in *Carmina*, and she kept moving too far downstage. I was standing in front of her trying to keep her in place. But the steps kept traveling forward, and I kept backing up, and pretty soon I was in the orchestra pit on my butt. Luckily, the pit was raised, or I might have broken my neck instead of my leg."

"You backed off the stage?" Lindy asked incredulously.

"It's hard to believe, I know, but Carlotta was so forceful. Everything is a power struggle to her."

"You think she did it on purpose?"

Biddy shrugged.

"What did Jeremy do?"

"Nothing." Biddy sighed. "Oh, he took really good care of me; paid for everything that insurance and workman's comp didn't cover. He's good that way."

"But he didn't put it to Carlotta?"

"Not while I was around, but Peter did. While we were waiting for the ambulance, he read her beads in no uncertain terms. I've never seen him so angry."

"He thought she did it on purpose?"

Biddy's hands shot into the air; the wine sloshed in her glass. "Nobody knows what Peter thinks. He was hired when Jeremy started up the new company, and he's been scowling ever since. He's efficient and uncomplaining, but stays completely to himself."

"And that's another thing. What's happened to him, Biddy? He looks eaten up. He would never have allowed a batten to remain unsecured in the past." Blood rushed to Lindy's stomach. "He's not . . . sick, is he?"

Biddy chewed on her lips. Lindy knew what she was thinking. Biddy had loved Claude faithfully for years with no reciprocation from him. He had finally "come out," and when he became ill, Biddy had nursed him and then buried him. His family didn't even come to his funeral. So many of their friends were dead. Please, not Peter.

"Biddy."

Biddy jumped, then shivered. "No, I don't think so. He's straight. Isn't he?"

"It's hard to tell in this business."

"No. I'm sure."

"Maybe, but, Biddy, this is not the Peter Dowd we all knew and loved."

"He's still wonderful with the dancers, cares about their comfort, and he always runs interference for them against Carlotta." Biddy's mouth worked spasmodically.

"Biddy, he's changed," said Lindy. "But, I guess, working around Carlotta could put a strain on the most benign personality. I just can't understand why Jeremy would keep her on. She should have retired years ago. She's awful and ugly, and—"

"And they love her in the suburbs."

"I can't believe it. Why?"

Biddy shrugged. "Why do they eat at McDonald's? She's been living off her reputation for years. If she weren't so awful, I'd feel sorry for her."

"Don't tell me Jeremy keeps her on because she sells in the burbs."

"Of course not; he's an artist. He cares more about the

work than satisfying the uneducated whims of suburbia."
Biddy clapped her hand to her mouth. "I didn't mean . . ."

"It's okay. We are pretty gauche out here in the hinterlands." Lindy leaned back against the couch. "So why doesn't he fire her?"

"Not a clue. They may like her on the tour circuit, but they'll crucify us in New York. He knows that."

"And why does he let her get away with talking to him like she did tonight, and in front of everybody? I would have fired her on the spot."

"So would I, but he just takes it, and doesn't even seem upset about it. She's going to ruin us."

"It's not some kind of game, is it?"

Biddy looked blank.

"I mean, we've all seen some pretty sick relationships in this business."

"Not Jeremy, he's not like that."

"Wasn't Carlotta a member of his first company?"

"I think so, but she should have retired even before that."

"People like Carlotta usually keep their jobs by sleeping with the director."

Biddy made a lemon-sucking face. "Yuck."

Lindy raised an eyebrow.

"He would never. He hates her. You'd have to be dead not to notice it."

Lindy raised the other eyebrow.

"Anyway, he's gay."

"Straight or gay, I can't see him diddling someone like Carlotta," said Lindy. She tried to remember what she knew about Jeremy. He had been the artistic director of a prominent New York dance company until about five years ago.

Then he abruptly quit and disappeared for several years. He had been talented, intelligent, and a savvy businessman, a perfect combination for success. Now, he was back. Why would someone with so much going for him let things get so out of hand?

Bruno padded into the living room as she was wrestling with the thought. He wagged his tail perilously close to the ice bucket.

Lindy reached over as it began to topple and righted it. "Bruno." He put his front paws on her lap and attempted to crawl up.

A head appeared around the corner of the archway to the hall. "Bruno, come." The voice was groggy with sleep.

"Glen, here's Biddy. Come say hello. I'll get you a glass." Lindy started to get up.

"Hi, Biddy," he said from the archway. "Good to see you. I'm beat," he said to the room in general. "Good night."

Lindy felt her cheeks tingle and sat down again. "He works long hours."

"Computers, right?"

"Telecommunications. Of the global variety." Couldn't he have at least made an effort at small talk with Biddy? He knew how close they'd once been and how excited she was seeing her again. Why did it suddenly strike her that Glen might be wiring the world, but had begun to tune her out?

"He's still cute."

"Yeah."

Biddy stared at the space where Glen had stood. "What am I going to do?"

The question hung in the air. Lindy poured the rest of the wine into the glasses.

"I need help." Biddy pulled her fingers through her hair, leaving wisps radiating from her face. "You and I were always a good team, weren't we?"

Lindy eyed her cautiously. "What are you getting at?"

"It's only a few weeks until the Joyce season."

"You want me to come to work?"

Biddy nodded her head in jerky, hopeful movements. "I'll arrange it with Jeremy."

"I'll be forty-four in November. I'm not in shape. I can't find my cheekbones much less my hipbones." Despite her protests, the idea of working with Biddy was growing like a bionic mustard seed in her brain.

"Just for a few days. I can't seem to manage this alone. I have to clunk around on these crutches, and I just feel overwhelmed." Biddy clutched her wineglass with both hands; her hair had maxxed out.

"I can't . . ."

"Please."

Lindy reached over and pushed away a strand of Biddy's hair. "Working for Jeremy is pretty important, huh?"

"Lindy, it's my life."

Well, how could she say no to that?

It was well after two o'clock when Lindy staggered upstairs to bed. Her head was reeling from wine, intrigue, and the possibility of actually having a job, even for a few days.

So much for a pleasant evening at the theater. The on-stage drama paled compared to what had happened back-stage afterward. Take one nasty diva, an impervious director, a brooding stage manager, and you had enough to tempt any mystery buff, or a desperate soap-opera writer. And then there was Biddy.

Glen and Bruno were snoring peacefully. Lindy tripped over a pair of shoes lying in the doorway.

"Ouch." Bruno lifted his head at the sound. "And get off my side of the bed, you mutt."

Bruno closed his eyes. Lindy groped her way through the darkness to the bathroom, feeling her allegiance drawn back into the past. She clicked on the light and began rummaging through the medicine cabinet for some aspirin. Just in case, she thought. She popped two into her mouth and stuck her mouth under the running water. It was a routine that she remembered well. Between aches, pains, strains, and the occasional hangover, Lindy had taken her share of aspirin over the years.

She threw her clothes in the hamper and pulled out a T-shirt from the top drawer of the bureau. When did we start wearing clothes to bed, she wondered as she pulled the shirt over her head. She looked at Glen, a little pudgier, a little pastier. He had been aggressive in his attentions to her, and after the nefarious Gianni, she was more than susceptible to his all-American, no-nonsense kind of charm.

He knew where he was going, what he wanted out of life. He wanted Lindy, and she had succumbed. And now he had just what he wanted and had gone where he wanted to go, but Lindy was afraid that he had left her behind somewhere along the way.

There was suddenly a hollow pit in her stomach. Probably the wine, she thought. She and Glen had made such grand plans, and they had achieved them. Or maybe, it was Glen who had achieved them. With Cliff and Annie away from home, it seemed like he hardly needed her **at** all. But Biddy needed her. She shivered. One phone call, one evening at the theater. Suddenly she didn't feel so sure of herself.

"This is not a good way to think," she said aloud and jumped at the sound of her voice.

"Aarghgh," came the response from the bed.

Lindy sighed. She couldn't even tell if the sound had come from Glen or Bruno.

She climbed wearily into bed, grabbed Bruno by the collar, and pulled him onto the floor. He made one of those baleful doggy yawns.

Lindy growled back and tucked her feet under the comforter. Glen turned over, facing away from her. Bruno jumped back onto the bed and after walking over her for a few seconds found a comfy spot between them.

"Pick up my laundry tomorrow?" one of them mumbled.

"You will not cry," she said silently over and over like a mantra until she fell asleep.

Three

When Lindy came downstairs the next morning, Biddy was on the phone. She motioned Lindy over. "Jeremy" she mouthed. She handed Lindy the phone. Lindy shook her head. She wasn't ready to make any decisions. She hadn't even had coffee.

"Hello, Lindy. It's Jeremy." His voice was a smooth, unruffled baritone, and her doubts melted into the receiver. "Look, I'm sure this is an imposition, but if you're available, I would consider it a great favor if you could help Biddy out for a while."

She swallowed hard. "Jeremy, I'm really flattered, but I haven't done this kind of work in years. I'm not sure I can even touch my toes."

"Lindy, it's like riding a bike."

Well, she could ride a bike, probably. Her doubts flew out the window, down the street, and into the next county.

Biddy added Lindy's name to the roster at the stage door and led her down the hall. She swung the door open. "This is ours. I'll go find Jeremy." Biddy smiled, eyes twinkling. "Make yourself at home."

Lindy walked into the empty dressing room and tossed

her dance bag on the makeup table. She stood in the middle of the room watching dust motes dance in front of the dingy window. Bats were slamming around inside her stomach. Damn. She had stage fright, and it felt great. She took a deep breath, held it, then exhaled slowly through her mouth. With a last look around the dressing room, she wandered backstage.

A group of girls was warming up onstage. (All dancers were called "girls," "boys," or "kids" until they retired, usually around the age of forty.) The boys would show up at the last minute. Some things never changed.

Dressed in a wild assortment of sweatpants, cutout T-shirts, sweaters, and leg warmers, four girls stood at a ladder in the center of the stage. The Jeremy Ash Dance Company was a contemporary-dance company, but the dancers were classically trained. A ballet *barre* was as essential to their day as brushing their teeth. They had reached *grande battements*, the high kicks that ended that portion of the warm-up, before they moved into more strenuous movements in the center. Their feet curved as their legs kicked to the front, side, and back, high above their heads.

Two girls were stretching on the floor, legs spread out in a straddle. Deli coffees sat on the floor in front of them, and they sipped and talked as they curved their backs right and left and forward.

Laughter came from behind her. The boys. They could afford to take it easier than the girls. Competition between men wasn't as tough; there were fewer of them to choose from. She heard the rustle of paper bags being opened: the ubiquitous tour breakfast, coffee and a hard roll. It felt good to be back.

"Seems like everyone's making a comeback these days."

Lindy looked over her shoulder and into the brown eyes of Peter Dowd. "Hi, Peter. I didn't get a chance to say hello last night. It's good to see you." Lindy stretched out her arms to give Peter the customary theater hug and kiss on the cheek.

"It was a busy night." The tone of his voice stopped Lindy midgesture, and she dropped her arms to her side.

"Never a dull moment, especially with you-know-who around?"

Peter made no comment but looked past her to the stage. Lindy was acutely aware of his body next to hers. It exuded an unsettling mixture of standoffishness and invitation, and he seemed oblivious to it. She longed to ask him what was wrong.

"Yeah, he seems to have made a slip there," he said after a moment. "He's out front with Biddy."

Lindy watched him walk onto the stage. Peter Dowd had missed his calling. He should have been on the stage, not backstage. Tall, lean, with thick hair the color of obsidian, and cheekbones to die for. A little makeup over those scars, and he'd be perfect, not a leading man, but the mysterious, dark stranger.

Lindy crossed to the front of the stage. Biddy and Jeremy were sitting in the front row. Biddy looked up and motioned her over.

In the past Lindy would have jumped down and gone out to the seats. She quickly evaluated the possibility of landing on her feet and walked over to the stairs that led down to the house from the side of the proscenium. All this company needed was two rehearsal directors on crutches.

Jeremy rose when she approached them. "Good morning. We'll start with the *Holberg Suite*. It's pretty straightforward. The *Prelude*'s in good shape, except for the spacing of the girls' trio. They keep cutting off the boys' entrance, and you could get fuller movement from the *Sarabande*."

Did he want her to take rehearsal now? Lindy frantically ticked off corrections and organized the piece mentally as he talked. *Prelude*, whole company; *Sarabande*, a sextet for three girls and three boys; *Gavotte*, group again; *Air*, adagio for Andrea and six boys; *Rigaudon*, fast paced and short last section. Okay. She could wing her way through the piece easily; the movement flowed perfectly with the music. All she had to do was fine-tune. She'd worry about *Carmina* later.

"Then we'll take a break while they set up for *Carmina* and do a couple of hours on it. That way the crew won't have to set up the cage twice."

"Sounds good. What do you want me to do?" asked Lindy.

"We'll introduce you to everybody, and then you can take the rehearsal. You might as well jump in."

She took several slow, calming breaths. "Okay, but, Biddy, what are you going to do?"

"Biddy can help me with some paperwork. I've got two grant proposals due in May, and I'm tearing my hair over them. Lucky for me, Biddy is good at everything; keeps me from having to hire a bunch of specialists."

Biddy beamed.

Lindy swallowed. Just like that. She was back at work.

"Well, let's get to it, then." Jeremy led them to the stage and pulled himself up over the edge. Biddy and Lindy took the stairs.

Jeremy called the company together. Most had finished warming up, but a few sauntered out of the dressing rooms. She would have to give a lecture on warming up before rehearsal. She had a lot of work to do, but first she needed to win them over.

Jeremy introduced her, giving the particulars of her career. A few of the older dancers seemed to recognize her name. They might have been starting their careers when she had retired, but most of them had still been children.

I could be their mother, she thought as she looked at the faces in the assembled group. Sixteen pairs of eyes looked back at her. At least, Carlotta wouldn't be coming in until later. It would give her an hour to build a rapport.

"Let's get started, shall we?" She gave them her brightest smile. "And those of you who still need to warm up, do so on the sly, please, and try to be a little earlier next time."

She turned and walked to the middle of the stage, legs shaking. "Let's take the opening section with music just to get the juices flowing, and then we'll stop and work on a few things."

The girls took their places quickly. Paul did a few last jumps and trotted off to stage right. A couple of the boys slouched off to the wings muttering to each other. Grumbling she could deal with, but if there was going to be an attitude problem, it would come from the one they called Rebo. She had noticed his name in the program. No last name, just Rebo.

He was a tall, muscular black man, long legged with a well-developed torso. He wore a red bandanna around his head and had a gold loop in one ear. He cocked his head at her, then moved indolently to his starting position.

What crap, thought Lindy. She recalled how he had burst onto the stage, gobbling up the space and standing the hairs of her forearms on end. Power, strength, rhythm, and good looks. And such an attitude. Well, she'd get through to him. He had too much talent to waste his energy on self-indulgence.

She pushed the play button on the boom box at the front of the stage. It was cued to the beginning. Thank you, Peter. She had enough to think about without having to search for music cues.

She let them dance the *Prelude*, then turned off the tape player.

"Good. Now I want to work on the girls' entrance, the three of you there. What are your names?" Mieko, Laura, and Kate. "Please bear with me. I'm trying to learn people and steps at the same time, so give me a day or two, okay?"

The trio looked at her pleasantly but didn't respond. Lindy took them through their steps, adjusting the spacing and directions so that the group stayed cohesive. Then they tried it to music.

"That's much better," volunteered Kate, or was it Laura? Mieko she could remember: Oriental features, straight black hair, petite. And a name like Mieko Jones tended to stick in your mind. "I could never make it to my place for the next cue," said Kate. "Now I have plenty of time."

If all of life could be so simple, thought Lindy.

Next she worked on the lift that she had seen Andrea and Paul practicing the night before, using two boys as "spotters" to catch her if she started to fall. When they got to a series of turns that lowered until the dancers were lying on the floor, Lindy stopped them.

"Not bad, but you need to open up your feet and lower

your turns gradually until the end. Like this." She took a deep breath and demonstrated for them. The turns were easy. She ended stretched out on the floor looking up at them.

"Okay, I got down here by myself; who's going to get me up?"

Quiet laughter rippled through the group. Rebo waltzed up and made an exaggerated kowtow. "Madame," he said and pulled her up with one hand so easily that she sprang onto her feet.

"Thanks, getting up would not have been a pretty sight."

Rebo granted her a wide, toothy grin. "My pleasure," he said.

Gotcha, she thought.

She started on the *Air*, the section for Andrea and six men. Their movement was seamless. Lindy just fine-tuned, adjusted an occasional handhold, shifted a position slightly so that it would read better from the audience.

They had reached the final movement, the *Rigaudon*, when Carlotta appeared at the side of the stage. She was wearing a fur coat and sunglasses. Honestly, thought Lindy. The woman had no taste. It was the middle of April; she must be sweating in the ridiculous thing. But she had probably had to save all her life to buy it. Might as well get her money's worth. Carlotta stopped for a moment, gave Lindy a haughty, appraising look, and went into her dressing room.

"*Brr-r-r.*" Rebo hugged himself and flashed Lindy a challenging look.

"Carlotta may be older than me," she replied innocently, "but I can handle her."

She gave them a fifteen-minute break. That would be long enough for Carlotta to get ready and for Peter to have the stagehands set up the cage for *Carmina*. She wandered back into her dressing room for the bottled water she had brought. There was no sign of Biddy and Jeremy. "When you walk through a storm . . . ," she sang under her breath.

She came out into the hall just in time to see Carlotta come out of her own dressing room, her hand on the shoulder of the costume mistress. Lindy reminded herself to ask Biddy what the girl's name was.

"It wasn't Peter's fault."

Carlotta patted her shoulder. "I know, dear." The girl looked gratefully up at the aging dancer and scurried past Lindy down the hall.

Lindy walked toward Carlotta and stuck out her hand. "Carlotta, Lindy Graham." She had slipped back into using her stage name automatically.

Carlotta looked at Lindy's hand like it was some unrecognizable object. Then slowly she shook hands. Her limp fingers felt like bird bones in Lindy's firm grasp.

"Oh, yes, Lindy Graham. I thought you retired to have children." She looked Lindy up and down as if counting the extra pounds.

"I did; now, I'm back." Lindy flashed her a smile. "When you're ready." She didn't wait for an answer but went through the door to backstage, heart hammering.

Peter was standing at the edge of the stage. "Cage is up, dancers are ready."

"Thanks." Lindy walked briskly onstage.

"Okay," she said. "Let's take it from the top. Where is Carlotta?"

On cue, Carlotta appeared. After one disdainful look around the stage, she took her opening position. Lindy hit the play button. Andrea looked out of the wings and shrugged. Rebo and two corps boys hurried out of the first wing. "Sorry." They took their places quickly, and Lindy recued the music to the beginning. A minute later, Andrea and the boys were draped on the cage, and Carlotta had flung out her arms. But when she started to lift Andrea, she promptly stopped. Andrea dropped heavily onto the metal bars. The two boys winced.

"Really," drawled Carlotta. "This is impossible. The girl is a lug; perhaps *you* can do something with her." Her eyes pierced Lindy's, and Lindy noticed for the first time, they weren't dark at all, but a dull gray.

Lindy gritted her teeth, then said nonchalantly, "Andrea, when you feel Carlotta start to lift you, just pick yourself up, please."

Andrea picked herself up, raised herself on point, and fell.

"And she's too close to me after her fall. David always told her to fall forward." Carlotta turned to Andrea. "Forward, dear, that's downstage, that way, toward the pit."

Andrea crawled downstage and glanced up at Lindy.

Lindy willed her to stay in control.

"Well, that seems to be settled. Could we please try to get to some dancing?" Lindy turned her back on them and spoke at the boom box. "Let's cut to the second section." She fast-forwarded the tape.

They rehearsed, but there was no energy. Movements were cut short, steps forgotten, entrances made late. It was amazing to watch the degeneration. An hour ago, the stage was rocking with exuberance. Now it was peopled by clumsy amateurs.

They moved on to the *pas de deux* for Paul and Carlotta. The kid was visibly shaking. He missed the first two lifts, and Carlotta turned on him.

"You incompetent little ... just like your father. Two untalented peas in a pod."

Paul glared at her.

"Take two minutes, everybody, but don't leave the stage," said Lindy. Paul was immediately led off by Andrea and Mieko.

Lindy faced Carlotta. "This is doing no good. Can we try to make this work, please."

"Dear"—the word dripped with sarcasm—"the poor thing couldn't dance his way out of a paper bag."

Lindy looked her straight in the eye. She had to tilt her head up to do it. Carlotta was a good four inches taller than she was. She needed to dye her hair; the lighter roots formed a line down her center part. Like a skunk, thought Lindy.

"He could if you would help." She raised an eyebrow. "We all need to keep our jobs, dear. Let's try to make this as painless as possible."

Carlotta's eyes widened, then narrowed, like a cat deciding whether the pounce is worth the effort.

Lindy turned back to the group. "We'll start the duet again. Be ready to make your next entrance." She recued the music.

Rehearsal limped along. Lindy was exhausted mentally and emotionally, as well as physically. As soon as Peter announced three o'clock, she cut them loose.

"Talk about time standing still," she said as Peter unplugged the boom box.

"It's really ten till, but you looked like you needed rescuing."

"You're a good man, Peter Dowd."

He wrapped the cord around the handle of the boom box and walked away. At the edge of the stage, he stopped as Carlotta appeared holding a crumpled piece of poster-size paper.

"Where's Jeremy?"

Peter shrugged.

Lindy walked up behind him. "Can I do something for you, Carlotta?"

"Look at this." She shoved the paper toward Lindy. As Lindy took it, she noticed the boys crowded into the door of their dressing room. She straightened out the paper; the crinkling sound seemed absurdly magnified.

Across the top were the words spelled out in block letters: NOW APPEARING, THE DIVINE SWINE. The head shot that Carlotta used for the program, and obviously taken when she was much younger, had been cut out and pasted to the body of a pig.

Lindy swallowed. Peter glanced at the paper, then walked away. The boys disappeared into their dressing room.

"Where's Jeremy?" Carlotta repeated.

"I'll deal with this," said Lindy. Her eyes met Carlotta's. An instant of wordless challenge passed between them.

"I doubt it." Carlotta snatched the poster out of her hand and headed toward Jeremy's office.

"Then I won't deal with it," said Lindy under her breath. Carlotta wouldn't accept sympathy, even if Lindy had found any to give. And she hadn't. All their old antipathies had resurfaced in that one brief look. She pushed the thought away. It was her job to remain neutral, and she needed some time to get her bearings before she started dealing with the company's intrigues. But a word of advice wouldn't hurt.

Lindy stopped by Paul's dressing room. The door was ajar. Paul sat at the dressing table arranging an already neat display of makeup. Rebo and two corps boys, Juan and Eric, were gathering their dance bags to leave for the dinner break.

"She acts like she was the queen of the Gypsies," said Eric.

"Bitch," whined Rebo. "Everyone knows I'm the queen of the Gypsies." He blew Eric a kiss and struck a pose, a broad-shouldered Venus de Milo with arms.

"Paul, do you have a minute?" asked Lindy.

"Sure, come in."

"Hey, catch you at the restaurant." Rebo led the others quickly out the door. Lindy heard their laughter as they walked away. "Too bad that batten missed her; we could be dining on pressed pork *au jus.*" Another eruption of laughter, and they were gone.

Paul began lining up makeup pencils in a row. "I didn't have anything to do with that," he said.

"That's not why I'm here." Lindy sat down on the edge of the table; it creaked under her weight. It was attached to the wall along one side with support legs at each end. The makeup lights surrounding the mirror were on, and Lindy felt their warmth through her shirt. "How about some advice from somebody who's been there?"

"You worked with Carlotta?"

"Hasn't everyone? But in those days she had more technique and less attitude."

Paul smiled slightly.

"Listen, there's someone like her in every company. They

only get away with it if everyone else lets them. You know what I mean?"

"I guess, but she doesn't ever let up." Paul fingered a container of pancake makeup, pushing it round and round in little circles.

"No, she doesn't. But my generation survived her. So will you."

"Why does she have to be so destructive?"

Lindy shrugged. "I guess it's the only weapon she has left. She invented her life. Spent all those years working as hard, harder, than everyone else, and they were still prettier, more talented, more lovable than she was. It's sad, really. She's at the end of her career. What will she have when it's over?" Lindy smiled at the boy. "She's finished, you're just beginning."

"You want me to feel sorry for her?"

"I just want you to take a step back from it."

"While I'm trying to lift her over my head?"

"You have a point."

"The really sick thing about Carlotta is that she treated my dad the same way."

Lindy blinked as she made the revelation. Allan Duke. Of course. "You're Allan's kid." She paused. "Sorry, that was the mother in me talking. You're not a kid, but a professional."

"Not much of one, considering the way I'm letting Carlotta get to me."

"Then stop it. If you don't buy into the power struggle, she won't have any power."

"It's not so easy. She's on her second generation of 'Duke bashing.' Dad used to have to partner her in Jeremy's old company. He'd come home mad as hell. He finally chucked it and retired."

"What's he doing now?"

"He and mom are in Cleveland. He's artistic director there."

A hint of an idea popped into Lindy's mind. "Paul, did he retire before Jeremy quit as artistic director?"

"About the same time, I think. I don't really remember. I could ask him when I talk to them." He blushed. "They like me to call them once a week, just to say hello and keep them up on the gossip."

"You might ask him if he remembers what was going on then."

Paul looked at her curiously.

"In the meantime, don't let Carlotta do this to you. You've got a great career ahead of you. Do what you have to do. Pretend she's somebody else." Paul blushed again. "Erase her, ignore her, and just dance your best."

"That's what Dad says. 'Dance around her, over her, or through her, just keep going.'"

"Smart dad."

"But I think she's doing it on purpose. She wanted me as her partner, like she wanted to keep punishing my dad. She's horrible. I hate her."

"Forget her." She pushed herself off the table. Another creak. "Paul, those guys didn't have anything to do with the batten falling, did they?" She looked at his face. "Of course not. Stupid thought. You'd better get something to eat."

Lindy sat in the audience, holding her breath. Her first day on the job and she already felt totally responsible for the outcome of the performance. The houselights dimmed. Biddy patted her knee. "Here goes."

"Easy for you to say."

"I'm sure you were a great success. They'll do fine."

The curtain opened. Smoke billowed out into the house as the stage lit up. Maybe there should be less smoke. Lindy opened her notebook and took her first theater note in twelve years.

It was easy after that. She wrote rapidly, keeping one eye on the stage. Carlotta reached to Andrea; the girl picked herself up. Lindy clutched her pen. Andrea rose on half pointe and fell forward—toward the pit. Thank you, Andrea, said Lindy silently. The *pas de deux* passed with only a few shaky lifts. The boys came on like gangbusters. Lindy began to relax. The final procession entered, their dark robes skimming the ground like phantoms. The last lift. Lindy crossed her fingers. Paul missed Carlotta but made a good save. No one in the audience would know that it had been a mistake. They climbed up the cage. The curtain closed, and Lindy snapped her notebook shut.

"Not so bad," she said to Biddy.

"They did great. Thanks."

"It ain't over till the fat lady sings."

Biddy opened her mouth.

"Don't you dare."

The curtain opened for the bows. The corps came forward, then the trio. Andrea stepped forward for her solo bow. Lindy held her breath. Carlotta replaced Andrea, reached both hands to the audience, and sank into a low curtsy, head barely lowering. The applause grew. Carlotta stepped back into line, and the curtain closed as the company took one final bow.

Lindy expelled her pent-up air. "Now, you can sing."

The *Holberg Suite* was danced impeccably. Jeremy was a master at his craft, blending the steps flawlessly with the music. When the audience left the theater, they were humming the last movement of the *Holberg Suite*.

Four

The next day, Lindy sat in the audience watching the dancers warm up. She hadn't slept well. Images of falling battens and outraged divas interrupted her sleep. Her body felt stiff. She should be taking a *barre*, too; give her muscles a chance to work properly, and take her mind off accidents and changed personalities. Or had she just gotten too soft to cope with the strains of tour?

All the dancers were onstage, even the boys. Maybe I'm doing something right, she thought. They seemed relaxed. Trained to be resilient, they had relegated the opening-night accident to the realm of interesting tour gossip, if it were an accident. I'm the only one still worried, thought Lindy. Just like a mother. She started rehearsal.

The company breezed through the corrections she had taken the night before. It was an intelligent and talented group. Jeremy really knew how to pick them. Except for Carlotta. Why would he hire her after putting together such a good company? Whatever talent she had in the past was gone. New Yorkers would go for her blood; he was asking for failure.

She gave the dancers a fifteen-minute break. She was watching Peter and the crew constructing the cage, when she saw the costume mistress watching her from the wings. It took her a minute to realize who the girl was; her manner was so self-effacing that she seemed to merge with her surroundings. When Lindy looked her way, she lifted her chin slightly. Lindy took the cue and walked over to the wings.

"We haven't met; I'm the wardrobe mistress, Alice Phelps." For someone who was responsible for so much beauty onstage, Alice was downright dowdy. Her brown hair, thin and straight, was pulled back from her face in a low bun. Strands had fallen from the clasp and hung limply over her ears. She was wearing a faded-blue smock that only accentuated her pear-shaped figure. Pins and threaded needles were thrust into the fabric of her pocket, and a pair of orange-handled scissors hung from a ribbon around her neck. The top of her head came to Lindy's chin.

"It's a pleasure to meet you, Alice. Did you need to speak with me?" Lindy asked softly, feeling an immediate compassion for the woman. Alice was one of the many anonymous workers who kept the dancers looking glamorous, and who never received any glory. Washing, mending, polishing shoes, and helping with quick changes made up the bulk of her life, and she looked it.

Alice made no reaction.

Honestly, thought Lindy, can we pick up the tempo a bit? But she smiled at Alice and thought about Walter Mitty. Perhaps Alice, too, had a secret life.

"Yes?" she prompted.

Alice began to speak as if she were unaware of the time that had elapsed since she had begun the conversation. "This probably isn't the time, but . . ." Her eyes were focused, not at Lindy, but on the stage. "I wondered if . . . I mean . . . well . . ."

"Well?"

"Someone is making a mess of Carlotta's costumes. Tying her shoes together, misplacing pieces. Like that. I'm sure it's just for fun. Like a joke. But with everything that's happened . . . Carlotta's not so bad . . . she just got off to a bad start."

Yeah, about fifty years ago, thought Lindy.

Alice's eyes were scanning the fly area above the stage. "I'm sure they aren't thinking about that, or they—But now, I practically have to dress Carlotta, you see what I mean. And maybe—it's not really your—you know—but I hate to bother Jeremy. Like that . . ." Her speech trailed off.

She glanced at Lindy for the first time since she had begun to talk.

Peter passed by them. "We're finished. Shall I call the dancers?"

"Please," said Lindy. She turned back to Alice, whose eyes were now following Peter into the backstage area. "I'll speak to the dancers when the time seems appropriate, okay?"

"Thank you." Alice's body turned and followed her eyes back to the dressing rooms.

Lindy turned back to the stage. Well, it took all kinds. Alice seemed to live in a fog. Not like the dresser they had when Lindy was still dancing. What was his name? Ari. She smiled at the memory. He was a wizard of poufs, coifs and flounces, mincing about with flying, efficient fingers. Ever present, always at your elbow when you needed him. "Dahlin', relax, let Ari take care of it." He was a far cry from this quiet creature who had drifted off backstage.

Peter called the dancers onstage. They reappeared quickly, but the rapport was gone. Before the break, they had been energetic, enthusiastic. Now, like Alice, they seemed to be looking anywhere but at Lindy.

This was so unfair. Lindy bent down to check the tape. When she looked up, everyone had taken their places for the beginning of *Carmina*. Only Carlotta stood at the side of the stage, weight thrust onto her right leg, hand resting on her hip. She looked her age this morning. Her skin was pasty. Two blotches of red sat on her cheekbones. She had eaten off most of the red lipstick that covered her lips, and her chin seemed longer than ever. Maybe she hadn't been sleeping that well, either.

"Places, please," Lindy said unnecessarily. Everyone was in place but Carlotta. She stared back at Lindy, grimaced, and walked lazily to the wing.

So that's how it's going to be, thought Lindy. Feets don't fail me now. She pushed the play button. Rebo and Eric brought in Andrea. Carlotta entered behind the music. She sauntered over to Andrea and yanked her off the cage. Andrea's head snapped back. Lindy tensed, but Andrea kept going. She fell forward away from Carlotta.

Carlotta began her solo. Lindy gritted her teeth. She was marking! The bitch. This was no time to relax. Paul entered for the duet. He missed the first lift. Carlotta shoved him away. He missed the second.

"Let's pull it together, you two. I don't want to have to stop the tape," yelled Lindy from where she stood. Carlotta hit him with such force on the third lift that the boy staggered backward.

"Okay, that's it." Lindy stopped the tape. "You're fighting

each other. Take a deep breath, and let's start the duet again."
She saw heads peeking out from the legs.

Carlotta turned and gave Lindy a withering look. "Maybe
you should cut to the next section, dear. The boy seems
incapable of dancing this morning."

"We'll take it from the beginning of the duet, please."
They started again. The dancers had moved closer to the
stage, watching. Paul missed the first lift and shot Lindy an
anguished look. Carlotta hit him from behind.

"Stop this," Lindy demanded.

Carlotta turned on her. The music continued in the background. "This is ridiculous." Carlotta spat out the words. "I
can't work like this." She lifted her chin like a spoiled child
and stalked off the stage.

No one moved. They looked at Lindy. She looked at Carlotta as she left the stage, and made a decision.

"Neither can we. Ordinarily I wouldn't let this happen,
but in this case—who's her understudy?" Andrea stepped
forward, eyes on the ground. "And who's your understudy?"

"Mieko." Andrea's voice was barely audible.

"Okay, fellas, let's take it from the top. Haul Mieko up
and bring her in."

"Yes, ma'am," boomed Rebo and hoisted Mieko effort-
lessly over his head.

It took a few minutes for the chill to wear off, but gradually the company began to recover. It was an incredible trans-
formation; Andrea and Paul made every lift. Lindy yelled
out corrections over the music. After several sections, she
stopped them to fix a spacing problem. When she turned to
the tape recorder, she saw Jeremy standing in the back of
the theater.

He turned and walked away.

Lindy's stomach shriveled and sank with a thud. She shook it off. It felt great to be working again. Paul and Andrea were a perfect match. Even the spacing seemed to fix itself. Surely, Jeremy could see that.

After another hour, Lindy turned off the tape player. "That's enough for today. You did great, but you have to keep it at this level. No matter what. Your job is to make it work, under any conditions, and, believe me, it's going to get worse before it gets better." She gave them a theatrically meaningful look and walked off in search of Jeremy.

How long had he been standing in the back watching? He probably had seen her confrontation with Carlotta, but surely, after seeing how good the dancers looked without her, he would be forced to make a decision.

She knocked quietly on the door of the dressing room that had been commandeered as Jeremy's office. Without waiting for an answer, she poked her head inside.

Jeremy was sitting at the makeup table, staring into the mirror that ran crosswise along the wall. The makeup lights were turned off, and the light in the room was dull and gray.

"Am I fired?"

He glanced up at her and smiled. It was a weary effort. The corners of his mouth barely turned upward, and fatigue dulled the usual liveliness of his blue eyes. "No," he said, looking back into the mirror.

"Jeremy, I barely know you, and it certainly isn't my business to tell you how to run a company. But you must have seen how the whole group pulled together after Carlotta walked off."

"I saw."

"And?"

He didn't answer, just sighed deeply as if he were about to recite a speech he had said too many times.

"Lindy, you don't—" He broke off. "It was like witnessing a little bit of heaven. Only we're stuck in hell, and even a glimpse makes it pure torture."

"Then why don't you fire her?"

"Because Jack insists on keeping her. Jack badgered me into starting this company when I didn't care about anything in the world. He saved my life. He made this all happen. He works hard, though God knows why. He wants her. She stays."

He turned back to the mirror and stared vacantly past his own reflection.

Who was Jack? His lover, maybe? She walked to the back of his chair and put both hands on his shoulders. "Sometimes you have to be ruthless, Jeremy, even when it hurts someone you care for."

She felt his shoulders tighten, then relax. He reached up and covered her hands with his. "Believe me, Lindy, I know that."

Lindy groaned and collapsed onto one of the double beds in Biddy's hotel room. Biddy looked up from the pile of papers spread on the table in front of her. She was sitting at a round table positioned near the only window; her cast rested on another chair across from her.

Lindy groaned again.

"Heard you the first time," Biddy said over her shoulder.

"Biddy, what are you doing?" Lindy propped her aching body up on her elbow.

"Grant applications. Easier to do them here than trying to make Jeremy concentrate on what he's doing. He's good at paperwork, but he sure doesn't like it."

"*M-m-m.*"

"Hey, you'd better pop into the shower, or you'll be stiff as a board in the morning."

"I'm all ready stiff as a board."

"Some shape you're in. I thought you worked out at a gym."

"I do, but there I ride a bike that doesn't go anywhere, walk into the wall for twenty minutes, and climb stairs that end where you started. I don't stretch, kick, turn, and jump with a bunch of younger, thinner professionals looking on. Maybe I should be doing a ballet *barre.*"

"I'm sure you did just fine." Biddy began to arrange the pile of papers into stacks.

"Actually, I was a dismal failure. Carlotta stormed out of rehearsal, and I let her go. Jeremy saw the whole thing. I think you have just witnessed the shortest comeback in history."

Biddy turned to look at her, a mixture of horror and admiration playing on her features. "Wow."

"Biddy? Has it occurred to you that there is something more sinister here than just one nasty diva?"

Biddy looked perplexed. Of course not. She had lasted in the business for years only seeing the good parts and ignoring the bad. Lindy felt a pang of envy.

"What if that batten falling wasn't an accident?"

"I don't quite follow you."

"Maybe someone is trying to help Jeremy get rid of Carlotta."

"That's a horrible thing to say."

"Or, maybe someone besides Carlotta is sabotaging this company, and using her as the catalyst." Lindy shook her head. "It all comes back to the same thing. Carlotta. Why does Jeremy put up with her? He doesn't need her, he doesn't like her, and he said that it was hell working with her."

"He did?"

"Yeah. It doesn't make sense. Jeremy comes out of seclusion and starts a new company. He's got talented dancers, good ballets, and a New York season on the horizon. Carlotta shows up, and he hires her just because somebody tells him to. He told me that much when I talked to him after rehearsal."

"You talked to him about Carlotta?"

"I told him to fire her. Do I have nerve or what?"

Biddy whistled. "Well, Jeremy said to jump right in. So you did."

"Just like always. I could never stay out of trouble, and I'm such a nice person. But doesn't the whole thing strike you as a little too much? Why is he letting her destroy the company?"

Biddy chewed her lip and passed her hands through her hair. "I've been trying to figure that out for the last three months. It doesn't make sense."

"No, it doesn't, not yet, anyway. And I doubt if I'll be around long enough to figure it out. I think I'll take a hot bath."

After the bath and room service, Lindy felt a lot better. She and Biddy dressed and headed to the theater for hour call. Most of the dancers had arrived earlier and were applying makeup and chatting lightly. Reggae, the Gipsy Kings, and Bach poured out of the dressing rooms, joining in a cacophonous symphony in the hallway. The stage crew was making last-minute adjustments to the lights, and Lindy could hear hammering coming from the shop behind the stage.

She and Biddy were sitting in their dressing room, the door ajar, when Carlotta arrived. Her complaining voice echoed as she passed them. Lindy cringed and peeked outside.

Carlotta swept past the door. A slight, but paunchy man in a dark three-piece suit shuffled hurriedly behind her. A boutonniere of freesias stuck out of his lapel. Thin strands of hair were combed forward over his balding scalp, and even in the shadowy light, Lindy could see the sheen of perspiration on his face. And then she recognized him.

She closed the door. "That's Jack."

Biddy nodded. "Carlotta must have called him. He never comes on tour. What's she up to now?"

"No. I mean, that's Jack Sullivan."

"Yeah, he's the business manager."

"Oh, Christ, Biddy."

"What?"

"He was Jeremy's business manager years ago. He was fired—for stealing money from the company. Surely, you knew that; I even heard about it in New Jersey."

"But—" Biddy's hands shot to her hair. "That was just a rumor."

Lindy shook her head slowly. "Oh, my kind and trusting friend. Jeremy, Jack, and Carlotta back together again? Biddy, I think this company is in deep shit."

* * *

That night's performance went well, in spite of Carlotta's aggressive dancing. The rest of the company seemed to have benefited from a day of rehearsing without her, and Lindy began to hope that they might be able to sustain it.

But she encountered a group of despondent dancers when she and Biddy returned backstage after the performance. They were standing in a tight group that virtually hummed with unhappiness.

"Now what?" sighed Biddy as she and Lindy approached them.

"Guess what?" exclaimed Rebo. "Still no paychecks, and Jeremy says we have to go straight to Connecticut instead of back to the city for our days off."

"Yeah, it stinks." Juan was standing safely behind Rebo's lean body, using it as a psychological shield.

Biddy faced the group. "You know, guys, Jeremy made this clear from the beginning. This is a tour, and we need to keep focused. We can't have people running back and forth to the city all the time."

"But, Biddy, we have things to take care of. I mean, we do have lives," pointed out one of the girls.

"Of course you do, but right now your lives belong to the company. *Capisce?*"

Rebo appealed to Lindy.

"Look," she said, "you know Biddy's right. So get something to eat. Watch TV. Bitch and moan, but be on the bus tomorrow."

"Are you going to be on the bus?"

"I've got my car, but quite frankly, I'm not sure I still have a job. Now get back to the hotel." They started to move away. "And be on that bus."

She turned to Biddy. "No paychecks?"

"Just the last week or two."

Lindy threw up her hands. "Unbelievable." She cast her eyes heavenward. Maybe it was just as well she was about to be fired. "I guess I'd better go face Jeremy. I'm sure Carlotta has put the screws to me by now."

"Do you want me to come with you?"

Lindy shook her head. "I'd rather be humiliated in private, if you don't mind."

The sound of voices came through the closed door of Jeremy's office. Carlotta's rasping screech was unmistakable.

"Do you really expect me to take corrections from that hausfrau?"

"That hausfrau happens to be ..." Jeremy's voice was low. Lindy leaned into the door but she couldn't make out the rest of the sentence.

"Well, I won't. You can try to sabotage me all you want, but I'm not budging."

Jack's voice rose in a thin plea. "Carlotta, be reasonable. No one is trying to hurt you. They're just kids playing games."

"They tried to kill me; I'm not even safe on the stage."

"Too bad they missed." It was Jeremy. Lindy jerked back from the door, horrified.

"Jeremy, really." Jack's voice.

Carlotta's laugh swelled derisively. "Jeremy, darling, you're pathetic."

"I'll buy out your contract."

"She needs this job, Jeremy." Jack. Imploring.

"I *want* this job. And I'll have it."

The sound of a fist slamming onto the makeup table, then Jeremy's carefully controlled voice. "How long are you going to keep punishing me?"

A silence. Lindy held her breath; her ear was resting against the door.

"I want her out. Get rid of her. Try acting like a man—for once." Footsteps across the concrete floor. Carlotta was making her grand exit.

Lindy managed to jump into the shadows as the door flung open, and Carlotta swept toward the stage door. Jack followed on her heels, leaving the door open behind him.

Lindy steeled herself and walked inside.

Five

She had a job. For some reason that was not at all clear, Jeremy had asked her to stay on. And for reasons just as unclear, she had said yes. Now, she just had to pack. And tell Glen. He could certainly survive a few days without her. He could probably survive without her completely, but that wasn't an option she was willing to pursue.

She attacked her wardrobe, choosing clothes for their look rather than their fit. She was sure she'd be dropping a few pounds with the schedule she'd be keeping. She gathered jeans, practice sweats, evening wear, and an assortment of shoes that ranged from her new four-inch heels to her oldest treadless Nikes and crammed them into her suitcase. Not the matching Samsonite luggage that she and Glen used for vacations, but the old green tour bag that she had whimsically saved and stored in the attic.

She spent the rest of the day canceling appointments and finding her replacement for the talent show.

At six o'clock she started dinner. She pounded veal until it was paper thin, floured it, and stuck it back in the fridge. A quick sauté and it would be ready. She cut tips off asparagus, washed lettuce and field greens. She pulled the wooden salad bowl from the top shelf of the pantry, wiped off the dust, and seasoned it with garlic.

At seven o'clock the dining table was set, complete with candles and her best wineglasses; the wine had breathed, but Lindy was holding her breath. She puttered around the table, straightening forks and refolding napkins. When Glen hadn't shown up by seven-fifteen, she went out into the garden and picked a few early daffodils and hyacinths and arranged them in a vase, sticking the stems down between crystal marbles to keep them in place.

At seven-twenty-five, Glen's BMW pulled into the driveway. A minute later, he emerged from the garage and walked toward the house. He was carrying a bouquet of flowers wrapped in the pastel paper of the local florist.

"Hi." He handed Lindy the flowers and gave her a peck on the cheek.

"Thanks, sweetie. What's the occasion?"

"Just because I love you, and," he added sheepishly, "because I wasn't very friendly to Biddy the other night. I was tired. I've worked ten days straight." He slipped his arms around her and gave her a more meaningful kiss.

Better get this over with, she thought. She led him into the house and poured out two glasses of Medoc, put the flowers in water, and took the veal out of the fridge.

"Speaking of occasions, this is pretty elaborate."

Lindy concentrated on the veal.

They were having after-dinner coffee when Lindy's nerves forced her to bring up the subject of her new job. Glen had loosened his tie and thrown his jacket over one of the extra chairs. He looked pretty good. She smiled at him.

"Jeremy asked me to come to work."

Glen puffed out his cheeks. It made him look like Dizzy Gillespie. "Who's Jeremy?"

"The director of the company Biddy works for."

"What makes him think you would want to go to work? Doing what?"

"Biddy's on crutches, for crying out loud. Do you know how hard it is to carry on a rehearsal when you can't jump up and demonstrate how to do things?"

"No."

"No, what?" Lindy held her breath.

"No, I don't know how hard it is. What did you tell him?"

"I said . . ." She exhaled slowly. "That I'd have to discuss it with you."

Glen smiled. "Sure you did. And how long is this little jaunt going to take? Surely, you don't really want to go back to work, especially now that the kids are out of your hair. You could start having some fun."

"Just for a few weeks until the New York season."

"Weeks? I don't get it. Is this some kind of midlife crisis or something?" His eyebrows quirked together above his nose. She could see the corners of his mouth beginning to tighten. Eyebrows and mouth together. His "I don't get it" expression.

"Sweetie, you're gone all day, and you're tired at night." She refrained from mentioning that he'd have the TV to keep him company. "I'm kind of bored. I thought it would be fun; you know, like a busman's holiday."

Glen leaned back in the chair. "Hell, why not? I'm hardly at home, anyway. Go and get it out of your system. Just don't stay too long, okay?"

And that was that. Monday morning she posted her itinerary on the fridge, threw her suitcase into the Volvo, and headed toward the Tappan Zee bridge.

Spring had come to the Northeast. It was one of those sunny, blustery days, the air crisp and vitalizing. Trees lined the highway like spectators at a parade, leaning in the April breeze as if trying to get a better view. Spires of evergreens punctuated the hillsides of lighter green, and their branches swayed contrapuntally to the quiver of budding maple, dogwood, and locust trees.

She sped along the Cross Westchester Expressway, humming along with a Mozart piano concerto that played from the radio. If it weren't for the number of cars on the road, you'd never believe that New York City was just a few miles away, thought Lindy. That's why the suburbs are bearable. You could be surrounded by trees and flowers, and just when it started driving you stark raving mad, you could escape. Civilization was only thirty minutes away.

Two hours later, she passed through the center of the quaint, but upscale, Connecticut town where the company would spend the next six days teaching master classes and performing at the University Theater on campus. Six days anywhere was a luxury. To fill out every week of a tour, companies sometimes had to book frightening excuses for theaters: old movie houses that had been converted into stages, dressing rooms that were no more than old storage rooms, one-night stands when time was so limited that there was only enough time for a quick spacing rehearsal, while the crew hung the lights. As soon as the performance was over, the crew would strike the sets, roll up the floor, and truck it all over to the next theater and set up for the next performance. The costume mistress would gather all the costumes, dry out the worst of the sweat with a hair dryer before packing them into the costume trunks, only to have to unpack them the following morning.

But Jeremy still commanded a good deal of clout on the dance circuit. He had managed, or Jack had, to book longer runs in the best theaters in the area. The company should be strong and prepared when they finally arrived in New York, and Lindy would be a part of it. She felt energized; she would even make Carlotta come around. It would be glorious.

She almost missed the turnoff to the Sheraton. A woman with a mission, she had passed right through the town without noticing it.

The Sheraton University Parkline appeared unexpectedly before her, its six stories rising like a squat monolith above acres of pastureland. In the distance, the grasses gave way to a line of trees. It was the only building in sight, but that was an illusion. The sprawling campus lay only five minutes over the horizon, and where there was a big campus and a convention-size hotel, there was bound to be a brand-new mega-mall, a tenplex movie theater, and other modern harbingers of rural death close by.

She walked into the lobby. It was spacious, with high ceilings. Modern upholstered chairs were grouped comfortably together in several places throughout the room. A restaurant showed through open doors across the hall from a bank of two elevators, and a bar with a separate entrance stood beyond. She walked across the terra-cotta tiles toward the registration desk; her steps sent up little echoes around her. She signed the registration card and took her key from the congenial desk attendant, a young man with thick glasses and a calculus textbook, which he had slipped quickly underneath the desk. An equally young and studious-looking bellhop took her luggage and followed her into the elevator.

Biddy was sitting at the table immersed in grant applications. "Hey, it's like I never left," announced Lindy as she handed the bellhop two dollars and dismissed him at the door.

"How was the drive?"

"Typical." Lindy threw her bag on the empty luggage rack. "Traffic at the bridge, and I daydreamed the rest of the way. Lucky for me, I'm not crossing the Canadian border by now. Anything scheduled for today?"

"Not unless you want to see the theater; the crew's loading in."

"Normal-size stage, number of wings, enough dressing rooms?"

"Old, but yes."

"I think I'll pass, though I thought we might take a drive over to the campus. My friend Angie Levinson teaches here. I want to say hello."

"Sounds good to me; I could use a break from these applications. They get more convoluted each year, thanks to the ever-changing status of National Endowments."

A few minutes later they were driving into the campus commons. They stopped at a little bakery in the row of brownstone shops at the base of the college.

"A pound of rugalach," Lindy said to the girl behind the counter. "Angie's downfall," she explained to Biddy. "We used to ply her with them in hopes of making her gain weight. While the rest of us filled up on rice cakes, Angie stuffed herself with sugar and carbos and never gained an ounce. Maybe she's gotten fat."

The dance department was located in an impressive new Movement Education complex: concrete, steel, and lots of glass. Angie was just dismissing a class as they arrived at the second-floor studios. She was as thin as ever.

"Some people have all the luck," whispered Lindy as Angie recognized her and came running over.

"My God, Lindy Graham, what brings you here?"

"I'm back on the road ... for a minute. Angie, this is Biddy McFee, and this is for you." She held up the bakery box.

"Still up to your old tricks, I see. Hi, Biddy. It's nice to meet you. You guys have perfect timing; I've got a fifteen-minute break before my next class. I'll make some tea, and we can pig out."

As they followed Angie out of the studio, Lindy noticed the slightest, almost imperceptible, layer of fat silhouetted by her shiny jazz pants.

Yes, she thought. Yes, yes.

Angie poured tea into mugs and handed them round. Each mug had a picture of a famous ballet dancer glazed on its side. She shoved a stack of theme books to one side of her desk and put her feet up.

"So how do you like my little enclave?" Angie shook her shoulder-length hair back from her face and dug into the box of rugalach.

"Impressive," said Lindy. "Do you have a big staff?"

"Three full-time, two part-time, and a bevy of teaching assistants. Dance is booming in the boonies, and I'm as pleased as punch about it. The politics, of course, are lethal, but I've developed a thick skin, a complacent attitude, and, all in all, I adore this cushy life." She reached for another rugalach and blew a strand of hair away as she leaned back in her chair.

"So what about you? Did you marry that charming Glen what's-his-name?"

"Haggerty. Yeah, we live in New Jersey."

"So what are you doing here?"

"Doing a brief stint with Jeremy Ash, giving Biddy and her broken leg a little assistance."

"It must be a bitch hauling that thing around a theater," Angie said.

Biddy smiled in agreement.

"And taking a break from fund-raisers, church bazaars, and movement therapy at the local nursing home," Lindy continued.

"Hey, you do that, too? I go over to Hollingwood Gardens twice a week myself, Tuesday and Thursday mornings. Keeps me sane, working with geriatrics and trauma victims. The least I can do."

"I know what you mean," Lindy agreed. "It's pretty satisfying stuff."

"It really is. Plus I visit Sandra DiCorso while I'm there, not that she's even aware of it." She shook her head thoughtfully. The brown strands swayed back and forth against her cheek, the kind of hair Lindy coveted. "Still, you know how easily you're forgotten once you leave the business, and what happened to her was such a tragedy."

"Sandra DiCorso?"

"Sure." She looked at Biddy. "If you're working for Jeremy, surely you remember her."

Biddy shook her head. "I don't think . . ."

"Sandra was the young dancer who had that accident a few years back. It was right before Jeremy dropped out of sight. A big to-do at the time, but now she's completely forgotten. A real shame. The only visitors she gets are me and Peter."

"Peter?" Lindy and Biddy exchanged looks.

"Where have you been? Peter Dowd. She's his sister."

"Sandra DiCorso is Peter Dowd's sister?" Lindy didn't even know Peter had a sister.

"Sure. DiCorso was just a stage name. A name like 'Dowd' doesn't exactly sparkle with glamour, now does it?"

Lindy turned to Biddy. To judge by the look of dismay on her face, this was news to her, too.

"Doesn't Peter work for Jeremy now?"

Biddy nodded. "But he's never said anything. Not that he would; he keeps pretty much to himself. But you'd think somebody would have said something. I mean, that's pretty insensitive of us."

Angie shrugged. "Well, he probably doesn't want anyone to know. He was really broken up after the accident. The two of them were *mucho* close. I was shocked to hear that he was working for Jeremy."

"Why?" Biddy's question came out in a squeak.

"Everyone blamed Jeremy for the accident. And then Jeremy left the dance scene but good. Nobody could find him. Everyone figured it was guilt."

Lindy heard Biddy choke back a cry.

"Oh," said Angie, looking at Lindy and nodding her head slightly at Biddy. "That's only what I heard on the grapevine."

She shook her head energetically. "Probably none of it is true."

"And where is the—what was the name of the nursing home?" asked Lindy.

"Hollingwood Gardens. It's about a twenty-minute drive from here, down Fox Hollow Road, right before you get to the mall." She put her cup on the desk. "Listen, it was a long time ago, and I've probably got my facts all mixed up. I wouldn't worry about it, Biddy." She stood up. "I've got to go teach; Beginning Jazz Dance, my fave, but it jacks up the enrollment numbers. I'll see you around campus."

Angie left them at the elevator and hurried down the corridor to her class.

Biddy was staring at the down button. "God, it must be awful to be forgotten like that. It's the worst kind of nightmare. And poor Peter. He never said anything. How can people who are supposed to be such sensitive artists be so cruel?"

"Because they get caught up in their own little worlds at the expense of everything else," said Lindy. "No one has ever called me to see how I've been. I could be dead for all they know. But in all fairness, I haven't given them much thought, either."

"But to be left like that."

Lindy touched Biddy's arm. It was a gesture of empathy. She felt compassion for Sandra Dowd, but what frightened her was the tiny crack that had appeared in Biddy's unquestioning loyalty to Jeremy. And how did Sandra Dowd fit into the current puzzle? Just another accident? It was too coincidental not to mean something. But what? Should she pursue it? Maybe it would be better for Carlotta to destroy the company, than for Lindy to destroy Biddy's faith in Jeremy. What had she started? And should she finish it?

"Do you think we should visit her?" asked Biddy.

"I think Peter would be furious if we did."

"Poor Peter."

"Wait here for a second." Lindy ran back down the hall to Angie's office, where she scribbled a quick note and taped it to the back of Angie's chair: I'd like to join you at the nursing home tomorrow if it's convenient. Call me at the University Parkline. Room 324.

Six

"Okay, I give up."

Lindy looked up from where she was clutching the bathroom doorknob. Biddy's head was hanging over the end of her bed; the morning sun set her sleep-disheveled hair into a blazing aureole. "What on earth are you doing?"

"A *barre.*"

"Like in ballet? And I suppose that's a *grande plié?*"

"Doesn't it look like one?" asked Lindy, sitting on her haunches, both knees turned out to the side.

"You look more like a frog waiting to snare the wallpaper. See any flies in that floral print?"

"Cruel, cruel," said Lindy, using the doorknob to pull herself back to a standing position.

"Try it again, and this time keep your back straight and don't sit on your heels." Biddy shifted around on her side like a break dancer until her cast hit the floor, and she came to a sitting position.

Lindy straightened her back and began the descent, keeping her knees out by her ears and stopping when her butt was a few inches from her feet. She straightened up with a creak.

"It's only eight-thirty," said Biddy. "Why don't you wait

until you're at the theater and can use something more substantial to hold onto?"

"And take the chance of anybody seeing me? When Swan Lake freezes over. Anyway, I have to meet Angie at Hollingwood Gardens at ten o'clock."

Biddy watched silently. Lindy moved on to *tendus*. They were a lot easier than *pliés*. Stretch out and close, four to the front, side, back and side, *en croix*, the shape of a cross.

"You still have the best feet I've ever seen," said Biddy.

"And you still have the greenest eyes that ever lied," returned Lindy beginning to sweat. "Why don't you order some coffee?"

Biddy scooted around the edge of the bed and reached for the phone; Lindy moved on to *rond de jambes*. It *was* just like riding a bike, she thought. After all these years, her muscles were still programmed to dance. She was feeling quite pleased with herself until she heard Biddy singing "Aloha-ee."

"Are you saying that my *derriere* is wiggling?" A trickle of sweat dripped off the end of her nose. She wiped it away with the back of her hand.

"Nice *port de bras*. And yes, it looks like you're doing the *pas de hula*," said Biddy. Lindy squeezed her butt and concentrated on the circular motion of her leg. "But you're doing better than me. I can't even get into fifth position. My cast is too big."

"Well, I can't get into fifth position because my thighs are too fat."

"You are a mess. Try *developé.*"

Lindy raised her foot to her knee, stopping briefly in *passé* position to rest before extending her leg out to the side. Then slowly she lifted her foot, aiming it shoulder level. She had almost straightened her leg when it began shaking and fell with a thud.

"Oh, God, is there any reason you can think of why a middle-aged, suburban housewife should be able to touch her knee to her ear?" asked Lindy, rubbing her thigh.

"Well, if I had a husband like Glen . . ." Biddy raised her eyebrows until they disappeared under the puffs of her uncombed hair.

"Arabida McFee, I'm shocked and horrified. That's a deliciously perverse idea." Lindy began kicking to the front.

"And an inspiration to go on with *'grahn bahttemahn.'* " Biddy drawled out the French pronunciation.

"God, you sound just like Madame Koussekovsky."

"Euw, yahz," replied Biddy, crumpling her torso into a Transylvanian pose. *"Yand a one."* Lindy kicked. *"Yand a tehoo."* Lindy kicked again. *"Yand a thre-e-e-e."*

Lindy kicked and collapsed with a giggle. "God, she was frightmare theater, and that was the dirtiest studio I've ever been in. You couldn't even stretch your feet for the cracks in the Marley. What were we thinking of when we left Maggie to take class with her?"

"It only lasted a week, and, thank God, Maggie was understanding enough to take us back."

"Yeah," said Lindy. "She was the best. She kept me on my feet when I was too tired to even feel my feet."

"Yep, there will never be another . . . ," Biddy began to sing.

Lindy finished the second side of her *battements*, and the coffee arrived.

* * *

Angie was waiting for her at the nursing-home entrance when Lindy got slowly out of the Volvo. Her legs were still twitching from her first *barre* in twelve years, and she nearly fell over when she reached back across the front seat to get the bouquet of flowers she had bought in the hotel lobby.

"How did you manage to get the morning off?" asked Angie. She was wearing the pinkest warm-up suit Lindy had ever seen. "Jeremy is the taskmaster of all taskmasters. Who are the flowers for?"

"Everyone is teaching master classes this morning, as you well know, and I thought I might drop these off for Sandra, get my volunteer fix in, and be back at the theater for twelve o'clock rehearsal."

"Indefatigable as ever, I see."

"Nature and me and the state of vacuums," Lindy said. "Of course, the only vacuums around me these days are of the cleaning variety."

Angie's laugh was a clear, soprano trill.

"Nice color," said Lindy, indicating Angie's warm-up suit.

"Bright colors are very cheering. Come and meet my old folks."

They entered through the double doors of the brick building into a comfortable lobby. A burgundy Queen Anne couch and wing-back chair stood at one side. Potted ficus graced each side of the couch, and an enormous chandelier hung from the ceiling.

Angie signed them in at the desk and led Lindy into a bright sun-room off to the left. It was cheerful, warm, and conspicuously free from the usual nursing-home odors. A row of wheelchairs were lined up across the room. Some of the patients slumped, asleep in the chairs, strapped in so they wouldn't inadvertently tumble out. Others waved feebly. A few actually seemed eager to begin.

Angie slipped a tape into a boom box that had been set up on one of the institutional tables that ran along one wall. She had chosen songs from the 1930s and 1940s, songs they might recognize. One lady, fragile and brittle as antique china, began singing along to "Slow Boat to China" before Lindy even recognized the tune. She was joined by the reedy voice of a corpulent gentleman a few wheelchairs away. The woman next to him started howling.

An attendant appeared at her side and took her hand. "Minnie. It's time for your exercising. It's all right, dear." She turned to Lindy. "Unexpected noises frighten her. She should settle down soon. If she doesn't, I'll take her away."

Angie was already in the middle of the room facing her audience. "Okay, everybody, hands in the air. And point your fingers up and down, wiggle them all ar-o-u-nd," she intoned in a singsong voice.

Lindy joined her, flexing her fingers along with the rest of them. Next they moved the wheelchairs into a circle, and the participants batted a balloon around to the strains of "I'm Looking Over a Four-Leaf Clover." It took some effort for Angie and Lindy to keep the balloon aloft. Some of the folks had surprising strength, but most only made feeble swipes at the balloon as it came near them. A few made no effort to play at all, and the balloon would settle into their laps or roll onto the floor. Angie would pick it up and bat it to the next person. The session ended with a fairly rousing rendition of "If You're Happy and You Know It" accompanied by hand clapping, feet clattering, and head nodding.

Before they left, Angie and Lindy stopped at each wheel-chair to say goodbye. Minnie started to cry, Lindy patted her hand, and the attendant whisked her away. Some seemed sprightlier after the exercise, but a few had not even awakened from their aged dozing.

"Whew," said Angie as she collected her tapes and waved a cheery goodbye to the room in general. "See you on Thursday, everybody."

Lindy picked up her flowers and followed her out. Several corridors and turns later, when Lindy was thoroughly lost, Angie stopped at a nurses' station. The nurse on duty smiled in recognition. "And you've brought a friend, how nice," she said as if continuing a conversation they had just been engaged in. "She's quite popular this week. I'm so glad, though I doubt if she even realizes it, poor thing. Daneeta will show you down."

Daneeta turned from the file cabinet with a stack of manila envelopes in her hand. She was a tall black woman in her early twenties. Without a word, she plunked her folders down on the counter and turned left down the hall. About fifty feet later, she entered a door on her right and crossed to the figure sitting in a wheelchair that was turned toward the window.

"Miss Dowd, you have visitors," she said in a melodious croon. She turned the chair around toward the center of the room.

There was not a hint of movement from the blank, but beautiful, features that faced them. Sandra DiCorso didn't move. Her head didn't lift. Her hands didn't catch the edges of the chair. Wherever her thoughts were, they were not in this room and not for her visitors.

Daneeta continued crooning as if she were having a conversation instead of a monologue. "It's Ms. Angie, your friend, and she's brought someone with her."

Lindy gazed at the seated girl. Black hair offset the stark whiteness of her face. Her features were fine, the cheekbones high, the mouth sculpted. Lindy knelt down beside the chair. "Hello, Sandra, I'm Lindy Graham. I work with your brother." Not a flicker from the dark lashes. "These are for you. Shall I put them in some water?" she asked quietly. Daneeta's tone was catching.

Daneeta took the flowers from Lindy and pulled off the paper covering. "Well, would you look at this?" Sandra didn't look, but Lindy and Angie did. "They're lovely daisies and pink pompoms. Won't they be fine on your dresser?" She turned to Lindy. "I'll just get a vase; be right back."

Angie had taken over the monologue. She was explaining about Jeremy's company being at the university, adding bits of related information as if she expected an answer. She didn't get one.

Lindy swallowed away the sudden tightening in her throat. God, what a waste. She looked desperately around the room, focusing on the contents in an attempt to quell the tears that had suddenly sprung to her eyes. The walls were covered in bright posters: Degas dancers, a New York City Ballet advertisement in primary colors, a kitten in a pink tutu bounding into the air while his companion chewed at the ribbon of a point shoe. A ceramic ballerina in a brittle tulle tutu balanced on one leg on the dresser. A stuffed bear with a red plastic heart was propped up next to the ballerina. An enormous bowl of white and yellow flowers was set on the bedside table.

Someone had taken pains to make this room special and intimate. Peter, of course. Efficient, no-nonsense, loving Peter. Lindy imagined his cut and scraped fingers unwrapping the delicate figurine, finding just the right place to display it, trying to reach the vacancy in his sister's face, and it broke her heart.

Daneeta returned with the vase of flowers, and Lindy pulled herself together. "Here we are. Aren't they pretty? Where shall I put them?" Daneeta looked directly at the girl who didn't look back. "How about on the dresser, next to Teddy?" She pushed the bear aside and placed the arrangement next to him. "I do think this is a perfect place, don't you?" Lindy wondered who she was talking to, but managed to mumble yes.

They said their goodbyes and followed Daneeta back to the nurses' station, where she picked up her files, smiled at them, and walked away.

"God, that was depressing," said Lindy.

"Which part? The seniors or Sandra?"

"Sandra, mostly. I mean, at least the older ones have had lives; now they just want to go home. Home to the past, or home to their Maker. But when you see someone cut off in their prime—"

"I know, you start thinking 'There but for the grace' . . . etc."

"Exactly. What's wrong with her? Will she get any better? I vaguely remember hearing about it, but I was in Jersey by then, and it didn't really touch my life, you know?"

"I know. She fell in a rehearsal. Only, for some reason she was rehearsing alone at night, and no one saw it happen.

Luckily, she was found by the custodian who came in to clean later that night."

"Yikes." Lindy shuddered. It was every dancer's nightmare. One misstep and your career was over. In this case, that misstep had taken more than a talented girl's career.

"Well, there's nothing you or I can do about it. Nor, apparently, the doctors, and we have some of the best trauma specialists in the country at the U. Hospital. I just come and talk to her. Maybe someday she'll get better. Maybe she even knows what's going on around her. You have to act like she does, just in case."

Lindy breathed away the lump in her throat. "Why do you think everyone blamed Jeremy for what happened? If she was rehearsing alone, how could he be responsible?"

Angie shrugged. "It was awhile ago. All I know is there was a big scandal. Questions about whether it really was an accident and about Jeremy's involvement; then *lots* of talk. Right after that, Jeremy dropped off the face of the earth. Then later, the business manager was fired. Even with a new staff, the company couldn't recover and was disbanded about a year later."

"Was Peter working there at the time?"

"I don't think so. Wasn't he at City Ballet then? Everyone moves around in this business so much, it's hard to keep track. Well, I'd better get back to campus and check on the master classes. You headed to the theater?"

Lindy nodded.

"It's a great old theater. One of the original buildings. A bit outdated, but lots of class. I'll hate it when they build the new one."

"They're going to tear it down?"

"The trustees want to; it isn't big enough for the current campus and too expensive to renovate. But there's a move to keep it intact as a part of the new complex and use it for student productions. I'd hate to see it go."

Lindy drove back to campus in a quandary. Jeremy, Jack, Carlotta, Peter. Why would people with such enmity toward each other work together? She couldn't begin to untangle their motivations. For all the mysteries she read, she had never learned to pick out clues unless the writer tap-danced around them, and those she recognized usually turned out to be red herrings. There was definitely a mystery here; she just hoped it wouldn't have the usual outcome. Most of the deaths in the theater world either occurred onstage, where the deceased rose from the dead in time to take his bow; or from AIDS, which was the ultimate and final curtain.

She was so lost in thought that she arrived at the theater without realizing it. It took a few minutes to comprehend the parking code: blue for handicapped, green for faculty, orange for students.

She parked in a black-lined visitors' space, unloaded her dance bag, and stopped for a minute to appreciate the ambiance of the old theater building. Even in the midday sunshine, its brownstone facade evoked images of a gaslit New England street. It was a massive box, not elegant, but inviting. The entrance was set off by Ionic columns, free standing in front and mantled into the brownstone around the doors. Rail balconies fronted two upstairs windows, and the whole of the structure was topped by a black slate Georgian roof.

Lindy walked around to the back. Jeremy was just going into the stage door.

"It's a grand old building, isn't it?" she said.

"Yes, very substantial." He looked down at a stage weight that held the door open. "Let's just hope the equipment isn't as ancient as the edifice. And let's just hope we can fill it for five nights."

"How are ticket sales?"

"Good for tonight, *ish* for tomorrow and Thursday, better for the weekend. The usual. If we get a good review, things will pick up. A lot of people will wait to see if the critics like it before they'll commit to leaving their televisions for an evening of live theater."

Lindy smiled. "Is that a hint of cynicism I hear?"

"Moi? Never. I'm as eager and optimistic as ever." He opened the door and followed her inside.

Why is it, wondered Lindy as they entered backstage, I can never figure out whether he is being serious, ironic, or just plain obtuse?

They were early. Only the stage crew was moving around in various states of lethargy. The trouble with using resident crews was that they rarely showed a sense of immediacy. With rehearsal only thirty minutes away, they were just beginning to roll out the Marley floor. If they didn't speed up, they would still be taping it down when the rehearsal began. Dance companies always traveled with their own Marley to insure consistency of the dance surface. It was heavy, took up lots of room in the trucks, and added a small fortune to freight costs when it had to be flown, but it paid off in the long run.

Lindy noted the unevenness of the old wooden floor of the stage. It was dry and splintery and would be disastrous for dancers who spent much of their time rolling, falling, and sliding as did the dancers of the Jeremy Ash Dance Company. The warped planks were broken up in several places by shorter squares of wood that fit unevenly into the floor like one of those children's sort games—squares in square holes, circles in circle holes; old-fashioned trapdoors used for entering ghosts and deus ex machina.

Peter almost knocked them over as he sped onto the stage. "Half hour, guys. Ralph, put another man on the Marley, and let's start focusing the sides."

Ralph grunted and rose from squatting at the first roll of Marley. Lindy looked away from the flabby skin that showed between his T-shirt and jeans. She had seen enough beer-enhanced stagehand flesh to last her until her next retirement.

"Thank God for Peter," said Jeremy.

"Yes, how did you get him?"

Jeremy shrugged. "When we started up, he came looking for a job. Beats me. He had a good job, but who can turn down more work, less pay, and a constant headache when you get the chance?"

"Maybe he missed touring."

Jeremy looked at her in disbelief.

"Some people do, you know. Or, maybe it was your winning personality." Peter seemed, if not exactly happy, at least content with his job. Did he blame Jeremy for his sister's accident? She certainly didn't see any signs of hostility, which, if he did, should be hovering pretty close to the surface.

"Definitely, my winning personality. And Alice came along right after that. What a team."

A team? Lindy had never even seen them speaking together. But they spent a lot of time in the theater. Familiarity could make for a smooth-running machine.

There was a rustle of activity behind them. The company

was wandering in, loaded down with dance bags and paper bags of food.

"Half hour," Peter called over his shoulder without taking his hands or eyes off the side light he was adjusting. "Dressing rooms are through that door or up the stairs."

Jeremy turned to Lindy. "Hurry the kids along, will you? I've got to check the box office."

A half hour later, the floor was laid, and the dancers were in place for spacing the *Holberg Suite*. It went so well that Lindy decided to move on to *Carmina*, hoping to have some time at the end to run the understudies through a few sections.

The cage was assembled and so were the dancers when they realized that Carlotta hadn't arrived.

"We'll space without her and use the understudies until she gets here," announced Lindy. They finished the spacing; Carlotta still wasn't there.

Peter was setting cues at the light board backstage left. It was a mammoth, archaic contraption that required two men to run the cues. And it was positioned so that anyone entering from the first wing had to detour around it. "I'll call the hotel." He disappeared into the darkness of backstage.

"Well, while we're waiting, let's try the procession. Andrea, stand in for Carlotta, will you?"

Andrea took her place center stage next to Paul. The other dancers exited stage left, picked up candelabras from the prop table, and formed a double line for their entrance.

"It's really important to keep exact unison on your turns," said Lindy. "Even the smallest discrepancy is exaggerated because of the lights. Let's try it with counts."

They entered slowly as Lindy clapped the rhythm. Each

foot hit the ground at the same time; strides were matched so that the whole line moved as one organism across the stage. They were beginning the slow, descending turns behind Andrea and Paul when the first hitch occurred.

"Okay, hold it. These candelabras should move around exactly at the same speed. If you get off, it looks terrible." She took one of the candelabras to demonstrate. Her arm dropped about six inches. "Heavy little monkeys, aren't they?"

"Yeah, your arm's dead meat by the end of the piece," complained Eric.

"This is what they mean when they say you must suffer for your art." Lindy smiled at him and handed back the candelabra. "Better you than me. Try to keep them even. And Eric, why does your group keep moving upstage here? It should be a completely straight line."

"Because Carlotta keeps moving in on us when she leaves Paul for the lift. Christ, it's scarier than the first act of *Giselle* back here."

"Yeah, she gives us the Wilis," added Juan, who punctuated the sentence with ghostly howling.

Rebo clutched his stomach and fell to the floor, writhing. "Bad joke," he groaned. "I'm having a bad-joke attack."

Mieko grabbed him by his shirt and pulled him up. "The Wilis are in the second act, bonehead."

"She loves me." Rebo tried to embrace the girl, but she ducked gracefully out of the way.

Lindy shook her head, smiling. They were actually having fun. And then she saw Carlotta standing next to Peter by the light board. Her smile disappeared.

"You weren't supposed to start *Carmina* until two." She faced Lindy with a stance of studied intimidation.

"The call was for twelve o'clock. If you want a dispensation, talk to the Pope."

Carlotta turned to Peter, who shrugged and turned back to the light board.

"Can you please hurry? You're keeping everyone waiting." Well, that wasn't exactly true. They hadn't even missed her. "We'll continue on until the end and fix this when Carlotta is ready." Lindy turned to the house to see if Jeremy was there. The house was empty. She really had to be more disciplined. She had worked with real divas before and had never lost her cool. She wouldn't let Carlotta be her downfall.

Carlotta returned faster than Lindy had expected, and it occurred to her that she had been in the theater all along but was waiting to make an effective entrance. They started with the procession. As Carlotta turned from Paul to take the final lift, the center of the procession moved upstage out of her way, destroying the unity of the turning lights.

Lindy stopped the tape. "Right here, guys, you're moving upstage. Carlotta, stay closer to Paul when you circle behind him. You're getting too close to the corps. It's throwing off the line."

Carlotta took a deep breath like she was being lowered into boiling oil. She began again, avoiding the line of candelabras by making grotesque contortions. It looked ludicrous.

"Thank you. That's so much better."

They broke at four o'clock. Most of the dancers returned to the hotel on the bus; a few opted for eating in the university shopping area and napping in their dressing rooms.

"Hey, Lindy." Paul's voice came through the open door

of the boys' dressing room. She poked her head inside. "I talked to my dad."

"How is he?"

"Fine, but he gave me the dish on Jeremy's old company."

Right. Lindy had almost forgotten their previous conversation. She came all the way in and closed the door. They were alone except for Rebo stretched out on the floor; a towel lay across his shoulders as a makeshift blanket.

Paul lowered his eyes. "Rough night, I guess."

"As long as he keeps his days together." Lindy gave Rebo a sidelong look. "He's talented, but he's on the road to burn out. I'm sure you guys will put it to him, right?"

Paul nodded.

"So what's the story from your dad?"

"He left a few months before the company disbanded. He said it had been a total disaster. Some girl fell at a rehearsal, and the police were questioning Jeremy about his whereabouts or something. They finally decided it was an accident, but then Jeremy left, and nobody knew where he went to. But, Lindy, Dad's sure it wasn't Jeremy's fault, and he said to only tell you and nobody else. That it shouldn't color how I feel about Jeremy, because he's a good guy, and he'll do right by us."

"Anything else?"

"Well, here's the funny part." Paul lowered his voice to a whisper. "Jack was the business manager. A few months after Jeremy left, Jack quit. Only the rumor was that he was fired because he was embezzling money from the company. Lindy, do you think he's taking our money, too? Is that why we haven't been paid? Why would Jeremy let him do that?"

And why had she gotten this kid involved? She wanted

to kick herself several times. She sat down in the chair next to him. He looked miserable.

"You know, Paul. Dance companies are like soap operas. Too much angsting without knowing the truth. By the time stories get passed around, the most innocent bystander can look like Charles Manson."

"But—"

"I'm going to look into things. I'm sure there's a rational explanation to our current money problem, and you are not to worry about it. Understand?"

Paul nodded, but he looked like a jurist who had just been told to ignore that last outburst by the witness. It was impossible.

"But I do think you should keep this to yourself. It won't help upsetting everybody."

Paul blushed.

"Who did you tell?"

"Nobody, but at the end of the conversation, Eric came into the room; he's my roommate. And he kinda overheard the part about Jack. He started pumping me, and it just sort of came out. Not the part about Jeremy, but the last part about Jack embezzling the money."

Lindy closed her eyes. Her neck muscles were gnarled and her shoulders hurt. Rebo snorted and turned facing the wall. He had probably heard the whole conversation. What had happened to her brain? All she needed was the entire company panicking.

"Rebo, are you listening?" Lindy asked sotto voce. "Open your eyes and come straight."

He rolled over to face them. "Not straight, anything but that." His grin was seductive. Huddled on the concrete floor, dance bag for a pillow, he looked like a desert sheik. He propped his arms behind his head and waited.

"Okay, I'm a total ditz for letting Paul talk while you were here."

Rebo sighed. "It's a good thing you're not a brain surgeon. The patient would be dead by now."

"I should just stick to fixing steps and spacing, huh?"

"And getting us a paycheck." He sat up and groaned.

"You should definitely stick to steps and spacing, my dear."

"You're right, you're right." He reached for a pack of cigarettes on the makeup table. "I'll go—not straight—but clean. Will that do?"

"It's a deal. You curtail your social life, and I'll get you a paycheck. And don't say anything about this conversation. Any of it. Got it?"

He tossed the pack back onto the table. "Got it. But, man, it's weird. These guys are a bunch of whacked-out masochists. They make me look like Julie Andrews."

"I'll talk to Jack, but erase the last ten minutes from your memory banks, I mean it."

She left them staring at each other in total silence. They wouldn't stay quiet for long. You couldn't keep secrets in a group that worked, lived, ate, and slept together. Her head ached, and her shoulders felt like they were growing out of her ears.

She found Jack in the lobby of the hotel. He was collecting phone messages from the front-desk clerk when she walked up beside him. He was wearing the same three-piece suit he was wearing the first time she had seen him. It was shiny in places and seemed too snug to button comfortably.

"Got a minute?" she asked.

He looked surprised. "Sure. Shall we step into my office?" He led her into the bar and to a booth off to one side. He ordered a scotch; Lindy ordered a seltzer. After the waitress had left the drinks, Lindy got down to business.

"Jack, I might be way out of line, but we need to pay these people. I'm surprised they haven't walked out already. What kind of trouble are we in?" She looked him straight in the face and tried to look businesslike. It wasn't easy. Her throat was dry in spite of the seltzer, and she kept expecting Jeremy to pop in at any moment. That would finish it. Ms. Buttinsky at it again.

But Jeremy didn't appear. Jack took a prim sip of his scotch and flicked the air with his fingers. The hem of his sleeve was frayed with age. "There's no real problem, just a sluggish cash flow. We've had some big expenditures lately. That *Carmina* contraption and the candelabras came in way over the estimates. A few late payments from sponsors; everybody is suffering from cash-flow problems, thanks to our illustrious, art-bashing congress. But it will all be sorted out soon. In fact, a big check just cleared today, and I'll have paychecks for everyone tonight."

He gave her a condescending smile, which wasn't at all convincing. "So," he continued with a shrug. "Nothing to worry about. Anything else on your mind?"

There was plenty on her mind, but she had accomplished the one thing she needed from Jack. She was sure he had

had no intention of paying anybody until she had confronted him. What she needed now was a long talk with Biddy.

"No," she said lightly. "See you tonight." She left him with the check and walked briskly out of the bar. She didn't see him slug back the rest of his drink.

Seven

Biddy was not in their room. The beds were neatly made; the grant proposals were stacked in two even piles on the table. Not even an empty soda can disturbed the cleanliness of the room. Biddy had obviously not returned since they had left this morning. Lindy spent a few minutes pacing from the window to the beds in frustration. When she finally heard the door click, she advanced on Biddy with unreasonable impatience.

"Where have you been?"

Biddy looked startled and a little hurt. "Teaching a Rehearsal Techniques Seminar to graduate students. Did you need me?"

Lindy smiled contritely. "I always need you. I'm bursting with gossip and haven't been able to share it. If you had come in much later, you would have found me exploded into little pieces."

"Nasty rehearsal?" Biddy dropped her bag and collapsed on the bed, hoisting her cast up with one smooth tug. The mattress bounced under its weight.

"Not too bad, though Carlotta was late. The usual stuff. But I went with Angie to the nursing home this morning. I saw Sandra Dowd. It was pretty awful. To end up like that." Lindy described the visit and what Angie had said about everyone blaming Jeremy for the accident.

"That's ridiculous. It wasn't Jeremy's fault."

Lindy ignored her reaction. "And the next part is, Paul talked to his father, and Allan said that there was actually an investigation before it was declared an accident. Jeremy was under suspicion."

"No, I don't believe it." Biddy's hands shot to her hair. "Jeremy is the most wonderful person, and he would never hurt anybody. You just don't know him well enough."

"Biddy, I don't think Jeremy would hurt anybody, not intentionally anyway. I'm just saying—I don't know what I'm saying. Let's try to think this out. I'm beginning to think that whatever happened then may in some way be responsible for what's happening now."

"You mean that Jack and Carlotta have some hold over Jeremy because of Sandra, and this has all been some sordid game?"

"Not a game, Biddy, but sordid and destructive." Lindy sat down on the bed and faced her. "What exactly do we know? One, Jeremy is in seclusion, maybe because of the accident or for some other reason we're not aware of. Two, Jack, after stealing from him, somehow convinces him to start a new company with Jack as the business manager. Jack would have to have a pretty persuasive argument, wouldn't he?"

"Maybe he really cares about Jeremy, or maybe he was desperate for work. I don't think anybody would hire him after what happened, do you? Maybe Jeremy felt sorry for him, or knew he was innocent?"

"And get saddled with Carlotta in the bargain? That would be a harsh sacrifice even for the most loyal of friends."

"But Carlotta didn't come until a few months ago." Biddy tugged at her hair.

"I realize that; I can't figure it out at all. I've read hundreds of mysteries, and I've never figured out who dunnit until the last page."

"And you think if we could figure this out, we could make everything right again?"

"Or destroy it."

"Lindy, you're scaring me. Maybe we don't want to find out."

"How long do you think the company can go on like this?"

"Oh, God," moaned Biddy and dropped her arms across her face.

"And I talked to Jack. He said he'd have paychecks tonight."

Biddy sat up. "I'm beginning to get a nasty feeling about this. I want to take a look at the books. I don't know how, but we'll have to figure out a way."

"My exact thought."

They spent a half hour piecing together what they knew about the convoluted relationships in the company: Jeremy and Jack, Jack and Carlotta, Peter and Jeremy, ending up more confused than when they started. They made plans for raiding Jack's briefcase, some practical and some hopelessly outlandish.

After a quick bite to eat, they drove to the theater. Lindy prepared herself to look at everyone in a new and unbiased light, but her resolution shattered when they entered the stage door.

Alice was sitting on a folding chair next to the prop table. Tears were dropping off her cheeks onto her smock. She must have been at it for a while; her face was swollen and blotched. The effect did not enhance her features. Peter stood next to her, his arm loosely draped over her shoulder.

"Carlotta's costumes are missing from her dressing room," Peter said. "Really, Lindy, this is going a bit far. A few pranks against Carlotta are okay, but it's hardly fair to do this to Alice."

"You're right. Call the company onstage, will you, Peter?"

A few minutes later, sixteen dancers stood before her. She had a good idea who was behind the practical jokes, but she didn't want to alienate any of them. "Look," she said, careful not to gaze at any one person too long. "Carlotta's costumes have been taken out of her dressing room. Alice is very upset. I know this is not what was intended, but when a little fun begins to hurt the wrong people, it has to stop. The four of us are going into the shop now. We'll be there for fifteen minutes."

The costumes were hanging in Carlotta's dressing room when Lindy came out of the shop. "Good show, everybody, for tonight and for this." She and Biddy went out to the audience early. Better to leave things on a positive note.

They were taking their seats when Biddy stopped her. "Don't look now, but there's Carlton Quick. The *Times* must have sent him. Wow."

"Oops, too late." Lindy pasted on a smile and walked down the aisle to where Quick was sitting. "Carlton, what an unexpected pleasure."

"Lindy, darling, it is you. You look divine. And Arabida McFee. Well, well, we've come full circle."

"Only we'll be sitting through the performance tonight," said Lindy. "And you, Carlton? Still sleeping through the boring parts?"

"Of course, darling." He gave her a fleshy, gold-speckled smile. "How else would I catch up on my beauty rest?"

"Well, I think we'll manage to keep you awake tonight. Have you taken a look at your program?"

"Just got here. Are wonderful surprises in store?"

Lindy flashed him an impudent smile. "Stay awake and see for yourself. See you later."

As they sat down a few rows behind him, Quick turned to face them. His mouth performed a series of Silly Putty expressions before it relaxed, and he turned back to the stage.

"He must have seen the program," said Biddy.

There were no major problems that night. Carlotta even managed to stay away from the candelabras, and the processional proceeded without mishap. Jeremy's piece was danced with joyful abandon; when a famous critic is in the audience, news spreads fast.

Quick managed to snag them before they could escape backstage after the final curtain. "Darling, I nearly had a coronary; you should put a disclaimer in the program in case anyone is frightened to death by the old bag." He put the tips of his fingers to his forehead. "Jeremy must have gone round the bend."

"So you did stay awake."

"I had to. Afraid of nightmares." He shuddered, jowls

vibrating. "But in all seriousness, darling, the company is fresh and talented. Dump the dreadful diva, and you'll be a hit."

"If it were only that simple," sighed Biddy as she clunked after Lindy.

Jack was handing out paychecks when they arrived backstage. "But only one?" Rebo said. "You owe us two."

"All in good time, boy." Jack turned and walked into Carlotta's dressing room.

"Did that asshole just call me 'boy'? I'll kill the motherfucker."

Eight

Lindy blinked her eyes open. Morning. A hotel room. Tour. It felt comfortable, familiar. She smiled and got out of bed, feeling only minimally sore from her first ballet *barre* in years. She climbed into her sweats and headed for the doorknob.

She was finishing *battements* when breakfast arrived. Munching on English muffins and squeezing the last drops from their grapefruit halves, she and Biddy reviewed the corrections from the previous night and decided what areas needed the most work.

Rehearsal began each day at noon. This gave the dancers the mornings for sleeping in, relaxing, and considering the general notes Lindy had given them the night before. The day started with Jeremy's *Holberg Suite* and was followed by *Carmina*. The break in between allowed time for the setup of the cage. It was a quick procedure considering the size and bulk of the metal tower. There were three major sections: base, middle, and top, which fit together and were stabilized by inserting cross bars into els; the crossbars also served as climbing rungs.

The rehearsals were beginning to take on a rhythm of their own. It was a satisfying feeling. If they could just maintain their work habits until the New York season, they would be assured of favorable reviews, in spite of Carlotta.

Carlton Quick's review was being circulated around the dressing rooms when Lindy arrived at the theater. Quick was one of the last critics who still made the midnight deadline for the next edition. Sometimes it took several days for a review to appear in the paper; not much help in boosting ticket sales for a short run.

Lindy walked into Paul's dressing room. A huddle of six heads bent over the paper. Eric looked up. "Review's out. They don't call him Quick for nothing, and it's good, mostly."

Andrea sat scrunched in a chair, arms folded over her head. She looked out from under them.

"Expecting a cave-in?" asked Lindy.

"She's going to kill me."

"Let me see." Paul handed Lindy the paper. She skimmed the complimentary paragraphs about *Holberg* and found the item she was looking for: a glowing accolade for the "golden-haired beauty that danced David Matthews's arresting chore-ography with grace and intuitive understanding." The only allusion to Carlotta was the very pointed statement that "unfortunately, all casting choices were not as successful as the choice of Andrea Martin in the supporting role. The critic hopes to see more use made of this talented dancer in the future."

"Well," said Lindy as she plopped the paper onto the makeup table. "Fasten your seat belts, guys . . ."

"Yeah, it's going to be a bumpy ride, but, Andy, look what happened to Bette in the end." Rebo writhed in top diva imitation, bulging his eyes and rolling them until only the whites showed.

"Right now I'd rather face Bette Davis than Carlotta. Oh, God." Andrea slumped down in her chair.

"We'll protect you from the 'Demon Diva,'" said Paul gallantly.

"Thanks, Paul." Andrea smiled at him.

"I'll beat her with my do-rag."

"Thanks, Rebo."

"Just like in *The Wiz*. The Scarecrow." He pointed Vanna White-style to Eric. "The Tin Man." He put his arms around Paul and gave him a sloppy kiss. "I guess that makes Jeremy the Cowardly Lion, 'cause I be Toto. Gonna bite de old witch on de ankle and steal her shoes."

Paul pushed Rebo away. "You're so full of crap, Rebo."

"Dat's why dey luv me."

"What would your middle-class, Midwestern mama say if she heard you talk like that?" asked Lindy.

"Madam, I never talk 'like that' when conversing with the grande dame, I assure you," quipped Rebo, and he pinched her on the butt.

"You're incorrigible."

"Like I said, that's why they love me."

"Let's get to work," said Lindy. "What time is it?"

"Don't know. Peter, that keeper of the timepiece, hasn't shown up yet."

"Well, get onstage and start warming up, please."

Lindy fetched the boom box from the prop room and plugged it into the floor plug at the front of the stage. Peter wasn't around, though he must be somewhere in the theater. He was always there before the others. Or maybe he had gone to visit his sister. They could get by without him for a while. She began the *Holberg* rehearsal.

It was during the *Air*, that Lindy first became aware of Peter standing in the wings. He was gazing at the movement onstage, a faint smile on his lips. Standing behind him, loaded down with dresses that needed to be steamed free of wrinkles, was Alice, also watching.

He must have felt Lindy observing him. He caught her eye momentarily, frowned, and turned away, bumping into Alice. The pile of dresses slipped to the floor. He didn't stop to help her; he seemed unaware of what he had done. Alice bent down, quickly gathered up the fallen dresses, and followed him backstage.

During the break Lindy watched the crew construct the cage. They lugged the middle portion onto the base and hammered retaining pieces into numbered slots. Peter was putting up the crossbars, slamming them vehemently into the fittings.

She wandered over to him. "How's it going?"

"Fine." He didn't look up, just banged another bar into place. His tone of voice and the sound of metal hitting metal had the same teeth-jarring grind.

"Five minutes more."

"Peter, is something wrong?"

"No."

"Peter."

He stood up so abruptly that she took an involuntary step backward. His long fingers wrapped around her upper arm and drew her toward him. "Why did you go there? Leave us alone. It's none of your business. Just leave me alone."

His face showed no emotion, but his voice was barely controlled. Rage. Lindy recognized the emotion immediately. He was containing it, but barely. Why hadn't she realized it before? His demeanor had always been calm, efficient, even caring, but she should have guessed from his physical appearance. His thinness could have been caused from stress, bad diet, even illness. But Peter wasn't ill, just sick at heart. Lindy's stomach flipped over and dropped. She had violated his defenses by visiting Sandra. How could she have been so unthinking? She hadn't even considered how he would feel. In fact, she hadn't thought about him at all.

Now, she could feel the years of pent-up frustration rumbling just beneath his veneer of icy acceptance. His anger was escaping now like air through the pinhole in a balloon. Aimed at her. Enough force and it would explode. She stood frozen, indecisive. She didn't know how to comfort him or diffuse his anger. With a jolt, she realized that she was afraid of him.

He had grabbed her arm so forcefully that her right side was crumpling from the pain. He glared at her with harsh, penetrating eyes.

"Peter."

Her voice must have sounded pained; he loosened his grip and stared at her arm in dismay. "Sorry." He released her. "Why shouldn't you be curious? God knows, I should welcome any show of concern. No one has even bothered to visit her in five years. Five years. Like she never existed. Jeremy has never been to see her. Not once. That cold-blooded bastard. I'll never forgive him."

She reached to touch him, to make some human contact, but he jerked away. "I'm sorry. I didn't know."

"Why should you? Just forget it, please." He picked up the last crossbar and banged it into position. "Ready."

Lindy turned away, ashamed at her insensitivity. Carlotta was standing in the wings, watching and smirking.

Damn the woman. The whole world might be a stage to Shakespeare, but this stage was becoming their whole damn world. Nothing was private; everything was magnified. Lindy felt sick. She'd like nothing more than to smother the old bag with her insufferable fur coat and walk away from the whole convoluted mess.

"Call the dancers, please."

Peter walked off toward the dressing rooms pointedly ignoring Carlotta as he passed her.

They started in the middle of *Carmina*. Lindy wanted to do as much work on the piece as she could before rehearsing any part that would bring Carlotta in close contact with Andrea. There was going to be a scene. Scenes were what Carlotta did best, and after the review praising the ingenue, she knew that Carlotta was just waiting to come in for the kill. For once, she wished Jeremy would appear at the rehearsal, but he had come in and gone directly into his office with Jack, closing the door behind him. He must be aware that things were going to be tough today, and Lindy was a little miffed that he left the situation entirely in her hands.

She couldn't keep the two women separated for long. There was too much interchange between the characters they were portraying, though what their theatrical relationship was supposed to be was a little vague. The younger woman representing the other's past exploits? The symbolism of dreams lost? It would make more sense for Andrea to carry the story line using Mieko as her alter ego. That's what Lindy would have done, but she didn't know what David Matthews had intended. He was supposed to come to the

Thursday performance. She would try to pin him down on certain dramatic situations that were still eluding her.

Her mind had been wandering for just a few seconds, but it was long enough for the rehearsal to slip from her control. Carlotta had gone into action. Lindy snapped to attention as the older woman gave Andrea a shove. Peter appeared from offstage. His presence was so immediate that Lindy looked unconsciously at the floor where the trapdoor lay hidden beneath the Marley. It was the perfect deus-ex-machina entrance: the god suddenly appearing to set things right in Greek dramas.

The cast looked on openmouthed as Peter grabbed Carlotta by both arms and lifted her off the floor. "Get this straight and get it now. There will be no disruptions like this on my stage. This is a professional company, and you will act accordingly. Understand?"

Carlotta's face was colorless as parchment, but whether from surprise, fear, or anger was impossible to tell. Peter shook her like a locked door. Her feet sputtered against the surface of the floor.

"Do you understand?" The words seemed to strangle him.

"Keep your hands off me, you miserable worm," she hissed. "Jack won't stand for this. You're finished."

"No, Carlotta, you're finished." The voice was low, calm, and melodious in spite of its directness. Jeremy stood at the edge of the stage. He didn't even have to raise his voice to be heard. Talk about your Greek gods. Lindy silently thanked the deities for his fortuitous appearance and for his total control of the situation.

Peter released his hold, and Carlotta stumbled backward. "There will be no more outbursts, Carlotta. Just do your steps and leave everyone alone." He glanced at Lindy and then turned to Peter. "What happened?"

"She pushed Andrea." Peter jerked toward Carlotta. "You could have hurt her. What if she had—" He stopped, then recoiled from her as if she were a venomous snake.

"Get back to rehearsal. And no—more—of—this." Jeremy turned, jumped over the edge of the stage, and sat down in the first row, dead center. "Carry on, Lindy."

Lindy reached for the play button with shaking hands. She hadn't reacted fast enough. Now Jeremy was sticking around to make sure everything ran smoothly. She glanced at him through lowered lids.

He returned her look with an encouraging smile. He settled back in his seat and draped his right leg over the armrest, the picture of studied calm.

Rehearsal plodded on. The troops were massing. Jeremy had given them an unspoken order to stand their ground. They kept their spacing, even when Carlotta moved too close. They danced past her if she moved too slowly. They effectively erased her from the stage. These tactics wouldn't work in the long run, but for the first time since Lindy had joined the company, she felt them embrace their own power.

Lindy's respect for Jeremy jumped way up the scale. He had gotten himself into an untenable position, but he was taking control. She felt a surge of optimism.

She fine-tuned the girls' trio, encouraged the boys to higher energy levels, demanded more drama in some sections, more subtlety in others. Carlotta caused no more trouble. She would later, no doubt of that, but for the moment, life seemed wonderful.

When she turned to stop the tape, she saw that Biddy

had joined Jeremy in the audience. Biddy smiled and made a surreptitious thumbs-up sign. They looked like a kooky, two-headed beast, sitting there together, Jeremy's right leg over his seat arm, Biddy's cast stuck out to the left.

Lindy turned back to the stage, wiping the smile off her face. "Let's cut to the end. I want to try something. Paul and Carlotta, that final climb seems a bit crowded to me. Hang back just a bit, Paul. Let her get a few steps ahead of you and then speed up a bit at the last minute. Not too melodramatic, okay? Just a bit of space." Paul nodded, Carlotta made no objection, and Lindy cued the tape.

Carlotta was on the fourth rung of the climb, when it suddenly gave way. One leg tangled in the metal as the rest of her hit the floor. There was a communal gasp from the dancers, but no one moved to help her. Finally Paul stepped cautiously toward her. Carlotta lay sprawled on the floor, trying to disengage her leg from the cage.

Then everyone seemed to move at once. Lindy rushed forward; Jeremy was, somehow, right behind her. Carlotta began shrieking and yelling obscenities at Paul, who was trying ineffectually to help her up. Lindy was vaguely aware of Peter running across the stage. Alice shuffled behind him, carrying an ice pack. Lindy could see Jack hurrying through the wings.

Carlotta had managed to untangle herself and was half standing, groping at the structure for support. She stood on one leg; the other leg hung limply from the knee. She knocked Paul out of the way and turned on Peter. "You did this. You and—" Her head spun to look at Lindy. "And her. You planned this. Jack! Jack!" Her voice was shrill and hysterical. "They planned this, just like the last time. Look at the bar. They've cut it so I would fall. She made me go up first."

Every head turned to look at the cage. The fourth rung dangled from one end. Peter stooped down and picked up the loose end. "The welding has broken through." He turned to Jeremy, confused. "I didn't do this. Look. The welding hasn't been cut, it's broken. It's hard to believe this could happen. Atlantic always does impeccable work."

"It's not hard to believe." Carlotta lunged at Peter. Alice, who had been trying to apply an ice pack to Carlotta's foot, tumbled backward onto her butt. Before Peter could react, a bloody trail from Carlotta's nails streamed down his face. Jeremy and Jack pulled her away.

"Carlotta, you're not acting rationally," said Jack. "Let's get you off your feet and assess the damage."

"Assess the damage, you fool!" She whirled around and grabbed him by the lapels. Freesia petals dropped to the floor, and the rest of Jack's boutonniere followed as Carlotta twisted the fabric in her fists. "I'm not some bloody piece of merchandise. You'll be doing the assessing soon, you little charlatan."

"Jack, maybe you should take her to the emergency room. Alice, give him a hand, will you?" Jeremy turned to Lindy.

"Right," she said. "Let's get back to work. Understudies. And stay away from the cage."

Peter came to stand beside her. His face was smeared with blood where he had tried to wipe it away with the sleeve of his T-shirt. "I'll check out the structure thoroughly. I've never had any problem with Atlantic's work before."

"Fine." Lindy touched his shoulder. "But first, get yourself a Band-Aid."

Carlotta was still screeching at Jack offstage. The sound shot through the wings and onto the stage. Lindy turned up the music, hoping to drown her out and return to some kind of normalcy. She had to force herself to concentrate on the dancing. She wanted to send everyone back to the hotel and check out the broken cage herself. If the structure had been weakened, wouldn't Peter or one of the stagehands have noticed? They set it up and dismantled it each day, storing it in the shop. Could someone have sabotaged it? But why?

Stop it, she demanded silently. Keep your mind on your work.

A few minutes later, she saw Jack and Alice helping Carlotta out of her dressing room. Jeremy watched them leave and then came over to Lindy.

"They're taking her to the emergency room. I don't think it's broken, but she'll be out for tonight." He paused for a minute, surveying the stage. "Get the understudies in shape. And Lindy, you're doing good work."

Lindy breathed a sigh of relief.

The cast was nervous at first. They were prepared for their parts physically, but to be abruptly pushed into performing without the psychological preparation would take its toll if Lindy didn't settle them down. So she started at the beginning and just let them dance their nerves away. They would find their stride; she was sure of it.

Biddy and Jeremy watched the last few minutes of the rehearsal from the wings. When they broke for dinner, Jeremy made a short speech, telling the dancers they had all worked hard, and he had total confidence in them. Lindy had stood through hundreds of similar speeches from many directors, but none had been as simple and eloquent and believable as

Jeremy's. She marveled at his ability to always turn a situation to the better, with such naturalness and ease.

While he stood talking to individual dancers, Biddy motioned Lindy into the wings. She had been looking at Lindy throughout Jeremy's speech with barely disguised excitement. Her hair was standing on end, an experiment in static electricity.

"I thought he'd never stop," she said breathlessly. "We've got to hurry."

"What?"

"The books. In the excitement, Jack left his briefcase. Maybe there's something in it. You know . . ." She prompted Lindy with an urgent look.

"Biddy, we can't rifle Jack's briefcase. What if he comes back to get it?"

"That's why we have to hurry. You said we needed to look at the books."

"I thought you said that."

"Well, you agreed."

"Okay, I did agree," admitted Lindy. "And I guess we have to do it. But we'll have to wait until the theater clears out and risk Jack's coming back. Let's just hope the local emergency room is really busy today."

"Excuse me, Lindy." Lindy and Biddy jumped guiltily.

"Yes, Andrea?"

"What about my costume?"

"What about it? You do have one, don't you?"

"No, they ran over budget, so they didn't have the extra one made up. There's fabric, but it isn't made. Mieko can fit into mine, and Kate can fit into Mieko's. But I guess Alice will have to alter Carlotta's for me, and Alice has gone with them to take care of Carlotta—"

"Don't worry," Biddy broke in. "I'm sure Alice will be back in plenty of time to take a few tucks. You'll be all right. Now get back to the hotel and rest." Andrea nodded and left them.

"Just hurry up, and take everybody with you," said Lindy under her breath.

They watched from the office window until the bus pulled out of the parking lot. Then they turned to the briefcase. It was open, surrounded by financial sheets. A blue ledger sat on top of the papers.

"This is the first time I've ever been glad of Carlotta's nasty temper," said Biddy. "Jack must have been too rattled to lock it before he left."

"Or there's nothing incriminating in it. I can't understand any of this," said Lindy, poring over the ledger pages.

"But I can. Thanks to some friend who badgered me into taking night courses in accounting."

"Thanks, but I didn't mean for you to use your math skills for breaking and entering."

"So it's a good thing the briefcase just happened to be sitting open on the table." Biddy handed her a stack of papers. "Bills, probably. See if you can find anything that looks suspicious." She had already opened the ledger, and her fingers were flying over the portable calculator on the table before her.

After a few minutes, Biddy looked up. She sounded disappointed. "All the numbers add up. Of course they would.

Maybe he keeps two sets of records. Isn't that what embezzlers do?"

"I guess, but I don't have a clue as to how it works."

"Me neither. They don't have a course in Doctoring the Books in night school."

"But maybe there's something here." Lindy pulled an invoice from the stack of bills she was holding.

They didn't hear him approach. He was suddenly there in the doorway, blocking their escape.

"Oh, God," whimpered Biddy.

"What the hell are you up to?" He stepped inside, closing the door behind him.

"Oh, Jesus, Peter. We must be in heaven 'cause you just scared the hell out of us."

"Funny."

"How are those scratches?"

"Forget the damned scratches. What are you doing?"

Biddy looked at Lindy; Lindy looked at Peter. "Well," she began. Her mind was blank. They should have thought up a believable reason to be here in case they were caught, but they hadn't. Could Peter be trusted? He already thought she was an insensitive busybody. How would he react to her snooping into company business? Especially in view of what she had just discovered. Or worse, could Peter be siphoning the funds, and not Jack at all? He might just hate Jeremy enough to weasel his way into a job and then destroy the company. She tried to see him as the villain, but it just wouldn't work. Maybe she was too damned naive, but she thought of Peter as one of the good guys.

"Have you taken enough time to come up with a good story? I'm not going to believe anything but the truth, but you can try." He leaned against the edge of the table and crossed his arms. Keep your mind focused, she pleaded with herself.

"Okay." She expelled a long sigh. "You caught us red-handed."

"Lindy." Biddy looked at her imploringly.

"It's okay, Biddy, I hope. We're looking through the books. Come on, Peter, something is wrong here. We all know that sponsors pay before the performance. Nobody lets fees trickle in after the fact, or we'd all be bankrupt."

"Right." He encouraged her to go on, but Lindy could see from his face that he was already several steps ahead of her explanation.

"The payments have been entered," said Biddy. "Every theater on the last tour has paid."

"So where's the money? Is that what you're looking for?"

"Yes," said Lindy. "Peter, I have to ask you this before we go on. Do you know where the money is going?"

His response was more of a bark than a laugh, but it took away one more doubt from Lindy's mind. It had the harshness of someone who wasn't used to laughing, but it was genuine.

"You're not very subtle, Lindy." Peter shook his head. "I don't know. Jack doesn't pay me, either."

"Then why do you stay?" Lindy cringed at her own stupidity.

Peter frowned. She could almost hear the gates locking around him.

"Sorry, I'm off the subject. Didn't you say something about Atlantic making the cage?"

"I always use them. They do excellent work, until now anyway, and are very reasonable for a union shop."

"Do you deal directly with them?"

"Yeah, I send over the specs. They call or fax if they have any questions. But we were on the road with the last tour when most of the construction was done. Jack stayed in New York, and he'd fax me the communications from the office. There weren't many; I went over it pretty thoroughly with Atlantic before I left. Why?"

"Because there is no invoice from Atlantic here."

Peter stuck out his bottom lip. He had very full lips. "Maybe it's in another stack."

"But there is an invoice from Barton Scenery for the construction of a metal frame: seventeen thousand dollars and change."

"What? Let me see that." Peter grabbed the invoice out of her hand. "That son of a bitch. I've never even heard of this company. The Atlantic estimate was eight thou with a twenty percent margin."

"You're sure the bid was supposed to go to Atlantic?"

"There was no bid as far as I know. Jeremy asked me who to use. I said Atlantic; he and Matthews agreed. Hell, I talked to the shop several times before I left."

"Could Jack have pulled it and given the job to this Barton company?"

"And get a little kickback for his effort? I guess. I only check the bills when there's a discrepancy. The paperwork I get is just a glorified packing list."

They nearly missed the sound of the car driving into the parking lot and coming to a halt just outside the stage door.

"Oh, no," cried Biddy. She began shuffling papers together and threw the ledger into the briefcase. She tore the paper out of the calculator and pushed it into Lindy's hand. Lindy crammed it into the waistband of her sweatpants.

"Is the stage door locked?" she asked Peter.

"No, damn it, I don't take the pig iron out until everybody's gone. Horrible for security, but it's better than running back and forth to open the door all the time."

They had barely returned all the papers to their approximate places when Jack came in. He gave them a startled look and glanced uncomfortably at the open briefcase.

"Oh, Jack, good," said Lindy. "We were just standing here wondering if you'd be back for your briefcase, or whether we should take it to the hotel for you."

"Uh, thanks. I'll take it." Jack slammed the top down and grabbed the handles. "I have to run."

"How's Carlotta?"

"Oh—she's okay. Just a bruise, the doctor said. She'll probably be fine for tomorrow." He turned and hurried out of the room.

No one spoke until they heard the car leave the parking lot. "That was close," said Biddy, turning from the window. They breathed a collective sigh of relief.

"Let's get out of here. We can figure out what to do later," said Lindy. "Want a ride to the hotel?"

"No, thanks," said Peter. "I think I'll stay around and check over the cage one more time. If this was done by some fly-by-night company, there's no telling what else might be wrong with it."

"We'll bring you a sandwich."

"Thanks." He smiled at Lindy for the first time since she had arrived.

Nine

The performance couldn't have been better. There were a few near misses and shaky balances, but the company danced with expression and dexterity. The absence of Carlotta was an instant panacea; the Jeremy Ash Dance Company had been released from an evil spell and had come back to life.

It had been touch and go until the curtain rose. Backstage before the show had been tense and jittery. Lindy went from dressing room to dressing room with bits of encouragement and words of advice. She had to be careful not to give too many last-minute corrections and overload their racing minds and nerves. She repeated the same words again and again. "Breathe, get into your legs, focus on what you're doing. Pay attention, you'll be fine, just do one thing at a time."

She had dropped into the costume room mainly because she had nothing to do. Alice was completing the alterations to the dress for Andrea while the girl squirmed and shook herself, trying to dispel a nasty attack of stage fright.

"Hold still, I'm working as fast as I can," said Alice through lips holding a row of straight pins. She deftly pulled the fabric between her fingers and secured it with the pins.

After a few minutes, she struggled up off her knees.

"There, you're done." She pulled the dress carefully down the length of Andrea's slender body, manipulating the fabric so that the pins didn't stick her as the dress fell.

It was forty-five minutes to curtain before Alice completed the alterations. Lindy was sitting in the girls' dressing room chatting with Kate and Mieko. Andrea was staring into a small makeup mirror, applying false eyelashes with trembling fingers. She looked up into the large mirror to compare her eyes and snatched off one of the lashes.

"I can't get it even," she moaned and started applying more glue to the strip of lashes.

"Clean off the old glue first, then reapply it. And let it dry a little before you put it on," said Lindy. "Relax. You've got plenty of time. How many times have you put on lashes? A thousand or so?"

"You're right. I'm being a nervous Nellie. I just wish Alice would finish with that dress. Paul and I haven't even tried the lifts with it yet."

"Alice will be done any minute. You worked the lifts with the corps dress, and they're pretty similar."

"She's even making me nervous," said Mieko to Lindy's reflection in the mirror.

"Ladies, you have heard a first." Kate raised her arms like a ringmaster. "The inscrutable, unflappable, 'don't let them see you sweat,' Mieko Jones has butterflies."

Mieko stuck out her tongue to Kate's reflection.

The distraction worked. Andrea's second eyelash was in place, and she moved on to applying lip liner. Her face had the perfect bone structure for the theater, prominent and finely chiseled. She didn't need to use the brown contour powder to accentuate the curve of her cheekbones. Her lips were full and expressive. Her face projected freshness and vitality even when covered by the heavy layer of stage makeup: pancake, mascara, blush, and heavily lined lipstick.

Alice slipped in through the door. The room was narrow, and the door banged back, hitting the wall opposite the makeup table. She squeezed past Lindy and hung the dress with the other costumes on the metal rack attached to the wall. The rack was rusty and had been covered with one of those plastic shower rods that opened along one side and then snapped back into place.

The whole theater was pretty shabby, Lindy mused, as Alice bustled around the costumes, fluffing some, smoothing out others. It was appalling how beautiful, old theaters were left to a slow death. Faded paint, rusted pipes, splintered stage, not even a sentry at the stage door. It was sad.

"I could have finished much earlier," Alice said, "but Carlotta wouldn't let me leave the hotel. If she wasn't so upset, she would realize that I had a lot of work to do."

"Alice, even when you're trying to be mean, you're nice," said Mieko.

Alice looked flustered.

"The old hag knew you had lots to do. She was putting the screws to you. Even in pain, she's busy orchestrating revenge."

"She's such a bitch. I thought people like her only worked for the opera," said Kate. "Here, Andrea, try this color." She tossed a tube of lipstick toward Andrea. She missed it, and the tube rolled toward the edge of the table.

Lindy caught it as it dropped and handed it back to her. "Okay, girls, no more diva dishing. Get those little muscles in working order."

Andrea quickly brushed the new lipstick onto her lips. The three girls rose from their chairs as one person and walked out the door, grabbing headsets, extra shoes, and leg warmers. Alice followed them.

Alone in the dressing room, Lindy looked into the mirror. Computer operators had nothing over the theater. You heard about people in the same room, talking to each other on screen instead of bothering to turn around to face each other. But the four of them had just carried on a conversation to each other's reflections in the mirror. Lindy pursed her lips and remembered just in time that it was bad luck to whistle in a dressing room. She bit her bottom lip instead. This was not the real world, or was it?

She stood in the back of the house during the show. Biddy had opted for sitting. It was hard to pace convincingly while lugging a heavy cast back and forth. She picked up one crutch and tapped Lindy on the butt.

"Merde," she said and made her way down the aisle. There were two empty seats beside her. Lindy wanted to be on her feet in case there was another disaster. And Jeremy was unable to hold still. She had seen him pacing in his office, pacing in the lobby, and now he was pacing in the small standing-room area in the back of the house.

He was immersed in his own thoughts. Lindy watched him at a distance, too nervous herself to wonder how Jeremy had ever gotten himself mixed up with two such destructive people as Jack and Carlotta. She could only worry about tonight and what Jeremy would think if she wasn't able to pull it off.

Stop being so self-centered, she admonished herself.

You're only one little piece of this. But egocentrism was the staple of their trade and a necessity if not taken too far. It was the quality that turned talented proficients into artists or failures.

Jeremy jolted to a stop when the houselights dimmed. He came to stand beside Lindy, the side of his arm touching her shoulder. It was a subtle appeal for comfort, and she didn't move her arm away.

It was the longest fifty-five minutes she could remember standing through. She did every step, every lift, every entrance and exit of every dancer on the stage. She was sweating, but smiling, when the curtain finally was drawn on the bodies of Andrea and Paul draped on the still intact and standing cage.

Relief replaced tension. Biddy turned in her seat, smiling radiantly. Lindy nodded back, but she was afraid to turn to Jeremy. She had tried to sneak a peek at his face on several occasions during the dance, but he stared straight ahead, his features immobile, and she couldn't read his feelings from his profile. They continued to stand side by side until Biddy joined them.

"Wow." Biddy bounced the ends of her crutches off the floor like a drumroll. She beamed at Lindy and beamed at Jeremy. "Well? Are you guys going to stand there in a daze, or what?"

Lindy shrugged her shoulders slightly and glanced sideways at Jeremy.

He opened his mouth and then closed it, took a deep breath and winced as if the act of breathing had hurt.

Lindy wanted to shake him until his thoughts tumbled out.

For once, Biddy looked like she wanted to shake him, too.

"Jeremy," she prompted.

He looked from one to the other of the expectant women in front of him. The audience was moving past them in a rush to the bar or outside for a cigarette. Normally, Lindy would have followed them, picking up comments in order to get a pulse on the audience's reaction. But right now, she only cared about Jeremy's reaction, and it was slow in coming.

"I'm such an asshole," was what he said when he finally chose to speak.

It was an odd response. Lindy expected ecstatic congratulations and a rush backstage. She could have coped with disappointment if he hadn't liked what he had seen. But "I'm an asshole" didn't leave much for her to work with.

She swallowed. "Would you care to elaborate?"

"Huh?" He shook his head slowly back and forth. "They've been ... I've let them ... I could have lost this." He looked back and forth at the two women.

It was Biddy whose patience finally broke. "Jeremy, what did you think of the performance?"

Jeremy's eyebrows lifted in mild astonishment, and then he grinned. "Wow." He draped his arms around both of them and started walking them toward the hall that led backstage. They had only gone a few feet, when he stopped.

"I know what I have to do. I shouldn't have let this go on so long. I owe Jack a lot, but ..." He paused; his face clouded over.

Biddy and Lindy waited expectantly, but he said no more. Except for the sounds of the cage being dismantled, backstage was completely silent. Lindy's heart constricted. She knew that feeling. They were waiting. Waiting for Jeremy's reaction. Every dressing room's door was ajar, but the light banter that usually followed a good performance was completely absent.

Jeremy walked to the door of the boys' dressing room. He didn't enter but braced himself with his hands on both sides of the door frame. He stuck his head in. "Great *Carmina*, kids. Pauly, very nice."

He spoke in a normal voice, but it carried to every door. The backstage exhaled in a big sigh of relief, like a woman being released from a too tight corset. He stopped at each door, giving praise, showing his pleasure. He was the perfect director: part demanding boss, part doting parent.

When he gave Andrea a hug, murmuring "Andy, good girl" into the top of her head, Lindy's eyes welled up with tears. Embarrassed, she turned away, only to see Biddy blubbering happily behind her.

"God, I love the theater. No stiff upper lip for me. Give me good old sloppy emotion any day." She ruffled Biddy's hair. "Let's get out front before we embarrass ourselves."

Lindy waited for Jeremy at the standing-room wall. When he appeared, his euphoria was gone. His shoulders were rigid beneath his silk jacket. The muscles at each side of his mouth tightened and relaxed, broadcasting his warring emotions like a blinking neon sign. He gave Lindy a cursory look before turning to the stage and leaning on his elbows on the half wall.

Lindy turned to the stage, too. The houselights blinked, and she watched the audience members hurry to their seats.

As the houselights began to dim, Jeremy spoke into the air before him. "It's my company. I have to do what is best for it, and that means Carlotta has to go. David will be here tomorrow. As choreographer, he has to be consulted, though I'm pretty sure what his reaction will be. He almost pulled *Carmina* when we insisted he use Carlotta. I don't think she'll go without a fight. I shouldn't have waited so long." He snapped his head toward Lindy. His feverish blue eyes held hers for an instant before their image faded as the lights lowered to black. "Lindy." She peered at his silhouette in the darkness. "Don't say anything. I want to talk to Jack first. I do owe him that." He jumped as the *Holberg Suite* began and turned back to the stage. "This is not going to be pretty."

The entire company gathered in the hotel bar after the performance. It was an impromptu celebration. Jeremy bought the first round of drinks and made an eloquent toast. The company had taken over the bar, standing or sitting at tables in animated groups. They congratulated each other, laughed at the near misses they had overcome. No one mentioned Carlotta, and Jack was conspicuously missing.

Toward the end, Peter entered the bar with Alice in tow. His hand rested fraternally on her shoulder as he guided her to the bar and deposited her between Andrea and Kate. He glanced toward Lindy and took his beer to the other side of the room.

By the time Lindy and Biddy retired to their room, they were both a little drunk. Biddy lumbered crablike down the hall.

"Can't find my key," she said, both hands stuck into the pockets of her dance bag.

"I've got mine." It took several attempts before Lindy managed to get the key into the lock and open the door. Her hand groped for the panel of light switches inside the door. She slapped at the panel, turning on several lamps and the entrance light. She stared, understanding coming slowly to her intoxicated brain. Biddy bumped into her and giggled.

"Someone has been in our room."

"Whad'ja mean?" asked Biddy, nudging her way around Lindy. She stopped. "I don' see anythin'."

The room hadn't been disarranged, much. Drawers weren't emptied onto the floor. Papers hadn't been thrown around the room; the beds were only a little rumpled. But it was clear that someone had been searching for something.

"Oh, m' God, have we been robbed?" Biddy fell toward the dresser and opened the top drawer. "No, my money's still here. I know you're not supposed to leave money in your hotel room, but you gotta trust people sometime."

"Whoever it was, wasn't looking for cash. Look at your grant proposals. You'd never leave them that messy. And everything else is just a little off." Lindy's brain was beginning to clear.

"Should we call the manager?"

"No—No, let me think."

"What if they're still here?" Biddy looked around in horror.

"Oh, shit." Lindy jumped away from the bed and looked underneath it.

"Don't, Lindy. What would you do if you found somebody under there?"

Lindy looked under the other bed. "Check the bathroom."

"I'm not going in there alone."

They both went to the door of the bathroom. Lindy stuck her hand around the edge of the door and turned on the light. "Nobody here, thank God."

"Whew. I wish I hadn't drunk so much downstairs; I could use a drink."

"Forget it. Who would be searching our room, and for what?"

"Jack." The name came immediately to Biddy's lips. "He wasn't at the theater tonight or at the party. He could have searched our room then, but what would he be looking for? We didn't take anything, did we?"

Lindy shook her head. "Only the calculator tape, and he didn't know about that." It dawned on her in a point of blinding clarity. "Did Peter return the Barton Scenery invoice?"

Biddy grabbed at her hair, balancing her crutches under her arms. "I don't know. Everything happened so fast. We were all throwing things back into the briefcase. But if he didn't put it back, that means Jack thinks we have it. But we don't. Or maybe—" She turned to Lindy slowly, a look of incredulity spreading across her face. "Oh, Lindy. You don't think Peter could be involved, do you? He didn't come to the bar until later. Maybe it was him after all, and he thinks we know something more than we do."

"Sounds like you've been reading too many mysteries. Maybe the maid dropped the papers and wasn't neat about putting them back. Maybe there's a perfectly reasonable explanation for this." Lindy didn't believe it, but she knew her brain was still too fuzzy to think clearly. She didn't want to think that Peter might be the embezzler, and she didn't want to worry Biddy. What she needed most were two aspirins and sleep; they could figure it out in the morning.

"You're right. It's probably just our imaginations. Too much excitement." Biddy babbled on unconvincingly.

"Let's get to bed. I'm beat."

Ten

The telephone was ringing. Lindy rolled over and groped for the phone. The receiver bounced off the bedside table and hung from its cord. She managed to get it to her ear.

"Hello," she croaked. The sun shone through the partially opened curtains, casting a rectangle of light across the ends of the beds; the rest of the room was dark.

"It's Jeremy."

Lindy sat upright, willing the rest of her body and mind to consciousness. "What's up?"

"My blood pressure. Jack left a message. He's gone to New York. He won't be back until tomorrow."

"Shit. Does that mean tonight won't be 'Dump the Diva' night?"

"I don't know. David is coming in this afternoon. Carlotta's already been on the phone to me twice. There's no way she's going to miss tonight's performance. How a woman with a brain that small has made it this far is astounding."

"She's managed to use what gifts she has pretty effectively."

There was silence at the other end of the line. Lindy cringed. "Well, never mind," she said lightly. "We'll let David take a look tonight and wait until Jack gets back if we have to."

"I know you think I'm being a wuss on this, Lindy. You're probably right, but I owe Jack a lot."

"I think you're wonderful. What's one more day in the scheme of things? We'll see you at rehearsal." She hung up the phone. One more day. It would be hell, but they had made it this far. What was one more day?

Carlotta was back in form. She showed up to rehearse early, limping slightly. No one suggested she take another day off. She lurched through her steps, mowing over Paul, pushing dancers off their spacing, getting in the way. Lindy didn't stop to correct her. No one complained. There was an unspoken conspiracy to let Carlotta burn herself out. When the procession entered carrying the candelabras, she moved uncomfortably close to them. They held their straight line, and she narrowly missed knocking them over.

Not a moth to the flame, thought Lindy. A behemoth, and she held her tongue.

Most of the dancers stayed around the theater after rehearsal. Biddy sent out for food. They ate quietly in their dressing rooms; no one turned on music. A few dancers sat on the stoop outside the stage door smoking cigarettes; their hushed voices carried back into the theater through the crack left open by the pig iron.

By seven o'clock the tension was unbearable. Lindy went through the motions of giving last-minute notes. She reminded them that the choreographer would be in the audience that night—as if they could forget.

Carlotta was the only person who seemed unaffected by

the change in mood. She called for Alice every few minutes. Everyone else dressed themselves, helping each other with zippers, snaps, and hooks and eyes.

Jeremy came in with David Matthews around seven thirty. Matthews was short, wiry, and energetic. They made the rounds, saying hello, and wishing everyone a good performance. The dancers' responses were demure.

At seven forty-five, Lindy could stand it no longer. She found Biddy and herded her to their seats in the audience.

Jeremy and David Matthews were sitting several rows in front of them. Matthews was studying his program. Jeremy made an occasional comment. Lindy was pretty sure they weren't discussing business; Jeremy had decided to let the action speak for itself.

"I just hope they dance half as well as they did last night," whispered Biddy, and Lindy realized that she had been so preoccupied over the break-in and Jeremy's call, she had forgotten to tell Biddy what he had planned and how Jack's departure had postponed it. Biddy had managed to sleep through the entire conversation.

The houselights went out. The music began, and the curtain opened onto the foggy stage. Rebo and Juan carried Andrea to the cage. Carlotta entered and picked her up. The girl collapsed onto the floor, straight down, not forward where Carlotta had demanded she fall. Carlotta walked forward, kicking the girl's feet out of her way as she did.

Lindy flinched. "Hold on, Andrea, hold on," she said under her breath. Biddy patted her knee without taking her eyes off the stage.

The boys entered. They were electrifying. Matthews's head turned toward Jeremy. The girls' trio followed. Their timing and spacing were flawless, and Lindy began to relax. By the end of the trio for Mieko, Andrea, and Rebo, she had almost forgotten that Carlotta was back.

She shouldn't have. Carlotta entered for her solo. She looked ancient compared to the girls. Was this what the choreographer intended? Lindy didn't think so. The corps entered behind Carlotta, moving to the right. Carlotta should have moved with them, leading the group, but she stayed dead center like some idiot opera singer rooted to the spot. What did the bitch think she was doing? She only made herself look bad. Surely, she couldn't be that stupid, or was she just so arrogant that she didn't care?

The corps danced right past her. They were doing what they were supposed to do. They wouldn't be to blame if things went wrong. If they just stayed determined and didn't start embellishing, Carlotta would finish herself off.

By the time the final procession entered, Lindy was exhausted from holding her breath. Biddy sat bolt upright; her hands clenched the armrests. And then it happened. The procession started its turns; Carlotta moved away from Paul and ran right into Eric's arm. The force of the impact knocked the candelabra out of his hand, but he kept turning. Rebo's foot caught the edge of the candlestick, and it skidded across the stage. Carlotta tripped over it, and the flickering light mercifully went out.

Lindy covered her face with both hands and peeked through open fingers. Pick it up, somebody, she pleaded silently. Mieko kicked the candelabra into the wings.

Carlotta managed to regain her footing but hit Paul with such force that he staggered backward. He fought to press her above his head, but he couldn't manage it, and Carlotta dropped heavily onto his shoulder.

"Shit," said Biddy.

The people in front of them turned around and stared. Lindy even lowered her fingers in amazement.

"Sorry," said Biddy.

Lindy didn't even see how Carlotta and Paul managed to get to the top of the cage for the ending. The curtain was closing before she knew what had happened. Matthews rocketed out of his seat as the curtain rose for the bows. Jeremy followed him, eyes straight ahead.

Lindy jumped out of her seat and climbed over Biddy's legs. "You're on your own." She raced after the two men, squeezing past the early risers making their way to the lobby for intermission.

Jeremy and David Matthews were standing in the hall near the door to backstage. The hall was empty; the audience exited up the aisles and through the back doors.

Lindy stopped short as she rounded the corner. Pressing against the wall, she peeked out at the two men. Matthews had turned back to face Jeremy. His face was contorted with anger. Lindy could see his right eyebrow twitch rhythmically even from where she was standing, and not for the first time, she marveled at how insignificant details could leap out to capture one's attention.

"I want her out. What's wrong with you, Jeremy? You've always been smart, intuitive. Have you lost your grip?"

No answer. Another string of emotional accusations. Jeremy didn't attempt to interrupt him.

"I don't know what hold that bitch has over you, but I'm pulling *Carmina* if you don't get rid of her. Now. Understand?

Fire her, bribe her, break her goddamned leg if you have to, but she doesn't go on that stage again. I mean it."

He turned toward the stage door, then spun around and strode back up the hall toward Lindy. Lindy ducked back around the corner. He marched past her without seeing her, jostled a few people in the lobby, and hurried out the front doors.

Jeremy waited for his exit before he looked up.

"Well . . ." He waited for Lindy to emerge from her hiding place.

Lindy peered around the corner. "I guess he'll get a cab back to the hotel."

Jeremy seemed to be unscathed by the barrage of insults he had just sustained. He merely quirked one side of his mouth, casually slipped his arm around her shoulders and walked her to the door.

And then she realized that he had orchestrated the events completely. Of course. He had made David give him the ultimatum. David was the bad guy. Jeremy had no choice, and Jack would have no recourse but to accept the decision. She wanted to throw her arms around him and tell him how brilliant he was, but she just walked beside him grinning like an idiot.

Jeremy opened the door, and Lindy stopped smiling. There was pandemonium backstage. Carlotta held one of the candelabras, swinging it inches from Eric's head. He had been right. It looked like a modern version of the mad scene from *Giselle*. It would have been funny if Lindy hadn't known how heavy those candelabras were. Jeremy moved with feline speed, but Peter was there before him. He grabbed the candelabra from Carlotta and slapped her hard across the face.

She reeled from the force of it. Andrea grabbed Peter, wrapping both arms around him and trapping his arms in hers.

"Don't, she's not worth it," she sobbed.

Peter dropped the candelabra. It landed with a thud at his feet.

"It's all right," he said, freeing his arms and enclosing them around the trembling girl. "It's all right. She's gone."

Carlotta *was* gone. The door of her dressing room was shut. No one had even noticed her exit.

Jeremy picked up the candelabra and put it back on the prop table. He turned to Eric, ruffled his hair, and slapped his butt. "Well, bold one, had enough excitement? I think I see a gray hair or two."

Eric started to cry. Jeremy enclosed him in a bear hug. "I'm sure Lindy has notes. Get onstage." No one moved. "Now, and if you hurry, I'll buy the drinks." He led Eric away toward the office.

"Last one onstage buys the next round," yelled Rebo, who bounded off through the wing. Everyone else followed.

"Let the kid compose herself," said Peter, still embracing Andrea. "I'll send her out in a minute."

Lindy nodded. God, she loved these people. Self-indulgent, pampered, competitive, they sure knew how to pull together when they had to. She followed the others onto the stage.

She hadn't taken any notes. There was no time to give any, even if she had. There was another piece to do, and intermission was almost over.

"Look, guys—" she began.

"Some serious shit just went down," interrupted Rebo, "but we be cool. Right?"

"That's all I ask. Some serious shit has gone down, as

you say, but it's going to be okay. Just don't let this screw up the next piece. Got it?"

They nodded.

"Then change costumes and get back out here."

She didn't return to her seat for the *Holberg Suite* but stood in the back. She saw Biddy hobble back down the aisle and sit down. She must have been out front listening to the audience's comments. Well, she'd get the whole story when they got back to the hotel. Lindy was too agitated to explain things now.

Carlotta's dressing-room door was still closed when Lindy returned backstage after the show. With any luck, she had gone back to the hotel already. Maybe Jeremy had fired her after all. No, he would wait for Jack to return— as long as he returned before tomorrow's performance.

The dancers were still onstage. No one seemed eager to leave the comfort of the proscenium.

She walked into the cluster of bodies. "That was pretty good. You really pulled together. *Carmina*, however, was a bust, and I have a few notes. These things happen. Sometimes the poltergeists get onstage with you, and there's nothing you can do but keep muddling through." She spent the next few minutes giving notes that didn't really need to be given. She just wanted to spend time with them.

"Boys, you got too far downstage in the quartet. Andrea . . ." But Andrea wasn't onstage. "Never mind, I'll give her corrections tomorrow." Maybe she's seeking comfort from Peter, Lindy thought; they would make a nice couple. "All right, that's enough. Get dressed and on the bus. I'll find Jeremy. He owes us drinks."

"But what did David Matthews think?" asked Mieko.

The air was rent with a loud wailing.

"That bad?" said a voice from the back.

"Oh, shit," said Lindy. "Now what have you guys done?"

"That's not Carlotta," said Rebo. He rushed off the stage followed by Juan and Eric.

Carlotta's dressing-room door was open. Rebo stopped suddenly, causing a domino effect as dancers piled up behind him. Lindy slipped under his arm and froze.

Carlotta lay on the cement floor, still in her *Carmina* dress. One leg was bent under her, the knee sticking out in a grotesque parody of a ballet step. One arm was flung dramatically out to her side. It was the last theatrical gesture Carlotta Devine would ever make.

Kneeling by her feet, Andrea rocked back and forth, keening in a heart-wrenching soprano.

"Get back, all of you," shouted Lindy. There was movement to her right, and she started. Alice moved jerkily from behind the open door.

"I—I came in to get Carlotta's costume, and she was there—leaning over her." Alice began to whimper.

"Oh, Christ. Rebo, get them out of here."

Peter skidded through the door as the others backed away. "I was—what happened? Oh, shit."

"You'd better call nine-one-one. No, first, do you know how to find a pulse? Should we touch her?"

Peter stood mesmerized by the sight. Blood oozed out around Carlotta's head in a black Rorschach pattern.

"Peter."

He jerked convulsively, knelt down, and placed his fingers

under Carlotta's jaw. "Nothing," he said without looking up. "I'll call." He rushed out.

Lindy backed out the door and into Biddy and Jeremy. She turned to them, her lip trembling. But they were both staring at the figure on the floor.

Eleven

Jeremy was the first to recover. "Is she . . . ?"

Lindy nodded.

"What happened?"

She shrugged. Her voice seemed to be buried under piles of rubble.

Jeremy turned to Biddy. "Call the company together. Quick."

Biddy turned away, then turned back and looked at Jeremy as if seeing him for the first time.

"Move." She hurried away.

"Someone's called the police?"

"Peter." Lindy mouthed the word. She noticed the sheen of perspiration on Jeremy's forehead. It had sprung out suddenly, the only evidence that he was upset. She wondered for a second if he was going to be sick. She certainly felt sick, and she couldn't gather her thoughts. They were floating around the top of her head, but she couldn't catch them.

He didn't say anything else, nor did he move toward the body. He took Lindy by the elbow, pulled her out of the dressing room, and shut the door.

"Don't fall apart on me now." She saw his mouth moving, but the words sounded far away. His hand enclosed her jaw in a viselike grip, and he turned her face toward his. "Lindy, for Christ's sake."

She snapped out of her shock. "Right." She followed him to the huddle of dancers waiting near the prop table. They were all there. Some were crying; some had their arms around each other. Peter was standing like a sentinel between Alice and Andrea, who were sitting on two folding chairs.

Jeremy spoke. His voice pierced through the charged atmosphere. "Listen, and get this right. The police will be here soon. They'll probably ask all of us a lot of questions. If you know something, tell them. Do not embellish, do not guess, do not try to impress them and, above all"—he looked directly at Rebo—"do not give them attitude."

His eyes roved the faces that looked out from the shadows. His voice softened. "We all like to tell a good story. That's what makes us artists. But do not try to be entertaining. Just answer their questions, don't add anything.

"Now go to your dressing rooms. Don't talk. Don't try to guess what happened. Keep your minds blank." The sound of sirens rose in pitch as the police cars pulled into the parking lot, then warbled down to silence, punctuated by the slamming of car doors.

Jeremy walked over to Andrea, who was rising slowly out of her chair, and knelt beside her. "They will want to talk to you and Alice. Try to be clear and only tell the facts."

"I know, Peter already told me."

Jeremy shot Peter a questioning look.

Peter turned away.

Three uniformed policemen came through the stage door followed by EMTs rolling a stretcher.

"In there." Jeremy pointed into the hall toward the closed door of Carlotta's dressing room.

The older of the policemen nodded and motioned to one of the EMTs, who followed him toward the door of Carlotta's dressing room. The officer's squat frame progressed like a bulldozer. His flesh bulged over the collar of his police jacket.

The two accompanying officers stood aside as they passed. They were both young and seemed nervous.

One pulled out a notebook and crossed to Jeremy. "You're?"

"Jeremy Ash, the director of the company." The young man nodded solemnly. "If you could just tell everyone to stay put, our chief is on the way. He was off duty," he added by way of explanation.

Jeremy nodded.

The chief of police arrived minutes later. He was dressed in jeans and a plaid woolen jacket; the smell of cigar smoke wafted around him. He was accompanied by a taller man, also in jeans, who surveyed the area and moved casually off to the side.

"Chief O'Dell," said the young cop who had spoken to Jeremy. "Williams is in there with the rescue squad."

O'Dell nodded and walked toward the dressing room. His companion stayed behind.

"Hey, Bill, is that you?" asked the younger cop, suddenly aware of the other man's presence.

"Hi, Rory. Yeah, it's me. What do you have here?"

"Don't know yet." He shrugged. "We haven't talked to anybody. We were waiting for Chief O'Dell. What are you doing back on home turf?"

"Playing poker with my brother-in-law until a few minutes ago. I wanted to get away from urban crime for a few days. I hope this isn't going to be a busman's holiday."

Lindy's dulled senses snapped to attention at the words. She had been standing out of the way, watching the activity of the police with a detached calm. Now she looked at the man who was talking. He was big: big-boned and angular. He towered over the curly-headed Rory. His voice was low but resonated across the air so that his words were clearly audible to Lindy where she stood in the shadows several yards away. His seeming nonchalance was a stark contrast to the bustling activity around him, but it didn't have a calming effect. Lindy's teeth started chattering. He emitted an air of urbanity in spite of the jeans and worn leather hunting jacket he was wearing. There was something in his manner that unnerved Lindy. She took several deep breaths and yanked her gaze back to the other officer.

O'Dell stuck his head out of the door. "Bill, do you mind coming in here for a minute?"

Bill shoved his hands into his pockets and moved laconically toward the dressing-room door. He was interrupted by the entrance of a cadre of campus policemen, who crowded through the door and looked expectantly into the room.

"Oh, Christ." O'Dell nodded to Rory, who moved to stop the newly arrived group. "I need a goddamned circus."

He lowered his voice as Bill reached him. "Hartford is sending us a Scene of Crime Unit, but it'll be a while. Would you mind taking a look?"

Crime? thought Lindy. Of course. Carlotta could hardly have bashed in her own head. She hadn't seen a wound, but the amount of blood around Carlotta's head couldn't have come from a fall.

O'Dell called over to the other officer, who seemed to be trying to melt into the shadows as Lindy had been doing. "Joe, you and Rory start some interviews. And make sure no one leaves." He looked around. "Hey, you, there."

Lindy jumped.

"Who are you?"

"Lindy Graham, uh, Haggerty." Lindy was suddenly aware that she was the only person who had not fled to a dressing room. There was no sign of Biddy or Jeremy. She was completely alone. "I'm the rehearsal director."

O'Dell looked at Bill.

"Like a unit leader."

"Oh." He looked back at Lindy. "Well, Ms. Haggerty. How many people are still on the premises?"

"Sixteen dancers," she began, "if you don't count Carlotta." She motioned to the door behind him. "And the crew and—about thirty people, maybe more in the front."

"Oh, shit." O'Dell rolled his eyes heavenward.

Bill laughed. It changed into a cough when O'Dell shot him a glaring look.

"Williams, get out here. It's going to be one hell of a long night."

O'Dell and Bill replaced Williams and the EMTs in Carlotta's dressing room and closed the door. Several more uniformed men had arrived and were talking to Rory. They dispersed, and Rory knocked on the door to Jeremy's office.

"Sir, would you ask everyone to come out here?"

Jeremy began tapping lightly on each door. Two of the new policemen went to the prop room and herded out the crew, Peter and Alice among them.

Williams faced the group that was now crowded into

the backstage area. He unbuttoned his jacket. "Maybe you should all sit out in the auditorium. We'll need to talk to everyone present. It may take awhile; there are so many of you."

Lindy followed the others through the side door and out to the house seats. Williams came out onto the stage and explained briefly about the procedure of getting statements from everyone. He looked self-conscious, like an understudy who hadn't had time to memorize his lines.

The houselights were on. The light was harsh. Most of the dancers had not had time to remove their makeup, and their faces stood out in garish, Fellini-like masks.

There is nothing less glamorous than a fully lit theater, thought Lindy. And then it hit her. Carlotta was dead. The rescue squad hadn't even tried to resuscitate her or rush her to the hospital. Could we have brought her back to life, if we had tried? Were we guilty of not trying? She jerked out of her seat when she heard her name called, and a uniformed man beckoned to her to follow him.

She was led through the backstage to a room near the prop room. It was a large dressing room used for the chorus of large-scale productions. The company hadn't needed it, since they were a small group, and it had been locked since their arrival.

Now, Detective Williams sat at a wobbly card table in the middle of the room. His jacket lay on one of the benches that ran the length of the makeup tables. Standing next to him was a tall, spindly policewoman. Her uniform seemed pinned to her shoulders and dropped straight to the floor without a curve. Lindy inanely recited "Jack sprat could eat no fat" as she tried to calm the bats in her stomach.

Williams motioned her to the chair that faced him across the table. "Ms. Haggerty?"

"Graham." She sat down. "I use Graham for the stage," she added. It was a stupid thing to say. Williams raised his eyebrows. They were very bushy, but short, barely extending to the ends of his eyes. "My married name is Haggerty, but I go by Graham here. It's my professional name." She should cram a fist into her mouth before she made herself sound more ridiculous.

Williams nodded his head gravely and said, "Yes, I see." He asked her about the position she held with the company, some background information, and about the events of that night.

She told him about the scream, finding the body, calling the police. She willed herself not to elaborate. She gave the bare facts as she knew them. She recited them dully, as unemotionally as she could. Surely, they didn't think anyone had deliberately hurt Carlotta. It must have been an accident.

He was asking about doors. She dragged her attention back to what he was saying. "Excuse me?"

Yes, the stage door had been propped open. Yes, anyone could have come in. But that didn't usually happen. Security? Alice always collected everyone's valuables and locked them in a theater case in the costume room. The door to the hallway? Yes, it was unlocked so the directors could come and go. Sometimes, friends or fans came backstage. Did she see anyone come back that night? No, she hadn't noticed. Peter usually kept the area free of unnecessary visitors.

"Did anything unusual occur backstage tonight?" The

question jarred her from her rote responses. Clammy fingers seemed to creep around her neck.

"No, I didn't see anyone that shouldn't have been there. Why?"

Williams shifted in his seat. The policewoman shifted her weight to her other foot. Her limp uniform shifted to her other side.

"Among the company members."

"Oh."

"Was there?"

What should she say? How could she make this man understand that what had happened at intermission was not that unusual.

"When?" she stalled.

Williams leaned forward in his seat. "Was there not an altercation between Ms.—" He glanced down at his notes. "Ms. Devine and some of the company members?"

"Oh, that. It was just Carlotta having one of her attacks. She does that sometimes."

"Attacks?" He raised his eyes to hers, his pencil poised above his writing pad.

"Diva attacks. She likes—" Lindy took a strangled breath. Carlotta was dead. "Or rather, liked to throw her weight around. Just emotional outbursts. She did it all the time." She knew she was beginning to babble. She bit the inside of her cheek to stop herself. She concentrated on the sweet taste of her own blood. It helped her to concentrate. She told him about Carlotta stabbing at Eric with the candelabra.

"It's a prop in one of the dances, but Peter took it away from her." Carlotta had gone back to her dressing room.

They had gotten ready for the next piece. No, she didn't notice Carlotta leave. The door of her dressing room was closed. She hadn't seen her again until they heard the scream and found her on the floor of her dressing room.

She felt herself trembling. Delayed shock, said part of her brain. Carlotta dead. Lying on the cold, hard cement, stretched out in that ridiculous pose.

The policewoman handed her a tissue. Lindy put it to her face and bit harder into her cheek. Don't fall apart on me now.

"Do you know of anyone who would want to harm Ms. Devine?"

He looked directly at her face, trying to read the answer. Well, she didn't have one.

She steeled herself and returned his look. "She wasn't nice. No one liked her. But she was a common type in the theater; we were used to her."

Williams stood up. "Thank you, Ms. Graham."

"Am I free to go?" She sounded just like some suspect on one of Glen's cop shows. She wished now that she had paid more attention.

"Yes, but we'll need you to come down to the station tomorrow and sign your statement."

Lindy nodded and walked on wobbling knees to the door. She reached for the knob and turned it. "It was an accident, wasn't it? I mean, you don't think that . . ." She didn't finish the question. The two police officers were bent over the papers on the table. They didn't look up, and she closed the door behind her.

Joe was waiting outside the door to accompany her back to the auditorium. Several more uniformed men and women had arrived and were now moving methodically about the hallway. A yellow tape cordoned off Carlotta's dressing room and the surrounding area. They skirted the edge of the tape and returned backstage.

The man whom she had seen entering with Chief O'Dell was leaning against the light board, apparently comfortable to wait and watch. One leg was crossed over the other, and his arms were folded across his chest. He looked like a mummy from the set of *Aida*.

Lindy walked slowly forward. He watched her openly, a slight smile on his lips. "Kurt Weill comes to Connecticut," he said softly as she passed him. She didn't look at him; his words had chilled her very soul.

Lindy spent the next hour shuttling dancers back to the hotel. Jeremy stayed on until everyone had finished being interviewed and returned on the bus. When she finally staggered out of the elevator to the third floor, she found Biddy leaning over her dance bag, her cast balanced out to the side as she rummaged inside the bag. Papers and unidentifiable pieces of clothing were dumped haphazardly about the floor.

"Biddy, what are you doing?"

Biddy looked up from her bag. Her face was red from leaning over. "I still can't find the darn key. I always put it in the side pocket, but with all the distractions, I just can't find it."

"I bet someone returned it to the front desk." Lindy raised her eyebrows and handed Biddy her own key.

"Jack." Biddy pushed a wild mop of curls out of her face,

took the key, and turned the lock. Lindy gathered up the mess, tossing everything indiscriminately back into Biddy's bag and took it inside.

Biddy stood hunched over her crutches, staring into the minibar. "What's the strongest liquor in here, do you think?"

Lindy sank into one of the chairs at the table and dropped her bag to the floor. "Beats me. Brandy, I suppose, for shock. They're always giving ladies a nip of brandy in Victorian novels. Even though alcohol is a depressant not a stimulant. I had forgotten how much we drink on tour. It will make me fat."

"How can you think about your weight when Carlotta has been murdered?" snapped Biddy. "Oh, I'm sorry. I didn't mean to yell at you. I'm just so, it's just so, oh, dear."

"We don't know she was murdered."

"Juan saw them putting one of the candelabras in a box when he was going for his interview."

"What?"

"Juan saw the police . . ."

"I heard you. Maybe he was mistaken. Everyone's nerves are pretty strung out."

Biddy shook her head slowly. "They think Carlotta was murdered. That one of us did it."

"That's ridiculous," said Lindy, pushing her own conclusions aside. "People don't get killed with stage props. The candelabras are heavy; they might give someone a concussion, but you couldn't bash somebody's head in with one of them."

Biddy's face turned a sickly shade of gray.

"How about that brandy?" Lindy asked.

There was a light tap at the door. "Now what?" Lindy rose wearily from her seat and opened the door. Rebo, Eric, Juan and two corps boys named Richard and John were crowded around the opening. "We be bad," said Rebo, with his head lowered penitently.

"Is this your idea of comedy relief?"

"Shit, no, we're in deep shit." His eyes flashed at her.

"Then you had better come in." Lindy opened the door wider, and the men filed inside forming a perfect semicircle in front of her.

"For crying out loud, sit down and tell me what this is about." She paused, a sickening feeling rising in her stomach. "You didn't kill her, did you?"

"Lindy," gasped Biddy. John and Richard dropped onto the bed. Juan, Eric, and Rebo began a chorus of denials.

"Okay, just one of you talk." Lindy's own nerves were painfully near overload. She slowed her breathing, willed her heart rate to lower, closed her eyes, then opened them.

Rebo began talking. "We played the tricks on Carlotta." He looked around at his comrades. There was no hint of his jive accent when he spoke again. "It was my idea. You know, a bit of humor to take the edge off the bitch. But we didn't hurt her."

"The candelabra?"

"I stuck it outside her door. So when she opened it, she'd see it."

Lindy shrugged, not understanding.

"There was a note." Rebo wiped his face, his strong fingers spreading across his features. "It said . . ." He seemed genuinely embarrassed. "It said, 'If you can't stick it to us, use it on yourself.' " His voice cracked on the last word.

"That's disgusting," blurted out Biddy.

"*She* was disgusting. We tried to get it back before the police came, but Jeremy had shut the door, and it wasn't outside. The note wasn't there, either. Then Juan saw them bring it out of her room. Someone must have used it to kill her, and my fingerprints are going to be all over it."

"Our prints will be all over that room. We were always doing stuff in there," said Juan. He was visibly shaking.

"Did you tell this to the police?"

They shook their heads in perfect unison.

"Well, I think we had better. The police are smart, I think. They'll understand."

"Are you sure?" The question came from John. He looked so young and innocent, Lindy wanted to pat his head.

"Pretty sure. But regardless, you have to tell them before they ask you. It will save them a lot of trouble, and I'm sure they'll appreciate it in the long run."

"They're gonna crucify my ass," said Rebo.

"Why?"

Rebo looked at her incredulously. "Black and gay? The note? I'm dead."

"The cops are not all thick-necked racists, Rebo. They are concerned with finding the truth."

"Shit, Lindy, what movies have you been watching?" He had a point. She only knew about policemen from books, television, and the occasional precinct scandal reported in the newspaper. But wasn't there always at least one good guy on the force who fought for truth and justice? If there was, she would find him and badger him into doing the right thing.

"Guys, there is nothing we can do tonight. Just go to bed.

I don't know what's going to happen tomorrow, but the first thing we're going to do is tell all. Jeremy, Biddy, and I will go with you." They stood up and clustered around her. She found herself in the middle of a group hug, silent, slightly swaying, comforting one another.

The telephone rang. The group broke up. "Okay, guys, outta here." Lindy walked around the bed to answer the phone. "Pour those brandies will you, Biddy?"

"It's Jeremy, are you asleep?"

"Hardly. Are you back at the hotel? What happened after I left? What did they say?"

Lindy heard him release a heavy sigh. "I'm at the hotel. I hope they finish looking for whatever they're looking for before tomorrow's performance. If not, we'll have to open one of the chorus rooms and camp out until the week is over. I'll try to get rehearsal space at the campus for tomorrow. It's probably best to keep the kids busy. They asked a lot of questions and were still working when I came home on the bus. Oh, God, Lindy, she would have been out of here tomorrow. I shouldn't have waited."

"Did you call Jack?"

"I just tried. His machine was on. I left a message for him to call me. Oh, Christ." There was a long silence. "You and Biddy had better get some sleep. We'll need to meet pretty early tomorrow and get organized."

"There's just one more thing, Jeremy." She told him about the visit from Rebo and the boys, and what they had confessed.

"Damn, damn. I should have stopped them. I knew who was doing it, but quite frankly, I was enjoying it."

"Give yourself a break, Jeremy. You're responsible for running a company, not being mother, father, and nasty nanny to your employees. They're adults, every one of them." She took the glass of brandy that Biddy was holding out to her. "We'll see this through. You get some sleep, too."

Twelve

A chorus of uniform-clad policemen moved across the stage and climbed up the cage, carrying candelabras. The stage lights changed colors at an alarming rate: blues, reds, ambers succeeding each other with dizzying speed. The uniforms turned as a group and marched forward. Keep your lines, you're out of line, she yelled, but they kept coming, replicating themselves as the music crescendoed. It was deafening. Lindy clasped her hands over her ears and woke up.

She lay in the dark, heart pounding, breath labored, stuck in the abyss of interrupted sleep. The numbers of the clock on the bedside table glowed 3:22 A.M. She sat up, drawing her knees to her chest. Carlotta was dead. That was it. It came back to her with horrible clarity—the body, the questions, the boys' confession.

She pulled her body out of bed and crossed to the window. The parking lot below was quiet. Evenly spaced lampposts cast dim cones of light onto the parked cars that formed a perfect line around the perimeter of asphalt. When the sun rose, people would get into those cars and drive away, going on about their lives, carrying their own set of tragedies and disappointments with them.

A black car pulled slowly out of the lot. He was getting

an early start. Probably anxious to get on with his vacation or back to his wife and children. Lindy envied him; she wished she were on her way home. Or did she? Glen would be working. Cliff and Annie wouldn't be there. They didn't even know she had gone back to work. In her excitement, she had forgotten to call them.

Lindy pressed her forehead against the window and watched the blinking turn signal of the car as it turned into the street. Cliff and Annie had their own lives now. Even the weekly phone calls had gotten further apart. If this was the empty-nest syndrome, she thought, why am I the one who feels left out on a limb?

No, it was better that she was here and working, even with a murder, than rambling around an empty house waiting for the next adventure. This *was* the next adventure. She'd call the kids tomorrow. She wouldn't mention the murder. The car disappeared around the corner of the hotel, and Lindy turned from the window.

She had to get some sleep. Keeping order would be up to her tomorrow. Don't fall apart on me now, she whispered. She crawled back into bed and pulled the covers over her head. The next thing she was aware of was daylight.

The bedspread had fallen to the floor. Biddy was tiptoeing around the room, and the smell of coffee wafted from a trolley, which stood in the middle of the room.

"Breakfast," said Biddy, her voice barely above a whisper.

Lindy blinked at her. Whoever said that things always looked brighter in the morning was right about the first thirty seconds. It took about that long for Lindy to remember what had happened the night before. She didn't feel better at all.

She threw her feet onto the floor and took the cup of

coffee Biddy handed her. Neither of them spoke. It was an awkward silence, but neither of them was ready to face what had to be faced.

Biddy walked back to the trolley, added sugar to her coffee, took a sip, and put the cup down. She turned to face Lindy. "Who did it?" Her voice held an accusing note.

"Well, I didn't."

"Don't be ridiculous. I know you didn't, but who do you think could have? Was it one of us? Maybe somebody sneaked in."

"I think that's probably what happened." Lindy didn't believe that, but she wasn't ready to contemplate the alternatives. She also felt uncomfortable talking to Biddy. She had a comfy suburban safety net to run home to. She had Glen. She would have lots of activities to keep her mind off what had happened. Biddy only had this life, these people. If one of them turned out to be a murderer, Biddy's life would never be the same. There was a good chance the company would fold, even if Jeremy or Jack weren't involved. The publicity alone could finish them. Lesser scandals had destroyed companies before.

"Biddy, I won't desert you." She blurted it out.

"No matter what?"

Lindy looked at her cautiously. "No matter what."

"Do you think it's too early to call Jeremy?"

Lindy shook her head. Biddy dialed his extension. The conversation lasted only a few seconds.

"He's coming over. The police want to talk to us again."

"All of us?"

"Just the three of us, and Peter, and Jack when he gets back, for now anyway. What are we going to tell them?"

"Whatever they want to know. First, about the boys and their tricks. And then . . ." Lindy shrugged.

"Not about what we found in Jack's briefcase," Biddy pleaded. "Don't even tell Jeremy. It might not have anything to do with Carlotta, but they would think the worst. Please, Lindy."

"They'll probably find out in the course of their investigation."

"Please."

"Okay, we'll wait for a while. Maybe Jack will have an explanation, though it seems pretty incriminating."

"It couldn't have been Jack. He wasn't even here. And not Jeremy, or Peter, or you, or me."

"Well, at least not you or me. Even if you had tried to brain her with your cast, I doubt if you could have kicked that high." Lindy sighed. "I guess that means I'll miss my morning *barre*. Let me get dressed before Jeremy gets here."

Jeremy was sitting at the table when she came out of the shower. He was drinking coffee out of a glass.

"Sorry," she said, grabbing clothes out of the dresser drawer and dropping the towel she had wrapped around her to the floor. "I meant to hurry, but I guess I went into a trance in the shower."

"It's okay, take your time."

She threw on jeans and a sweatshirt and sat down. Her jeans felt a lot looser. "So now what? How many cups of coffee have you had?"

"A few. Do I seem a little hyper? I've been waiting for someone to wake up."

"You could have called us," said Biddy.

"I know, thanks. Chief O'Dell called. He has some more questions, though I can't imagine what more we can add."

Biddy gave Lindy a warning look.

"Where does he want us?" asked Lindy.

"Down at the station. I told him we'd come this morning, get it over with. I may sound callous, but my main concern is getting on with this tour, keeping everybody on an even keel."

It was an unceremonious morning. The station was located in the middle of the historic downtown, but it was a new brick building, one story with a flat roof. It looked pitifully small and mundane to Lindy. Of course, her knowledge of police stations came only from mysteries and television; both sources seemed terribly inaccurate.

They were interviewed separately. Lindy told about the boys' pranks, speaking the words into a tape recorder. While they were waiting to sign the typed statements, they compared notes, except Peter, who sat glumly in one of the metal and plastic chairs, a conspicuous distance away from the others.

It had taken two hours, but now they were driving back to the hotel. They had all lapsed into silence. Lindy considered turning on the radio, but decided it would be in poor taste. Instead, she began humming a Noël Coward tune under her breath, "Why must the show go on?"

"Oh, no, the dress."

Lindy slammed on the brakes, pulled the car to the curb, and turned to look at Biddy. Peter and Jeremy were staring at her, too.

"We don't have a dress for Andrea. The police have Carlotta's, and there isn't an extra one."

Lindy sighed deeply. "You just about scared me to death. We'll get Andrea something to wear."

She maneuvered the car back into traffic. Leave it to Biddy to be thinking about a costume at a time like this. Even distracted by murder, she was the consummate professional. The show must go on. Chief O'Dell had given them clearance to use the stage, though they wouldn't be able to use the downstairs dressing rooms. In lieu of the radio, Lindy began to hum again.

"Alice brought the extra fabric. I'll see if she can pull something together," said Peter. "She's probably already at the theater. Very efficient, that one."

It was the first time he had spoken to them that morning. After a curt "hello" when he met them at the car to go to the police station, he had maintained a preoccupied silence. When he hadn't offered information about his interview, no one had pressed him to talk. Lindy would have to talk to him later. She had a few questions of her own.

They dropped Biddy and Jeremy at the hotel to round up the company and bring them to the theater for rehearsal.

"It seems strange that we are being allowed back into the theater so quickly, don't you think?" she asked Peter as the two of them drove toward the theater.

Peter was staring out the passenger window. "Probably finished doing whatever it is they do."

"Do you think they'll let us go on to Hartford on Sunday?"

"No idea. I've never been in this kind of situation before."

Lindy kept her eyes glued to the road ahead. "When Sandra was hurt, wasn't there an investigation?" She heard

his intake of breath, but she didn't move her eyes from the
white line of the highway.

"How—" He gave up. "Yeah, there was an investigation.
It was ruled an accident."

"But you didn't believe that?"

"What are you getting at? You think Jeremy goes around
bashing dancers on the head? That's not funny," he added
in a harsh whisper.

"Jeremy?" Did Peter actually think Jeremy had killed
Carlotta? "If you blame Jeremy for the accident, why did
you come to work for him, Peter?"

"Leave me alone. I didn't kill the bitch."

She shouldn't have been so abrupt. It was cruel and
counterproductive. She began a more circuitous line of questioning.

"Do you think Alice will be able to finish a dress for
Andrea by tonight?"

"Probably. Like I said, she's efficient."

"Jeremy was lucky to get both of you."

"What's that supposed to mean?"

Lindy shrugged. "Just that Jeremy was lucky to lure
Alice away from a higher-paying, secure job at the ballet."

Peter looked blank. "He didn't lure her. When I signed
on, she asked me if I thought they needed a costume mistress. I said maybe, and that was it."

"Why would she want to leave her job?"

Peter rubbed the back of his neck. "I never thought about
it. The costume shop was big there. She probably was stuck
with menial jobs. Seniority and all that. She's duller than
dishwater, but she's good with fabric. With a smaller company, she gets to be her own boss, I guess."

They arrived at the theater. Peter jumped out of the car as soon as Lindy pulled into a parking place. "I'll find Alice," he said as he slammed the door.

He had outmaneuvered her. She had gotten off on a tangent about Alice and hadn't learned anything that would help her find out who was stealing from the company, or why Peter hadn't returned the invoice to Jack's briefcase. She slammed the door of the Volvo and followed him across the parking lot.

Peter was banging on the stage door when Lindy caught up with him. After several minutes, the door was opened by a policeman, who asked their names before he allowed them to enter.

Lindy stopped just inside the door. She was not prepared for the scene inside the theater. Yellow tape had been drawn over every door. It closed off the entrance to the hallway where all the first-floor dressing rooms were located. It was blocking the door to the prop room, the costume room, and the shop.

Peter strode over to the door of the shop. He was stopped by a policeman, whose frame barred the way in.

"What's going on?" asked Lindy, coming up behind Peter.

"They won't let me in. How am I supposed to set up for rehearsal when I have no access to the sets or props?" Peter threw his hands in the air.

"Sorry, ma'am, but we're still working in certain areas. As soon as we're finished, you'll be able to get back in." The officer looked at Peter. "The sooner you accept that, sir, the sooner I can get this area cleared. And you can thank the president of the university for even letting you continue with the show. It makes our work that much harder."

Peter growled and turned away.

They found Alice at a portable sewing machine set up in the chorus room, which had been used for the interviews the night before. Pieces of chiffon and gold lamé were draped over the benches and the back of the chair she was sitting on.

Alice looked up when they entered and smiled vaguely. "I'm working on a costume for Andrea. I realized that we might not get the, um, other one back, so I decided . . ." Her voice trailed off. "But they wouldn't let me in. That means dirty socks for tonight, I guess. And every time I need a straight pin, I have to ask, and someone brings them to me. It's going to take all day. But I don't mind," she added.

Peter rolled his eyes and left.

"Thank you, Alice. I knew you would have everything under control. Good work."

"Thank you," Alice murmured, looking out the door.

The company arrived a few minutes later. They entered single file through the stage door, each giving his or her name to the policeman on duty. The dancers who had dressing rooms on the second floor climbed wordlessly up the stairs.

"Be onstage in fifteen minutes," called Jeremy. He turned to the others. "Now, to find a place for the rest of us." By doubling up in the usable rooms and commandeering the chorus room, Jeremy and Lindy settled everyone in.

"They can't get to their makeup or the costumes," said Jeremy. "I hope these people step it up."

"Why did they close off all the rooms?" asked Biddy. She looked like she might burst into tears at any minute. "It's just not fair."

"I know it's hard for you to believe, Biddy," said Jeremy. "But life is not fair."

Biddy's bottom lip quivered.

"Pull yourselves together, you two. It's going to take a lot to get through today," said Lindy.

"Sorry, Bid." Jeremy kissed the top of her head.

Dancers began to move past them on their way to the stage. Lindy followed them. Peter was at the lighting panel, throwing on the stage lights.

"I think we'll run the music through the house system today instead of using the boom box. We could use the extra energy, if you don't mind running tape for me."

Peter shrugged. "Might as well, there's nothing else for me to do."

Lindy scanned the faces of the dancers as they warmed up. There wasn't much to read in the concentrated expressions on their faces. But their body language betrayed them. Tense, morose, scared—Lindy saw it all and steeled herself for the hours to come.

"When you're ready," she said to the stage in general and walked to the front. She said a few words. The speech was not thought-out, she was just anxious to get started. Moving was the only way to dispel the gloom.

She had to stop the music three times within the first couple of minutes.

"Come on, this is pretty lame. When the curtain opens, I want to see energy, vigor. You can do it. Take your places. Lift up. Get the weight out of your butts, or you'll end up looking like suburban housewives."

They lifted up. Well, it was a start. Mieko led the girls'

dance with precision. She is unflappable, thought Lindy. We could use a few more like that.

Andrea, however, was a mess. She fell out of balances, missed her turns. She moved through the steps like a somnambulist. Lindy pulled her aside. They started again. It went a little better.

The music filled the theater, louder than usual because there were no bodies in the house to absorb the sound. That helped. The dancers were pulling themselves together, slowly.

"Hold it. Peter, run the tape back to the beginning of the *Sarabande.*" She turned to the sextet. "Deep into the music, please. You're skittering along the surface of the notes. It makes your movement look superficial. Make it sensuous, draw it out. Lag slightly behind the beat." They began again.

"That's better, but there's something wrong with the spacing. Hold on a minute." Lindy jumped off the edge of the stage and jogged backward up the aisle surveying the spacing of the dancers. "Kate, pull over to the quarter mark. That's right. Try to make it there by the second phrase. Eric, does that throw your spacing off? No? Then let's try it."

The music started again.

"You're good at this, aren't you?" The voice came from behind her to the left.

Lindy looked back over her shoulder. It was the man from last night, Bill. He was stretched out comfortably in a seat a few rows behind her.

"Getting people to do what they're supposed to do, even under extreme conditions," he continued.

"The theater is one long, extreme condition," she replied. She turned away from him and walked back to the stage.

She hoisted herself up over the edge. What was he doing here?

She gave the dancers a break. She needed to move onto *Carmina*, but she dreaded it. She was sure that everyone else dreaded it, too. Just get them back on the damned horse, she told herself. The cage was released for use by the policeman in charge. Peter and one other stagehand assembled it. The other stagehands had been sent home.

Lindy looked at the dancers; nobody was moving to their places.

"Let's go," she said. They took their opening positions.

Mieko was deposited on the cage. Andrea picked her up without emotion. When Mieko's arms dropped to her side, Lindy saw her give Andrea a reassuring smile.

They managed to get through the piece. It wasn't a superb effort, but it was a hard-won attempt. Lindy dismissed them for dinner.

Bill was still sitting in the audience, slouched slightly in his seat, elbows resting on the armrests.

All right, let's just see what you want. Lindy braced herself and jumped off the edge of the stage. Hey, she thought, I can land on my feet. Not bad for being back to work for a week. She walked up the aisle, a thinner, stronger, more confident Lindy, and sat on the arm of the seat in front of him.

Bill straightened up. He didn't look like a policeman. His hair was short on the sides and in back. Brown with traces of lighter hair, gray maybe, laced through the longer hair on top, too long for a regulation haircut, surely. Did policemen still have regulation haircuts? And his face was too classically defined, and too pleasant-looking, to have spent his days with mayhem and murder. Prejudice, prejudice, thought Lindy as she perused his face. That's like saying all male dancers are raving queens; you should know better. But for so large a man, his features seemed too refined. He looked more like a director than a policeman.

He sat patiently watching her and then asked, "Are you linked up to a computer?"

She must have been staring at him longer than she realized. She felt her cheeks heat up, but knew her complexion wouldn't register the blush.

"Who are you?" she asked back.

"Bill Brandecker." He flashed her a wide smile and held out a big hand.

Lindy's hand disappeared into his. "Lindy Graham, unit leader."

Bill laughed. It was a hearty reverberation.

She waited for him to continue, but he just sat there, an expression of easy humor on his face. The kind of humor a person acquires by always standing a step away from the situation they're in, she thought.

"Are you a policeman?"

"Yes, no."

"Well, that about covers it."

He laughed again. "Yes, I'm a policeman of sorts, but no, I'm not working on this case. Not my, um, field."

Field? Didn't he mean jurisdiction? "Oh." Lindy slid off the armrest and onto the seat. "Just here for the show?"

"If you mean, do I get my kicks from watching other people's pain, the answer is no."

Now she blushed. Anger had that effect, and she was

more angry with him for turning her words around than embarrassed. She tried frantically to think of something nasty to reply, but her mind wouldn't cooperate. "Then why are you watching?"

"Because I'm here. Because Dell has been up all night trying to finish up so that the show can go on, as they say. Because I'm not burdened with finding the facts. Sometimes you learn a lot more just by watching."

Lindy felt chilled. "So you *are* working on the case."

"I'm just satisfying my curiosity. Do you mind?"

Of course she minded. It was the most heartless thing she had ever heard of. But she didn't say so. "Well, I hope we don't disappoint you," she said through clenched teeth.

That smile again. "Oh, I'm sure you won't."

Lindy gave him her best glare and left. That was a bust. In the old days she could have charmed the man into telling her whatever she wanted to know. But this guy seemed impervious to her. Maybe she wasn't in such great shape after all.

She practically crashed into Biddy, who was flying around the corner of the back hallway. Lindy caught hold of her to keep her from falling.

"Jack's back. He's really hysterical. He's going to upset everybody."

"Get everyone on the bus. I'll deal with Jack."

Lindy heard them before she saw them. They were standing in the stairwell. Jack had Jeremy backed into the wall.

"You're a Judas kiss; everything you touch, you destroy."

Jack's voice was shrill and hysterical. His face and lips were drained of color.

Lindy grabbed the man's shoulder. "For the love of God, Jack, control yourself. It isn't Jeremy's fault."

Jack looked at her, unseeing, and shook her hand away.

"It is his fault, and even you can't fix it, can she, Jeremy?" He grabbed his briefcase from the floor and rushed out the stage door.

"I guess I deserved that," said Jeremy mildly.

Lindy shook her head. How much abuse was the man willing to take? She turned away. Brandecker was standing a few feet away. His back was to them, but she recognized his silhouette. And she knew he had heard.

The performance was sold out. Jeremy had even relinquished their seats to the box office to be sold. Lindy stood next to Biddy along the half wall that separated the audience from the standing-room section. Jeremy stood on the other side of the aisle. Jack was next to him, an uneasy distance between them.

"Nothing like a little murder to fill a house."

Lindy turned slowly. "Hello, Mr. Brandecker. I didn't know you were a dance fan."

"Oh, I have all sorts of interests. Have the bosses made a truce?" he asked with a nod toward Jeremy and Jack.

"Biddy, this is Bill Brandecker, a 'sort of' policeman. This is Arabida McFee."

"A pleasure. Call me Bill."

Biddy nodded in some confusion. Bill settled himself next to Lindy. "The only thing I don't really like about live theater is that they don't sell popcorn."

"Well, at least you can get a beer at intermission."

Bill smiled his wide smile. "I'm a wine drinker myself."

Of course, you would be, thought Lindy. The man was infuriating.

"I'm always amazed at the public's thirst for blood," he continued. His voice seemed to carry to the balcony. "This crowd is particularly festive, don't you think?"

Lindy gritted her teeth. Biddy was staring at him in openmouthed disbelief.

"I bet a third of them just came out of morbid curiosity."

"You're wrong." Lindy choked on the words.

"Why else leave their cushy suburban homes, their big-screen televisions, their Surround Sound . . ."

"Oh, God, Glen. I forgot to call him, he'll be frantic." Lindy shoved her notebook at Biddy and ran backstage to the phone.

"Who's Glen?" Bill asked.

The machine picked up the first time she called. "Glen, I know you're there. Pick up, please." She hung up and called again. This time Glen answered.

"Hi, hon." The sound of sirens wailed in the background.

"Glen, I'm sorry I didn't call before, but so much has been happening."

"Hmm, yeow. Gruesome body."

"It was. It was just awful. And the police think it's murder."

"Of course they do, the guy's face was blown off."

"What?"

"Pretty graphic stuff, even for prime time."

Lindy blinked. Twice. How could he confuse a television

show with what was happening to her, here, now? "Glen, I mean here. A murder."

"I told you, you wouldn't like going back to work. Hey, do you mind calling me back when this show is over?"

"No. I don't mind." She blinked again. This time to cut off the incipient tears that stung her eyes. "I love you."

"Love you, too."

Lindy stared at the receiver. What she needed was a big hug and some sympathy. What she got was a rain check. She hung up the phone with more force than was necessary. It clattered around the hook before it finally settled down. She turned on her heel and stalked back to Biddy and Bill Brandecker at the back of the house.

Biddy handed the notebook back. "Things okay?"

Lindy nodded. If Brandecker didn't stop smiling, she was going to hit him. She could see the headlines of the local paper: BRANDECKER DECKED BY EX-DANCER. She didn't find it amusing.

The houselights dimmed, and the curtain opened to a smoke-filled stage. Bill stifled a laugh. Lindy stepped on his foot.

The phone was ringing when Biddy and Lindy opened the door to their hotel room. Lindy grabbed for it.

"Murder? What the hell are you talking about?"

"Hi, Glen." Lindy told him everything that had happened.

"You're coming home right now. Tonight."

"I can't. The police won't let anyone leave."

"Then I'm coming there."

Thank God. He really had been paying attention.

"I can't believe you got yourself into such a mess."

Lindy felt a wave of disappointment. He was coming to bail her out. And he was annoyed.

"Thanks, but I don't think that's such a good idea. One murder suspect in the family is enough."

"That's not funny, Lindy. Surely, they don't think you did it?"

"I don't think so, but you couldn't really do any good. I'll keep you posted, okay?"

"I guess. I do have a pretty important meeting tomorrow, but if you want me to come, I will."

"No, but thanks." She hung up the phone. She could handle this on her own; she was just out of practice. She had dealt with some pretty disastrous tours before. Of course, none of them had involved murder. . . .

"Is he coming?" Biddy handed her a glass of brandy.

"No." Lindy sipped at the brandy and grimaced. "At the rate things are going, maybe we should just buy a bottle of this stuff."

Biddy sat on the edge of the other bed. Their knees were almost touching. "What are we going to do?" Her face was the color of blanched almonds. Her hair stood out at bizarre angles.

"We're going to make a list. We know a lot more background than the police do at this point, and maybe we can figure out what we don't know."

"And do it before Wednesday?"

"Wednesday? Oh, Hartford. Surely, they'll let us go to Hartford. It's only an hour away. They can't expect everyone to stay neatly in place every time they have to investigate a murder."

"Even if we all had motives and opportunity?"

"Oh, Christ, Biddy, this isn't some book. Though if it were, I'd be tempted to turn to the last page and forget the suspense."

"Me too."

"I wish I had read more police procedurals, but they're just so boring. In the books I read, the police are either bumbling idiots or sophisticated, urbane gentlemen."

"Like Mr. Brandecker?"

"Hardly like Mr. Brandecker."

They moved to the table with paper and brandies before them and began to make a list of names and circumstances.

"For now, let's rule out you and me and the dancers on the second floor. That leaves the first floor. Paul."

Biddy wrote down his name. "His father was Carlotta's partner. She was mean to both of them."

Lindy frowned. "Seems pretty insubstantial, but write it down."

"Rebo?"

"Hmm, he did orchestrate those tricks, but leave a blank."

"Eric. Carlotta threatened him with the candelabra."

"Yeah, but, Biddy, the kid was petrified. I can't see him sneaking back and clubbing her with her own weapon. But write it down."

Biddy listed the others. Juan, Kate, Mieko. "Andrea? Ingenues have killed to get parts before."

"Only in the movies, but write it down."

"Jack? If he is stealing the money, and if Carlotta found out about it, then—"

"Exactly, add another column for things to investigate. For example, where is the money going? Certainly not to clothes or cars. That black Buick must be eight or ten years old. And the only wardrobe expense he has is that ridiculous boutonniere. Even out of season freesias can't be that expensive."

"I forgot, Jack was in the city that night."

The image of the parking lot appeared in Lindy's mind. A dark car, pulling out onto the street. It was a black car. She could still see it clearly in her mind.

"Maybe, write it down."

"Peter?"

Lindy considered, swirling the brandy around in the water glass. "He blames Jeremy for his sister's accident."

"What?"

"It kind of slipped out in a conversation we were having."

"But he's always nice to Jeremy. Why would he want to work for him if he hates him?"

"Exactly. And did he return the invoice to Jack's briefcase? I never got a chance to ask him. And if he didn't, why didn't he, and where is it? What if he's skimming the money and not Jack? And who broke into our room?"

"You're going too fast." Biddy was writing furiously. She stopped, pen poised in the air. "But what does all this have to do with Carlotta?"

"Beats me."

"I know, write it down."

"Alice."

Biddy shrugged. "She did leave a good job to come to work here. But I thought maybe she, well, sometimes she seems to like Peter."

"So she followed him here to be close to him? Kind of

pitiful. He hardly knows she exists. And he seems to favor Andrea."

"I think Andrea reminds him of Sandra."

"Sounds more like a soap opera than a murder."

"They do murder each other on soap operas."

"Oh, Biddy, you don't . . ."

"I spend a lot of time in hotel rooms. There's not much else to do. Usually."

"Well, your expertise may just come in handy. That leaves Jeremy."

"No, he wouldn't. I know him."

Lindy waited. Slowly Biddy wrote his name.

Gently and quietly Lindy said, "Carlotta was wrecking his company, but he was planning to fire her today."

"He was? But he didn't say anything."

"He told me not to tell anyone until he spoke to Jack. It was last night during the intermission. I overheard him talking to David Matthews. David was furious, but Jeremy had already decided before that. He would have told you, Biddy, if things hadn't happened the way they did."

"Then he would have no reason to kill her," Biddy said defensively.

"No. But I can't help thinking that it's all involved somehow. Jack comes to him and gets him to start a new company. Part of the deal must have been that he had to take Carlotta, but why?"

"He would never have agreed to that."

"But he did. Maybe not right away, but she was here. And Jeremy obviously hated her. What the hell could that relationship be? He would never have taken her for a lover, even if he weren't gay. Not his type."

Biddy blushed.

"I know, it is a disgusting thought, yuck."

"So now, what do we do?"

"Get some sleep. And tomorrow we start asking questions, subtly. And if the dance pixies stay with us, we'll be on our way to Hartford before Wednesday."

Thirteen

Lindy didn't remember dreaming. That was about the only good thing she could say for the morning. She had hoped for subliminal understanding while she slept, but she only felt confused. Maybe she should stay in bed and watch television. How bad could soap operas be? She rolled over, but years of discipline had resurfaced, and she couldn't drift back to sleep. She got up, walked over to the dresser, hoisted her right foot to the dresser top, and leaned over it, stretching. She changed feet and stretched again. Her mind began to clear.

She concentrated on *pliés*, forcing any thoughts about Carlotta's murder out of her head. Biddy groaned in her sleep. Lindy held her leg out to the side. By her last *grande battement* worry had begun to seep back into her consciousness. She picked up the phone and dialed room service, then lay down on the floor and began her sit-ups, thinking how lucky Biddy was to be able to sleep.

"Twenty-four, twenty-five, okay, that's it." She looked over to the huddle underneath the blanket. "Get up, Sleeping Beauty."

Biddy groaned. "Just a few more minutes."

"Coffee's on its way, another twenty-five sit-ups, and we're going to the mall."

"Shopping?"

"It's good therapy, remember? I think better when I'm spending money. Anyway, my clothes are getting too big."

"You can't have lost that much weight. You've only been here a week."

"If you don't have to struggle to get into your jeans, they're too big. Better a tight eight than a comfy ten."

"Oh, all right." Biddy rolled out of bed.

The mall was new, big, and surrounded by pastures. "It probably replaced some beautiful, old farmhouse," said Biddy as they drove into the parking lot.

"Or several beautiful, old farmhouses," returned Lindy. "Where shall we start? One of the big stores on the ends or the smaller ones in the middle?"

"We might as well start at one end and work our way through."

They took the escalator to the second floor of Neiman Marcus. "Head straight to the clearance rack," said Lindy.

"You still shop the clearance racks?"

"Old habits."

"But doesn't Glen make lots of money?"

"Sure, but anybody can look good in a three-hundred-dollar dress. It takes talent to find a good sale item."

"I doubt if I can even afford the sale items," said Biddy as she stopped in front of two long rows of dress racks marked "Additional 30% off."

She frowned. "The problem with shopping in big stores

is there is so much to choose from, and the clothes are so crammed into the racks that it's hard to see what's there."

"Just like the rest of our life. We've come to the right place."

"How about this?" Biddy pulled a slinky black pants suit from the tangle of clothes.

"No black pants suits and no stretch pants. I didn't wear them when I was twenty and weighed a hundred and five pounds, and I'm not going to wear them twenty-something years, and pounds, later."

"Okay, so we're at the mall, let's think."

"This isn't bad." Lindy held up a floor-length floral dress with a halter top. "It would look great on you. See if you can find it in a size six."

Biddy made a face.

"Too overstated? Maybe . . ."

"Lindy."

"Oh, all right. We have a murder. Nobody liked"—Lindy gulped—"the victim. There are plenty of motives, what about opportunity? It had to have happened sometime after Carlotta's outburst and before we heard Andrea scream. That's intermission, *Holberg*, and a few minutes of notes— less than an hour. I'll stay backstage after the intermission tonight and see who is where."

"That's a good idea, but what if it was an outsider?"

Lindy heaved a section of clothes backward to make more space and started searching through them. "Biddy, I think you had better give up on the outsider theory. I hope the police do catch some psychotic diva-hater that was seen lurking around the theater on Thursday night, but until then, we had better start piecing some ideas together. I don't like it any better than you do, but consider. If we tell the police about the missing money, they're going to blame Jack or Peter. If we tell them about Sandra's accident—well, you get the point, right?"

"I get the point."

"So concentrate on shopping; it will clear our heads."

They carried armloads of clothes into the fitting rooms. "So when we get back today, we'll start conducting our own interviews," Lindy said through the slats of the dressing cubicle's door. She stepped outside. "How's this?"

Biddy stuck her head out of the swinging door. "Too matronly."

"I thought so. What have you got on?"

Biddy stepped out into the aisle wearing a silk striped miniskirt with bolero jacket.

"Not bad, except for the cast. When does it come off?"

"Soon, I hope. I've got an appointment with the sports doctor after Hartford, if there is a Hartford," she added under her breath.

"Buy it. You can wear it opening night at the Joyce." If there is an opening night, she thought.

"Don't you think it's a bit . . . ?"

"Exactly, buy it."

They returned to their respective cubicles and came out in new outfits.

"Wow. That's perfect," said Biddy.

"And a size eight with plenty of room, almost." Lindy tugged at the waist and twirled around. Shots of silver thread sparkled against the muted patterns of gray and pink. The dress was cut high across the neck and plunged to the waist in back where the bias-cut skirt cascaded to the knee. "And I can even wear my new stilettos."

"Better you than me."

"Well, at least there's one advantage to breaking your leg."

They made their purchases; Lindy threw two pairs of size-eight jeans on the counter.

"Don't you want to try them on?" asked the silver-haired clerk.

"They will fit," said Lindy. "I will them to fit."

Biddy giggled. Some of the color had returned to her cheeks.

They stopped on the first floor, browsing at the jewelry counter. "So are you going to save the dress to wear for Glen or maybe wear it for a certain good-looking police person?" asked Biddy as she slowly turned a display case.

Lindy ran her fingers over a pair of dangling earrings, working at keeping the corners of her mouth from turning up. A vision of her wowing Bill Brandecker rose up in her mind. Maybe a new conquest was just what she needed; maybe Glen could use a little competition.

The thought of Glen brought her back to earth with a thud. There was no way she was going to screw up the last twenty years for a temporary fling, no matter how enticing. "Certainly not. I'm a happily married suburban housewife." She plucked the earrings from the rack, giving play to the last of a fantasy that would never be acted on. "I think these earrings are perfect." She bought them. "There goes a week's salary. I can't afford to work."

Biddy's face clouded over. "Speaking of salaries."

"Okay, forget shopping; let's get to the theater. I'll try to pump info out of Peter, and maybe talk to Alice. You take Paul and the boys."

The stage door was still locked. Once they were let inside, they separated. Lindy found Alice folding laundry in the costume room.

"They finally let me back in," she said without looking up.

"Maybe they're going to finish up today," said Lindy. "There seem to be more uniforms but less tape."

"Do you think so?" It was the most animation Lindy could remember seeing from Alice. She sat down on a trunk.

"It must be pretty hard working like this."

No response from Alice.

"Having to make a new dress on such short notice. I wonder why they didn't have an extra one made up already."

"They ran over budget, I think. Anyway, I just added some lamé to the inside of Andrea's robe. There wasn't enough fabric to make a new one. And I constructed a pattern for the dress from one of the corps dresses and adapted it."

"Carlotta must have been hard to work with."

Alice's mouth tightened at one corner. "I didn't mind her."

"She could be really nasty, though."

"She didn't bother me much. Saved it for the others, I guess."

Lindy settled in for the long haul. She watched Alice's face. "She really put it to Andrea, didn't she?"

"She was jealous," Alice said, lowering her eyes to the socks she was holding. She began folding them into a ball, tossed them into a basket, and retrieved two more. "Andrea is pretty and talented, but Carlotta was stupid. The way she treated her only made Andrea seem even better."

That was certainly true. Just about everyone had been ready to throw down the gauntlet for the young ingenue. And pretty astute of Alice to be aware of it. She was always in and out of dressing rooms, backstage, collecting costumes—always around, never noticed. What else could she have observed? At this rate, it would take Lindy all day to get information from the stolid costume mistress.

Lindy leaned back on her hands and tried to look relaxed. "She sure had Jack on a nose ring."

Alice threw another ball of socks into the basket, then her face lightened. "She was horrible to him. The things she called him . . ."

"In front of you?"

Alice nodded. "I didn't mind."

Lindy held her breath. How could the girl be so damned complacent? She willed Alice to keep talking.

"She was always threatening him. 'You'll never get rid of me.' Stuff like that. I mean, if somebody wanted to kill her . . ." She left the rest unsaid but gave Lindy a meaningful look. It was the first time she had made prolonged eye contact with Lindy. It was unsettling. Alice dropped her focus back to the laundry basket. "But then, when I came in and saw Andrea leaning over the body—well, like, that makes sense, too."

"You think Andrea might have killed her?" Lindy asked incredulously.

"Well, I hate to think—you know, but she could be pretty

high-strung, and that's what the police think, isn't it? That it's the person who discovers the body, like?"

God, the whole world was watching prime-time cop shows, thought Lindy, and Alice works nights.

"I have no idea. Well, I better get to work." Lindy walked out of the room, her head spinning. Too many suspects, too many motives, too complicated for me, she thought despondently. I hope the police are better at this than we are.

She ran into Peter in the hallway. He was wiping his hands on a paper towel and looking murderous. His eyes narrowed when he saw her. He twisted the paper in his hands until it was a tight roll and tossed it toward the trash can. It hit the rim and bounced onto the floor. "Now they're fingerprinting everybody in the chorus room. Better get it done."

He walked past her, shoulders rigid, and Lindy felt a lurch of compassion. Stop it, she thought. No favorites, keep your mind objective. She entered the room. Rory looked up from his clipboard and motioned her to a table covered with cards, ink pads, and metal boxes.

Lindy remembered taking Cliff and Annie to the local police station to get their prints taken as part of a Protect Our Children Campaign. She missed them terribly. Annie had cried when they took her fingerprints. She was only seven, and she was afraid the ink wouldn't come off. She didn't want her friends to see her black fingers when she played her cello in the school orchestra.

Glen had laughed and gone to wait in the car, but Cliff had wiped each finger until the ink faded to gray, then took her into the men's room. While Lindy stood guard at the door, Cliff scrubbed Annie's hands until they glowed pink.

Rory rolled the tips of her fingers across the ink pad, pressing each one into the appropriate box on a piece of white cardboard. Ten boxes, ten fingers.

The procedure didn't take long, but her hands were shaking the whole time. She felt guilty. Did she look guilty? And what about the others?

She tossed her paper towel in the garbage and finished wiping her fingers on her jeans. Peter wasn't in the shop or the costume room. She found him in the small storage room at the end of the hall. The room was about ten feet square, dim, and smelling of dust and machine oil. Two walls were covered by rusty metal shelves that held wooden crates of hand props. Each box was labeled in broad black letters: LANTERNS, REVOLVERS, FANS, CANES. A row of stage rifles lined a cabinet on the opposite wall.

Lindy cleared her throat. Peter whirled around at the sound, and she yelped in surprise. He was holding a long military sword; the tip was pointed at Lindy's solar plexus.

"Planning a duel? I think one of the guns would be more effective." She pulled the crate of revolvers out a few inches and looked inside. "Colt forty-five? No, you don't have a ten-gallon hat. Derringer? Only for saloon girls. What's this?" She held up a snub-nosed pistol with a pearl handle.

"Beats me; props aren't my expertise."

"Maybe the sword would be better. More romantic. The sound of metal clanging in the ears of some fair damsel as her lovers fight to the death."

Peter shook his head and slid the sword back onto the shelf. He smiled faintly. "Sometimes, Lindy, you are so . . . so absolutely . . . ."

"I know, that's what they all say," she said lightly.

"Have a seat? I know you're going to badger me until you get your way, and I'm getting tired of trying to avoid you." He upturned two truncated stools, the kind used by milkmaids, and they sat down. Peter's knees stuck up by his ears; he stretched his feet out in front of him. "I like this room. Cozy, in its own way, surrounded by the spirits of past plays. I find it comforting."

"Let's cut to the chase, shall we? Who do you think murdered Carlotta?"

Peter's eyes widened, the brown irises dark and arresting and deep. A woman could get lost in those eyes, thought Lindy.

"Not Andrea."

"But who?"

"Jack or Jeremy. My bet is Jeremy. It wouldn't be the first time he had—" He stopped. Lindy watched his Adam's apple twitch spasmodically.

"I know this is hard for you, but you have to help me with some background. Why do you blame Jeremy? Sandra's fall was an accident."

"That's what they finally said. But they suspected him at first. She had to have hit the radiator with such force, somebody must have pushed her or thrown her, but they couldn't prove it, or they didn't try." Peter dropped his head into his hands. His long, pale fingers made tracks through the black strands of his hair.

"But why would he want to hurt her?"

Peter looked up, templing his hands in front of his lips like a child praying. "I don't know. I was on tour in Europe when it happened. He always seemed to adore her. But then she fell in love. She wrote me that she wanted to get married.

Maybe he didn't want to lose his best dancer. She was good, not just a technician. She had such energy, such joy. By the time I got back she was—it was—damn it, Lindy, don't make me do this."

"All right." She dropped to her knees and pulled his hands from his face. "Why didn't you return the invoice to Jack's briefcase?"

"How did you know that?"

"Someone searched our room."

"When?"

"The night after we rifled Jack's briefcase. Wednesday, I think."

Peter stood up and pulled Lindy to her feet. "You and Biddy, be careful. Did you tell the police?" His thumbs were digging into her upper arms.

Lindy hesitated only for a moment. "No, Biddy made me promise not to. She's trying to save this company, but it's just a matter of time. Peter, why didn't you return the invoice?" Gooseflesh had broken out on her arms, and her scalp was charged with fiery fingers of electricity.

"Because I wanted to make sure. Check with Atlantic."

"And did you?"

"Yeah, the company pulled the order during the last tour. Told them that *Carmina* had been postponed, and they wouldn't need the structure. Atlantic returned the specs and took the normal cancellation percentage. Just a few hundred dollars, nothing compared to what Jack or Jeremy made on the deal with Barton. I called them, too. They're a body shop."

"You mean for cars?"

"Exactly. They barely spoke English, and when I mentioned Jack's name, they forgot what little they knew." He seemed to have forgotten that he was holding Lindy by the arms. His grip had drawn her up on tiptoe from its intensity.

"So it was Jack."

"You thought it was me." His face wore an expression of bleak disappointment.

"Not for a minute."

Peter's fingers loosened, but still he held her in front of him. "I wouldn't do that to the company; I care about them. It's Jeremy I hate. Obviously, I had an ulterior motive for working here. I thought if I was around, if I could watch him, he'd slip up, and I'd finally know for sure what happened to Sandra. I don't know why it's so important to me. It won't change anything. Nothing will."

He swallowed. "There's one more thing. Remember the night the batten fell? It—" He glanced past her shoulder and shut his eyes. "Shit." He released her and strode out of the storage room.

Alice was standing in the doorway.

Lindy caught up with him at the prop table. She had forgotten about the rehearsal completely. Dancers were already on the stage; a few were coming out of the chorus room wiping their hands. "Peter, what about the batten? We have to join forces on this. It's everyone's livelihood."

"We're not necessarily on the same side, Lindy." His whole body went rigid. "Onstage, everybody." He brushed past her and headed for the stage.

Lindy turned around and let out an exasperated sigh. "Bill, how nice to see you."

His expression was unreadable, but he certainly wasn't smiling. "Talking shop? Or doing a little amateur sleuthing?"

"Excuse me, I have to start the rehearsal."

"Leave it to the police, Lindy. They know what they're doing. That's why they get paid."

Lindy turned away and lifted her chin. Her back was to him, and he couldn't see her face, but maybe he'd pick up on the body language as she walked away. She heard Biddy come up behind her.

"What's he doing here?"

"Making me uncomfortable, for starters."

"Do you think he's being paid to keep an eye on us?"

Lindy considered. "Maybe when he said 'sort of' policeman, he meant he was a private investigator. That would make sense."

"Yeah. Anyway, I found out an interesting piece of information from the boys."

"Tell me. But look like you're talking shop so he won't try to read our lips."

"Do you think he can do that?"

Lindy shook her head. "I wouldn't put it past him. What did you learn?" Lindy leaned over to cue the boom box.

"The boys think Jack gambles. Juan overheard Carlotta saying to him that his little compulsion had wrecked lives and was going to finish off the company."

"That's something I hadn't thought of. It would explain where the money was going. From the way he dresses, he must lose a lot. What did Jack say to her?"

"Juan didn't stick around to find out."

"Well, that casts a new light on things. Carlotta concerned for somebody else? Do you think she was trying to convince him to stop?"

"Juan said she sounded like she was putting the screws to him."

"That sounds more like Carlotta. But it does add a whole new twist to the problem." She stood up. "Places, please." She turned to Biddy. "All we need is another element to grapple with. We're drowning in too many possibilities already."

Before Lindy had a chance to begin the rehearsal, Jack appeared at her elbow. "Sorry for interrupting, but can I have a couple of minutes with the company?"

Lindy nodded and called the dancers over.

"Some good news in all of this," said Jack in a dry voice. "The bank has cleared our checks, and I have paychecks today. Those of you who have direct deposit have already had your checks deposited."

There was an approving murmur from the group. They all looked a bit haggard; maybe today would turn things around.

"Thank you, Lindy." Jack's eyes were black slits surrounded by puffy skin; his whole face seemed to sag. His jacket hung limply around his rounded torso, and he hadn't bothered to put on his boutonniere. But when he walked away, Lindy noticed there was a spring to his ordinarily frenetic stride.

"Wow, he must be upset," said Biddy. "I think this is the first time I've ever seen Jack without a flower in his lapel."

"Or maybe the florist couldn't—" Lindy stopped in mid-sentence. "Freesias." She was such a dolt. Or maybe it was just a coincidence. That was more likely. "Freesias," she said again to no one in particular.

"What . . . what?" asked Biddy, a look of concern spreading across her face.

Lindy ignored her. "All right, everybody. Give me lots of energy. We'll have a short rehearsal. Give you some time to spend those paychecks."

"What?" Biddy repeated.

"It may be nothing, but you and I are taking a little drive after rehearsal."

Two hours later, having successfully eluded Brandecker, or so they hoped, Lindy and Biddy were driving down Fox Hollow Road on their way to the Hollingwood Gardens Nursing Home. Lindy hadn't explained what they were doing. It was too nebulous at the moment. Ideas, events, relationships were popping around inside her head like hundreds of corn kernels. With luck, they might settle into a pattern that made sense.

Lindy led Biddy through the front lobby.

"Posh, isn't it?" said Biddy. "Do you think Peter pays for it? I don't think they have family left. Maybe insurance?"

"Something else we need to find out."

"Good day, ladies, could you please sign our guest register?" Behind the reception desk sat a wizened lady in a pink floral wrapper. Her eyes twinkled like blue glass, but the effect was spoiled by the crust that had formed in each corner.

"Mrs. Harrell, thank you, my dear, for helping me out. I'll take over again." Mrs. Harrell was replaced by a carefully coifed woman in a tasteful tweed suit.

She turned to Lindy and Biddy with a pleasant smile. "Every time I leave my station, she pops right in. I hope she didn't say anything, well, you know. We have some real characters here."

Lindy had signed the register before it occurred to her to use a false name. If Peter found out she had been back, he would not be happy, and she felt a certain trepidation about provoking him into anger. She guessed that once that nearly implacable facade cracked, the emotions released would be intense and possibly dangerous.

As she and Biddy walked down the hall, Lindy tried to retrace her path from her first visit. All the hallways were painted a pastel blue beneath steel handrails and were covered with flocked fleur-de-lis wallpaper above. Lindy couldn't find any features that distinguished one hallway from another, and she wondered how often patients roamed the halls without a clue as to where they were. She was about to concede that she was lost when she caught sight of Daneeta coming down the hall. An orange-and-black University jacket was thrown over the shoulders of her uniform, and the strap of her shoulder bag hung over the jacket. She must be getting off work.

"Daneeta." The woman slowed as she reached them, then recognition showed on her face.

"You're Miss Angie's friend. If you're looking for Sandra's room, you sure are lost."

"I thought we might be. This is my friend Biddy. She's also a friend of Angie's."

"Nice to meet you." Daneeta began walking back the way they had just come. "Just turn right at this next corridor, then left at the next, and you'll see the nurses' station. Keep going straight, and her room's on the right."

"Would you mind terribly taking us there? We're pretty

bad at directions. I know you must be in a hurry to get home, but I'd really appreciate it."

Daneeta didn't answer but led them down the corridor to the right. The nurse on duty looked up as they passed. "People to see Sandra Dowd," Daneeta said.

"Oh, her brother's here. I think he took her down to the solarium. It's such a nice day."

Daneeta nodded. "You can see the solarium from her window. Save you the trouble of chasing around after them."

"Would you mind going with us?" Daneeta must think she was an idiot, but Lindy needed to talk to her alone.

Daneeta shrugged and led them down the hall.

Lindy's heart began to pound against her ribs. Please don't let us run into Peter, she petitioned to no one in particular. Biddy's face was blotched with pink patches. Like the Cowardly Lion meeting the great and powerful Oz, she looked like she might bolt and run at any moment.

Lindy slowed as they reached Sandra's door, then peered inside. Empty. She stepped inside. The bowl of flowers sat on the bedside table, an enormous arrangement of yellow and white freesias. She touched Biddy's arm and indicated the arrangement with her head.

"What?" whispered Biddy. "I don't understand."

They moved inside the room. Daneeta seemed to have lost her urgency to get home.

"What?" she asked.

"Daneeta, does the nursing home provide flowers for their, um, guests?"

"No. Oh, you mean these? They're beautiful, aren't they. He sends them every couple of weeks. So thoughtful. You wouldn't believe how many folks here are just out of sight, out of mind. He's a good man, Mr. Peter. He takes care of his own."

"Her brother sends them?"

"I guess so. No one else visits her."

"How could we find out?" asked Biddy.

Daneeta's face screwed up. "Why do you want to know?"

Lindy waffled for a second and said, "It's important. It's hard to explain, but something is going on in our company, and we think it has to do with the flowers."

"Why don't you just ask her brother?" Daneeta moved to the window. "They're out there now."

Lindy looked past Daneeta. The solarium was about twenty feet away, glass-enclosed and planted with potted shrubs and drifts of spring flowers. Peter and Sandra sat in full view, separated from them only by the plate glass of the solarium wall. She shrunk back. Biddy stared mesmerized by the scene before her. Peter was sitting in a white wrought-iron lawn chair, leaning forward toward Sandra's wheel-chair. He held her limp hands in his. His thumb moved gently across the knuckles of her sculpted fingers.

"We shouldn't be watching," cried Biddy. "I didn't know. How awful."

Lindy dragged her away from the window. Tears had sprung into her eyes and trickled down the groove between her nose and cheek.

Daneeta handed Biddy a tissue and said gently, "Why don't you just wait here for them? It's her dinnertime. They should be coming back in a few minutes. You could ask about the flowers then."

Lindy fought with the unreasonable panic growing inside

her. "Look, Daneeta. We don't have much time. Someone who works with us, with Peter, has been murdered."

"I read about that in the papers. That was you?"

"Yes, and we need to know who sends those flowers. It could be really important."

"You mean they think that Peter might have killed that woman? Never." Daneeta's face screwed up again. She seemed to have only two expressions, benign smile and distorted worry.

"We don't know what the police think, but we have to find out before they do."

"Then come with me." Daneeta was out the door before Lindy could grab Biddy and follow.

She was standing over a computer, fingers running rapidly over the keyboard, by the time Lindy and Biddy caught up to her. The computer took up the entire space of the records office, which seemed to be a converted storage closet.

"Armstrong Florist. It's local. But no name of the sender is listed." Daneeta turned abruptly and screwed up her face at them. "I hope you're not up to something bad. Those two people have been through enough."

"We're trying to help," said Biddy.

"That's all right, then." Daneeta's face returned to its smile. "Let's get out of here before someone sees us and starts asking questions."

Lindy grabbed a pen and copied down the number of the florist on her palm. "You've been a great help, Daneeta. Just keep your fingers crossed. Now, where can I find a pay phone?"

The pay phone was placed unobtrusively in an alcove off

the main lobby. An arrangement of silk flowers sat on a small telephone table; beneath it were a pen and a writing tablet bearing the name of the nursing home. Lindy dialed the number. This time she remembered to use a false name.

Her cousin was a patient at the Hollingwood Gardens Nursing Home. She had just come from Indiana (well, why not) to visit her, and she was wondering who sent those lovely freesias. She wanted to thank them for their thoughtfulness. Sandra Dowd. Yes, I see. Yes, he's always been so kind to the family.

Biddy shifted from one crutch to the other as she listened to the one-sided conversation. Her head darted from side to side as she kept watch for Peter, who would have to pass them as he left the nursing home.

Lindy hung up the phone. "It's Jack. He has an account there."

"That's really . . ." Biddy searched the air. "Kind?"

"Weird is more like it," said Lindy with forced patience. "Doesn't it strike you as a little ritualistic? He sends her freesias, and he always wears one. Like some lover's symbol."

They stared at each other. Was it possible?

"That's pretty farfetched," said Biddy, shaking her head. "I can't see Sandra in love with Jack. I mean, he's nice but not exactly the type that young, beautiful girls go for. And, anyway, what could this possibly have to do with Carlotta? Unless, she was in love with Jack. No, impossible. He doesn't fit the image of—"

Lindy raised her finger to her lips and closed her eyes. "Don't move." She mouthed the words at Biddy.

Biddy froze.

It would only take a few seconds for him to pass from their view. But time had slowed down as it tended to do in bad dreams and embarrassing situations. Peter passed the reception desk moving in freeze-frame slowness. Lindy held her breath. Why were they sneaking around like this? She should have just told Peter what they were doing. He probably would help them. If he could be trusted. But could he?

Peter's movements and Lindy's thoughts snapped back into real time as the figure of Daneeta appeared, her body blocking the view of the pay phone. She chatted animatedly to Peter as she led him to the door. She waved him a friendly goodbye, then turned and wiggled her fingers in the direction of the phone and left by the front door.

"Thanks, Daneeta, we owe you."

The house was sold out again that night. Instead of staying away, the audience packed the theater, and there was a definite "festive" mood in the air. Though Lindy was loath to use Bill's description, she had to admit that Carlotta's death had been good for business. So far, anyway. Hopefully, the whole sordid affair would be cleared up without doing permanent damage, except to Carlotta, of course.

She rushed backstage while the dancers took their bows for *Carmina*. She watched as they filed off the stage, deposited the candelabras back onto the prop table, and went through the door to the hall and back to the dressing rooms. The police tape had been removed, and everyone was back in their original rooms. Carlotta's room was still taped, and a padlock had been added to keep everyone out.

Everyone was where they should be. Dancers dressed for the next piece. Toilets flushed. One of the boys called for

Alice. She shuffled into their dressing room with a pair of socks and exited, tossing a used pair into the garbage can next to the door.

Peter was overseeing the demolition of the cage. It would be completely dismantled so that it could be loaded into the truck the next morning for the move to Hartford. The night of the murder it had just been removed to the back of stage right, out of the way of entrances and crossovers.

Jeremy wasn't backstage. Lindy had left him talking to Biddy in the back of the house. On Thursday night, he would have been in his office with Eric. But Eric would have had to leave to dress for the next piece. Lindy looked through the door to the hall. From where she stood, she could see the door of Carlotta's dressing room and part of the opening to the boys' room.

Across the stage, two stagehands stood along the rail. They began to pull the ropes of the counterweight system, hand over hand like sailors hoisting a sail. The backdrop for *Carmina* rose into the fly space above the stage, and the scrim for *Holberg Suite* lowered to replace it.

Peter had returned to the lighting panel and was speaking into a headset to the follow-spot operators in the booth located at the back of the balcony. He would call the show from the board, while two lighting men ran the cues next to him.

None of the equipment in the theater was computerized. Old-fashioned, unwieldy, and slow, it would take everyone's full attention to get through each piece. So who would have time to leave their station and kill Carlotta?

Peter called five minutes. Dancers began to take their places for the next dance. Lindy moved out of the way to the far side of the light board. A stagehand readied himself at the front curtain, waiting for his cue. Two others manned the light board. The others drifted back into the shop to wait for the end of the piece when they would be needed again. The hallway was empty; everyone was focused on the beginning of the *Holberg Suite*.

"Places, please." Lindy heard Peter's steady voice give the cue. "Warn on blackout. Warn on curtain. Blackout, go." All light went out onstage. Only a small lamp on the light board illuminated the panel. The rest of the backstage area, as well as the stage itself, was engulfed in darkness. "Curtain, go."

Lindy heard the curtain being pulled. The stage was effused with a bright, warm light. At the same time, the music began, the sound of violins bouncing into action. Backstage became even darker and then gradually came back into shadowy view as the stage lights spilled into the offstage area.

Lindy had to pull her attention from the stage; it was such a beautiful effect. Lights, music, costumes, graceful bodies. It was mesmerizing. Backstage, everything appeared as it had before the blackout. There had been time for someone to sneak past the door and enter Carlotta's room without being seen. But who?

All the dancers were in both pieces, except Carlotta. The memory of a Tunisian vacation popped into Lindy's mind. She and Glen had been sitting at the horseshoe bar in the hotel when the lights suddenly went out. When the emergency generator had finally restored them, Glen swore that the people sitting across from them were not the same people as before. For the rest of the night, they had made up stories of innocent tourists being shanghaied from the bar during power failures.

But everything here was just as it had been before. No one could have moved that fast. It must have been someone out of the stage area. Only Jeremy was unaccounted for, but maybe he had already gone back out front. That's what he would have normally done, but had he done so that night? He hadn't returned to his seat in the theater, and he hadn't joined her at the back. There was only one way to find out. She would ask him as soon as the performance was over.

And then what? She refused to think about it. He had to be innocent. She couldn't make herself imagine Jeremy bludgeoning Carlotta to death. And there hadn't been any blood on him, had there? She would have noticed. He would have had time to enter Carlotta's dressing room during the brief blackout, but he would have had to come out after the lights were back on, and someone would have noticed. Lindy looked around her. Everyone was intent on their job. Peter watched the stage, his voice calmly giving cues into the headset.

The music changed tempo; the *Gavotte* had begun. Lindy caught snatches of flowing costumes as the dancers passed from her view. She moved toward the back of the stage, slowly trying to see things in a new perspective. Catch any little thing that wasn't quite right, just like in rehearsal. It was usually just a misplaced hand, weight shifted to the wrong foot, a step taken a second too quickly. The smallest quirk could throw off an entire movement, or a stage full of performers. But nothing here caught her eye. She was at the prop table when she noticed someone standing in the wings.

The music had changed to the *Air*. The melody was bewitching. The men were lifting Andrea, handing her from one to another in a floating reverie, passionate, yet serene. Like the choreographer, thought Lindy, classical structure with a longing romanticism just below the surface. Lindy wrenched her gaze from the stage and looked at the person in the wings. The blue smock flared out over Alice's ample bottom.

Lindy moved up beside the costume mistress. She was standing with her arms folded in front of her, one of the robes from *Carmina* draped over her elbow.

"I love this music," said Alice, staring dreamily toward the stage.

"Me too." It couldn't have been Jeremy. No one who could create such beautiful movement would be capable of destroying a life. In the back of her mind, she knew that wasn't true; great artists were often selfish and destructive, but not Jeremy. She wouldn't believe it.

She took a few steps backward, trying to detach herself from the spell being woven by the dancing. Peter had slipped off his headset; it rested around his neck. His head was turned toward the stage.

Lindy walked toward the door to the dressing rooms. No one seemed aware of her presence. She turned around abruptly, shooting one arm into the air. One of the lighting people glanced up briefly but then looked back to the board. Anyone could have walked right past.

Peter popped the headset back over his ears. "Warn on cue seventeen. Warn on curtain." In a minute or two the curtain would come down on their last performance at University Theater. The *Rigaudon* music was bouncing to the end. Everyone was in action. The music ended, the curtain closed, and the dancers got ready for the curtain calls.

The entire cast lined up across the width of the stage for the first bow. After bowing, they split center and exited to both sides of the stage. The demi-soloists, then the soloists took their bows, and finally the entire cast again. The curtain flew in and settled in a pool of fabric.

"Houselights, stage lights. Thanks, everybody." Peter dropped his headset onto the light board and left the stage.

"Do you want to talk to us?" Kate was one of the first dancers offstage.

"Uh, no, but I think Biddy might have taken a few notes. Hang on." Lindy took the time to watch everyone as they began leaving the stage, where they went, who was talking to whom. Was it like this on the night Carlotta was killed?

Biddy came backstage, Jeremy walking beside her.

"Have any notes for the cast?" Lindy prompted.

"Uh, no," said Biddy, looking surprised.

"All right, you guys, you're cut loose. Good show." Lindy watched the path that everyone took. It had been several minutes before they had heard Andrea's scream. Everyone but Andrea had been onstage.

"Was I supposed to take notes?" asked Biddy.

"Huh?" Lindy shook her head without taking her eyes off the retreating dancers. She followed them into the hall and watched as they disappeared into dressing rooms, closing doors behind them.

It was no use. Carlotta must have been dead by the end of the piece. Lindy stood in the empty hallway. Empty, except for her and the yellow tape that stretched across Carlotta's dressing-room door.

Fourteen

A hotel lobby had never looked so inviting. Lindy had filled Biddy in on what she had noticed backstage during the last part of the performance, carefully editing out her fears about Jeremy. She could feel the tension that emanated from her friend, and she knew she would have to be very careful when she finally broached the subject.

"Guess who's here," Biddy said in a voice that underscored her tiredness.

"Oh, God, why us?"

Bill Brandecker, the ever present, was walking toward them. Lindy readied herself with several bons mots to hurl at him while she continued slowly forward.

"He does look kind of elegant."

"For crying out loud, Biddy. He's wearing jeans and a flannel shirt."

"Maybe he's lonely."

"Then he should go home and start looking for another poker game." Lindy braced her shoulders, fixed her eyes on the ground, and decided to walk past him without acknowledging his presence.

"Good evening, ladies."

"Good evening," they both mumbled. They even sounded

guilty. Lindy looked up with the most dazzling smile she could muster. It wasn't very effective. She was sure the expression was more like a razor cut than a smile. She showed more teeth.

"Why, Mr. Brandecker," she began, then gave up the pretense. "What do you want now?"

"I thought I might buy you a drink."

Right, if he thought he could weasel information out of her—but then, the game did work both ways. "We'd love to have a drink with you." She smiled sweetly—she hoped.

Biddy looked at her in amazement. Her eyes widened; warning emanated from them like lighthouse beacons in a storm. "Not me, I'm really tired tonight. Thanks anyway." She moved around him so quickly that she barely missed hitting him in the shin with her crutch.

"Some other time, perhaps." He gave Biddy that disarming smile. Lindy braced herself. "And you?"

"Actually, I'd love a drink, thank you."

Biddy had stopped behind Bill and was pantomiming to Lindy, slicing her index finger across her throat. Lindy ignored her.

Biddy gave up and retreated toward the elevator.

Bill led her into the bar, which was surprisingly quiet for a Saturday night. He stopped at the booth where she had sat with Jack just a few days ago. Lindy walked past it and said, "How about here?"

Bill shrugged and sat down, watching as she slid into the upholstered bench across the table from him.

"Mr. Brandecker . . ."

"Call me Bill, please. 'Mr.' makes me feel a little anti- quated. And what shall I call you? Belinda, Lindy, Haggerty,

Graham? Do you have any other names I should know about?"

"Sacco, Vanzetti? You can call me Lindy."

"It's an odd world, the theater. Everyone's name seems to end in a y or ie, or some other diminutive. Or they use something totally fictitious. Doesn't anyone get called by their real name?"

"Hardly ever, and then, like children, only if you're really mad at them."

Bill laughed. It was disarming, like his smile. But Lindy wasn't fooled by it. Brandecker, she was sure, could indulge in conversation complete with witty comments and apparent charm, while taking mental notes, complete with crossed t's and dotted i's. She would have to be careful.

"Take Carlotta Devine, for example." Well, he had moved onto that subject smoothly enough. "Do you know what her real name was?"

Lindy shook her head. "I've never thought about it."

"Carol Schwartz."

"You're kidding. Well, that's appropriate."

Bill looked puzzled.

"Isn't *schwarz* German for black?"

"That bad, huh?"

"Oh, yes." Lindy tried to survey the minefield that lay ahead. "She was a hideously nasty person, but I'm sure you've heard that from everyone. I suppose I'm sorry she's dead, but I find it hard to work up any compassion for her. She made everyone's life miserable when she was alive, and she seems to be continuing the tradition now that she's dead."

"So, everybody hated her?"

"No," she said a little too quickly. "I wouldn't say 'hate.'

There's one like her in every dance company, probably in every secretarial pool, too. You just learn to cope and say really catty things about her behind her back."

"What did people say?" Well, so much for trying to lighten the conversation.

" 'Divine Swine' was my favorite." She smiled in spite of herself.

Bill smiled. Thousands of tiny alarms went off in her head. Don't be cute. Pay attention.

The barmaid interrupted them. Lindy ordered a glass of white wine, which Bill immediately changed to a bottle of French chardonnay. He thinks I'll get drunk and confess, she thought. She changed tactics.

"Since you obviously invited me here to talk about the murder, do you mind if I ask why?"

Bill leaned back and looked at her, but didn't speak.

"If you're just 'sort of' a policeman, and this isn't your 'field,' why are you going to all this trouble? Are you a private investigator?"

"Do you remember everything people say? Pretty observant."

"I'm trained to be observant. It's my job. Are you a private detective?"

"No."

"Look, I don't feel like playing twenty questions tonight. Can you just tell me why you are doing this?"

"Because I'm here. I used to be a policeman. Now, I teach at John Jay."

It took her a second to assimilate what he said. "A professor?"

"Yeah, don't I look like one?"

She looked at his flannel shirt, opened at the collar. She tried to study his face, but the lighting in the bar was too dim. "But you used to be a policeman."

The barmaid returned with the bottle of wine and set it in a standing ice bucket. She made a show of pouring it out, carefully turning the bottle to keep it from dripping. It was probably the most interesting thing she would have to do all evening, and she was making the most of it. "Enjoy," she said and walked away.

Bill watched her leave, his eyes focused on the hem of her black satin miniskirt. "I used to be a policeman, but now I teach criminology. I got sick of the violence and the gore and the pain."

"So now you just deal with theories instead of criminals?"

Bill leaned forward and crossed his arms on the table. "I now try to look at the reasons people turn to violence, maybe someday add my little bit to prevent violence instead of always cleaning up after it. Maybe even train a few people to go out and do a better job than I did. You think that's a, pardon the pun, cop-out?"

"Not at all," said Lindy, startled by the chink she had so easily stumbled upon. "I think it's very altruistic and a bit idealistic. Decent qualities in a man. Do you think it's a cop-out?"

He started to speak, then changed his mind. Then slowly he said, "What I think is that you have a pretty nasty situation here. Dell is good, but he hasn't had much experience with artistic types. Most of his cases revolve around drunk drivers, domestic disputes, and burglaries. There's a surprising lack of murder or art, here, even for a college town."

"And do you have experience with artistic types?"

"I've known a few. I'm not just some flat foot with a degree. I can tell the difference between Puccini and Mozart, *Swan Lake* and 'Slaughter on Tenth Avenue.'"

She had annoyed him, and she felt smugly elated. Some other time she would have loved to delve into the inner workings of the man, but she needed other information from him now. There were more serious matters at stake.

"So you've graciously volunteered to kibitz on the investigation. I thought policemen were fanatically territorial."

"They are, and I am not kibitzing."

"Oh? Then why are you showing such an interest in all of this? Deriving a new theory at our expense?" Her tone was aggressive. She couldn't help herself. "And on your vacation. Isn't that taking your work a little too seriously?"

He laughed. "That's the same thing my ex-wife said when she showed me the door. Though she didn't state it quite so sympathetically."

"Sorry." Why was he telling her this? He didn't strike Lindy as the type of man who spilled his guts to every woman with whom he drank wine. He must be leading her somewhere specific.

Bill seemed to realize the subtle shift in her attitude. "It was a long time ago. Police work, at least mine, and family don't seem to mix. And you?"

His question had caught her off guard. With two words he had subtly regained his control of the conversation.

"What about me?"

"Does your work and family mix?"

Lindy blessed the dim lighting and her olive skin. If she had Biddy's complexion, her ambivalence would have colored her face.

Bill's eyebrows rose. He was waiting for a response.

"I'm really retired; I've just been back a week. Biddy asked me to help her." She stopped talking abruptly. She had almost told him why Biddy had asked her to come back. She had to be more careful. Her glass was almost empty. "It was hard for her with her broken leg. I wasn't busy, so I came to help them out until the New York season. It's a good company, and I was glad to help. They're good people; they're just caught in bizarre circumstances."

She was talking too much, clumsily trying to lead the conversation away from the details of Carlotta's death. She was out of her depth. God, what an amateur; she just hoped she wasn't digging herself into a hole. She concentrated on her wineglass, twirling it around with her fingers. "They're emotional and self-indulgent sometimes," she said without looking up. "Tempers flare up quickly, and then it's over. They're supposed to be dramatic. People who express their feelings all the time don't have the energy left over to do really terrible things. Even in the real world, isn't it always the bottled-up types who go on a rampage?"

"Don't you consider this life the 'real world'?"

That was not the question she had anticipated, and it took her a second to answer. "Some people do."

"But not you?"

She stared past him, her eyes following the pattern of gold squiggles on the mirrored wall tiles. "I did once. Maybe I will again."

"Maybe living in this make-believe world of fairies and princes has warped somebody's sense of reality."

"We don't do fairies and princes. We're a modern-dance

company." Lindy heard her own words, how she had shifted from "they" to "we."

Bill's face was blank. He topped off their wineglasses. She realized that he had been goading her.

"You have a devious mind."

Bill lifted his wineglass and took a sip. It was a peculiarly refined gesture from a man of his size.

"Why don't you people look outside the company? She probably had a private life; most people do."

"I'm sure the police are considering all options."

"Don't you know?"

"I'm not privy to confidential information, even if my brother-in-law is the chief of police. I'm strictly unofficial, as I keep telling you."

"But what kinds of options?" She threw subtlety to the wind.

"Well, it's an old saw, but usually true."

"I know—lust, greed, and I forget the other one."

"Revenge." He tilted his head.

Revenge? Bill's eyes seemed to penetrate right through to her stomach. Her face felt clammy, and for one dizzying moment, she thought she might pass out. His words droned on. "I'll tell you one thing. The police are looking into her finances as a possible motive: bank accounts, insurance policies, inheritance."

Lindy relaxed slightly.

"But I think it's closer to home."

She tensed again. "You're wrong."

"You've told me that before."

"I'm sorry. But you were right when you called it 'home.' It *is* like a family. This kind of work consumes your life. It becomes your entire world. Dancers make terrible salaries, when they're paid at all. They're constantly being squeezed between management and the unions. We depend on each other, support each other . . ."

"Protect each other?"

Lindy fought with the growing lump in her throat. "When we have to. But not like you think. I know it sounds melodramatic. That's just the way we express ourselves."

"You're not their mother, Lindy."

"No, that's Biddy's job. I'm the Dutch uncle." She smiled. He poured out the last of the wine. "And don't try to get me drunk. I never get drunk. I always fall asleep first. And I'm not going to confess to being a mass murderer with bodies buried all over the state of Connecticut."

"Personally, I don't think of you as a serious suspect. Not very objective thinking for a policeman, I realize. But Dell will not be so easily swayed."

"Then why are you being so nosy?" To hell with it. She took another sip of wine.

He smiled. He smiled a lot. Only this wasn't his usual variety. It seemed more gentle. It was also fleeting. His voice became more direct. "Because I think you're interesting. I also think you're holding out on the police. If you know something, Lindy, tell them. Withholding evidence is not only a crime, it can be very dangerous."

"I don't know who killed her."

"But you know something. What is it? Who are you trying to protect?"

Lindy felt herself wavering. Bill was leaning across the table; his right hand was resting close to hers. His eyes were penetrating. She felt flustered. She tried to pretend he was

one of those two-dimensional fictional detectives, easily out-
foxed. But she felt herself succumb to his intensity. It was
tempting, but dangerous. His hand moved slightly. It was
close enough to grab hers.

She moved her hand back. "I just know that I didn't kill
her. Trust me. If she caused me that much trouble, I would
have jumped into my station wagon and headed back to my
comfy home in the suburbs. I wouldn't have bashed her head
in."

"But someone did. Someone beat her to a bloody pulp
with a prop, for Christ's sake. Someone who is willing to
sacrifice the rest of you, to save himself."

"It isn't one of us. It can't be. No one would do that."

"Lindy, you've got a brain. . . ." He left the rest unsaid.

"Anyone could have come into the theater. The stage door
was open. There were sixteen candelabras sitting on the prop
table in full view. Even a stranger would have seen them.
And anyway, how do you know it was the candelabra?"

Bill shrugged lightly, or was it a twitch?

"I thought you weren't privy to confidential information."

"It's obvious," he said, looking into his wineglass.

Lindy felt every muscle contract. They'll think it's Rebo.
He had said they would, but revenge? Brandecker was trying
to confuse her. She could feel that. How much of what he
was saying was the truth, and how much was fabrication?
She couldn't trust him. Too bad; she needed his help.

"Well, wouldn't the killer be covered with blood if that
were the case? I mean, doesn't it spray all over the place,
leave traces or whatever?" She felt queasy. "Listen to me,
nobody was covered in blood. I would have noticed. That's
not something you could miss."

"You were all pretty upset. A person doesn't always notice details under those circumstances."

He didn't move away. His voice was gentler but his body held its intensity.

Lindy felt smothered by his closeness. "I do. I'm always astonished by the kinds of detail that jump out at you when you're under pressure. I know they didn't find blood on anyone. Did they." It wasn't a question, but a demand.

"Not that I have knowledge of, but consider what happened after Carlotta's body was discovered. Jeremy sent everyone back to their dressing rooms. Most of them had changed into street clothes before we arrived."

"That's why they taped off the dressing rooms? They were looking for—" She couldn't continue. Bill's hand moved closer to hers but didn't touch it.

"What did they find?" She could barely make the words audible. He didn't answer, and she thought that he must not have heard her. "What did they find?" she repeated. She didn't care if she sounded hysterical, and she was sure she must. Bill's face loomed before her; the rest of the room went out of focus. Maybe she was drunk after all.

He wasn't going to answer her. "You're full of shit with your 'busman's holiday' and 'not privy to,' Bill Brandecker."

Bill pulled his hand back. His mouth had tightened into a straight line across his face. The interview was over. Police had a way of indicating that without saying a word, and Bill was still a policeman at heart, even if he called himself a professor.

He pulled some bills out of his wallet and plunked them on the table. "I'm sure they will cover all the angles. I'll walk you to the elevator."

He led her across the lobby to the elevator, holding her rigidly by the elbow. He pressed the up button with his free hand and turned her toward him. Her elbow was beginning to throb, but she didn't try to free it from his grasp. He leaned down, his face inches from hers. For one terrifying moment Lindy thought he was going to kiss her.

"Be very careful, Lindy. And if you ever decide you can trust me—" He shoved her abruptly into the elevator, and the doors closed. She leaned back against the rail, relieved and just a little disappointed.

Fifteen

Lindy awoke to the buzzing of her travel alarm and the blinking message light on the phone by the bed. She slapped off the alarm and ignored the light. She needed to talk to Jeremy.

She found him in the weight room in the basement of the hotel. Surrounded by computerized exercise machines, Jeremy was the sole human occupant. She stopped at the observation window and peered in.

He was sitting at the pullover station on the Universal circuit. Dressed in baggy sweatpants and a loose-fitting T-shirt, cut away at the neck and sleeves and truncated above the waist, he lowered the weight-encumbered bar to his lap. She could see his abdominals ripple as he slowly released it upward. His biceps strained with the effort, but his face was impassive. A dancer's training. Never let the work show in your face. The audience doesn't want to see the exertion, just the magic. Jeremy was perfectly disciplined.

And, of course, he would go to a gym. She had never seen him exercise, except for occasionally demonstrating to the dancers how a step should be executed. She had tried to imagine him in his hotel room, dressed in tights, giving himself a *barre* while he corrected his placement in the hotel mirror. She couldn't picture it. In fact, she never really thought of him as a dancer. He had been good in his day. She had seen him onstage a few times during her own career. But he had retired early to take over the directorship of an established company, and he had clothed his dancer's muscles in street clothes ever since. He even rehearsed in slacks and collared shirts. It was a smart move. It separated him from his peers, who, at first, were not much younger than himself. He had an instinct for the nuances of leadership.

Now watching his bare arms straining with the effort of weight lifting, the sweat trickling down into the waistband of his sweats, she was struck by his vulnerability. She even felt a little embarrassed watching his enforced regimen. He was in great shape for someone who must be well over forty. It inspired her to watch him, reminded her to stick to grapefruit for breakfast when her taste buds cried for pancakes and bacon. She stood by the door admiring his physique unabashedly, until he finished and motioned her over.

"Staying in shape is hell," he said from underneath the towel he had thrown over his head. He scrubbed his hair and slipped the towel around his neck. "Getting old is a bitch."

"I know," she said. "I've let myself go pretty badly in the last few years."

"I did, too. Now, I'm paying the price." He set up at the next station, impaling several, different-size weights onto a metal pin and straddled the bench. He curled the weights upward. She watched the sweat trickle down his forearms and drop off onto the floor. It suddenly struck her what a solitary figure he was. Of course, he would keep in shape by working with weights, competing with the machines, with his own weaknesses, alone. Always in control, never breaking down in front of others. He hadn't really asked for her help, only said that Biddy needed her. What did he need, she wondered.

"The local police seem determined to keep us here for a few days," he was saying. "Even though I imagine the state police will be taking over the investigation. They are probably more equipped to deal with something like this."

He was carefully avoiding that one word: "murder." They both knew it was just that. *Murder.* No way to get around it. To ignore it. Carlotta wouldn't be getting up from her pool of blood to take her curtain call. But he was loath to say it. And so was Lindy.

"What do you want to do in the meantime?" she asked. She sat down on the plastic cushion of some machine that reminded her of an obstetrician's table, padded braces for feet and knees. She crossed her legs.

"I talked to Angie Levinson this morning. Offered to do a lec-dem for her students tomorrow morning," he said between grunts. "Figured we might as well keep the kids busy. Better for their minds to be occupied with their work and not with this stupid tragedy. Peter's left the sets and floor at the theater. No need to load up and wait around for someone to rip off the truck. The sponsors in Hartford are a little anxious about us making it in time, but ticket sales have skyrocketed." He laughed harshly as he dropped the weights for the last time and threw his leg over the seat. "I've assured them we will be there by Wednesday at the latest. God, I hope I'm right." He walked toward her until he stood above her, looking down. "Who the hell could have done this, Lindy?"

Lindy swallowed and said as calmly as she could, "I was going to ask you the same thing."

He looked at her for a few seconds without answering. She felt uncomfortable. She didn't think he had done it, but she thought that he thought she did. His cheeks were flushed from the exertion of exercising; he looked vulnerable, not sinister.

She jumped in. "I've been doing some snooping, for a good cause, I hope. Peter's sister is in a nursing home nearby; I went to see her."

Jeremy rubbed his face with his towel, hiding whatever reaction he had to her statement.

"I can't help thinking that Carlotta's death is tied up to what happened in the past. Can that be possible, Jeremy? What exactly happened to Sandra?"

Jeremy turned from her without a word, walked through the door to the waiting room, and sat down on the Naugahyde couch. Lindy followed him and sat next to him.

"You want the whole story, I suppose."

"That would be nice," she said encouragingly.

"I despised Carlotta. She destroyed my life. I'm glad she's dead."

Lindy tried not to let her jaw drop.

"But I didn't kill her, if that's what you're thinking."

"I wasn't thinking that," she mumbled. She wished he'd elaborate, but he sat staring at a coffee spill on the carpet, and she knew she would have to drag the story out of him piece by piece. "Then why did you keep her on?" she asked.

Jeremy shrugged. "Jack."

"What does he have to do with it?"

"I'm not sure. He wasn't forthcoming, but he insisted that I hire her, so I did."

"But why?"

"Jack pulled me back from the lunatic fringe. I was killing myself—drugs, booze. He stepped in and badgered me into pulling myself together, starting over. He got the funding, the bookings, everything. I owe him."

"Jeremy, what happened that made you quit in the first place? I know it isn't really my business, but the police will find out, and they may get the wrong impression. They don't understand us. If it could have anything to do with Carlotta's death, please tell me."

"I don't want to remember it, Lindy. It's taken a long time for me to forget it."

"Jeremy."

He cradled his head with his fingers, digging the heels of his hands into his eye sockets. When he finally spoke, it was to the coffee-stained floor. "Sandra DiCorso. She was a promising young dancer in the company. So talented, so beautiful. I liked her . . . a lot. You know what I mean?" He looked at Lindy over his fists.

"You mean like . . . ," she stammered.

"Yeah, like . . ." He began to massage his forehead with his fingers. The only sound in the room was the buzzing of the fluorescent light above them. Then Jeremy let out a deep sigh. "I know everyone thinks I'm gay because of the way I look and because of my profession. They just assume, and I never tried to dissuade them. It's good for business, or at least a good cover. I just never got into other guys. Well, a couple maybe, but I never needed sex enough to die for it."

Lindy nodded, knowledge of what he was saying dawned on her slowly.

"Anyway, she didn't care for me, that way."

Lindy wondered why he couldn't say it. He had loved Sandra DiCorso. Did Peter know? Did Jack? And, more importantly, had Carlotta?

"I was supposed to rehearse her in a new role after the rest of the company had finished for the day. We had a fight. She told me she was quitting dancing; getting married. But not to me. I went berserk, stormed out, and she went on rehearsing alone. She must have fallen, hit her head. She's never recovered. I visited her once, but I couldn't stand it. She's locked in some world that no one can reach. I just couldn't take it." His voice cracked, and Lindy realized that if he hadn't been so well trained, he would cry, and she ached for him. But she pressed him to continue.

"If I hadn't been so self-indulgent, if I had stayed . . ." He shook himself and steadied his voice. "But I didn't. Instead I went out to a club and drank myself under the table. Carlotta showed up. She always had a way of finding you at your most vulnerable and putting the screws to you. She came on to me. She was disgusting. I said some horrible things to her, I think. I was pretty out of it."

"So, crippled with guilt and feeling sorry for yourself, you quit and went on a binge of self-destruction," Lindy continued for him.

"You make it sound so—"

"It just doesn't sound like you."

He glanced at her from the corner of his eyes. The rest of his body was immobile. "There's more." He lifted both feet to the couch and hugged his knees.

Lindy focused on the ragged ends of his shoelaces. She hoped she could handle this. You should never try to get people to face things they don't want to face unless you're equipped to deal with their reactions. It was too late to worry about it now. She waited.

"It was finally declared an accident, but first there was an investigation. It was questionable whether someone could hit her head with such force without being pushed or thrown. Something like that. I was the prime suspect for a few agonizing days. I had an alibi; Carlotta was all over me at the club; she wouldn't take no for an answer. But when the police talked to her, she denied having been with me."

Lindy's stomach shriveled to the size of a walnut. "Didn't anyone else see you?"

"You know how those places are. Everyone loaded on something or on the make. People thought they remembered seeing me, but they weren't sure when."

"God, Jeremy."

Jeremy didn't acknowledge her. He didn't even seem aware of her. He was now citing facts as if reciting a litany. Lindy guessed that he must have repeated the story, asked himself the same questions, day after day, night after night, and getting no answers, except that he had been betrayed, and his life was in shambles.

"I tried to get back to work, but the looks, the innuendoes, my own guilt. I couldn't hack it. I finally opted out."

"Until Jack kicked you back in?"

"Right."

"And Jack insisted on Carlotta?"

Jeremy nodded.

"And she wanted this job to punish you for rejecting her."

Lindy was thinking out loud, but she thought Jeremy needed to hear it. "That's just like her. And you kept her on, not just because of Jack, but because you wanted her to keep punishing you, because you can't forgive yourself."

Jeremy dropped his head to his knees.

She was being cruel, and she hated it. But it was time to get things out in the open. "And you don't let everyone think you're gay because of the image. It's to keep everyone confused. Men think you're being discreet, and women think you aren't attracted to them. That way they won't get close to you. So you can't hurt them—"

"Stop it." Jeremy's voice was ragged with pain.

She had gone too far. He wasn't ready to face it yet. She touched his hair and watched his body tense. "Okay, so what about Jack?"

Jeremy turned his head to look at her. "What about him?"

"It's hard to believe that Carlotta orchestrated all this. She may have taken advantage of the opportunity to get back at you, but Jack really needed a job for his own survival. He approached you, made you feel obligated to him; he needed you in order to save himself. He was accused of embezzling, in case you've forgotten. And now, the same thing is happening again. The company isn't paid on a regular basis . . ."

"Cash flow or something. I let Jack handle the money. It's a relief not to have to deal with everything."

"Get a grip, Jeremy. You know as well as I do, if a sponsor doesn't pay, you don't perform. I've sat through hour-long intermissions waiting for final payment before continuing to the last act."

"Only in Italy or Mexico, maybe. It isn't the same in the States. We don't usually have to resort to such extremes."

"But we always get paid in advance. We looked at the books, Jeremy."

"What?"

"Biddy and I looked through Jack's briefcase, the day Carlotta fell. He left it behind when he took her to the emergency room. Peter was there, too. Jack hired an unknown company to construct the cage, instead of the one Peter had recommended, at twice the fee. Jack is skimming, and you had better face it."

"Why would he do that? If he needed money, I would have given it to him. I owe him everything. He kept me from killing myself."

"Do you pay any attention to the books?"

"No. That would be admitting that I didn't trust him. When he wants me to sign, I sign."

"I'm not blaming you."

"But it's another of my little failings."

Lindy ignored his self-contempt. "Some of the dancers think he gambles."

"Jack? Ridiculous."

"Juan overheard a conversation between Jack and Carlotta about his 'little obsession.' "

"No, I don't believe it. Surely, I would know that at least. Oh, God. I've made such a mess of things. Maybe I should disband the company."

"And go back to drinking and drugging? You can't disband. You won't. You're tougher than you think, Jeremy. We'll see this through."

An involuntary shudder passed through his body. "I suppose. But, Lindy, we'd better hurry."

* * *

Hurry. She knew she had to, but part of her recoiled at the thought of what she might find. There was nobody she was willing to sacrifice in order to find the truth. Jack, maybe. She didn't really like him. He would also be the easiest person to replace. But life didn't usually work out that way, and she felt guilty for being so willing to throw him to the dogs.

Jack was taking the money. She was sure of that. But what was he doing with it? Carlotta must have known. How else could she have gotten so much control over him? Maybe she was threatening to expose him. That might be a motive for killing her. Maybe she was even demanding some of the take. She couldn't have afforded that ostentatious fur coat on a dancer's salary. If she had known about his original stealing—could prove it—she could have forced him to hire her when no one else would. That would make sense, but was it possible?

If Jack had killed her, the company could continue without too much disruption. It was too convenient, maybe. And how did the freesias fit into it? Why would he continue to send flowers all these years? Initially, he might have sent them as an official company gesture, but for five years? That seemed a bit extreme.

All she had were questions. She needed some answers, but she had no idea of how to find them. If the police found out how Jeremy felt about Carlotta, they would arrest him for sure. He was alone in his office, once again without an alibi. History repeating itself. He even admitted that he hated her. Maybe he had been waiting for years to get back at her. That's the way the police would see it.

She had left Jeremy sitting on the couch. She needed to think, to hurry, but instead she wandered aimlessly across the hotel lobby. She stopped to look into the darkened gift-shop window. The shop was closed. Maybe Connecticut had a blue law. Who would want to buy this stuff anyway? University sweatshirts, stuffed animals, key chains, the flotsam of a weekend spent in a hotel.

"Ms. Graham." Lindy jumped. The desk manager motioned her over. It was the same young man that had been on duty the day she had arrived. He had been gracious then, had welcomed her with a smile. He was churlish now. Having possible murder suspects in your hotel couldn't be good for business. Policemen, even in plain clothes, would be upsetting to the guests. The staff probably looked at each of them as possible murderers. This man certainly had that look on his face.

"Yes?" She walked over to the counter.

"Messages for you." He barely looked at her as he handed two memo sheets across the registration desk. As soon as she took them from him, he turned and began straightening the keys in the room boxes behind him.

"Thank you," she said to his back. She looked down at the messages: "9:15 A.M. Glen Haggerty. Call home"; "10:05 A.M. Bill Brandecker. Meet him at the theater as soon as possible." Lindy crammed the message from Glen into the pocket of her jeans and headed for the parking lot.

Strange. Why would Brandecker want to meet her at the theater? Why would he want to meet her at all, after last night's conversation? Maybe he had found something. Would he actually share it with her?

She turned the Volvo out of the hotel parking lot. Please

let it be good news, she thought. Her mind was racing. She arrived at the theater without being aware of the drive.

There were no cars in the lot. She realized she had never seen Bill's car, but he must have one. The company truck wasn't even there, but the stage door was held open with the pig iron.

She went inside. It took a few moments for her eyes to become accustomed to the darkness after the brilliance of the daylight outside. She walked to the shop. The door was ajar, but no one was there. The cage had been dismantled and was packed in cases stacked near the loading-dock door. Rolls of Marley lay against the wall, ready to be loaded into the truck.

"Bill?" she called tentatively. No response. Well, really, why was he being so enigmatic? Where was he? Did he have something to show her that could only be seen at the theater? Had he really found something? More questions—where were some answers?

She called again. Her voice echoed down the hall, but still, there was no answer. For a man who has no respect for theater life, thought Lindy, he sure has a flare for the dramatic. She walked down the hall to the dressing rooms. They were all locked. She didn't go near Carlotta's; the tape was still in place. She went through the door to the stage. It was even darker, and she hit the side of the prop table with a thud. Holding her aching hipbone, she oriented herself in the direction of the light board and walked carefully forward.

The back of her neck began to prickle. She had been in dark theaters hundreds of times and felt totally comfortable, but she had also read hundreds of mysteries. If she had been reading this one, she would be screaming at the heroine: "Go back, you ninny." But this wasn't a book. She groped her way to the lighting panel and threw a lever.

A deep-blue light washed across the stage from the side lights, blinding her momentarily. The curtains seemed to waver as bright light sliced through the darkness surrounding the stage.

She looked out across the stage and called, "Hey, Brandecker. Is this a remake of *The Phantom of the Opera?* Do I have to sing?" There was still no answer. She couldn't see anything past the lit stage. Shadows thrown by the light across the stage dissolved into total black. She walked onto the stage.

It lay bundled up in the middle of the floor. At first it looked like a body, draped in a piece of curtain fabric. She rushed forward. It seemed too small for Bill, but who? She knelt down and reached toward it. The material sank underneath her touch, just a pile of fabric. It slipped through the gaping hole in the floor. The trapdoor had been lowered.

"What?" She hadn't heard anything. The push came totally without warning. Not strong, just enough to throw her balance forward. Instinct took over, and her arms stretched out before her. Her elbows hit the edge of the opening, sending sparks of pain all the way to her teeth. The flesh beneath her sweater tore as her weight hurled her into the darkness below. Her fingers clutched at the edge, barely breaking the momentum of her downward fall. Her body automatically landed on both feet absorbing the shock with a deep *plié*. She curved into a backward roll, off to one shoulder to protect her spine.

I did a lift like this once, she thought. Then blackout.

* * *

She heard her name, over and over, from down a long corridor. She was missing her entrance. She couldn't get to the stage on time. She tried to sit up. Heavy material was draped around her body, and the more she tried to move, the more tangled she became. The sound of her name was louder now, but it still had an echo effect. She'd wake up soon. It was just one of those nightmares where you heard your music but couldn't find your way to the stage. Those happened all the time. She couldn't move. No matter, it would be over soon, and then she would wake up. Breakfast maybe.

"Lindy!" This time the sound was loud and right above her. She tried to look up; her shoulder hurt like hell. She didn't usually feel pain in a dream. A head appeared in the sky, surrounded by a square halo of blue. The gods speak from the heavens. As a Greek god, Bill looked kind of funny, and his costume was terrible. She started to giggle.

"For Christ's sake, don't try to move."

It really was Bill.

"Bill." They should have done better dialogue. This wasn't very clever. Her body ached everywhere, dull pain accented by sharp.

"Don't move, I'm coming down."

"Not this way, we haven't got the kinks out yet. Try the stairs."

Bill's head disappeared, leaving only the shining blue box. Pretty good special effects, she thought drowsily and drifted off.

The next thing she knew, Bill was kneeling beside her. It wasn't as dark now. He must have found the light switch.

She hurt everywhere. This was no dream. Someone had pushed her through the trapdoor. She jerked up and let out a groan.

"Don't move."

"You said that already. Where the hell were you?"

His hands were running along the length of her body, her arms, and her legs. It would have felt good if she didn't hurt so much. "Ouch!"

"Of all the stupid . . . what did you think you were doing?"

"I came to meet you; where were you?"

"What are you talking about? You probably have a concussion."

"I got a message to meet you here. Wasn't I supposed to meet you?"

"No."

"Then why are you here?"

"I was following you. And it's a good thing. You're impossible. Is anything broken?"

"I don't think so. Somebody pushed me."

"Obviously. I didn't think you jumped down on purpose."

"You don't have to be so mean."

"See if you can stand up." Without waiting for her to move, he pulled her to her feet. She meant to stand up, but her knees buckled and she slumped against him. Strong arms caught her. She leaned into his body. She felt safe, but her head hurt. She could feel his heart beating through his windbreaker. For a second she forgot that she was a happily married suburban housewife. Then her brain cleared with frightening speed. She pulled away. "Thanks. I'm okay."

"Yeah, right."

"Are you annoyed with me?"

"Yes." He looked like he wanted to finish the job someone else had started.

"Why?"

"Because I can't believe you fell for such an obvious trick."

"I fell down the hole, didn't I?"

His eyes closed and he shook his head like a father who had just been told his kid had screwed up again. "Let's get you cleaned up. You're bleeding all over my jacket."

He helped her toward the stairs. The storage room made her skin crawl. Dust and cobwebs covered everything. The single lightbulb that hung from the ceiling didn't cast much light, and for that, she was grateful. Years of discarded objects littered the surface of the floor, and cardboard boxes were stacked in haphazard piles along the walls. Cleaning buckets, broken chairs, mildew-covered rags vied for space. Lindy kept her eyes focused on the rickety stairway and the open door above her.

Bill led her into the shop, pulled a folding chair over to the industrial-size sink, and eased her into the chair. Lindy touched her throbbing cheek and pulled away sticky fingers.

"It's just a scrape; face wounds always bleed a lot. It'll look nasty for a few days, but probably won't scar." He cocked his head. "Do you want to go to the emergency room?"

"No." He thought she was vain. Well, she didn't care what he thought. It was clear to her that she would need his help, regardless of how he felt about her or the rest of the company. And he had said he was following her.

"Why were you following me?"

Bill held a not-too-clean towel under the tap, then wrung it out. He dabbed it gently at her cheek. Big hands, light touch. The towel felt rough, but cold and soothing.

"Because you need following, obviously," he said, continuing to clean her face. "I knew you would get yourself into trouble. After you gave me the slip yesterday afternoon, I figured I'd better get serious. I've been camped out in the hotel lobby all morning. I saw you go into the weight room; I saw you leave the hotel." He handed her the towel. "And now I want some answers. Everything."

She had no choice. She needed his expertise. "Okay, but promise you won't jump to any conclusions, keep an open mind."

"Damn it, Lindy. I always keep an open mind. I'm the professional, remember? Now, start talking." He pulled another chair across the floor; its metal tips screeched across the concrete. He swung it around so the back was facing her and straddled it, leaning on his arms across the back.

"I'll make a trade," she said, nestling her cheek in the wet towel. "I'll tell you what I know, and you tell me what you know."

"When· is it going to sink into that pea brain of yours, that this is serious. It's not some stage show. There won't be any applause at the end, and you won't forget the plot when you leave the theater." His voice thundered across the space between them. It made her head pound.

"You don't think much of us, do you?"

"What I think is that you're all a bunch of self-indulgent, pampered children that live in a dreamworld. Somebody in your little family has lost their grip on reality, what little they had in the first place. And I'm going to find out who it is. Do I make myself perfectly clear?"

"Perfectly," she said calmly and then added, "I bet your wife was in the theater, right?" She looked at him blandly and knew she had hit the mark.

"Actress," he said. "Now, I've told you something; it's your turn."

"My arms hurt." Lindy began to pull her arms gingerly out of the sleeves of her sweater.

"Stop stalling. I'm beginning to lose my patience."

She started with Biddy asking for her help, about searching Jack's office. "We think he's stealing from the company, and Carlotta knew it."

"He was accused of embezzling before," he said.

"How did you know that?"

"The police know a lot more than you imagine. They've done a background check on everyone involved, including you. They also know that Jeremy was investigated over the injury of a young girl in his former company. That makes him a prime suspect in this case."

"No. He didn't cause Sandra's accident or this one."

"Carlotta's death was not an accident. It was plain, old, unadulterated murder. No one saw him during the last part of the performance that night."

"But he had decided to fire her. He told me."

"Who else did he tell?"

"No one. He didn't have time."

"That won't help him much. It's hearsay."

"It's not hearsay. I heard him. Unless you think I'm lying," she challenged.

"It doesn't matter what I think. Keep talking."

"The girl who was injured, Sandra DiCorso, is Peter's sister. She's in a nursing home near here. Jeremy would have never hurt her. He—" She stopped herself before blurting out that Jeremy had loved her. Somehow that fact might make Jeremy even more suspect. "It's Jack who's been sending her flowers ever since."

"Sullivan? Why?"

Lindy shrugged. "I don't know."

Bill pulled out a notebook and pen from the pocket of his windbreaker.

"I did bleed on you." Lindy nodded toward the spots of blood across the right side of his jacket. Bill ignored her and scribbled into the notebook. "Bill," she said slowly. "Wouldn't there have to be blood on the killer, on his clothes? The police must have found something, if it really was one of us."

Bill looked up from his writing. His eyes were a pale blue, or maybe not. It was hard to tell in the light; the lighting seemed to be dim whenever they were together. She couldn't even describe his features; they were always partly in shadow. She felt an urgent need to see his face in daylight.

"Come on, I've been doing all the talking. It's your turn." She waited.

"I can't tell you."

"But why not? How are we going to figure this out if you're not honest with me?"

"*We* are not going to figure this out. It's a police matter, and you're going to butt out."

"Then I'm not going to tell you the rest." She threw the wet towel at his head. It settled on his shoulder. She shouldn't have done it, but it was a gesture of her frustration. She waited for his temper to explode.

But it didn't. He smiled. "See? Self-indulgent." He tossed the towel back to her.

She pressed on, ignoring his sarcasm. "If they found the clothes, why haven't they arrested someone?" Fragments of ideas darted across her mind. "Because they don't know who they belong to." She was thinking out loud, but she had nothing to lose. "A costume. No, they all have the dancers' names in them. Something of Carlotta's. Her coat, maybe." She looked for a response from Bill. Nothing. He was waiting for her to figure it out. "It would have to be big enough to cover the person, but then they would have to have had time to put it on and then hang it up again. Or at least throw it over . . . the candelabra? It would absorb any spray of blood. Right?" She sank back in the chair. "But if the candelabra was covered, it wouldn't be hard enough to kill her or cause blood. Bill?"

"Stop guessing. Do you have anything else to tell me?"

Lindy shook her head.

"Then you'd better get back to the hotel and a hot bath. That's what you people do for stress and strain, isn't it?"

He drove her back to the hotel in her car. The sun was shining, and Lindy took the opportunity to memorize his face. Brown hair streaked with blond and gray. Eyes, definitely blue—a light, clear reservoir of blue. And he didn't seem so big outside. Not over six feet two and rather thin. It was his manner and voice that were so overpowering.

"I'll see you to your room. Just to make sure you don't try to sneak away again."

They were walking through the lobby, when Paul, Eric, and Rebo came out of the restaurant. They separated, and Rebo walked toward the front door.

"I think I'll just have a talk with that boy," said Bill, setting off in the direction of Rebo. "Go upstairs."

Lindy followed him toward Rebo. "Don't call him 'boy.' "

Bill stopped. "I didn't mean it like that."

"I know, but he takes it like that."

"Jesus, what happened to you?" Rebo stared at the side of her face.

"Where have you fellows been for the last two hours?" Bill countered.

Rebo stepped forward. His normally rich-chocolate complexion had an ashy gray tint to it. Must have had a wild night last night, thought Lindy. "Self-indulgent" echoed at the back of her mind. Time for another little lecture.

"Having lunch." He was being surly. Lindy narrowed her eyes at him, and he took the hint. He lightened his tone. "For the last hour, and hanging out before that."

"All three of you?"

Rebo nodded. "What happened to Lindy?"

"Someone pushed her through the trapdoor at the theater. Knowing your penchant for pranks, I thought you might know something about who did it—"

"Bill," Lindy interrupted.

"Shit, no, I'd never hurt Lindy; you know that." He appealed to Lindy. "Or anyone else," he added to Bill.

"I know that, Rebo. Mr. Brandecker is just a little edgy." She knew it was the wrong thing to say before she had finished speaking, but it was too late. She *felt*—more than *saw*—the change in Bill.

"Maybe not Lindy, she's so lovable," Bill said through gritted teeth. "But you did threaten to kill Jack Sullivan. Maybe you settled for Carlotta instead?"

Rebo looked at Bill incredulously. He turned on Lindy. "Is that what you told him, Lindy? I'd expect that attitude from a lot of people. But not you."

"I didn't."

"Thanks for the vote of confidence. You want to arrest me? Go ahead. If not, stay out of my way." Rebo pushed between them, shoving Lindy to the side, and headed to the door.

"That was real professional."

"Go upstairs, Lindy," Bill said wearily. "You throw me off my game."

Sixteen

It was a long afternoon. The bath didn't help, only made her abrasions sting more. She pulled on sweats, limped down the hall to the ice machine, and had barely eased herself onto the bed when Biddy walked in.

"The grant proposals are finally ready to be mailed. I hope a murder won't shed unfavorable light on our—Good Lord, what happened to you?"

Lindy looked out from under an ice-filled towel. "Fell in a hole."

Biddy threw her crutches on the opposite bed and sat down next to Lindy. She pulled the ice pack away and cringed. "Aloe. I've got some in the bathroom." She pushed herself off the bed and started dragging her leaden leg toward the bathroom. "Oh, damn. I hate these crutches." She leaned back at a precarious angle to retrieve them. "I feel so useless."

"I know just how you feel." Lindy closed her eyes.

Biddy returned from the bathroom and gently spread the cream on Lindy's battered cheek. "Tell me what happened."

Lindy told her about the note, about going to the theater and being pushed down the trapdoor. Biddy's eyes ballooned with each new fact, growing larger and larger until they looked like they might burst. "Then Bill found me, and . . ."

"Bill?"

"You know, Brandecker. He's been spying on us. I told him what we knew."

Biddy's eyes grew even wider. "Not about the books!"

"Yes, I'm sorry, Biddy. I had to. We're in way over our heads. We need his help."

"Do you trust him?"

"Not for a second, but he's the best we've got. He doesn't like us much, probably resents the fact that we ruined his vacation, but he's smart. I also told him about Jack sending the flowers."

"Do you think Jack pushed you? He might be getting desperate if he thinks we're onto him."

"Possibly. We have to be careful. The police probably already know a lot about his finances, and with what I told Bill, they'll want to talk to Jack again."

"Brandecker's going to tell the police everything, isn't he?"

"I'm pretty sure he will. He doesn't have much of a choice. I made it clear that some of the things I told him were in confidence, but I don't think that means diddly to him. He's like a hound on the scent. Not very attractive."

She continued with the details of her conversation with Bill, carefully editing out the parts about Jeremy. She felt uncomfortable about considering the possibility of Jeremy's guilt in front of Biddy. She couldn't protect her forever. She might have to face losing Jeremy soon enough. Biddy's loyalties ran deep, had always run deep. She was loyal to the company, but more than that to Jeremy. It seemed to be her lot in life to be attached to someone who couldn't commit as much to her. First Claude, and now Jeremy. But then, Jeremy wasn't gay. Well, Biddy didn't need to know that yet.

Lindy felt tiredness numb her mind. She couldn't juggle a murder investigation and everyone's emotional involvement at the same time. "There's one more thing, Biddy. Bill knows about Sandra's accident. I guess the police have checked everyone's background." She yawned. It hurt her jaw. "They know that Jeremy was suspected of causing it."

Biddy began to protest.

"I know," said Lindy as her body plunged toward sleep. "It may get nasty before this is over. We've got to be strong."

"I've always been strong. It isn't much fun."

Lindy placed a heavy hand on Biddy's and fell asleep.

It was dark when Biddy shook her awake. Her body felt incredibly heavy and sluggish.

"I've been to see Jack."

Lindy sat up. Jolts of pain shot out in every direction. "Are you crazy? He's still here? I haven't seen him since he yelled at Jeremy in the theater."

"I couldn't stand it any longer. We have to push him into making a move. He must be the murderer."

"Yeah, and he could kill you next."

"I'll take the chance. I told him I had looked at the books; I didn't tell him that you and Peter were there. And I didn't mention the trapdoor."

"What did he say?"

"He denied everything, of course. He tried to blame

Peter for the over expenditures. But I didn't buy it, and he knows it."

"So you set yourself up as his next victim, is that it?"

Biddy lifted her chin. "I'm not afraid. I'll do what I have to do to save this company. And you'll have to do what you can to save me."

"Oh, Biddy, I was bored in the suburbs, but I didn't need this much excitement."

"But you do need something to eat. I'll call room service. Some soup, maybe?"

"The hell with soup, how about a bacon cheeseburger?"

"What about your diet?"

"To hell with that, too."

It was delicious. Lindy knew if she were ever to face a firing squad, however unlikely, her last wish would be a bacon cheeseburger. They sat across from each other at the table by the window.

Biddy pointed a French fry at Lindy. "It used to be that after a show, we'd come back to the room and paint our toenails and talk about boys." She took a bite and pointed again with the remaining half. "Now we just talk about murder."

"All the boys are younger than we are now." Lindy took a bite of burger.

"Jeremy didn't do it."

Lindy's mouth was full, and she couldn't cut Biddy off. She waved her hand. She wasn't ready to deal with this, but Biddy continued before she could swallow and guide the conversation away from Jeremy.

"I know you're trying to protect me. You don't think I

can act rationally because of my loyalty to him. It's not like with Claude. I was really in love with him; I thought in time, he would love me, too. Jeremy is talented and sensitive, and I respect him a lot, but I couldn't stand it if you thought I was just, you know, some fag hag. The dancing is what's important to me. Maybe, because I came from a family of eight children, getting married hasn't been too appealing to me. Nor that kind of emotional commitment. But I'm not perverse." She shoved another fry into her mouth.

How could she eat after a speech like that? Lindy forced her mouthful down with a large gulp of seltzer. "Biddy," she began, and that was as far as she got. Biddy had guessed exactly what she had been thinking.

"I just wanted you to understand," said Biddy matter-of-factly.

"I do, I really do. After a few years of marriage, commitment changes to a kind of peaceful coexistence. *Your* life is a lot more creative. I just worry about your retirement."

Biddy laughed high in the back of her throat and stabbed a pickle with her fork. "I won't have a job long enough to retire from if we don't solve this murder." She chewed slowly and swallowed. "The thing I keep wondering about is, well, there was a lot of blood on the floor, right? Wouldn't the murderer have blood on him? That's the way they catch them on TV."

"Carlotta's coat."

"Her coat?"

"I kept asking Bill about the blood. He wouldn't tell me, but he let me keep stabbing around until I came up with the idea of the coat. The murderer could have worn it; the blood would be on it, not his clothes." Lindy stood up and looked around her. She pulled the plug on the table lamp and wrapped the cord around the base.

"Oh, no, you don't," said Biddy.

"Where's your bathrobe?"

"In the bathroom."

Lindy went into the bathroom and returned wearing the robe. "Something just isn't right, Biddy. So, in the tradition of famous detectives, all of whom were smarter than we are, we're going to 'reenact the crime.' Stand up, please."

Biddy popped another fry into her mouth and stood up. "Which one am I?"

"Carlotta. Come out into the middle of the room. Turn around."

Biddy turned away from her, and Lindy touched the lamp to the back of Biddy's head. "So I hit you with the candlestick, and you fall. . . ." Lindy started laughing.

"Forward." Biddy lowered herself to the floor. "Onto my face, but Carlotta was on her back."

"So I bash you a few times and turn you over." Lindy demonstrated. "But that would still leave my hands and face exposed. Or, what if I bash you on the head, turn you over, throw the coat over you . . ." She took off the bathrobe and threw it over Biddy.

"Be careful," said the muffled voice underneath the robe.

Lindy picked up Biddy's head and carefully touched it to the carpet several times. Biddy wrestled out from under the robe.

"The coat would cover everything," said Biddy excitedly. "And it also takes care of the fact that the candelabra isn't heavy or sharp enough to draw blood, but the concrete floor would be."

"Exactly." Lindy helped Biddy to her feet. "But how does that help us?"

There was a light tapping at the door.

"Jack?" asked Biddy.

"Maybe," said Lindy, picking up the lamp from the floor. "Oh, this is stupid." She put the lamp back onto the table and went to open the door.

Paul, Eric, and Juan stood side by side. They stared dumbfounded at Lindy's face. She stared back at them, relieved.

"Oh," said Paul. "We shouldn't have come."

"Well, you did, so come in." Lindy opened the door wider, and they entered single file, lined up again, and stood mutely waiting.

"This looks like your rendition of bad ballet," quipped Lindy.

No one laughed. They turned to Biddy.

"Rebo's gone," said Paul.

"What do you mean 'gone'? He has a lec-dem tomorrow. You mean 'out'?"

"Out, but he said if he didn't come back, just to throw his stuff in his suitcase and put it on the bus."

"I'm going to beat him senseless when I get my hands on him," said Lindy, and then she cringed at her own words. So did Biddy. "Tell us everything."

Juan began. "He was really upset when he came back to the room this afternoon. Said you had told that cop that's been hanging around that he killed Carlotta."

"I hope you don't believe that."

"Of course not, you know how he gets. He's complicated. Like he can't decide whether to get famous or kill himself, instead. He just sort of flipped, raved about how they were going to blame Carlotta's death on him, 'cause he was an easy make. That nobody really cared about him, all that old shit."

"Do you think he went back to the city?" asked Biddy. "They'll just find him, and it will be worse for him."

"No, some guys we met came to pick him up."

"What guys?" asked Lindy.

Juan looked at Eric, who inhaled deeply and took up the story. "Last night these guys came backstage. They knew some people we know and invited us out after the show."

"Go on."

"They drove us into New Haven to a bar."

"You went all the way to New Haven for a drink?" asked Biddy.

Eric looked at Lindy. "A gay bar. It was the closest one. Rebo got really wasted and was ready to hang with these guys all night, but we made them drive us back."

"So do you know how to get in touch with these guys?"

"No. We kind of only remember their first names, but they seemed to be regulars at this place, and we thought maybe they might go back there tonight."

"On a Sunday?" asked Biddy.

"And we thought, maybe, you would loan us your car," said Juan, ignoring Biddy. "We'll be really careful, and we could get him back before he gets into more trouble."

"And he thinks nobody cares, poor thing."

"We know he's a jerk sometimes," said Paul. "But he just can't seem to reconcile his various lifestyles. Black, but from the Midwest; rich, but black; gay, but . . ."

"I get the point," said Lindy. "I'll go with you."

"You don't have to. We'll be really careful with the car."

"I'm going. Biddy, you'll have to go down and distract Brandecker if he's still in the lobby. Tell him anything you want, except what we're doing. Just give us time to get away. And then come back and lock yourself in. *Capisce?*"

It took more than forty-five minutes to find The Grind. The boys were a little vague about its location, and it wasn't exactly the kind of place you could ask directions to from a gas station's attendant. They were cruising the warehouse district when Juan pointed to an old diner. "There it is."

Lindy pulled the Volvo into the parking lot. The faded silver facade of the bar looked dull in spite of the colored floodlights that focused upward from the ground. The windows had been painted over, and the door was a black hole, no illumination marking its entrance.

"You'd better wait here," said Paul.

"Not a chance," she returned.

"Maybe you both should wait here," said Eric.

"I know how to say 'no,' " said Paul huffily and got out of the car.

Eric and Juan gave Lindy knowing looks. "He's so straight. How did he ever get into this business?"

It took a little convincing before the bouncer let Lindy in. She had thrown on a pair of jeans and a shiny shirt. Her face was bruised and ugly, but she tried to look jaded and seductive at the same time, showing her best profile, in this case, the undamaged one.

The music was deafening; it throbbed into every corner of the crowded space. The original counter served as the bar, but all the booths and tables had been removed to make room for a dance floor and dark corners where other things went on.

They moved slowly along the bar, looking for Rebo. Men stood three deep, pressed together, arms entangled, hands resting on denim butts. It was impossible to tell where one body left off and another one began.

Lindy received more than one appraising look, and Eric was fondled by a pair of pudgy hands attached to a man who looked like he had just arrived on his Harley. Maybe he had.

Rebo was on the dance floor, a glass in one hand, his arm draped over the broad shoulders of a tall blond. For a frenzied second, Lindy thought it was Jeremy, but when the man turned to nuzzle his head into Rebo's shoulder, the similarity vanished. He was young and handsome, but not healthy. Lindy's stomach constricted.

"Get him out of here."

Juan sidled across the dance floor, hips swaying, until he was next to the couple. He put his arms around Rebo's waist and separated him from the other man.

Lindy saw him whisper into Rebo's ear, then Rebo's eyes met hers. He swayed slightly. Juan kept one arm around his waist, caressed his chest with his other hand, like a lover come to claim his own, and led him to where the others were waiting.

The lights and music were pounding. The heat of too many, too needy bodies stifled the air.

"The bouncer's watching," warned Eric. He laced his arms around Paul and Lindy and started slowly toward the door, laughing. Juan followed with Rebo, who let himself be led away.

Just as they reached the door, Eric slipped his tongue into Paul's ear and groped him erotically. Paul stood bolt upright. "Fresh, but cute, isn't he?" Eric winked at the bouncer, who looked bored and turned to peruse the room. Juan and Rebo had slipped through the door.

"God, that was disgusting," spat Paul as soon as they had reached the parking lot. He threw Eric's arm from his shoulders.

"Sorry. I've always wanted to do that. Won't happen again. Forgive me?"

"I guess."

"It was for a good cause."

"Oh, all right. But never, never do that again."

"Methinks the boy doth protest too much." Rebo grinned. His eyes were glazed. That was obvious even in the dim light of the parking lot. His body leaned on Juan in rubbery abandon.

"Get him in the car," said Lindy. "And don't throw up on my backseat."

They stopped at the first McDonald's they came to, and Lindy ordered large coffees for everyone, two for Rebo, at the drive-through window. He was about halfway through the first cup when whatever he was on started to wear off. "You shouldn't have bothered," he whined from the backseat.

"And leave you there to wallow in self-pity? You have a lot of nerve. Your life just isn't that bad."

"I thought that you—"

"Bullshit. You know I didn't tell Brandecker that you killed Carlotta. It was just an excuse to go off on a binge. Kill yourself if you want to, but not on my time."

"You're really pissed at me, aren't you?"

"Yes." She screamed the word. "I'd like to . . ." She had had enough of violent expressions. "To . . . spank you."

"That would be yummy."

Lindy's anger dissipated into laughter. It was impossible to stay mad at him. "Well, I just might. Especially if I thought it would keep you home."

"Home," Rebo repeated.

"Lindy," said Paul. "There's a car following us."

"Ignore it. Brandecker probably eluded Biddy. I don't feel like adding a chase scene to an already overloaded night. Just don't talk to him when we get back."

But the car continued straight when they turned into the hotel. They hauled Rebo, who had fallen asleep during his second coffee, out of the backseat and through the lobby. The night clerk glanced up, but returned to the paperback he was reading with a look of disgust.

She left them at the door of Juan and Rebo's room. "Don't let him leave. And make sure he's on the bus for the lec-dem at nine-thirty. I hope he feels like shit in the morning."

Seventeen

Rebo was not the only one to look under the weather on Monday morning. Lindy's face was purple, scraped and swollen on one side. The contrast of the untouched skin on her other cheek only made it look worse. Biddy's complexion was blotched from restless sleep. The dancers filed gloomily onto the bus. Dark clouds hovered low above them, but rain refused to come. Wind swept around in little cyclones without managing to find a single dried leaf or stray piece of trash to kick about.

"I think it's time for a company meeting," Lindy said quietly to Biddy as they watched the others embark.

Biddy rolled her eyes.

"Company dinner?"

"That's a better idea, but I'm so tired. I don't think I can stand an 'angsting' session."

"We'll keep it light. Want to drive over with me?"

"No, I think I should go on the bus."

"Then I'll go, too."

It had been a long time since Lindy had been on a tour bus. She stopped by the driver and looked down the row of seats. It was like peering into a diorama, the kind schoolchildren made for book reports. Seats made of folded cardboard. Paper people pasted to the front of each one. *Belinda Graham Goes on Tour* would be the title. It would be about a young girl whose dream in life was to be a ballerina. After a few earth-shattering problems, which would be cleared up rapidly before the final pages, the girl would be the star of the show and have gotten her man, as well.

But these were real people. They may be called kids, but they were full-fledged adults with their own sets of dreams and disappointments. Headsets had come out; faces were buried in paperbacks. A few dancers were already dozing. It didn't matter if they were going five miles or five hundred, they were at home.

And what about her? Was this her home, too? An old, familiar feeling gurgled up from some hidden recess inside her. It was just like the old days: when she was at work, feeling guilty about leaving Glen and the kids; and when she was at home, feeling guilty about not concentrating on her work. Some things didn't change. Where the hell did she belong?

Biddy nudged her from behind. "Are you going to stand all the way to the lec-dem?"

Lindy sat down in the first seat. The high back of the seat cut off everyone else from her view. For the first time since leaving New Jersey, she felt utterly alone.

Biddy stood in the aisle, counting heads, then dropped into the seat beside her, clutching her crutches in both arms. "I'm sorry I got you into this."

Lindy dragged her attention back to the present.

"I just thought you could help me deal with Carlotta. I didn't know she was going to get murdered. We were in New

Jersey, and I automatically thought of you. You always knew exactly what to do when things got tough."

"Biddy, you didn't get me into this. I wanted to come. I thought I was perfectly content until that night at the Endicott. It kind of jostled my perspective of things. I didn't realize before how much I missed this. Silly, isn't it?"

She had given up her career because it was too hard to juggle work, husband, and kids. "I'd already retired as a dancer before I left."

"But you were a great rehearsal director. Still are."

"Yeah, but I wanted to be a great wife and mom, too."

"You are." Biddy squeezed her hand.

Lindy squeezed back. "I guess." God knows she had tried hard enough. While she attempted to shape and mold and enhance the lives of her husband and children, her own life had flown by like a giant desert sandstorm, leaving Lindy in its wake.

Sitting here on a bus in Connecticut, it seemed to her that once she had settled them into the house of their dreams, it was Glen who had taken off. Now, Cliff and Annie had taken off, too. And where did that leave her?

It left her right here, and it was about time she got her act together.

"Really, Biddy, except for the murder and getting pushed down the trapdoor, this has been the most fun I've had in years."

A few minutes later, the bus pulled up in front of the Movement Education Building. A few comments wafted toward her as she gathered up her dance bag.

"Wow, the twentieth century."

"My kingdom for a dressing room with lights that work."

"Cushy."

"The theater in Hartford has been totally renovated," Biddy said primly over the tops of their heads.

The dancers filed off the bus. They moved sluggishly. Well, no one really loves an early-morning call, thought Lindy, but she felt uneasy. Things were beginning to fall apart. Jeremy had removed himself from everyone, like he was waiting for the final blow. This was no time for vacillating. She needed to take control.

"Definitely in need of a company dinner," she said to Biddy. "Where is Jeremy? I'll ask him if it's okay."

"He and Peter came earlier with Angie. Peter has to teach a Stage Craft seminar. He was not thrilled. Talking for a whole hour is not exactly his style."

Angie met them in the upstairs hall. She looked distracted. "Hi, everybody. Girls' dressing room is here, and the boys' is down on the left. Yell, if you need anything." She turned to Biddy and Lindy and led them farther along the corridor.

"The police are here. They took Jack in for questioning this morning, and now they've asked Jeremy to come to the station. There's more than one of them, and they look pretty serious. I hope things aren't getting worse."

Biddy gasped. Jeremy was walking down the hall between Detective Williams and another officer. His face was completely drained of color, but he appeared calm and not surprised at being led away.

A group of girls came out of the door and stopped abruptly, their conversation dying midsentence. They all watched the procession move toward them. Jeremy slowed as he reached the group of worried faces.

He nodded slightly to Biddy. "You'll have to do the lec-

dem. The tapes are in the studio. Peter will be here soon."
And then they were gone.

The girls disappeared back into the dressing room. Lindy
could hear their frantic whispers through the closed door. It
wouldn't be long until everyone had heard. There would be
another round of suspicion, fear. The company was disinte-
grating. She was failing Jeremy, and Biddy.

"You shouldn't have told him, Lindy," Biddy sobbed. "He'll
destroy us. It's your fault." She spun around and hobbled
into the studio.

Angie put her arm around Lindy. "She didn't mean it. I
don't know what's going on. I stayed away because I knew
you'd call if you needed me. She'll be all right."

Lindy choked back a sob. She was a stranger again. Jeremy had turned to Biddy to carry on. He had cut her out of
what she loved most. She skulked down the hall feeling like
the traitor Biddy thought she was. She groped her way around
the corner and pressed her forehead to the wall. Do not fall
apart on me now, she begged.

Crying is a great catharsis—witness the popularity of
tragedy in the theater—but Lindy knew she didn't have time
to cry. That would come later. Tears of relief or wretch-
edness—at this point she didn't care which. She just wanted
it to be over. She'd go home to New Jersey, where she
belonged. She wouldn't complain if Glen watched television
all night. She'd even watch it with him. She banged her forehead on the wall. No, she wouldn't. Pathos. Really, Lindy.
No, bathos, it's even worse. Let's try the stiff-upper-lip routine. She straightened herself up and marched down the hall
and into the rehearsal studio.

* * *

They made it through the lec-dem, answering the usual questions at the end, like, "What do you eat for breakfast?" and "What's touring like?" Not like this, Lindy thought bitterly.

She took her place on the bus; Biddy moved to the back. It was Peter who sat down beside her. They stared out at open fields, new growth bending in the wind, as the bus carried them back to the hotel.

"Now, what?" asked Peter.

Lindy looked at him. His cheekbones stood out like ledges over the hollows of his cheeks.

She leaned her head back against the seat and closed her eyes. "I don't know."

"I've hated him for so long. Now I just want it to be over."

"Me too."

Lindy lingered in the lobby until she saw Biddy go into the elevator. She didn't have the energy or the courage to face more incriminations. There was no news from Jack or Jeremy. She followed the last group of dancers into the elevator and rode up to the third floor.

Biddy was lying facedown on the bed. She made no sound except for an occasional shudder, but her back heaved with silent sobs.

Lindy threw her bag on the floor and sat on the edge of the other bed. And waited.

After a few minutes, Biddy lifted her head from the bed. "Glen called. The message light was on when I got back. I thought it might be word from—" That was as far as she got before she broke down again.

Lindy reached for the phone and pressed the numbers mechanically. Glen answered on the first ring.

"Where have you been? What's going on there? You never return my calls."

Lindy glanced at the top of the dresser and the pile of message slips that had accumulated there. "Yes, I do. Eventually."

"You sound really depressed. Are you okay? Did they arrest anyone yet? Are you safe?"

"Yes, no, yes. I'm just really tired."

"Good. No, I'm serious. Tired is better than a lot of alternatives I can think of. Remember that meeting I told you about?"

"No."

"It was the night of your murder. Anyway, it's definite. They've offered me an overseas consultant position. What do you think?"

Overseas. Like in international travel. More days and nights away from home. Lindy mentally kicked herself. This was a great step-up for him. He deserved it.

"Well? What do you think?"

What did she think? She was . . . envious. "That's great, Glen."

"Big pay increase. A lot of travel, but you can come with me, sometimes. I'll be really busy at first, but after that, we can mix business with some pleasure. What do you say?"

"If it sounds good to you, it sounds good to me."

"Then, I'm going to accept it. I wanted to talk to you first."

"I'm really proud of you. Congratulations."

"Gotta go. Love you."

"Love you, too."

Biddy had raised herself onto one elbow. "What was that all about?"

"Glen just got a promotion. Overseas consultant, whatever that is. Lots of travel. That will be fun," Lindy said without much enthusiasm. A string of lonely nights with only Bruno as company stretched before her. A nice, warm, hairy body that snored, shed, and had doggy breath. Great.

"You'd be traveling with him?"

Lindy shrugged. "Sometimes. It will be nice to go back to all those places I never got to see the first time around. The inside of a theater looks the same in any country. Dark. I'll enjoy being a tourist for a change."

"Oh."

"What?"

"I was kind of hoping that you might stay on."

"Biddy. You're the most changeable creature I've ever met. I thought you hated me."

"I'm not changeable," said Biddy. "I'm just resilient. There's a difference. Anyway, I don't hate you. I was upset. I lashed out at the safest person. I knew you'd forgive me. Right?"

Lindy moved over to Biddy and gave her a hug. The telephone rang.

"Glen," said Lindy as she picked up the receiver. "Hello." A pause. "What do you want?"

Biddy sat up and mouthed the word "Who?"

"Listen, Mr. Brandecker. I don't need to talk to you. I don't want to talk to you. You've got what you wanted, now leave us alone." She slammed the phone down. "The nerve of the guy." The phone rang again. "Don't answer it."

It kept ringing. They sat, unmoving.

"How long do you think he'll keep this up?" asked Biddy.

Lindy shrugged. The ringing stopped. She grabbed the receiver and shoved it under her pillow. "This should take care of any more phone calls." They sat on Biddy's bed, staring at Lindy's pillow, nerves on edge.

Biddy squeaked when the banging on the door began.

"Don't answer it," commanded Lindy.

"Lindy, he could keep pounding on the door all day."

"Then I'll call security."

"You think security is going to tangle with a policeman, and one that big? Maybe you should hear him out and then get rid of him once and for all."

"You get rid of him. I'll hide in the bathroom."

Biddy erupted into giggles. "It's a ridiculous idea."

"It worked in Brussels, didn't it? Oh, all right. But I'm not going to be nice."

Bill Brandecker had no intention of being nice, either. Before Lindy had the door open, he pushed his way through and slammed it behind him.

"I know you think this is my fault," he bellowed at her. A vein in his temple pulsed. Veins always pulsed noticeably in fiction. Lindy had never actually seen one pulse in real life, and she found it fascinating.

Not getting any reaction, Bill stopped yelling and looked at her. "What are you looking at?"

"The side of your head."

A growl rolled from deep in his throat. He turned to Biddy, who cowered back against the headboard. "How can you stand her?" He turned back to Lindy, who still stood by the door. "If you ever—could get control of your wandering thoughts, even for a second—you might—just might—organize them into an ordered thought process." The sentence had taken several breaths and had ended in a near roar.

Lindy knew this trick. Attack before they have time to attack you. She'd wait him out and then let him have it.

"Are you finished?" she asked calmly. "If you are, I can recommend a good theatrical agent. You need a little fine-tuning, but a few lessons should do the trick."

She very methodically opened the door. "Good day."

Bill looked stunned. He eyed her intensely for a few seconds and then walked out the door.

Lindy leaned back against it. "I've always wanted to do that exit. Just like in the BBC version of *Pride and Prejudice* where Eliza gives Lady Catherine the boot."

"I feel a little sorry for him," said Biddy. She pulled the receiver from under the pillow and replaced it on the table.

"I can't believe you. Just a few hours ago, you were saying he had destroyed our lives. And now you feel sorry for him?"

"He doesn't seem so bad in person. He's so loud and big. But I think he, well, respects you."

"Just remember that he ratted on us."

"He didn't really have much of a choice."

"I know. I shouldn't have confided in him. I just didn't know what else to do."

"I didn't mean all those things I said. You did the right thing."

"So what *are* you saying?"

"Maybe you should talk to him if he calls again. Maybe he'd be willing to help if you ask nicely."

Lindy bared her teeth. "Like this?"

The telephone rang.

It was the "I'm sorry" that did it. Lindy wasn't used to men apologizing, straight out with no extenuating reasons tacked on. They usually turned it into being your fault: "Sorry, but you know I had to work late ... Sorry, but all the other moms ... But if you had only—I would have ... Sorry, but you always ..."

That simple "I'm sorry," period, nothing else, had left her momentarily nonplused. And before she could recover, she had agreed to meet him downstairs.

Bill was sitting in one of the overstuffed club chairs in the lobby. He rose when he saw her. He seemed to tower over her. He didn't look contrite, and for a second, Lindy wished she had sent Biddy in her place. She had expended the last of her energy in the confrontation upstairs. She felt claustrophobic.

"I suppose it's too early for a drink?" he asked.

"Let's walk. I can't stand it in here." She headed toward the front door. Bill stuffed his hands into the back pockets of his jeans and followed her out.

"There's an access road down on the left," he said.

She turned to the left. The day was still overcast, but the clouds had lifted and the sky had turned a light gray. Still no rain, but the air was chilled. She crossed her arms in front of her.

"Cold?"

Lindy shook her head. Bill seemed to have shrunk to normal size in the outdoors. Open space was a better background for him, she thought. He was more approachable.

She felt sorry for his students, who probably cowered in their seats during his classroom lectures.

"The police knew everything. Nothing I told them had much bearing on their decision to requestion Jeremy."

"I thought you would help us," she blurted out, her anger making a brief resurgence.

"I'm trying. But what do you care more about? Saving your friend or finding the truth?"

"He didn't do it," she snapped, but her voice lacked the conviction she wanted to feel. "What about Jack?"

"They've released him for now."

"Why?"

"He admitted to skimming the books, but he implicated Jeremy in that, too. He said that Jeremy forced him to take the money, and out of loyalty, he did."

"That's a crock."

"I think so, too."

"You do?" She looked up at him expectantly. His eyes were definitely blue. "Then are you going to help us?"

"It isn't that simple. You know absolutely nothing about the way an investigation is carried on, do you?"

"No. I've never even had a parking ticket. Well, except once when—"

"Don't get started." He smiled.

She shut up.

Bill took her arm and steered her down the access road that skirted the parking lot and led to the back of the hotel.

"Let me explain a few things," he said pedantically, and Lindy braced herself for a big dose of condescension. "I shouldn't tell you anything. I wouldn't know anything about the case myself except Dell sees me as some kind of expert on the waywardness of arty types."

Lindy started to speak, but he stopped her. "Jeremy has means, motive, and opportunity. Carlotta refused to alibi him for this previous accident. It's all in the records, if you have access to them. Then his life falls apart. You can see how that might fester until he was driven to get his revenge."

"Circumstantial, right?"

"Alone, but coupled with the fact that he can't account for his whereabouts at the time of the murder, that the choreographer was pressuring him to fire her, and his fingerprints were on the candlestick ..." Bill turned his hand, palm up, in a gesture that said fait accompli.

"But he picked it up after Carlotta threatened Eric with it. Everybody saw him."

Bill nodded, but Lindy knew there was more coming. "They're hoping they can get a confession."

"Even if he's not guilty? You make it sound like a police state."

"They don't torture people, Lindy, just manipulate them into telling the truth. I shouldn't have told you this, but I owe you one for being honest with me yesterday. You can send cookies to my jail cell if they find out I've talked to you."

He had made the last statement casually, but Lindy didn't miss the enormity of its implication. "You were a lousy cop, weren't you?" she asked gently.

"Yeah." He looked over her head into the distance. "You get caught up in people's lives, then go about systematically destroying them. It wasn't so bad with the hardened criminals, but you'd be surprised how many homicides are committed by normally decent human beings."

They had cut off the access road and were walking down a heavily overgrown dirt track, an abandoned tractor path that was no longer needed since the surrounding fields no longer supported working farms. Shoots of new grass mixed with the dried stalks of old, their height virtually blocking out the view. Only the top of the hotel was visible.

Lindy felt her head begin to clear; her body relax. Fresh air had a way of doing that. "What if Sandra's accident really wasn't an accident?"

"That would make it worse for Jeremy."

"No. Not Jeremy, but someone else." She had been wrestling with an idea for days. It was out of reach still, but maybe the two of them could ferret it out. "What if, say, Jack was involved, and Carlotta was blackmailing him?"

"Go on."

"I mean, Jack has been sending flowers all these years, every two weeks. That seems a little extreme unless, maybe, he was responsible for the accident."

"An interesting idea, but it doesn't help with the current murder. Jack didn't return from New York until the next day."

"But he did."

"What? How do you know, and why didn't you tell the police?"

"Hearsay."

"You're getting your terms mixed up."

"Everything is all mixed up, but I know he was back. I saw his car leave the parking lot. It was late, around three in the morning. I couldn't sleep. I was staring out the window and I saw his car drive away. I didn't make the connection at first. I was preoccupied with everything else, and I didn't expect to see his car because I thought he was in New York. It was a dark car. But now that I think back, I'm sure it was Jack's. Old, big, black. That would mean he was here and could have murdered Carlotta."

"I think you're stretching facts to fit into the scenario you want."

"Are they sure Jack was in New York all that night? Maybe he came back, then left and came back again."

Bill looked amused. "I'll see if I can find out, let's turn back."

"I know you're just humoring me," she said as they began retracing their steps. "You think I'm totally dizzed-out, but I'm not. It's more instinct than intelligence, but I know I'm right."

He reached for her shoulder and swung her around. "You may be right, and I'll help you if I can, but do not act on this yourself. I don't want to investigate your murder." He pulled her toward him and kissed her. A major kiss, arms enfolding her. A wave of fascination, then something stronger, rushed up her body. Heady stuff. It had been a long time since a man had come on to her so abruptly and so . . . thoroughly. She had no choice but to respond. For a minute.

She broke away. What the hell was she doing? "Don't."

Bill gazed out over the tops of the surrounding grasses. "I know. But I figured it was the only chance I'd get."

She felt the blood rush up her neck and into her cheeks. How could he stand there with that distracted half smile on his face? *She* probably looked awkward and embarrassed . . . and eager. She looked away.

"We'd better get back." Bill shoved his hands back into his pockets and began walking toward the hotel. She fell in step beside him, neither of them breaking the silence.

They returned to the access road. The pavement felt hard and secure beneath her feet. "Can you find out if Jack was really in New York?" Her voice only sounded a little shaky.

"I'll try, but I have to get back to the city. They'll probably release you to go on to Hartford tomorrow with or without Jeremy. But you and Biddy had better start thinking about what to do with the company. Jack will be arraigned on embezzling, if Jeremy files charges. If they have enough on Jeremy, it will go to trial. Somebody will have to deal with the business end."

"Biddy can handle that if she has to." She was ridiculously close to tears. "I'll handle the rest, but . . ."

"I'll contact you in Hartford if I find out anything."

"Thanks. I'm sorry we ruined your vacation."

They finished the walk back in silence.

"He kissed me."

"I knew it," cried Biddy triumphantly. "And on a scale of one to ten?"

"Biddy, it's not funny."

"Lindy, if you're going to get back out in the world, you've got to be prepared for men falling in love with you. They always did, remember?"

"But it was fun then. This wasn't fun."

"But was it good?"

Lindy shot her a menacing look. Biddy stood with one

hand on her hip, that saucy "tell me every detail" expression on her face. One lift of her eyebrow, and Lindy was ready to confess. She sank onto the bed.

"Delicious."

"Oops." They both started to laugh. "So what are you going to do about it?"

"What any red-blooded American girl would do—forget it ever happened."

Biddy frowned.

"We've got too much to deal with already without adding adultery to the pot. But, oh, Biddy."

"So what did you learn?"

"That you sleep in the bed you make."

"About the investigation."

"Oh." Lindy straightened up. She ran through the conversation with Bill, explaining her dawning ideas about Jack.

"Wow, that makes perfect sense."

"If only it were true. Bill also said that they'll send us on to Hartford tomorrow, and we'd better be prepared to carry on without Jeremy."

Biddy didn't even flinch at the suggestion. She had readied herself for the fight. Lindy felt a sudden surge of hope.

Eighteen

They moved on to Hartford the following morning without Jeremy. Biddy rode on the bus; Lindy followed behind in her car.

The bus maneuvered down the narrow city street and double-parked in front of the hotel, a building dating from the 1920s, which was flanked by two rows of smaller boutiques. Lindy pulled up behind the bus and was relieved of her suitcase by a waiting bellboy, and of her car by a parking valet. "If you need your car, call the front desk, and it will be driven around. The parking garage is around the corner and very secure." He drove away.

She walked through the double wooden doors, held open by a uniformed doorman. The lobby could have been used for an F. Scott Fitzgerald set. Tall potted palms rose on each side of the chestnut registration desk; the entire lobby was paneled in the same polished wood. The atmosphere was warm and rich, and evoked the insouciance of another era.

Lindy could have appreciated the ambience if she hadn't been so preoccupied. She longed for the serenity that her surroundings promised, but knew there would be no peace for any of them until one of them was declared a murderer and removed from this life forever.

She shuddered involuntarily and followed the bellboy up the curving staircase to her room.

"I've called a company meeting for six o'clock. The hotel can put us in one of the banquet rooms," announced Biddy as she pulled clothes out of her suitcase and tossed them haphazardly into drawers. "We'll feed them, but we'll have to let them know what's going on."

"And what is going on? I saw you talking to Detective Williams at the hotel this morning, but I didn't want to interrupt," said Lindy.

"They haven't arrested Jeremy yet. Just held him over-night for questioning. I guess they have to arrest him or let him go."

"And how are we going to find that out?"

"When he shows up in Hartford, or doesn't."

"Then, we'll just have to stick it out. In the meantime, you have some nervous sponsors to meet."

"In two hours. I hope you'll come with me. I think I can convince them not to cancel, that we can carry on. There'll be a lot of loss on both sides if we can't deliver."

"We'll deliver, and, of course, I'll come."

The rest of the afternoon was spent reassuring the Hartford Arts Association. They met at the theater, which was only a block away from the hotel. It wasn't an easy meeting. There were a few members with extremely cold feet, but Biddy was convincing, and even Lindy was swayed by her seeming confidence.

There was a telegram waiting for her at the desk when she and Biddy returned to the hotel.

"I haven't gotten a telegram since my last opening night." She tore open the envelope. "It's from Bill. Quaint, but more private than leaving a message."

Lindy read it through and then crumpled it in her hand. "Jack's clear. He charged gas at ten o'clock going north on I-ninety-five."

"I'd still like to ask that rat a few more questions," said Biddy.

"So would I, but I doubt if he'll make another appearance. I wouldn't dare show my face if I were in his place. It's your baby now."

They barely had enough time to shower and change before meeting the dancers downstairs. They mulled over how to approach the meeting while choosing what to wear. They discussed what to say, and more importantly what not to say.

"I guess we've seen the last of Bill Brandecker, too," said Lindy.

"Are you sorry?"

"No, not really. But it doesn't seem like him to just walk away. Though he's spent more time on us than we have any right to expect." She pulled a pair of shoes out of the armoire that served as the closet.

"Maybe you should have encouraged his advances."

"It was not an advance, more like an experiment."

"Maybe you should have encouraged him to experiment more." Biddy finished pulling a green velour sweater over her head. "All right. Sorry. I was just trying to make a joke."

"Laugh so we won't cry. Nice try."

"Oh, come on, Lindy. Married people play around all the time."

"Not me."

"I know, not you. But don't you miss it?"

"Not until now."

"Well, it wouldn't be the worst thing in the world. People do it all the time."

"And we know what happens to those people. Marriage is like that finger in the dike thing. Relax your vigil for a second even, and you might drown in the results."

"Sounds too complicated to me."

"Like the war on drugs, you just say no." Lindy slipped her arm over Biddy's shoulder and they hurried downstairs.

The company was assembled in the smaller of two banquet rooms, tastefully refurbished like the rest of the hotel. The waitresses and busboys seemed happy enough to accommodate the group at the last minute. Lindy wondered how long it would take before she saw suspicion in the faces of that well-trained staff.

Peter looked up from a huddle of dancers. Lindy noticed that Andrea was among them. Could anything good come out of this mess? Peter, if no one else, deserved some respite. "We've loaded in, floor's down," he said as Biddy and Lindy approached the group. "Is it a go?"

Lindy watched Biddy assume her "business face."

"Yes, it's a go." She turned to the rest of the room who had stopped their conversations in order to listen. "We're continuing on. Jeremy has been delayed in order to clear up a few loose ends, but he'll be joining us soon. You're all free to leave as far as the police are concerned, but I hope you'll stay on. It's been a frightful experience, and, unfortunately, it isn't over yet. We've been through more than a lot together, but we have something good here. I can feel it. I know you can feel it. Let's not lose it now, when we're so close."

"But, Biddy, what if they arrest Jeremy? Are we still going to have jobs?"

She turned in the direction of the voice. "We're contracted through the Joyce season. That gives you a paycheck through May. Beyond that, I don't know. It will depend."

"What's going to happen to Jack? We heard what he's been doing. You're not going to let him back, are you?"

"Jack won't be working here any longer. I don't have the authority to fire him, but I'll make sure he doesn't touch another penny of the company's money."

"But he signs all the checks," said someone else.

"Not without Jeremy's accompanying signature, or in Jeremy's absence, mine."

Lindy looked at her in astonishment. When had she managed all of this?

"I want you all to take time to consider before you make any decisions. I hope you'll decide to stay. Now, let's eat."

Talking broke out again as the dancers moved toward the tables.

"I'm staying." Rebo's voice resounded from the crowd. "I don't have to think about it. If you want me, I'm staying."

"Thanks, Rebo." Biddy's voice was tremulous. "We want you."

Lindy sat next to Biddy. "When did you get the power to sign checks?"

"I've always had it, in case we needed a check and one of the two signers wasn't available. It's a normal formality."

"Oh," said Lindy, impressed.

They proceeded through dinner: salad of field greens with balsamic vinaigrette, a main course of above-average chicken Marsala with julienne vegetables. It was not the lively affair that most company dinners were, but at least they were together. Nothing like breaking bread to put things back on an even keel.

The room was set up banquet style, tables pushed together to form a U. Lindy and Biddy were sitting at one of the sides. Lindy watched Rebo spread his arms in front of his dinner companions. Jesus at the Last Supper, she thought and bobbled her wineglass. There was a burst of laughter, and the image faded.

She had regained her composure and was half listening to Biddy recounting some tale of tour when Mieko and Kate burst into the room.

Mieko looked wildly around until she zeroed in on Lindy. "He's here, that bastard," she exclaimed breathlessly. "Jack. We saw him in the lobby. We were coming back from the bathroom. He looked like he was checking in. I can't believe it."

"Biddy, what are we going to do?" asked Kate. "Should we try to stop him?"

"We'll take care of Jack." Rebo sprang from his chair. Paul, Eric, and Juan started to rise, but Peter already had his hand on Rebo's shoulder.

"I'll take care of it." He pushed Rebo back into his seat and started toward the door.

Alice jumped up, turning her chair over, but Andrea had

already followed Peter out. Lindy and Biddy followed her, with the rest of the company behind them.

Peter had stopped Jack on his way to the stairs. The desk clerk was looking on nervously.

Jack's voice was low and spiteful. "You're wasting your energy, Peter. There's not much you can do at this point."

"I can keep you away from the company, and I will."

Jack snorted and turned away; Peter's hand caught him by the shoulder. Jack responded by swinging his briefcase into Peter's ribs, doubling him over. Andrea was knocked down by the impact of Peter's weight hitting her.

Biddy rushed past them. "You're finished here, Jack. You can wrap up whatever business you think you have tomorrow and then leave."

"That's exactly what I plan to do. There is no company. They'll arrest Jeremy for Carlotta's murder, and that will be the end of this little travesty." He pushed past her and rushed up the stairs.

"You can't stop us, Jack," cried Biddy to his retreating form. "We're going to make it."

The faces behind her had plunged once more into hopelessness. Lindy was glad that Biddy was staring up the stairs. "Let's get back to dessert, shall we?" The group moved back into the banquet room. Andrea was attempting to help Peter, but he pushed her away and lunged for the stairs.

"Peter, no." Biddy's voice stopped him at the foot of the stairs. He seemed to waver, then turned and strode across the lobby, out the front door, and into the street.

Andrea stared after him. Lindy put her arm around the girl. "He just needs some time to cool off. He'll be back."

Andrea bit her lip and quietly shook her head. "I don't want to go back in there."

Lindy led her over to one of the paisley-covered love seats that sat at each side of a square glass coffee table. The front door was hidden from their view by a large potted palm; a few of the bottom fronds were turning brown.

"Why can't he open up? Trust someone?"

Lindy watched the girl twist the tails of her knit shirt into a ball. She wasn't prepared to give advice to the lovelorn. She felt terribly out of her league. "I don't know."

"Alice says he's completely devoted to his sister and never looks at another woman."

"Well, he doesn't look at Alice, anyway."

Andrea laughed softly. "I almost miss Carlotta. When she was mean to me, he always stood up for me. I thought that maybe ... but I guess I was wrong."

"I wouldn't be so sure." Lindy looked furtively around. If Peter would just make an entrance, she could wrap this up. But Peter wasn't accommodating.

"When I found the ... when I found ... her, he was so gentle. He told me what to tell the police, and how to—"

"He told you what to say to the police?" Lindy interrupted.

Andrea nodded. "He said, if they pushed me, to tell them I heard a noise, and that I went in to see what it was."

"And did you?"

Andrea looked at her blankly. "Did I what?"

"Did you tell the police that you heard a noise?"

"No. I couldn't lie. I know Peter was trying to protect me." She sighed deeply, a shiver running across her shoulders. "At least, I thought he was. But now he hardly even speaks to me."

"So you didn't hear a noise?" Why hadn't she questioned Andrea more closely?

"No. I went in to tell Carlotta what a bitch she was and to leave us alone. I had had enough. When you took everyone back to the stage at intermission, Peter followed her. She said the most awful things to him. Said he was useless; that he couldn't even help his own sister. I could have killed her when I heard her. And stuff about Sandra, vicious things. She was insanely jealous of everybody, even a poor girl who will never dance again."

"Did you see him leave?"

"What?"

Lindy grabbed the girl by her shoulders and faced her directly in front of her. "Was Carlotta alive when he left her?"

"Of course. He stormed out and back to the light board, and she slammed the door."

Lindy let out a momentary sigh of relief. "And did you see Jeremy then?"

"No. He was still in his office with Eric."

Lindy released Andrea's shoulders and jumped up. "Look, I'm sure things will work out. Peter just needs some time to figure it out. So much has been happening. Why don't you stay and wait for him?" She practically ran across the lobby in her rush to find Biddy. As inconspicuously as she could, she dragged Biddy away from her coffee and cheesecake and led her to the stairs. Andrea was sitting where she had left her. Lindy hoped she wouldn't have too long to wait.

"What—what?" asked Biddy as Lindy closed the door to their room.

"Peter saw Carlotta alive during the intermission after the fight, a little tidbit, he forgot to mention, at least to me. Andrea just told me. I didn't even think to ask her. I am such a dolt."

"But how does this help Jeremy?" Biddy held up her hands. "I know, write it down." She grabbed hotel stationery and a pen out of the desk drawer and plopped onto the bed.

"Carlotta was alive during the intermission, and after I released everyone, there was a rush to get ready for the next piece. People were all over the place. So it had to happen during the *Holberg Suite* or during notes afterward."

"So we've narrowed the time down about ten minutes. What now?"

Lindy sighed with disappointment. "We keep narrowing, eliminating possibilities until we get it right. I want to talk to Peter." She picked up the phone and rang the front desk.

"Andrea's gone. What are the chances that she and Peter . . ."

"And if they are, should we interrupt them?" added Biddy.

They were interrupted by a knock. Exchanging glances, they both went to answer the door.

Not Peter, not Jack, but Jeremy. Smiling.

"Thank God, how did you—what did they say?" Words tumbled out of Biddy's mouth in an avalanche of relief.

Jeremy responded by gathering her up, crutches included, and giving her a hearty hug.

Hmm, thought Lindy, and then she was gathered up, too.

Their levity didn't last long. Jeremy pulled away. He looked tired and disheveled. He had changed clothes, but

Lindy could tell he hadn't paid much attention to what he had put on. She could see tiny lines of fatigue around his mouth and eyes.

"You look beat. Sit down and tell us what happened, if you can stand to."

Jeremy moved away from them, shrugged out of his jacket, and threw it across the bed. He sat down in the boudoir chair next to the window. He was much too big for the chair, and it took a few seconds for him to find a comfortable position. Biddy and Lindy sat next to each other on the end of Biddy's bed facing him.

"The upshot is they had to let me go, momentarily at least. They didn't want to; we're now in somebody else's jurisdiction, but they couldn't put all the 'maybes' together enough to actually arrest me. And I wouldn't oblige them by confessing to something I didn't do." He looked from Biddy to Lindy and back again, waiting for a reaction.

It was Biddy who spoke. "You big idiot. Don't you dare look at us that way. We know you didn't do it."

Jeremy looked down at his hands, then at Lindy. She shook her head slightly. Men, she thought. Jeremy was worried that she had told Biddy about Sandra and him. He was sitting here, suspected of murder, and he was embarrassed about an old love affair.

"Jack's here."

Jeremy vaulted to his feet. "Him, I could kill. He implicated me. Told them that I had made him steal the money. What an imbecile. All they had to do was look at our bank accounts to know that was a lie. What's he up to, I wonder."

"I'm going to find out right now." Biddy heaved herself off the bed. Her crutches clattered onto the carpet.

"Sit down, both of you." Lindy was exasperated beyond endurance. "It's worse than the opera around here. Comic opera, if it weren't so tragic. No one is what they seem. Skeletons in every closet. Misguided lovers. Threats and chases and trapdoors." Biddy and Jeremy were staring at her, eyes round. "Sit down."

They sat down.

"Now, we're going to start again. Take it one step at a time." She felt like a schoolteacher facing two dull students. "Jeremy didn't kill Carlotta. Biddy didn't kill Carlotta. I didn't kill Carlotta."

She was interrupted by a knock on the door. "Oh, God, not again. It's worse than New Jersey." She dropped onto the bed and threw her arms over her head. Jeremy and Biddy broke out laughing.

"No, stay where you are, I'll get it," offered Jeremy, still laughing. He looked at Biddy, and she broke out into a new round of giggles.

Peter was not laughing. "I heard you were back." He looked at Jeremy, but didn't step inside.

"Come in, Peter. Welcome to Bedlam." Jeremy clapped him on the shoulder and moved him through the door.

The realization hit Lindy like a bolt of proverbial lightning. Jeremy had no idea of how Peter felt about him. She could hardly believe it, but Jeremy seemed entirely comfortable with the other man. Was it possible that they had spent this much time together without him picking up on how Peter felt? It seemed incredible. Well, maybe it was time he found out. The action in the room continued without her. Doubt fought with certainty in her overloaded brain.

She took the chance. "Jeremy, Peter thinks you injured

Sandra." She was vaguely aware of Jeremy stopping, his arm still around Peter's shoulder. Peter stared at her, eyes blazing. Biddy turned to her, face frozen in an unfinished laugh. Gee, people really do move in slow motion, she thought.

"I think it's about time the two of you had a little chat." She turned to Jeremy, who still hadn't absorbed her outburst. "Everything, Jeremy." She turned to Peter, who hadn't moved. "Hear him out. And don't do anything stupid. Biddy and I are going for a walk, a long walk, maybe we'll find an all-night grocery store. Peruse the cabbages. Take as long as you want, but get it done."

She walked to the armoire and grabbed two jackets indiscriminately off the hangers. "Come on, Biddy." Biddy scrambled for her crutches and followed her out.

There were no all-night grocery stores. There were no all-night anythings. The neighborhood was dark and deserted. She didn't want to talk to Biddy, and Biddy, for once, didn't seem inclined to ask any questions. They stopped in front of a jewelry store, staring through the plate-glass window at empty velvet display cases.

Lindy couldn't calm her ragged nerves. She stared at the velvet until it began to dance in front of her unfocused eyes. She felt deflated, alone, and she missed . . . Bill. Damn Brandecker. Why did he have to kiss her? But it was more than that. It was the camaraderie, the working together. Well, at least the promise of it.

She did a quick edit. Glen—maybe she should call Glen. But unlike Bill, he would never understand what was going on. How could he? Everything in his life worked perfectly to schedule. All the way up the corporate ladder, he had never had more than minor setbacks, quickly overcome. She envied him in a way. He was comfortable with his life, with their life. After all, they had spent eighteen years building a marriage—or maybe she had been doing the building. He never seemed to have to work at anything. And once Lindy had agreed to marry him, he didn't even have to work at that.

She felt a tear slide down her cheek. Not now, she thought. She never felt comfortable anywhere. Her life was all over the place, the highest highs, the lowest lows. Never anything in between. Why couldn't she just be satisfied with the way things were. Another tear joined the first.

"What's the matter?" asked Biddy without turning to look at her.

"Life is so stupid," she croaked.

"Don't I know it."

They continued to roam the empty streets for an hour. They had passed by the hotel three times when Lindy turned into the door. "That should do it."

Their room was empty. "Well, no sirens. Maybe they worked it out." She still hadn't told Biddy what it was all about.

Nineteen

The next morning, Lindy and Biddy walked to the theater. Almost a week had passed since Carlotta had been found dead in her dressing room, and they were still no closer to finding out who had killed her. Every day had brought new possibilities, new suspicions, and then had dead-ended. Jeremy still wasn't in the clear, as far as the police were concerned. Jack was gone. Maybe they should have found a reason to keep him around for a few days. If he had killed Carlotta, he would walk away free, and they would never know for sure.

The sun beat down, warm and reassuring. Lindy listened to the one-two rhythm of Biddy's crutches along the sidewalk. A new theater. Maybe the change would help, but there could be no going back, no attempt to reconstruct the time sequence, no looking into unexplored crannies for clues that had eluded them. They hadn't even been admitted into Carlotta's dressing room to pack her things. Only Alice had been allowed to retrieve those items belonging to the company, signing for them. The rest had been packed away and taken by the police.

Hawthorne Theater had been part of a massive regentrification of downtown Hartford. Not the new high-rise district, but the picturesque, dying old town. Constructed of brick and stone, its Federal-style facade stood out hopefully among boarded-up shops and storefronts waiting for renovation. Across the street, two restaurants accommodated the theater patrons; one, an Italian coffee bar, the other, a nouveau bistro. They were closed now, not opening until late afternoon.

Biddy and Lindy had used the main entrance for the meeting with the Arts Association. It had taken place in an office, which still smelled of new carpet. Now they turned down an alley on the side of the theater toward the stage entrance. The sun immediately gave way to a cool, dark passage. The theater rose several stories on their right; the old savings and loan building, soon to be a shopping mall, matched its height to their left.

The alley was narrow, and they had to walk single file past the newly painted fire escape, which reached to the upper levels of the theater. Lindy paused, her eyes following the black iron grids upward.

Biddy pulled up short behind her. "Let's stick to trapdoors, okay?"

"My exact thoughts." Lindy brought her attention back to the alley. She intended to memorize every detail of the walk; she planned to scope out the entire theater. If something was going to happen, she would be prepared. But what was she expecting?

They had reached the metal stage door; it swung open. A shiver ran through her. She walked inside.

"Mornin', miss." An ancient, frail man wearing a security uniform was sitting on a rickety stool. He looked up from a clipboard that lay across his lap. "Name's Sal, and you are?"

He finished the question by squinting his eyes at them, glinting eyes encased in a landscape of deep wrinkles.

"Graham and McFee."

His fingers scrolled down the list. "Right." He nodded them in.

Security guard, noted Lindy. Phone on the wall behind him. Outside line. She reached for the inner door. There was a buzz, and it opened. She looked back at Sal. His hand was touching the wall to his right. She began to feel easier.

They walked into a hallway and through another metal door to stage right. Brand-new curtains separated the wings. She walked onto the stage and peered out into the house. The houselights were dimmed, and an enormous crystal chandelier created a halo of light over the red velvet seats. Fabric covered the walls of the auditorium; it would wreak havoc with the acoustics. The ceiling was covered by painted scenes in the Rococo style: helmeted gods riding on clouds; reclining women, with Greek gowns draped suggestively around their voluptuous figures.

"Wow," said Biddy, her head tilted back regarding the scene.

"Let's see the rest."

The dressing rooms were upstairs behind the stage. Directly underneath them were the shop, costume and prop rooms. They climbed the concrete stairs to a landing, then took the turn up another flight.

"You'll get your exercise here," said Lindy as she watched Biddy rattle up behind her.

"Another week and I'll be out of this darned thing, I hope." The sentence bounced out as her crutches hit each step.

They turned down the hall to the left. Lindy made a note of the fire exit to their right. The dressing rooms had been unlocked. They were plain, but sparkling clean. New plumbing had been installed. She hit the light switch inside the first room, and bright makeup lights outlined nondistorting mirrors. The walls had been stripped to the brickwork and shone with a layer of polyurethane. A full-length mirror was attached to the wall next to the tiny window that looked out over the street behind the theater.

"Very nice. Now I think I'll check out the rest of the theater before everyone else gets here."

"Not me." Biddy dropped into a chair. "I think I'll just take a rest before making the descent."

Lindy returned below and peeked into the costume room. Alice was on her knees, steaming the chiffon *Holberg* dresses. The dresses were lined up on hangers like empty doll clothes. She continued on. Open space doubled as the shop and loading dock. To her left, sunlight poured through the half-raised door. She looked to her right. The wall behind the stage was mounted on rails so that it could be opened to move scenery directly from truck to shop to stage and then closed again. Very efficient use of space, she thought. Smaller metal doors on each side led to backstage. The backstage extended all the way to the outside wall. She went in the stage-left door.

Peter was on headset, setting lighting cues. He nodded to her. "I could get lazy in a theater like this," he said between instructions.

She smiled. He seemed relaxed. She wondered if he and Jeremy had come to an understanding. She doubted if she would ever know what they had said to each other.

She wandered onto the stage. The pit was up, but it was

separated from the audience by a brass rail. She went offstage and through the door to the house. She slipped through the curtain that hid it from view by the audience and sat down in the first row, center. It was quiet, except for the occasional clank of metal as the crew unpacked sections of the *Carmina* cage. Lights popped on and off, faded and grew brighter, then changed as Peter tested the next cue.

This was her favorite time in the theater, when everything was still before you. Planning, focusing, imagining the reviews. If she concentrated, she could forget the turmoil of the week before. But it wouldn't go away: images of Carlotta's hair stinging Jeremy's face; the fall from the cage; Carlotta lying contorted on the floor, mixed with scenes of gay bars and hotel bars; Jeremy walking between two policemen; Biddy crying; Jack's briefcase knocking Peter off balance; Alice, standing backstage, saying, "I love this music." They were all wound in a tangled mess in her head. If she could just find the thread that would unravel it, like the thread that when pulled released the hemline of a dress, it would all fall into place, wouldn't it?

The sound of dancers entering the stage door brought her back to the present. She got up wearily and went to show them to their dressing rooms.

The rehearsal started off brightly. Everyone seemed to have pulled together in spite of Jack's brief resurgence last night. Spacing for *Holberg* went quickly since the University and Hawthorne Theaters had standard-size stages with the same number of wings. Lindy called out her corrections from the house. After an hour, they changed over to *Carmina*.

Jeremy stood at the side of the stage, looking on. They

began the run. Andrea threw the cloak open, and he stepped forward motioning to Peter in the wings to stop the tape.

"Do you mind, Lindy?" He turned to where she was sitting in the audience.

"Not at all," she replied in mild surprise. It was the first time she had seen Jeremy take an active part in a rehearsal since she had arrived.

He walked over to Andrea and spoke to her. She flashed him a huge smile, then closed the cloak around her and opened it again, this time with more flourish. "Better, try it again and this time . . ." He moved behind her and wrapped the cloak and his arms around her, holding her by the wrists. "Now." He curved his body over her, making her contract to the right and then threw her arms open. The train of the cloak swirled around her feet, entwining them. The lamé lining shone brilliantly on each side of her willowy body.

He looked out to Lindy for confirmation. She leaned back in her seat. Perfect. She nodded happily. Maybe they were on their way back.

Jeremy stayed on stage, maneuvering groups, shaping individuals, repeating sections. Lindy sat back watching. He was really good at this, and he was finally free to work again. And then the feeling came back. It wasn't over. She had to make it right. There was no one to depend on but herself.

Jeremy gave the dancers a ten-minute break. Lindy walked backstage. Jeremy was talking to Peter, head cocked slightly to the side. She could sense the new understanding between them.

She felt a bright future hanging precariously before her, but danger seemed to be lurking in every wing. Melodramatic, she thought disgustedly. Get a grip. Think logically. She surveyed the backstage area intently as if by looking hard enough she could draw the answer from the walls. But these were new walls with no memory of what had happened. She gave it up and went back to her seat.

Biddy joined her. "I heard that Jeremy was taking rehearsal this morning. I hope I haven't missed it. He's good, isn't he?"

Lindy nodded.

The dancers took their places. Jeremy was back onstage; he was having a great time. She and Biddy watched in silent admiration until Lindy felt someone slide into the row behind them. She turned around.

"Bill, where have you been?"

He looked tired and rumpled, and he was wearing a suit. His shirt was unbuttoned at the neck, and Lindy could see the end of his tie hanging out of his coat pocket. She had never seen him wearing anything but jeans before. A suit, even a wrinkled one, gave him an air of . . . competency.

"We thought you had deserted us," Lindy began.

"Don't give me a hard time, Lindy. I've just spent two days and nights badgering New Yorkers, and I'm tired and—"

"Cranky," she finished for him.

"And cranky. I didn't desert you. I was doing some research."

"What kind of research?" Biddy turned around in her seat.

"Looking at records from Sandra's accident report, what little there was of them. Picking the brains of anybody who was still around who had worked on the investigation, and spending half of last night in search of Sandra's old boyfriend."

"Wow," said Biddy.

Lindy just stared in amazement. "You're a genius," she finally murmured.

He smiled slightly, looking at her with sleep-deprived eyes. "Thanks, but actually, it was just legwork. His name was mentioned in an otherwise useless report, and I figured he might just remember something that would help. A bartender," he snorted. "It took a few bars before I could locate him. He works all over the place. I finally found him in a neighborhood dive on East Ninety-third Street. What I don't get is, why you girls keep falling for the pretty-faced, vapid types."

"Bill, please keep to the subject. What did he say?" Lindy hunched on her knees, facing Bill over the back of her seat.

He crossed his arms and leaned back with a complacent yawn. "What would you say to a love triangle?"

"What?" Biddy and Lindy gaped at him.

"Sandra, Jeremy, and Jack," he said slowly.

"But Jeremy's gay," said Biddy, unbelieving.

"He wasn't then, if what Devon"—Bill enunciated the name, rolling his eyes—"says is true, and I think it is." He brushed Biddy's stuttering aside. "Jeremy and Sandra had been lovers, but then Devon came along. They were planning to get married, but she was having a hard time breaking it to Jeremy, who was still in love with her, according to the boyfriend. In the meantime, she was always telling him, Devon, about how Jack was coming on to her, trying to give her things, and being generally slimy and whining, saying he loved her, asking her to marry him, et cetera, et cetera."

Lindy glanced at Biddy, who was staring into her hands. "But Jack is gone. He showed up last night for a hideous moment, but—"

"Jack hasn't checked out of the hotel yet. And he'll be stopping by here before he leaves town."

"How do you know?"

He smiled. "I left him a note."

"You didn't."

"Yep, only I signed Jeremy's name. Told him I wanted to talk after the rehearsal. Maybe we could come to an agreement. I think he'll show."

"But there's a security guard at the door."

"I left Jack's name with Sal."

"You *are* a genius."

"A genius in deep shit if this doesn't work."

"I'll bake you cookies every week, I promise." Lindy wanted to hug him, but she didn't.

They sat through the rest of the rehearsal: Lindy grinning; Biddy staring at her hands; Bill snoring lightly.

As soon as Jeremy dismissed the dancers, Lindy woke Bill, roused Biddy, who had been sitting like a statue since Bill had dropped the news about Jeremy's sexuality, and hurried them backstage. While Bill apprised Jeremy of his plan, Biddy and Lindy cleared the theater of dancers. The stagehands had left immediately to grab a bite somewhere nearby. Hopefully, Peter would be with them. Alice was the last one out, and Lindy breathed an audible sigh of relief as the door closed. "Do you go on break now, Sal?"

"No, I get a dinner break at five-thirty, then I'm back. Then I'm gonna watch the show."

"We're expecting someone."

"I know, I'll be sure he gets in, and I'll send him upstairs." Sal shifted his bony bottom on his stool and prepared to wait.

Lindy returned to the others. Jeremy and Bill were deep in discussion like two boys in a football huddle. Biddy leaned against the prop table, pulling absentmindedly at a strand of hair.

"Everyone's gone. I didn't see Peter. He must have gone with the stagehands."

"Let's hope so," said Bill. "The man's a loose cannon. We don't need him screwing this up."

They climbed the stairs and left Jeremy in the first dressing room, door ajar. They took their places in the next room and pulled the door closed, but not latched. And they waited.

"I feel ridiculous," mumbled Bill. "Even if it was my idea, especially, since it was my idea."

"Just think of it as a stakeout," whispered Lindy. She was beginning to worry about Biddy.

Bill put his finger to his lips. Lindy had heard it, too. Someone climbing the steps. Crepe soles on concrete. They moved closer to the door.

"You wanted to talk?"

"Come in, Jack." Jeremy's voice was as mellow as ever. "I thought we should have a little chat."

"There's nothing to say. They'll arrest you soon enough. You can try to sue me from jail."

"I think not. The police know that Carlotta was blackmailing you, not me. And when they find out why, I think they'll manage to get around that receipt from a gas station. Perhaps you'd be interested in making a little deal."

Jack's response was cut off by the sound of the door banging into the wall. Bill sprang into the hall, with Lindy right behind him.

"Oh, shit," said Bill, stopping just inside the door.

"Oh, shit," echoed Jeremy.

Oh, shit, is right, thought Lindy, looking around Bill and into Peter's furious face.

"What deal, Jeremy?" His voice started low, strangled, barely enough air escaping to sound out the words. But it was rapidly growing in pitch. He turned on Jack. "Why was Carlotta blackmailing you?"

Jack backed away from him.

Peter advanced on him. "Tell me, you simpering, little toad." He accented each word with a shove that finally landed Jack sprawled against the costume rack. "What did you do that gave Carlotta such power? Everyone knew you were a filthy embezzler, so it couldn't be that." One hand had slipped around Jack's neck. With his free hand, he lifted the man up and pinned him to the wall.

Jack was turning red. "Help, somebody, get him off me."

Lindy started to move. Bill's arm thrust out across her, blocking her way. She looked up at him, shocked. Sweat trickled down his temple from his hairline past his ear. He was staring at the two men.

"Why?" Peter knocked Jack's head against the wall.

"It was an accident, I swear it." Jack's tongue was protruding between purpling lips.

Peter loosened his grip slightly. "What was an accident?"

Jack lurched aside, but Peter brought his head up against the wall. "Tell me, while you still can."

Bill's arm was still rigid across Lindy. She watched impotently.

"Sandra. It was an accident. I only wanted to talk. She was so beautiful."

Peter reeled, but didn't loosen his grip. "What happened?"

His voice was ominously low. His knuckles grew white as his grasp tightened, and Jack made a horrible choking sound.

Lindy felt Bill stiffen, but still he didn't move.

"Keep talking, or I'll break your neck."

Jack looked wildly about him. No one moved to help him. Jeremy was leaning against the makeup table with an air of detachment.

"It was an accident, I tell you."

This time the blow was harder.

"I just wanted to talk to her. She wouldn't stop dancing. I just wanted her to stop. To pay attention to me. I grabbed her arm, but she broke away and hit the radiator." His confession ended in a gurgle. "Jeremy, for the love of God." His plea was barely a whisper.

Jeremy didn't budge. "You let me take the blame, let everybody turn against me. Carlotta must have known it was you. You destroyed Sandra, and you nearly destroyed me."

"I've been trying to make it up to you ever since."

"Peter can kill you as far as I'm concerned."

Peter took the cue and tightened his grip. Bill lunged forward and pulled him away from Jack, then shoved him toward Jeremy, who surrounded him with both arms, part restraint, part consoling.

"So you left her there to be found by a custodian." Bill's voice was grim, and for a moment, Lindy was afraid that he was going to strangle Jack himself.

Bill turned to the door. "I think you can make that call now, Sal."

The old man stood in the doorway, unruffled. "Already did, sir. Soon as the yellin' started."

Bill pushed Jack into a chair and stood guard. Jack buried his face in his hands sobbing. "It was an accident."

"And was Carlotta an accident, too?"

"Carlotta?" Jack blubbered. "I didn't kill Carlotta. I didn't kill her."

It was a long five minutes before the sound of sirens split the air. Peter had pulled away from Jeremy and was sitting on the windowsill. Jeremy watched Peter from the makeup table. Biddy watched Jeremy from where she clung to the door frame. Bill stood over Jack, his hand firmly on the man's shoulder. Lindy leaned against the wall watching them all, the scene etching itself permanently in her memory.

Then she heard the rush of feet on the stairs. Two uniformed officers were taking Jack away. "You have the right . . ." Another man wearing a suit walked over to Bill.

"Brandecker."

"Monroe." Bill returned the greeting.

"O'Dell called me this morning, but what exactly are you doing here, Bill?"

"Getting a little culture."

"Like hell. I'll have to get statements from all of you. But after that, you'd better keep a low profile. Go home if you can tear yourself away from the ballet. You'd better hope we get a confession from this guy."

And then he was gone. No one else moved. They sat where they were, in the charged atmosphere, incapable of leaving. Then Peter slowly got up and walked out of the room. They watched him go.

"Is it too early for a drink?" asked Biddy quietly.

* * *

"But what I don't understand is why the police didn't figure out that it was Jack's fault in the first place," Biddy said. They were sitting in the bistro across the street, the first customers of the day. Looking for Peter, Jeremy had gone once more to the pay phone to call the hotel.

"Who knows? We probably won't. Maybe they investigated Jack, as well. There didn't seem to be that much emphasis placed on Jeremy's involvement from what I could find out. It was probably what happened in the company afterward that led to his defection. What you people do to each other." Bill shook his head. He was drinking scotch. He looked like he needed it.

"Not just us people," said Lindy, looking directly at Bill. "All kinds of people hurt each other, not just dancers and actors."

Bill returned her look with a stony stare, but his reply was interrupted by Jeremy's return. "Still no answer. Maybe he's back at the theater. I'll go check."

"Not yet," said Bill. "In spite of the vast entertainment I've enjoyed in your presence, I'm going to have to leave you. There are a few things you need to be prepared for."

Jeremy sat down.

"Jack will probably try to worm his way out of this. He was rather coerced into confessing his involvement with Sandra's accident, and he still denies killing Carlotta."

"But he did kill her, didn't he?" Biddy's voice was soft but imploring.

Bill shrugged. "Probably. But they'll have to drag it out of him. I think he'll talk, eventually. You'll all have to make a statement. Peter did attack him, and Jack might just have the wits to bring charges against him." He stopped their questions with an abrupt gesture. "It shouldn't come to much, but Jeremy, Peter does need some serious therapy. His nerves are stretched to the limit. Arresting Jack is not going to make that fact magically go away."

"I'll take care of him."

"Professional therapy." He shot a glance at Lindy. "He won't get this behind him with hugs and kisses and 'we love you' from his coworkers."

Lindy glared back at him. He was making them sound like idiots, but she bit back her reply. She recognized that tone of voice; she had heard it often enough. He was goading her, and he knew she wouldn't retaliate; they owed him too much. Okay, Bill, she thought. Get it out of your system.

"But it is over, isn't it?" asked Biddy.

"For you. The police will take care of it from now on. You'll have to sign some papers, appear in court, possibly. But I think you can start 'picking up the pieces,' so to speak. And I have to get back to my classroom." Bill pushed his chair back and stood up.

"I don't know what to say." Jeremy stood up also. "How can I—"

"You can buy my drink." They shook hands formally. "Ladies."

Lindy watched his retreating form with a growing agitation. "Bill, are you coming to the theater tonight?"

"Thanks, but I think I've had enough culture for one vacation."

Twenty

Some secrets are hard to keep, and the news of Jack's arrest was common knowledge by hour call. Shock and dismay gave way to acceptance and relief. Music again blared from the dressing rooms. Corps girls ran in and out of each other's rooms trying new shades of lipstick, making plans for after the performance.

Lindy strolled down the hall and stopped at each door to smile and chat. She felt a little guilty at her immense relief. Jack would go to jail. A terrible thing, but he had done it to himself. Why shouldn't they celebrate at being released from his destructive grip. She took the stairs slowly, letting the last of her pent-up tension pass from her body out into the air. She pushed open the metal door leading to stage left and went backstage.

Less than an hour to curtain; the first time since she had been back that the curtain would rise on a company free of suspicion and guilt. She looked out onto the stage, where stagehands were putting the last bars of the cage into place.

Peter was standing in position just off the first wing. He removed his headset and hung it on a peg on the podium, where his cue book was placed.

Lindy eased up beside him. "How are you?"

"Okay." His shoulders tensed, his mouth tightened, and he looked deep into her eyes. She hugged him. Okay, it wasn't professional therapy, but it *was* a start. "I feel a little sick," he said. "I think I could have killed him."

"I don't think so."

"I'm leaving after Hartford."

Lindy pulled away. "Why?"

"I've found out what I came to find out, and I doubt if Jeremy will want me hanging around reminding him of the past. She never told me about Jeremy. I was really wrong."

"But why leave now? You and Jeremy have worked things out, right? I know you can make better money elsewhere, but you've got a life here."

"Some life, built on deceit and hate."

"What about Andrea?"

Peter turned away. "I guess she'll have a great career."

"You and Andrea. I mean, it's a little obvious how she feels about you."

"It is?"

"I'd say so."

"She's appreciative. I just tried to keep Carlotta off her case." He turned suddenly. "She acts like an air head sometimes, but she's really sensitive and intuitive. And young."

"Not that young. How old is she? Twenty? Twenty-two?"

"Twenty-four."

"Old enough to know what she wants."

"And she wants me, right?"

"Why not? You're intelligent, caring, good-looking, especially if you'd smile a little."

Peter's lips tightened to a thin line.

"That's a start."

He grunted.

"But you'll have to work on the laugh."

Then he smiled. His face transformed, and Lindy felt a little twinge of titillation herself.

"She's going to be noticed; she'll have her pick."

"I think she's already made her choice. Stick around long enough to find out, okay?"

"Yeah. Now let me get back to work."

Lindy sat contentedly in the audience, her notebook and pen resting in her lap. *Carmina* looked great, even for a revival of an already overused ballet. Jeremy's hand was evident in the vitality of the dancers, the nuances of the movements. Andrea handled the cloak with confidence. Each detail that Jeremy had worked on added a new depth to the interpretation. Biddy and Jeremy sat next to her. Theirs was another relationship that would have to work itself out, but Lindy knew they would handle it. Life was looking pretty good.

The boys were romping through the quartet. They were having fun. Andrea reappeared onstage. She had shed the cloak and was clothed in wisps of silky gold chiffon. Her golden hair reflected the light as she turned. The cloak.

Lindy jerked in her seat.

Biddy's head turned toward her. Lindy shook her off. The cloak. Carlotta's cloak hadn't been returned by the police with the rest of the company's possessions. Alice had had to adapt Andrea's cloak in its place. Why? Carlotta was still wearing the dress, so they had to keep that; it was probably ruined anyway. But why keep the cloak? She wasn't wearing it. She only wore it for the beginning of the piece and didn't put it on again.

Lindy made herself picture Carlotta's dressing room on the night of the murder: Carlotta lying on the floor; Andrea leaning over her; Alice coming from behind the door. Carlotta's fur coat was hanging on the dress rack. She could see it in her mind. And the cloak was, where? She couldn't recall. It must have been in the room, because it was gone. The police had kept it, or had they?

Lindy's mind was racing. Had they kept the cloak because it had been used in the murder, or was it missing?

Bill could have told her, but Bill was gone.

A growing uneasiness replaced Lindy's relief. She looked at Biddy and Jeremy. Relaxed. The bitterness of years erased from his face. The fear of loss gone from Biddy's. She couldn't bear to break their happiness by telling them of the doubt that had suddenly leapt into her mind. If only Bill had stuck it out one more night, but he had had enough of art . . . and of her. She was back on her own, like always.

As soon as the curtain lowered on *Carmina*, Lindy rushed backstage. Biddy and Jeremy headed to the lobby.

She slipped through the curtained arch to backstage and pounded on the door. Peter opened it; she rushed past him. Andrea's cloak was lying on the prop table, just like Carlotta's would have been. She slowed down; she would wait and watch. She leaned back against the wall. Intermission passed. The dancers took their places onstage. The cloak was still lying on the prop table.

The lights went to black. She tried to focus on the table, but she couldn't see anything. The music started. The lights popped on. The cloak was still there.

And next to it stood Alice.

She was staring at the stage. "I love this music," she had said the night after Carlotta's death when Lindy had stayed backstage. It had been during the *Air*. She was watching from the third wing with the cloak—Andrea's cloak—folded over her arm. But before Carlotta died, it would have been Carlotta's cloak that she was holding; her job to take it back to the dressing room and hang it up. And halfway through the *Holberg Suite* she still had the cloak.

Lindy stood paralyzed by the understanding that whirred into her brain, like the fragmented pieces of a kaleidoscope suddenly made clear—painfully, violently clear. But why had she done it? That didn't make any sense at all.

Alice picked up the cloak, her eyes still riveted to the stage. Then she turned and shuffled away.

Lindy looked wildly around her. Peter was calling cues. Everyone was either onstage or waiting for an entrance. All attention was directed at the dancing. No one had noticed anything unusual the night Carlotta was murdered. *No one ever noticed Alice!*

Fear constricted her throat, but Lindy forced herself to follow Alice out the back door. She saw her feet round the landing and go up the second flight of stairs. She followed. Her heart was pounding so loudly that she was sure that Alice would hear it and turn around, but Alice was disappearing into Andrea's dressing room when Lindy reached the second floor.

She needed just a peek to be sure. Hugging the wall, she crept toward the door of the dressing room. The music of the *Sarabande* was playing through the intercom. Mieko would be beginning the girls' adagio. She looked inside.

Alice was hanging the cloak on an oversize hanger, smoothing it with deft fingers. She would have been in Carlotta's dressing room that night, during the *Holberg Suite*, just like tonight. Lindy pulled back, but Alice had seen her reflection in the mirror.

Stupid, she thought, and she poked her head back inside the door. "I've lost my notebook. Thought I might have left it here when I was talking to the girls." The blood was roaring in her ears.

Alice glanced at the table covered with makeup, dance clothes, and soda cans. "I don't see it."

"Oh, well, maybe I left it backstage." Lindy started to back away.

"Why are you following me, Lindy?" It was said in the same mild tone in which Alice always spoke, but Alice's eyes were fixed on hers.

"I wasn't—I lost my notebook."

"I saw you, you know." Alice stepped forward, her eyes unwavering. Her gaze was mesmerizing.

Lindy stopped. "Saw me, where? In the mirror?" What was the girl talking about?

"In the prop room. With Peter. He was holding you."

Lindy thought back desperately. In the prop room? "Oh, you mean with the sword."

"He was holding you."

"He was helping me to my feet," Lindy said, not understanding. Sweat began to roll down her armpits.

"Carlotta said you would try to take Andrea's place. I didn't believe her until I saw you. First Andrea, then you. You couldn't leave him alone, either of you. But he isn't interested in you. He only cares about Sandra."

"I'm sure you're right, Alice." Lindy stumbled backward over the doorjamb.

Alice pulled at the ribbon that hung around her neck, her eyes boring into Lindy's. "You shouldn't have tempted him. I'm the only one who understands him. Carlotta knew that, and she was jealous, jealous of me."

Her hand continued to pull the ribbon until the orange-handled scissors slipped out of the pocket of her smock. "She was ruining everybody's life. She deserved to die." She caught the scissors in her right hand; her fingers gripped the handles.

Lindy backed into the corridor; Alice was only a few feet away.

"It's all right, Alice. I understand. It wasn't your fault." She tried to recall scenes like this from those hundreds of mysteries she had read. There was always a scene like this, but her mind couldn't retrieve a single one.

The *Gavotte* began in the background. Four minutes had gone by. Lindy backed away slowly, trying to think. She could scream, if she could scream, but no one would hear her. She made a frantic calculation. Another twelve minutes for the piece to end. A few more minutes to take the bows and get offstage. Could she keep Alice occupied for another fifteen minutes? She backed farther along the corridor. Maybe she should just run like hell.

"I thought she liked me. She seemed so understanding. She said she would help me."

Lindy's eyes were held by the glint of the scissors.

"I should have killed you when I pushed you down the trapdoor, but I thought I could scare you away. Why didn't you go away and leave us alone, Lindy? With Carlotta dead, we could have been happy." Alice lunged forward, stabbing the scissors at Lindy's face. Lindy barely managed to jerk her head away.

"I love him." Fat tears coursed down Alice's face.

Lust, greed, revenge. Love? This wasn't love. Alice had gone round the bend, and no one had even noticed.

"I'm sure he cares for you, too." Lindy managed to whisper the words.

"He did. When he left the ballet to come here, I followed him. But then Carlotta came and began destroying everything. At first, I didn't realize what she was doing. She was supposed to be my friend. But she kept attacking Andrea so that he would feel sorry for her. Pushing her at him and laughing about it the whole time, laughing at me with those big, yellow teeth." The tears were coming faster now; Alice's eyes, pools of desperation. "And then you, throwing yourself at him. Carlotta knew, she saw you. She told me and laughed. Didn't you think I knew what you were up to?"

Lindy's mind was reeling. Alice in love with Peter? She certainly hadn't shown it. There was the way her eyes followed him whenever he was around. But her eyes seemed to follow anything that caught her vision.

Now, those same eyes held Lindy's trapped in their terrible gaze.

"Alice, believe me. I don't want Peter. I'm sorry if you got that impression. I assure you, Peter doesn't want me, either. We're just friends."

Alice shoved the scissors at Lindy's chest. Lindy stumbled backward until she was against the wall. Alice was blocking the stairs to her left. The fire exit. If she could just get to the door. It must only be five feet away. It would swing outward onto the fire escape. She could make it to the alley and back into the theater, with Sal and the telephone.

"That night when she went after Eric with the candelabra—Andrea ended up in his arms. And then when I took the cloak back, it was sitting there on the floor. Just waiting for me. I knew what I had to do. But it didn't kill her. She started moaning. Looking at me with that face, that ugly face. I couldn't stand it. Why did she do it, Lindy? I had her cloak. It hid that horrible face."

Lindy wanted to cover her ears, shut out Alice's garbled confession. Oh, God, please don't let me be sick. She inched along the wall. The *Gavotte* music was still playing. Surely, it had been close to three and a half minutes. She was almost to the fire door. Only a few more feet.

"It felt good, Lindy. Once I started bashing her head into the floor. Over and over. I couldn't stop. I didn't want to stop."

Alice lunged toward her. Lindy sprang toward the door and threw herself against the release bar. Alice fell against the wall where Lindy had been. She staggered a few steps before she regained her balance.

It gave Lindy just enough time to get out onto the fire escape. But not enough time to shut the door. Alice was outside, too.

Lindy turned and ran down the metal steps two at a time. She had made the first landing, when Alice slipped off the stairs above her and fell, knocking her against the rail; the scissors shot past her ear. She pushed against Alice's unwieldy body, but the girl was heavy, and struggling to get another try with the scissors.

"Lindy!" It was Bill's voice. To the rescue again! The man

had an incredible sense of timing. Through the iron rails she could see him running down the alley from the street. She gave Alice a violent push; Alice fell back against the rail. Lindy fled down the stairs.

Bill had already started up the steps of the fire escape. Lindy was racing toward him, when she realized Alice wasn't following her. She looked up in time to see the ends of the blue smock vanish inside. "Use the door," she shouted to Bill and followed Alice back up the fire escape.

The final notes of the *Gavotte* blared down the empty hallway. Ten or so minutes to go. Lindy was breathing hard; she was scared, but the thought of Alice attacking unsuspecting dancers drove her on. At least Bill was here. On cue, Bill reached the top of the stairs.

"God, you're good."

"I may kill you myself. Where did she go?"

"I don't know. Is Sal calling the police?" She followed him down the hall as he pushed doors open and looked inside. The *Air*'s haunting melody filled the air.

"Sal wasn't there. Probably watching the damned ballet."

"Then how did you get in?"

"Don't ask."

They were at the end of the hall where the second stairway led down to the stage. They took it at a run.

"Go call." He shoved her forward. She began to run across the open shop to the stage door. She got as far as the costume room. The door was open. Alice was leaning over the trunk where valuables were kept. Her hair had come loose from its clasp, and it hung limply over her profile. Then she stood up, leaning on the edge of the trunk for support. She held a tiny pistol in her hand; she pointed it at Lindy.

Bill had caught up to her. He stopped abruptly.

"You're not going to fall for that old trick," said Lindy. "It's just a prop. She probably took it from the last theater. Peter and I were looking at them. She saw us."

Alice fired. The bullet hit the metal wall with a deafening clang and ricocheted. Bill threw Lindy against the wall, covering her with his body and driving her breath out of her. She felt her ribs creak under his weight.

"Deadly prop," he said.

Peter bolted through the door to their right. "What the hell was that?"

"Alice has a gun. She killed Carlotta. She's in there." Bill indicated the costume room with a nod.

"Alice?" He took a step forward.

"Call the goddamned cops, Peter, and take Lindy with you."

"Sal's calling."

"Who's calling the show?" Lindy's voice was muffled under Bill's body.

"Screw the show." Peter moved toward the door of the costume room. "Alice, what are you doing?" He spoke calmly in the same voice he always used with the dancers when they needed to be calmed down. "Put the gun down, Alice. I won't let them hurt you."

Alice moved through the door into the hallway; she seemed to waver, but kept hold of the gun.

"Move back, Peter," she said in a flat voice. "It's too late now. I killed her for you. She wouldn't let us be happy."

"Bad dialogue," whispered Lindy. Bill pushed her farther into the wall.

"What's she talking about?" asked Peter, staring at the tip of the gun.

"She's in love with you," Lindy managed to say around Bill's shoulder.

"You're kidding."

Alice moved forward, backing Peter to the wall. "I have to leave now. It won't work out. I see that now. I'll have to go."

The final movement of the *Holberg Suite* was drawing to an end. Bill lessened his weight against Lindy. He was about to make a move. But Alice swung toward him, aiming the gun at Lindy. "Move back. Lindy will have to go with me."

Bill moved out of the way. "Just do what she tells you, Lindy."

"No!" Peter yelled. Alice turned at the same time. The gun was aimed at his chest. In blind terror, Lindy leapt from the wall and aimed her best *grande battement* at the hand holding the gun. Alice yelped as Lindy's foot hit her hand; the gun flew into the air and clattered to the floor.

Bill grabbed Alice. The music ended. Uniformed men came through the door, and the audience broke into applause.

Peter laughed, more like a squawk. "No one would ever believe this."

"And I, for one, am never going to tell them," said Bill.

They were sitting in the waiting area of the train station. Jeremy and Biddy had picked them up at the police station when they finished giving their statements, and Bill had insisted on being dropped off instead of taking a room at the hotel. It was after three in the morning, and the station was deserted except for one black custodian pushing a broom between the rows of benches.

"I can't believe you kicked the gun out of her hand." Biddy's voice echoed around the air. Lindy noticed that she had combed her hair.

"Pretty ridiculous, I know."

"Effective, anyway," mumbled Bill, looking like he might nod off at any minute.

"But in love with Peter? I never had any idea. How can we live with someone that closely and not know them? It's really awful."

"We get so caught up in our own little worlds, Biddy," said Jeremy. "Oh, hell, no one ever noticed her. That doesn't say much for her, or us."

"I certainly didn't notice," said Peter.

"She told me that you had liked her before you left the ballet," said Lindy.

"I hardly ever talked to her. I'm sorry I brought all this on you, Jeremy. I should have confronted you at the beginning. None of this should have happened."

"Bullshit, Peter. You can't take the responsibility for everybody's actions; leave a little guilt for me."

Biddy shook her head. "Boys, let's leave the guilt for Carlotta, Jack, and Alice, though Alice, poor thing, can't be in her right mind."

"No," said Bill. "Obviously not in her right mind. I suppose as long as she thought Peter only cared about Sandra, she could keep her fantasy intact. But once he showed interest in Andrea, and then Lindy came along. . . ."

"But I—"

"I know, but in Alice's warped perception, she saw you as a threat."

"And Carlotta reinforcing her fears and making fun of her . . ." said Lindy.

"She cracked. She just couldn't juggle it all anymore."

"Thank you, Dr. Freud. I told you it was the repressed types who always went off."

He only nodded but gave her a look that made her tremble. "I should have seen it earlier," he said slowly. "The police had their suspicions. No one could really pin down her movements for the night of the murder, though her story was pretty convincing. She had access to Carlotta's dressing room, but they hadn't come up with a plausible motive yet. If someone had bothered to mention how she felt about Peter—" He shifted in his seat. "They would have arrested her eventually."

"Even if I hadn't bungled my way into that last confrontation," said Lindy. Why did she feel so uncomfortable? "I didn't mean to, and if you had been there, I would have told you what I thought, instead of running after her like an idiot."

"Right."

"But thank goodness you did show up," said Biddy. "And in the nick of time, like the cavalry. That was incredible. How did you manage it?"

Bill shrugged. "I was just coming to say goodbye when the show was over. I guess I was a little early."

"With timing like that, you should be on the stage," said Jeremy.

"Lucky for us, he wasn't," said Lindy. "I do appreciate it, Bill." He wasn't looking at her. "But you let me think it was the fur coat. You must have known that they kept the cloak. Why didn't you tell me?"

"Because you can't stay out of trouble, Lindy. You're exhausting. Dell only let me in on all of this because he thought I could better cut through all the drama and get to the truth. And before you get huffy, no, I was not working for the police. I just got caught up in the melodrama."

Was that all it was to him, a melodrama? "Could you tell me just one more thing?"

"Just one?" He smiled.

She ignored her reaction to his question. In a few minutes, he would be gone. It would all be over. It would be better that way.

She cleared her throat. "How did you get into the theater if Sal wasn't at the stage door?"

"I think it was a ballet step."

Lindy grinned. She felt like crying. "I don't know why you did all this," she began. A train whistle moaned the approach of the 3:24 to New York.

"Yeah, you do." Bill got up. "That's my train. Back to the grind. I've already missed three days of classes."

Lindy felt a familiar jolt of panic. It was just like coming to the end of a successful run. That letdown after the final glorious curtain. The emptiness that replaced the excitement.

She missed the goodbyes, the handshakes, the hugs. She was too busy trying to relax her mouth; it was threatening to twitch. And if she allowed that, she *would* cry. She knew the signs.

She followed Bill across the waiting room. He was walking out of her life as easily as he had walked in.

They stopped at the base of the stairs that led to the platform. "I've done a lot of stairs since meeting you," he said.

Lindy looked at the ground. So this was it.

He lifted her chin with his knuckle. "Maybe in some other lifetime."

"That would be nice."

And then he was gone.

Twenty-one

The New York season was met with rave reviews, an adoring audience and the interest of several potential sponsors. Peter had stayed on, they had a new costume mistress named Rose, who "took shit from no one," and had hired a new corps girl to fill the spot left from Andrea's and Mieko's promotions.

Biddy appeared opening night wearing a tailored pants suit and sneakers.

"Free at last, free at last," she sang. "Not a great fashion statement, but I'm on my way."

"I'll miss you clunking around in that cast. It was becoming part of your persona."

"Well, I won't. Wow, Lindy, you look great."

Lindy was wearing the gray-and-pink dress from Neiman Marcus. The waist was loose, not a bulge marred its shimmering surface.

The first person they met on their way to the audience was Carlton Quick. He pecked Biddy on the cheek and congratulated her on her recovery and then turned to Lindy. "You look marvelous. You must have dropped two dress sizes since I saw you last. Nothing like a little murder to kick start a diet."

They made their escape.

"I thought Glen was coming tonight," said Biddy.

"A last-minute meeting. Another evening with an empty seat beside me."

"Well, don't look at me. I'm too nervous to sit. I'll just pace backstage."

Lindy found her seat and sat down, feeling not nearly as glamorous as she had intended. Alone on opening night. How typical.

The houselights began to dim. Almost every seat was filled. She should have released Glen's ticket back to the box office to be sold.

"Is this seat free?"

She recognized the voice. She didn't even try to stop the tingling sensation that coursed through her. Bill sat down in the seat beside her.

"I thought you had had your fill of the theater."

Bill shrugged. "I decided to give it another chance."

"And?"

Bill gave her dress an appraising look. "It's growing on me."

The houselights faded to black.

Lindy didn't see him again. She had left him in the lobby after the performance. She walked down the stairs to the dressing-room door, feeling his gaze on the back of her neck. She wasn't ready to decide what kind of relationship they might have. She needed more distance—give her feelings time to segue him into the role of friend, or let him take a final exit. She was married. She was a mother. And anyway, she had a New York season to deal with. With one hand on the doorknob, she took one quick look back. She couldn't help herself. A fleeting smile from Bill and she shut the door behind her.

The rest of the week had raced by: rehearsing, dining with patrons, watching Biddy and Jeremy making plans for the company's future. And then it was over. On her first free day back in New Jersey, she was invited to see the videotape of the talent show she had abandoned.

She sat in the chairwoman's rec room drinking decaf coffee and munching gourmet cookies that tasted like cardboard. She was okay for the first half hour. She even made it through the Torville Family Puppeteers: mother, father, and two scrawny children mincing about behind their duck puppets and lip-synching to "Splish, Splash (I Was Taking a Bath)." But when Arthur Klein, his bald head topped with a red-and-white striped stovepipe hat, and his wife, Edith, her ample figure draped in the American flag, began to tap-dance to "God Bless America," Lindy suddenly remembered an appointment and fled, all the way to Rome.

For two glorious days she and Glen trekked through the Colosseum and Forum. For the next four days, he hobnobbed with executives from a multinational company, whose name had so many initials Lindy couldn't remember them all, while she wandered the streets alone. She made the rounds of museums and famous statues. She stared at the restored ceiling of the Sistine Chapel, which had been covered with scaffolding the last time she had visited. Finding herself at Trevi Fountain, she tossed in a coin.

In the afternoons, she haunted piazzas she had known.

Sitting at a table for one, she sipped Campari and soda and watched the heads of lovers at nearby tables, all young, beautiful, and thin. Sometimes she would join Glen and his clients for dinner, or else she would eat at the hotel with her latest mystery beside her and then go outside to watch the seven hills light up around her.

Glen had gone directly to the office from the airport. The limo let her off at the kitchen door; she dumped her suitcases in the middle of the floor. She looked at the pile of mail and *Times* bags stacked on the table, where they had been left for her perusal by the housekeeper. The phone rang.

"Seems like old times," she sang. She picked up the receiver and reached for the *Times*.

"Hi. It's Jeremy."

Lindy dropped the paper onto the table, unopened.

"Listen, I know you probably just got back. But I've got great news. We've lined up a West Coast tour for October. We'll have to start rehearsing right away; they want two different programs. I'll do another ballet and maybe a revival. Then there's a possible six weeks in Europe in February."

"Congratulations. That sounds wonderful."

"Thanks. I've convinced Peter to stay on. He's going to be okay. Andrea's making him see a therapist, though he doesn't like it much. And that new costume girl is a bitch on wheels, but funny. I think she'll work out. And then . . . " He paused.

Lindy waited.

"Well, actually, Biddy has consented to take over the business end. She's artistic, as well as financially savvy, and honest. So, the reason I'm calling is, would you at all be interested in coming along as rehearsal director?"

Lindy looked around her at the stacks of mail, the polished kitchen counters, her suitcases lying in the middle of the sparkling floor.

"Thanks, Jeremy, I'm already packed."

Please turn the page for an exciting sneak peek
of Shelley Freydont's newest
Lindy Haggerty mystery
HIGH SEAS MURDER
now on sale wherever hardcover mysteries are sold!

The evening drew to a close. The Farnsworthys retired; the deWinters wandered off to the casino. Rebo began to table-hop.

The room had thinned out considerably when Peter dropped into an empty chair beside Lindy. She slipped her aching feet back into her shoes.

"You don't have to do that for me," said Peter. "Is it over yet?"

"I saw you waltzing out there. Not bad for a stagehand."

"Hmmph."

Several dancers came up to the table. "We're off to the Cabaret for some real dancing," said Juan. Beside him stood Paul Duke, the sandy-haired, lead dancer with the company. Next to him, Mieko looked dead on her feet.

"You want to come?" asked Andrea Martin, another one of the company's dancers, looking at Peter.

Peter smiled up at her. "I've got work to do, you go ahead."

"No, that's okay. I don't really care about going." She looked disappointed.

"Go ahead."

"Are you sure?" Andrea's golden hair cascaded over her

shoulders. Even in a black velvet dress, cut low at the neck and high at the hemline, she looked like a child waiting for permission.

Peter nodded.

"Okay, then. See you later." She hurried out with the others.

"Oh, dear, is the *blumen* off the *rosen?*" asked Lindy.

Peter's eyes followed Andrea to the door. "No." He turned to Lindy. "She's sweet, but I think it's a limited engagement . . . for both of us." He settled back in his chair, twirling an empty glass that had been missed by the waiter. "She needed somebody, and I needed somebody to need me—someone who could show it."

Lindy touched his arm and gave it a gentle squeeze.

"It's been good, but I think we're both ready to move on. She's much too social for me, and I think I stifle her. She's talented and intuitive and loving."

"But not enough?"

Peter shrugged. "Don't worry. Neither of us will come out of this with a broken heart." He heaved himself to his feet. "Well, now I have real work to do. I meet with their tech guy in the morning." He kissed Lindy lightly on the cheek. "Good night."

Love. I must be getting old, thought Lindy. Working in a dance company was like living in a fish bowl. On tour, you were constantly thrown together: continuous travel, long hours in the theater, eating together, rooming together. It was like that Fred Astaire song, "Change partners and dance with me." There were only so many combinations. And it was tough for the girls. There were an equal number of men and women in the Ash Company, eight of each, but considering that half of the men were gay, the odds didn't seem quite fair. Of course, some people had lovers and spouses who didn't tour, but most of the time, those relationships were short-lived. It was too hard to be away from each other all the time and still remain a couple. Lindy had seen more than a few relationships killed by touring. And it was worse for the ballet companies, where the percentage of straight men was even smaller.

Put them all together on the "Luv Boat," and they were bound to furnish enough intrigue to fill an entire Enoch Grayson book. And opera singers were notorious for their illicit liaisons. Maybe the Mozartium Quartet would add an element of decorum to the next ten days.

The Mozartium Quartet was burning up the slot machines in the casino when Lindy passed through on her way to the Cabaret. She just wanted to remind the gang not to stay out too late. She had turned forty-four on her last birthday, but she could still remember the days when she would party all night and then drag into rehearsal the next morning. Now it was her responsibility not only to keep the ballets looking clean and well rehearsed, but to make sure the company was in good enough shape to carry out her corrections.

Music rumbled out into the hall through the open doors of the Cabaret. Lindy stopped inside the door to get her bearings. A rotating mirror ball flicked lights over the tables that surrounded a crowded dance floor. Colored spotlights lit the dancing couples and reflected off the windows that flanked each side of the room. Outside the windows, an occasional silhouette appeared and then passed from view as passengers strolled along the deck.

She recognized Paul and Andrea among the crowd of couples pulsing to the reverberating bass of piped-in music. Rebo and Juan sat at a table with several of the ballet boys. Rebo waved her over.

"Hi, Mom."

"Just checking," she returned.

"Yeah, Suzette will be popping in any minute now," said one of the boys. "She actually thinks she has us on a curfew. Imagine." He shook his head in mock disbelief, then looked toward the door. "Voilà, like Von Rothbart at the wedding."

Suzette was standing in the entrance. Where had she been all evening? Lindy walked toward her.

Suzette started when Lindy reached her. "Oh, hi, Lindy. Checking up on yours, too?"

Lindy nodded. Suzette looked terrible. Her face was pale; of course, the colored lights that flashed above the dance floor didn't help. But it was her nervous manner that got Lindy's attention.

"Have you seen Dede?"

"No, but she's probably in the crush on the floor. Are you okay? I didn't see you at dinner."

"Oh, I guess sailing doesn't agree with me. I was feeling, um, queasy, so I just stayed in my room."

Not very good politics, thought Lindy.

"Oh, there she is." Suzette made a beeline for a table where Dede sat talking to a young man, their dark heads bent toward each other over the table. Dede looked up when Suzette approached them. The young man stood up. After a moment of dumb show in which Suzette looked agitated,

Dede looked mutinous, and the man generally confused, Suzette grabbed Dede by the wrist and led her away.

"Good night, Lindy," said Suzette as she pulled Dede toward the door. She didn't even look at Lindy as she marched out, her daughter in tow. Dede had begun to cry.

Oh dear, thought Lindy. She followed them out and watched them step into the elevator.

Lindy wandered through a passageway that led out onto the deck. She steadied herself, holding onto a stair rail that led up to the Coda Deck. She really should get to bed. She was dead tired, and her feet were killing her. The deck was quiet, lit only by the moon and the lights that reflected from the inner rooms. Moonlight bounced off the light teakwood; only amorphous shadows reminded her that she was not entirely alone.

She slipped out of her shoes. No one could tell she was barefoot; her dress was long enough to conceal her feet. It was so serene. She could feel more than hear the music and laughter from inside. She walked away from the lights and leaned against the rail, wondering momentarily if anyone ever fell overboard. Even though the rail came above her waist, it would be easy enough to lean over and . . . with that gruesome thought, she turned to leave and rebounded off the front of someone's tuxedo. Her shoes fell to the deck with a clatter.

"Oh, I'm sorry," she began.

The shocked face of David Beck stared back at her. Without a word he bent down and retrieved her shoes.

"Thanks," she said. "Not very ladylike, I realize, but my feet were killing me. Four-inch heels, pinched toes—you have no idea." Or did he? Had she read somewhere that he was a cross-dresser? No, that was David Bowie.

They stood there for a moment, attached by her shoes. Beck had handed them to her, but had not let go.

"I'm Lindy Graham, Jeremy Ash Dance Company. The rehearsal director, not a dancer. I retired years ago." He hadn't said anything; she was talking enough for both of them. "Well, thanks again." She wrenched her shoes away and turned to leave.

"David." A pause. "Beck," he added in a hoarse whisper.

"Nice to meet you." How was she supposed to react? David Beck looked about as skinny and nervous as a greyhound. Did he expect her to gush and ask for his autograph? He looked like he might bolt for his kennel if she did. Should she act as if she didn't know who he was?

"We're neighbors, aren't we?" asked Lindy.

David Beck closed his eyes the way children do when trying to think of the answer to a hard question.

"The Callas Deck. We're across the hall," she prompted. "Oh."

She couldn't help it. She started to giggle. "Do I frighten you?"

"A bit," he mumbled. But he stood his ground, or rather, he leaned back against the rail. The moonlight washed his pale skin into a silver sheen, his eyes into gray prisms. It made him look slightly extraterrestrial. He didn't say another word.

A basket case, thought Lindy, *but an appealing basket case.*

"So, why aren't you in there?" She pointed over her shoulder to the window of the Cabaret. Her voice sounded raspy.

"I hate that music."

So he could put a whole sentence together. "Isn't that rather like biting the hand that feeds you?"

"I can feed myself, thank you, and all my friends and relations." His voice had reached a natural cadence. It was a velvety baritone. Very appealing. No wonder David Beck was so skittish. Women, and men, must fall over themselves whenever he opened his mouth or even looked their way. He was looking her way now. She could feel the music pulsing from the dance floor. Or maybe it was her own pulse.

He took a deep breath, but if he had decided to continue the conversation, he didn't get the chance. A shriek, followed by the flying form of someone running toward them, interrupted him. He jumped back violently, and Lindy caught the figure as it careened into them.

Suzette's wild eyes stared up at her. Strands of hair had fallen loose and whipped crazily about her face. "Murder," she gurgled. "He's dead. Oh, my God, he must be dead."

"Who?" asked Lindy.

"Him."

Lindy rolled her eyes. This wasn't getting them anywhere. "Where?"

Suzette pointed behind her without looking. She was gulping in air. "The stairs—at the bottom of the stairs. He fell—right at my feet."

Lindy shoved Suzette toward David and began to run toward the stairs. She skidded to a halt, shoes still in her hand. There was no one there.

David staggered up behind her, attempting to hold up Suzette, whose hands clutched at the lapels of his jacket.

"There's no one here, Suzette."

"He was there. I saw him." Suzette pointed with jabbing motions toward the base of the stairs. With each jab, David jerked back like a man feeling the recoil of a shotgun.

Lindy pried Suzette away from him. "Who did you see, Suzette?"

"Danny. It was Danny Ross."

"Well, he isn't here now. Maybe he slipped. A few drinks and these stairs could be pretty treacherous."

Suzette collapsed heavily onto Lindy, all arms and legs. Lindy looked at David for help, but he had lost what little color he had and looked like he might faint.

Great, she thought, *one hysterical ex-dancer, a wilting rock star, and no sign of the body.*

ABOUT THE AUTHOR

Shelley Freydont has toured internationally as a professional dancer with Twyla Tharp Dance and American Ballroom Theater. She has also choreographed for and appeared in films, television, and on Broadway. She now lives in New Jersey with her husband and two children. She is currently working on the third Lindy Haggerty mystery.

<u>BOOK YOUR PLACE ON OUR WEBSITE</u>
<u>AND MAKE THE</u>
<u>READING CONNECTION!</u>

We've created a customized website just for our very
special readers, where you can get the inside scoop on
everything that's going on with Zebra, Pinnacle and
Kensington books.

When you come online, you'll have the exciting
opportunity to:

- View covers of upcoming books

- Read sample chapters

- Learn about our future publishing schedule
  (listed by publication month *and author*)

- Find out when your favorite authors will be visiting
  a city near you

- Search for and order backlist books from our
  online catalog

- Check out author bios and background information

- Send e-mail to your favorite authors

- Meet the Kensington staff online

- Join us in weekly chats with authors, readers and
  other guests

- Get writing guidelines

- AND MUCH MORE!

Visit our website at
http://www.kensingtonbooks.com

It is the hour of War.
It is the time of the Apocalypse.
It is the End of the World.

First came Death—and men and women slaughtered each other without a second thought. Then Famine devastated crops and livestock. Plague struck as a mutated smallpox virus that killed in hours.

Most of the survivors have no idea that the world is about to end at the hands of the Four Horsemen of the Apocalypse. But a precious few, whose ordinary lives vanished under direct assualt of one of these terrible, evil, supernatural figures, know the truth.

These are mankind's only hope: A preacher given the power to stop Death. Two teenagers who can see the truth in anyone's heart. A mother and her two daughters, who saw the man they all loved sacrifice himself to save them from Plague. A writer whose young son became the embodiment of Famine.

With the Four Horsemen preparing for the final destruction of the world, it seems futile to stand against them. But even now, in humanity's darkest hour, there is hope, and love, and faith in the hearts of these heroes. They will stand against evil.

Unto the very last man, woman, or child.

CHARLES GRANT

RIDERS IN THE SKY

TOR®

A TOM DOHERTY ASSOCIATES BOOK
NEW YORK

RIDERS IN THE SKY

Copyright © 1999 by Charles Grant

A Tor Book
Published by Tom Doherty Associates, LLC
175 Fifth Avenue
New York, NY 10010

www.tor.com

Tor® is a registered trademark of Tom Doherty Associates, LLC.

ISBN: 0-812-56286-0

First edition: December 1999
First mass market edition: August 2000

Printed in the United States of America

0 9 8 7 6 5 4 3 2 1

For Nancy:
spellcaster, vampire-slayer,
gambler on the moon;
with great respect, and love.

PROLOGUE

He stands at the end of a long rough jetty, nearly one hundred yards from the safety of the shore. Rhythmic explosions from twenty feet below as the cold December sea tears itself apart against the uneven boulders. His hands are in his pockets, only once in a long while slipping away to clear the cold spray that drips from his face. He wears a black denim jacket over a thick dark sweater; faded jeans, worn sneakers. With no hat for protection his hair ducks and twists in the wind.

He faces the horizon and looks at the water and sees nothing but waves rolling steadily toward him. Rising as if taking his measure, falling as if needing less distance before they can rise again, and crest, and drive him at last into the slick and jagged brown-black stone.

Clouds low and heavy.

Feathers of rain in the distance.

Every few minutes, a flare of lightning, and thunder warns.

He has been here for hours, since the winter sun first

rose, and finally there's a long deep breath, a long and slow exhalation while his eyes close and his shoulders slump and his lips move in a silent prayer he fears won't be answered.

His name is Casey Chisholm, and he knows he's alone.

Far behind him, on the beach, people wait, huddled and shivering. Watching. Afraid that he won't turn around, that he'll forget they are there, that he will instead take that next step. Into the sea. That after all this time and after all he has told them he will be lost to them, and they'll be lost.

Yet none move to stop him, and none move to speak to him, and none move to help him because there is nothing they can do. They can only stand there. Waiting. And watching. While the cold stiffens their limbs and discolors their faces and takes their breath and turns it into ghosts the wind blows back into their dark and fearful eyes.

Every few minutes someone will look at someone else, a raised eyebrow, a pulled-in lip, a tilt of a head, a confused shrug. With nothing to say to the man on the jetty, they have nothing to say to each other as well. Not now. Not anymore. It's all been said and it's all been done, and there's no sense in doing anything else.

Just wait.

Ignore the bloodstains, ignore the cuts and bruises, pay no attention to the rough bandages and heavy cast and deeply aching muscles and sharp aching bones and the sure and certain knowledge that what they've been through so far can't possibly shine a light on what they know is to come.

A tall man, lank and bowed, turns to stare at the trees that line the miles of sand that face the ocean. Nothing moves there but the branches, needled or bare. Nothing moves but clumps of violently trembling sawgrass that tops the few dunes he can see from where he stands. Nothing moves, and he turns back, expecting nothing more, a quick smile and a soft grunt when the woman beside him slips her arm around his waist.

Two children, young girls, flank a woman who wears a veil over her face, only her eyes exposed. The three hold hands and dare the wind to knock them down.

A young man and a young woman stand close without touching.

There are others. Not many.

And apart from them all is a woman who holds the neck of her thin coat closed at her throat. A scarf over her hair flutters as if trying to break loose and fly. Of them all she is the only one whose eyes are red and puffed from weeping. Yet her back is straight and her chin is up, and alone among all the others she has no trouble with a smile.

Alone among all the others, she seems to know, and she is ready.

His name is Casey Chisholm.

And despite the people who wait and watch and whisper prayers of their own, despite the town that lies beyond the trees, despite his years of dreams, despite the nightmares that once had been true . . .

His name is Casey Chisholm.

And he is alone.

Part 1

1

1

Almost autumn; just past noon.

A light warm wind that nudges damp leaves along gutters and bats them fitfully across lawns; clouds merge in a vast blanket drawn over the horizon, drawn over the sky, smothering the light to a dark dusky haze; porch lights and streetlamps, headlamps and traffic lights; neon in store windows, too bright for the hour, too brittle for comfort.

Grey ghost pedestrians, scowling at each other, scowling at the weather, wishing the storm would hurry up and break, get it over with and get gone; in offices and shops no one speaks, hardly working, watching the windows, waiting for the storm; in schools children twitch and shift, cats' tails, while teachers do their best to hold their attention while watching the windows, checking the wind, waiting for the storm.

2

In a field to the south, a small carnival breaking down, preparing for the next day when it will head south for the winter.

Where it will unpack and die.

The owner has had enough. Throughout the season his games were always crowded, his rides and attractions always filled, but it was the faces that had finally made up his mind—desperate adults and hungry young ones, weary of the plagues, of the famines, of the deaths that had besieged them over the past three years, demanding happiness now, and a few moments of joy. But when they left the grounds their faces were weary, sullen; it was just too damn hard to be happy these days because when they'd get home there would always be reminders—of the plagues, of the famines, of all the damn death.

A few lights high on a half-dozen guy wire–propped poles along the edge of the midway, and a woman named Claire Sultan who walks through the shadows, one hand in her hip pocket, smelling the distant fading summer as the wind touches her cheeks and whispers through her hair. She is the daughter of the man who owns this portable, and too fragile, link to an earlier time, a time when she was young and knew how to laugh at a clown and sigh at a trained bear and shake her head without moving it at the young men who tried to impress their young women by throwing softballs into peach baskets and firing rifles at paper targets and holding their hands too tightly while the Octopus soared and twisted.

It's almost over now, and she has no idea what she'll do once they reach Florida and the equipment is sold and the carnies scatter and she's left with her father, who can't stop staring out their trailer window, wondering what had happened.

The crew has worked hard. The Ferris wheel is already down, the small tents already packed away on the trucks, the fences and gates and food stands and poles and flags and cheap gifts and cheap food long gone.

Only the carousel is left.

She takes her time getting to it, because once she does, it's definitely all over. She'll walk round it and pet the animals and sit in one of the benches and run her hands along a bronze pole or two, then give Marco the signal to make it all vanish. Her job. Her ride. Her life.

Her nostrils twitch, she smells rain, and she can't put it off any longer. With one hand in that pocket, the other running down the back of her short dark red hair, she blinks away all memory and makes the carousel the only thing she sees in the haze.

Once this is gone, she thinks, I'm going to have to learn how to make a living. That frightens her. Terrifies her. No romantic, yet she still lives for the carnival; for all its scams and tricks and cons and temptations, it's all she's known for twenty-seven years, and all she's ever wanted to know.

Marco has asked her to marry him, says he has enough saved up to keep them until he can find another job. Forever if necessary, he had told her with a shy smile under those summer-blond curls that seldom stay where they're brushed; I'm not all that smart, but I know how to save money. I'll be good to you, Claire, I swear to you, I'll be good.

He's ten years older, has worked for the Sultans for twelve years, off and on, and she thinks she actually loves him, but right now she isn't sure. He's strong, he's kind, but he doesn't love the life the way she does.

He doesn't love the life she's about to lose.

Don't be afraid, he told her; don't be afraid, I'll take care of you. Really. I'm not as dumb as I look.

Maybe not.

But he doesn't understand.

3

The carousel's ridged circus tent top has one light at the apex, a large and bright tulip-shaped green bulb that catches bits and sharp hints of itself in the flakes of gold paint years of weather haven't yet peeled away. Beneath, her pets wait for her good-byes—a pair of strutting llamas, a pair of strolling giraffes, a lion in full roar, an ostrich in full gallop; two old-fashioned sleighs for those who can't take the up-and-down; red horses, black horses, white horses, gold and bronze and speckled horses with hand-carved manes and hand-painted hooves and bared teeth she touches up with a small brush every year.

She is alone now because the others know and keep their distance.

They're also on the lookout for trouble, for the gang of young men and women, almost two dozen strong, who had swept through the grounds late the night before, swaggering through the crowds, taunting the acts, daring roust-abouts to fight, scattering with high-pitched laughter when the police finally arrived, leaving behind broken whiskey and beer bottles and a few cuts and bruises.

They left the carousel alone.

"Well," Claire says, grabbing a pole, swinging up to face a one-eyed llama. "Well."

Twenty-seven years old, she could pass for thirty-five. Older. Hard lines from a hard life she wouldn't have had any other way. A life that had driven her mother into a distant memory when Claire was only five. A mother Claire had stopped wondering about a long time ago. Gone is gone; what's left is the life.

With a twitch of a grin she slaps the llama lightly on its frozen rump and moves on to the ostrich, running a palm along its wood-feathered flank and across one raised leg.

"Well."

The smell of oil and sweat and thousands of children's rumps and grown-ups' feet and sneakers and babies who cried all the way around in the circle that a philosopher might say never ends; but she knows that riding the horse, or the lion, or that tiger on the other side never takes you in a circle. It's forward; always forward, through a kaleidoscope dream that lasts for as long as the number of tickets in your hand.

"Oh . . . hell," she mutters at a sudden tear on her cheek. A swipe more annoyed than angry takes it away, and she dries her hand on her hip.

What she wants to do, what she wants desperately to do, is open the hidden door in the fat center column covered with mirrors and painted faces, slip inside the control room, and turn the switches on.

Lights. Music. Up and down.

One more time.

One last time.

Let the music reach the town and let the children hear and dream, while she rides her favorite lion. Forward. Into a dream.

But she can't, and she knows she can't, because it would break her too-old young heart.

Instead she leans up on her toes and plants a silly kiss on the underside of a giraffe's stiff lifted chin; she stretches out on a sleigh and stares at the underside of the canopy, at the struts and bars that lift the animals up and down, searching for the clown faces she's sketched up there, one for every season, her notches for surviving another year.

She can't see them; not yet the middle of the afternoon, and it's already too dark up there.

A sigh, a quick laugh at herself, and she swings to her feet and yelps, "Jesus!" when she sees the man watching her.

"Sorry." He steps into the green light. "Didn't mean to startle you."

He's not very tall, wearing old western boots scuffed to hell and back, jeans so old that what blue is left looks like patches, a long-sleeve black shirt under an open vest decorated with what she thinks are Indian designs of some kind. He has a low-crown black western hat that hangs down his back on a beaded string. When he steps closer she sees his hair, parted in the center and gathered into a ponytail reaching just above the middle of his spine, a little grey in brown-red, gleaming as if it has just been washed and brushed. His face is thin, a sharp nose, chin and cheeks hidden by white-and-brown-red stubble, thicker on the chin where it almost makes a beard.

Despite the light, she can't really see the color of his eyes.

"We're closed," she tells him with an apologetic shrug, dusting a nervous hand over her jeans. "Sorry, sir, but you'll have to leave."

"Oh, I intend to," he answers. A smile, wide enough to show white teeth, quick enough to make her wonder if he really smiled at all. His voice is soft and thin, some kind of accent she can't quite place. Maybe Kansas, maybe Texas. He nods at the carousel. "This is special, you know."

"I know."

"Don't see many like it anymore." Another step, the breeze takes on a chill, and she can hear rumbling in the dark distance. The clouds bringing rain that will make leaving tomorrow a royal pain in the butt. He reaches out to touch a pole. Caresses it. The now-you-see-it smile again. "Been a long time since I rode on these things."

"Mister, look, really, I don't want to be rude or anything, but I've got a lot of work to do. I can't—"

His hand drops, tucks into a front pocket. "Sorry again. I guess I shouldn't bother you." Soft voice. Thin voice. Gentle voice. He squints as if in thought. "Hear you're closing up shop. For good, I mean."

She nods ruefully. "Soon as we get to Florida, it's all gone."

"Kind of sad."

"Not 'kind of' at all," she says, suddenly angry. "It damn well is sad."

Sawdust slips across the ground ahead of the wind; pieces of straw; scraps of paper.

He glances at the sky as faint lightning flares through the belly of the clouds. "Then don't end it," he tells her, scuffing a heel along the ground. "Keep on."

"Yeah, right." She jabs a finger at the dark. "Those damn people out there, they wouldn't know a good time if it bit them in the ass."

"Been rough the past few years, you oughta know that."

"Yeah, so? So they gotta curl up and die?" She moves to the edge of the platform and leans against a pole. "Have you seen the kids, mister? My God, they're older than their parents." She forces a shiver. "You should hear them laugh. Like they've never done it before in their lives."

He nods, rubs one cheek with a finger.

She shakes her head, the disgust she's felt all season moving into her throat. She doesn't understand why, and why now, but she can't stop it.

"The last month we've been in Michigan, Illinois, saving Ohio for last because it was always the best. I can't tell you why, but it has been, for as long as I can remember." A halfhearted kick at the air. "It's been like traveling through a desert, man, like traveling through a desert."

He watches her; patient.

"And last night those . . . those . . ." She can't find a word that wasn't born in the gutter. A deep breath. An apologetic smile, a lift of her eyebrows. "Sorry." A hand across her brow, and it pushes up through her hair. "We had some trouble last night."

"So I hear." He scratches under his chin, closes an eye as he looks at the sky. "You take care of them?"

"No. Cops came, scared them off."

"Ruined that farewell performance."

She nods, anger wrapping an iron band around her chest once again. "It would have been nice, it really would have been nice to go home on a high." Another deep breath doesn't calm her. "Bastards. Cops . . . man, are they useless, they said they were just letting off steam, being Saturday night and all. We shouldn't take it personally." Her eyes roll. "Jesus. Not take it personally."

The smile. "Spare the rod."

She looks at him, wondering. Blinks and says, "Not that I expect any better. I mean, we do all the work, and we're always the bad guys, you know what I mean?" A rueful grin. "Traveling guys like us, carnivals and whatever, we don't have the best reputations in the world."

Far to her left, the shouts of the crew cramming the last of the gear into the trucks, trying to beat the rain. They sound anxious, and probably are. Once done, and the animals bedded down for the night, there would be a final blowout. Usually a celebration with a touch of melancholy, this time it would be a wake.

She catches rain on the wind again, lightning in the clouds over the town four miles distant, and a soft rumbling, like something out there waking up.

The old man reaches over one shoulder for his hat, and as he puts it on, he looks down the midway. A tumbling piece of paper, a few leaves, dust passing through the fall of light from those half-dozen poles the town had insisted on putting in for some unspecified safety reasons. He stands just on the edge of the carousel roof's sharp shadow, squaring the hat, flicking the brim with a finger.

"Mister, really, I have to—"

"Red," he says, not turning around. "The folks I know, they call me Red." He half turns then, smiling at her sideways as he brushes a thumb across the stubble on his chin. "At least they used to, when this was the right color. Rusty sometimes, but mostly it's Red."

"So what do they call you now, Red?"

He lifts one shoulder; his voice softens. "Lots of things, Claire. Lots of things."

Another shout, it might have been her name, and she swings easily down to the ground. It sounds like Marco, and it sounds as if he's losing his temper. "Look, it's been nice, Red, but you really do have to leave." She doesn't tell him it's time to take the carousel down; that's none of his business, and he's already ruined her final farewell. "I don't want to be pushy, but . . ." She shrugs her regret.

That smile, and a quick outward push of his chin, like an old bird in a silly hat. He salutes her with two fingers to the brim, nods, and walks away, hands in his pockets.

Weird, she thinks, watches him for a moment, then heads for the trucks where the others will be waiting. She knows that more than one of them figures she's a little short in the sanity department, but she doesn't mind, as long as they do what they're told.

Then she groans an "Aw, shit," when the rain, not wasting time with a let's start with a gentle shower, suddenly slashes at her on the wind. She sprints for her trailer, home eight months of the year, and grabs a slicker and floppy hat from their hooks just inside the door.

"Taking her down now, Daddy," she calls, and leaves without waiting for an answer.

Silver rain where it passes through the lights on a sharp slant, emerald where it passes through the carousel's glow. Head ducked and tucked, shoulders hunched and stiff, she starts toward the ragged clump of old trucks and old trailers where the men await her signal, and she tells them with sharp gestures there's no sense in it right now, get dry, this won't last, we'll do it later.

Then she looks back over her shoulder, and stops. Frowning.

That man, Red, stands in front of the carousel, turning to instant shadow when lightning turns the afternoon a swift colorless white.

"God damn," she mutters, and vacillates—go right to him, or get some of the guys to watch her back? He's old, and she's strong, but she's seen too much not to know that looks can be camouflage. The decision is made for her when he steps onto the platform.

"Damn," she yells, and races toward him, boots splashing through mud puddles, eyes squinting nearly shut as the wind takes her head-on. This is too much. Last night, and now this. Son of a bitch, she's gonna kill that old bastard. Goddamn old people think they got more rights than anyone else. Well, not this time, and not that old man.

She's more than halfway there when, abruptly, everything stops—wind, rain, thunder.

One faint lightning flicker.

And silence.

She falters, licking her lips, wiping the back of a hand across her face, swearing that if he touches just one of her precious animals, she's going to rip his face off, the creep son of a bitch.

"Hey!" she shouts. "Damnit, get the hell away from there, you hear me?"

But she can't move any faster than a hurried walk. Feet splashing through puddles, through slops of thick mud. She doesn't want to move any faster, because she can see him drifting among the animals, a shadow in the dark where there shouldn't have been a shadow at all.

A sudden loud pop startles her—one of the pole lights has blown out. As she looks, another one explodes, starlike white sparks spraying to the ground.

She's heard no gunshots, no air rifle sound, maybe it was a slingshot, and another bulb disintegrates while she watches.

Oh, boy, she thinks, and swallows, and nibbles at her lower lip; oh, boy.

It's not so much the how and why of the exploding bulbs that unnerves her; it's what's left when it's over—a single shimmering pool of vague white halfway between the carousel and the exit, and the green light that slips over the carousel's roof and reaches the ground, where it turns darker, almost black.

When the wind finally returns, she's grateful; it had grown too warm suddenly, and the chill is welcome; when the rain returns, she's tempted to take off the floppy hat and let her face feel the drops, just to wake her up.

Lightning over town.

Thunder through the dark.

She's tempted again, this time to check her watch, knowing it's way too early to feel so late. Hell, she only had lunch an hour or so ago. But an hour or so ago the clouds hadn't yet made their way from the horizon, and there was still autumn-warm sunshine and the familiar sound of the crew laughing and cursing as they broke the carnival down; an hour or so ago, she had said to her father:

"I think you're wrong. Honestly. I think we ought to go into town and file a complaint. We've got damage, Dad, and they should pay."

Craig Sultan had looked up from behind the folding table he used as a desk and shook his head as if it weighed a ton. "Why bother, hon? We aren't going to repair it, just sell it, for God's sake."

"It's the principle," she'd insisted.

"It's a waste of time," he'd answered.

No, she'd thought then, and thought now as she remembered; it's not a waste of time. They got away with it. They'll do more. They need to be taught a lesson, the sons of bitches. They need to be taught.

She grimaces at the heat the thought rushes to her face, dripping rain from chin and nose. It must be because it's over, she decides, because she's never felt this way before. Other times, in other years, she was never so quick to vengeance. It must be because it's over—the carnival, her life.

Instead of weeping again, she snarls and stomps through the mud to the carousel.

She doesn't care why; she can only taste the rage.

4

She can see Red more clearly, rubbing a hand along the neck of one of the horses, and she wonders if maybe he's not such an old creep at all, if maybe he really does understand what this all means, that if, like her, he's saying good-bye.

She slows, rage momentarily dampened, shoulders hunched against the rain, the wind.

An old man who's seen who knows how many carnivals in his time. Memories that stretch back who knows how many decades. And now he comes upon one of the last, and it's no wonder he disobeys her and comes back. One last time. Because he'll never see another one again.

She stops.

The wind causes some of the rain to scatter into ribbons of mist; near the carousel the rain has turned to emeralds, a beaded curtain of tiny flaring emeralds that makes looking at her animals confusing, because emeralds and animals shift and shimmer in the wind. Movement without the carousel spinning.

Old man or not, though, he has to go.

She takes a step, opens her mouth, and . . .

. . . the rumbling she had heard beneath the storm earlier grows louder, low trapped thunder in a great cat's throat.

Red tilts his head up and looks at her from beneath the brim of his hat.

She raises a hand to beckon him away.

He smiles that smile and swings onto the back of a white-speckled horse.

She stares stupidly at her hand and lets it drop heavily to her side.

He reaches for the reins and settles in the saddle, boots

slipping into the stirrups while one hand rests on his thigh.

She wants to weep, this time for his memories, maybe a summer afternoon when he was a kid, waiting for the bell to sound, the warning bell that sends the parents laughing off the platform, the bell that signals the beginning of the ride and the music and the reach for the brass ring that will keep the ride going.

Forward; always forward.

When he tugs lightly on the reins and the horse slowly, stiffly, turns its head, Claire knows it's the way the slanting rain distorts what her eyes try to see; when he leans forward a little and whispers something and the horse's legs straighten until its hooves touch the platform, she knows it's the way the rain and mist have confused her vision; and when the horse shakes its head and she can hear above the storm the sound of a bridle and a snort and a sharp stamping hoof, she knows it's the rain.

What she doesn't know is why she can see the horse turn, pulling away from the brass pole that once pierced its shoulders and pinned it in place.

What she doesn't know is why it can, with a flick of its reins and a word from the rider, toss its head and bare its teeth and step down off the platform without hesitation while the rain washes each little white speckle from its flanks and leaves only gleaming black behind. Tail snapping side to side, mane ruffled and fluttering as the storm eases from downpour to shower.

They stand there, horse and rider, caught in the pale green glow.

They stand there, and Claire's mouth opens for a word, perhaps a scream, and nothing comes out but a short terrified whimper.

They stand there, and she checks fearfully over her shoulder, thinking she should call Marco and the others, one call that would have them armed and running even though, suddenly, she believes without reason that she is in no danger.

A short sharp shudder she blames on the day's chill.

The shower is little more than drifting mist now, lightning and thunder confined to the clouds, and with a careful deep breath she takes off her hat and, as she approaches the carousel, lets it fall to the ground. One eye on horse and rider, ready to bolt if they so much as look at her cross-eyed, she pulls herself onto the platform and examines the pole that had once held the horse. The brass is cold against the palm and fingertips that slide along it, searching for the break, knowing she won't find it but reason demands she look anyway.

When at last she turns, so slowly she can almost feel each muscle working, she attempts a questioning pleading smile, but the attempt is so feeble she nearly cries. Nearly screams. Nearly falls.

But she does scream, short and sharp, when the green tulip bulb explodes high overhead into emerald sparks that fade quickly and for a moment leave nothing but darkness behind.

She holds her breath, some part of her ashamed at her reaction, some part of her angry because she doesn't understand.

A swallow, an exhalation, a step toward the edge as the light on the pole in the middle of what is left of the carnival's last midway allows her to see him again. He's watching her, she knows it, but she can't see his face beneath the brim of that hat.

Watching her.

Not smiling.

Mist curling lazily around the horse's legs, creeping across the mud, swirling up onto the carousel and curling cold around her ankles.

The horse bobs its head and steps backward, water splashing silently from beneath its hooves. Its mouth works the bit, its tail lashes the air, and the one eye she can see is wide and white and staring.

"Hey," she says hoarsely, knowing what's about to happen and demanding an explanation.

Red makes a clucking sound with his tongue, and horse and rider turn away, walking slowly toward the exit and the road that lies beyond.

"Hey!"

She feels stupid, standing there so helplessly, and that angers her. She wants to know who the hell he is, she wants him to bring back her horse, she wants him to tell her how he did it, she wants him to tell her there's nothing to be afraid of despite the deep-throated big cat thunder that rolls over the field and the lightning that snaps at tree-tops and distant rooftops like the tongue of a dark dragon.

He stops and looks over his shoulder.

She still can't see his face.

But she can, this time, catch a glimpse of his eyes, and they're green. Not emeralds. Not jewels. Not glowing.

Just . . . green.

Not smiling.

Although there is the storm, and the distance between him and her, she can hear him as clearly as if he were whispering in her ear:

"Spare the rod, Claire," he tells her. "You know the rest."

They ride through the light from the single bulb on that high pole, and she isn't amazed and isn't frightened and isn't the slightest bit bewildered when she thinks she sees the light pass through them both, thinks she sees tiny flares of scarlet fire splash from the hooves, thinks she hears those hooves striking the earth as if it were dry and laced with iron.

Thinks she sees them vanish before they reach the other side, nothing now but the mist, twisting, curling, drifting away into the dark.

It's the rain and the wind; it's the lightning and the thunder; it's the rage she feels at the bastards who've ruined her final good-bye.

So she leaps from the carousel and races toward her men, screaming at them, shrieking, ordering them to get moving, find weapons and get moving because no one, especially not a bunch of drunken half-witted sons of bitches is going to take away the only thing she has left.

Her good-bye.

Her farewell.

And when Marco asks her what she wants done when they find those hick freaks, she looks back toward the midway and she doesn't hesitate at all when she says, "Kill them, Marco. Kill them all."

2

1

Almost autumn; just past noon.

A light warm wind that carries the scent of sea and pine, a faint touch of mudflat and marsh, just the slightest hint of a flower that has bloomed past its time; a high afternoon sun bright but not bright enough to haze the color of the sky, a handful of high island clouds that take their own sweet time drifting west to east; gulls in the air, pelicans on wharf pilings, a young blue heron picking its away across shallow water beneath gnarled cypress and twisted mangrove, while something dark shifts in the reeds, and the surface ripples.

A single story, wood-and-stone schoolhouse, its windows open, the voices of teachers and children; several score houses, mostly wood, a few brick or stone, windows open, the voices of radios and televisions, here and there someone on the phone; pedestrians on the main street, pleased they can still wear shorts and short sleeves, taking their time, no hurry at all, while the locals count their blessings there are any tourists at all.

Camoret Island, in the eye of the storm.

2

The Camoret Sheriff's Department was housed in a single-story brick building on the north corner of Midway Road and Landward Avenue, a T intersection that marked, within a yard or two, the geographic center of both town and island. The recessed entrance was trimmed in scalloped wood painted white, with double glass doors propped open to lure the sea breeze inside. Above the arched lintel was a sign that announced the building's function in fancy gold letters outlined in black. There were no windows in front, or on either side. In back there were six: one for the sheriff's private office, two for the main room, and below them, along the top of the high reinforced foundation, there were three, narrow and barred, one for each of the cells in the basement.

Sheriff Vale Oakman figured that after fifteen years he knew the place so well he could be struck blind tomorrow and still find his way around without once barking a shin.

Today, however, he could see all too well.

He stood to one side in the entrance recess and pressed his lips together in order to stifle a decidedly unprofessional groan. For a moment he considered retreating to the street, pretend he hadn't been here. But it was too late, and his eyes closed in a brief silent prayer that this isn't a sign of how the week was shaping up.

It was Monday, and Mondays were supposed to be reasonably peaceful, a natural extension of Sundays when, in the main, nothing happened at all. It was supposed to be a time to shift out of his weekend gears, a gentle and painless transition into the rest of the week. A time for paperwork. For checking the wanted notices the state and Feds piled on his desk like slush, marking the trails of the gangs that had begun to swarm out of the cities across the landscape.

For working out, lately, the details of his retirement.

It was not, by God and first thing after a big leisurely lunch and his monthly attempt to charm the apron off Gloria Nazario, for seeing the likes of for God's sake Dub Neely.

Y'know, he thought, still unable to bring himself to step over the threshold; you know, it's not like you couldn't squash him if you wanted. I mean, it's not like you couldn't pound the jerk through the floor.

Oakman was a man of average height who seemed to be constructed out of nothing but spheres and cylinders, head to torso, arms to legs, with a loose-fitting tan uniform that made him appear even larger. But only strangers and tourists ever considered him overweight; everyone else knew that most of that round was muscle, not fat. At least it was something they liked to believe. And for the most part, it was true.

Thinning black hair barely long enough to lie down, greying black eyebrows, and a small sharp smile that barely moved his cheeks at all. A twinge in his left knee now and again when the damp settled in, especially in winter; his night vision when driving not quite up to par; a tendency to be short of breath when he climbed too many stairs or walked for too long.

But Jesus, Vale, you can still squash the little creep.

Or get the hell away.

From where he stood in the recess, no one could see him from either of the high-back benches set along the walls left and right. Beyond a waist-high gated railing were four blondwood desks, the first and largest facing the doorway—Verna Dewitt's, and it was her job to give him any one of a number of signals they had developed over the past dozen years, most of them warnings to turn around and get gone, trouble's brewing and you're not gonna like it.

Usually it was Mayor Cribbs on his high political horse, or some agitated outraged tourist, or, on occasion, some joker reporter from the mainland who wanted to know, like they all wanted to know, what the real scoop was, the real deal, what it was really like to be the sheriff in charge of a whole damn island.

Once in a great while it was Norville Cutler, looking for a sly favor or uncirculated news or just a few minutes alone to pass the time of day . . . and to remind him, mayor or no mayor, law or no law, who was really in charge of the way things went.

On Mondays it was *never* Dub Neely.

The world, he decided sourly, is coming to a goddamn end.

So, resigning himself to the inevitable, he lowered his head, blew out a slow breath to keep his temper in check, and finally stepped inside.

"Morning, Sheriff."

Verna greeted him brightly, too loudly, with a big old smile only he knew was mocking. She was a thin woman, close enough to skinny not to make much difference, whose uniform was never without unnervingly sharp creases. She wore black-frame glasses attached to an elastic cord, a different color every day, and today her hair was bundled into a clumsy chignon that only served to accentuate the hard angles of her face and the length of her neck.

Her desk was the largest because it also held the dispatch radio connecting the office to Vale and his three deputies. And when she kept it turned down, like it was now, the faint static buzz sounded like summer flies endlessly batting themselves against a window pane. A lazy sound. For Vale, the perfect description of the way things ought to be.

Except, apparently, today.

Verna hadn't warned him about Dub because Dub was already waiting impatiently at the gate, leaning hard against the waist-high railing. His clothes were a direct contrast to Verna's uniform, especially where his belly pushed against a shirt that might once have been white and obviously hadn't seen an iron in a couple of weeks. A water-stained suede vest, a sloppily knotted tie yanked away from his neck, and sand-and-mud smeared clodhoppers that always seemed to want tying.

If you didn't know him by sight, you definitely knew him by smell—personal hygiene wasn't his strong point, but liquor or beer on his breath was. Neither was so overpowering that you couldn't stand to be near him; the smell was more subtle than that, and therefore more unsettling. Oakman knew that half the time you couldn't help wondering if maybe it was actually you who desperately needed the wash or the toothpaste.

"Dub," he greeted flatly, taking off his Stetson, nodding as he wiped a thumb across his brow.

Neely nodded back sharply, his pallid face mottled, brow and cheeks red with anger. "Sheriff. About damn time you got here. I want to report a crime."

"Hey, we all got to eat sometime, Dub." Oakman patted his stomach. "Some of us more than others."

The small joke didn't work.

Neely sneered. "Place could go to hell and you wouldn't know it. I'm a taxpayer, you know. My hard-earned money pays your salary. And your goddamn food bills."

"Then I want a raise."

That didn't work either.

"Damnit, Sheriff, I'm here to report a crime and you're making fun of me."

"No," Vale told him patiently, "I'm not, and I'm truly sorry if I come across that way. I'm still shaking off the weekend, you know how it goes." He shifted his stance, hat at his waist, an attitude of respectful, serious listening. "Go ahead, Dub. What's the problem?"

"Not a *problem*, it's a *crime*, damnit, ain't you listening? She,"—Neely swept a grime-streaked hand toward the deputy receptionist—"insisted I had to wait on you. Wouldn't do it herself."

"Well, *she*," Vale reminded him curtly, "is Miz Dewitt to you, Dub." He edged the shorter man aside with a well-placed hip, unlatched the gate, and was through and had it closed before the shorter man could follow. As he glared down at an uncontrite, fighting-hard-not-to-giggle Verna, he said, "What kind of crime we talking about here?"

"Murder," Neely answered, his voice low.

Vale closed his eyes, sighed, turned, and said, "Whose murder, Dub? Where?"

"Don't remember his name. The guy who came here a summer or two ago. The giant. He's on the beach." Neely frowned, moistening his lips as he concentrated. "Wasn't breathing, best I could figure, and there was blood all over the place." He shuddered. "Awful stuff, Sheriff. Awful. You should have seen it." He lowered his voice again. "I think a gang got him, you know? They're hiding in the marsh. I told you about that a hundred times. They're hiding in the marsh, and now they done us murder."

Vale made his way around the desks to the back of the room, where a large area map hung on the wall between the two windows whose blinds were at half-staff. From a distance, Camoret Island resembled a large blunted arrow pointing toward Spain, its somewhat crooked shaft aimed toward the Georgia coast just north of Savannah. He traced its curved outline without speaking. Nodded thoughtfully. Grunted softly. Looked over his shoulder and said, "Dub, we got umpteen miles of beach here, not counting the marina and the wetlands. You want to tell me just where you found this alleged body?"

Neely frowned as he squinted across the room before, at last, he shrugged helplessly. "Don't remember."

Of course not, Oakman thought; that would be too easy.

"Think you can show me?"

Neely shrugged again and began to fuss with his tie. "Think so. Maybe. Yeah. Maybe."

"Verna, anyone else report a one-man massacre this morning?"

"No, sir, Sheriff."

"I ain't lying, Sheriff," Neely snapped. "I know what I saw."

"I know, Dub, I know. Like the camels you saw around South Hook last June."

"Well—"

"And the UFO over North Beach. They was fixin' on an invasion, as I recall."

"Yeah, but—"

"I won't bother to remind you about the giant."

"Well, damnit, Sheriff, you know that one is true. I *was* lying down, and he *is* damn big, scared the living hell outta me, coming up on me like that. How the hell was I to know he was just looking for work?" He patted his chest gingerly with two fingers. "My heart ain't been the same since, you know. Least little thing gets it racing so bad I see spots and nearly fall over. His fault. All his fault."

The sheriff nodded. "And now you say he's murdered."

"Blood, too. Don't forget the blood."

"Aw, Jesus, Dub." Vale shook his head, slapped his hat back on, and told Verna he was taking Dub and the Jeep for a ride on the beach. Then he shoved Neely through the doorway none too gently, and said over his shoulder, "And if by some miracle Chisholm drops by, tell him he was murdered last night and would he have the decency to stick around so Mr. Neely here can make an ID when we get back."

As Verna sputtered into high-pitched laughter, he squinted at the late September sun and sighed yet again.

Mondays.

Son of a bitch, he didn't even have his Mondays anymore.

3

Midway Road wasn't exactly the most imaginative name in the world for a street, but Vale was glad it at least wasn't called something like Rising Surf Avenue or Wafting Breeze Boulevard. That sort of nonsense was prevalent enough in the coastal towns; the one thing he didn't need here was what Gloria called cutesy-poo for the tourists. There was plenty of that already in the dumbass names of some of the shops, half of which start with "Ye" or had *e*s at the end of words that never had them in the first place.

Still, he didn't half love this town, and a good part of that had to do with the drive.

A half mile from his office the shops and trees gave way to houses and trees, and lawns still green, gardens still blooming. Few of the buildings were big this close to town center, but none were ramshackle, none in desperate need of repair or paint. Enough shade speckling the road to keep the temperature at a decent level, a decent breeze to cool the sweat when the shade didn't work.

It was the same in the other direction, and a good enough excuse to keep him out of the office as much as he could.

"Where we going, Dub? Come on, you gotta give me a hint, okay?"

"The whales, I think. Yeah, I think it was at the whales."

"You sure?"

"I guess."

"And you're sure it was Casey Chisholm."

Neely didn't answer, and Vale didn't press him. The man might be a royal pain in the ass, but somewhere inside those mismatched clothes and under those streaks of dirt and God only knew what else was a man who used to be a teacher, or a college professor. At least that's what the word was, and once in a while Vale heard something that made him believe it. Why he'd come to Camoret, why he was what he was now, no one knew and no one asked. His business if he wanted to drown; even Lyman Baylor, pain-in-the-butt preacher that he was, had stopped trying to save him.

A few minutes later Dub began to squirm a little in the passenger seat, and Vale grinned. The pudgy little man didn't care for not having much but roll bars and struts between him and the blacktop; more than once he'd declared Jeeps and their cousins dangerously unnatural, quite possibly demonic. But a mile down the road he settled himself, squinting into the wind that slipped past the sun visors Vale had snapped up over the windshield's top frame.

"Funny, ain't it," Neely said, rubbing the side of his nose with a finger.

"What? Your murder?"

"No." A hand waved west, toward the unseen mainland. "You know. All that shit going on." He sniffed, and rubbed his nose again. "We been lucky, you know? Camoret ain't had none of that sickness went around last year, had pretty much plenty of food. Only a few of them bastards coming out to raise a little hell." He squinted at the brick schoolhouse as they sped by. "Like we was blessed or something, you know what I mean?"

Vale looked at him, surprised the dope had even noticed. Any other day, he would swear nothing ever got through the man's alcoholic haze but the price of his next drink. "Good a word as any," he agreed.

Dub nodded solemnly. "Like them kangaroo folks."

"The what?"

"You know, them people that live with the kangaroos?"

"You mean Australians?"

"Well, who'd you think I meant? The Chinese? Jeez, Sheriff, pay attention here. They got no kangaroos in China, you oughta know that."

"Right," Vale said. "Right."

"They ain't blessed is what I'm talking about. What I read, they's getting ready for a shooting war pretty soon."

Now that the sheriff already knew. Sometime around midsummer, some drunken and drugged-up Indonesian

sailors had hijacked a patrol boat and shot up a small cruise
ship tooling around the water near someplace called
Queensland; he never heard of it but that didn't matter.
When it was over, a dozen or so Australians and New
Zealanders had been killed, a couple dozen more badly
wounded. Words had been exchanged. Diplomats recalled.
Fuss and bluster in the UN. Maneuvers and high-visibility
training on both sides.

"'Course, it's no skin off my nose," Dub said, bracing a
hand against the dashboard as Vale swerved to avoid a gull
squatting insolently in the middle of the road. "You just
get tired of hearing of it, you know what I mean? If it ain't
the kangaroos, it's them guys over in Africa beating the
crap out of each other." He shook his head sadly, scratched
through his hair, then used the end of his tie to dab some
sweat off his neck.

"We had lots of killing before," Vale reminded him.
"That year, remember? Seemed like half the country was
going up in smoke."

Dub shook his head again. "That was killing, Sheriff.
This time we're talking war."

The houses were fewer, the trees thicker, live oak and pine,
willows house-tall and taller. Not long before the road
began a long and slow curve to the west, they passed a
clutch of undistinguished homes flanking the blacktop, and
Vale squinted over to the left, hunting for signs of
Chisholm at his house. The smart thing would be to stop,
knock on the door, look around the place, but Neely had
gotten under his skin, and he decided to go on, he could
always check the house later.

Less than a mile farther north, sidewalks and houses
ended. Sand drifted across the blacktop. Reeds and weeds.
Just before the road straightened again, Vale swung the
Jeep hard to the right and followed a wide sandy trail
through the trees, marked by a sign that told him he was

heading for North Beach, No Dogs, No Bicycles, Bonfires
by Permit Only.

Ten minutes later they reached the sea.

And the whales.

4

As far as anyone knew, there had been no Indian population on Camoret when the Spanish discovered it on their
way to Florida; as far as anyone knew, they stayed only
long enough to build a few huts and some graves before
moving on, without leaving any recorded reason why they
had abandoned their find. It wasn't for lack of fresh water,
good soil, protection from the elements, or proximity to
the coast for trade and military purposes; Camoret had all
of that, but the English didn't stay either, their records just
as brief and puzzling as their predecessors'.

No one knew, then, who had given it its name.

No one knew, then, who first stood on the clean wide
beach and looked back across the Atlantic toward home.

Or who first discovered the whales:

Six huge boulders in three pairs worn smooth and
grooved by wind and sea, white-streaked grey, so deeply
set that no one had ever been able to dig beneath them to
measure their actual size. The three largest resembled the
great heads and humps of whales about to sound, behind
each a smaller boulder, nearly flat on the back side, one of
them split on top to give imagination reason enough to call
them flukes, the tails up and ready to slap at the surface.

The lead whale's head was eight feet high, twelve feet
long, with a nine foot tail; the others, each slightly behind
and inland of the one in front, weren't quite so imposing,
but all were taller than a tall man.

A family it was: Daddy the largest, Baby the smallest,
Momma firmly planted in the middle, holding the group
together.

By the time Camoret town was firmly, permanently established, no laws were needed to protect the site. It was a given: do your mischief elsewhere if you need to let off steam, but vandalize the whales at your peril.

They were climbed, of course, and played on and around; there were picnics and trysts, games invented that used the boulders as bases, photographs taken and a magazine layout about ten years ago, but the only damage done was by the wind, and the sea.

Wishing he were somewhere else and moving up his retirement date because he couldn't stand this crap anymore, Vale parked off to the side of the trail's end, in a spot where countless other vehicles had tramped and hardened the sand into a makeshift parking lot. An empty trash barrel stood at each corner. A small sign on a canted post warned drivers not to go any farther.

"Where?" he asked as he pulled a pair of sunglasses from his shirt pocket and put them on.

Dub moved to the front of the Jeep, a hand rubbing the small of his back, eyes narrowed against the glare off sand and water. The nearest whale, Baby, was fifty yards away; he pointed to the lead whale, another twenty farther on.

"Okay, then. Let's do it."

Although he didn't for a minute believe Neely's story, he couldn't help a slight anticipatory tightening of his stomach, couldn't help leaning to one side as if he could see through the boulders to the place where the body was supposed to be. Those men Dub had claimed had only raised a little hell had in fact done more than that—two break-ins, a severe beating, an attempted arson.

Word was, it was Cutler's boys, not mainland strangers. Stump Teague and his brothers, who lived in separate houses at the edge of the marsh.

Another reason why retirement was looking better every day.

Neely didn't speak.

The only sound was the crunch of their shoes on the sand, the hiss of the wind across the surface of the beach. The voice of the surf didn't count—it was there all the time, and the only time it was noticed was when it grew louder.

As Neely swerved around Baby's tail, his right hand automatically, absently, reached out to stroke it. For luck. Touch wood, on stone.

Vale moved in a wide arc, keeping the boulders on his right. The beach was nearly two hundred yards wide along the full length of the eastern shoreline, dotted with clumps of dried kelp, smashed shells; a gull feather twitching where it had stuck in the sand, a pine cone quivering in the depression of a footprint. The tide was out, but he could still see plumes of spray where waves struck the massive teeth of rock jetties that had been built out into the water. The earliest colonists had recognized the danger of erosion from storm and ordinary tides, and every spring and autumn Camoret continued what they had begun—hauling the largest rocks and boulders they could find to add to each jetty's bulk, repair the winter's damage. One every quarter mile, and so far it had worked.

"You know," Dub said, sticking close to Vale's side, "sometimes you kind of feel like Robinson Crusoe out here, you know what I mean, Sheriff?"

Vale did.

There were no buildings anywhere on the beach, no homes, no shops, all forbidden by law. Waves, then sand broken here and there by sawgrass-topped dunes, then a heavy line of trees and underbrush. An unbroken sky. No ships on the horizon. Stand long enough, quietly enough, and you'd never know there were several hundreds of people back there, thousands in the right season. It was as if no one lived here, or ever had. Ever.

When they reached Daddy's head, Vale took off his hat, wiped his face with a sleeve, and said nothing.

The sand was empty.

No body, no blood, no stains.

Just to be sure, he checked the other side, checked the rest of the family, then walked along the treeline for fifty yards in either direction. When he returned, Dub had plopped himself on the ground, his back against the boulder, hands on his knees. Staring at the water.

"Dub."

"Don't say it."

Vale blinked, cocked his head. That wasn't Neely's usual voice. No whine, no apology, no sputtering preparation for a story that would explain how the body and blood had vanished. This was Neely's other voice, stone sober, something he had heard but only three or four times a year.

"Must've been the light," the little man offered, flatly.

"Must've been," Vale agreed, no accusation in his tone.

"That guy must've been taking a nap or something. Slept on the beach all night, maybe. I think he does that a lot."

"Probably. Lots of people do, the weather's nice and all. Do it myself sometimes." He wiped his face again, replaced his hat, adjusted his sunglasses. "Yep. Can see that, Dub. You're probably right."

Neely rocked to one side so he could extricate a dented hip flask from his back pocket. He held it against his chest with both hands, licked his lips several times, finally said, "Do you have any idea what it's like to be a drunk?"

Vale didn't know what to say. This was suddenly way beyond the boundaries of their relationship, such as it was.

"For one thing," Neely said, looking up at him with a squint and a half smile, "you see things that ain't ordinarily there, ordinarily."

Vale hesitated, then nodded as if he understood; what the hell else could he do?

"For example"—and Neely nodded toward the place where he'd thought the body had been—"that giant—"

"Chisholm. Casey Chisholm. For crying out loud, Dub, the guy's a little strange but he does have a name."

"Yeah." Neely returned his gaze to the sea. "He don't have a car, you notice? He's got this old bike instead, never goes anywhere but where he lives, once in a while I see him in town. But far as I can tell, he never goes off-island, you ever notice that? Thought at first maybe he was on the run, you know? Did something bad and was using us to hide out."

"And . . . now you don't think so?"

"Nope." Neely unscrewed the top, took a drink and coughed, took another, and screwed the top back on. "Another thing about a drunk is, people don't pay you no attention except to kick at you once in a while, get you the hell out of the way. So you see things, you know? Hear things." He laughed silently. "Don't always remember what it is, but it happens."

Vale rolled his shoulders against a light chill that rode the breeze. Now this was more like it—Neely not making any sense.

"So, uh, what did you see, Dub?"

"Ain't seen nothing, not really."

"Then what did you hear?"

Top off, another drink, longer this time, and this time, no coughing.

"I'm sitting right here last night." He smacked his lips. Another drink. "Communing with the stars, you know what I mean? The meaning of life, Sheriff. The meaning of life. Kind of an existential haze sweetened by a good red wine. Anyway, that giant comes walking up the beach. Moon's big enough, but I'm sitting right here, so he don't see me. So he's walking along, got his hands in his pockets, just out for a stroll."

"So what?" Vale said impatiently. "Jeez, Dub, you eavesdrop on him or something?"

"Nope, that ain't what I heard."

"Dub, damnit, if you don't tell me, I'm gonna smack you into the middle of next March."

"Horses."

Vale barked a laugh. "Horses? Christ, Dub, we don't have any horses on the island, you know that as well as I do."

"Don't care, Sheriff. That guy's walking along the beach and he gets a little way up there, and all of a sudden I hear horses. Kind of walking slow, but I hear them."

Wearily Vale massaged his brow with two fingers, adjusted his Stetson, rubbed his brow again. "Hell, I'm going back. You want a ride?"

"No. Thanks anyway, I think I'll just sit here a while. Commune, you know?"

"Whatever," Vale said and started back to the Jeep.

"I'll tell you something else," Neely called after him.

Vale lifted a hand over his shoulder, an I-don't-care-see-you-around gesture.

"He heard them too," Neely called. "Didn't see jack, but that Chisholm guy heard them too."

3

1

Almost autumn; long past noon.

A light warm wind that still carries dampness from a brief storm just passed, pushing ripples across puddles, nudging raindrops from sagging leaves; a dead branch lies in the slow lane of the interstate, and the occasional car swerves around it, lifts a wave, each time pushing it a little closer to the shoulder; the smell of mud and wet grass and oil smeared to rainbows on the north-to-south highway; a crow in the left land, tearing at the bloody body of a cat.

The interstate is divided by a wide grass median slowly turning brown, with an infrequent run of young trees in the process of shedding yellowed leaves; beyond the deep ditches that line the outside of the road, steep weedy embankments topped with fences, some wood, some wire, sagging here and there, rusted here and there, while cattle graze and horses drink and a tractor makes its way across a rolling fallow field.

And once, only once, the distant echo of gunfire.

2

His name is Reed Turner, and he's much too young to be so old.

Once tall, he trudges along the highway with a stoop to his shoulders, too much weight there for him to stand upright. His face, once smooth, has dark lines at the corners of his eyes, the corners of his mouth, lines that have little to do with the road dirt that has settled there. He has long since lost what little baby fat he had left when last he bothered to look in a mirror. Really look. Really see what stranger would look back at him.

He is, now, just a year and a few months past the last of his teens, but when people look at him they think they see a man twice as old. Twice as tired. Twice as beaten.

Her name is Cora Bowes, and she's much too young to be so old.

She wears a baggy pair of sun-bleached jeans, a baggy denim shirt, and in her right hand she holds a gnarled length of wood she's learned to use as a club and walking stick. Her hair has been lightened by months on the road, is pulled back into a ponytail but still looks ragged where she's cut it herself. When she's relaxed, when she can find a good reason to smile, she is attractive in a way that puzzles others into wondering why. Nevertheless, she is. When she's relaxed. When she can find a reason to smile.

She is, now, only fifteen months past her nineteenth birthday, and once in a while she wonders exactly how old she looks. Whatever it is, it's too old, and she knows it, and sometimes, at night, she wonders where it's all gone.

* * *

They have been together since the day and night their world blew up. Three years, too many months, too many days since almost everyone they knew, everyone they had known, had perished in a firestorm battle that had left nothing standing but a church whose bell tolled every night though no one pulled the rope. Far too long since they had seen—and took years to really believe they had actually seen it—the only man they had ever trusted struggle with a woman in the bell tower, heard the screams, heard the explosions, saw him fall. Believing him dead, they had run. Nowhere in particular, just . . . away.

When they heard he had lived, had actually survived the fight and the fall, they went back to find him, and have been searching ever since.

They sit on a log at the side of the road, lifting a thumb at every car and eighteen-wheeler, making frantic angry gestures that have them giggling when every car and eighteen-wheeler takes a look and passes them by.

Finally Cora drags a backpack from under her legs and zips it open, reaches in and pulls out a chocolate bar. Slowly she turns it around in both hands, smacking her lips loudly, as if preparing her stomach for a grand Thanksgiving meal.

"Cora, for crying out loud."

"What's the matter? I want to appreciate this, you creep. We're almost out, in case you hadn't noticed."

"If we're almost out, don't eat it."

She sticks her tongue out at him and peels half the wrapper away, passes the bar under her nose as if testing a fine cigar. "I hope this is the right way."

"You're supposed to eat it, dope."

"I mean where we're going, Reed. God."

He doesn't answer right away; he's too busy squinting up the hilly road to check for traffic. They've been walking for weeks, with only three rides to ease the aches and blisters on their feet, and they're headed south now, because of a dream.

"It's right," he says at last. His voice, once high, has deepened a little.

"If you say so."

"I do, Cora. I do."

"Want a bite?"

"Nope."

"We're almost out."

"You eat it. I'll be all right." He rests a hand against his chest. "Don't mind me. I'll manage." His other hand pulls a piece of dark bark from the log. "This'll do just fine. I don't mind. It's roughage."

"Creep."

"Dope."

They smile but not at each other; they don't have to, not after all this time. Not after all they've seen.

Cora chews and swallows, the production so exaggerated he can't help but laugh.

"What day is it?" she asks.

"Tuesday."

"What year?"

Reed shrugs. "Who the hell knows?"

Their first plan after they'd left home the second time, for the last time, had been to head for the South, because that's where their friend, Casey Chisholm, had come from. But they hadn't realized how large a place the South really was, especially when they had little money, no transportation of their own, and not a clue where in Tennessee, or anywhere else for that matter, he might have gone to ground. It took them a while, but they soon learned how to talk to strangers, how to sift through rumors, how to judge a face and a smile and a tone and a gesture. That made the searching easier, but it didn't make it successful.

And every time they think they see a huge, white, gunboat Continental with a silver hood ornament shaped like a charging horse, they go to ground themselves. They made it through the famine, were untouched by the plague, had been hassled and attacked and several times nearly separated, but the only thing they really fear is the sight of that Lincoln.

Death drives that car.

They know it.

They have seen her.

3

By sunset it's clear they won't get another ride today, so they pick up their backpacks and sleeping bags and trudge away from the road, into a stand of trees at the edge of a small farm. They don't bother with the farmhouse because they have nothing to trade in exchange for a bed and meal. Besides, Reed thinks as they bat aside branches in search of a dry clearing, the last time they had stopped at one, the farmer had spent the whole night reading to them from the Bible, trying to save them before it was too late and the world ended and they were damned.

And doomed.

It was tempting to tell the well-meaning old man not to bother, thanks but no thanks, they had already seen part of the End.

They had already seen the first Horseman.

Reed didn't, though. The old man wouldn't have believed him, and would probably have run them off at the business end of a shotgun for being blasphemers or something. It had happened before; Cora had a scar on her right thigh to prove it.

Water drips on his hair, splashes in his face. The earlier Reed, the one who lived in Maple Landing, New Jersey, and lusted after Cora, who wouldn't give him the time of day, that Reed Turner would have lost his temper and started screaming, kicking at the trees and cursing everything that moved. This Reed, however, only wipes the water away.

"Just think," he says as he follows her around the lower boughs of a fat pine, "that the guys who settled this place back in the old days, they had to live like this all the time. Pretty amazing, don't you think?"

"Pretty stupid," she answers, stepping into a small clearing and dropping her bags. "I would've stayed home and let someone else do it."

"Some pioneer you are."

"I'm not a goddamn pioneer," she snaps. "I am a goddamn orphan, and don't you damn forget it."

He starts to say, *well thanks a lot, what about me?*, but he doesn't. She's in one of her moods, and even a grunt would set her off, and he'd have to put up with her temper for the rest of the night. Not that he blames her. More times than he wanted to count, she had almost convinced him to give this up, that Chisholm was a lost cause and they'd never find him unless they suddenly got a hell of a lot luckier than they had been. A miracle; it would take a damn miracle.

But the hints and clues kept coming, and he couldn't ignore them: a huge white-haired man dressed in black seen in this small town, or in that place barely large enough to make it on a map. Because they had no real time reference for the sightings, they had just about covered every state east of the Mississippi and south of the Mason-Dixon; because they kept hearing stories about the giant who preached wherever someone would listen, they kept moving.

They have nothing else to do.

They have nowhere else to go.

Cora digs the pit for their evening fire; he sets out the sleeping bags and rummages through what's left of their larder. Pretty skimpy, he realizes, deciding on a couple cans of vegetables and one can of soup. Tomorrow they'd have to stop at the next town and, if it wasn't battened down against strangers, see what they could do to pick up more. If necessary, get a job for a week or so. They have gotten good at that, too.

"Steak," he says.

"What?"

He winces, not realizing he's spoken aloud. He fusses with the contraption he'd made a long time ago, a collapsible cooking frame that fits over the fire for their one small pan, their one small pot. "Sorry. Just daydreaming."

"Some day," she tells him, making it sound like a promise.

They eat, they don't speak, they make sure the fire is out and the utensils cleaned and put away before crawling into their sleeping bags to stare at the sky.

He's almost asleep, when Cora whispers, "That guy."

"Huh?"

"That guy we met last year. The one in West Virginia, remember? Broken arm? Looked like he'd fallen down a mountain? We gave him some money. Remember?"

He does; he doesn't want to.

"You . . . you said he was different. Like Chisholm."

Even though she can't see him, he nods. "Yeah."

"Why, Reed? Why was he any different than us?"

"I've told you a hundred times, Cora, I don't know. Soon as I saw him I just knew."

Something dark flies under the few stars they can see; in the trees something shifts, it sounds like feathers.

His left hand nudges her hip, and she slips her right hand into his. It's the way of it these past few months, falling asleep holding hands. For reasons they can't explain, it's better than an embrace.

A car on the interstate backfires twice, and she squeezes his fingers suddenly and so tightly he has to bite down on his lip to keep from making a noise. It's something they've never gotten used to, the guns that came out when the famine was at its worst and people all over defended their pantries, when the plague mushroomed with neither rhyme nor reason and the guns came out to keep the odd-looking away.

He's almost asleep again, when she whispers, "It's changed, Reed. It's not the same out there. Or is it just me?"

A hopeful note he sours when he says, "No. I know what you mean."

And it *has* changed.

What there is now, everywhere they've been, from everything they've seen in newspapers and on television, is an intensity that's almost terrifying in its strength. It didn't take some people long to put together the several disasters that had occurred over the past half decade, then fit them together and come up with some version of Armageddon. Even the doubters learned to keep their opinions to themselves, and those who urged calm and reason have at last run out of reasons why death and famine and plague and war have nothing to do with prophecies that aren't confined to any one religion's Bible.

A simple thunderstorm sends people screaming into the streets, cowering behind locked doors, pouring into houses of worship not necessarily Christian.

And it's all one step away from a violent explosion.

"Reed?" Cora says, a little girl voice.

"Yeah?"

"Where is he?"

"An island, Cora. That's all the dream says—he's on an island. And he's close."

4

1

Almost autumn; just twilight.

Streetlights and porch lights make Camoret seem very much smaller under a sky that has turned on every star it can find; a comfortably cool breeze that gives just the right touch to the season without forcing sweaters or heavy jackets out of the closet; cats making their way through the trees toward their prey; the muffled cough of a gator at the edge of the swamp; the muffled sputter of an old engine as a small boat made its way around South Hook to the island's only public marina.

All under a moon more white than silver.

2

Along the one-mile business district on Midway Road an alley separated every office and shop, bar and restaurant; behind each building was a shallow parking area for owners and employees, widening onto another paved alley that ran the length of each block. The buildings themselves tended more toward wood than brick, but all were sturdy, decades of reinforcement against the storms that blew in from the sea or across from the mainland.

Across the street and two doors south of the sheriff's department, the light from a nearby streetlamp sparkled off a hand-painted arc of Old English lettering whose metal-flaked gold paint had been specially designed to glow as if afire. The script was difficult enough to read in the first place; most days, once the sun began to wester, it took sun-glasses and some hard puzzling to figure out that the letters spelled *Camoret Weekly*.

Tonight a man stood in the window, hands clasped behind his back, his pointed chin up. Lean without appear-ing frail. His solid grey hair, which nearly matched his grey suit, was thick and brushed straight back from a smooth high forehead split by a widow's peak. Deep-set eyes. Thin dark lips pursed and ready for debate. The only color on him was his bow tie, and it was a suitably subdued maroon.

A glance to his right, at an antique brass pendulum clock on the wall, and Whittaker Hull shook his head in resigned disapproval.

He'd been standing here for nearly an hour, and not once had he seen a patrol car or that ridiculous white Jeep of Oakman's pass in either direction. He had, on the other hand, seen a handful of tourists already half in the bag and it wasn't even nine, a gang of teenagers streak past on skateboards that seemed to have rockets attached, and one thunder-loud drag race between a vintage Ford and some-thing that looked pieced together from the worst scrapyard in the state.

It was a crime.

Hell, there'd been several crimes, and not a single sign of the Law.

He rubbed his chin thoughtfully, wishing absently as he did that he hadn't shaved off his beard. He had hoped it might make him look a little younger; all it did, he was sure now, was make him look like a corpse.

Suddenly Dub Neely appeared on the sidewalk in front of him. Standing at attention, eyes front, chest out, stomach in. An abrupt broad grin, a mocking salute, and he marched away, arms swinging stiffly, lips pursed in an unheard whistle.

Now that, Whittaker thought, is a damn crime on two wobbly legs. Remembering seeing the fool being driven away by the sheriff two days ago, he automatically began to write his next editorial.

There was property and people to protect, a standard of conduct to maintain, and Oakman had been with what could only be called the town drunk, the community disgrace, no doubt taking the rest of the afternoon off to hunt for flying saucers or talking dolphins or whatever else Neely's pickled brain had conjured this time.

"Do you realize," he said, his voice graveled and deep, "that the world is going to hell in a custom-made handbasket, yet still we must continue to cater to society's dregs lest we be called heartless, inhumane, and without a single divine drop of human compassion?"

No one answered.

He tipped back on his heels, rocked forward, tipped back.

"Were this an election year, we might better understand Sheriff Carnivale Oakman's interest in the demented ravings of a man who, if rumors are correct, was once considered an esteemed educator somewhere deep in our heartland, but is now little more than a walking and most persuasive advertisement for the immediate repeal of the repeal of blessed Prohibition."

No one answered.

He tipped back, rocked forward. Cleared his throat.

"But it is not an election year, and we must therefore puzzle over the sheriff's priorities. War has broken out in this fragile world of ours, a war that pits the decent against the indecent, the law-abiding against the law breaker, the

moral against the immoral. We are under siege here on
Camoret Island, our families in peril, our businesses on the
verge of bankruptcy, our society on the verge of dissolu-
tion. With alarming frequency the dregs of the mainland
make their way to our haven, yet our law enforcement
guardians persist in pursuing the trivial, investigating the
inconsequential, and ignoring the pervasive danger, thereby
flushing our hard-earned tax dollars straight down the
drain.

"Explain yourself before it's too late, Sheriff Oakman,
before the voters of this island take a second searching
look at the real man behind the badge."

He sniffed, nodded once, and turned away from the window just as his stomach began to growl, reminding him
that supper was long overdue, and once again he hadn't
bothered to stop work for a bite to eat. The newspaper may
only be a weekly, but unlike his predecessor, he did not
treat his position like a hobby.

For all the trouble it causes him with local merchants
and politicians, he believes in what he does.

The room was knotty-pine paneled and comfortably
small, just large enough to hold the room-wide counter for
customers who wanted ads or subscriptions, a roll-top desk
and padded swivel chair, a handful of filing cabinets. A
green-shade lamp on the desk provided the only light. In
the back wall an open doorway that led to his private office
and the stairs that climbed to his apartment above.

"So what do you think?"

"Pompous," a voice called from the back. "Pompous as
all hell."

"Of course," he answered. "But will they like it?"

"Vale will string you up."

"He understands my position. He will not take offense."

"Not after he strings you up, he won't."

Hull rolled his eyes and stepped behind the counter,
lowered the flap, and finger-dusted the smooth polished
top. "You overestimate the power of my humble words."

"Good. I'll put that on your tombstone."

He turned as a tall young woman glided into the office doorway, snug jeans and loose tartan shirt, red hair in rich waves settling like a cloud on her shoulders. If she wore makeup, it was too artfully applied to notice, and she looked so much like her mother that he sometimes had to hold his breath in case she was a ghost.

In her right hand was a small tape recorder, which she looked at with distaste. "Seriously, Dad, you really expect me to transcribe all that hot air?"

"I do." He leaned back against the counter.

"And what about Mayor Cribbs? That makes him look bad, too. Stupid, even, for backing Oakman all these years."

"If the shoe fits," he answered with a shrug. "Jasper is too cowardly to add to the department. Probably because Cutler won't let him." His expression twisted in disgust. "Oh, God forbid we should upset the blessed monied tourists who visit their little kingdom."

"Later, then," she said, and grabbed the door frame so she could swing back and drop the recorder onto her desk. As she did, he realized she wasn't wearing anything on her feet.

"I can afford shoes, you know, Ronnie," he said dryly.

"It's still officially summer," she reminded him, pulling a windbreaker from a peg just inside the door. "You know I don't wear shoes in summer. Never have, never will. Besides," she added, "they'd only get messed up anyway." Another reach around the door, lower this time, and she held up a pair of well-used rubber wading boots. And grinned.

Hull straightened. "No."

"Sure. Why not?"

He lifted his left hand, counted off on his fingers: "Snakes. Gators. Tetanus. Quicksand. Malaria." Lifted the other hand. "Typhus. Did I mention snakes? Did I mention the Teague brothers? Did I mention," he added with a pointed look at his watch, "that it's getting dark out there?"

His daughter grinned again, crossed the room, and kissed his cheek wetly while she gave him a near-suffocating hug. "You're sweet, Daddy," she whispered, "but I can take care of myself. And there are no gators, it's a saltwater marsh."

"The Teagues," he repeated when she pulled away. "Stump is a Neanderthal who's just discovered fire, and his kin are worse. I'm surprised they haven't sent someone over from Emory to study them."

"I do have a gun, Daddy, you know. And the day I couldn't shoot better than Stump Teague is the day I marry Dub. Okay? Okay."

It wasn't okay. It was never okay when his only child took herself into that damn wetland without someone along to watch her back. But she did it regularly anyway. She worked part-time for some damn office or other in the Department of the Interior, her job to keep track of the wildlife in the marsh. Hell, marsh; it was a goddamn swamp, he didn't care what she said. All year round she tagged and counted the birds and the critters, noted the effects of the tides on water and salt levels, noted the damage done by hurricanes and winter storms, and wrote up enough reports every year to paper a barn.

A hell of a thing that she's more comfortable in there than she was in town. Or with him.

"Your dinner's in the oven, it'll be done in ten minutes," she called as she headed for the back door. "If I'm late—"

"If you're late," he called back, "I'm going down to Betsy's, eat enough grease to explode my heart!"

Her laughter was cut off when the door slammed, and he looked to the ceiling as if, for a change, there might be some guidance up there, if maybe her mother had a ghostly word or two for him. A wince when he heard her gun the engine of her pickup, another when he heard tires screaming as she shot down the alley toward the side street three buildings down.

I take it back, he thought; she'll never make it to the swamp alive.

But he couldn't help a smile as he walked into the office, or a chuckle as he switched on his computer and waited for everything to get in its place. He had little idea how the thing actually worked, but Ronnie had showed him enough to allow him to search the world for the stories he printed every week.

The local stuff he gathered himself.

And right now, he didn't much care about the world, no matter what the editorial would say; right now, he was more concerned with the island.

He opened a file only his daughter knew about, and scrolled through it slowly. It wasn't as if his memory needed refreshing; he practically had it all memorized. But seeing it there on the screen, seeing it on paper whenever he printed it out, gave it a legitimacy that somehow didn't exist when it was kept in his mind. Where it lived every night. In dreams. Fever dreams that infected his sleep and had him waking with sweat chilling the sheets, puckering his chilled skin, tasting like saltwater as it snaked past his lips.

In dreams not even his best sour mash could suppress.

His chair was on casters, and he pushed away from the desk. Stared at the screen, at summaries of reports he had picked up from the wire services and television. Wondered if he could turn that data into a graph, some kind of visual aid to make it more dramatic:

Sunday night in Ohio a carnival troupe had ridden into town and attacked a group of kids, some of whom had run wild through the carnival the night before. A small army, the police had said. It was like a small army had blown through, and they were helpless as the townspeople formed an army of their own. They were still counting the dead;

On Monday afternoon, in Louisville, a gang no one had known existed erupted in a bizarre turf war. Bizarre because they'd raided various stables in the area and did most of their fighting from the saddle. It lasted most of the night. They were still counting the dead;

A state police substation besieged by a gang coalition just outside Houston; a service club in Tulsa turned a fund-raiser blood bank drive game into a test of weapons and ammunition.

They were still counting the dead.

Just this morning Ronnie had reminded him that in any given year over the past decade there had been frequent outbursts of pocket violence, and he hadn't been able to convince her that this was somehow different. He couldn't prove it, he could only feel it, but this wasn't the same.

Just as he knew that Camoret wasn't the same either.

It had nothing to do with Cutler and his pet, Mayor Cribbs; nothing to do with whatever they were up to.

He didn't know how, but the island wasn't the same.

He didn't know why, but he was fairly sure he knew when it had changed:

It was the day Casey Chisholm had walked out of the sea.

At the end of the alley Ronnie turned right, barely slowing down, stopping only when she came to the Midway Road intersection, and that was only because there was a pedestrian couple stepping into the crosswalk. She smiled brightly at them, received a warning glare in return, and wondered as she waited if maybe she ought to stay home for a change.

Daddy had been acting a little strange lately. More intro-spective than usual, and more testy, if that was possible. It had nothing to do with his latest crusade against Sheriff Oakman; that had been going on for the past ten years. Not even the increasing harassment from Cutler and his boys had stopped it. Besides, if it wasn't the sheriff, it would only be something else. Development of the shoreline, dredging the bay at South Hook to allow larger ships to dock, new motels, the sorry state of the school . . . he'd once, only half-jokingly, suggested building a wall across the series of causeways that connected the island to the world, thereby preventing Camoret from being, as he'd put it, despoiled.

She had once laughingly and lovingly called him "Crusader Rabbit," which had hurt him deeply until she realized he'd thought it a comment on his ears, not a reference to a TV show now in repeats on cable.

Lately, however, his heart didn't seem in the fight. He was just going through the motions.

Daddy, don't tell me you've caught this Millennium bug, too.

Don't be foolish, child, that's a fiction, I deal in fact.

But still, she wondered; and in wondering, worried.

A rap on her window made her jump, hold her breath. When she looked, she saw a man in a deputy's uniform step away from the pickup, grinning as he mimed rolling the window down. She did, reluctantly.

"Evening, Miss Hull." He hooked one thumb in his gleaming black gunbelt, the other hand tipped his hat.

"What do you want, Freck," she said wearily.

"Well," said Billy Freck, looking back the way she'd come, looking ahead across Midway, "I was wondering if you were counting on setting up housekeeping here. I do believe there's a law against that."

A number of comments came to mind, all of them bordering on the outright obscene, but she hustled them back where they were born and made a contrite face instead. "Sorry, Deputy, but I was thinking."

He stepped closer, the grin now a smile as smooth as his youthful face. Even with his black hair slicked back and shining, she had to admit he was a fairly good-looking man, muscles in all the right places, courteous as all get-out, with all the right words.

She couldn't stand him.

He reminded her of a snake oil salesman she had seen

once in a Western, charming money and virtue from all the town's ladies without suffering even a minor twinge of conscience. His goal was conquest, not love or even friendship, and the harder he worked on her, the more stubborn she became.

A glance into the pickup's bed. "I see you're heading for work there, Ronnie."

"That's right."

"You need some help maybe?" The Serious Concern Look, now. "Swamp's no place to be poking around at night. It's Wednesday, you know. The Teague boys'll be looking to get some spending money for the weekend."

"Why, thank you, Billy," she said, "but I'm not going in very far. Just a scouting mission for a change." She blinked rapidly, close to batting her eyelashes. "But if you know those boys are going to be out, why aren't you there waiting for them? Be a feather in your cap, I'd guess."

The smile slipped away for just a second, and when it returned it was as if it had never left. "Why, don't you worry, Ronnie, I got things well in hand." Another check of the streets before he leaned a little closer. "Thing is, you see, I got a plan."

"Ah." She nodded and, unable to stop herself, sat a little straighter, smoothing out her shirt just enough to make him strain to look without staring. "Sounds dangerous."

He shrugged. "Nah, not really. Stump's a blowhard, we all know that. All talk, no action, you know what I mean?" He braced his hand on the roof. "Tell you what, when you get back from your scouting, why don't I treat you to something sweet at the Teach, tell you about it? To be honest, I could use a little of your swamp expertise. Secret paths, stuff like that."

And damn if he didn't wink.

A moment of feigned consideration before she shook her head ruefully, actually gave him a little pout. "Sorry, Billy, but I promised Daddy I'd be home right after. You know how he gets when the paper's coming out."

"No problem, Ronnie, no problem." He stepped back and tipped his hat again. "You take care, hear? I'll catch you another time." ·

Not while I'm still living, she thought, smiling as she pulled away, laughing aloud as she swung around the corner and headed north for Landward. If nothing else, he got points for never giving up; and she checked the rearview mirror, just in case he got it into his little head to follow.

That wouldn't be good.

If he did, she actually would have to go to the marsh, and do some pretending-to-work until he went away. She felt badly enough, lying to her father; she definitely didn't need Billy Freck finding out what she was really up to.

Freck settled himself behind his cruiser's steering wheel, not bothering to watch the bitch take the next corner practically on two wheels, not even pausing for the blinking red traffic light hanging over the street. He didn't care. Tonight wasn't to be, that's the way it goes, win some, lose some.

It wasn't as if he was exactly starving for affection.

He set his hat carefully on the passenger seat, pulled down the sun visor, flicked on the vanity light, and checked his hair, making sure there weren't those stupid indentations along the sides of his head. A wink at himself, the visor back up, and he made a careful U-turn and headed south at a near crawl.

It being the middle of the week, there weren't an awful lot of people out, taking air. Mostly tourists looking for bargains at the shops that still kept late hours, and a few kids no doubt trying to pass their fake IDs at every bar on the Road. He smiled and nodded, or gave a short wave, to those he knew, kept Mrs. Gumber's too-dumb-to-live dachshund from climbing a tree after a cat, watched a couple of black-mask gulls squabbling over a hamburger bun and wondered why they weren't nesting down at the marina, took a tour of some of the side streets, checked in with Dwight Salter, who was working dispatch tonight, and finally, just after eight, pulled into the graveled parking lot at the side of the Edward Teach Bar and Grill, parked in the one spot the outside lighting barely reached, turned off the engine, grabbed his hat, and slid out of the car.

Hitched up his belt.

Polished the toes of his black shoes on the back of his trouser legs.

Then he hauled open the heavy oak door and stepped inside, holding his breath against the smoke, the smell of liquor, waiting for his eyes to adjust.

Along the front and down the right wall were a dozen high-back booths, a dozen round tables stretching to the back in the floorspace on his right; the bar was on his left. The walls were paneled in rough dark cedar and cluttered with crossed sabres, netting, and prints of famous pirate ships. A low, raw-beamed ceiling, a pair of pool tables in back, dart boards on the back wall, sawdust on the bare-plank floor. Behind the bar, a huge skull-and-crossbones flag, and the thing he hated most—a six-foot gold cage that housed Pegleg, a grumpy, mangy parrot that dared people to feed him so he could bite their fingers off.

One of these days, he promised himself, he was going to blow that friggin' bird's head off.

A slow look around—not much to see, just a few drinkers, a few diners, no one at the games in back—a friendly nod to Ben Pellier, the owner and bartender, and when he was sure the general sobriety was high enough to preclude trouble for now, he moved to the bar, where Pellier met him. They exchanged polite greetings as the bigger man reached under the bar to pull out a paper bag slightly stained at the bottom.

"Best fries in town," Freck said, making sure the bag didn't touch his uniform.

"Glad you think so, Deputy."

Freck grinned, gave him a mock salute, and left. Took a welcome deep breath of the night's cool air, returned to his patrol car, and before he slipped in, opened the bag and reached in, rooting among the greasy fries until his fingers touched the thick envelope at the bottom.

Well, Ben, he thought, it looks like you get to live, you stupid bastard.

He closed the bag and got in.

A woman sat in the passenger seat.

"Hey," he said, tossing his hat and the bag into the back seat, checking the area to be sure no unwelcome eyes were watching.

"Take me in, Deputy, I've been a bad girl."

After wiping his hand on a rag, he started the engine and backed quickly out of the lot. "Not as bad as you're gonna be, honey."

"Don't bet on it," she said, and when he finally looked over, he realized she wasn't wearing a stitch.

Ben Pellier scratched vigorously through his thick black beard, adjusted the black patch over his right eye, counted to thirty just to be sure Freck wouldn't be returning, then ran a palm over the freckled hairless pate he washed and burnished every night before coming on duty, and said, "Mari Cribbs."

The four men at the bar gaped, then whooped with laughter. Money changed hands. High-fives were offered and accepted. One of them headed for the men's room, staggering because he was laughing so hard. Two more settled their bill, wiped their eyes, and left. Still laughing.

The last one counted his bill's change as if it were all he had in the world, then carefully tucked it away in his jeans pocket. "How did you know?" he asked, sliding off his stool.

Ben grinned and reminded him that less than an hour ago, there had been three women in the Teach, each of them alone. "They drink, two of them leave, Mariana said she's afraid her daddy's on the prowl tonight, can she use the back way." He spread his hands—easy deduction. "I happen to know, though, that Daddy is on the mainland sucking up to the governor. And this is about the time Freck comes in every night. She was probably tucked in by the Dumpster."

"You're amazing."

"No, Rick, I am just a humble proprietor of a humble tavern who happens to have an eye for his customers."

The parrot squawked.

Rick Jordan laughed again and waved over his shoulder as he headed for the exit, a faint limp in his right leg.

Ben watched him go, sorry to see the young man leave so early. He liked Rick. A hard-working kid who just couldn't seem to catch a break. Unlike that arrogant, son-of-a-bitching deputy, who was panting so hard for the sheriff's job Ben was surprised Oakman didn't have to change his uniform twice a day, just to get rid of all that drool.

On the other hand, life ain't fair, especially these days.

At least he was shut of Cutler for another month. Assuming Freck didn't do something stupid with that money.

After filling an order for one of his waitresses, he walked to the low end of the bar and stared at Pegleg. One black eye stared back at him.

"What?" he said softly, sticking a scarred finger through the bars to stroke the bird's back. "What's the matter, Peg, you ain't said a word all day."

All week, for that matter, he thought as he turned away. The vet claimed nothing was wrong, the old bird was just fine, but Ben knew better. Pegleg was one of the main reasons folks came in here, but no one had been able to get a rise out of him for days. Not even Billy Freck, who didn't need to say a damn word, just walk in.

Working on automatic, Ben washed glasses, checked the draft kegs, checked the levels of the liquor, wandered into the kitchen where he joked a while with his cook,

Senior Raybourn, until Alma, his blessed wife, chased him out with a flap of her apron.

The thing was, he didn't want to stay behind the bar tonight.

The thing was, if he did, he'd sooner or later have to look at that bird.

Who would be sitting on his top perch. Still as an old statue.

Staring at the door.

Squawking softly to itself.

3

"Gone," said Senior Raybourn, standing at the back door, watching the patrol car peel out of the lot, spitting gravel. He wiped his hands on his apron.

"Good." At the griddle Alma Pellier flipped a hamburger patty over and pressed it down, squeezing out the grease. "Can't stand the man."

Raybourn agreed but kept it to himself. It didn't always pay for the help to voice an opinion around here. Especially an old coot like himself. Especially an old black coot. It wasn't that he didn't trust Alma or Ben; he did, without question. It was habit, that's all; strong one, like breathing. Get to talking out of turn, you might do it in front of the customers, and the wrong person might hear. Like Mr. Deputy Kiss My Feet Freck. The Pelliers understood, and they knew him well enough to know what he was thinking anyway.

Alma, her hair so pale some thought it was white, turned away from the stove and wiped a cloth over her face, sighed loudly, and headed for the front. "Keep an eye, Senior, okay? I want to talk to Ben."

Senior nodded, took his place at the stove, glancing over the order sheets, making sure everything was on track. No microwaves here. Ben insisted the food be cooked right,

not warmed over, one of the reasons Senior liked working
here. Some had called his skills magic, and that pleased
him. Wasn't magic, of course, just a lot of years' practice.
The real magic had been in Luella's hands, but she was
long gone now, trading recipes with angels; it was just him
and his boy, Junior. He just plugged away best he could,
and if folks liked what he done, praise the Lord, that was
just fine with him.

Check the griddle, check the oven, check the stove.

Stubby fingers, short arms, a stomach that signaled he
tested his cooking a little too often, a thin horseshoe of
white hair around a perspiration-bright bald pate. A face
scarred under the eyes and across the broad nose, signs of
a time half a century ago when a Birmingham gang wielding razors had caught him alone in an alley.

He and Luella had found the island by mistake. She'd
called it God's plan, and he hadn't argued, and hadn't left
since. Now she was gone, only Junior to remind him she
ever existed, and now he was afraid he'd lose the only real
home he'd ever known.

"Senior?" Alma at his side, tugging his elbow, concerned. "Senior, the burger's charring. You okay?"

"Yes, ma'am, sorry," he said, shaking himself back.

No, ma'am, he thought; I ain't right at all.

4

There are three ways to get to Camoret Island when the
weather is decent and the sea doesn't mind:

There is no airstrip, but seaplanes often land on the bay
at South Hook—businessmen whose companies have the
wherewithal and the ego, a handful of weekly tour excur-
sions, and once in a while a private aircraft;

by the sea itself, in chartered ships and fishing boats and
those touring the Inland Waterway;

and by the three-stage Camoret Causeway.

The causeway's first stage leads from the mainland to Hawkins Island—barren, mostly rock and scrub, a half-mile wide west to east. The second stage crosses the water to St. James—barren, mostly rock, a long, low pink-painted Quonset hut on either side of the road, both of them named Cutler's Last Stop in script neon on the roof. If it can be made out of shells and the bleached bones of washed-ashore fish, Cutler sells it, and they serve as foul weather way stations for those who don't want to take the last leg in rough seas.

One lane in either direction, each half again as wide as an ordinary highway lane. The first two legs rise in easy humps over the water to let all but the highest seas pass beneath it; the third leg is nearly flat, nearly a mile long, with sixty feet of rock and cement for shoulders, each shoulder's oceanside edge bordered by fencing made of outward curving, thick iron pipes theoretically able to break up damaging waves before they swamp the road and wash it clear.

On a grey day, a foggy or rainy day, if you sat at the western end, the traffic looked for all the world as if it were climbing out of the sea, speckled with water, straining for solid land.

"Do you know how long it's been?" Ronnie Hull said, sitting cross-legged in the bed of her pickup, a blanket around her shoulders, a wool cap pulled down snugly over her hair. So far, a steady breeze had kept insects from her face and hands, but she doubted that grace would last much longer.

Beside her in the roadside clearing, Rick Jordan sat on the lowered tailgate of his own truck, a much more dented, scratched, and beaten version of hers. "Haven't a clue."

"A month," she told him, then forced herself to cough to clear an obstruction in her throat. "At least a month."

They faced west, parked just out of reach of the two

goose-neck streetlamps fixed on either side of the cause-way's end. The clear sky allowed them to see the low arc of mainland Georgia's glow at the horizon, as if it were burning. Between here and there, however, there was only the night, and the longer they watched it, the more it shifted and rippled, a black satin curtain that rose out of the sea.

Invisible waves slapped against the rocks and fallen trunks that lined the shore. Trees that lined the road whis-pered to themselves; something splashed in the marsh behind them; something flew overhead.

Night noises.

"Impossible," he said.

She glanced over, could barely see him. Working his boat had darkened his skin, sun glare and wind and the life that he led had added a few lines. Not yet thirty, four years younger than she, and he looked ten years older. Seemed that way, too, sometimes.

"You can see for yourself." She waved a clipboard at the causeway. "Almost a month, and once the sun goes down no one comes over."

He grunted.

Her eyes narrowed. "You think I'm wrong?"

"I think I don't see what difference it made." He shifted. "Who cares? So what?" He shifted again, and the truck creaked, softly. "Ronnie, it's a scary drive in the dark. I don't do it myself when I can avoid it."

"You don't get it, do you?"

"Guess I don't."

"Rick, pay attention—when the sun goes down, the island's cut off."

He said nothing for a long time, then: "Actually, you're wrong, you know."

"I'm not."

"What about the newspaper?"

She glared at him and looked away. "Okay. So the paper gets delivered. But nothing else, Rick. No one else."

When he didn't respond right away, she pulled the blanket closer around her shoulders and stared at the causeway. Four times in the past five months, the delivery truck made it this far before, according to the various drivers, a bunch of drunks whooping and yollering stopped it and grabbed most of the bundles. No one was hurt, and one, of the drivers even thought it was kind of funny.

She didn't.

No delivery meant no sales, and no sales . . .

Finally, after the last incident, she had made it a point to bring herself and her rifle here each delivery night. If the Teagues tried it again, they were going to be in for a seriously unpleasant surprise.

And Rick, the poor sweet dope, had volunteered to keep her company.

"Spooky, though," he whispered.

"What?"

He nodded toward the causeway.

Yes, she thought, it is.

But it's not so spooky that somebody, some time, wouldn't make the trip.

Night noises:

In a patrol car parked behind a dune on the beach, squeals and giggles and a long muffled groan;

In the kitchen above the newspaper office, the soft ticking of an oven clock and the buzz of a cooking-done alarm;

In the sheriff's department office, the mutter of static on the dispatch radio, and cards slapping on a desk, a complicated game of solitaire that's been running for weeks;

At the marina, boats rock and creak at their moorings;

On the beach, the steady paced crunch of boots in the sand;

Over the island the distant rumble of an airliner heading for Atlanta;

In the Edward Teach, an old parrot in a gold cage, staring at the door and squawking softly to itself.

5

1

Almost autumn; close to midnight.

A cold wind blows off Lake Erie, hushing through stunted grass that fights to live a little longer; an arrowhead of geese calls under the stars, soon followed by a flock of ducks whose calls aren't quite so lonely; a streak of pale smoke from a wood stove, a curling plume from a fireplace, a stubborn mist that floats at the base of a dead tree, resisting the wind, shredding anyway.

An L-shaped motel on a small country road not far from a small town that crawls up a small hill; twelve units in all, slowly filling with hunters asleep long ago after filling the bar; one open door, one light in a room large enough for two beds, a chest of drawers, a table and chair, no more; backed to the door is a large dusty car, its trunk open, the bulb burned out six months ago and never replaced; the interior roof light is on because the passenger door is open, and exhaust puffs from the tailpipe in time to the soft grumbling engine.

And on the car radio, barely loud enough to hear, a man sings of cattle whose brands are still burning and whose eyes are made of fire.

2

A tall man the dark contrives to make much thinner than he is slams the trunk lid shut and winces at the sound. A silent apology to no one in particular, and he slides in behind the wheel, rubbing his hands together, adjusting the dashboard vents to catch as much warmth as he can.

The room light turns off, the door closes, and a moment later a woman takes her place beside him and watches their breath begin to fog the windshield.

"Are you sure, John?" she asks, Louisiana clear and smooth in her voice.

"I don't know. Maybe it's just the pizza. I ate too damn much."

They watch the road beyond the parking lot, but nothing passes, nothing moves.

"I have to tell you something," she says, still looking straight ahead.

"Okay."

"I think . . . I think I'm more scared now than I was before."

He doesn't answer; he can't.

They watch the road, listen to the geese.

"John."

"Lisse, I couldn't tell you any more than I already have."

"It's been almost two years."

"Ah." He reaches out, takes her hand, squeezes it, lets it go. "You want to know why now, right?"

"I want to know why anytime."

"I couldn't answer that one either."

He reaches out, turns on the headlamps, turns the parking lot grey. Waits for her to tell him to turn them back off, unpack the car, let's get inside where it's warmer, where we can go to sleep and forget about driving in the middle of the night to a place we've never seen except in a dream.

His dream.

If she asks, he will do it.

And he knows she won't.

She won't because they've seen too much together, been through too much, watched too many people die in more ways than one; she won't because she's seen the carrion crows with the bright blue eyes; she won't because she's seen what a nightmare can do when it doesn't wait for sleep.

She won't because she's listened to the tapes John had made while writing his book. Interview tapes of murderers waiting to die. Tapes of murderers who killed dozens, friends and family and strangers, for no other reason than just because they were in the mood.

One of them was John's father-in-law.

"Well." John rubs his eyes, rubs his shoulders, pretends to slap himself awake. "Into the breach, I guess."

"Whatever you say, Prez."

He snarls.

She laughs. His height, the way his unruly hair strikes his brow, those deep-set eyes and slightly high rasping voice . . . once, in college theater, he had been given the part of a young Abe Lincoln, and the resemblance had been so uncanny he had been tagged "Prez" until he graduated. He probably wouldn't have minded, but she's seen how people look at him oddly once in a while, trying to place the face, thinking they know him, or somebody like him.

Untrue.

As far as she knew there is nobody in the world like John Bannock.

Who else, she wonders, has a son who causes famine?

He puts his hands on the steering wheel, thinks again about not going, and shakes his head. Not because he has no choice. Not because he's as frightened as Lisse. Not because he believes he's finally gone insane.

He has a choice, but it doesn't matter.

There's only one place to go, and once he finds it he knows that he'll find explanations. That's all he wants. Peace, and explanations.

Finally he leans over awkwardly and kisses her cheek, settles himself and releases the brake. The car drifts onto the highway, drifts almost silently in its lane until at last he feeds it gas, and the motel is left behind.

Lisse turns off the radio; there's nothing there now but murmuring static. "Will he be there do you think?"

"He better be."

"Will he know you? You only met him . . . what, twice?"

"Something like that." He grins. "Terribly auspicious. It was on death row, in Rahway Prison, in the lovely and hospitable Garden State of New Jersey."

"Now there's a recommendation."

What he doesn't remind her of is the phone call, the one at the hotel in New Orleans where he had met her, when Casey Chisholm called him and said, "God help you, John. God help you, you're marked."

And disappeared.

Until last night, in the dream, and John saw him again and couldn't explain why, but he knew they had to leave.

Miles later she yawns and groans and whispers, "I love you."

He glances at her in mock horror. "Uh-oh, that means trouble."

She punches his arm. "No, that wisecrack answer means you got to tell me the truth."

"Who said?"

"An old bayou tradition. You don't say 'I love you' back, you got to give me an answer and it's got to be the truth."

"I've never lied to you, Lisse."

"Good."

"So what's the question?"

No sound but the engine, and the old tires on the road.

"Are we going to die?"

6

1

Almost autumn; between midnight and dawn.

   Two different cars on two different roads—one moving slowly, the other taking its time. One travels in moonlight that's lifeless, cold, and damp, the other through a rainstorm that produces no wind; one crosses a prairie speckled with early snow, the other climbs a wooded hill while the valley below burns end to end.

They travel at an hour that has no real name. Some call it Saturday morning, the rest call it Friday night.

   It didn't matter.

   It's the dead time.

2

The prairie doesn't seem quite so wide in the dark, its expanse not so forbidding.

A good thing, too, because the driver is bloody sick and damn tired of looking at a horizon that's always too damn far away. Her fingers are stiff from gripping the steering wheel, her butt is numb from sitting so long, her brain is on automatic because she dares not think too hard about too much. She and her companions have been on the road for just over a year, spending almost all their money, taking jobs to make more to spend more, finally returning to the city they had fled. Just in case. Just in case she was wrong.

She hadn't been.

In fact, she knew she hadn't been, but for months all that thinking and dreaming and wondering and grieving for the loss of her husband had almost convinced her that she had made a huge mistake. That she, and those with her, were truly destined to remain in Las Vegas, let the rest of the world take care of itself.

Wrong.

Dead wrong.

The dreams, when they began, were at first only unnerving. Then frightening. Then terrifying. Then . . . revealing and oddly comforting.

On the road again, she sings silently to herself; I can't wait to get back on the road again.

A bitter snort of a laugh. A fearful glance around to see if she's disturbed the others. A self-pitying sigh because no one asks her what's the matter, are you okay, Beatrice, is everything okay?

No, she answers anyway, everything is not okay, but thanks for asking.

Beside her a woman sleeps, her head resting against the window. Her face is covered with a soft cotton veil that begins just below her eyes, and every so often, in her dreams, she twitches, moans, a finger brushing the veil as if making sure it's still there. In the backseat are two girls, one now twelve, the other now thirteen, with the most improbable names the driver has ever heard in her life— Moonbow and Starshine. Equally improbable is the way they've managed to sleep for so long, curled tightly against each other, making no noise at all.

The driver smiles, flexes her fingers, ducks and twists and tilts her head to stretch and ease her neck, rubs each shoulder in turn.

Once in a while, although not so frequently anymore, she turns to say something to her husband, and it isn't until she sees the veil that she remembers that her husband's gone. That she's a widow. That he was murdered.

She blinks each time, and bites softly on her lower lip. These days there are no tears; they were shed and are gone. These days there's only anger, the only reason she's in the car, forever driving.

In the morning the girls will wake and want to know if they're there yet.

In the morning she'll have to tell them that she doesn't know.

She has to force herself to remember how long it's been since they left Las Vegas for the second time, and most of the time she doesn't bother because it doesn't matter. A month, a year, who cares, her husband is dead, and so is the man who tried to save him, and all that's left now is the progression of the sun, rise and set, and the procession of traffic that passes them every day, and the wondering if this town, this city, this farm, this crossroads, will be the place.

If her husband were here, he'd know.

But he's not.

All she can do is head east.

And trust the dreams.

3

On the far side of the hill, the sky glowing above it in spite of the rain, the road becomes a switchback, and the driver takes it slowly, carefully, wondering why in hell they just didn't make the thing straight. Up and over, none of this twisting and turning and mentally crossing a few fingers that some idiot isn't barreling down on her from the opposite direction because, really, there's no place to pull over. No shoulders, just trees, and a narrow two-lane road.

Actually she doesn't really mind it, but it seems such a waste, all that work following someone's pioneer winding trail instead of heading directly into the next valley, no curves, no obstacles; they haven't even named the road, so the pioneer's work was all for nothing.

She sighs.

She sniffs.

The rain eases, and mist begins to form tiny clouds that drift between the tree trunks onto the road.

Beside her, a large woman bundled in a green coat hums softly in time to the windshield wipers' sweep. Some kind of gospel tune, the driver supposes, but she doesn't know what it is, and she doesn't want to ask because Eula Korrey, for some damn reason or other, expects them to know the name of every blessed tune in the book, and spirals off into a pouting huff when she discovers they don't.

And don't particularly care.

A soft noise behind her, and she checks the rearview mirror. She can't see very well, there are no lights along the road, but she can make out a small figure tucked under a blanket. On the back shelf is a cowboy hat; she has a feeling the little guy has left his boots on.

"Be dreaming," Eula says quietly, white-gloved hands folded in her lap.

"I guess so."

"You know what he dreams of?"

"No, and I don't ask."

Eula shifts, and the driver, whose name is Susan, sees a flicker of pain across the woman's gleaming black face.

"You still aching? It's been over a year."

Eula nods carefully. "This ain't the way it's supposed to be, getting all banged up like that." She shakes her head in anger, in confusion, brushes a finger across the green felt hat that lies between them. "Ain't the way, nossir. Not the way it was written."

"It doesn't make any difference how it was written," Susan answers calmly. "It's written a lot of different ways. Sometimes they get to fight us, and sometimes they get to win. For a while."

"Maybe. But I'll bet none of them talk about us getting all banged up."

Susan grins, suddenly laughs and catches herself quickly before she wakes the boy up.

The last turn at the bottom is the sharpest, and she slows the car to the pace of a fast walk, is ready to stomp the accelerator to shoot across the valley, when Eula straightens and says abruptly, "Look."

It takes a moment, but Susan finally sees, and brings the car to a halt, leans back, and says, softly, "Joey, wake up. Come on, cowboy, rise and shine."

The headlights have pushed some of the dead time to the side, and at their farthest reach she can see a lone figure waiting in the middle of the road. He sits on a great black horse, rain dripping from his hat. He doesn't squint at the light, he only nods and leans over the animal's neck, pushes a hand through its long mane and sits upright again. The horse bares its teeth, works the bit, and begins to move slowly toward the car.

Eula fusses with her grey hair, pulls the hat into her lap. "Sit up, boy," she tells Joey without looking around. "Sit up, now, child. Time to pay attention."

Feeling oddly at ease, and just as oddly anxious, Susan stares straight ahead as horse and rider pass the car; she looks in the rearview mirror to watch them turn around, the red glow of the taillights reflected in the horse's large eyes. When they stop beside her door, she presses a button and the window slides down.

"Evening, ladies," the rider says, touching two fingers to his hat brim.

The boy says nothing; the women nod, mutter, "Good

evening, Red," and wait, paying no attention to the cold rain that bounces through the open window. He doesn't bend over, they can't see his face, but they can hear his voice and that's all that matters.

Red ignores the rain as well, peering into the dark beyond the headlights. His left hand holds the reins; his right hand rests on his thigh. The horse snorts and tosses its head, steam in clouds from mouth and nostrils.

"He knew," Red says, sounding pleased, patting its neck. "Soon as he saw me, he knew."

"I want to ride him," the boy says, his voice loud in the silence.

"Hush," Eula scolds.

"Well, I do," Joey says, pouting.

Red swings easily out of the saddle then, and for just a second they can hear the sharp sound of sharp spurs. And the stamp of a hoof. Susan isn't positive, but she thinks she caught the brief reflection of a single flame in the windshield.

Red pushes back his hat, and rests his arms on the window's shelf. A quick grin for the boy, and a shake of his head. "Not now."

The boy slumps dejectedly, head down.

"Sit up," Eula snaps. "Pay attention, child."

The boy does what he's told, but it's clear he's still pouting.

"Nice automobile," Red says to Susan, nodding his appreciation. "Good way to travel. If you have to travel this way."

The car is an old and long, white Lincoln Continental, with a hood ornament in the shape of a charging silver horse. The engine is nearly silent.

"I like it," she answers stiffly. She doesn't look at him. She doesn't want to see his eyes. It's bad enough she can feel his breath on her cheek.

"How're you feeling, Miz Korrey?" he asks. "You healing up all right?"

Eula purses her lips, unsure, before she answers, "It ain't supposed to hurt. I still got bruises, you know. Susan here, her face ain't healed yet either." She turns her head. "Ain't written that way."

Quick grin, here and gone.

"No, I don't guess it is," he tells her gently, so gently she stiffens and looks away. "But that's the way it is. That's the way of it." A long pause. "You understand, Miz Korrey?"

"Yes sir, I do," she answers. A smile of her own. "Don't gotta like it, though."

He laughs and nods. "It'll get better," he promises. "Much better." He steps back from the car, and before they realize what he's done, there's the sharp ring of his spurs and he's in the saddle again.

And all they hear is that voice.

"It's almost time."

Susan can't help herself; she has to know: "How?"

Another pause; the sound of rain on the roof.

"We ride in, we take over, just the way it's supposed to be." A pause that might have been a silent laugh. "Don't fret. I'll tell you when."

"Are we alone?"

"We're always alone. But no, there'll be some help, I think. Gotta check that out directly."

"Will they fight us? Again?"

"They'll try," he says, a quiet laugh in his voice. "Won't be much fun, otherwise."

At last Susan smiles, confidence returned. "But we'll win, Red, right? This time we'll win."

He doesn't answer.

He rides away.

Mist on the road, rain skating down the windshield, and she watches him ride away, droplets of scarlet fire splashing from the horse's hooves.

Part 2

1

1

Deep autumn; Tuesday; just past morning.

High clouds and a slow breeze and a sun already drifting past its peak; waves and tide are high, the last fierce signs of a hurricane just gone, one that shied away from the coast but left its winds behind; small twigs on the roads, a handful of dead branches, here and there a few shingles trapped in a gutter; a road crew working on the hanging traffic light at Midway and Landward; the sound of chainsaws; the sound of hammers.

A handful of surfers gather on the beach, gauging height and courage and the size of their boards; two beachcombers with metal detectors, each with a burlap sack flung over a shoulder; gulls swarming the flotsam the waves have left behind, dropping shells onto the jetty rocks, then scrambling for the meat; photographers still and video do their dances for the right angle, an impromptu party ranging across a pair of dunes, a child crouching intently over a tide pool while his father looks on, smiling.

A dead bird in the woods; still twitching.

2

The house wasn't the smallest that Casey had ever lived in, but sometimes it felt like it. It was a two-story, low-ceiling square of no particular design, with a screened-in porch that faced Midway Road, and a slightly canted chimney above a peaked slate roof. What faded paint was left on the clapboard looked either blue or grey, depending on the sun, on the rain, on the way the trees gave or took away the shade. The yard, while not garden magazine lush, was at least neat—front, sides, and back—and there was a hedge along the road with thorns an inch or two long, thick as a man's thumb.

He hated trimming that damn hedge, and he had the bandages to prove it. It was, he reckoned, a continuing test of his resolve, and his threshold of pain. Still, he decided as he stepped back and let the pruning shears swing idly at his side, it looked pretty good. Fairly even along the breast-high top, the corners as crisp as they were ever going to get, and most of the leaves still hung on.

A point in his favor then: he hadn't killed the stupid thing yet.

All in all, a decent morning's work.

His free hand reached over his head in a bone-snapping stretch; a satisfied groan, a handkerchief across his face to take the sweat away before he tucked it back into his hip pocket. Several cars passed the house in both directions; he didn't recognize them, and none greeted him. A police cruiser drifted south with a quick press of its horn, and he waved without looking, halfhearted at best.

Discouraging visitors—a skill he wasn't exactly proud of, but he'd also gotten pretty good at it over the past couple of years, here and elsewhere. He was, and had been for a long time, no longer the local curiosity, just some kind of weird guy who preferred his own company.

He snorted, shook his head at a major understatement—
at most, he went into town once a month, to stock up on
groceries for the next three or four weeks . . . and spoke to
no one; at most, the only people he saw out here were
those who drove past or those who rented the houses under
his care . . . and he spoke to them only when courtesy
demanded it.

He knew little of what went on around the rest of the
island, and until now, he hadn't particularly cared.

Alone was what he had wanted, and alone was what he
had achieved.

He wasn't sure why, but now that had changed.

His place was one of a cluster of eight, all the same save
their colors, four on either side of the road, and the only
one occupied at the moment, which meant his work was
pretty much done for the day. He could, of course, hit each
house one by one, see what cleaning had to be done, if his
latest repairs still held or if something new wanted fixing,
but that would imply an initiative he didn't feel like tapping into just now. It wasn't that he was lazy, and it wasn't
that he wasn't a little proud of how he had handled the
responsibilities he'd been given.

It was just that he didn't feel like it.

Not today.

Today was for lazing.

like hell, Chisholm, give it up, you're stalling.

Today was for hanging out, for appreciating the weather
and the scenery and the constant smell of the sea in the air.
For laughing at the gulls as they squabbled over nothing,
maybe walking over to the marsh to watch the herons strut
their stuff in the shallows, maybe hike on over to the
beach, sit on Daddy Whale's head and watch the silhou-
ettes of fishing boats skimming slowly across the horizon.

Whatever he would do, though, work wouldn't be it.

stalling

It was, all in all, a pretty sweet deal, this job of his. He was, for the most part, his own boss. As long as he did what he was supposed to do, when he was supposed to do it, days like today could be taken without guilt.

His landlord had proposed the arrangement when Casey had been sent to him to inquire about a rental. In retrospect, it must have looked like a bizarre conversation. Norville Cutler barely came up to Casey's chin, yet he acted as if he were a good foot taller.

"No sweat, I think I can help you. Man, you're a pretty big guy. Handy at all?"

"I'm no expert, not much good at plumbing, but . . . I can work, yes. If it matters, I learn fast."

"Good. Got some places up on Midway, that's the main street in case you ain't figured that out yet, the only one that goes one end of the island to the other. They aren't much, the houses, but they pay their way. Had a guy, stupid son of a bitch, couldn't find his ass with a map and a flashlight, he cut out on me last month, the stupid bastard, didn't even give me notice. So I'm figuring . . . you want to work, keep them in shape, keep the tenants happy, you know the kind of stuff I mean, you can use one for yourself."

"Sounds good to me."

"It is, mister. It's damn good. Better'n most deserve. Best part is, I won't bother you hardly at all. I'll know if you're not doing the work, don't have time for inspections, but you know what I mean. You do your bit, I'll stay outta your hair."

"I get a choice of places?"

"Hell, no, I'll show you which one. Except for the tenants, and that's only late spring to maybe October, the only neighbors are behind you. Some old lady, a couple of nig—black guys, an old man and his son, they won't bother you at all, you won't even know they're there most of the time. You're not from around here, am I right?"

"Right."

"Kentucky . . . no, Tennessee, am I right? You spent some time elsewhere, but I figure . . . yeah, Tennessee."

"That's not bad."

"What do you do?"

"What?"

"You made a living before here, right? You didn't just pop out outta the ground, right? So what do you do?"

"I . . . nothing. I don't . . . nothing."

"The law after you?"

"The law? No."

"Well, Mr. I Don't Know Nothing, you take care of me, I'll take care of you. Off the books, the whole nine yards. Just don't stiff me, pal. People around here, they'll tell you, I don't like it when someone stiffs me."

A cool breeze touched his face, and Casey was grateful for the slight shiver it caused, and he was suddenly tempted to forget the walking, the beach, and just go inside, take a nap, let the rest of the day slide by. Like all the other days since he had arrived on the island. Let them all slide by and behind him, forget him, make it seem possible that he had never been anywhere else, never done anything else but slap paint on walls and hammer nails into boards and rake yards and replace shingles and wash windows and weave mesh patches into screens torn by age and nosey squirrels.

And when he awoke, it would be nearly dark, time to begin the process of trying to get a good night's sleep.

Without the dreams.

Without the nightmares.

of a church bell tolling, no one at the rope

A process that generally began with supper. Out of a can or out of the microwave. Then, weather permitting, a half-mile hike through the trees to the beach, and another hike along the wet apron. Listening to the ocean, listening to the birds, dodging the waves trying to snare and soak his feet. Once in a while, if the tide was low, climbing clumsily out to the end of a jetty where he could see nothing but water ahead of him, nothing but sky above.

Where he could be alone.

Where he could feel small.

Too small to matter.

explosions.

He was close to five inches over six feet, his shoulders and chest broad, arms and legs to match. His hair was thick and long, brushed back and curled black to his shoulders. High cheeks and a dimpled chin, heavy brows and a nose that time had left something less than sharp. A face, all in all, that made no apologies for the beatings it had taken, physical and otherwise, and was all the more imposing for it.

Or so others had told him. He wasn't sure about the imposing part, but he had often used the size, and a grumbling voice that sounded born in a deep canyon, to good advantage in his former life.

the law after you?

No, but my dreams are.

maybe so, but you're still stalling.

a ghost-white car gliding out of the fire

He grinned and shook his head.

Stalling indeed, and making a bad job of it, too.

He slapped his leg lightly with the shears, told himself there was no need to rake up the debris he'd snipped from the hedge, told himself there was no need, right now, to oil the hinges on the porch's screen door, and certainly no need to sweep the porch itself. Or vacuum the living room. Or dust what little furniture he had.

By the time he was upstairs he was laughing aloud; by the time he had taken a shower and changed his clothes, he was almost excited.

For the first time since he had exiled himself to this end of Camoret, he was going into town with no other purpose than to walk among the living.

He stood in front of the low, white pine chest of drawers in his bedroom, hairbrush in one hand, checking his reflection in the slightly warped mirror hanging on the wall above it. He had gotten used to the distortion. Somehow it seemed to fit.

The idea for the trip had come to him only last week, as he returned from the grocery store with his latest batch of provisions. With virtually all the tourists gone until spring, the only people he had seen were locals. And something about them had sparked his curiosity: a feeling of tension, unease, behind the faces that either smiled blankly at him or glanced at him with no more than a passing curiosity. For days he had passed it off as his starved imagination; and for days he had been unable to forget it.

Yesterday he had actually straddled his bike and ped-aled a hundred yards down the road before anxiety turned him around in a spray of dust and pebbles.

None of your business, he'd told his shadow as he raced back for home; none of your business, and you're probably wrong anyway, so let it go, keep on keeping on with what you're already doing.

Hiding.

This morning he had stood at the sink in the tiny kitchen and said, "From what?"

During each monthly grocery run, he usually treated himself to lunch at either Betsy's or the Tide, where he eavesdropped unashamedly and, if he was lucky, grabbed an old copy of the *Camoret Weekly*. This way he was able

to pick up some of what was going on around the island.
So, as far as he could tell, there had been no unusual spike
in the death rate, violent or otherwise, the famine had evidently had little effect here, the plague had mercifully left
them untouched, and thus far they had escaped the current
turmoil that swept across the mainland.

From what? he asked the reflection, and it gave him a
disgusted look that told him not to be so stupid, he knew
damn well from what.

ghost-white

Nevertheless, it was time.

Well past time.

He put the brush down, ran a hand across his chest, and
reminded himself this was only an experiment, not a complete change in habit. The recluse was only checking the
landscape, not surrendering the safety of his cave.

He hurried out of the room to the landing, and paused at
the top of the narrow staircase. His bedroom was on the
right, in front, a second bedroom on his left. Behind him,
on the right, was the bathroom, and on his left, another
room he used for storage.

The door was ajar.

"Damnit," he muttered harshly, and took a step down,
trying to ignore it.

He couldn't.

He returned to the landing and pushed the door open,
stepped over the threshold and looked to the right, where
another door, a closet, was open as well.

His eyes closed briefly and he took a deep breath. The
house was poorly constructed, he knew this. Doors sometimes opened on their own, the frames weren't always true.
Once he'd understood this, he was determined not to read
anything into it. Yet, as he kicked the closet door shut and
for good measure whacked it with the heel of his hand, he
decided it was past time to nail the damn thing shut.

He didn't need this.

He didn't need this at all. Especially not today.

The first thing he had done after Cutler had shown him around and left, was drag his rope-bound suitcase into the storeroom. There he had emptied most of it into the closet, and hadn't been back since.

Except to close the goddamn door.

He glared at it now, daring it to defy him, then left the room, slammed the outer door behind him, and took the stairs down one at a time. Five minutes later he was on the bike and on his way. He grinned into the faint wind of his own making; he laughed at a blackbird that tried to hop beside him, gave up, and soared away; he coasted and laughed again and wished he had done this a long time ago.

It was an odd feeling, this good feeling; not until now did he understand how much he had missed it.

How much had been lost by being so alone.

3

Between the sheriff's department and a redbrick building that served as town hall and courthouse was a large pocket park, grass and high trees and a public bicycle stand where Casey locked up his bike. Wiped nervous hands on his jeans, scolded himself for acting like a kid on his first date, and headed south.

Three blocks later he stopped.

Unlike a number of other eateries on the island, Betsy's didn't pretend to be anything other than what it was—a simple sandwich shop, no frills, no fancy summer prices. A few tables, a few booths, a short counter along the left-hand wall for those who wanted nothing more than a slice of pie and a cup of coffee. A pine forest mural along the back wall that had always amused Casey because whenever someone popped out of the kitchen, it seemed as if they were walking out of a tree. Open at six for breakfast, closed at seven. Having established it just before the turn of the century, the original Betsy and her family were long gone, her several successors not bothering to change the name.

Gloria Nazario was the current owner, a pleasantly rotund Cuban refugee whose brother, Hector, did most of the cooking while she did most of the serving and a black man named Junior Raybourn did most of the sweeping up.

Casey sat on the first stool nearest the door. Although the room was nearly full, no one had done more than glance up when he'd entered, which was fine by him. Today he wanted to listen as much as eat; with his back to the room, he was, he figured, about as invisible as someone his size could get. And with the long mirror on the wall behind the coffee urns and other counter paraphernalia, he was able to watch most of the room without having to stare.

The waitress, a too-thin young woman with too much makeup and bottle-blond hair that needed touching up at the roots, took his order without speaking, despite his awkward attempts at conversation. She wrote, she checked a price on the menu, and walked into the kitchen.

Not a word.

Not a look.

All right, he thought; so I'm a little out of practice.

Yet he couldn't help a check in the mirror, just to be sure he still looked presentable. There had been a few times, after pedaling home, when he'd noticed things sticking in his hair—bits of leaves, once a spider, once a feather that the wind had tucked behind his ear. The image of what people must have thought had made him laugh then; he didn't laugh now.

There was nothing wrong that he could see.

All right, no problem, she's having a bad day.

Nevertheless, as he waited for his lunch, he was puzzled by the glances people gave him when they thought he couldn't see them—not really unfriendly, just . . . wary.

Suspicious. Not that the reactions surprised him very much—he was, after all, the stranger who lived among them. Curiosity was to be expected when he sidestepped his routine.

Still, he was more than relieved when the meal finally came and he was able to concentrate on fueling his body, not his imagination.

Not to mention, he reminded himself, a little judicious eavesdropping if he could, picking sentences and fragments out of the conversations that filled the shop.

It wasn't that difficult; it was as if he weren't there.

In the booth by the entrance three men, suits and ties and briefcases, argued about the Ausso-Indonesian War, debating the moral ambiguities of New Zealand desperately trying to keep herself neutral despite the deaths of her citizens in the initial incident. Other island-cluster nations had begun to declare for Indonesia. China was concerned. Australia was puzzled that no one, yet, had officially declared for her. Race rather than right had entered the propaganda, and the continent nation couldn't understand why she had been left to stand on her own.

A friend passing the booth suggested the three ought to concern themselves more with North Korea's massing troops a few miles north of the Demilitarized Zone. "We're gonna get sucked in," he said bitterly. "Just like the first time. You watch, we're gonna get sucked in."

From somewhere else:

"You really going to sell?"

"Hell, I'm tired of having to do the causeway route every time I want to see a damn movie."

"You get an offer?"

"Sort of, yeah."

"Don't tell me . . . Cutler."

"Eat your dessert, we're late the judge'll kill us."

* * *

"Goddamn Freck says I shouldn't have been out so late. Jesus, it was only nine o' goddamn clock. Who thinks they're gonna get mugged at nine o'clock, for God's sake? Here, for God's sake."

"Dumbass deputy couldn't arrest a jaywalker, the stupid son of a bitch. So . . . what, he say you were asking for it?"

"As much as."

"Stupid son of a bitch."

"Tell me about it. I swear to God, I can't wait to get out of here."

". . . have to pry that boat out of my cold dead hands."

"So you're not selling?"

"You deaf, boy? I'd rather sell my wife."

Casey slid a month-old copy of the *Weekly* toward him, scanning the headlines and sighing without a sound. A fragmented Yugoslavia continued to tear itself apart; revolutions in Brazil, Chile, plus a half dozen more across Central and Southern Africa; India and Pakistan glared at each other across mountain passes, exchanging random artillery fire, raising banners; Japan altering its constitution to allow for a full-blown, full-time army and navy.

All of this he had already seen on television, but seeing it in print, no matter how briefly covered, somehow made it worse.

He picked at his french fries, flipped over a page, and glanced through several articles that were, in essence, ill-disguised editorials, righteous rants against the growing number of households leaving the island because of "hooligan activity" and "bald political pressure," all not so vaguely attributed to an "unholy alliance" between Norville Cutler's various businesses and Mayor Cribbs's alleged greed, the purpose of which was neither hinted at nor explained. Casey had the feeling that were he a regular reader he'd already know. He also sensed an angry desperation here, a warning of some kind that time was running out for whatever the editor felt was on the way; and it didn't, he figured, have anything to do with the problems on the mainland.

I really ought to get out more, he thought, and ate, read, after a while frowned because there was something about the tabloid-size newspaper that didn't seem quite as it should be. Blatant editorializing in what were supposed to be ordinary news reports was one thing, the weekly newsmagazines did it all the time, but as he flipped the pages back and forth randomly, he suspected the answer was right there in front of him. Something to do with . . . frowning deeper, he turned to the back page, then to the classified section, the want ads, the garage sales. Another page or two at random, and he finally realized what it was—advertising. There were hardly any ads, display or otherwise, and while he was no expert, he was fairly certain that ad revenue was what kept a newspaper in business.

Especially this time of year. The Monday before Thanksgiving, a few weeks before Christmas, the paper should be bulging with holiday sale announcements, even if many of the seasonal shops had already shut down.

"You have to go to the office for a new one," Gloria said as she slid his bill toward him. Her hair, long and black, was caught in a hairnet, her face touched with lines drawn by the work she did. Large black eyes, watching him, not smiling.

"You don't sell it anymore?"

She shook her head. "Not worth it." A glance toward the door. "Not to no one hardly anymore."

He laid his money next to his plate, a gesture to indicate he didn't want the change.

"You work for him, don't you?" she asked as he pushed off the stool.

"Who?"

"Mr. Cutler."

He shrugged. "I guess so. Yes."

She nodded once. "Okay. So don't come back no more, okay? Go somewhere else."

He stared in disbelief, but she had already turned her back, fussing with coffee cups, fiddling with one of the urns. A deliberate, and fearful, dismissal that made him want to at least ask for an explanation. But the set of her back, the way her hands darted at doing nothing changed his mind.

Avoiding the gazes of the other customers, he left, stood on the sidewalk, squinting until he grew accustomed to the bright afternoon sun. Until the surge of anger that followed him outside subsided. Not enough, however, to completely quash the temptation to walk into another shop to check the owner's or clerk's reaction. He almost did it. He almost turned into the gift shop next to Betsy's on the right, or the photo shop on the left. Just to see. The problem was, even if he was asked to leave, or treated coldly, he still wouldn't know why. He was only a handyman, for crying out loud, and hadn't seen Cutler more than a handful of times since he'd taken the job. His pay was usually picked up at Cutler's downtown office—only twice had Cutler brought it out himself, and that was because the man wanted to check on his properties, not because he was the kindly employer who cared about his people.

What the hell was the guy doing that for God's sake hired help should be tarred with the same brush?

It was, if he thought about it long enough, almost amusing. He had heard of people being barred from bars before, but never from a sandwich shop. Begone, you weirdo, and never darken my mayonnaise again.

With an imperceptible shake of his head, and a fleeting one-sided grin, he started up the street, hands in his pockets, telling himself that he was undoubtedly overreacting. Gloria had problems with Cutler, that much was obvious;

no reason to believe that anyone else would treat him the same. Hell, most of Camoret didn't even know who he was, much less who he worked for. But each time he paused to enter another store, another shop, he changed his mind and moved on.

Halfway up the next block he reached a cedar-shake building no larger than a small bungalow set well back from the sidewalk, as if distancing itself from the businesses on either side. A white picket fence divided concrete from grass and two large cherry trees slowly and at last dropping their leaves. He knew there were only two rooms inside—a small waiting room, and a large office behind it. Norville Cutler Enterprises, and the only person he'd ever seen there was Mandy Poplin, the receptionist he assumed doubled as a secretary. He supposed he could always ask her what was going on; not that she would tell him. Each time he picked up his pay, an envelope filled with cash and a receipt, their conversation was little more than formally polite.

Here's your pay, Mr. Chisholm.

Thanks, Mandy. Nice weather we're having.

Yes, it is. We'll see you next month.

He walked on, annoyed less at his treatment now than at the deflation of his adventure. All that buildup, all the anxiety, all the reasons why he shouldn't get involved in town life again, all for nothing.

Abruptly he stopped and looked over his shoulder.

Gloria Nazario had already known he worked for Cutler. She had asked him several months ago, and it hadn't seemed to bother her then. So what had changed?

Go back, be polite, be deferential, ask.

He couldn't do it.

Instead, he crossed the street and walked another block, absently checking the Christmas decorations in some of the windows, Thanksgiving displays in others. What he would do, he decided, is pick up the latest *Weekly* edition, see if there was something in there, something new, that would give him more information. Maybe even ask the editor himself. Assuming, he thought with a quick sour grin, that the man didn't toss him out on his ear.

A quicker step, another block, and he hesitated only a second before entering the *Camoret Weekly*'s office. The door had barely closed behind him before he wondered if · he hadn't made a mistake.

4

The outer room was empty, a stack of new papers on the counter, still bundled. A wall clock ticked loudly. A man's voice in back, raised in anger.

None of your business, Casey cautioned. He grabbed a paper, fumbled in his pocket to produce a dollar bill he dropped on the counter, and turned to leave.

None of your business; until he heard another man cry out and the sound of something large crashing onto the floor, followed by the distinct sound of breaking glass.

Don't, he ordered as he lifted the flap; asking for trouble, he warned as he dropped the paper where he'd found it, crossed the room hurriedly and opened the door just enough to stick his head through.

An old man leaned heavily against the left-hand wall, panting, one hand over his heart. On the floor at his feet a scattering of folders and papers, and a computer monitor, its face shattered. A short man in jeans and brown leather jacket, heavy beard and tight curly hair, stood in the middle of the room, arms folded across a chest so large it made him seem deformed. A much taller man in denim coveralls, whip-lean and stringy dark hair, sideburns down to his jaw, had his hand on a printer as if ready to sweep it off its stand.

For an instant the three stared at Casey as if he'd dropped in through the ceiling.

Casey looked at the old man and said, "Trouble, Mr. Hull?"

"Who the hell are you?" the short one demanded. "Get lost."

Casey ignored him. "Mr. Hull?"

The editor blinked rapidly, head trembling. Although his hair was mussed, his bow tie askew, he didn't look as if he'd been hurt, just scared half to death. His lips worked, but made no sound.

"Damnit, Cord, stuff this jerk somewhere, I ain't got time for this shit."

The tall one grinned. "Whatever you say, Stump." He sniffed loudly and shook his head. "Ought to know better," he said to Casey. "Ain't right, butting in."

A brief unanswered prayer to be somewhere else, and Casey nudged the door all the way open with his foot as he stepped onto the threshold, letting them see him all for the first time. Cord Teague stopped before he'd taken two steps, his fisted hands unsure what to do next.

"Aw, Christ," Stump said. "Shit, I know you, you're that retard at the houses."

Casey didn't move; he just stood there.

He wasn't about to start anything himself, but he'd been in enough fights in his life to know the signs—the bluster, the doubt, the wonder just how tough this big man was. Sometimes there was good advantage to looking the way he did.

"Well, goddamnit, Cord, I got to do everything myself?" Stump reached to a nearby desk and picked up a length of pipe. He brandished it at Casey, one last warning. "Stupid retard."

Deliberately, slowly, Casey let his face go blank. Nothing there but the eyes. Slightly narrowed. Watching.

"Stump," Cord whispered, backing slowly toward the alley door, unable to take his gaze from Casey's face.

Casey straightened, just enough, and filled the doorway

side to side. Still no fists, no warning glare. He just stood there. Watching.

Cord grabbed the doorknob. "Stump." His hand slipped off, and he tried again. "Stump, let's . . . come on, Stump, leave it be."

"I told you once, I told you a hundred times, you stupid son of a bitch, we can't let—"

"Just leave," Casey said, his voice quiet. Rumbling. The mutter of thunder on the far side of the horizon.

Stump blinked at him, frozen for a moment before he raised the pipe as if ready to club him, but he couldn't stop his hand from trembling just enough to betray his nerves.

"Leave," Casey repeated. "You've made your point. Get out."

Cord yanked the back door open and stepped into the alley. "Come on, Stump. Jesus . . . come on."

Stump was clearly torn between giving ground and losing face in front of his brother. A warning glare at Hull, and he kicked viciously at the papers by his feet, whirled, and made to take one last bash at the printer Cord was supposed to have tipped over.

Casey was faster.

He grabbed Teague's wrist and hauled up, nearly pulling the shorter man off his feet. Off-balance, Teague cocked his free arm to throw a punch, teach this meddler a lesson, and stopped when he saw Casey's expression. Didn't resist when Casey wrenched the pipe from his grip. Said nothing when Casey dragged him to the door, dangling like a small child about to be punished, and shoved him gently outside.

Closed the door and locked it.

Hull sagged shakily into a wheeled leather chair, hand still on his chest, the other ineffectually swiping at his hair. His face was pale, eyes bright with either shock or tears. His left couldn't seem to stop jumping.

"You all right?" Casey asked again, gently, setting the pipe down on a desk behind him.

Hull nodded mutely, hesitantly.

"Okay." He started for the door, paused and said, "I'm taking a paper, okay? There's money on the counter."

The editor didn't respond save for a weak gesture of thanks, and Casey left, picked up his newspaper, and went outside. Across the street he saw Deputy Freck leaving the sheriff's office. He called out and waved, checking for traffic as he trotted to the other side.

Freck, hands on his hips, eyes hidden behind dark sunglasses, waited impatiently.

"Might want to check over there, on Mr. Hull," Casey told him, pointing with the paper. "He had some trouble with Stump Teague and one of his brothers."

"Is that so?"

"Nearly wrecked his office."

"No kidding."

Casey didn't know what to say next. He glanced over at the *Weekly* office, muttered, "Just thought you ought to know," and started for the park, half expecting to be stopped. When he reached the bike stand, he fiddled unnecessarily with the combination lock, using the time to see what the deputy would do.

Instead of checking on Hull, the deputy watched him, hands still on hips, and what might have been a smirk on his lips.

A gust of anger, a temptation for confrontation, before he dropped the newspaper into the deep wire basket behind the seat and wheeled the bike to the curb. Once there he paused for a trio of cars to pass, then pushed off, waiting until he was steady before looking back again.

Freck hadn't moved.

The anger returned, and he pedaled hard, leaning over the handlebars, letting the wind nearly blind him. It wasn't Freck that bothered him, it was the shame he felt for not staying to make sure the old man was all right.

Not your business, he told himself harshly.

No, he answered, but it damn well used to be.

2

1

Deep autumn; Tuesday; late afternoon.

Norville Cutler considered himself a decent judge of a man, a fairly canny businessman, and someone who could measure the size of a customer's wallet and its willingness to be emptied even before that customer took off his sunglasses so his vision could adjust to the deliberately dim lighting of either of the causeway shops. It was for the latter reason that most of the time he could be found in the *Cutler's Last Stop* on the westbound side. He didn't give a flying fart who left the damn island; he only cared about those on the way to it. They were the ones with the most money to spend. He also kept at least two people on duty at all times—a woman pretty enough to convince any man in Bermuda shorts that a genuine Caribbean shark's tooth was just the thing to add to a key chain, and a man with just enough flare and exotic danger about him to convince most women in large hats and rhinestone sunglasses that a genuine Puerto Rican coral necklace was the perfect thing to accentuate that marvelous tanned cleavage.

All of which had made him a comfortable living. But what had made his fortune before he'd reached fifty came after he had taught himself the finer points of real estate management—buying and selling, appraisal, and making sure that what he wanted was on the market when he was ready to buy it, and not a moment before.

Obstacles were only hurdles, not impenetrable walls.

"I don't believe it," he said. "One stinking old man, and you can't even handle that."

A man of average height, an easy living paunch, and a three-piece tailored suit with French cuffs and gleaming Italian shoes, he didn't for a minute believe in the Good Ol' Southern Boy image. His idol was the shark that used to belong to the large bleached jaw mounted on the wall behind him. He also didn't believe in getting too close to his off-the-books employees, which was why he stood behind the display case, hands spread on the glass top.

"I don't understand."

Outside, a rising sea slammed against the causeway walls and barriers. A slow wind hummed around the building's corners. The sun just past its zenith; the long front window reflecting the interior in cold pale grey despite the brightness outside.

Stump and Cord Teague stood in the wide aisle, hang-dog, and not a little afraid.

"He busted in," Stump told him flatly. "We was in the middle of the message when this guy busts in."

"Chisholm," Cutler said.

Cord, half a step behind his brother, nodded, his hands trying to find a place to hide.

Cutler stared at the rings and necklaces, bracelets and pins in the case under his hands. A part of him thought that no one knew Mandy Poplin made most of them; another part wondered why the Teagues had to become such a problem, especially since he was so close to the end. Three brothers, none as stupid or thick as they made out in public, parents long since gone, no wives or steady girlfriends, living in raised shacks on the edge of the marsh. They were his pet project, and he was, now, beginning to regret it.

"You tell him anything? Chisholm, I mean."

"No," Stump answered, insulted. He swiped angrily at his beard. "We was just startled, that's all."

"Big," Cord whispered. "Sumbitch is big."

Cutler knew exactly what he meant. It was one of the reasons he'd hired the man—someone that big lurking around, the tenants were less apt to cause him grief.

"Hull knows anyhow," Stump said with a sharp nod. "He didn't get hurt, like you said, but some of that computer stuff ain't working so good no more." When he grinned, his long teeth seemed startlingly white amid the black mustache and beard. "We didn't finish, but I know he gets it."

Cord wandered off, peering in the cases, grunting to himself, staring at the walls where stuffed marlin and shark, sea bass and barracuda were mounted on polished pine shields. "Tall," he said, his voice quiet, barely heard. "Was tall, that retard."

Cutler ignored him. "Look," he said to Stump, "if he understands, that's fine. Real fine." He raised a finger. "But I don't want one more issue of that rag on this island, you hear me? If that damn daughter of his, or any of her friends, try stopping you stopping the next truck . . ." He sniffed, looked at the ceiling. Shook his head slowly. "He's been sniffing around Atlanta, Savannah, Mr. Teague. For an old man he sure gets around, sure knows a lot of people he shouldn't. It just isn't healthy." Abruptly he gripped the sides of the case and leaned forward, forcing Stump back a step. "You know the old saying, that Sixties thing? War is not healthy for children and other living things? Something like that?" His eyes narrowed. "This is war, Mr. Teague. We've won some, we've lost some. But if you know what's good for you, we won't lose any more."

He straightened.

He smiled.

A gust of wind slapped at the building, the ceiling lights flickering, just for a moment.

He took an envelope from his jacket pocket and laid it on the glass. "You're getting rich, Mr. Teague, you and your kin. Make sure you live long enough to spend it."

2

It didn't take long for Whittaker Hull to clean up. Once the papers had been piled on his desk, a broom took care of the glass, and a spare monitor kept in a closet replaced the one Teague had smashed.

He couldn't stop shaking.

He stared at the pipe lying on Ronnie's desk and knew it had been meant for his leg, or his arm, but only after it had been used on the rest of the office's equipment. He reached out, and pulled his hand back. He couldn't touch it.

He couldn't stop shaking.

He sat, he stood, he opened the alley door carefully to be sure the Teagues had gone; he went into the front room and saw the dollar bill Chisholm had left on the counter.

The sheriff, he thought; I'll report this to Vale and let him handle it.

"Oh . . . Christ," he whispered, half in disgust, half in defeat. He leaned heavily against the counter, one hand absently fussing with his tie. Sure, let good old Vale handle it. Each time the delivery truck had run into trouble, he had reported it, and each time, Oakman had assured him he would get right on it. Handle it personally.

Nothing had happened.

Hull didn't think Vale was in Cutler's pocket, but it didn't matter. The sheriff's growing lack of courage had, over the past couple of years, become legendary. No, infamous. Make peace at all costs had become the man's motto, and to hell with the next election, he was on his way out anyway, why rock the boat, stir the pot, make waves.

He sighed loudly and lowered his head.

He couldn't stop shaking.

He couldn't banish the image of Chisholm standing in the doorway, appearing out of nowhere. For a second Hull was positive he had seen anger there, close to rage, and had actually, momentarily feared for the Teagues' lives. Chisholm could have crushed them without half thinking, but he hadn't.

That voice had done it for him.

He closed his eyes, in shame for his own weakness, for not putting up a fight no matter the consequence, and in remembering that voice.

"Dear Lord," he whispered.

He couldn't stop shaking.

3

Being a minister in a community of such flux and flow in population was a challenge Lyman Baylor had accepted with enthusiasm. He hadn't cared that many of his colleagues, and most of his family, considered this tantamount to exile; he hadn't cared when his father had questioned his sanity, since the alternative had been a thriving congregation in New Orleans.

"But that," Lyman had argued, "is already established. All I'd have to do is go there and fit in to something that's already running. I wouldn't be much more than a mechanic, making sure everything gets oiled.

"But this . . . this is going to be work. Hard work. And I don't mean the accounts and the politics and all the rest of that business. This is souls, Dad. I'm talking about souls."

Five years later, close enough to thirty to count the hairs on the back of its head, he was still excited. Still smiling

each morning, still writing each sermon as if it were his
first, still delighted each time he picked the hymns for the
church's electronic carillon. He knew that half his congregation, mostly the staid and the elderly, hadn't yet stopped
thinking of him as a mere child, just a caretaker preacher
until a real one came along, but he didn't care. He had
never missed a service, never missed a call on the sick and
the shut-ins, never missed an opportunity to be seen in
every quarter of the island.

"They'll think you're a pain in the butt, Ly," Kitra had
cautioned in the beginning. "They'll call you a Bible-
thumper."

"You mean a religious man."

"No, you know full well what I mean. An extremist.
That's not the same. And they'll avoid you, Ly. They'll
think you're a nut and they'll make our lives miserable."

Not anymore.

On official duty, as he called it, he wore his light grey
suit and maroon shirt, white cleric's collar; off-duty, he
dressed in his civvies and spent time on the docks talking
with the fishermen about tides and fish and baits and seasons; spent an evening or so a week in one of the town
bars, the more respectable ones at first, talking and listening and playing a little pool or a few games of darts; took
Kitra to the restaurants and got to know the owners, the
waitresses, the waiters, the busboys; visited the few
remaining steady members of the parish and got to know
their lives.

Never pushing.

Never apologizing when asked his profession. But
always . . . always making sure the people he spoke with
knew when services began on Sunday morning.

"You know," Ben Pellier had once said, "no offense, but
you sure don't act like a preacher."

Lyman had paid his bill and said, "Well, actually, Ben,
yes, I do."

And he was official today as he backed out of the rectory driveway, first on his way to Whittaker's office to drop off the church's ad, then over to Mayor Cribbs' office to demand a reason why Geraldine Essman's murderers had not yet been apprehended. It had not, of course, been reported as murder, but Lyman knew in his heart it wasn't anything else but.

Mrs. Essman had lived in a small bungalow on Draper Street, a block in from Midway Road. The place had been burgled the night before Halloween, the last straw in a long stretch of incidents the old lady had suffered since the beginning of the year. Word was, she had been mildly beaten and locked in a closet. Word was, the moment Deputy Salter had opened the closet door she demanded the name of the best real estate agent on the island.

Two weeks later, after prowlers had broken a kitchen window, a massive heart attack put her in a grave behind Reverend Baylor's church.

Lyman had known her well.

Left untouched and undisturbed, she would have lived to be a hundred.

He smiled at the image of her, sitting as always in the front pew, watching him carefully, daring him to err either in Scripture quotation or interpretation. A tough old bird who deserved much better. As a matter of fact—

And he cried out when something slammed into the side of the car.

He jammed the brakes on, switched off the ignition, and looked worriedly to his right, in time to see a bicycle wobble backward and fall against the curb. Oh, Lord, he thought, licked his lips, touched his heart briefly, and moved as fast as he could around the rear bumper.

Oh, Lord, he thought again when he saw the big man sitting in the street.

"Mr. Chisholm," he said, kneeling beside him. "My goodness, Mr. Chisholm, are you all right? I didn't see . . .

I was . . . I'm so sorry, I should have been more careful. Are you all right, sir? Are you injured?"

Chisholm closed his eyes tightly, snapped them open and stared at him, clearly dazed, A hand brushed across his forehead, then back through his hair.

Lyman, fighting to regain some use of his lungs, put a hand on the man's shoulder. "You wait right here, Mr. Chisholm. I'll phone—"

"No." Chisholm shrugged the hand off, and winced, inhaled sharply. "No, it's . . . I'm okay." He managed a smile, then a waggle of his hand, a help-me-up gesture Lyman was slow to obey. But once on his feet, the big man brushed grit and dirt from his legs and smiled again. "My fault."

Lyman wanted very much to believe it, found it easier when he saw the two six-packs still in the bike's carrier basket. "I was thinking," he offered by way of weak apology.

Chisholm nodded. "Yeah, so was I." He took an unsteady step back, half closed one eye, and examined the car's back door, right hand absently massaging his left shoulder. "At least I didn't dent it."

Lyman couldn't help it—he looked as well, and felt a flush when he heard Chisholm laugh. "Yes. Well." He pointed at the bike. "Will it work, do you think?"

"I sure hope so. It's a long walk, otherwise." The big man took a step toward the curb, froze a moment when balance seemed to leave him, then leaned over and hauled the bike upright. A swift examination, and he nodded. "Looks fine." He straddled the seat and took a deep breath. "Listen, Reverend, I'm sorry. It really was my fault. I would have seen you if I hadn't been so preoccupied."

"That's all right," he said, relieved. He started for the car, hesitated, looked back, a pointed stare at the beer. "Listen, Mr. Chisholm, if you, uh . . . I don't know, want to talk or something . . . you . . . well, you know where to find me."

Chisholm's sudden smile made him uncomfortable; there was no humor in it at all. "No thanks," the big man said gruffly, and pedaled away before Lyman could say anything else.

Curious man, he thought as he stood by the driver's door and watched Chisholm go. Kitra swore he was hiding from the police, and a few of his parishioners had suggested he was just a simple man, as in simple in the head. Lyman didn't believe either theory, but he was intriguing, no doubt about it. Perhaps an unscheduled visit . . . whatever the man was, it was clear he was troubled. A grimace, then, as he chided himself for not insisting Chisholm see a doctor immediately, if for no other reason than to further dampen his conscience.

He shook his head, was about to slide in behind the wheel, when suddenly he straightened and looked over the car's roof. Squinted. Looked back the way Chisholm had gone, and shook his head again.

Odd, he thought.

For a minute there he could have sworn he'd heard the clear sound of hoofbeats.

Nerves, he decided immediately; the aftershock of the accident, and a good dollop of guilt.

Nevertheless, as he backed the rest of the way into the street and turned the car toward the center of town, he checked the rearview mirror just as a strong gust of wind rocked the vehicle and lifted a cloud of dust and dead leaves from the street.

For a minute there he heard the hoofbeats again, and saw in the swirling cloud the hazy figure of a riderless dark horse walking slowly away.

He gripped the steering wheel tightly until the wind died and the dust settled, and there was nothing left in the road but Casey Chisholm on his bike.

Guilt, he decided as he drove off, shaking slightly; most definitely guilt.

4

Jasper Cribbs loved politics. He had no illusions about his place in the larger Georgia scheme of things, but considering the hoops those boys in Atlanta had to jump through just to get something done in their districts, he wouldn't change places with any of them for any amount of money. He'd rather be a big fish in a little pond, a bullfrog in a spit puddle, than some self-important, I-got-higher-ambitions asshole's lackey.

He considered being mayor of Camoret Island much like being in the entertainment business, and he was one of those slash people that Hollywood was so fond of these days. Actor/director. Writer/producer. Fact was, he was probably a double-slash man these days—acting the part of the small-town Southern mayor, complete with the hick name and the suspenders and an ample belly, directing the town's welfare from his position of power, and producing the whole thing from behind the scenes, where very few knew what the hell he was up to.

Which, considering what he was up to, was the best place to be these days.

The perks weren't so bad either.

Being who he was, and making the money he did, he was virtually guaranteed that Mary Gwen was always happy. Nothing more that woman liked than to spend his money, run a few committees, and stay out of his way. In his eye, the perfect marriage.

It gave him a house on the bay at South Hook, a miniature antebellum, four-acre estate already paid for, and something else to keep his wife happy, and out of his hair.

Daughter Mariana was another matter entirely. How such a child could have sprung from his loins was a continuing mystery. He loved her dearly, but he sure didn't understand her. She did and said the right things at the right times, of course, he wouldn't have it any other way. A beautiful child, looked just like her mother when her mother could still fit into that honeymoon bathing suit, but the girl was as stubborn as a stump. Still, unlike her mother, she had the instincts of a barracuda, and that made him proud.

Most days, though, the most satisfying part of the job was his office. Sitting on the top floor of the town hall in his brown leather swivel chair, doing all his acting and directing and producing. Healthy leafy plants in big pots, nice paneling, pictures of him and whoever on the walls, nice carpet, a desk big enough to be the mayor's but not so big as to intimidate the little folks.

But the best feature was the lightly tinted fan-shaped window, near high as the ceiling, divided by white-painted wood strips into something that looked like a peacock's tail, curved at the top, all joining at the base.

At three stories, Town Hall was the tallest building on the island except for the watch tower on the ridge at South Hook. So he could swing his chair around, put his feet on the low sill, and look down at Camoret without anyone knowing he was up here. It wasn't a great view, not the bay or the fancy houses, not even high enough to let him see the ocean, but it let him see the people who elected him. Keep an eye on them, so to speak, help him more than once prepare for surprises.

Like just a few bits ago, watching that caretaker lunk come out of Whittaker's office, not looking all that happy. He spotted Deputy Billy and nearly ran across the street, did some pointing with a newspaper back at Hull's office, and Jasper figured he already knew what was going on. A point for the deputy—he never moved. A nod, a couple of words, and the next thing Jasper knew the lunk was on his way out of town, pedaling like the Devil himself was after him.

Good work, he had mouthed, and as if Freck had heard, he kind of glanced up in the mayor's direction, gave a small salute, and walked away. Not going, Jasper had been pleased to note, anywhere near that old man's place of business. A minute or so later one of those damn little Japanese or Korean or some damn thing cars comes hauling ass up the street, turns onto Landward without stopping for the light, and vanishes.

He recognized the car as Stump Teague's, and had grinned. Message delivered.

Things like that just made his day.

He sighed contentedly, checked over his shoulder to be sure he really had finished all the work his secretary had piled on his blotter, then hooked his thumbs under his green tartan suspenders and pulled them away from his chest, dared himself to snap them loose, and chuckled when he refused. Mariana had done that enough when she was little; he didn't need to revisit that kind of pain.

Against the far wall by the room's only visible door, a grandfather clock chimed the hour. He checked it against his watch, sniffed, scratched absently around the beginnings of his jowls, and pulled lightly at his second chin as he squinted back down at the street.

A slow humorless smile.

Wouldn't be long now. Deadline was the end of the year, and he didn't see many problems meeting it. Probably do it early, as a matter of fact. He had done some checking just that morning, had taken a surveyor's map from his safe and looked over the extent of his and Cutler's project. There were only six properties left, and three of those abutted Cutler's rental shacks, mostly easy pickings. One of the remaining was already in negotiation, and the other two . . . well, people do change their minds once in a while.

He grunted a laugh.

Hardest one, he figured, would still be Senior Raybourn. That man couldn't, wouldn't see reason. Hell, he was only a goddamn cook, for God's sake, but he held onto that stupid little house like it was some kind of gold mine. Cribbs could make him rich with one stroke of his gold-tip fountain pen, but that old black bastard wouldn't sell. And after the Essman woman's death, they had to move carefully. Quietly. Besides, he sure as hell didn't need some sniffing-around, civil rights fancy suit jackass lawyer kicking up dust. The fact that the Raybourns were the only blacks on the island made them too conspicuous. For now. Later, though, if push came to shove and he had to move in a hurry, all the damn marches in the world would be a world too late.

What he needed now was peace. What he needed was to make sure Hull didn't sniff out the truth. That old man, and who would have thought it, had already stirred a few embers that threatened to become a fire. Damn editorials had some important people talking. If today's little message didn't sink in . . .

Maybe it was also time to see that others didn't get to feeling bigger than their britches, as his daddy used to say. Time to make sure Oakman doesn't develop a sudden case of conscience and an affinity for upholding the Law; time to have a quiet word with Billy Freck, make sure he truly knows who runs things around here, and it ain't, no disrespect intended, that little dandy, Norville Cutler.

His and Norville's silent partner would not take lightly to such a situation.

He squirmed a little at the thought.

Not from guilt; he hadn't minded taking the man's money at all. Especially when it was clear there were tons of it to go around.

He squirmed because he wished, devoutly wished, he knew what the man looked like. So far it had only been a voice on the telephone, a special delivery package, an unexpected deposit in one of his bank accounts. Norville, of course, didn't give a damn as long as the checks didn't bounce. He, on the other hand, liked to know who he was dealing with. Want to look into a pair of eyes, see where the lies hid, see where the truth kind of bent and twisted a little.

One of these days, he decided, not too strenuously; one of these days he was going to demand a meeting.

He laughed aloud.

"Jasper, don't you have better things to do than looking to behead the golden goose?"

Like, it was probably time too to see what could be done about the Reverend Baylor's increasingly disturbing Sunday sermons. That Bible wimp had been listening to Whittaker too much. Jasper didn't think it would take too much to back him down, but—

He straightened, and scowled.

"Well . . . hellfire," he muttered. "Speak of the goddamn devil."

Lyman Baylor's car came to a lurching halt right down below him. A minute later he climbed out of the car and hustled across the street, right into the *Weekly* office.

"Whittaker," he said quietly, "you know what's good for you, you'll keep your damn big mouth shut.

And he sighed when the preacher soon stormed outside and marched back across the road, ignoring a van that nearly ran him down, nimbly dodging a scatter of kids sweeping by on their bikes. He held his breath until Baylor vanished inside the sheriff's office, expelled it in a silent whistle. The call would come soon enough, Oakman asking what he should do; meantime, there was a breather. A chance for him to think a little.

The wind picked up, strong now; he could almost feel the chill through the glass. The shadows were growing long, the day's warmth slipping away with the sun. He watched as a few leaves blew over the rooftops across the way, spilled out of the alleys and tumbled into the street. The traffic light swayed.

A faint shiver; he rolled his shoulders.

Directly opposite was the barbershop, an old-fashioned,

sit-in-a-high-leather-chair-and-let-the-man-do-his-work place, not one of those new-style salon things that catered to both men and women. He loved that barbershop. A place where a man could unwind, let old Farelli or his son do all the talking while you nodded and dozed and forgot the world for a while. Jasper touched at his thick dark hair, thinking maybe it was time for a trim. Time to pick up on a little gossip.

He blinked.

The roof, like all the roofs on the island, was slightly peaked to let the rainwater rush off. A lot of leaves up there now, spinning and lifting. Same with the gift shop just to the left, with the drugstore between it and the newspaper.

He frowned, not quite sure what he was looking at.

The wind picked up in a brief roar, enough to startle him, enough to send all those leaves flying.

One plastered itself against the window, and Jasper stared at it, amused, studying its underside, the points and the veins. Watched as it was joined by another. By a dozen. By a score of them, and more. Pinned by the wind to the glass-feather panes. Light dimmed in the office, and movement made him look up, and look behind him.

The shadows of the leaves trembled on the walls around him, magnified, shifting.

Crawling, he thought, and abruptly laughed aloud.

When he looked back at the window he could barely see outside. The leaves, dead and all colors, left hardly any glass uncovered, and above the wind he could hear them as they vibrated against the panes, shifting as though seeking firmer purchase, seeking a way in.

He could hear them.

Scratching.

His imagination, of course, yet he couldn't help stretching out a hand toward them, feeling the cold seep through the glass, almost feeling how brittle, how frail the leaves were.

Scratching.

He pushed the chair back slowly, not stopping until it bumped up against the desk.

Scratching.

The room nearly dark.

He licked his lips, tried to smile, wished someone were in here with him, just to see what he saw. Hear what he heard.

All those leaves, and their faint, insistent scratching.

Suddenly a handful fell away right in front of his eyes, and the light that broke the wall nearly blinded him. He put up a hand to shade his eyes, realizing the wind had calmed, watching as the leaves skittered down the panes and vanished below the sill, leaving only a few behind.

It took a long time.

And when a soft voice said, "Mayor Cribbs?" he yelled and jumped to his feet, tripped over a leg of the chair and nearly fell against the window.

"Mayor Cribbs?"

He stared dumbly at his desk, panting, touching his face with the fingertips of one hand, while the other shook so hard he had to clamp it against his chest.

The intercom; it was the intercom.

"Sweet Jesus on His throne," he whispered, and dropped heavily into the chair, leaned heavily against the desk, and fumbled a bit before he pressed the right button.

"Mayor?"

"Yes, Mrs. Grummond," he answered, acutely aware of how high his voice sounded.

"There's a call for you, Mr. Mayor," his secretary said. "Sheriff Oakman."

"I'll call him back, take a message."

"He says it's important."

"Take a message, Milli. I'm busy right now."

He took his finger away and placed his hand on the blotter, pressing down until the trembling stopped. Breathing deeply. Smiling uncertainly. Staring at the desk because he didn't want to look at the wall and see a small shadow there, crawling slowly toward the ceiling.

Toward him.

A good ten minutes later he leaned back, shook his head, and decided to call it a day. There was nothing that would keep him in this office one second longer. He'd call Mary Gwen, have her meet him in the restaurant of her choice, and spend the next few hours listening to her gab and fret and complain and eat, while he did his best to drink himself to sleep.

Once decided, he relaxed.

A touch of the real world, that's what he needed. The perfect solution. Maybe he'd even tell Mary Gwen about it, let her laugh at him a little, make a little fun.

Just what he needed.

Briskly he rubbed his hands together. He adjusted his jacket, smoothed his hair, made sure there was nothing on the desk that needed signing, and stood. Posed for a moment for an invisible audience, practiced a smile, and went to the coat tree next to the grandfather clock, where he took down his topcoat, draped it over his shoulder, and opened the office door, not once looking back at the glass-feather window.

An automatic touch to his breast pocket, and he scowled when he realized he'd left his good pen on his desk.

"Damn," he muttered, turned and headed back.

Stopping halfway across the room when he stepped on something, looked down, and backed away.

There was a leaf on the carpet.

Dead, and trembling.

5

Casey sat on the front porch, cigarette in his right hand, legs stretched out and crossed at the ankles, and wondered, not for the first time, what it was about this island that allowed such warm afternoons so late in the year, yet let the temperature take a relative nosedive once the sun had set over the mainland. Maybe it had something to do with the Gulf Stream, maybe something to do with the water that remained warm most of the year and kept the sea breeze warm as well. Or maybe, he thought with a lopsided smile, he didn't know what the hell he was talking about.

The house's shadow had finally reached across Midway Road, the sun low enough not to reflect in the windows on the other side of the street. The air was still. Lightly chilled. With no inhabited houses nearby, the neighborhood was dark, and silent. Motionless.

It was getting on time for supper, but he wasn't about to move. Despite an ice pack and some chewed aspirin, his shoulder was still sore to the touch, and darkly bruised, but not nearly as bruised as his ego. He hadn't stopped beating himself over the head since he'd returned, a constant berating for being so blind stupid as to not see that car, and for practically running away when all Reverend Baylor had wanted to do was lend him a hand.

Stupid; really, really stupid.

Not to mention the still churning anger over what had happened in the *Weekly* office, and afterward, with that smug deputy sheriff. If he had had any brains at all, had had a lick of sense, he would have insisted the deputy go check on the old man, not taking no for an answer. And he should have gone with him, instead of taking off like that. Hell, for that matter, he should have stayed with Hull for a while, let the guy vent a little if he'd needed to, or checked the man himself to be sure he wasn't hurt.

But he had left—don't get involved—he had given his conscience a pat on the head by dutifully talking to the law, then stopped at the liquor store for his beer, and compounded his nonsense by good God almighty hitting a car backing out a driveway. A minister's car, yet.

"A *minister's* car," he whispered, and shook his head.

Some days it just didn't pay to get out of bed.

Some days it just didn't pay to get half-baked ideas like testing himself to see if he could still function around people.

Some days it was hardly worth taking a breath at all.

"Oh, now, there you go," he said sourly to the self-pity waiting to pounce. He had had enough of that already, and except in a dream now and then, he'd hoped he'd gotten over it.

Right, he thought; sure.

He recognized the signs: the time of day, the stillness of the air, the retreat of the sun . . . the darkening of his mood. A beer would go down good about now, but he held off deliberately. One now, when he really craved it, and it would be one a little while later, one a little while after that, another and another until the fridge was empty, and he was crawling into bed.

A hangover in the morning, and it wouldn't stop the dreams.

Tempting, though; awfully damn tempting.

lying in a hospital bed a thousand miles north, bones broken and muscles torn and drugs to soothe the pain, but Lord there wasn't enough to prevent him from seeing that ghost-white car gliding out of the fire, the dead in the streets, the explosions and the rain and the open mouths, screaming, the open mouths, demanding answers, the children . . . the dying children . . . and listening to the sound of hoofbeats on the road.

He crushed the cigarette under his heel and closed his eyes. Only for a moment.

The sputtering sound of a small motor made him sit up; the twilight bright beam of a single headlamp made him wonder; and when he saw what it was, he couldn't help a grin.

An old red scooter, and it moved very slowly.

With a silent groan, he pushed stiffly out of the chair and opened the screen door, leaned against the frame with his arms folded, and watched as Junior Raybourn putted up the road, passed the house and, to Casey's mild bemusement, made a slow wide turn before parking at the curb at the foot of the walk. Junior wore a screaming red helmet, aviator goggles, an old high school football jacket, heavy pants, heavy boots, and padding on his knees and elbows.

But he never wore gloves.

He cut off the engine and sat for a few seconds, head cocked to one side as if listening to the echoes. Bouncing slightly on his seat. Fingers dancing across the handlebars as though he were playing a piano.

Casey watched, but said nothing. He knew enough not to speak yet, because Junior didn't much care for conversation; it confused him sometimes, and sometimes made him cry—no tears, just pursed trembling lips and a hound dog sadness around his large dark eyes. He was, as far as Casey could tell, Senior Raybourn's only child, if a man nearing forty could still be called a child. He had no idea what had happened to the mother or what had caused Junior's condition; he only knew that Junior and his father lived on Draper, the street behind Casey, one house down, and that Junior worked at Betsy's and sometimes ran errands on that scooter of his. Never traveling more than twenty-five miles an hour, hugging the curb all the way.

Not once in two years had they ever come calling.

On the other hand, he had never gone to their place either, or even, when he was at the Teach, passed a word with the old man.

Finally Junior stood and very carefully took off his helmet and goggles and placed them on the seat. His hair was short and shot with white, his features broad, his skin much darker than his father's. Long legs, long torso; a whippet of a man, and just as skittish. A second while he examined the sky, then pulled a bright red wool cap from his jacket pocket, and pulled it on. Smoothing it with his palms. Folding it up in front and measuring with his fingers to be sure it was even all around. Finally he unlatched the rear compartment and took out a large paper shopping bag, stared at it for a moment, then clasped it gingerly to his chest. When he walked slowly toward the house, his gait was awkward, small steps, then widening his stance as if he were a fat man distributing shifting weight.

Halfway to the house he realized Casey was there, and he stopped. Blinked very slowly, his lower lip out.

It took Casey a while to realize what was wrong—him. Standing at the top of the steps, practically looming over the yard. A smile to dispel menace, and he slipped his hands into his pockets and stepped down to the walk.

"Evening, Mr. Raybourn." Friendly, and soft.

Junior nodded quickly and hurried the rest of the way, stopping just before he collided with Casey. He held out the bag, nodded again when Casey took it without looking inside. He didn't have to; he could smell herbs, spices, chicken.

"Mrs. Nazario," Junior said, looking at the sky, not Casey. His left arm was bent so his fingers could stroke his left shoulder. "She said. She said I should tell you." He shifted his weight awkwardly from foot to foot. Nervous now, afraid he'd forget. "She said. She said sorry she was that way with you. Today. At the place where I work." He swallowed hard, sniffed, fingers at his shoulder looking as if they were plucking guitar strings. She said you was to eat that." He nodded at the bag. "For supper."

"Well, thank you, Mr. Raybourn."

Junior grinned. "She said. She told me. This week is Thanksgiving, you know."

"I do know that, Mr. Raybourn, yes."

"She said you was, if you could, you was to come to Betsy's for dinner." He grinned again, still staring at the sky, fingers leaving his shoulder, strumming the air. "Thanksgiving dinner. We have real special food then. She said. You was to come. That's—" He frowned, bit down on his lower lip. "Day after tomorrow."

"Well, you know, that's very kind of her, Mr. Raybourn. I'll—"

"No," he said, shaking his head rapidly. "No, my name is Junior. Call me Junior. Mr. Raybourn. He's my daddy, don't work with me, I work all by myself. I got the scooter, you know. It's Junior's scooter. My name is Junior."

"Okay, sure. Then you call me Casey, okay?"

Junior shifted his weight again, scanned the sky, the roof, nodding as he thought about it. "Okay."

Casey smiled. "Great. And thank Mrs. Nazario for me, will you please?"

"Yes, sir, I surely will." Junior took a step back. "I have to take my scooter now. Suppertime."

Casey nodded, and held out his hand.

Junior stared at it, fearfully, suspiciously, before reaching out to take it with a firm grip. He shook it once, nodded sharply . . . and suddenly moaned soft and deep in his throat.

No, Casey thought; Lord, no.

A brief intense blast of cold, followed immediately by heat close to furnace fire.

Junior snatched his hand away and rubbed it hard against his chest, a wide-eyed stare while his lips worked, a tic in one cheek, one eye blinking.

"Junior—"

"Scary," Junior said and hustled away. "Scary."

Casey didn't try to stop him, didn't try to explain because he wasn't sure himself what had happened. Only knew that he had felt that cold before, and that heat; only knew that some had claimed, in the life he had left behind, that he had used it to bring a man—

"No," he whispered angrily, and went back inside, only half listening to the scooter fade down the road. The next time he saw him, he would tell Junior a good one, the best lie he could come up with that would make sense to the man. Or maybe he wouldn't say anything at all. Ignore it. Forget it.

"Son of a bitch," he said harshly to the empty house. Not angrily now; wearily. "Son of a bitch. Just . . . leave me alone."

He ate the meal, he had a beer, he walked upstairs to fetch a fresh pack of cigarettes from his bedroom and stopped in the hall, looked into the storeroom.

The closet door was open.

Not just a little.

It was open wide.

3

1

Deep autumn; Wednesday; early afternoon.

Reed Turner sits on a bench in a riverside park. Not
much of a park actually; barely wider than the road that
runs behind it, and high enough above him that drivers
probably couldn't even see him there, under huge trees
whose limbs are almost as fat as their trunks. One day
before Thanksgiving, and his jacket is folded on the seat
beside him. Crazy. It's crazy. Just a week ago he and Cora
had been in Atlanta, and though it wasn't exactly cold
there, it had been damn chilly. Here, not all that far away,
it felt warm enough to be late spring. Crazy.

The South hadn't turned out to be anything like he'd
thought, like he'd read about, like he'd seen on TV.

But then, nothing was anymore.

He scratches a cheek that needs a shave; after a vigorous
push through tangled hair that needs washing, he spreads
his arms along the back of the bench, stretches out his legs,
watches the sluggish water drift past him, toward the sea.
He's been here for almost two hours and hasn't seen a sin-

gle boat come up from the port at the river's mouth. Yesterday, at this same spot, a cabin cruiser had grumbled west, half a dozen people on deck, holding drinks, listening to music, dressed as if they were going to dinner at a restaurant so fancy he couldn't begin to imagine what it looked like inside.

Cora had sneered at them, telling him they were obviously pretending nothing was wrong.

"They should see what we've seen," she'd said bitterly. "Stupid bastards, they don't care."

But maybe, he thinks now, they have seen and they don't want to see anymore.

Atlanta had not been fun. A week before they arrived, the city had been torn up by outsider gangs hunting for fresh turf. It had taken what was left of the Georgia National Guard and some help from Alabama to drive them out, blood and bodies left behind, and every paper he read made some kind of hand-wringing reference to the Civil War and General Sherman. They'd left after only one day, afraid of the roadblocks and checkpoints, the uniforms, and the stares.

Savannah, so far, has been quiet.

It is, he thinks, like being in another time. The old houses, the once in a while passing of a riverboat, the trees large and heavy-limbed, the cobblestones, the way the people he'd talked to so far didn't seem to care about the skirmishes in eastern Europe, the war in the Pacific, the wars he'd stopped counting in Africa and the Middle East.

For that matter, he doesn't much care now, either. He has more important things to worry about.

He thinks . . . he fears that Cora is going to leave him.

Since the middle of September she's been making comments about the futility of their search. Not her usual sarcasm; bitter now, and venomous. The last time they believed they were on the right track was last spring, early April. Since then, they've been going on the strength of his dreams. His dreams, not hers.

Last night she said, "Walking on water? You saw him walking on water? Tell me again, Turner. One more time."

He didn't want to. He recognized the tone, the expression, the set of her lips. Belief turned to doubt had finally curdled into mockery.

"I don't know where I am," he told her anyway, "but I'm standing beside this huge bird, and I can smell stuff—fish and oil and . . . and sea air and . . . and like it smells around mudflats, you know? I'm looking over a hill of some kind, really low, and I can see him . . . I know, okay? I know it sounds dumb, but it looks like he's walking on water, out to some kind of island."

He'd glared at her, daring her to make fun, but all she'd done was give him a look—pity or disgust, he couldn't figure out—and walked away, back to the cheesy motel room they'd rented. With, she reminded him, the money she made doing the waitress thing. Her money, not his; his dream, not hers.

He watches the river, eyes half closed. She wants to stop. She's had it, she doesn't care anymore, she wants a place to stay that has more than one room, that has more than a view of a beat-up highway, that doesn't smell of all the people who have slept there before.

He pulls his arms to his sides, grips the edge of the bench seat. Is it his fault there were all those islands out there? How the hell was he supposed to know that? It was why, at her insistence, they had gone inland, to Atlanta. She was sick of the ocean, sick of water, sick of everything that even hinted at something nautical.

And the night they fled the chaos, he had had the dream again, and only with a promise, a swearing, that if they didn't find him by Thanksgiving he'd give it up would she go with him on the road one more time.

Two more days.

When he'd looked at a local map and saw all those islands off the Georgia coast, he'd almost cried.

Two more days, and it'll be over, and he'll lose her,

because after all this time, in spite of his promise, he knows he can't stop.

And she can.

She will.

He sits up, lowers his head, lets his hands dangle between his knees, feels the sun on the back of his neck, and thinks, angrily, Jesus Christ, it's practically winter, why the hell isn't it cold?

Nothing's right anymore. Not even the weather.

His eyes close. He rocks slowly back and forth. For the first time in months he thinks of his mother, of his nearly always drunk father who never hit him, just pretended he was sober, of the house in Maple Landing, burned to the ground, vanishing into the surrounding forest weed by weed, sapling by sapling. Of his friends, all of them dead; of his family, all of them dead; of the people he didn't really like, all of them dead. Of the houses he's seen here, many of them painted or trimmed with an odd shade of blue—to keep the ghosts away.

It may work for these people; it doesn't work for him.

He rocks back and forth, listening to the river, and the traffic above and behind him.

Suddenly, so suddenly his eyes snap open, he realizes that he's tired. Worse than tired. And he knows this to be true: that without Cora, no matter how he feels, he won't go on.

The chase is over.

That his dreams were probably nothing more than hope born of the ashes of what used to be his life. That Chisholm, as he always had, would somehow make it right.

Funny thing; he probably ought to cry, but he hasn't the strength. What the hell. It's over.

He sits up, takes a deep breath, rubs his eyes with the heels of his hands, stretches until one shoulder pops, picks up a stone and flings it into the water, wonders if Cora will stick around when he tells her.

When he hears her footsteps on the grass behind him, he can't decide if he should smile when he tells her, or be solemn. When she touches his shoulder, he says, "Cora, we have to talk," as he stands and turns.

And sees her face, flushed and bright, and sees the man and woman standing behind her.

"Me first," she says, her voice trembling. "Holy shit, Reed, me first."

2

Junior Raybourn stands motionless in Betsy's kitchen, holding a broom, staring at the oven.

Hector Nazario, stained white apron, thick black hair grey-dusted at the temples, thrice-broken nose, watches him warily, wondering if maybe he should get Gloria in here. Raybourn, he was all right most of the time, but sometimes he acted as if the world wasn't here, and that spooked him.

"Junior," he says quietly.

Junior blinks very slowly and points at the round face of the thermometer fixed to the oven's side. "Mr. Nazario, is that Fahrenheit or centigrade?"

Hector gasps so loudly Junior drops the broom. Its clatter sounds like snapping wood.

"Oh, no," Junior says, fumbling for the broom, backing away at the same time, face contorted as if he's ready to cry. "I'm sorry, Mr. Hector, I'm sorry. Did I say something bad?"

3

Earlier, only a few minutes past noon; under a soft blue sky and small wandering clouds and a breeze comfortable in the sun and winter-cool in the shadows:

Cora soon enough grows weary of walking. She's been walking for what seems like hundreds of years, and all she wants to do now is find a place, a cave, a hideout, a *something* that will let her sit down for more than a couple of hours at a time, to lie down for more than one lousy night. She doesn't bother trying to figure out just when the end came; it doesn't make any difference. One day she was working out ways to pick Chisholm out of a zillion people in a city, the next she's ready to pack it in and go . . . away.

Not home.

There is no home.

She's left Reed on the bench, unable to look at him anymore, knowing that he's finally realized she's reached the brink. He'll have to work it out for himself, whatever it is he's going to do. She, however, is done. Finished. Over. Through. It had taken them a while to understand that Chisholm wasn't just running, he was hiding, and whoever first said this was a big country didn't know jack shit, because it wasn't a big country, it was a goddamn monster, and two ordinary people haven't got a hope in hell of finding someone in it if that someone doesn't want to be found.

The worst thing is, she knows Reed will try. He'll really try to pretend that he's given up, too, and that he'll go wherever she wants. In the end, though, he'll still be looking, and she'll know it, and sooner or later they'll have the fight to end all fights, and she'll lose him.

"Oh, God," she whispers. "Oh, my God."

She's left the riverside tourist area, all those old warehouses made into something else, all those new sidewalks and streets and signs and stuff; what she sees now are buildings of brick and wood and a couple of them mixed, and they look as tired as she feels. No tourists here. A guy on a street corner, leaning against a lamppost, drinking out of a brown bag; two guys in the doorway of a barred-window liquor store, arguing quietly; little old ladies, most of them black, hustling with heads up and shopping bags in hand; a few kids cutting school, earphones on, jiving—did they still call it jiving?—to whatever music they have stuck in their pockets; the smell of old beer and old urine and old vomit, exhaust and rubber and once in a while the sickening wash of fresh paint.

No one gives her more than a glance.

It doesn't take a genius to figure out she looks as miserable as they do.

This, she thinks, is a bitch of a way to spend her formative years, and she giggles. Aloud. High-pitched, almost keening.

And still no one looks.

She hesitates, not wanting to go too far, not wanting to get lost. Across the way is a low and clean yellow building whose entrance faces the corner, its windows bricked over, and on the roof a neon cross in blue and red. There's a sign over the door, but she can't read it clearly, Tabernacle of Something Something. Passing it is a tall black man, and a child who barely comes to his waist, colorful bows in her hair. They're laughing, the little girl skipping ahead and waving her arms, then racing back and grabbing the man's hand and holding it for a while before rushing off again, examining store windows or the warped stained plywood where store windows used to be, finding something in the gutter and tossing it away as soon as the man scolds her.

Cora watches, and is surprised to feel something she hadn't felt in a long, long time: envy, and she wonders if Reed ever thinks about Maple Landing, about his family, about their friends. Lately she has, all except for the family part. Tries to anyway, except for the family part, but *he* keeps popping up.

Cora, get supper; Cora, what the hell you doing wearing clothes like that, you look like a slut; Cora, come here, girl, you're in real bad trouble; Cora, come here. Come here, girl, Daddy won't hurt you. Goddamnit, Cora get your ass—

The unexpected blast of a horn makes her jump, eyes wide and a hand to her chest as she realizes she's stepped off the curb, almost into the path of a dusty old car. Reflex brings her free hand up in a screw-you-watch-where-you're-going gesture, but she can't catch a breath as she backpedals to the sidewalk, and she bends over for a moment, hands on her knees, mouth open, gulping and swallowing, glaring at the automobile and wishing, in that same moment, the damn thing had hit her.

Her vision is blurred, not quite tears filling her eyes, but she can see a man leaving the tabernacle, and her mouth opens even wider.

Damn, she thinks; damn.

He's tall, broad, long wavy black hair, dressed in black. By the time she straightens and slaps the tears from her eyes, the man has walked away, moving down the side street, his back to her.

"Oh my God," she whispers, and without thinking, without looking, dashes across the street.

"Hey!" she screams. "Hey, wait up, it's me, Cora!"

At the same time, the car that nearly hit her darts to the curb and a man scrambles out, clinging to the open door. He calls, "Casey! Hey, Casey!" and Cora stumbles to a halt not far behind him.

"Casey! Hey, it's me!"

The big man looks back over his shoulder, puzzled, and Cora sags.

It's not him.

Of course it's not him, you idiot. You think he's gonna show up out of nowhere, out of some stupid yellow for God's sake sidewalk church just because you're feeling sorry for yourself?

The man from the car shrugs an embarrassed apology, the big man in black waves a *no problem*, and Cora decides she'd better head back. Reed is probably worried half to death about her, and she might as well get this it's-over stuff over with. Then the man from the car turns to her, and she can't help herself—she stares.

Wow, she thinks; he looks just like—

"Excuse me," he says, moving toward her slowly. He's tall, lanky, heavy brows and unruly hair. "Did you say your name was Cora?"

She backs up warily. Doesn't nod, doesn't shake her head.

"Cora Bowes?" He stops, glances at the car, looks back at her. "Bowes, is that right? Cora Bowes?"

Far up the street, the little girl laughs, and her father laughs with her.

"Who . . . who wants to know?" she demands.

"I . . ." The man shakes his head, pushes a shock of hair off his brow. "You thought" he jerks a thumb over his shoulder—"you thought that man was Casey Chisholm."

She can barely breathe; she can barely see.

A woman steps out of the car, stares at her over the roof. "John?"

The man holds out a hand, palm up. "I'm not going to hurt you, Cora. But . . . you did think he was Casey, right?"

She nods before she can stop herself.

He smiles, a broad and relieved smile that makes her grin in return. "That," he says, pointing to the woman, "is Lisse Montgomery. My name . . . I'm John Bannock, and if you're really Cora Bowes from New Jersey, then I think you and I have to talk."

4

Deep in the eastern Alabama hills a stout black woman stands in front of a shack whose foundation is a series of cracked and stained cinder blocks. At her feet lies a young man, not much more than a boy, whose skin is cracked and red, pustules covering his face and arms, eyes swollen shut, streaks of dried blood spreading from his nose. In the shack's doorway lies a girl child, naked, skin so taut it seems every bone in her body is trying to break through.

A little boy in a cowboy suit stands in the middle of what used to be a hardscrabble garden. Most of the plants have withered, and when he touches the last one with a finger, it vibrates and snaps, its leaves black-brown before they hit the ground.

"This is boring," Joey says, pushing at his cowboy hat until it hangs down his back by a thin rawhide string.

"I know, child," Eula says, pulling on her white, lace-cuff gloves. "I know."

They look to Susan, who leans against the long white Continental, arms folded across her chest. She watches the sky; she says nothing; but she's frowning.

Red had come by to see her; her, not the others. Met her deep in the woods and told her he had things to do, a couple of things to see to, some arrangements to make.

"What kind of arrangements?"

"Want to make things easier, that's all. Even the odds a little."

She had almost lost her temper. "Even the odds? Against us? What kind of talk is that?"

He had leaned over from his saddle, that awful smile there and gone. "You were beaten once. They were too. Kind of like to make sure that don't happen again."

"But it can't." She had looked fearfully to the sky. "How can it?"

He had straightened, creaking leather, his voice low and deep. "You were beaten," he said again, and there was green fire in his eyes. That smile. She had backed away and watched as that great black horse took Red into the woods.

Now she watches the sky. Frowning. Wondering.

Even the odds a little.

The idea makes her nervous.

5

In the Edward Teach, Ben Pellier is trying to explain to Mariana Cribbs—who is too damn distracting in her tight jeans and a T-shirt that's cut off just above her navel—why he's put a cover over old Peg so early in the day.

"That's silly," the young woman says. Her blond hair is piled in curls and ringlets around her head, something she saw in the movies last week.

Ben figures she's used at least two cans of hair spray to keep it all up there. Has to be; not a single strand has moved since she walked in.

She sashays down to the end of the bar, tries to look up under the bottom of the floral cloth draped over the cage. "He's lonely, Ben. He wants to see his friends." She lifts the cloth a little. "Hey, bird. Hey, Peg. Pretty bird, you want some light?"

Ben says nothing. He waits until Mariana suddenly gives up, dusting her hands on her hips, looking at him with a strained smile. He nods.

She hears.

Old Peg, sitting in his cage.

Squawking softly to himself.

6

John Bannock can't believe his luck. One day before Thanksgiving, and out of an entire city . . . hell, an entire section of the whole entire country, he runs across not just one, but two people searching for Casey Chisholm.

And to make things even more incredible, they just happen to be from where Casey used to live.

Once all the introductions had been made, the exclamations of surprise and shock, he had taken the kids—and they surely weren't much more than that—to the small hotel west of town where he and Lisse had booked a room. He could tell they were hungry, and by the way Lisse had fussed over an impatient Cora, he had known they were nearing the end of their rope. A decent meal was in order, some peace, some normality, so they had sat in the restaurant, and he watched their reluctance, and their suspicions, give way to the temptations of the menu.

As they ate, he noticed that Reed was the one who told most of their story, while Cora was the one who kept asking questions he didn't yet want to answer. An interesting pair. He couldn't figure out how they'd stuck together for so long.

The only time, in fact, that Cora's smile seemed genuine was when Lisse called him Prez, and the girl had said, "That's it! You look like Lincoln a little. You know that? Bet you're sick of hearing it, too, right? Boy. Hey, Reed, doesn't he look like Abe Lincoln?"

By the time their second helping of dessert had been cleared away, however, Cora had grown silent and Reed hadn't done a very successful job of trying to hide the yawns that threatened to split his cheeks wide open. Without asking, John had booked a second room, hustled them off without much more than perfunctory debate, and after splashing a little cold water on his face, brought Lisse to the hotel bar, where they found a booth shadowed enough to be private, close enough to the bar itself so he could keep an eye on the large-screen TV near the center of the back wall.

He can't believe his luck.

Lisse, a sweater draped over her shoulders, turns a mint julep slowly in her hands without picking it up. "They never make them right," she complains mildly, nodding at her drink. "You get outside the Deep South, they look awful pretty but they taste awful."

"I thought we were in the Deep South."

She snorts. "John, you got a lot to learn. Louisiana is Deep South. This place . . . it's way too North. Too many people from the North living here."

He smiles, touches her arm.

She is luck too. Fate, maybe. Maybe Destiny. She had been a waitress in a New Orleans hotel when they'd met, and somehow—even now he couldn't really explain it—they'd ended up traveling together. Nearly dying together. She could have left him any time over the past couple of years, but she hadn't. And that's something you just don't question.

A trio plays desultory jazz in a corner—bass, drums, keyboard—but not loudly enough to muffle the TV, which shows news footage of a riot outside an arena in a city he didn't catch. Cops and kids. And the kids seem to be dressed pretty much the same; a uniform of sorts. Like an army.

"I've been thinking, Prez," Lisse says, sitting back, arms extended to keep hold of her glass.

He looks at her and rolls his eyes, moans, looks to the ceiling, and mouths a fake prayer. Looks back at the auburn hair dusting her shoulders, curls and waves that shift and shimmer in the dim light.

"Oh, hush," she says lightly. "We got those kids now, we got to start making a plan."

"I thought we had a plan."

"Oh, some plan—look in every pissant town and holler in the universe for a guy who clearly doesn't want to be found." She inhales, sighs. "Case you hadn't noticed, it's getting on toward the end of the year."

He nods; he's noticed.

"So I'm thinking, tomorrow we find a place that'll feed us Thanksgiving dinner until we're nearly dead. Then, on Friday, we check those islands out there," and she waves vaguely eastward. "I mean, how many of them can there be?"

"You believe Reed's dream then?"

She looks at him as if he ought to know better. "I believe yours, right?"

A shrug—okay, you win.

"I'm just hoping he isn't somewhere in the Caribbean, you know what I mean?"

That thought had occurred to him once, but he doesn't think so now, and tells her so. The only explanation he has is that it doesn't feel right, Casey being somewhere that far away. It just doesn't . . . feel right. Not, he realizes sourly, that he's been exactly one hundred percent on the mark thus far. If he had been, they wouldn't be here now, watching a battle on TV and drinking mint juleps.

He almost laughs.

A group of men come in, boisterous, name tags on their suit jackets, swarming the bar, convincing the bartender that the game, whatever it is, is on another channel. The battle is quickly replaced by a commercial, but the noise level remains high, and Lisse slips closer, one hand fussing at her hair, twirling a strand around a finger. Nothing coy; just a habit.

"You didn't tell them about you," she says.

"Nope."

She bumps him with her shoulder. "You afraid they'll run off?"

"They'll think I'm nuts."

"Oh, for . . ." She takes a long drink, makes a face, and pushes her glass away. "John, they have been on the road for nearly three years, looking for a man they know did something special. Something kind of like what you did. What in God's name makes you think they're gonna think you're nuts?"

He doesn't answer.

He can't answer.

Even now, all this time later, he wakes up in the middle of the night and sees his young son on the back of a huge palomino, a little kid in a cowboy suit who isn't a kid at all, trying to ride him down. Trample him. Kill him. That the boy was adopted doesn't make much of a difference in the middle of the night—Joey is his son, and his son tried to kill him.

"I've been thinking something else," she says, briefly leaning her head against his shoulder.

"Spare me."

"Hush."

"You're thinking in threes, I'll bet."

She nods, and winces when one of the name tag men yells at the jazz trio to shut it down, are they drunk and blind, can't they see there's an important game going on?

"If Casey is one, and I'm another, and we're talking about Death and Famine . . . who's the third?"

She hesitates before answering, "I've got a better one for you: If there's three, and it's what we think it is, who's the fourth?"

7

"Lady Harp?"

"Yes, dear?"

"Do we really have to go?"

"Yes, dear, I'm afraid we do."

"But I like it here. The school's neat, and Star's got a boyfriend, and Momma, she even goes out again."

"I know, dear, but we have to go."

They stand outside a small Missouri cottage, the girl scowling, the woman searching the stars for something to guide her.

"I like it here," Moonbow says softly.

Beatrice Harp can't respond to that. She likes it here, too. After all the driving, all the hunting for something to which she could not put a name, it was nice to settle down for a while, to pretend all was well, that once the new smallpox had run its course, all, in fact, would be well.

If it hadn't been for the fighting, she might have actually come to believe it.

But whatever it was that had driven her and her late husband to help a young man fight his demons in the desert, whatever that had been had returned, and she could no more ignore it than she could ignore the way the moon looked bloated and ready to burst.

"Tomorrow's Thanksgiving," Moonbow says miserably. "We should at least have Thanksgiving dinner."

"We will."

"At a diner or something, right?"

"I don't know. But we'll have that dinner if it means so much to you."

The girl shrugs. Maybe it does, maybe it doesn't, but Lady Harp should at least give them a chance to find out.

A movement at the front door turns them around.

"Momma?"

In the doorway Jude Levin stands in her nightgown, her veil still on, her hands twisting the fabric as if trying to keep it on and yank it off at the same time.

"Momma?"

"There's a man," says Jude anxiously. "I couldn't sleep. every time I closed my eyes I saw a man."

Beatrice keeps her gaze on the stars. She wonders which man Jude is talking about—the one who seems so awfully big and awfully dark, or the one who rides the horse whose hooves give off tiny fire.

8

"Cora, please, I'm begging you—go to sleep."

"Aren't you the least bit curious about this guy? For all we know he could be a pervert or something."

"Come on, you think he's a pervert?"

"Well . . . no."

"Then go to sleep."

"He never answered my questions."

"He was trying to feed you a decent meal, Cora. The first decent meal we've had in I don't know how long. And these beds are the nicest beds we've slept in for months. You looking a gift horse in the mouth?"

"I'm looking, Reed, to find out what the hell's going on here."

"Cora."

"Okay, okay."

"Don't okay. Lie down. Sleep."

"Okay, okay, I'm lying down. You happy now? I'm lying down."

"But you're not sleeping."

"Well, how can I sleep? You're talking all the time."

"Cora—"

"For God's sake, Reed, how many times do I have to say I'm sorry?"

"But—"

"Shut up, Reed. Just . . . shut up."

9

Sheriff Vale Oakman likes to visit the harbor at night. Water slapping softly against hulls and pilings, lights from nearby houses reflected in the water, the hollow sound of his shoes on the planks of a pier. The smell of salt and fish, brine and oil, damp wood and old paint. A boat moves cautiously around the Hook into the bay, running lights like the lights of a large Christmas tree. From across the water, at the base of the hill, he hears music, splashing, and someone laughing, wonders who'd be so stupid, or drunk, to be swimming this late at night, this late in the season.

He makes his way past the fancy boats whose owners are preparing to put them in dry dock; he listens to a radio in a houseboat, not quite muffling the sounds of someone having a damn good time in bed; he hunches his shoulders against a gust of wind that slips through cracks in his leather jacket, ruffles the heavy fur collar, makes his nose run.

There is a small gap then, one that requires that he leave the long boardwalk and take a few steps across a rock-and-sand beach raked clear of debris. The next pier belongs to the working men. The fishermen. The charters. The boats not nearly as sleek or large or smelling of money. Five minutes, taking his time, and he reaches the berth for the *Lucky Deuce*, a boat he figures has about two more seasons in her before she sinks to the bottom before she leaves the bay.

Rick Jordan sits on a butterfly cleat near the bow, Ronnie Hull standing beside him, both in fleece-lined denim jackets and baseball caps, Rick smoking a cigarette, Ronnie with a beer in her hand.

"Very romantic," Oakman says with a smile.

Ronnie looks at him, startled, not smiling at all, not pleased to be interrupted. "I suppose you came all this way just to tell me you've arrested the Teagues, right? For all that crap they're doing to my father and the paper?"

The sheriff shakes his head. "Sorry, Ronnie."

She looks away across the water; he doesn't exist for her any longer.

"What's up, Sheriff?" Rick says.

"Want to remind you it's your time in the Tower. Four days, starting Monday."

Rick stares evenly at him. "You came all this way just to tell me that?"

The boat in the bay sounds a horn and is answered by one on shore, half a mile up.

"I like the walk," Oakman answers truthfully. "Cool, clear night, all those stars, a shooting star or two. Nothing better, right?"

"Except," Rick says sourly around his cigarette, "if you're stuck in the damn Tower."

The bay that's formed by Camoret's southern hook is usually fairly calm unless the weather is particularly fierce.

The Hook itself is higher than the rest of the island by several hundred feet and is heavily wooded. A south wind generally blows straight across, and what slips down the steep hillside is weakened by the trees it has to pass. The houses there, in several tiers formed by several narrow roads, are large. Expensive. Each on at least a two-acre plot. A splendid view of the mile-wide bay, the white beaches below, the docks that moor the boats and yachts that belong to the houses.

No one lives along the top of the ridge. Even if the land were wide enough to hold a house, building there would invite certain disaster from hurricanes and winter storms, but there's a watch tower there, in the middle, a steel-and-wood lattice beneath a round metal cabin open on all sides from waist-high to the eaves of the conical roof. The volunteers who work there in six-hour shifts are hired and paid by the town, not the state, to look for fire and to track storms when the alert has gone out. Not half bad in spring and summer, a bitch of a job when even the Gulf Stream can't blunt the worst of the cold.

At the start of every season, it's the sheriff's job to round up the volunteers and set the rotation. In late autumn, in winter, that meant the fishermen, and the shopkeepers who close down until spring—those, that is, who don't flee the island for someplace warmer. And anyone else who happens to feel the pull of civic duty and the chance of adventure.

Rick snaps his cigarette into the water. "I'll be there," he says at last.

"Good. Thanks."

"No problem."

There's nothing more to say, and he walks away, hands in his pockets, listening to the water. The boat is still out there, its lights smaller as it heads toward its berth. An airliner flies over, high enough to be little more than a speeding star that leaves a rumbling behind it as it heads for the coast.

"Sheriff."

He stops. It's Ronnie.

"One more thing happens to my father, or the paper, I'm going to the state."

He doesn't turn. "No need, Ronnie."

"He was nearly killed. If it hadn't been for that Chisholm guy, he would have been killed."

Oakman does turn then. "Tell me, Ronnie—if all this stuff is going on, why doesn't he file a report? I can't do much if he doesn't file a report."

"Reverend Baylor did."

"But your father denied it. Specifically said it was all a misunderstanding." He walks away. "Get him to stand up, Ronnie. Get him to do more than blow hot air in those editorials of his, and I'll see what I can do."

He keeps walking, a sudden churn of acid in his gut making him wince. One more year, he thinks; one more year and I'm out of this job and off this island. He'd even spent half the day showing Verna and Salter those Arizona brochures.

"Jeez, Vale, why Arizona?"

He had pointed at all the photographs. "Look closely, Verna. You see any damn water?"

Deputy Salter, face covered with enough freckles to make him look diseased, told about a cousin who had moved there and near died from the heat. "Dry heat, Sheriff. Not like we got here. Sucks the water right outta your body, leaves you looking like a mummy."

Oakman had directed a pointed look at his own hefty build and spread his arms wide. "Jesus, Dwight, you think I'm worried about losing a few pounds? No water, weight loss, sounds like hog heaven to me."

He doesn't hear Ronnie's footsteps until she's grabbed his arm and yanks him around.

"Well, tell you what, *Sheriff*," she says, making his title sound like an obscene curse, "the next time Stump

Teague or any of his brothers walks into my place of business, I'm going to shoot first and file a report later, you hear me?"

"Now, Ronnie, no call—"

"I'm going to kill him, Sheriff. I'm telling you right now I'm going to kill that little snake before he kills my father."

10

The living room is spare. An old couch and an easy chair face an old television set, a table between them that holds an ash tray; a brass floor lamp in the corner, faded prints on the walls, faded carpet on the floor. Against the back wall a low bookcase, filled with magazines and books and three different Bibles, all of them well used.

Senior Raybourn has taken some time off; Ben didn't give him any trouble, told him to take as much time as he needed. Senior appreciated that because something's wrong with his son, something he can't figure out. It would be easier if the boy would talk, but Junior won't come out of his bedroom to explain, has been there since last night. He sits on his bed and rocks back and forth, humming softly, left hand at his shoulder, fingers weaving the air. As far as the old man can tell, his son hasn't been hurt, no bruises or scratches, but nothing Senior has done has made the boy speak, and now he paces the living room, gnawing lightly at his lower lip.

Please, Lord, he prays; please, Lord.

All Hector told him was that Junior had come back from a delivery, had said something remarkable about some thermometer in the luncheonette's kitchen, then wouldn't do any more work, only whisper-pleaded for his father.

The delivery was to the big man who lives in the house on Midway Road, off right and behind Senior's backyard.

Senior wants to be angry, but what's the point? He's old,

he can't fight, and that man is a giant, could swat him down like a fly.

Please, Lord.

The last time he had seen Junior like this, it was years ago, when they had been walking along the beach and a whale breached out beyond the jetty. Scared the poor boy half to death, gave him fits and nightmares; he wouldn't eat for two days, wet his pants, wet his bed. The clinic doctor—damn toad Alloway with his thick glasses and fat lips, eyes that looked like a fish about to die—he couldn't do nothing for the boy, started talking about sending him away, put him in a place where people knew about things like this. Senior had never talked so hard and fast in his life, finally convinced the doc that he could take care of his son better than any stranger. Alloway, reluctantly, finally agreed, and Senior had prayed and cleaned and held his son and it wasn't long before he was back to himself.

He wasn't so sure now, though, he could handle another time like that. He was old. His back wasn't so good anymore, his knuckles ached after working all day, and his eyes weren't so good either.

If anyone found out Junior was this way again, they'd take him away for sure.

They'd take him away, and Senior would die.

Please, Lord, please.

A footstep in the hallway stopped the pacing. He turned just as Junior reached the doorway, stood there looking around until he saw his father.

"Daddy?"

"What is it, son? Are you all right? What is it?"

"Scary."

Senior swallowed the urge to cry. "What is, boy? What's scary? What that man do to you, huh? That man do something to you, son?"

Junior shook his head quickly, shifted his weight from foot to foot, then crossed the room to the bookcase, hands on hips, scanning the shelves.

Senior closed his eyes briefly. "Junior."

Junior picked up a magazine and sat on the couch, flipped the pages front to back, looked up and smiled. "I like this," he said.

"I know, son. Pretty pictures."

Junior shook his head, His lips moved for several seconds before he said, "No, Daddy, pretty words."

"Junior . . ." Please, Lord, give me strength. "Junior. Son." He dropped into his chair, did his best to keep his old eyes from tearing up. Gripped his knees with his hands to keep the fingers from trembling. "Son, words aren't pretty, not like the pictures. You can't look at them like that, son."

"But they say pretty things, Daddy."

Oh, Lord.

"Junior . . . Junior, how do you know that? You can't hardly read."

And Junior said, "Yes, I can, Daddy. Sure, I can. Every word. You want to hear?"

11

Norville Cutler stands by the register in the eastbound Last Stop, opening and closing the drawer. He can hear the sea trying to tear at the barriers between it and the building. Can feel the building shudder slightly when the waves are high.

One light overhead.

No lights outside.

Not a car or truck has passed in at least an hour, in either direction.

The fish mounted on the walls seem larger, their eyes not so dead, not so black.

He should be home now, listening to Mandy taunting him from upstairs, her voice husky as she tells him what she's wearing, or what she's not wearing, what she's going to do to him once he gets into the bedroom. Or the hall. Or the top of the stairs. He should be home, but he doesn't need the distraction. He needs to think. He needs to think hard, because he's beginning to feel it's all on the edge, ready to fall one way or the other, and he doesn't like the feeling that it's going to fall the wrong way, come apart before he can do anything about it.

Nothing specific, not really.

Just a feeling, and after all these years, his feelings, his instincts have seldom led him wrong.

The farce with Hull and Chisholm was a sign of it, he was sure. That should have been a done deal, no problems, a simple matter of a few well-placed bruises as a taste of what might be in the old man's future. But his boys screwed it up, and now he has to worry what Hull is going to put in the next edition. He had no doubts—there would be another edition, no matter what he tried.

A shade less than six weeks to go; he needs assurances nothing else will go wrong.

Trouble was, there was only him and Jasper, and Jasper was so damn sure there was nothing wrong at all that there absolutely had to be something out there aiming to gum it all up.

Cutler doesn't consider himself a superstitious man, yet he never deliberately tempts the Fates either. That would be stupid. It's like going to church once in a while. Cover your ass. Just in case. You never know.

So when things go without a hitch for as long as this deal has, he can't help himself; he just has to worry. Not because there's bound to be a disaster, but because the folks involved tend to grow complacent, and that's when serious mistakes are made. Law of averages, he once told Jasper; it's the law of averages.

He isn't sure yet how big a mistake Teague's failure is, but he feels he has to do something, and do it soon. Just in case.

He closes the cash register drawer.

He opens it.

He decides to get hold of Teague and tell him to hold off on what they'd planned for Senior Raybourn. Give it another week, maybe two. That would be cutting it awfully close, but everything else should be in place by then, and if Senior doesn't sell . . . hell, ain't no one around here gonna miss a fat old cook and his halfwit son.

The drawer slams shut.

He listens to the sea, and he smiles.

Hell, if the ocean hasn't gotten to him after all these years, why in God's name should he be worried about some old fart's newspaper that isn't even heavy enough these days to kill a damn fly. He's got no proof, and Jasper keeps reminding him they can always shut him down with a good old lawsuit.

A laugh.

A shake of his head.

A puzzled frown when he hears something moving across the gravel parking lot in front. He moves away from the display case toward the window, wondering if he should get the gun in the register drawer, gets halfway across the room when the door opens, the wind slams inside and sets the light to shaking, and he sees someone standing on the threshold.

"Closed," he says. "Come back tomorrow."

"Don't think so."

It's an old man, kind of lean, wearing tired old jeans and scuffed old boots, an open vest with some kind of Indian designs on it, a low-crown western hat tied loosely under the chin by a beaded string, and his hair is in for God's sake braids that hang down his chest.

"Mr. Cutler?" The man smiles. A quick smile, here and gone. Not much else to see beneath the hat's brim.

"Who wants to know? I told you we're closed." He looks out the window, up and down the causeway. "Jesus, man, where's your car? You walk the hell out here?"

That smile again.

Cutler wishes the guy would move closer; he can't see

much of his face, just that flash of a smile. He clears his throat. "Look, if you're a salesman, I ain't buying."

"I ain't selling, friend," the man answers. "But I sure could use some of your help."

He takes a step in—the sharp ring of spurs—closes the door behind him, and there's nothing inside now but the sound of the sea, and the light above their heads almost too dim to cast a shadow. Shimmering a little, making the dead fish look as if they're trying to twist off the walls.

"Got a proposition for you, Mr. Cutler. Something I think just might ease your troubled mind."

Cutler wants to laugh, wants to throw this geezer out on his ass, wants to get home to Mandy and whatever's she's planning for him tonight, because for no reason at all, right now the last place he wants to be is in this place, right here.

With the grizzled old man in the Indian vest.

"I don't get it," he says hoarsely.

"Oh, you will, Mr. Cutler. Believe me, you will."

12

Kitra Baylor had known full well what she was getting into when she'd married Lyman. Her uncle had been a preacher, her grandfather, a close cousin. She'd known their wives and had seen firsthand what a fish bowl they lived in. Yet it hadn't deterred her when she'd met that ordinary-looking guy with the thinning blond hair who burned to a crisp every summer before settling into a meager, hardly-worth-it tan, grew red-faced every fall when the Falcons blew another game, and whose moral outrage at every injustice had him pacing through the night, trying to figure out what could be done to make it right.

When they're alone in the rectory, she calls him the Lone Ranger, and she knows, despite his protests, that he's secretly pleased.

Tonight, in the kitchen, she stands back from the stove

and draws a wrist over her forehead to clear it of perspiration. Another pie finished, one more to go. Tomorrow morning, after service, she'll take most of them to those parishioners who don't have a whole lot to be thankful for on the holiday; the remaining three are for her husband, who can eat a gallon of ice cream, or three pumpkin pies over the course of two days, and not gain a stupid ounce.

"My Lord, you are beautiful," Lyman says from the doorway.

She blushes and waves at him—*go on, tell me another*.

Once, in another lifetime, she had won a beauty pageant in North Carolina, and the experience had excited and terrified her so much she'd never done it again. But her looks had stood her in good stead, as a grade school teacher, and as the preacher's wife. While it raised some minor problems, it smoothed over a whole lot more.

"Listen, dear," Lyman says, standing behind her, arms around her waist, hands clasped at her stomach, "I'm thinking of taking a look in at that Chisholm fellow up the road. I'm pretty sure he hasn't seen a doctor."

"Ly, you worry too much."

"I can't help it. I mean, Kit, he slammed into my car!"

"I know, dear. You've told me a hundred times."

She covers his hands with one of hers and squeezes gently. "Leave him be, honey. Leave him be."

He sighs into her hair. "I suppose."

They stand for a long while, silent and still.

"The horses," she says at last, disengaging herself from him, fussing with her apron.

"What?"

"If you want to do something useful, find out who's been riding those stupid horses up and down Midway all night. You know there aren't—" She stops when she sees the expression on his face. "What, Lyman? What's the matter?"

So he tells her what he had seen after the collision with the big man, Chisholm, how he'd passed it off as a combination of adrenaline and shadow, a freakish spurt of imagination.

"But that's not the same," she tells him, shaking off the shivers his story had given her. "What I hear is real, and I don't like it."

"I know, dear," he says. He takes a second. "I've heard them, too."

13

The tide slams against the jetties, artillery fire from the mouths of deep-bore cannon that seem too loud to be natural. Foam bubbles in cracks; water boils over the boulders; the moon has turned everything a lifeless silver, except the black clumps of seaweed scattered across the sand at the farthest reaches of the waves. Sawgrass trembles away from the wind. Sand hisses down the slopes of the dunes. A candy wrapper bounces and twists along the beach until it bumps into a shoe torn at the toe, coming apart at the heel.

Dub Neely reaches down, picks the wrapper up and stuffs it clumsily into his coat pocket, and walks on, into the trees and along a narrow path worn by those who sought the sun in summer. His head is down, his gait unsteady, moonlight reaching the ground in fits and starts as bare limbs sway and pine limbs quiver, and it isn't long before the off-and-on light makes him dizzy, makes the beer in his empty stomach begin to work its way up to his throat.

He doesn't bother to fight it; it's only a matter how far he can get before he has to stop.

Ten yards before he grabs hold of a bole with one hand and vomits, closing his eyes as his throat turns raw, wiping his mouth with an already stained sleeve. Ten minutes before he moves on, shuffling, ignoring the tiny knife points of sand that dig into his soles through the gaps in his shoes, thinking only of the cot he has waiting in the empty house near the swamp and the blanket that will cover him and protect him against the cold. Nearly tripping over an exposed root. Scraping his shoulder against a trunk that has no business being where it is, so he slaps at it angrily, snarls, spits, and walks on, concentrating on not stumbling, because if he falls he knows he won't get up until the sun rises again and his bones will ache and his head will swell and he'll be in no condition to beg for Thanksgiving dinner. Which, if he's lucky, will be more than a few scraps. And when he stumbles again, he decides the hell with it, the hell with Thanksgiving and the hell with food and he might as well die now because there's no sense anymore, there's just no sense. He'll end up as he should, like that tiny skeleton over there, the skeleton of a small bird that lies beside a pile of other tiny bodies, more birds the insects and crows have cleaned to the bone.

When they move, he isn't surprised.

He's more drunk than he's been in months, so it makes perfect sense that those little skeletons can move, can rise on skeleton legs and skeleton claws and waddle and hop toward him. In and out of the moonlight. No eyes. Just beaks and bone. A fascinating example of biology gone mad, and he grins as they gather at his feet and begin to peck at his shoes.

It isn't until the first one draws blood that Dub Neely begins to scream.

Part 3

1

1

It had been a long time since Casey had been in a church, and it wasn't nearly as uncomfortable as he'd feared. A little strange, perhaps, but not uncomfortable. At least there were no signs of impending lightning or other manifestations of Divine disapproval for his absence. For which, he supposed, he ought to be grateful, all things considered.

The church was crowded, and experience had taught him to arrive early so he could sit at the far end of the back pew. Unfortunately that allowed him to become the target of curious stares, a few cautious nods and, to his guilty delight, three outright glares of hostility as the three Teague brothers filed in, each wearing a blue serge suit a good full size too small. Mayor Cribbs and his family were there, Norville Cutler and Mandy Poplin—the woman from his town office—Hull and his daughter and a young man Casey didn't know, but from his gait appeared to be more at home on a boat than on land.

The others, most of them, were just faces. Faces he recognized but had no names, or names that did not come readily to mind; faces of strangers; but the faces he enjoyed the most were the faces of the children. Clearly most of them didn't want to be here. It was Thanksgiving. They were supposed to be home, taking in the smells, stealing nibbles from platters, annoying mothers in kitchens, ready to eat and watch football and maybe play a little touch or tackle in the yard before the sun went down. They definitely weren't supposed to be in a stuffy old church.

He smiled to himself, and now and then lowered his head to hide the pain memories set upon him.

For the life of him he couldn't explain why he was here. It had just happened. He'd awakened, showered, and found himself dressing in the best clothes he had. Not a suit, but decent grey slacks and a white shirt and dark tie, and shoes he hadn't worn in . . . too long. Too long. A dark windbreaker, not the denim jacket, and the next thing he knew he was outside in springlike sunlight, walking south, taking his time, standing for a long while outside Baylor's church before sighing, shrugging, and finally going in.

Candle wax and polish; a vaulted ceiling whose thick exposed beams represented the hull and keel of Noah's ark; several tall windows down each side—frosted, not stained glass; above him, a gallery for the organist and choir; whispers and coughs and the creak of wood.

As he sat there, alone despite the couple squeezed in beside him, he tried to remember the last time he'd been inside a church; two years, at least. He tried to remember the last time he'd held a Bible; two years, at least.

I don't belong here, he thought suddenly, but suddenly it was too late.

The organ sounded the first note, the congregation rose, and the service began. The hymns, some familiar; the prayers, some familiar; the faces of the strangers, and the faces of the children. Sprays of wheat and trays of fruit and gleaming vegetables; warm sunlight through the high, wide window behind the simple wooden cross suspended

from the ceiling; autumn flowers and a large pumpkin and
the faces of the children.

I don't belong here.

Reverend Baylor was a curious, pleasant contradiction.
He seemed stiff, almost formal, until he sang; he seemed
uncomfortable until he climbed into the pulpit, looked out
over his congregation, and gave them such a smile that
Casey nearly wept.

I don't belong here.

Lord, he thought, I think I know what You're doing, but
You know as well as I do that I don't belong here.

Not anymore.

The sermon held no admonitions, no threats of hellfire
and brimstone, although Casey had to admit that's exactly
what he had expected; it was brief, humorous here and
there, somber in a plea to pray for those souls under attack
physically and otherwise. No mention of the Millennium,
but he didn't have to say the word, just caution his flock
that a little introspection as the year comes to an end would
do no harm, a little acceptance of the man who had hung
upon the cross would help in the coming times.

Casey didn't know the hymn that ended the service,
knew only that it was anything but solemn, a loud and joy-
ous prayer of thanks that in a smaller church in another
place would have had the congregation clapping and swaying in time to the music.

He was out of the pew before the last note had faded, out
of the church and into the fresh air before anyone else
thought to move. He hurried down the walk toward the
street, breathing heavily, deeply, trying to decide if he
should go home for his bike or just head on into town to
take advantage of Gloria Nazario's kind invitation. There
was no temptation not to go; she had offered, and he would
accept, and with luck be able to apologize to Junior for
scaring him like that.

He looked right and saw Midway Road stretch too far
north. Nope; no bike. By the time he got home he'd be

sweaty and unfit for civilized company, and a shower and change of clothes would get him to the restaurant too late. Better just to go on; it wasn't all that far, maybe he'd get lucky and someone would offer him a ride. And if he was too early, it was a beautiful day; he could stroll around a little, take in the sights, check out the seasonal decorations.

Behind him the chatter of the congregants leaving the church, the cries of impatient kids to hurry up, some laughter, someone clapping an order to a child. He didn't turn to look; he didn't want to see.

"Mr. Chisholm!"

Damn, he thought, but he couldn't ignore it.

As he turned, Reverend Baylor waved from the top step, a request to wait a while, until he'd finished greeting his people. At the same time a young woman strode toward him, stunning and blond, a smile just for him.

"Mr. Chisholm?" she said, holding out her hand.

He took it and nodded. "Yes, ma'am."

The smile broadened. "I'm Kitra Baylor. My husband almost killed you the other day." And she laughed.

Casey couldn't help staring, and couldn't help noticing that she didn't seem to mind the rudeness; he realized immediately she was used to it.

"Are you all right?"

"Yes, ma'am, I am," he said, just barely stopping himself from scuffing a foot on the ground. "A little bruise on my shoulder, that's all, nothing serious."

People flowed past them, and Kitra greeted with ease those who greeted her without once making him feel as if he were being ignored.

"Have you seen a doctor?"

"No need, Mrs. Baylor. Really, I'm fine."

"Well, you should have," she scolded lightly, a shake of her head. "You never know about these things." She leaned closer, lowered her voice. "Lyman is feeling so guilty, I'm hoping you'll stay a moment and ease his mind. That is, unless you have an appointment?"

He grinned. "No, ma'am, I sure don't. Not for a while, anyway. I think, though, that—"

He stopped when the Teagues came up in a phalanx behind her. Stump and Cord in front, the third brother behind. Casey knew that one had to be Billy Ray, as tall as Cord but bulldog thick rather than whippet thin. They had the same stringy dark hair that tried pathetically to look halfway combed, the same narrow-eye stare meant to intimidate and cower. They looked enough alike to be twins.

He touched Kitra's arm to encourage her to move her off the walk and out of their way, but surprisingly she wouldn't budge. A simple nod, a simple, "Good day, Mr. Teague," to Stump, and she turned back to him and said, "Do you have dinner plans, Mr. Chisholm?"

Cord and Billy Ray moved on and waited by an expensive-looking small sedan with a handful of dents in the passenger door and along the rear fender. They folded their arms loosely, arrogantly, across their chests, tucked in their chins, paid no attention to the kids who raced by and stared. Stump, however, brushed past Casey, paused, looked up, and said, "Well, well, well, look what crawled out of his cave."

Kitra's face went blank. "Mr. Teague," she said coldly.

"Didn't figure you for a churchgoer," Stump said, showing his teeth. "Thought you'd be stinking by now, you know? Thanksgiving beer and all that?"

"Mr. Teague," Kitra snapped.

"Ain't talking to you, lady," he said without looking at her. "Talking to the big retard here."

Casey looked over Kitra's head and saw Reverend Baylor watching them anxiously as he spoke with the mayor's family. Then, before he knew what he was doing, he took hold of Stump's arm and pulled the man toward his car. Teague tried to yank free, but couldn't; tried again, and Casey, still smiling for those who were pretending not to stare, said in a low voice, "Keep it up, Teague, and I'll pull it out of its socket and beat you over the head with it. Go home, get drunk, I don't care, just get the hell out of here before someone gets hurt."

He released Teague just as the man tried a third time to get free, which made him stumble into his brothers. Cord caught him clumsily; Billy Ray straightened instantly, his arms hanging loose and ready at his side.

With a careful shake of his head, Casey warned them not to be foolish. "Gentlemen, this is a real bad time, in case you hadn't noticed." He looked straight at Cord, who couldn't hold his gaze. "Go away, boys. Don't ruin these nice people's day. You got a problem with me, you know where I live."

He turned his back, still smiling, and returned to Mrs. Baylor's side, softening his expression to tell her everything was all right, there'd be no trouble.

"Mr. Chisholm," she began.

"I think I'd better leave, ma'am," he told her. "I'm having dinner with the Nazarios, and I don't want to be late."

Tires squealed; someone shouted an angry warning at the driver.

"Please tell your husband that really, I'm okay, no need to waste a doctor's time. Thank him for his concern. I really do appreciate it." He shook her hand. "You have a good day. I hope I'll see you and your husband again soon."

Without giving her a chance to reply, he cut across the lawn, long strides and swinging arms, clumsily dodging a chaotic game of tag, grinning at a red-cheeked baby in the arms of her mother. Once on the street he kept to the grassy shoulder to let cars pass, was grateful neither Mrs. Baylor nor the reverend tried to catch him.

His chest was tight; breathing didn't come easily.

You, he told himself, are a goddamned idiot.

"You know where I live," he whispered, mocking the deep voice he had used, and he grimaced. "Good Lord, man, are you nuts? You think you're some kind of cowboy?" He shook his head at his foolishness, pushed a hand through his hair, sensed a car pulling up and moved onto the grass.

The automobile, glaring gold in the sunlight, paced him. He finally looked.

Mandy Poplin gave him a polite smile and a quick wave, while Cutler just stared, the shadow of a smile under narrow watching eyes. If it was a signal or a message, Casey didn't get it, and didn't try; instead he nodded, smiled back briefly, and looked away.

The gold car paced him for another twenty yards.

Casey resisted the urge to look again, to demand an explanation; instead, he stopped. Gently massaged his left shoulder. Rubbed the back of his neck. Checked the painfully blue sky, saw a single dark bird riding a current, the shape of its wings telling him it was a hawk.

The car moved on, slowly, Cutler watching him in the rearview mirror until Mandy nudged him and he returned his attention to the road.

See you, Casey thought, sighed, and walked on.

Another hundred yards before the curbs and sidewalks began. He moved off the road, still disgusted at the way he had behaved back there.

you know where I live

Good Lord, what an idiot.

He hadn't just asked for trouble, he had begged for it, dared it, waved a red flag, thumbed his nose, did just about everything but take a swing at the jerk right then and there just to get things in motion. Hindsight suggested that's exactly what Stump was after, that he had no intention of taking the first step. A setup a blind man could have seen coming a mile away.

If he were smart, then, he would turn around and go home, prepare as best he could for the company he'd no doubt be having sooner or later—and probably sooner; if he were smart, he'd pack his bag, get on the bike, and get the hell off the island, because any chance of things stay-

ing the same now had been reduced from slim to none. He
never should have gone into town, never should have
butted in at the newspaper; he never should have thought
he could live a normal life again.

He couldn't; not now, not here.

He almost turned around, but with a one-sided smile he
figured that no, he wasn't all that smart. For the time being
the threat of crisis was over, and there was no sense worrying about what might come later. This was now, it was a
beautiful day, and after all, there was a Thanksgiving meal
waiting for him down at Betsy's, prepared by virtual
strangers who had asked him in without knowing who or
what he was.

Not smart, maybe, but he knew what was right.

2

The sun was warm, the breeze comfortably cool, and his
mood lightened considerably as he passed the houses that
marked the real beginning of town. Kids on the lawns,
grandfolks on the porches, a touch football game in front
of the school with boys and men some not yet out of their
Sunday best, leaves scooting along the street, a few birds
in the sky.

It was, he judged, almost ridiculously perfect.

When a hand touched his shoulder, however, he stiffened instantly, went cold, and braced himself as he looked
back angrily, readying for a fight.

"Mr. Chisholm," said Whittaker Hull, dropping his
hand, stepping back quickly.

Casey cleared his throat, managed an apologetic smile.
"Sorry. I was expecting someone else."

His daughter was with him, her red hair up and bound
behind her head, an autumn dress and a sweater, stockings
and pumps. He thought, for some reason, the outfit didn't
look natural on her. "Miss Hull."

Hull waved a long-fingered hand, settled it on his tie. "I never did thank you for your intervention, Mr. Chisholm. It was rude of me. I should have done it sooner. I should have called or come out."

"You should have beaten the hell out of them," Ronnie said to Casey, her face lightly flushed.

"Now, Ronnie," Hull said, a touch to her arm. A weak smile. "She has a temper."

Casey cocked an eyebrow and answered, "So I see," as he walked on, Hull on his right, Ronnie on his left.

"You should have," she insisted. "They deserved it." She frowned at him. "More, if you ask me."

Hull sighed. "They haven't scared me off, though, have they, dear?"

"No, but that's only because you're too stubborn to take a hint."

Hull laughed loudly as he sent a playful poke at Casey's arm. "She doesn't tell you, of course, that it runs in the family. With, I might add, a few extra notches of intensity."

Casey, only vaguely aware of what they were talking about, kept silent. Although curiosity wanted him to ask why the Teagues had been in the office in the first place, he said nothing. Curiosity killed cats, not to mention other things. A quick look around, but he didn't see the young man who had been with them in church. Another question he refused to ask.

Hull slipped his hands into his pockets, suit jacket pushed behind him. He kept his gaze straight ahead. "We don't see much of you around here, Mr. Chisholm."

"No."

"A fortuitous visit, then. The other day, I mean."

"Yeah. I guess you could call it that."

Ronnie made a face. "Awfully coincidental, if you ask me."

"Ronnie, please."

"Well, Dad, he could have done more than show them

the door. My God, they trashed the office, remember? They were going to beat you up."

"Ronnie, that's enough."

"Dad, he works for Cutler. It just seems to me—"

Casey stopped suddenly, and the Hulls moved a few steps beyond before they realized he wasn't with them. Whittaker lifted a hand in apology for his daughter's temper and accusations; Ronnie just glared.

"For one thing," Casey said, keeping his voice low and calm, "I really don't appreciate being talked about as if I were invisible. And for another, Miss Hull, I'm not much more than a glorified handyman. I hammer nails, I rake leaves, I throw a paintbrush around. Cutler pays my salary, such as it is, yes, but if you don't mind me saying so, I think you're way out of line here, if you're trying to put me in the same company as the Teagues."

She wouldn't back down, staring at him as if her expression alone would break him into telling the truth—that he'd gone easy on the Teagues because they all worked for the same man.

"Ronnie," said Hull sharply, "I think that's quite enough. Mr. Chisholm extricated me from a dangerous situation and for that, Mr. Chisholm, I am eternally grateful. If there's anything I can do . . . please. Name it."

Casey only shook his head, and made it clear by his stance that he wasn't moving until they did. And he wouldn't be joining them.

Ronnie didn't seem to care. One last stabbing jut of her chin as if to punctuate her remarks, spoken and unspoken, and she walked away. Hull passed a hand over his forehead, fumbled for something else to say, an apology, an explanation, and finally hurried after her, catching up only when she began to cross the street at the next corner.

Well, Casey thought, you sure could have handled that better, don't you think?

Maybe he could have . . . hell, he certainly could have. The young woman only wanted to protect her father, and wanted his protectors not to stop halfway. It was understandable, her reaction, but he wished she hadn't picked today of all days to confront him.

He was beginning to regret not going straight home. It seemed as if the world was out to get him, one way or another, either in punishment for leaving the house, or for not leaving it sooner.

Less than a minute later, however, the day and the neighborhood soothed his mood once again. Still, he couldn't help wondering just what it was he had missed, burrowing himself away out at the end of Midway Road all this time.

In the old days he would have made a pest of himself, asking around, looking for reasons why Stump Teague and his brothers were out to get an old man like Hull; in the old days he would have used his influence, if he could, to find out exactly what Norville Cutler had to do with it—he doubted very seriously that the Teagues were acting on their own. He didn't think they were stupid, not by any means, but he doubted they left their home in the marsh to hassle and frighten folks just for the hell of it, for free.

Which made him recall that deputy's reaction to the news of the attack, and that threatened to set his temper off again.

In the old days he would have marched that smug little man by the scruff of the neck over to the newspaper office himself, badge or no badge.

In the old days . . .

A noise much like a growl deep in his throat. The old days, he reminded himself sternly, were exactly that—old. Past. Gone. If not forgotten, definitely irretrievable. He was a different man now. He was a nobody, exactly as he'd planned it. Exactly as he wanted it.

Yet he couldn't rid himself of Ronnie Hull's disdainful voice, or the sneer that had split Stump Teague's thick scruffy beard on the church walk. It nettled. It grated. It was, in many ways, a familiar itch he couldn't avoid scratching.

Okay, so maybe it wouldn't hurt to ask a question or two once he reached Betsy's. It wouldn't be laying the ground-work for interference; it would be a simple information gathering exercise, so he'd know better who to avoid. A way of protecting himself, so he wouldn't get sucked in.

But it's tempting, Case, ain't it, he thought as he pushed open the sandwich shop door; you gotta admit, it's awfully damn tempting.

3

It was a simple meal, just the basics—turkey, mashed potatos, fresh-baked bread, dressing, vegetables. A bottle of inexpensive wine for each table. Portions average, not huge. The food good, not exquisite.

He was placed at a table near the back, Gloria and her brother fussing silently around him, embarrassing him when he finally understood that they had heard what he had done for Whittaker Hull. Treating him, for some rea-son, like some kind of local hero. Junior apparently wasn't working today, and there weren't many other diners, mostly old men and old women who obviously had no desire to stay at home, eat alone on Thanksgiving, and the Nazarios treated them like family. From the greetings, the mild banter, this was evidently an annual tradition.

There was quiet laughter, then, and soft conversation, and it didn't take long to see that the register had been locked up; today there would be no money exchanged. And though he got the occasional glance, no one spoke to him, which was fine until he had finished his dessert and realized how badly he missed it sometimes—the conver-sations, the good-natured teasing, the arguments, the debates . . . the contact.

In the old days.

This, he decided glumly, was turning out to be a really bad idea.

Still, he took every opportunity to do a little shameless eavesdropping and, as Gloria or Hector cleared away the tables, ask a few questions he hoped sounded harmless. It was Hector who gave him the most information once all was done, sitting with him for a while to have a cigarette break, a glass of wine, cool off from being in the kitchen all morning.

Bad times, you know? Bad times, Mr. Chisholm. I am speaking only what I hear, you understand. People talk, I can't help it if I have big ears. But you must see it too, Mr. Chisholm, out where you are. Nobody lives there except you, yes? One by one the houses are sold, and they don't get sold again, true? A place like this, all the ocean and the beach so close, they could be sold for a lot of money, I think. Even the little ones. But they don't. They just sit there now, empty, falling apart. Even Junior's father, they want him to sell, but he won't. He say he got no place to go, but still they try, always they try. Once, I hear, they came after him with some clubs and things, and he chased them away with a shotgun, maybe a rifle. They still bother him, but they don't get so close anymore.

Now some people say there gonna be a big casino out there, maybe a hotel, maybe a lot of big fancy houses like down at the Hook. Drain the marsh, you know? Fill it in, that wouldn't be too hard, it ain't that big. Nobody knows for sure. The mayor say he don't know nothing about it, he too wants more people living here to help the business places like ours. But he's a rich man, Mr. Chisholm, and like all rich men he wants to get richer. Maybe him and that Cutler, they want the island to themselves, I don't know.

But some people don't like that, they talk about it, they get hurt sometimes. Mrs. Essman, you don't know her, I think, they bother her so much she die, but nobody say it's anybody's fault. And Mr. Hull and his paper. Mr. Hull, he keep saying we in for big trouble, and they keep trying to

stop him, but they can't do that yet. Some day, maybe, they
will. I think it will happen that some day it will come.

"Hey," Gloria said, giving her brother a playful slap across
the back of his head. "You retiring? You clean the oven
already? All the dishes done?"

Hector laughed heartily, shook Casey's hand, and hustled back into the kitchen, a good-bye wave over his
shoulder.

Casey sensed then it was time to leave. He rose, patted
his stomach, and thanked her for her kindness and for the
delicious meal. It was, he told her, the most pleasant
Thanksgiving he had had in a long time.

"You just come back," she told him, walking with him
to the door. "And I am very sorry for the way—"

"It's all right," he assured her. "Really. I think I'm
beginning to understand."

"Maybe," she answered doubtfully. "You just come
back, I'll be nice next time."

When the door hissed shut behind him, he inhaled
deeply, smelling the warmth and the sea, feeling the comfortable weight of the meal in his stomach. He walked
slowly northward, the streets empty now, a pleasant
autumn silence broken only by the sound of a light wind in
his ears.

He tried not to think about what Hector had told him. It
was, at the least, none of his business. Land speculation,
the little guy getting forced out, big fish in little ponds
maybe thinking to get bigger—old story. A very old story.
Big city, little town, nothing changed, and certainly,
absolutely, nothing to do with him.

He passed a little gift shop and glanced in the window,
at a display of humorous cards touting the approaching
Millennium, at a pyramid of books—some novels, some
nonfiction—predicting the various miraculous changes or
unmitigated disasters the new Millennium would bring.

There didn't seem to be any middle ground. It was either a new Eden or the Apocalypse, pick one and live with it, pick the other and prepare to die.

He walked on.

None of it had anything to do with him.

Not anymore.

By the time he reached the Landward intersection, the blinking red light pale in the bright sun, he began to wish he had brought the bike anyway. Still a good three miles or so to go, and his legs were already feeling a little wooden. As he reached the town hall he glanced over his shoulder, hoping to spot a car heading in his direction. Another block had him praying for a newfound ability to fly.

A piece of work, Casey; you're one piece of work.

A grunt, a self-pitying sigh, and he moved on, passing a wide empty lot thick with trees, although the weeds near the sidewalk had been recently cut down, their stalks left to rot on the ground. He had almost reached the far side, when movement near a low shrub made him pause.

Soft burbling, like birds muttering in high branches.

The paperlike rustling of wings.

Curious, he sidestepped until he could see past the shrub, and it took a few seconds for him to understand—several large black birds stood around something lying in their midst. Pecking at it. Tearing at it. Ripping pieces of it away and raising their heads to slide those pieces down their gullets. He could see red, some white, and what looked to be fur. When he took a step toward them, they stopped their feeding and looked up.

Good Lord, he thought, and pressed a hard hand to his stomach.

They were crows or ravens, he wasn't sure which, but he was pretty damn sure neither had bright blue eyes like these birds did. Before he could decide whether it was actually true or just the light under the trees, one of them puffed its wings and strutted toward him, cocking its head, ordering him away. At the same time, another hopped backward pulling at something pink and stringy, just far enough for him to see the squirrel's head. Its blinking eyes. Its trembling mouth.

He swallowed hard and quickly backed onto the sidewalk, suddenly turned and grabbed a lamppost, leaned heavily against it, swallowed, and gulped air in a desperate effort not to lose his dinner.

The squirrel was still alive.

They were eating it alive.

He could hear the crows' soft voices, almost as though they were talking to themselves, could hear the flutter of wings, one annoyed squawk, the snap of a beak. He shoved away from the lamppost and nearly ran up the street. Swallowing. Gulping air. Blue eyes and a live squirrel—please, God, it had to be the light.

When he looked back from the next corner, he couldn't see them, couldn't hear them, and told himself there was no question but that it had to have been the light.

A few yards farther on, his stomach finally calmed, the taste of acid in his mouth gone when he spit twice into the gutter and wiped his lips with the back of a hand.

Blue eyes? he thought; oh, brother, what next? They going to wear top hats and tap dance for you?

He didn't notice the cruiser until it pulled over to the curb.

"Need a lift?" the sheriff asked, window rolled down, elbow on the ledge, sunglasses on.

Casey didn't think twice; he nodded, and the back door opened as if a switch had been thrown. "Thanks," he said gratefully as he slid in and pulled the door closed, stiffened when he realized Deputy Freck was in the front, too.

Oakman pulled away, swinging into the proper lane, keeping to the speed limit. A glance in the rearview mirror: "Hope your friends don't see you," he said with a chuckle. "Looks like you've been arrested."

"A chance I'll have to take," he answered with a shrug.

Freck looked at him through the mesh that separated

front seat from back, his sunglasses dark. "Your friends," he said, "are troublemakers, you know."

"What?"

"You hang around with the wrong crowd, Chisholm. Got to be more careful, you know what I mean?"

"I don't hang around with anybody," he said, suddenly wishing he could see their eyes.

Freck grunted, faced front. "Good thing."

They rode for a few minutes in silence, until the sheriff, smiling tightly, said, "You planning on staying? On Camoret, I mean."

Casey didn't get it, the comments and the questions; he didn't like them either. "Unless you know something I don't about my job, Sheriff, I guess I probably am."

Oakman nodded. "Good. We like new people, like them to be happy."

"I'm not exactly new."

Oakman lifted a shoulder. "No, but you kind of keep to yourself, you know? New is when you first get involved, you know what I mean? Meet people, talk to them, visit them, make friends. That's good. That's real good."

They passed the school, the church; the trees moved in and hugged the roadside, dappled shadows on the tarmac. The cruiser abruptly picked up speed, pushing him back against the seat and didn't slow again until the sheriff made a sharp, squealing U-turn and parked in front of the house, keeping the engine running. Relieved, Casey left the car as fast as he could without, he hoped, seeming rude, walked around the back, and stopped at the passenger-side door.

"Thanks," he said, looking past Freck toward the sheriff. "Appreciate it."

"No problem, glad to help," Oakman said. Still smiling. "Just keep your nose clean, son, that's all we ask around here."

Casey didn't know whether to be angry or just ignore

what he couldn't help thinking was a not-so-subtle threat. A nod, and he walked away, and stopped again when Freck's lazy voice said, "You don't vote, do you?"

"What?"

No eyes, just the sunglasses. "You want to be a good citizen, you got to vote. But you don't."

Puzzled, Casey nodded. "That's right. I don't. Not that it's any of your business."

Freck's lips parted in a shark-smile. "Yeah. Well, damn, I'm sorry, Chisholm. You know, truth is, I just plain forgot. Ex-cons can't vote, can they?" He picked at something on his upper lip. "Don't hardly got any rights at all, the way I understand it."

Warm sunlight turned winter cold; Gloria's meal turned acidic and boiled.

"Thing is," he heard Oakman say, "I do like to know who lives on my island, you know what I mean, Mr. Chisholm? Something like that—a conviction for robbery and attempted murder, for example—I need to know these things. Keeps me up to date. Helps me in my job." Oakman leaned over then, to peer around his deputy. "Like I said, Chisholm, keep your nose clean. You done all right so far. Let's not screw it up."

Freck grinned and faced front, still picking at his lip.

The cruiser roared away, trailing exhaust that lingered before the wind took it.

Son of a bitch, Casey thought. Son. Of. A. *Bitch*.

4

For the rest of the day he slammed through the house, kicking at air, cursing his shadow, trying to sit and failing, trying to relax and failing.

How did he know?

How the hell did he know?

He's the sheriff, you idiot, and he has computers, you jerk.

But it's been two years; why bring it up now?

Who cares? He did.

He switched on all the lights, turned on the TV and watched the news until he couldn't stand the sight of fighting anymore, not caring that some of it was as close as Savannah; he grabbed his windbreaker and started for the beach, hoping to walk it off, but before he was halfway there he realized the day's warmth was gone and the windbreaker wouldn't be enough to keep out the cold that would be settled on the beach; instead he walked, practically marching, around the curve toward the marsh, lashing out at stones, picking up rocks and throwing them as far as he could until his shoulder began to ache; he tripped when he reached a depression in the road and nearly went down, his left hand out to stop him, his car-struck shoulder flaring fire into his neck.

Son of a bitch.

there's a great violence within you, a man had told him once; *it's a frightening thing.*

Tears of frustration blurred his vision as he made his way home. He didn't bother with the road now; he cut through the yards of houses that were empty, some of them for several years, and he yanked at the branches of dying bushes, bulled his way through a rotting wooden fence.

a frightening thing

Years ago he had been cold, and hungry, and broke, and lost.

Years ago he had stood at the counter of an old convenience store, one great fist trembling in the air, apologizing as he demanded the clerk give him money. Just for food, that's all, he told her; that's all he wanted, just food.

The cop who came in just at that moment nearly shot him where he stood.

He slapped at his eyes with the backs of his hands to

drive away the tears, drive away the image of the cop and the girl and the ride to the station and the walk to his cell.

By the time he reached Draper Street, his rage was so great, his breathing so tight, he felt as if he were going to pass out. He stomped across the blacktop, figuring on cutting through Mrs. Essman's yard to his own just beyond, when he heard someone calling.

Scowling, jaw set so hard it was nearly trembling, he looked to his right and saw Senior Raybourn on the sidewalk, a faded racing cap on his head, open topcoat, baggy trousers. One quivering finger pointed straight at him.

"What did you do?" the old man demanded.

It was almost too much: anger, frustration, confusion, the need to weep, and the urge to strike out.

It was almost too much.

So much so that Casey nearly laughed aloud at the hysteria he felt at the sight of old Raybourn shaking that crooked old finger, his scar-circled eyes squinting myopically, his bandy legs shifting and jerking as if he couldn't decide whether to get closer or not.

"What did you do to my boy?"

Casey shoved his temper down, raised a hand, shook his head. "Nothing. I didn't do anything."

Raybourn's voice rose hoarsely. "You did something, damnit! He . . . you did something!"

The street was empty, the only car parked in Raybourn's drive. There were more stars than light in the sky; only one street lamp worked, and it was halfway down the block.

Go slow, Casey; go slow.

"Mr. Raybourn," he said as calmly as he could, "I didn't do a thing. He delivered something to me day before yesterday, a package from Mrs. Nazario, and I—" He shook his head again, slowly. "We shook, Mr. Raybourn, that's all. After he gave me the package we shook hands, and we both got a little shock. Like static electricity." He lifted his shoulders. "I swear to you, sir, that's all that happened."

Raybourn's lips worked furiously, and he took a stiff step forward, shook himself hard as though driving off a chill. "You touched him."

"Yes, because we shook hands," Casey repeated, calm beginning to fray. "I took the package, I thanked him, and we shook hands. That's it."

"More. There was more," the old man insisted.

"Damnit, no!" Casey said, voice deep and loud in the empty street. So loud, so deep, it backed Raybourn up. It was Casey's turn to point. "I did not do anything to harm him, Mr. Raybourn. Not one damn thing." His turn to take a step. "Go home, Mr. Raybourn. Go home and ask him again. Ask him again and leave me the hell alone."

Raybourn resisted for a moment, then wheeled about and hurried off, muttering loudly. Casey watched until the old man reached his porch, looked over his shoulder, and angrily pushed the front door open.

The slam was loud enough to create a faint echo.

I don't believe it, he thought as he stomped into Mrs. Essman's yard, stomped around the house; I just do not believe this.

He kicked and slashed his way through the hedge fence at the back, and strode around the side of his house with one arm swinging, desperately wanting to tear something down, rip something out of the ground and hurl it into the sea.

He shouted wordlessly, took a shadow-punch at the house, and shouted again.

He didn't feel any better.

Especially when he reached the front and saw Stump Teague and Cord standing on the porch steps, lounging as if they were waiting for an old friend.

"Well, well, well," Stump said, hands clenched at his sides. "Evening, retard."

Casey glared at them, his shoulders hunching, his head

lowered. "Believe me," he said with a slow shake of his head, "you do not want to do this now."

"Yeah, we do," a voice said behind him.

He turned quickly, just in time to see the fist, and the brass knuckles it wore.

2

1

Twenty years ago, Magnolia Court was one of the first hotels drivers saw as they approached Savannah from the west. A simple, low, four-story rectangle set beneath full-grown trees, its sandstone walls looking cool, inviting, peaceful, promising a haven for those who wanted to visit the city but not sleep there. Then the visitors grew scarce, most of the Court's trees died, stain and neglect discolored the walls, and by the time Savannah had begun its renaissance, it was too late. The Court was already more than halfway in its grave.

John Bannock didn't care.

Magnolia Court was convenient, reasonably clean, and it was cheap and better than staying in some two-bit motel.

"I think," Lisse said as they took the elevator down to the lobby, "you're going to have to talk to those kids today."

"I will, I will."

"They're going to leave, John, if you don't. Cora is, anyway. She's had it."

He faced away from the doors and examined himself in the mirror that was the back wall. His face had become shadows and hollows, his posture more slumped than usual, and there wasn't a whole lot of meat left on his bones. They hadn't starved, he and Lisse, but their appetites had shrunk each time their island search had come up empty.

She, on the other hand, looked as good as ever. She'd cut her hair once—he had thought it made her face and neck look too long—but it was back to her shoulders now, and its deep auburn seemed to flicker tiny flames in the elevator's indirect lighting. Slender to begin with, her weight looked to be the same as when they'd started out; only the angles of her face had grown slightly sharper.

She grinned at his examination. "Too late, Prez, you had your chance before we got dressed."

He felt heat in his cheeks and turned around. Even after all this time, all that had happened, he still wasn't used to her being so forward.

The doors opened.

The dark-slate lobby floor gleamed with fresh cleaning; the tall potted plants shone with recent misting. Muted voices held a conversation somewhere, but he couldn't see anyone but a bored clerk at the registration desk.

"John—"

"After dinner, Lisse, okay? I'll talk to them after dinner."

She grabbed his arm, yanked it gently. "That'll be too late."

"You're a pain, Montgomery."

"Yeah, I know."

She led the way to a couch near the entrance, a low table in front of it, armchairs on its flanks; she sat him down and headed for the gift shop, not knowing if the local paper had a holiday edition or not. He watched her go, the simple dress hugging her hips in a way that reminded him of her waitress's uniform, and the way she used to exaggerate the roll of those hips to get his attention. He had thought it simple flirting then; now he knew better.

A soft chime, the elevator doors slid open, and the kids walked out. Stiffly. Not touching. Space between them widening as soon as there was room. It didn't take a psychic to know they'd been arguing again. When he raised a hand to get their attention, it was Cora who saw him, and he didn't miss the hesitation in her step before she poked Reed in the side and nodded in John's direction. They wore clean shirts, clean jeans, but they walked as if they were trudging barefoot across sharp stones.

End of the rope, he thought; Lisse is right. They've reached the end of their rope.

He stood and smiled as they approached, asking about their night, their sleep, reminding them as Cora took the chair on his left, that he'd made reservations for Thanksgiving dinner in the hotel restaurant.

"Some Thanksgiving," Cora grumbled as she shifted and draped a leg over the arm.

"Better than eating beans out of a can," Reed snapped. Grimaced. Looked an apology at John.

She made a face and stared out the glass wall behind the couch. The hedge-rimmed parking lot was practically empty, save for a single police car idling near the hotel's two-lane entrance. "Maybe we'll see the march or something," she said, as if that could only be the most boring thing in the world.

John frowned. "March?"

"It was on TV," Reed explained when Cora didn't seem inclined to answer. "Some people are protesting today. They're supposed to march into town and have some kind of rally by the river." He tucked his hands between his knees. "You know—stop the violence, where are the cops when you need them, peace on Earth, stuff like that."

"They're going to start way out here?"

The boy shrugged. "I guess. Somewhere out here, I don't know where."

"Heck of a march."

Reed shrugged again and slumped back, didn't move when Lisse returned empty-handed. Cora only gave her a halfhearted wave.

Another patrol car moved into the parking lot and stopped beside the other.

"It's supposed to be cool, you know?" Cora said, foot bouncing, one hand folded atop the other on her stomach. "It's Thanksgiving, it's supposed to be cool. This sucks. I went out before, and it's like seventy degrees out there." She turned her head slightly. "Who the hell *are* you, mister?"

"Cora," said Reed angrily.

"What's the problem? He knows about us, we don't know jack about him."

Her voice sounded brittle and hollow in the empty lobby. The desk clerk looked up for a second before returning to his paperwork. A family of five spilled out of the elevator, the two youngest children racing across the lobby, chasing each other in circles. Their laughter seemed too loud; their parents made no move to hush them.

John pushed forward until he was on the edge of his cushion, a thumb stroking his cheek. Lisse sat back, smoothing her skirt as she tucked her legs under her. He looked at her, and she nodded.

"What?" Cora demanded.

"Cora, please," Reed said. "Look, Mr. Bannock, I got to admit, I'm pretty curious myself. But for me, as long as we know the same guy, I guess that's all right with me."

Cora scowled. "Not for me."

"No kidding."

"Hey," Lisse said, not raising her voice. "Y'all keep pecking at each other like that, you'll bleed to death before John gets in a word."

Reed blinked, then grinned; Cora pouted and sank

deeper into her chair. Foot bouncing. Hands pressed to her stomach.

John cleared his throat. He wasn't sure this was the right thing to do, that he still might scare them off no matter what Lisse believed. He pulled absently at the skin under his chin, left hand patting his knee as if he were keeping time to a slow marching song.

Then he looked to the high ceiling, the faded tiles, the embedded lights, and said, "My son is a killer."

2

I was writing a book, he said, refusing to meet either Cora's or Reed's astonished gazes. Believe it or not, I used to do people's taxes and accounts, but a friend of mine, a pretty popular nonfiction writer, knew how I hated that job and talked me into working on something he had set up for me. What it was, was a series of in-prison interviews with mass murderers and serial killers. Men, women, a couple of kids not much older than you guys.

My wife, Patty, and I . . . we had split up, partly because of that, the writing, the traveling, partly for other reasons. There's no sense giving you all the details, most of them wouldn't make sense to you anyway. But I learned pretty quickly from talking to all those killers that, unlike what the textbooks and profilers say, they were, all in all, pretty ordinary people. Families not perfect, but they weren't horribly unusual either. No abuse, no rape, no beatings, nothing like that. These killers did what they did just because they felt like it.

Because they were in the mood at the time.

What I couldn't find out was why. At least I didn't find out right away. It was the famine time, you see, and things were, as the saying goes, tough all over. It didn't occur to me until a whole lot later that not having a lot of food was only part of the famine's structure. The rest, the biggest part, I think, had to do with the fact that a lot of people had few emotions anymore. Not real ones, anyway. They reacted the way they did because it was expected of them—crying and laughing and acting guilty or sorry—it was a false front, an act, a mask they put on and took off whenever they felt like it.

They really didn't feel a damn thing.

Not when they held their children, not when they cut someone's throat or dumped poison into their food or pushed them off a cliff.

And even when I figured that out, sort of, it still didn't make much sense—the why of it, you know?—until . . .

Joey is my son. He's adopted. At least, I used to think he was adopted. I mean, I used to think we chose him, Patty and I, to be our son, until I realized too late it was actually the other way around. He chose us . . . he chose Patty because he needed a way to get around the country. So he could see people. So he could touch them. Literally touch them. Sort of drain them, I guess, or turn off the switch that makes emotions real, that makes people care, that . . . damn, I don't know.

Anyway, Patty helped him move from one place to another, but I don't think she really wanted to. I think today she had no choice. A little kid in a cowboy suit can't really . . . oh, hell, that doesn't make much sense either.

Patty's dead now.

Joey isn't.

I'm pretty sure he's still alive.

I have no idea where he is, not at this moment, but I have a bad feeling I know where he's going.

See, there was this horse he . . .

Oh, hell.

Listen, you two, I know we're all looking for the same guy, okay? We've all experienced something, I don't know exactly what you'd call it, but we've experienced *something* that's making us do this. And we know we have to do it by the end of the year.

Casey called me once, after all the troubles you guys had at home, back there in New Jersey. He told me I was marked, or something like that. I didn't know what that meant, I thought he was nuts, until Joey . . . until I had to . . .

Let's just say that I thought at the time that I had killed him. My own son. My Joey.

I'm sorry, but it's hard. My son isn't my son, yet I can't help calling him that. I can't help it. Patty loved him. I loved him.

Listen . . . I don't care who out there believes the Millennium is the End, and who thinks the Millennium is just another turn of a stupid calendar page. It doesn't matter. You know Casey better than I do, you know what happened better than I, but you know that he's different somehow, that he was able to stall or put off track or whatever the hell you want to call it whoever it was who caused all that death and destruction back then.

I did the same thing.

Lord help me, I did the same thing, and now it's all coming to a head and if we don't find Casey . . . I don't know. I don't know what we're supposed to do, I don't know if what we're supposed to do is going to do any good, but right now, I can't see that we have any choice.

We eat, we rest, tomorrow we get in the car and we try to find him.

I mean, what the hell else can we do?

3

"Susan," Cora said softly.

John blinked, looked up. "What?"

"Her name is Susan, and Casey fought her, but not

until . . . you know." She rubbed a finger harshly under her nose. "He almost died. We, uh, went to the hospital and his hair had turned all white and we didn't think he was gonna live, you know? We didn't think he was gonna live, so we left. There was nothing left of home, so we left. We were scared. I guess." A shrug. "We came back, and he was alive, and he was gone." Another shrug. And, surprisingly, the biggest smile John had ever seen on her face as she looked across the table. "So we aren't alone, huh, Turner?"

Relieved, Reed smiled back. "Nope. Guess not."

She giggled, though her eyes shone wetly. "You thought we'd think you were nuts, right?"

John admitted it.

"Well, we are, don't you think?"

Lisse sat up slowly.

"I mean, of all the people in the world, we're the ones who know what's going on. I mean, for sure. And we're weird, right? Reed's got his dumb dreams, and I just follow along." She shook her head, chin trembling, foot bouncing harder, faster. "I don't like it. I want to go home." Her voice rose a little. "But I can't, can I? I can't go home, because there ain't no home to go home to. And even if there was—"

"Honey," Lisse said gently, "you ever do any waitressing, traveling around like you did?"

Startled, Cora frowned. "What? Sure. Yeah. We needed money, so . . . yeah, sure."

"You ever have some bad-tooth wonder make a grab for your ass?"

Cora snorted. "Hell, yeah, lots of times."

"You ever slap his hand?"

She shook her head. "Didn't want to lose my job. But what does this have to do with anything?"

Lisse uncurled her legs, straightened her skirt, fussed with her hair. "Nothing. Just wondering. Besides, it's after noon, and I'm hungry."

She grinned, and winked.

Cora opened her mouth, closed it, shaded her eyes with one hand, and her shoulders began to shake. At first John thought she was crying. Until he heard the quiet laughter, saw her other hand wave as if batting something away from her face. When she hiccupped, her laughter exploded, filling the lobby, making the desk clerk grin uncertainly.

"You're . . ." Cora swallowed air, hiccupped again. "You're crazy, lady."

"Like you said, girl. But that doesn't change the fact that I'm hungry, and John here is buying." Lisse stood, reached out a hand until Cora took it, then pulled the girl to her feet. "It may not seem like it, sugar, but you think about it, we got a lot to be thankful for. We haven't been raped, we haven't been killed, we can still walk, and John still has a wallet full of money. The rest of it, that doesn't matter today. Okay?" She looked at Cora sternly. "That doesn't matter today."

Arm in arm, then, they walked off toward the restaurant.

John lifted his eyebrows, tugged at one ear, and stood.

"What happened?" Reed asked, looking around as if he'd missed something vital. "I don't get it. What happened?"

"Mr. Turner," he said with an exaggerated shrug, "don't ask me. I'm just the funny-looking guy with the wallet full of money."

4

The restaurant wasn't large, but pale walls and white table-cloths, the white uniforms of the waiters, white flowers in milk-glass vases, glass walls on two sides made it bright and seem cavernous.

The two dozen diners seemed lost in all that space.

There was plenty of talk, rattling of silverware and glasses and plates; music from hidden speakers, the occasional squeak of a heel on the bare floor, the scrape of a chair leg, a mild scolding of one of the children, a braying laugh. Yet the room seemed almost silent. Hushed.

John and the others took a table near the front window, which gave them a view of the parking lot and its shaggy hedge wall. He faced the glass, Lisse across from him, the glare putting her face in veiled shadow. They didn't need to order; there wasn't a menu. Dinner with all the trimmings was what the hotel had promised and what it delivered, no substitutions, take or leave it.

The family of five sat two tables over, the parents grimly determined to give their children a good time. Over by the side wall another family, two children this time, and John wondered what had brought them here, of all places, to celebrate a holiday best celebrated at home. The other diners were mostly singles, only three or four couples; since there were no meetings posted on the message board beside the elevator, he guessed they were probably mostly in sales of some kind. Real tourists generally stayed closer to the riverfront, where all the supposed action was.

It wasn't until he'd finished his salad that he realized the others were looking at him.

"What?" he said.

"This isn't a funeral, John," Lisse told him, scolding mildly. "You want misery, go to the front desk and look at our bill."

He grinned, rolled his eyes. "Sorry."

Another moment of awkward silence before Reed said, "There was this lady at home, she wanted to get married in a spacesuit or something."

Lisse laughed. "You're kidding."

Cora giggled, swore it was true, that the woman in question, when she wasn't running her small grocery store, spent half her time looking for alien landing spots in the woods around the town, which there wasn't much of since the place was in the middle of the wood. Or she signaled them with flashlights in the middle of the night, and spent the rest of her time trying to convince everyone that the aliens were already walking around and we had to do everything we could to make them feel welcome.

"I think she figured that getting married in a spacesuit would bring them out in the open."

John laughed, more at the animation in the young woman's face than at the story itself, and watched with admiration as Lisse unashamedly goaded them on, demanding more information with whoops of delight.

Over her shoulder he could see four cruisers at the entrance now, two of the cops dragging riot gear from a trunk as they joked with the others.

From a table in the middle of the room, a fat man in a rumpled suit complained about the sun, why couldn't someone pull a curtain or a shade, he could barely see his food.

"Listen," Lisse said, thickening her bayou accent, using her hands, "you think that's something? I worked at this hotel, the Royal Cajun, near the Mississippi, in New Orleans? You ever been there? No? Too bad, you ought to go, it's like no place you ever seen in your life. Anyway, we had this guy used to come in once in a while, he weren't much taller than a good spit, he used to talk to the river."

"Yeah, right," Cora said. "So what?"

"So what? Honey, the river talked back. Told him what to order, what to wear, told him once that he should go into a casino and bet everything he had on number four."

Reed, his mouth filled with turkey, giggled. "Did he?"

"Damn right. Bought the hotel, made me manager, told John there he didn't pay his bill, his ass'd be on the street before he took another breath."

They looked at him.

John nodded solemnly and crossed his heart. "True. All true."

"So . . ." Cora frowned. "So what did you do?"

John snapped his napkin open, draped it over his lap. "What could I do? I married him. Hell, he was rich, right? You can do stuff like that in New Orleans, they don't care. That made me her boss, so I fired her ass when she wouldn't bring me breakfast in bed."

Reed choked, Cora coughed into a laugh, and he saw in the distance what looked like flags and banners moving along the highway. The march, he thought; I'll be darned, they're really doing it.

"There was this guy once. In Kentucky? He wanted to make me a hooker. Said I'd make lots of money. Reed said go ahead, he was tired of begging."

"I did not."

Lisse reached over and covered Cora's hand. "Did you kill him, sugar?"

"Kicked him in the balls."

Lisse nodded her approval. "Good choice, dear. Men are like that, you know. You hit him in the head, he wouldn't feel a thing."

"Hey," Reed protested, and Lisse rapped a spoon against his skull.

John could see the marchers, a hundred of them, maybe more. He couldn't hear what they sang or chanted, could only see them from the chest up because of the hedge. They seemed to be having a pretty good time. The parking lot cops were gone, joining a score or more others he could see who were lined up on the shoulder. They didn't appear very concerned. A couple of the children spotted them and clamored to go outside to see the parade.

The fat man complained again, louder, telling his waiter that he didn't much appreciate eating in a fish bowl.

"He was my favorite customer," Lisse said, nodding at John. "I knew he was kind of sweet on me because he kept tipping me half the stupid bill."

"You did?" Cora said.

John nodded. It was true. Almost, anyway.

"Took me on a picnic on a ferry boat. One that goes across the Mississippi, down by the hotel."

That was true, too.

Lisse sat straight, fluffed her hair. "Defended my honor when a scumbag from hell tried to deflower me."

"Tried to what?" Reed said.

"Wow," Cora said. "Kind of romantic, huh?"

Another truth, but not all of it. Not by half.

"Hey, come on," Reed protested, "I helped you out a lot of times."

Cora blushed fiercely, suddenly, and became fascinated with the slice of pie the waiter slid in front of her. Her cheeks fairly glowed.

They're in love, John decided; they're in love, but they're afraid. He didn't blame them.

The marchers, evidently confined to a single highway lane, began to pass the hotel. Several children pressed against the restaurant wall to watch, calling to their parents, who called them back to their tables to eat their dessert and stop making a scene.

Lisse looked over her shoulder, watched for a few seconds, and looked back with a disinterested shrug, then grimaced when the fat man demanded to see the manager. John made a face that made her smile; Cora and Reed suggested several things the fat man could do to take care of the sun, none of them even remotely physically possible.

A young boy appeared at John's side, fair hair slicked back, clip-on tie decorated with tiny spacemen and a few drops of gravy. "Mister?" he said. "Mister, can I have your grapes?" and he pointed to the table's centerpiece.

"Edward Pearl," the woman at the next table scolded, "you get right back here, young man. Now, hear? And stop bothering the nice man."

"But Momma—"

John plucked a few grapes from their stem and handed

them over. "Better git, Eddie," he said in a low, man-to-man voice. "Your mother's a little mad."

The boy took them quickly, stuffed them in his mouth as he hustled back to his table.

"I'm sorry," the woman said as she gave the boy a half-hearted swat on the rump.

"No problem," he told her. And almost said, *I know how it is, I have a son of my own.*

It was an effort to look away; it was an effort to pick up his fork and cut himself a piece of pie; it was an effort not to dress Eddie Pearl in a cowboy suit.

"John?"

He didn't look up; he didn't dare; he was afraid the bright sun would put a tear in his eye.

"John."

He waved his left hand—I'm okay.

"You know," Reed said, "there was this woman, I forget where, Carolina or something, she—"

"Oh, please," Cora said. "She was drunk, okay?"

"She was not. She liked me." He looked to Lisse to plead his case. "We were in this little town—"

He stopped when one of the kids called to her parents across the room at the top of her shrill voice, flapping her arms excitedly, telling them to come look at the other parade. Edward Pearl immediately climbed up on his chair and pointed confirmation, neatly swiveling a hip away from his grasping mother. The commotion instantly sent the other children running to the side wall, pressing against the glass, waving and shouting.

John half rose to see what all the fuss was about, but Reed beat him to it when he said, "Holy shit."

Crows, John thought; oh my God, it's the crows.

crows in a flock, bright blue eyes, tearing out the throat of his—

He blinked, rubbed his eyes hard and blinked again.

"Damn," he whispered.

It wasn't the crows at all.

A dozen people, maybe more, wearing dirt-smeared black dusters and stiff cowboy hats, bright blue bandannas tied across their faces, only their eyes exposed, running full speed toward the hedge wall in front, spreading out quickly and expertly, their backs to the hotel.

Ten paces away they reached into their coats and pulled out shotguns and rifles.

"Lisse," John said.

The fat man rose and slammed his napkin onto his table. "I have had just about enough of this," he bellowed. "Where the hell is the manager?"

The first shot turned a handful of the police around, and a flagbearer dropped below the level of the hedge, screaming, but not before John saw her spitting blood.

There was no single second shot; it was a fusillade, from both sides.

One of the black-coated raiders turned sideways as he ran, ignored the march, and aimed at the hotel.

When the first bullet shattered the glass wall near the top, John grabbed Cora's arm and yanked her from her chair, yelled to Lisse and Reed, and spun around, intending to make a run for the lobby. At the same time, the other customers panicked, parents racing for their children, others for the exit.

The wall exploded inward in half a dozen places.

A waiter went hard to his knees, fumbling at a spear of glass embedded in his side; more shards brought a woman down, draping her facedown across a table, the glass sparkling in her back; the children scattered, shrieking, screaming, stumbling over upended tables and toppled chairs, while hands frantically grabbed for their arms; at the back of the room another waiter slumped against the salad bar, gleaming red hands clasped across his stomach;

the fat man plowed through tables and chairs toward the exit, still bellowing, kicking aside a crawling man, stepping over another.

The screams inside matched the screams outside.

John saw two men fall near the exit, knew he'd never make it, and threw Cora to the floor behind a long serving table, tipped it onto its side, and dropped beside her with a heavy arm across her back. He couldn't see anything now, not without lifting his head, not without taking his arm away as Cora lay there, shrieking, kicking her legs.

Pitchers and vases exploded, knives and forks danced and spun, a light fixture in the ceiling flared and threw sparks, and there were sirens inside and out, blaring above the explosions, above the gunshots, above the screaming.

He looked to his left, over Cora's head, and saw Eddie Pearl's mother sprawled on her back, arms outstretched, one hand clutching a napkin, nothing left of her face; and next to her he saw the boy, staring at the ceiling, legs twitching, a gaping hole in his throat and blood drowning his clip-on tie; he looked to his right and saw a little girl hobbling as fast as she could into the lobby, one shoe off, her white sock bright pink, while behind her a heavyset man tried desperately to scoop her up with one arm, the other hanging dead at his side.

He couldn't find Lisse.

Wood splintered over his head, and he felt needles slam into his back and the backs of his legs.

"Reed!" Cora shouted, and scrambled out from under his arm and to her knees, trying to see over the table, a cut on her cheek running red to her jaw.

"Down!" John yelled. "For God's sake, get down!"

He pulled at her hip, but she shook him off. "Reed! Reed, where are you?"

When he lunged for her and missed, he cursed and grabbed the table's edge, hauled himself up, and squinted through the bright sunlight.

Into silence.

A long, deep, warm silence.

No flags or banners left on the highway; bodies in the parking lot; bodies in the restaurant.

When the moans began, he thought he'd go deaf; when the crying began, he staggered to his feet and stumbled across the floor, not caring about the wounded, not looking at the dead.

"Lisse," he said. "Lisse?"

Cora screamed.

He whirled, nearly fell over, and saw Lisse standing dazed just inside the lobby, the sleeve of her dress torn at the elbow, her hair falling disheveled over her eyes. Swaying. Someone's blood fresh on her shoulder and the side of her neck. Calling to him without speaking, pointing mutely at the body that lay at her feet.

"Reed!" Cora screamed, and began to run. "Reed!"

3

1

Moonbow Levin was supremely unhappy.

First, she had, a year or so ago, lost her best friend in the whole world. She had been his princess, her mother was going to be his queen, and they were going to live in a seriously large castle someplace that wasn't anywhere near the desert, and he would fight dragons and demons every night just for her.

Then she had lost her home in the desert, because she and her family had to run away from things she still wasn't quite sure she really understood. Only that it cost her the best friend she'd ever had.

Then Starshine, the stuck-up creep, had turned thirteen only a few weeks ago, and suddenly she was this high and mighty hotshot, smartass teenager who was, to hear her talk, the greatest thing that ever walked the earth on two legs, and Moonbow had suddenly become the baby of the house.

Then . . . and then there was her name.

Moonbow.

Living in the desert outside Las Vegas, it didn't matter. People may have looked at her a little funny once in a while, but no one ever really made fun of her. Not even in school, where some kids had names as truly weird as hers. There was one kid named Goldust, for crying out loud, and another who called himself Snakeyes and swore it was his real name. So she was who she was, and was called what she was called, and no one cared, no one bothered her.

Once Nevada had been left behind, however, everyone . . . just *everyone* looked at her and Starshine as if they'd crawled out of some big old mountain cave in the middle of the night, and she was getting real sick of hearing them say, "Hey, kid, your mother a hippie or something?"

Last week Starshine announced that she wanted to change her name to Tiffany, and it was the only time Moonbow ever saw Momma lose her temper as bad as that. She'd grabbed Star by the shoulders and shook her, hard, and yelled that she had to be proud of her name, that it was what made her special, and if she ever even thought about changing it, Momma was going to whomp her within an inch of her life.

If Moonbow hadn't been so scared, she would have laughed at the terrified look on her sister's face.

The memory didn't change the fact, though, that she was still awfully miserable.

She sat on a log on the bank of some stupid river she didn't even know the name of, shivering a little in the coat that was too long, the one Beatrice had bought for her just last week. Her jeans were new and so they were too stiff; her sneakers were new, and they were stiff too, and would probably give her blisters before they were broke in. Their Thanksgiving dinner had been in a nice little restaurant that had cut-out turkeys and Pilgrims and Indians on the walls, and it was all right, she supposed, for a store-bought meal, but it wasn't the same as having Thanksgiving at home.

Which she didn't have anymore.

In serious misery, then, she hugged herself, watched her

breath float away in the sunset's golden light, and hunched her shoulders when her sister sat beside her, buried in her own too-long coat. She wore a baseball cap pulled as low as she could get it, trying to hide the haircut she'd given herself the night her mother had lost her temper.

Somewhere out there, some kind of strange bird made some kind of strange noise; Moonbow didn't think it sounded very happy at all.

"This," said Starshine, "sucks."

"I know."

"Big-time sucks."

"Yeah."

"I mean, who does old Harp think she is, ordering us around like that?"

"Momma's dream. That man, remember?"

"Screw Momma's dream, and screw the man, too. We all have dreams, Bow, but they don't take us all the way across the country." She stomped her feet to keep them warm. "This really sucks."

They watched the sluggish water lose its rippling sunset streaks, watched mist rise from the surface and slide into fog that crawled and puffed along the banks. The trees on the other side hardened into an uneven dark wall; a flock of geese called their way south overhead. Behind them, the dirty white wall of the lousy motel turned grey, then brown, then black, with only lighted windows to mark the fact that there was a wall there at all.

They listened to the river; they listened to their heart-beats.

"I'm gonna run away," Starshine said at last.

Moonbow gasped, shook her head violently. "You can't, Star. God, you can't do that."

"I'm thirteen, I can do what I want."

"You're *only* thirteen," Moonbow told her. "If they don't catch you right away, somebody else will and they'll . . . you know. You know?"

"I don't care. I can't take this stupid crap anymore. I

want to stay in one place, Bow. I want to take Momma's gun and go back to Missouri to that place we had, and I want to stay there forever. And if anyone tries to make us move, I'll blow their stupid heads off."

They heard voices in the distance, men laughing. Moonbow figured they were going into that crumby-looking bar across the road from the motel. She didn't remember what it was called, but there was nothing but old pickups and vans in the hard-dirt parking lot when she'd left the room to come out here, and the neon stag over the entrance was missing two legs and an antler. She had overheard Beatrice say something to Momma about how this motel maybe wasn't such a good idea after all, and that had only added to her misery.

"If you go," she finally said, "I'm going with you."

They shifted closer to each other, bumped shoulders, and maybe, she thought, Star wasn't really so bad after all.

The fog rose and slipped into the trees.

A honky-tonk bar band blasted the night each time the bar door opened.

"Damn," Star said, kicking at the ground. "It's freezing out here. Let's go inside and watch some TV."

"They only get three channels. I checked."

"Better than sitting out here, freezing our butts off."

"Momma still mad at you?"

Star didn't answer.

Quiet footsteps behind them, and when a long leg in jeans stepped between them, they moved aside to make room for their mother.

"It's cold out here," Jude said, rubbing her arms even though she wore a heavy coat. "You girls should come in where it's warm."

Her hair was waist-long and unbraided tonight, but her weighted veil was still on, only her large dark eyes showing, shining in the dark. Moonbow knew that sometimes, when it was real hot, she took it off when she was in bed. Never anytime else. Not even when they were the only

ones in the room, not even though they'd often told her
that they wouldn't mind it if she did.

Momma never showed her face to anyone.

Not even to the man who would have made her his
queen.

"So," Jude said, clasping her hands in her lap. "What do
you think?"

"About what?" Starshine asked sullenly.

Jude shrugged. "I don't know. Anything."

Starshine stamped her feet again and yanked on her
cap's brim. She muttered something Moonbow didn't
catch, but she figured it wasn't too bad, because Momma
didn't start yelling again, she only rapped a knuckle
against Star's thigh.

Star said, "Ouch," but she didn't move away.

A car backfired on the road.

They could hear a pair of male voices raised in drunken
argument.

"Nice place," Star said, her sarcasm thick.

"We'll be out of here in the morning, dear."

"And then where, Momma? Then where do we go?"
Starshine pushed off the log and walked to the riverbank's
edge, swatting at the reeds that grew up to her waist.
"When are we going to stop, Momma, huh? Is this what
we're gonna do for the rest of our lives?"

Moonbow tried to signal her sister to shut up, but it was
too dark now, and the fog too thick. If it hadn't been for the
window lights, she wouldn't be able to see her at all.

"Darling," her mother said patiently, "I know you're
tired. I know you're disappointed about leaving all your
new friends. But—"

"I'm not disappointed," Star said angrily. "I'm sick,
Momma. I'm sick of it all. I want . . . I want . . ."

"To go home," Moonbow whispered. She leaned against
Jude's arm and sighed loudly. "It isn't fair, Momma. You
know this isn't fair."

"But . . ." Jude's hands fluttered helplessly across her lap, through the air in front of her face, back to her lap again. "But we have to do this, kids. We *have* to. It's important."

Starshine yanked a reed out by the roots and flung it as far as she could into the river. "Please, Momma, don't tell us about the stupid dream again, okay?"

Jude's voice hardened. "It isn't stupid. Believe me, it is not stupid."

"Enough, Momma, okay?" Star said wearily, and she trudged back to the log, sat next to her sister. "Enough. We don't want to hear it anymore."

"Is that true, Bow? Is that really true?"

Moonbow shuddered at the pain in her mother's voice, but she couldn't deny that Star was right. They had been dragged across more than half the country, no say at all in where they were going, what they were going to do. In the beginning it was kind of fun, an adventure, like one of those quests she saw in the movies and read in her books.

It used to be fun, staying out of school, living in a different place every day, eating in diners and fast food restaurants and real restaurants every day; it used to be fun, until they had settled in Missouri and were reminded of what it was like, how nice it was not to be moving anymore, how nice it was to be able to come back to the same room, the same beds, the same house.

Every day.

"Oh, Lord," Jude said, and pushed herself to her feet. "Oh, Lord, dear God, what the hell have I done?"

2

Beatrice, hands cupped under her head, lay on a queen-size bed that sagged almost comically in the center. She would have moved to the other one, but that mattress had a depression at the top that made it feel as if her head were hanging over a great hole. The ceiling, stained and peeling and sagging itself a bit near the far wall, appeared to recede when she stared at it too long, but there was nothing else to look at in this miserable little room. The television barely worked, the furniture was barely adequate, and when she'd looked through the mildewed drapes a few minutes ago, all she could see was that horrid little bar across the road.

If she could sleep, it would solve everything. At least for the time being. If she could sleep, she'd be shut of the children's complaints and Jude's silent protests and her own persistent doubts that somehow she had made a terrible mistake.

Sir John, she thought, I think I'm going to stop.

My dear Beatrice, he answered, his form thin and shimmering in front of the chipped and streaked door, you know you can't do that.

Yes, I can, dear. Believe me, I can.

And what will you do, then?

She sighed, shifted, and said aloud, "I'll go back to that lovely place we just left. The children love it there, nobody bothers Jude, and I think I can get my old job back."

Darling, really . . . selling houses?

"I was getting damn good at it, I'll have you know."

Yes. Perhaps you were.

"And I'll get better, believe me. And when we have enough money, we can move to a bigger place, with more people, more things to do, and I'll sell even more houses, John, and . . . and . . . do whatever I want and not have to worry about a bloody damn thing."

The ghost—if it was a ghost; she couldn't be sure, and she really didn't give a damn—smiled wanly, shook its head sadly.

My dear, you can dream about selling castles in Wales

for all I care, but it isn't going to change a thing. You cannot go back. You must go on.

A series of backfires made her jump, loud voices and stumbling footsteps had her squinting to be sure she'd put the latch on the door.

"John—"

I'm sorry, my dear, truly I am. Besides, how will you ever find someone else to love if you go back to that dreadful Missouri place?

"John, don't be silly."

I'm not, Beatrice, I'm not. In case you haven't noticed, I'm rather dead, and you're too young to be in mourning for the rest of your life.

"John, you haven't even been gone two years, for heaven's sake. It would be . . . I don't know, unseemly."

Two years, two centuries, what difference does it make?

"Two centuries would mean I'm dead as well."

The figure smiled broadly, touched the side of its nose, and pointed at her with a long trembling finger.

Temper, my darling, temper.

Beatrice rolled onto her side, facing the wall.

That won't do it, you know, Bea. I'm still here.

"Don't I know it, you old goat," she muttered.

Sounds of a scuffle outside had her rolling over and sitting up quickly, feeling her heart beating hard, feeling a ribbon of cold encircle her neck.

Go on, my dear, the ghost told her gently; you really don't have a choice, you know. It's coming. Coming soon. And you have your part to play.

"Damn you, John Harp, I wish you were really here so I could strangle that scrawny little neck of yours."

What, and have to die all over again? I think not, my dear. I'll just stay in your imagination for a while longer, if you don't mind. It's so much safer.

She grinned, shook her head, and pushed a rough hand through her short brown hair, grimaced and raked her fin-

gers through her bangs. She must be getting dotty, that's
the only explanation, arguing with a ghost and threatening
to kill it. Dotty, and tired, and not a little afraid.

"Sir John," she said.

And someone hammered on the door.

3

Moonbow watched her mother pace in front of them,
hands gesturing helplessly, mumbling, looking up now and
again to the sky.

"Star," she whispered.

Starshine shook her head sharply, an order to be quiet.

Not fair, Moonbow thought; Momma believes and we
don't. It's not fair.

Pinpricks of damp cold as the fog drifted over her face;
the cry of a mournful bird deep in the woods across the
river. In one of the rooms behind her someone turned on a
TV, music and voices blending harshly and loudly. A car's
engine. A truck's rumbling. When she checked over her
shoulder, the window lights were smeared and fading.

"Momma? Momma, maybe we'd better go inside now."

"I need to think," her mother said. "I need a minute to
think."

"There's nothing to think about," Starshine told her.
"We're tired, Momma. We're sick of it."

"No," Jude answered sharply, harshly. She spun around,
faced them, and the girls recoiled. "You think I'm not
tired, Star? Do you really think this is the way I dreamed of
bringing up my girls?" She took a step closer, lowered her
voice. "Do you honestly believe that *this*," and she spread
her arms, "is the way I want us to live?"

Moonbow felt her sister trembling, grabbed her hand,
and squeezed it hard to stop her from answering.

"Trey Falkirk died so we could get away, and don't you
ever forget it," Jude said, each word the crack of a fierce

barbed whip. "He loved us all, you know that more than anyone, and he did what he had to do so we could do what we have to do." A hand lifted quickly. "Don't ask, Star, don't ask, because I don't really know. All I know is, Lady Beatrice agrees that we have to keep on, we have to find that man I saw. We have to find him soon." The hand dropped as if it were too heavy to hold up. "After that . . . I don't know. I do not know. But I do know that if we stop now . . ."

She looked up, looked back and touched the weighted bottom of her veil with one finger. "If I can live with *this* for the rest of my life, you can live with *me* just a little while longer."

"Not fair," Star said quietly. "That's not fair, Momma."

"No," she said flatly. "It isn't."

Moonbow was surprised. This wasn't like Momma, not like her at all, using what had happened to her face to make them do what she wanted. She'd never, ever done it before, and it was more than a little frightening now.

"All right, Momma," she said, giving Star's hand another squeeze, more gently this time.

Starshine slumped in defeat and said again, quietly, "It's still not fair."

"I'll make it up to you," Jude said, dropping to her knees in front of them, a hand on their knees. "I swear to God, I'll make it up—"

The first scream stopped her.

The second one brought the girls to their feet.

"Lady Bea," Starshine shouted, and jumped over the log, sprinted for the motel.

Moonbow and Jude were right behind her when they raced around the corner, right behind her when she reached the concrete walk that stretched the length of the building. They reached the door to their room together, and Moonbow froze.

Lady Beatrice was on the far bed, skirt bunched up around her waist, a nearly bald, pot-bellied man standing beside her, leaning over her, pinning her arms down by leaning on her wrists. A long-haired man with a backward-turned ball cap on knelt on the mattress, his jeans bunched around his ankles, ignoring her thrashing as he tried to rip her panties off her hips.

Starshine shrieked and charged into the room, leaped on the kneeling man's back, and began to pummel his head with one hand while reaching around to claw at his eyes with the other. The man roared in surprise, then laughed, and with one arm flung her off and against the wall. She hit hard and didn't move and all Moonbow could think of was that she looked like a broken doll.

Momma didn't run, didn't yell.

Moonbow watched, unable to move, as she walked over to the suitcase by the TV, opened it, and reached in.

"Hey, bitch," the second man said with a near toothless grin, "you don't have to—"

He shut up when he saw the gun.

"Damnit, bitch," the kneeling man said, then punched Beatrice twice in the face. "Hold still, damnit."

"Get off her," Jude ordered calmly, and pulled the hammer back.

The second man blinked stupidly; the kneeling man punched Beatrice again and looked over his shoulder. "Aw, Jesus," he said in disgust, "go to hell and wait your turn, huh? I'll be done in a minute."

Moonbow clamped her hands over her ears when Momma pulled the trigger; she turned away when the kneeling man snapped upright with a strangled gasp and a large red stain spread across his upper back; she leaned against the wall and didn't move, didn't make a sound, couldn't hear anything but shouting and firing and sirens and voices, and one kind voice that kept asking if she were all right, it's over, don't worry, hey, kid, hey, are you all right, did he hurt you?

She saw whirling lights that stained the fog red and blue, an ambulance that had backed up to the walk, men in uniform strutting around, people standing like dark ghosts in the fog watching and pointing, a man standing over her putting a blanket around her shoulders, someone on a stretcher covered head to toe with a sheet, Lady Beatrice huddled in the backseat of a police car talking to a lady cop, Starshine on a stretcher, oxygen mask over her nose and mouth.

Momma in handcuffs, taller than the two policemen who led her away.

That's when she decided she couldn't take anymore; that's when she decided it would be better if she went away for a while. Somewhere in the dark where it wasn't so cold; somewhere in the dark, without any fog.

4

*S*carlet fire and emerald sparks.

No one is left in the houses around the deep Ozark lake, all the boats pulled up and taken away, or placed high on saw-horses and covered with tarp. Windows are either boarded or shuttered, doors bolted, all tools and playthings locked away for the season. The water is smooth, not a ripple on the surface. The sky high and pale as the moon rises above the mountains. The air sharp and cold, a razor waiting to be used.

Scarlet fire.
   Emerald sparks that blur through the sky like comets.

Susan stands at the top of a grassy slope that leads down to the water, arms folded, chin tucked. Below, Joey stands with Eula on a short dock, the boy excitedly pointing at shooting stars and the old woman nodding, though she's seen it all before.

There is no wind.

There is no sound.

Until Joey giggles at something Eula has said and runs off the dock, up the slope, and circles Susan three times before stopping, hands on his hips, panting and grinning. Eula follows much more slowly, her head down, white-gloved hands clasped at her stomach, purse dangling from a strap over one wrist.

"I saw a movie today," Joey says, squinting at the stars.

"Did you," Susan says, her tone impatient.

"There were these guys on these really really big horses. They had cloaks and hoods and spears and everything. There was smoke and clouds and they were riding really really slow, and there was all this awful loud music." He scratched his forehead vigorously and frowned. "I think that was supposed to be us, right?"

Eula slipped but didn't fall.

Susan said, "Yes, they were supposed to be us."

"So how come we don't look like them, huh?" He looked up at her. "How come, huh? They were neat."

"Don't matter, child," Eula said, joining them, taking deep breaths, patting the back of a hand across her cheeks and brow. "We are what we are."

"Yeah, but they were neat."

A mountain on the other side of the lake cuts a black hole in the sky, and above the hole, just for a moment, there is scarlet fire and green sparks and the sound of explosions that make the trees tremble.

"It ain't fair," Joey pouts, standing downslope from the women, hands still on his hips. He uses his chin to point at the mountain. "He's having all the fun."

"Isn't," Eula corrects absently. "It isn't fair."

"That's what I said."

Susan can't help it—she shakes her head and laughs, and Eula laughs with her.

"What?" Joey says, demanding. "What did I say that's so funny, huh? You're making fun of me again."

"No, child," Eula tells him, reaching out a hand to touch his shoulder. "No, child, we're not."

"Then what are we waiting for?" he wants to know. His voice deepens as only a child's can. "He hurt me. That man hurt me and I want to hurt him. I want to hurt him now."

"Patience," says Susan.

Joey turns and stamps a booted foot. "I'm out of damn patience."

Eula straightens.

Joey glares at her for a second before bowing his head. "Sorry."

"Better be."

"I am."

Susan grins. "No, you're not."

Joey looks up and grins back. "Nope. I'm not."

"But you will be," she says, "if he finds out." And she points to the lake, and Joey turns and moans and backs up slowly.

The great black horse rides easily across the water.

Not a ripple, not a splash.

Scarlet fire drips from its hooves, emerald sparks dance from its nostrils and hit the water and turn to steam that turns to fog that rises and spreads in a slow-rising wind.

Red sits easily in the saddle, hat pulled low, one hand on his thigh, the other holding the reins. His head bobs side to side as if he was singing to himself, and when he reaches the shore, he looks up, and he's smiling.

Slowly Susan lowers her arms. "Yes?"

Joey runs down the slope and stands to one side so he

can pat the horse's flank while he walks. Red leans over, pulls playfully on the boy's hat.

"Yes?" Susan asks again.

"I saw us on television," Joey says excitedly. "We had hoods and stuff, and there was lots of neat smoke and stuff, and there was like these big wood things with pointy things on top." The horse stops when Red's eyes are level with the women's. "So how come we don't have those things, Red? How come, huh? Are we gonna get them?"

"Hush, child," Eula scolds.

Joey looks at her as if he's going to disobey, then mutters, "Yes, ma'am," and spends a few seconds taking care of his hat.

"You feeling better, Miz Korrey?" Red asks the black woman.

"Yes, sir, I am. All healed, all better."

"Good. That's good. And you, Susan?"

"Fine," she says shortly.

Red grins at her—it's there and it's gone.

The horse lowers its head, sweeps it around abruptly to stare at Joey, who gasps and backs away so quickly he falls on his rump, nearly rolls down to the water. He jumps up, muttering, brushing at his jeans, straightening his gunbelt, fussing again with his hat.

"Here, child," Eula says, and pats her leg until he stands beside her. One arm goes around his shoulder; she hugs him once, tightly.

Red pushes his hat back, crosses his hands over the saddle horn, leans over, and whispers something when the horse shies and stamps and lashes its tail. When it's quiet, he smiles—there and gone—and takes a deep breath.

Closes his eyes.

Opens them and says, "Be pleased to know it's time to hit the trail."

Susan says nothing, but her expression is smug; Eula nods; Joey whoops and hollers and breaks into a war dance until he slips on the damp grass and nearly knocks Eula down. This time she grabs the back of his neck and holds him at her side.

Red's face is impassive. "You know where you have to be. You know when you have to be there. There is no rush. We have plenty of time. I took care of a few things." He sniffs, rubs the back of his neck. "Don't believe I'll see you again before then."

"Even the odds?" Susan says.

Eula looks at her, puzzled.

"Maybe," Red says.

"What do you mean, maybe?" Susan isn't pleased. "Either you did or you didn't."

Eula draws herself up. "What are you two talking about? What odds?"

Red gives her the smile. "Just trying to make sure you don't get all bruised again, Miz Korrey."

Eula's expression tells him she's not sure if he's mocking her or not, but she says nothing, only grunts softly.

"And on the way?" Susan asks. "On the way?"

Red frowns at her. "You know."

She scowls back. "That's not right."

"It's the way it is. What can I tell you, but it's the way it is."

"My palomino," Joey says, impatiently shaking off Eula's hand.

"Waiting on you, pardner."

Joey nods thoughtfully. "And can I hurt him? Can I hurt John Bannock?"

Red grins. "Son, when it's time, you can do all the hurting you want to. Any way you want to." He holds up a finger. "But nothing before then, you hear me, son?" His head turns. "You hear me, Susan? You listening? Nothing before then."

The horse steps back, snorting, tossing its head.

Red's voice lowers, the sound of a dark wind blowing before thunder. "It's *my* time, you understand?" Staring hard until she has to look away. "You'll have yours again, but now it's my time."

A tug on the reins, a clucking noise, and the horse begins to turn down the slope.

"Red," Eula says.

He looks over his shoulder, nothing visible under the brim but cold green eyes.

Eula glances at Susan, then straightens her shoulders. "How is it written? How will it be? I wasn't supposed to get no hurting, you know. It wasn't supposed to happen. So how is it written?"

No one moves.

No one speaks.

Until at last he says, "There is no written, Miz Korrey. There is no written."

"But the Book—"

"Man writes," he told them all, "but it's only words. They mean nothing. Not to us."

"That's no answer," she complains.

And he says, "Oh, yes, Miz Korrey. Oh, yes, it is."

He rides across the water, not a ripple, not a splash.

Scarlet fire in scarlet ribbons wind from the great black's hooves.

Emerald sparks from its nostrils scatter over the lake.

This time the water boils.

Part 4

1

1

An autumn wind blows across a Tennessee hillside, husking through the dying grass, slipping around headstones whose words are worn, whose surfaces are laced with spider-leg cracks. Dead flowers on distant graves shudder and lose their petals. Sharp blue sky and clouds like thin smoke. Trees in their colors spinning leaves into the air.

Casey stands alone beneath a weather-bent sycamore, hands in his pockets, shoulders up against the wind, hair stabbing at his eyes. White hair, not black, but still thick, still barely reaching his shoulders; he's long since given up trying to swipe it away.

He watches a small group of mourners standing beneath a sagging faded canopy. A few old women huddled in black, a few old men in black suits or dark suits, their ties knotted, their faces reddened, hair slicked, old shoes polished as best they could be. No young ones; no one younger than fifty. There are chairs, but no one uses them. The time has passed to sit in the presence of the dead.

Their bodies block what he knows is there—a coffin none of them, or the woman inside, could have afforded in this life. On the gently curved lid, a trio of flowers picked from the dead woman's garden only that morning, having lasted this long some said just to be where they are. A simple wreath propped on a wobbly tripod stand wrapped in green paper. A spray of lilies in a cheap glass vase that's much too short for the length of the stems.

On the far side of the grave, a giant of a man in a black frock coat and gleaming black boots, his face masked by shifting shadow, holds in his left hand an open Bible, his right hand passing tenderly over the coffin now and then. He doesn't look at the Good Book; he doesn't need to, he only holds it for the others. His voice reminds Casey for no reason at all of a river that flows in the lightless recesses of a cavern—deep and slightly rough, musical without song. He gestures toward the valley, toward the mist-covered hills that make up the horizon and the mist that covers the green valley floor; he gestures, and he speaks, and the old men and the old women nod, and whisper, "Amen," and close their eyes against the tears they thought they had already shed.

Casey orders himself to turn away, that he doesn't need to see this, that he's seen it already, but he doesn't turn and he doesn't stop listening and somewhere below his heart he feels the twisting of a knife.

I don't need this.

I don't want this.

The wind grows stronger, the mist dances and thins, settles and thickens, and the air is streaked with a thousand flying leaves like a flock of tiny birds determined to peck the eyes from his head. He ducks away, hisses when a sharp edge lays open a cut on his cheek. And one on his forehead. And another over the thick eyebrow above his left eye.

"I don't need this!" he yells, and one old man dressed in

old black looks over his shoulder, scowling, shaking a finger, and looks back to the grave.

"Damnit, I don't want this!" Casey shouts, and an old
woman dressed in the best black dress she owns looks over
her shoulder, sunken cheeks quivering, the scarf around
her head fluttering in the wind. She says nothing, but she
doesn't have to, and Casey snaps a curse at her, shows her
his back, and glares at the valley that dares look so peaceful on a day like this, with a wind like this.

While the leaves dart at him again, and again cut his face.

Finally he protects his eyes with his hands and leans
against the tree, listening to that voice, to the soft sobs and
the soft moans and far up the hillside the not-so-soft sound
of horses racing down from the crest.

Don't look, it's only a dream.

The voice, the sobs, hooves pounding the turf.

Don't look.

He can't help it.

"Lord, no," he whispers, and begins to run, slapping
away the leaves, leaning into the wind, because there is a
herd up there, one hundred or more horses of all colors
and breeds, stampeding down the slope, kicking over
headstones, digging grass up in great spraying clumps,
heading straight for the funeral under the faded canopy
over there.

He calls a warning, but no one listens.

He stumbles, spins in an awkward circle, runs again
and wonders why the living hell they can't hear the
beasts that are only a few yards away, heads tossing,
manes rippling, steam puffing from their nostrils and
foam bubbling from their mouths. He waves his arms and
yells; he waves his arms and the leaves blind him; he sees
a stump and veers around it, doesn't see the exposed root
that scrapes along his ankle, causing him to falter, to fall,
and for a few feet he's on all fours before he's up again.
Still running. Still yelling. Until something happens to

his legs and he's on the ground again, sprawled and watching helplessly—

While the herd sweeps through the funeral, snapping the canopy posts, trampling the wreath, shattering the vase, slamming aside the old men and the old women, swallowing them in their midst, and all he can see now is a red-tinged cloud and the horses and falling shadows, and all he can hear are the women, who are too old to scream for very long as they're broken.

Blood on his face and agony in his legs, he watches the herd continue headlong down the hill and vanish into the valley covered by the mist.

I don't need this, he thinks.

I don't want this, he begs.

And when the wind takes the dust, there is nothing left but the canopy lying torn and twisted on the ground, covering the mourners, who don't move at all.

The coffin is gone.

The man in black is gone.

Casey knows he can walk, but he crawls instead, keeping well away from the flapping canopy shroud, wincing as the leaves continue to shred his cheeks; swallowing bile, swallowing blood, until he reaches the lip of the fresh open grave. He knows that if he looks he'll see either the man in black or the dead woman's coffin, or, he thinks, he'll see himself.

Down in the mist a horse screams, and there is thunder.

He settles back on his heels, searching the sky, refusing to give the dream the satisfaction of showing him the all too obvious.

The wind pushes trickles of dirt into the hole.

The canopy ripples, its edges snapping like frayed pennants.

The smell of fresh-turned earth; the stench of crushed flowers.

He searches the sky, bows his head, leans forward, and looks.

The grave is empty.
I don't want this.
Nothing's there.
I don't need this.
And a voice says, "Yes, you do."

2

"No," Casey protested.

"You need it," the voice insisted, and he felt something cool and wet slide into his mouth.

He choked, swallowed the water, and said, "Damn."

The voice laughed softly, and he opened his eyes and saw above his head the familiar mottled ceiling of his bedroom. He blinked rapidly and hard because the light was bright and it was difficult to see anything but shapes and shadows moving around the room. Something fluttered by the window that overlooked the front yard; he concentrated on it until it focused into the old white curtains ruffled by a breeze. Beside the window he saw an IV stand, an empty plastic bag hanging from a hook, clear plastic tubing draped over the top.

A good start, he thought, and turned his attention to his water bearer.

A moment later he recognized her face. "Hi," he said, abruptly ashamed at how weak he sounded.

"Hi, yourself," Ronnie answered. Red hair pulled back, away from her brow and ears, a size-large checkered shirt that puffed and molded when she moved. "How do you feel?"

His eyes closed momentarily as he took careful, fearful stock—his face felt stiff, as if it were mildly sunburned, cotton batting had been crammed into his head, his chest didn't feel quite right, and his left leg had clearly been carved out of old wood.

Deeper, far deeper, there was a suggestion of great pain.

"Strange," he decided, somewhat surprised. "Okay, but strange."

"Good enough." She gave him another sip of water, cautioning him with a look not to drink too much at once.

"I'm home." He knew he sounded stupid, clearing his throat several times because it felt lined with iron shavings.

She nodded as she held the glass to his lips. "Yep, you are."

"So I'm not dead."

"Nope. Beat all to hell, though."

His eyes closed again.

He remembered, and held his breath for a long time, dampening the turmoil combination of anxiety and rage that made his neck muscles bulge, his head tremble slightly. He could sense Ronnie's unease and forced calm upon himself; a truce, momentary and fragile.

Then he slowly folded the sheet down and away from his chest, noting as he did the welts and bruises on the backs of his hands, the tiny cuts. When his torso was exposed, he couldn't see much, but he saw enough. More scratches, and a vast multicolored bruise that spread side to side and down to his stomach; he couldn't help thinking how much like mold it looked. He didn't bother to prod it, test it. It should hurt like hell, it didn't, and he let well enough alone.

"Damn," he muttered, voice rasping.

What he thought was: Why the hell aren't I dead?

He used his right hand then to examine his face, felt padding and rough edges down to his neck, up into his hair. "Do I want a mirror?"

She laughed silently. "Probably not today, no. You've got twenty or thirty stitches, and a ton of mummy bandages." She gestured toward his chest and legs. "The good news is, there's nothing broken."

"Small favors, I guess." He tried to sit up, groaned, and gave up when something long and hot flared in his spine. When his eyes closed, the pain eased.

"Dr. Alloway says you're supposed to take it easy," she

told him. "Not that you haven't figured that out already."
She called, "He's awake," over her shoulder and put the
glass on the nightstand, next to a trio of drugstore pill bottles. "Sorry," she said, keeping her voice low. "They
insisted."

A few seconds later a man's voice in the doorway: "Mr.
Chisholm, I'm so pleased you're back with us."

Another man, much younger: "Thank God."

Quiet footsteps across the floor, a faint rocking motion
as Ronnie settled gingerly on the edge of the mattress.

"We were awfully concerned, Mr. Chisholm." Reverend
Baylor, at his left side. "I hope you don't mind, but we had
some prayers for you at service."

"Whatever works," Casey answered, and sighed at how
flip his response sounded. "Thanks."

"Are you hurting, Mr. Chisholm?" Whittaker Hull, from
the foot of the bed, speaking gravely.

For an instant Casey saw the brass knuckles, the fist, the
face behind them, and he flinched before he realized that
he didn't hurt much at all.

"No," he said, amazed.

"That," Ronnie said, "is because you're all doped up.
When it wears off . . ."

3

He stands in the modest belfry of a modest church, and
Hell boils below him—houses burning, glass melting,
buildings exploding, trees afire all the way to the horizon;
people running and crawling and screaming and dying, or
dead already, faces turned to the night sky, blind to the rain
and the lightning.

A shotgun blast.

The sound of an ax meeting the back of someone's skull.

An automobile strikes a tree and adds fuel to the fire.

A cry for help.

A cry for mercy.

The flames are too bright in the middle of the night, and he can't see anymore what's real down there in the midst of flickering sliding shadow; he can't find his friends to see who's still alive, and he can't find the woman who brought all this to the town that was his home.

A boy far below looks up at him in horror.

He stiffens and rage takes him—the woman is right behind him.

A voice in his ear: "Believe it or not, we're on the same side."

4

He had questions, but he couldn't stay awake long enough to ask them all, sometimes asked them twice because he couldn't remember the original answers.

So the answers came in spurts and soft whispers, as the light dimmed and brightened and dimmed again, as the pain made its way to the surface on the tips of jabbing spears and lances, fighting the medication, fighting his sense of time and place.

"Who found me?"

"Senior Raybourn," said Reverend Baylor. There was amusement in his tone. "He said he was coming back to take care of you, whatever that meant. He had his shotgun, so I can imagine you must have . . . well, never mind. It doesn't matter. He found you on the walk, said there was more blood than skin, and thought you were surely dead. I think, Mr. Chisholm, that disappointed him somehow. At any rate, he called the sheriff, Gloria Nazario, and me. By the time I got here, Sheriff Oakman had already arrived."

"The Teagues. It was the Teagues."

"So you've said. A number of times."

* * *

Chilly.

The furnace loud.

Fresh sheets, a clean blanket, someone gave him a sponge bath because he couldn't stand, couldn't walk, and would be damned if he'd crawl.

"What day is it?"

Ronnie grinned. "Maybe you should ask what week it is."

Gloria Nazario brought him soup, fed him over his feeble protests, dried his chin with a napkin, all the while looking as if she'd murder the first person who looked at her sideways. She had taken over his care, and no one argued. Not even Hector, who sometimes stood in the doorway, staring at him as though trying to figure out what he was.

Gloria had no gossip, no news. All she said was, "Eat."

When she had to leave for Betsy's, Kitra Baylor took over, sitting in a corner armchair, reading, checking to be sure his pills were administered on time. When he tried to talk to her, all she said was, "Sleep."

Whittaker Hull had more questions than answers, and Casey had a bad feeling he was going to show up on the *Weekly*'s front page. Thank God, the man hadn't taken any pictures.

As far as he knew.

"Are the Teagues in jail?"

"No."

"Why the hell not?"

"Why did they attack you, Mr. Chisholm? Do you think it's because you helped me, is that what it was? Did you say something to Stump at church Thanksgiving morning?

I saw you talking to him, with Mrs. Baylor, and later, when you took him away. Well, I saw what you did; I don't know if you talked to him or not. He has a rather nasty temper. It doesn't pay to have it aimed at you. As you've already found out. What did you say to him, Mr. Chisholm? May I call you Casey? What did you say to him, Casey? What did you do? Do you know something? Do you know what's going on?"

A strong night wind that prowled around the house, voicing its displeasure at not being able to get in.

Once, the sound of rain snapping at the window, and the night seemed much darker.

A chubby man, with thin strands of short brown hair that refused to lie down properly across a tan-mottled scalp. Heavy lips, pale eyes, ears that stood out from the side of his head. Glasses in thick black frames.

Clark Gable ears, Casey thought, and must have said it aloud because the man scowled and shook his head with impatience.

He had a needle; he used it.

Casey drifted forever each time the man left.

"What day is it?"

"Eat."

"What day is it?"

"Sleep, Mr. Chisholm, sleep. It's the best thing for you right now."

*   *   *

"Why aren't they in jail?"

"Sadly, Casey, it's the way of it here. You haven't been around. You saw it in my office. Now you know."

Sometime, he didn't know when, but he still couldn't sit up without nausea spinning out of the dizziness that spiraled along with it . . . sometime during the next few days, Sheriff Oakman came to see him, full uniform, without the sunglasses. Perched on the foot of the bed, hat pushed back, gunbelt leather creaking each time he shifted. He said nothing about the last time they had spoken.

Casey couldn't think very straight, drug and pain at constant war, yet it didn't take long for him to catch on:

"So you say it was the Teagues, Mr. Chisholm?"

"I don't *say* so. It *was* them. Billy Ray hit me first. I don't remember much after that."

"So you don't really know if Stump and Cord took their licks, too."

"Don't think they just stood around, Sheriff. Stump was pretty ticked at me."

"It was near dark, that right?"

"Yes."

"Near dark. You told me before, you said that you were angry at something. Senior Raybourn, for one."

"Yeah, I was."

"And it was near dark."

"Like I said."

"So you were blind angry, it was near full dark, no streetlights, no moon, and you saw Billy Ray clear as a bell. That right?"

"I saw him. Yes. I said something to Stump, who was on my steps, and Billy Ray said something, and I turned, and he hit me. With brass knuckles."

"Well, I don't know about that, Mr. Chisholm. Doctor Alloway says those injuries aren't consistent with the use of brass knuckles. For one thing, your jaw isn't broken."

"Okay. Maybe it was just his knuckles. What the hell difference does it make?"

"Makes a lot of difference, Mr. Chisholm. The way the light was, the way your mood was, can't really believe that you saw what you claim you saw."

"I don't claim anything, Sheriff. I saw what I saw."

"Almost full dark, no—"

"Sheriff, I don't really give a damn what you think just now, okay? As soon as I can walk and think straight, I'm coming down and I'm swearing out a complaint, and you're going to arrest those sons . . ."

"Mr. Chisholm, you okay?"

"Unless it'd give you pleasure to see me throw up my lunch, Sheriff, you'd better leave now."

He resented all those people trampling through his house. Poking through his things. Making themselves comfortable on what little furniture he had. Walking in and out as if they owned the place. Every so often he could hear laughter downstairs, that hushed kind of laughter heard in hospitals and sick houses, joy muted in deference to the ill and injured.

A doctor came by several times—Alloway? Calloway?—but he could barely remember the man's face from one visit to the next, only that he was going bald and doing a lousy job of hiding it.

He was angry. At himself for being ambushed when he had been expecting it, and at the world for refusing to just leave him the hell alone.

He thought it was morning; it was certainly bright enough. And he could smell the sea.

Someone stood in the doorway.

He squinted, shaded his eyes.

"Mr. Raybourn," he said. Pulled at his throat with two fingers, hoping he wouldn't sound too hoarse, wishing his eyes would work better—focus was blurred, light was vaguely hazed. "It looks like I owe you a pretty large debt, sir."

Senior Raybourn stepped into the room, baggy pants and suspenders, his cap in one hand. "Don't owe me nothing."

"Yes, I do. You saved my life."

Raybourn's lips pulled at one corner. "To tell the truth, I was going to shoot you."

Casey smiled in turn. "Yeah. I kind of heard that."

"My boy . . ."

Casey waited, praying the old man wouldn't start up again about the handshake.

"I went home last night, he was looking at a magazine." Two hands at the cap now, twisting it. "Night I saw you, he was reading it, Mr. Chisholm. Stories and everything. The boy can't read all that well, but that night he was reading it like he'd been reading all his life."

"Look—"

"Last night he looks up at me and he says, 'I like the pictures, Daddy, all these pretty pictures.' "

Casey didn't get it, and frowned to prove it.

"Couldn't read worth a lick, Mr. Chisholm. The boy couldn't read no more. Whatever you done, it didn't stick." He slapped the cap on. "Couldn't remember that he did, either."

Casey spread his hands—*I don't know what to say.*

Raybourn backed out of the room, turned to leave, and looked back. "He's my only kin, Mr. Chisholm. You do something to him again, next time I'll finish it. I swear by God, I'll finish it right."

A week after he woke up the first time—maybe it was longer, he couldn't tell, time meant little or nothing and he really didn't care—he lifted his T-shirt and looked at his chest, and the bruise had shrunk dramatically and was so faded it had turned pale grey, little more than a shadow lurking under his skin. There were still a couple of bandages on his face, but the stitches had been taken out, assurances given that he probably wouldn't have any scars. None, that is, that would scare anybody.

He supposed he ought to feel good about that.

He couldn't figure out why he didn't.

The doctor—it was Alloway, not Calloway; a small victory he relished—instructed Kitra and Gloria that Casey was to take the medication only with his meals, but not to skip or skimp the dosage. Very important for the healing process, he declared; vital.

"I don't want anymore," Casey protested that evening.

"You heard the doctor," Gloria said.

"I don't care."

Hands on her hips, she watched until he swallowed, and he hated her for it.

The sheriff returned.

"Had a talk with Stump Teague," he said.

Casey frowned, shook his head to drive off the cobwebs. It almost worked.

"Says he was on the mainland, him and his brothers. They got a bartender to swear to it."

"The bartender's lying."

"Your word against his, Chisholm, and he don't have a record."

"No, but I've got the bruises."

"No kidding? Can't hardly see them from here."

"Get out, Sheriff."

"Why? You gonna throw up again?"

He stayed, trying to chat with Kitra Baylor, but she insisted he leave, Casey needed his rest.

"Rest?" Oakman snorted. "Man's been lying on his fat back for two weeks, give or take. He gets any more rest, he'll be dead."

Eventually, what few visitors he had only came by in the evening. They had jobs, and his condition wasn't life-threatening; he wasn't dying. They didn't stay long, either, and he didn't encourage them to. He couldn't figure out why they had bothered in the first place.

Eventually they stopped.

The quiet was a relief.

He used the time to practice sitting up, then walking, not doing very well at either and cursing himself for it; he used the time to stare out the window and watch the season slip closer to winter. It was still pleasantly warm when the sun was out, but there were days when clouds killed the warmth, and the wind had a touch of ice on its breath.

Rick Jordan brought him a portable radio, spent an entire afternoon telling stories about what could be seen from the fire tower on the ridge. About the people he could see with his high-power binoculars, and what they were doing. Casey laughed, but he didn't know why. The young man was so earnest in his attempt to pass the time, Casey didn't have the heart to ask him to repeat whatever it was he'd just said.

When he left, Casey pounded the bed in frustration, glared at the pills, and decided it was time to stop. The hell with Alloway, the hell with Gloria and Kitra and their Mother-knows-best looks. He was tired of living in a shifting cotton fog.

After dinner that night, he tucked the pills under his tongue, drank the juice Gloria handed him, and closed his eyes. Listened to her move around, straightening the sheet and blanket, turning off the radio and the Christmas carols it played, whispering with Kitra and Hector in the doorway.

He kept his eyes closed until he heard her leave the room, then spit the pills onto the bed; he kept his eyes closed until the front door closed and he heard two cars pull away.

When he was sure he was alone, he used elbows and palms to sit himself up, keeping his eyes half shut because opening them, even this time of day, let in too much light and made his head ache. Next, using bed and nightstand, he pushed carefully to his feet. Swayed. Swallowed. Used the bed to get him close to the door, then lurched across the floor and grabbed onto the frame.

There was no pain.

Just that damnable fog.

A few deep breaths, a few curses for encouragement, and he shuffled down the hall, bracing his hands against the wall, refusing to lift his feet because he knew he would fall.

Once in the bathroom he turned on the light, groaned, and grabbed onto the smooth round edge of the sink.

The mirror on the medicine chest door was streaked with leftover cleaner, but he could see his reflection well enough, and it made him grin.

"Mummy bandages," he muttered. "Lord, she wasn't kidding."

His knees weakened.

He snapped them rigid, splashed cold water on his face, drank from his palm until the cold stung fingers and throat, then splashed water vigorously over his head.

The fog almost lifted; it would have to do until all the medication was purged from his system.

Then, with fingers that disobeyed him half the time, he peeled the bandage patches from his forehead, his cheeks, from his left temple and the blunt of his chin, tossing them aside, not caring who might find them. He couldn't manage to lift the T-shirt over his head, so he grabbed a pair of manicure scissors from the cabinet and patiently, fumbling, cut it off.

When he was done, he stepped back as far as his arms would permit while one hand still held on to the basin.

"Lord," he whispered. "Good . . . Lord."

There were splotches of dried disinfectant—iodine, something else maybe, he really couldn't tell—and there were dark lines here and there the adhesive had left behind.

Nothing else.

No scars, no signs of the gashes and the cuts; no scratches, no bruises, no fresh-looking skin, and when he tested his skin with a rough finger, no tenderness.

I was hurt, he thought; damnit, I know I was hurt.

The fog settled, and his legs slowly lowered him to the cool tile floor.

I was hurt.

He crawled back to his bed. It might have taken him all night for all he knew, but when he awoke at dawn, there was a powerful thirst and his bladder screamed at him, so he half crawled, half walked back to the bathroom, closed the door and took one more look in the mirror.

Nothing.

Nothing.

5

"Son of a bitch!"

He looked at the date on the *Atlanta Journal* someone, probably Mrs. Baylor, had left at the foot of the bed.

It was Monday. Only five days until Christmas.

Three weeks, maybe a few days more, of living in that damnable fog.

Five days.

Enough time for all that to heal, vanish, as if it had never existed?

I don't know.

No.

6

Hector called his name as he came up the stairs, and Casey was ready, sitting on the edge of the mattress, bathrobe draped over his legs.

"I'll bring you breakfast," Hector said, surprised to see him up. "You don't—"

"I'll come down," Casey told him with what he hoped was a reassuring smile. "Just give me a hand here."

"I don't know. I—"

Casey grabbed the robe. "I'm coming down. Just make sure I don't fall on my face."

"Gloria's gonna kill me."

Casey smiled, and with the man's hand on his arm, managed to get to the kitchen without stumbling. It took a while, the fog was thin but there, but he made it. When he sat at the table, it was like sitting on a throne.

Hector fussed, worrying about what his sister would say, every so often glancing at Casey's face, puzzled but too polite to ask any questions.

Casey lifted his shoulders in an exaggerated sigh. "Man, I am *starving*."

That pleased the cook. "A good sign. Good sign." He made a large meal, and Casey ate it all—the eggs, the toast, the cereal, the bacon. His stomach suggested it was too much too soon; he didn't care. He needed strength, and what he usually received wouldn't do it.

After he finished, he sat back and sighed, loudly. "You are a genius, Mr. Nazario, a pure genius."

"Gracias," Hector said as he washed the dishes. "I get your pills in a moment."

"I'll take them later."

"But the doctor—"

"I'll take them later, Hector, don't worry about it. Soon as I get back upstairs."

Hector shrugged. "Okay. Then I—"

"By myself."

A few seconds passed before Hector turned slowly, dish towel in one hand.

"You have no idea how grateful I am," Casey said. "Without you and Gloria, the others . . ."

It was a gamble, and he knew it. Offense could be easily taken.

Hector studied him for a long time before dropping the towel onto the counter. "It is difficult, I know, for a man who has been alone to suddenly have all these people."

Casey nodded.

"It would be nice to be alone again. At least for a little while."

Casey thanked him without a word.

"Gloria," the man said, "is still going to kill me, though."

They grinned at each other before Nazario, in silence, insisted on finishing his cleaning. When it was over, Casey asked him if he could get in touch with Rick, there was something that needed done. Again Hector studied him, shrugged, and nodded. Didn't leave until Casey assured him a dozen times that he could indeed get back upstairs on his own and that if anything went wrong he'd get in touch immediately.

"How?" the man asked. "You don't got a phone."

"I'll tie a message to a sea gull."

Hector almost laughed, then picked up his coat and left without looking back.

It took a while before Casey realized he was truly alone, that the silence was a comfort, that he was finally on his own. Almost. Then, weak-legged and slightly nauseous, he made his way back upstairs. An hour later he was on the living room couch, in jeans and shirt; he hadn't bothered with shoes or socks, he wasn't going anywhere and the house was warm. He was proud of himself. He had managed to dress without falling over, to shave without slitting his throat, and to get back down the stairs without breaking his neck.

He kept a small towel beside him, every so often mopping the sweat from his face and neck, sometimes his arms. It wasn't the furnace, he finally decided, it was the last of the medication slipping from his system. Not fast enough, though; not nearly fast enough. He still felt as if he were a ghost in his own house, insubstantial and incapable of thinking in a straight line for very long.

He figured patience, in this case, was the greatest virtue he had.

The greatest gift, right now, was the silence that told him the house was empty. He had no idea why, suddenly, all those people had volunteered to care for him. Maybe it was his standing up to the Teagues, maybe it was the us-against-them feeling they seemed to have. It didn't matter. It had been welcome. For a while. Now it was not. One last thing, and it would be time to put up the walls again. Not quite so high, maybe, but high enough.

One last thing, and he could return to what he had been.

No; to what he had become.

He dozed.

He dreamed.

He woke up with a start, face covered in sweat, legs trembling as if they had run a long way.

In the dream he had run from window to window, peering out at a night that had no business being as dark as it was, looking for the source of the hoofbeats he heard. Slow and measured, they circled the house, as slow and measured he had heard them on the beach that night last summer.

They didn't stop until the dream did.

"I'm not yours," he whispered harshly, rubbing the towel roughly over his face, turning his skin pink. "Damnit, I'm not yours. Leave me alone."

He reached for the television's remote control, figuring it might be a good idea to catch up on what he had missed. No one had filled him in except for comments about the weather. Of course, there was always the chance they had, in fact, talked to him, but he'd be damned if he could remember anything. Pretty much anything at all.

The set snapped on to an incomprehensible commercial just as a pickup drew up in front of the house. He watched the truck, tense, until Rick climbed out of the cab, hitched up his jeans, and trotted up the walk.

He knocked.

Casey loved him for it.

"Open," he called.

The younger man pushed the door open slowly without entering, and when he finally stepped in, Casey laughed and said, "You expecting me to jump you?"

Rick grinned and ducked his head, embarrassed. "Sorry. Hector didn't tell me what you wanted, I didn't . . ." He grinned again. "Sorry."

"No problem." He cleared his throat, wished he had brought something to drink from the kitchen. "Look . . . look, I have no right to ask you, but I need a favor."

Rick shrugged. "Sure."

Careful, Case; careful.

"I, uh . . . it's got to be between you and me. No one else."

Rick looked around the room, at the ceiling briefly, and shrugged. "No sweat."

When Casey explained what he wanted, Rick thought for a moment and suggested a better way. It was as if he did this sort of thing every day, and Casey had to restrain himself from asking why the unquestioned agreement. He didn't want to blow it, to say something wrong.

After a brief argument about payment—"It's a favor, Mr. Chisholm, let's leave it at that, okay?"—Jordan left, and Casey switched to a news station, turned up the volume.

Not that he needed to.

The images were sufficient to tell him that little had changed. What made him groan aloud, however, was the rumor that Australia, faced with the possibility that China might enter her conflict with Indonesia, had raised the flag of nuclear weaponry. The newsman suggested it was only a stand-back-this-isn't-your-fight warning, and it was, after all, only a rumor. What he didn't have to say was that China wasn't a nation that took well to bluffing.

Meanwhile, in San Francisco, another gang war had ended at the intervention of the National Guard.

Meanwhile, in Athens . . .

My God, Casey thought; my God, it's really starting.

He turned the set off and stared out the window.

Not me, he thought.

Not me.

Leave me alone.

2

1

The Lighthouse Hut was just shy of seventeen miles east of Savannah. In its day it had been a fun place to travel to, to get fine lobster, a decent steak, halfway good small combo jazz, and drinks that were generous to a fault. In its day its side parking lot was always full from sunset to past midnight, and drivers heading south along the coast couldn't help but listen to the music that refused to stay confined within its uneven clapboard walls. It wasn't even close to resembling a lighthouse, and it didn't have such a great view of the ocean because the land it was on was lower than the road that passed in front of it, but no one minded because after the sun went down there was nothing out there to see anyway.

A new highway killed it. With no nearby exit ramp, drivers could only look and wonder as they went by, and only the faithful made the effort to get off. But even they eventually gave up, and the paint peeled and the parking lot tarmac cracked and the signboard on the roof quickly faded and, during a hurricane in '88, was blown to the ground.

The only thing that remained, really, of the old Hut was the large and gaudy, somewhat comical plaster statue of a gull on the wing that stood near the entrance.

It was the first thing Reed Turner had seen when John got lost trying to find the entrance to the Camoret Causeway.

"That's it!" he had yelled, practically deafening everyone in the car. "Cora, look, there's the giant bird!"

John had asked no questions. He pulled into the lot and parked, facing east, hadn't even taken his hands off the steering wheel before Reed was out of the car and moving stiffly toward the road. His left arm and shoulder were still swollen from a slam it had taken when he'd fallen over a table during the fighting.

He stood there until the others joined him, then pointed toward the sea. "Look," he said quietly. "That truck, you see it?"

Despite the low clouds, the dim light, John saw it. Not much of a truck in the distance, a pickup whose color was as dull as the air around it, but because of the angle and the low pitch of the land, it looked for all the world as if it were riding on water.

Reed took Cora's arm and tugged on it. "That's it," he insisted. "That's what I saw. Remember? The dream? That's where he is." His face was flushed, his forehead slick with sweat, and when she put an arm around his waist, he sagged gratefully against her. "I know it, Cor. I know he's out there."

"You're sure?" Lisse asked him.

He nodded, a grin more like a grimace.

"Well, hell, why not?" John said. "It's the only damn place we haven't looked, right? So let's get back in the— well, damnit!"

A few drops at first, a brief warning before the wind rose abruptly, the clouds split, and the storm began.

An hour later they were still in the parking lot, still in

the car. John kept the engine running so the heater would work, the only light the green glow of the dashboard that lay shimmering green ghosts on the windows. Lisse was asleep; he didn't wake her. It was, in fact, a miracle she was here at all. The blood he'd seen on her at the hotel he had immediately assumed had been Reed's.

It wasn't.

It was hers.

A piece of the window had sliced neatly through the side of her neck. No sooner had he reached her, and reached for her, than she had collapsed, lying across Reed's legs, while Cora knelt and screamed for help.

He had taken off his shirt and wadded it against her wound, did his best to staunch the blood that flowed from Reed's upper chest and back, did his best not to scream himself when, as the paramedics arrived, he became convinced they were both dead.

Even later, at the hospital, fending off reporters while, at the same time, trying to accommodate the inquiries of the police, he was positive that when it was over, only he and Cora would be left. And for the first couple of hours, Cora in the emergency room on a gurney, sedated for her hysteria, he wasn't so sure he wouldn't be the only one.

When a nurse finally grabbed him and sat him on a bed, he protested until she pointed out the dribbles and runs of blood the glass and splinters had caused.

"You are not," she said sternly, "going to bleed to death on my watch, mister."

For the better part of half an hour, she plucked wood and glass needles from his back, the back of his head, the backs of his hands and arms. She kept telling him he was lucky, all things considered, and he kept telling her she didn't get it, that his friends were out there somewhere, probably dying.

"Well, you're not going to do them any good like this," she said, slapped on disinfectant and a few bandages, and pushed him back to the overcrowded waiting room.

He had learned rather quickly the truth of the cliché of a waking nightmare.

The smell of blood, the smell of terror; voices raised and voices pleading; weeping and moaning, loud arguments and denunciations, hysterical laughter and not a few mordant jokes; people wandering dazed in torn clothes, in hospital gowns; the staff clearly near the end of its tether, doing its best to hold on.

The hospital was far too small to handle all the victims. Not enough operating rooms, the staff overburdened. He found Reed just as the young man was in the process of being transferred somewhere else. Cora had insisted on going with him; John hadn't argued. In the chaos, despite the best efforts of the increasingly harried nurses to keep track of all the admissions, all the treatments . . . despite the families that refused to sit down and wait patiently, their demands growing shrill, fear feeding upon itself . . . despite his determination once Reed was safely on his way . . .

He lost Lisse.

Three hours of roaming, paying no attention to suggestions and commands, sitting only when he was threatened with eviction by a cop . . . three hours, maybe more, he didn't bother to note the time because it no longer had meaning, he found her in a tiny windowless room on a different floor. With no idea how she'd gotten there, and not caring at the moment, he'd stood over her, staring at her bloodless face, at the thick dressing that wrapped halfway around her neck.

He held her hand.

He whispered to her.

He followed the drip of the IV attached to her right arm.

He had listened to voices in the hallway, but couldn't get anyone to come in and tell him how she was, how she would be, only that she had been in surgery. At the nurses' station he was told she would be all right. Blood loss had been replaced on the operating table, the vein sutured, the sliced muscle repaired.

Well past midnight a resident came in to check on her, told him her blood loss had indeed been severe, but it looked as if she would be left with little more than a scar on her neck.

"You shouldn't stay."

"I have to."

The doctor didn't argue. He shrugged, made notations on her chart, and left.

John never saw him again.

The only time he left her side was when he went in search of a chair, found it in a room whose signs warned of oxygen use, and carried it back. Sometime before dawn he fell asleep. Sometime later he woke up with a startled gasp, took several seconds to understand where he was, and saw Lisse.

Her eyes were still closed, but she was turned slightly toward him. She had moved, and that made him cry. Silently, one hand pressed to his eyes until he couldn't stand seeing the body of little Eddie with that hole in his throat anymore. Relief. And exhaustion. And a dreadful, certain feeling that he hadn't seen the last of the blood, or the dead.

Lisse's first words had been: "He's after us."

2

The Morlane County prosecutor shook his head sadly and said, "Your Honor, much as I can sympathize with the young ladies' plight, I cannot in good conscience see how we can even think of entertaining such a foolish notion, considering the seriousness of the charges and the clear risk to flight on the part of the accused."

The judge, an elderly man whose robes were obviously meant for a man twice his girth, rapped a pencil idly on his desk. "Crawford, save the fancy talk for the courtroom, would you mind? I've got a kicking mule ulcer going here and I want to go home before I die."

"Okay, it's a stupid idea, Judge."

"That's better."

"Then you agree."

The judge shook his head. "Not so sure about that, Crawford." He leaned back and tented his fingers under his chin, the pencil clamped between his palms, tip aiming at his lap. "Mrs. Harp, I'm going to ask you one more time to find yourself an attorney. Granted, what you've done thus far is first-rate, but being a lawyer in your own country doesn't really amount to a hill of beans over here. The systems are too different. You're a solicitor, not a barrister, if I understand the distinction correctly. You've never argued a case in court. You're treading on awfully thin ice here, ma'am, and I don't want to see your client pay for your mistakes."

Beatrice smiled. "Your Honor," she said politely, "if we could stick to the matter at hand, please?"

The judge's chambers was a small room, bookcase-lined, the desk old and scarred between the areas of high polish; all in all, not very imposing. But then, as Judge Trueax had explained earlier, it didn't have to be.

Beatrice wore a simple grey suit, and what she had told the girls were sensible shoes. The only jewelry, a small gold pin on her lapel, in the shape of a winged bird.

"Your Honor," she said, "may I assume you have . . . seen Mrs. Levin?"

Judge Trueax nodded gravely.

She gave him points for not wincing.

"Then where would she go? How could she hide? Her veil is on at all times, and without it . . ." She spread her hands. "I don't see the harm, and the children miss her. They need her, Your Honor." A self-deprecating smile. "I am not exactly the motherly type, and they need mothering right now. Now, more than ever."

"Your Honor," Crawford Marlbone protested mildly, "I admit this is an unusual case here—as far as the accused is concerned, that is. However, she has—" He stopped when he saw the look on the judge's face. "She's killed a man, Judge."

"Saving me," Beatrice reminded him.

"Doesn't take away from the killing part, ma'am. The public deserves—"

"From what I read in the local paper, Your Honor, the public thinks Mrs. Levin has done the world a favor."

"Maybe yes, maybe no," the judge answered, "but that's not for us to decide."

"She's not going to run," Beatrice insisted. "In point of actual fact, she has nowhere to go."

"Doesn't matter," said the prosecutor.

"In her condition, it matters quite a bit."

"Judge, we're talking precedent here. You want to start something you can't stop down the road?"

The judge leaned forward, let the pencil drop to the desktop. He pulled a tissue from a box, blew his nose, tossed the tissue into the overflowing wastebasket beside him, pulled out another, and mopped his brow. "We got Christmas barely around the corner, it ain't all that cold outside, why the hell do they keep the furnace blowing like this? I swear, I'm going to catch pneumonia before the year's out."

"When the year's out," Marlbone said with a laugh, "it won't matter. We'll all be dead, remember?"

"How could I forget? Every damn TV show and magazine's been telling me the same thing ever damn day—damned, no matter what the hell I do."

"Then perhaps," said Beatrice quietly, "you ought to listen."

The two men looked at her carefully, not sure if she was serious. Neither, however, was sure enough to smile.

"One night," she said, as if making a final offer. "The motel's two blocks away around the corner. An armed guard—"

"Judge, this isn't Mobile. We haven't got—"

"At the door. There is no exit, you can seal the bathroom window if you wish." She looked at Marlbone. "No one has to know, Mr. Marlbone."

"Trust me, Mrs. Harp—they'll find out."

"By then it'll be too late. It will be tomorrow and she will be back in court, and back in her cell afterward." A corner of her mouth pulled slightly. "It's not as if we're Donnie and Clyde, you know."

The judge fumbled with his pencil, then leaned back and aimed a loud laugh at the ceiling.

Bea frowned until Marlbone leaned over and tapped her knee. "That's *Bonnie* and Clyde, Miz Harp. *Bonnie* and Clyde."

"Ah. Yes. Well, the point is the same, you see. We're not a gang. We are two women and two children. I hardly think we pose a serious threat to society. At least," she added as the judge wiped tears from his eyes, "not for one short evening. As I understand the procedure, the trial may not even begin before Christmas. One night, now, could absorb a lot of the sting."

"I must admit, I'm tempted, Crawford."

Marlbone puffed his cheeks, rubbed his jowls thoughtfully, hooked a thumb in his vest pocket. "Judge, if word of this gets out before we pick the jury . . . I don't know. Mrs. Harp here is a clever woman. Accused murderer of a scum-of-the-earth bastard allowed one night with her children because she won't be home for Christmas, said scum-of-the-earth bastard killed while trying to rape the accused's lawyer." He shook his head. "You really think I'll be able to find a fair jury after that?"

"Then don't let it get out," Bea said reasonably. "I'm certainly not going to say anything."

Judge Trueax pointed the pencil at her. "One word, and you're in a cell with your client."

Marlbone rolled his eyes.

"You have my word on it, Your Honor."

"If we work this right, Crawford, there's no precedent."

"If we work this right," the prosecutor said sourly, "it'll be a damn miracle."

"Well," said Beatrice with a sly tilt of her head, "it is the season for it, isn't it?"

The judge opened the center drawer and dropped the pencil in. "See to it, Crawford, will you? And Mrs. Harp, you make damn sure I see you both here first thing in the morning. I will not be made a fool of, do you understand? Be grateful you found yourselves in this county, not somewhere else. We're small, my dear lady, but small doesn't mean we're stupid. One wrong move, and your British ass is mine."

The room, Moonbow thought, was much nicer than that other one. The TV worked, the beds were comfortable, there was no smell in the bathroom, and they couldn't hear anyone in the adjoining rooms. It would have been a lot nicer if Momma would talk, but all she did was sit on the edge of the bed, her head down, her hands still in her lap.

Star wasn't much better. She spent most of the time in the bathroom, like always, trying to make her hair look good. That was impossible. The way she'd cut it, it'd take weeks for anything to happen so she didn't look like one of those orphans in the old movies.

"Lady Beatrice?"

Beatrice stood by the bed farthest from the window.

She was packing.

"Lady Beatrice?"

"What is it, dear?"

"I don't understand."

"It's quite simple," she answered, keeping her voice low, staring pointedly at the door so Moonbow would do the same. "We're going to leave as soon as we can."

"But how?" She pointed at the door. "There's a—"

"Oh, for God's sake, Bow," Star said from the bathroom door. "Will you can it, huh? You've been yapping all night, you're giving me a headache."

Moonbow stuck her tongue out at her sister; Starshine did the same and sat beside their mother.

"Momma? Momma, you ever going to talk to us again?" She winked broadly at Moonbow. "Are we going to have to learn sign language?"

"Oh, no," Moonbow declared in mock horror. "I can't learn that. I can barely talk good as it is. Momma, please don't make me learn that finger stuff. I'll make all kinds of mistakes and Star'll make fun of me."

"Will not."

"Will too."

"Girls," said Beatrice softly.

Jude looked up then, and Moonbow could sense the smile behind the veil, could see it in those large dark eyes. Her mother was in one of her long loose dresses, the kind that flowed and danced like water when she walked. Her hair had been braided, and it hung down to her waist, so thick that Star had said she could have clobbered the guard with it and run away.

The smile vanished.

"You must never forget, girls," Jude said, "that I've killed a man."

"Momma," Starshine said angrily, hands on her hips, a scowl on her face. "Momma, that man was trying to rape Lady Harp. He threw me against the wall, and could have broken my neck." She touched the side of her head where the edge of bruise crept out from under her hair. "He would have killed you, Momma. He would have killed you."

She clapped her hands and rubbed them together.

End of story.

Moonbow watched her mother's eyes, but for the first time in a long time she couldn't read them, couldn't figure out what she was thinking or what she would say.

Then Lady Beatrice closed the suitcase and snapped the locks in place, slapped the lid, and said, "Get your coats, don't forget whatever money you have left."

Moonbow lifted her hands. "But—"

"Now listen to me, child," Lady Beatrice snapped, "I've no time to argue, and certainly no time to explain. Just do as you're told and we'll soon have your mother out of here."

"But—"

"What are you," Starshine said, "a billy goat? We're gonna bust outta here, see? We're going over the wall. Ain't that right, Lady Bea? We're hitting the road, leaving the narcs in our dust."

Beatrice opened her mouth, closed it, and shrugged defeat. "Whatever you say, Starshine. Just be ready when I come for you."

"What?" Jude twisted around sharply. "What do you mean? You're not leaving?"

"Yes, dear, I am. Just for a minute." She beckoned, and the girls came close. "Now listen to me—and no questions, Moonbow, just listen—I want you to make noise. Happy noise, as if you're so glad to see your mother you can't stand it. Not too loud, but loud enough that the gentleman outside will hear and be pleased. You understand? While you're doing that, you put on your coats. Jude, be ready to take the suitcase."

She crossed the room and put on her coat, buttoned it to the neck, and put her hand on the doorknob.

Moonbow saw her take a deep breath and close her eyes, and would have sworn she heard her whisper, "Sir John, this is crazy," before she opened the door and went out.

Starshine immediately began singing a nonsense tune, and her mother laughed. Not loudly, but loud enough.

Once the door closed, they kept up the noise while

scrambling into their coats, kept up the noise while they sat side by side on the bed and stared at the drapes that covered the window.

Holding hands.

Waiting.

Moonbow thinking that unless Lady Beatrice had a really really big gun, this was going to put them all in jail for the rest of their lives.

When the door opened again, they shut up instantly.

Lady Beatrice poked her head in, nodded her approval, and said, "Time, ladies. Please don't dawdle, I'm not as good at this as my husband was."

The next thing Moonbow knew she was outside, and it was dark, the fog as thick as it had been the other night, and the cold felt good on her face as she followed her mother and sister along the front of the building to the parking lot on the side. She wanted to look around, to spot the cops she just knew had to be watching, had to have them all their sights, but she didn't dare. She just walked, and prayed, and, when Lady Beatrice opened the doors of an automobile Moonbow had never seen before, she didn't hesitate—she climbed right into the front seat, closed the door, put on her seatbelt, and hunkered down as low as she could.

It didn't occur to her until Lady Beatrice had started the engine that she hadn't seen the guard who was supposed to be stationed outside the door. She turned and stared, and after a moment she saw his fog-dimmed figure—sitting in a chair on the far side of their room, hat down over his face, hands clasped across his stomach.

"Is he dead?" she asked fearfully.

"Don't be foolish," Lady Beatrice answered as she pulled into the street. "He's just very tired and needs a good night's rest."

The fog spun whorls and webs as a light wind pushed down the street ahead of them.

Traffic lights and streetlights and store lights were

smears of white and color, and when she looked over her shoulder she couldn't see the motel anymore because the fog had swallowed it.

"Thank you," Jude said from the backseat.

"Don't thank me yet," Lady Beatrice said. "We still have a long way to go, and we don't have much time."

"They'll come after us, you know."

"Then," Lady Beatrice said as she pushed the accelerator all the way to the floor, "they'll have to learn to fly."

Moonbow dozed, woke up once, and looked at the woman who drove the car. "I know you," she said sleepily.

"Do you now?"

"Yes. You're an angel."

3

Rick Jordan hated driving in a storm. His boat was more predictable than the handling of this damn pickup, and by the time he reached Hawkins Island he was ready to pull over and wait it out. The problem was, there wasn't anything on this miserable piece of rock to protect him, so he took to the next causeway stage and made his way slowly to St. James, gripping the wheel so tightly his fingers threatened cramps.

The last time, he thought sourly, he'll do a favor for someone he hardly knew. Next time, the guy can drive his own damn self.

A huge wave slammed into the rocks on his left, shaking the roadway, making him hold his breath and pray the structure would hold. A few seconds later another one struck the northside barrier, and a sheet of sea water slapped the pickup into a sideways skid. He yelped involuntarily, prepared himself to get out in case the truck toppled, and didn't relax a whit until the causeway touched St.

James. Immediately, he pulled over into the Last Stop's parking area, and sat there, trembling, sweating as hard as it was raining outside. He would have stayed until the storm passed, but the engine decided it had had enough and conked out, leaving him without heat or the radio.

"Well, shit," he muttered. He supposed it could be worse; he supposed he could be stuck in the Tower, exposed to every drop, every ounce of wind, plus the thing would be swaying a little, enough to make a man seasick.

It wasn't much consolation.

He slid over to the passenger side, yanked his cap down tight and zipped his jacket up to his neck, then shoved open the door.

"Shit!" he yelled when the cold rain hit him, and he ran for the entrance, pushed inside, and stood dripping on a narrow piece of rubber welcome mat. Panting. Wiping his face with one hand, while he opened the jacket with the other.

There were only a couple of overhead lights on, one at the end of the building to his left, one right above him. To the right the display cases and walls were uncomfortably indistinct, as if the fog had turned black.

"Bad time to be on the road," a voice said, and Rick turned his head so fast he felt a painful twinge in his neck.

Cutler stood behind the last case, a gleaming, stuffed barracuda on the wall above him. His coat was on, he held a hat in one hand. "If you're thinking of buying, I'm closed."

"Just getting in out of the rain," he said. "Can't last long, not at this rate."

The building vibrated.

The surf sounded like thunder.

Rick slipped his hands into his pockets and turned around, to look through the glass door. He could barely see the truck; he couldn't see Cutler's car at all. Just his luck Mandy wasn't working here today—she was a whole lot easier on the eyes than this jerk.

"Heard you got real friendly with Chisholm," Cutler

said, his tone making easy conversation, two guys caught with nothing to talk about.

Rick shrugged. "Helped him pass the time, that's all." He didn't like the way his reflection faded in and out, the way the rain struck the glass, shattering into starbursts. But he didn't want to look at Cutler, either. He was sure that pose under the fish was deliberate, and if he thought about it long enough, he'd probably start laughing.

Cutler wouldn't like that.

Not that he'd do much about it. Not physically, anyway. The man usually picked on people who couldn't really fight back. The fishing community, such as it was, was pretty tight. Go after one, you go after them all. Even Stump Teague wasn't that stupid.

Of course, there were other ways of fighting—a whisper to the bank here, a word to the mayor there . . . a friend of his tried to get friendly with Mandy a year or so back, next thing the guy knew the sheriff and Freck were climbing all over his boat. Violations up the ass that drove the man first into bankruptcy, then off the island.

Still, standing under that dead fish, those sideburns puffed, that hair so salon perfect . . . he wished Ronnie could be here to see it.

"You like helping ex-cons, do you?"

Rick closed one eye, turned his head. "Ex-con?"

"Yep. Attempted murder, grand larceny. North Carolina, I think it was."

He looked back to the storm. "Huh."

"Gotta be careful, you know." Slow footsteps; the back light went out. "Some folks don't like to charter with folks who run with ex-cons."

The air lightened outside, less like night now than late afternoon. The wind had stopped.

Rick tugged at his cap. "You know, Cutler, if I didn't know better, I'd swear that was a threat." He looked over again, and Cutler was still at the last display case, no definition now, just a form in the dark. "No kidding."

Cutler laughed quietly. "Purely an observation, my boy. Purely an observation. Perception, Mr. Jordan. It's all in the perception." The snap of a cigarette lighter. "Just a word to the wise, that's all. Businessmen like ourselves, we have to watch that perception."

Rick grunted a laugh. "Cutler, the only things that perceive me are the fish, and they don't give a damn because they're already practically dead anyway." He brushed some condensation off the door. "No offense, but I talk to who I want."

"So I notice."

The center light went out.

Rick took his hands from his pockets, flexed his fingers, leaned closer to the door, squinting as he looked east. The rain had eased to a heavy drizzle, and he could see breaks in the clouds.

And something else: "Hey, looks like someone's coming."

From right behind him: "Tough. I'm closed."

He jumped, jumped again when a hand reached around him and pushed the door open.

"Any time, Mr. Jordan. Any time."

Another tug on his cap, his jacket closed again, and he hurried to the pickup just as a car pulled in behind it. And as much as he wanted to get out of here, to get home and call Ronnie, tell her what Cutler had said, he walked over to the passenger side just as the window rolled down.

Four people in there, and Jesus, he thought, they look like they've been through a goddamn war. Bandages and bruises, the guy in back with his arm practically molded to his chest, the lady in front with a small bandage on her neck, not enough to hide the fading bruise there that ran practically all the way around.

"Hi," he said, leaning over so he could see the driver better. "The place is closed, sorry."

The driver, a clump of dark hair falling into his eyes, smiled wanly. "Just our luck." He glanced into the backseat, rapped the steering wheel a few times, and nodded. "So . . . maybe you can help us."

"Whatever I can." He just wished the guy'd hurry up. The rain was dripping down his neck, and the damp was beginning to seep into his bones.

Cutler's automobile pulled out of the lot, just short of spitting gravel and grit.

The driver watched it for a few seconds before: "We're . . . we are on the right track for Camoret Island, right?"

"Oh, yeah." He straightened and rubbed at the small of his back. "Don't want to disappoint you, though," he said, raising his voice so the man could hear him. "We're just about closed down too, for the season." A polite smile for the woman. "The days are still kind've warm, but the beach is still pretty chilly when the wind gets blowing."

The man said something he didn't catch, and the woman, looking as if she was afraid to turn her head, said, "Motels or anything?"

"None that are open." He squatted then, fingertips of his left hand balancing him against the door. "You're Louisiana, huh?"

Her smile was bright, though her skin was sickly pale. "That's right. You from there?"

He shook his head. "Nope. Had a girlfriend once, though, she was from Baton Rouge. She—"

From the back an impatient cough.

Rick took the hint, figured it was the girl, not the guy in the sling. "Anyway, if you folks are needing a place to stay, I really don't know how to help you. The guy that just left, he's got about the only office that stays open all year." He wiped a hand over his face, shook the rain off. "I can tell you how to get there, if you need to."

"I'd sure appreciate it," the driver said. "We've been a long time getting here, and from the looks of it, that's no small island you have there."

Rick never thought of it as small, or large, or any size at

all. It just was. Shining wetly now as the sun rammed gaps in the swift-moving clouds.

Then the young guy said something, and he frowned. "What?"

"Casey Chisholm," the guy repeated. "You know a man named Casey Chisholm?"

Rick stared at him for a moment. "Well, as a matter of fact, I kind of do, yeah."

He didn't think he would have gotten a more astonishing reaction than if he'd up and handed them each a million-dollar bill. The girl in back started crying, the boy whooped, the driver closed his eyes and grinned, and the woman with the auburn hair took a sharp deep breath and started to laugh. Her hand waved an apology, but she couldn't seem to stop, and he rose slowly, not sure what he was supposed to do next.

"Hey," the boy said, leaning over to see him better, "can you tell us how to get there? To where he lives, I mean. Can you show us?"

Rick wasn't sure. It was pretty obvious these people had nothing to do with Cutler, so that was all right. On the other hand, Chisholm was far from being a hundred percent, and maybe didn't want surprise visitors just now. But the looks on their faces, the kind of look usually saved for that big Christmas present in the corner, that made him think again.

"Tell you what," he said. "I'm fixing to go over there now, as a matter of fact. Why don't you just follow me. It isn't hard, but . . . just follow me."

Without waiting for a response, he returned to the pickup and slid into the cab. Once inside, he yanked off the cap and tossed it aside, told himself he smelled like a dead wet fish on a hot dry morning, and started the engine.

He didn't want to think about what he was doing.

He wasn't looking forward to seeing the expression on Chisholm's face.

Nevertheless, he had a pretty good feeling about this. A pretty good feeling that he was doing the right thing.

And if he wasn't . . . hell, it was no skin off his back. Chisholm wasn't a friend, wasn't a neighbor; he was just someone Rick had helped out a little because Ronnie had asked him to. He'd just go there, deliver the message the mainland pharmacist had given him, and go home. Call Ronnie. Have dinner with her. Let her pump him for information.

He grinned as he pulled onto the road, checking the rearview to be sure the strangers were following.

So Chisholm gets mad at him. So what?

Ronnie was going to be awfully happy about what he knew, and he knew just how to dole it out.

Damn, he thought, laughing aloud; damn, sometime I just step in it, you know what I mean?

4

"Because I watched them, Jasper, that's how I know . . . follow them? How the hell was I supposed to follow them? My car's the only gold one on the island, Jordan would have spotted it in a minute . . . Jesus, Mary, and Joseph, Jasper, he turned left on Midway and waved for them to follow along. The only reason he'd go that way is to see Chisholm . . . no, I don't know who they are . . . no, I didn't talk to them, I was already gone . . . Good Lord, you are the most . . . no, I didn't count them, for God's sake, it was raining! There's a passel of them, though, I could see that much . . .

"Look, Jasper, you're not getting the whole picture here. Think about it: they were *not* supposed to get this far. We were assured they'd already be taken care of, and Chisholm would be on his own. Assuming our boys hadn't already stomped his ass into the next century, that is. So now he's not alone, and I don't think our friend is going to be very happy when he finds out. I think maybe you and I, we ought to get a little creative around here . . . you know damn well what I mean, and if you're taping this, Jasper, so help me God, I'm gonna skin you bald, you hear me?

"All right, all right, don't get all huffy. Just watching my back, same as you, and don't tell me you're not. The thing is, we got exactly two weeks, am I right? Now surely we can come up with something in two lousy weeks. Put your brain on the boil, partner, see what you can come up with. Meanwhile, we got another problem . . .

"Right. Exactly right. Our friend doesn't want to wait any longer. Time to stop screwing around here, time to make that old black bastard see the light. If you know what I mean. Can't use Stump again, he's got no finesse. We gotta have finesse this time, and I think I know just the man.

"Best thing about it is, partner, the son of a bitch works cheap."

3

1

The minute the rain stopped, Casey grabbed his jacket and left the house. He didn't intend to go very far, only wanted some clean fresh air and a good strong walk to help clean out his system.

As soon as Jordan had left, he had made his way back upstairs, stripped, and stood under a hot shower, bracing himself against the tiled wall with one hand, letting the heat and the steam do its work. He stayed there for so long his skin began to redden, but he gave himself no complaints. It felt good. Almost sinful.

Afterward, he shaved, brushed his hair, and dressed. He sang loudly to the empty house. He walked from room to room and looked out the windows, not to see anything in particular, just to walk, to give his legs some exercise. The storm frustrated him, but it also allowed him time to sit for a while between his wanderings, for which he was grateful. He knew that if he'd gone out right away, he would have walked himself right back into bed—too much, too soon.

He ate as large a lunch as his stomach would take, bemoaning how much better Hector's touch was.

He considered a cigarette and changed his mind, walked the house again instead, taking his time, working up a sweat that had him back in the shower—no luxury now, purely utilitarian—and into a fresh set of clothes.

That was okay.

He felt good. He felt clean. He felt somehow less vulnerable for feeling so . . . good.

Once he stood on the porch steps, feeling the light breeze feather-touch his face, he realized he was in danger of being convinced he was back to normal.

Still, the rain-cleared air smelled wonderful. Intoxicating. Cold enough to make him rub his hands together, not so cold that he had to fetch gloves or a hat. Brisk, he decided; he and the air felt brisk.

And it reminded him, suddenly and powerfully, of the day he had left that North Carolina cell for the last time, the day he had walked through that high, sliding, pocked-with-rust iron door into the free world. The same intoxication, the same feeling of power, the same feeling of such immense giddy relief that his knees had almost buckled.

A feeling of such immeasurable sadness, for the time he had lost and could never regain.

He adjusted his coat, pushed stubborn hair away from his brow, and strode down the walk to the street. An automatic look left, a check right, and he crossed over, angling toward the narrow path that would, if he had the strength, take him to the beach.

No hurry, he cautioned; no hurry, Case, either you get there or you don't.

No hurry.

He rested under a fat-bole evergreen whose lower branches had been stripped away, those remaining looking as gnarled as a man's arthritic knuckles. There was no wind, just the sand and the tide marks and the roll of the surf.

A sky too large and too high, too clear of clouds after such an abrupt and nasty storm.

He could see the stone whales a hundred yards off to his left; to his right a tall dune that, he seemed to recall, had been much taller when he'd first arrived on the island. A pair of gulls strutting on the wet apron, wings out and legs dancing whenever a wave swept its foam toward them. Broken shells. The faint darkened rim that marked a long dead bonfire from a long forgotten party.

He wanted to go out to the jetty, feel the ocean's power beneath him, but he knew he wouldn't make it. The sun was on its way down, the sawtooth shadow-line of the trees crawling toward the darkening water. So he leaned against the tree and listened to the sea.

After a long time, he whispered, "I know what you want, but I can't do it. You know I can't do it."

The unbearable sadness of something never retrieved.

He didn't turn, didn't start, when he heard cautious footsteps behind him, softly crackling over the dead leaves and needles that lay thick and thin on the ground.

Even here, he thought; even here, I can't be alone.

Eventually a man came up beside him, barely reaching his shoulder, his oversize coat too thick for the weather, his hair unkempt beneath a pushed-back watch cap that looked as worn as his face.

"You listening for them?" asked Dub Neely.

"For what?" Casey said.

The faint smell of liquor.

Neely smacked his lips loudly. "They got me, you know."

Casey did look then, and looked down. The man's shoes were wrapped and wrapped again with duct tape, but he could see dark stains on the bottom of the trousers, and when he took a step away from the trees onto the sand, dark stains spotting his bare ankles.

"Looks like you walked through the briar patch."

Neely shook his head. "Them birds is what it was." He looked over his shoulder, eyes rimmed red and pouched. When he smiled, there weren't many teeth. "Them birds got me."

Casey didn't understand and didn't ask.

"Dead birds," Neely said, as if that would explain everything. "Walking bones, you know? Came right at me." He lifted one foot a couple of inches off the ground. "Damn near bled me to death."

Casey nodded, tilted his head, pulled his lips briefly between his teeth so he wouldn't smile.

"The thing of it is," Neely continued, facing the ocean, idly flicking something off a sleeve, "I wasn't as surprised as I ought to have been once I realized what was happening. An astounding bit of nature gone hog wild, and it was, in its awful morbid way, rather fascinating. The prerogative of a drunk, Mr. Chisholm; being able to observe the impossible without losing his mind."

"Is that so?"

"Damn straight." Neely rolled his shoulders, smoothed his cap down into place with both palms. "Son of a bitch, you look at that?" He pointed toward the water. "Some fool, looks like he left a perfectly good can of beer out there. Idiots don't know what they're missing, you know what I mean? Ain't got no sense the good Lord gave them, and what they do got they ain't got a clue how to use it. Stupid bastards. Hell of a storm. Had to hide under somebody's porch, man. Could've gotten pneumonia, something like that. Hell of a storm. The phrase, I believe, is gully-washer, right? No matter. A hell of a storm."

He reached into his coat pocket and pulled out a flask, shook it next to his ear to gauge its content, then twisted off the top and took a quick drink.

"Hell of a storm, man. Walking bones. Damn near killed me, but I got away. Close thing, but I did get away."

He took another drink and put the flask away.

"Weird shit, man. A perfectly good can of beer all by its lonesome."

Casey, saying nothing, pushed off the tree with his shoulder, put his hands into his pockets, and started down the trail toward home. The treetops had begun to blend with the sky, lowering it, and the tide on its way in had begun to snarl and roar. Considering the way weariness had begun to slip over him, it would be a good idea to get home before full dark.

"Hey!" Neely called.

Casey ignored him. He needed to sit. He needed to eat. This would be the longest half mile he could ever remember, but he wasn't about to stop to rest. Not now. Or stop to have a conversation with a drunk.

"Hey!"

He would sleep hard and long tonight. Tomorrow he would decide what he would do about the Teagues. Since the sheriff obviously wasn't going to do anything on his own, Casey had to make up his mind how far he was going to push this. Make the complaint and force the law into at least making a show of caring? Wait a couple of days and maybe do a little peace-keeping of his own? Forget the whole damn thing and hope there wasn't a recurrence?

"Hey, I'm . . . I'm talking to you!"

Whittaker Hull wanted to know what he knew, but he didn't think he knew anything. What was there to know? What did it matter to him anyway? Did he really give a damn?

"The horses, goddamnit!"

He stopped.

"I want to . . . I want to know if you was listening for them damn horses again!"

Ah . . . hell, he thought; oh . . . hell.

But when he looked back, Dub Neely was gone, nothing at the end of the trail but a faint glow from the water, and a darkness that looked all too much like a wall.

2

By the time he reached the edge of the woodland, twilight had turned to dusk, and he had used up all the curses he knew, aimed at the stupidity for walking so far so soon after he'd left his sickbed. His breath came in short gasps, pockets of sweat gave him shuddering chills, and his eyes weren't working quite the way they were supposed to. As if he had to walk through a world just out of focus enough to give him a headache if he looked at it too long.

Slowly, unsteadily, he passed between two of Cutler's rental houses and grinned at the sight of Midway Road. Nothing spectacular, it hadn't been miraculously paved while he'd been gone, but it meant that, if he had to, he could crawl the rest of the way home and not lose too much skin in the process.

A bonus, then, when he saw Rick Jordan's truck parked at the shoulder in front of his own place. Jordan himself sat on the lowered tailgate, legs swinging lazily, cigarette in one hand, his head drooped low as though he might be napping.

"Rick," he called, and winced at how weak he sounded.

Jordan dropped to the ground, arms slightly away from his sides as he searched for the voice. Nodded when Casey called him again, and wandered over, a hand in his hip pocket, the other flicking the cigarette away.

"No answer," he said, nodding toward the house. "I thought maybe you got yourself snatched or something, and holy shit, Chisholm, where the hell have you been, you look like holy hell."

Casey shrugged nonchalantly. "Just went for a walk on the beach."

"The beach?" Jordan stared at the houses, the trees beyond, measuring the distance. "You out of your mind?"

"Yes," Casey said, and laughed. "Come on inside, I have to sit, and sit fast. You can tell me—"

"Can't," Jordan said. "I have a date with Ronnie, and if I don't get cleaned up in a hurry, she'll sink me in the marsh."

They stopped at the pickup's hood, Casey resting a hip against it.

"So?"

"So, I don't get it."

"You don't have to, Rick. Not yet anyway. Did you find out?"

Jordan pulled a bottle of pills from his jacket pocket and handed it over. "Supposed to be antibiotics and painkillers and stuff, right?"

"Right. That's what . . ." He scratched under his chin. "Alloway? Yeah. That's what Alloway said."

Jordan took off his cap, slapped it lightly against his leg before jamming it back on. "Now I really don't get it."

Casey looked at him hard.

Jordan flinched apologetically. "Hey, sorry." He pointed at the bottle. "Valium."

"What?"

"That's what the man said. Valium. You know, it—"

"I know what it is, Rick," he said sharply. "What I don't know is how it did what it did."

"Hell, that's easy. There's enough there to make you stupid for the rest of your life. Kind of." He shook his head, kicked lightly at a tire with a heel. "Man, I didn't know half of what the guy was talking about. I always thought it was, you know, what shrinks gave you to calm you down. You know, nervous rich lady stuff. I didn't know it helped if you were having a fit or something, things like that."

Casey turned the bottle over and over in his hand. "Neither did I, Rick. Neither did I."

"That dose there, though, it's enough to . . ." He laughed

shortly. "Hell, I already said that, didn't I? So how come, huh? Why'd the man lie to you?"

Casey didn't know.

Jordan started for the truck door, stopped, and shook his head. "You really don't know?"

"Nope."

"You find out, you tell me? I have to admit, I'm awfully curious."

"You and me both, Rick. You and me both." He tucked the bottle into a palm, rolled it back and forth. "And thanks. Thanks for doing this. I owe you one."

"Nah. No sweat." Jordan opened the door and climbed in, then stuck his head out the window. "You might want to move over there, Casey. You don't need being run over on top of everything else."

Casey moved, but slowly.

More questions, and he was getting angry because he was too exhausted to think them through.

"Something else," Jordan said after he started the engine.

"What?"

Jordan pointed up the road.

Casey turned and saw, almost hidden in the dusk, a car parked at the bend.

"They came to see you," Jordan explained. "From the looks of them, they got themselves beat up pretty good, too."

"Who are they?" he demanded. "Rick, who—"

But Jordan had already pulled the truck into a tight U-turn, the engine and muffler too loud for talk. A hand waved over the roof, and the pickup was gone. Casey stared after it, the pill bottle tight in his hand, then stared at the car until a door opened, and a man slid out.

"Casey?"

He couldn't see clearly, didn't recognize the voice. Too tired to be tense, too confused and suspicious to answer.

The only thing he was sure of was that Rick wouldn't have left him if there was any threat.

He hoped.

Then he heard another voice: "Casey? Reverend Chisholm?"

Oh my Lord, he thought; oh my sweet Lord.

He reached out with his free hand for something to hold on to. All it found was air, and it was still fumbling when Cora Bowes exploded from the car and ran toward him, crying, hands and arms flapping, until she fell against his chest and he had no choice but to hold her.

"Cora," he said, his voice deep and husky. "My God . . . Cora."

a lifetime ago in a world dead and buried, three kids pulling a prank, and he'd caught them and lectured them and laughed and sent them on their way and one was dead and two were . . .

  two belonged to a lifetime ago
  in a world dead and buried.

He held her tightly, too stunned to speak, too many things abruptly awakened. Anger and joy and despair and the realization that he was about to fall. He held her more tightly, looked over her head, and saw someone hurrying toward him, arm in a sling tight to his chest.

His eyes widened.

He grinned despite the wail of failure that begged for his attention.

"I'll be damned, Reed?"

Reed Turner, heedless of his injury and ignoring Cora, fell against him too, clumsily, his good arm trying to encircle the larger man's back. He wasn't crying, but he couldn't speak.

Too much, Casey thought; this is too much, I don't . . . dear God, I can't—

"Casey, it's good to see you again."

The man was tall, lank, and once he was close enough and Casey could see his face and that jumble of hair, he squeezed Reed and Cora so tightly they gasped and squirmed and squeezed him back.

"John," he said flatly, no emotion left in him.

Bannock nodded, almost sheepishly. A half turn to indicate the woman waiting hesitantly near the car. "That's Lisse Montgomery, Casey. She and I . . . well, we kind of had an adventure. We, uh . . . we . . . you were right, you know. When you called that time? You were . . . hey, are you okay?"

He wasn't, and he wasn't about to play the role.

"The house," he said, blinking heavily. "I think you guys had better help me to the house."

4

On a mountaintop in Tennessee he sits on the great black and scowls at the twinkling lights of a large town spread across the far horizon, at the lighted roads that lead to it. He pushes at the brim of his hat until the hat rests above his forehead. His old-leather gloved hands are folded over the saddle horn. Leather creaks when he shifts. The bridle sings when the black bobs its head.

Beside him the long white car idles almost silently.

The driver's window is down.

The passenger window is down, and Joey, his hat off, sticks his head out and frowns.

"I felt something," he says.

Red nods. "Yep."

"It didn't work, huh?"

"Doesn't look like it."

"How can it not work?"

Red brushes a thumb over the pale stubble on his cheek. "Sometimes it just don't."

"That's stupid." And Joey yelps when Eula smacks him

across the back of his head, yanks him back inside, and forces him to change seats with her.

"I apologize for the child," she says.

Red nods. Just once.

"Still, it seems . . . odd, don't you think?"

A gentle criticism that makes him swing his head around. There is no expression on his face, and she looks straight ahead, hands in her lap. Waiting for an explanation.

The black stamps a hoof and backs up until Red and Eula are even.

"We've been doing this a long time," he says.

She nods. Just once.

"Maybe . . . don't rightly know, but maybe we've kind of had it a little easy."

No reaction.

Joey whimpers.

"Maybe . . . maybe we tend to forget we are what we are. We ain't no more than that."

She looks at him for a long time before, at last, she nods, reluctantly, the possible truth of it.

"Maybe," he says quietly, "I was wrong."

No response.

None at all.

Then Susan says, "Together."

The black shies.

emerald sparks and scarlet fire

"No more trying to even the odds, okay? because there aren't any odds, Red. There's only us. There's only them."

He takes a slow deep breath, and when he exhales fog is born on the ground, curls around the black's hooves, rises in patches and puffs above the white car's tires, spreads down the mountainside and soon smothers all the lights of the city and the roads.

"Yep," he says, and pulls his hat down. "Yep."

"Good."

He smiles. Not quick now; it lasts.

And Joey scrambles over Eula's lap, looks up at him, and says, solemnly, "I want to play."

When Red laughs . . .

. . . down in the city, a thousand people scream.

5

1

Early Wednesday afternoon, Lyman Baylor stands in the center aisle of his church, imagining the pews filled for Friday's Christmas as they had been on Thanksgiving, imagining himself up there in the pulpit, his words of such force and conviction that no eye is left dry, no soul left lost, no lips left without a smile.

So what do you think, Dad? he thought; you think I'm throwing it all away now?

The sun has reached the front of the building, slips into the nave from a small round window over the choir gallery, taking his shadow and stretching it toward the large cross hanging from the ceiling. There is little warmth left; the church is damp and chilled, but he's used to it, that's part of the building's character—no matter how hard the furnace works, there's always someplace that doesn't quite get the heat.

Behind him the front door opens.

"Ly?"

"Here," he answers.

Kitra, in a light topcoat that matches her red scarf, comes up beside him, takes his hand. A scan of the empty pews, and she chuckles, hugs his arm, sweeps her free hand across the nave. "You remember?"

He does.

The wedding had been a disaster. Not content with being scornful of his mission, neither had his family been silent about his choice of mates. Too beautiful, they said; turn too many heads, they said, and you know that means temptation; too stubborn, they warned, too sure of herself; her mind doesn't think the way yours does, son, and she'll have you in grief before the honeymoon is over.

They said.

As a result, his side of the aisle had been sparsely attended, while hers was hardly attended at all. Her family, although they liked him well enough, couldn't see the winner of an important beauty pageant spending the rest of her life tending to the needs of a cleric and his charges. And a Methodist, for God's sake, her despairing father had said; couldn't he at least, her mother said, couldn't he at least be one of those rich Episcopalians?

The outdoor reception had been rained on.

The honeymoon reservations in Bermuda had been lost, and it took two of their six days before they were able to regain their room without threat of having to move somewhere else.

And he had gotten so sunburned on the beach that he couldn't lie on his back for almost a week.

He squeezes her hand. "They're right, dear. It can't last. I'm sorry."

"I know." She kisses his cheek. "What a pity."

"So where are you off to?"

"I'm going to drop in on Mr. Chisholm. I can't believe he sent everyone away like that. How will he manage?"

Lyman looked at her, frowning. "You haven't heard?"

"Heard what?"

"He has company."

She steps back, a hand to the flat of her chest, and he wonders why she's gone ever so slightly pale.

"Company? Who?"

"I don't know, not exactly. Whittaker told me that Ronnie told him that. . . ." He laughs. "Sounds like a game of telephone, doesn't it?"

Kitra's smile is so clearly forced he can't help but wonder again.

"Anyway, I think there are four of them. Two couples. Rick Jordan met them on the causeway and brought them in. And that," he says with spread hands, "is all I know, dear. Torture won't get you anywhere."

There is a moment, a heartbeat long, when the silence is too loud. Then she takes his elbow and says, "Well, then, I guess you'll just have to take me to dinner, Ly. I'm all dressed up with no place to go."

"You," he tells her fondly, "are strange."

A swift kiss, which makes him look guiltily toward the altar, and they walk side by side to the door.

"I think I'll talk about friendship on Sunday."

"Yes?"

"Sure. This time of year, so many feel so despondent, so alone, as if they don't have any friends, and they always forget the best friend they ever had."

Kitra hugs his waist. "You're amazing, Lyman."

"Not really."

But he's pleased. Very pleased that the color is back in her cheeks.

"I'll meet you at the car," he tells her on the stoop. "I just have to lock up."

Just as she reaches the bottom step and he has taken the key from his pocket, they hear a slow, rhythmic, soft screeching. With no idea what in heaven's name it is, he rushes back inside, stops at the head of the aisle, and grabs for the back of the nearest pew.

The cross has begun to swing over the altar, its brass chains scraping against the eyehooks that hold them to the beams overhead. Although practically new, they sound centuries rusted, and Lyman can't help but think of an old ship on the ocean.

From the doorway Kitra says, "Lyman, tell me it's the wind, all right? Just tell me it's the wind."

2

Ben Pellier has finally finished wiping down the tables, laying out the half-dozen sets of darts near the board, and with Alma, making sure all the salt and pepper shakers are filled, the sugar packets are on the tables, and the individual silverware settings are all rolled up in their wine-colored cloth napkins. Senior is sweeping the floor, humming quietly to himself.

Opening in three hours, and he's ready for business, early for a change.

From the kitchen door, Alma says, "See if he's hungry, dear."

Ben nods and dusts his hands on his apron as he approaches the bar. As he scratches under his patch, he says, "Hey, you old fart, you ready to eat?"

Pegleg stares at him, then bobs his head several times. "Ready to eat," the parrot answers. "Ready to eat."

Alma laughs. "He's always ready to eat, that one."

Senior sweeps the last of the dirt out the front door, takes a swipe or two at the steps, and leans the broom against the wall as he pulls a pack of cigarettes from his shirt pocket. There's a light wind blowing in from the ocean, and his lighter fights him until he finds just the right angle of cupped hand and bent back.

"Those things'll kill you, man," Ben calls as the wind slips inside, stirs the fresh sawdust Senior has spread over the bare wood.

"Too old to worry about it," Senior tells him with a broad grin.

"And that makes the place look bad, you standing out there like that," Ben adds.

"Why? Because I'm black?"

"No, because you're old and funny-looking, you'll scare all the women away."

They laugh, shake their heads, and Senior returns to his smoke while Ben mimes for him to shut the door, then turns to see that Pegleg is okay. The old bird hates the wind, hates the breeze, will go nuts if anybody blows in his face. A story has gone around that it's because the bird doesn't like being reminded of his younger days aboard a ship that sailed the Pacific.

The truth was, Ben bought the stupid bird near fresh from its egg, but the story makes for a better story, and he's never contradicted it. He has no idea why Peg doesn't like the wind, and he really doesn't care. If it bothers his old friend, then it bothers him.

"Alma," he calls, "hurry it up, will you?"

Peg stares at him from his cage.

Ben laughs. "Oh, don't look at me like that, huh? It ain't my fault she's slow."

Peg spreads his wings as if stretching, then pecks once at the cage. He lifts his head as if testing the wind, says, "Ready to eat, Ben. Ready to die."

3

Billy Freck sits at his desk in the sheriff's office, legs propped on the edge, toothpick hanging out of the corner of his mouth. He's back near the window so he can see the parking lot behind the building, as well as straight across the room to the entrance. Verna is at her desk, straightening up before she goes home, once in a while answering the radio, giving instructions.

There are strings of red and silver stuff he never knows the name of looped around the walls, cutouts of snowmen and reindeer on the window, and a small Christmas tree at the end of the visitors bench.

As if, he thinks, that's gonna make anyone cheer up.

Oakman has already left so he doesn't miss dinner at Betsy's.

"How's it look out there, Verna?"

"Quiet."

"Too early for any excitement, I guess."

"I guess."

He takes the toothpick out, examines it, puts it back. "Heard the ex-con's got some of his gang up there on Midway."

Verna doesn't answer. She sweeps her blotter clean with the edge of her hand, adjusts her glasses, takes her purse from the bottom drawer.

"You think they'll rob the bank or something?"

"Or something."

"You don't care, do you?"

"Billy," she says without turning around, "right now, all I care about is getting out of here and not coming back until first thing in the morning."

He grunts.

She stands and stretches, keeping her back to him.

"You do your Christmas shopping yet?"

She nods.

"You buy me anything?" he asks around a grin.

She lifts a hand slowly over her shoulder and gives him a languid wave before stepping around her desk, checking it one last time, and pushing through the barrier gate. She points to the radio on her way to the exit. "Keep an ear out, will you, until Salter comes in?"

She doesn't wait for an answer.

Billy salutes her back. "Yes, ma'am, I surely will. You can count on me. Absolutely, you tight-ass bitch."

He swings his legs to the floor and saunters over to her desk, drops into her chair and begins to search through the drawers. He's never found anything there yet, but there's always a first time. Besides, it makes noise. The office is too quiet, and he doesn't like the quiet. No one in the cells below, he's the only living thing left in the building, and the more noise he can make without making a racket, the better he feels.

The radio snaps and hisses quietly, as if it were muttering to itself.

When, not surprisingly, there's nothing for him to find, he concentrates instead on the meeting he's got set with Mariana later tonight. Her old lady's got some damn dinner party or other, so Mariana can't get out until that's over. Then he's going to meet her down at the harbor, and with luck make a few waves of his own.

He's no fool. He knows she's only using him when she's got nothing better going on, but he has no intention of being the one to end it. Whatever "it" is. At least not until he gets his final payment from Cutler. Once that's tucked away in the bank, he's going to walk into Oakman's office, throw the cheesy tin badge into his fat old face, tell him a thing or two or three, and get the hell off this island.

He's not sure yet where he's going, but with the money he's saved over the past couple, three years, there won't be many places he won't be able to afford.

He rolls the chair back, has one leg ready to rest on Verna's desk, when the radio's speaker light winks on red and he hears someone whispering.

"Shit," he says, grabs the mike, and thumbs it on. "Salter, damnit, speak up, I can't understand you."

He listens.

"Dwight, that you? Whack your mike on the dash, it ain't coming through so good."

The whispering grows a little louder, but he still can't understand it.

"Sheriff, that you? Can't understand you, Sheriff, this speaker's gone all to hell." He raps the top of the speaker with his knuckles. "Sheriff? Salter?" Now he whacks the speaker with his palm, hits it again, and tosses the mike on the desk in disgust. "Goddamn cheap shit."

He listens a while longer, head tilted to one side, listening hard now because he thinks there's more than one voice he's hearing. Maybe not, but he sure knows what it sounds like—all those sons of bitches in high school who used to talk about him behind his back, stuck-up snobs who think you ain't a whole person if you don't have a whole family. Whispering about him in the cafeteria, in the halls, talking about his momma, how she run away one night and never came back; talking about his sister, how she'd climb under the sheet with any man or kid who asked her; talking about him because he only had three shirts and two pairs of jeans and all of them were made of old cotton.

Talking about him, how he'll end up in the gutter, just like the rest of the Frecks, just like the whole damn family.

"Damn," and he shakes his head, wondering where the hell all that came from. He glances over the radio's face until he finds the speaker switch and, not caring if Oakman bitches or not, flicks it off.

Maybe what he'll do is, he'll call down to Rick, the guy is an asshole, but he's damn good with things like radios and stuff. Maybe he can come on up, take a look, see what's wrong. To do that, though, he needs a telephone book, and after failing to find where Verna kept hers, he grunts to his feet and, stretching his arms over his head, looks around the room. He knows there has to be one here somewhere.

When he finds it he laughs. Wouldn't you know, it's right out there in the open, on top of Dwight's desk. He grabs it up, lets the cover fall open, and turns when he hears the radio whispering at him again.

"Christ," he mutters, and stamps over, kicking aside a chair on the way, reaches down to snap the switch off, and freezes.

It is off.

So is the speaker's red light.

But the whispers still slide from behind the speaker's grill, and he knows, he just knows, they're talking about him.

4

"Well, I'll be damned."

Rick kneels near the bow of the *Lucky Deuce*, staring at the water. There's the usual amount of flotsam there—plastic rings, some kind of food, bits of plants—but he also counts at least a dozen dead fish.

He stands, looks around, then walks to the end of the dock and follows the boardwalk along the water's edge.

"Damn," he says with a shake of his head.

He doesn't bother counting the number of dead fish.

He couldn't anyway; there are too many.

5

Norville Cutler sits on a park bench, arms spread along the back, topcoat open, hat on the seat beside him, watching old man Farelli fuss with the string of Christmas lights that outline the barbershop window. From down the street he can hear the tinny sound of carols carrying on the easy wind. Gold spiraled streamers are strung across Midway Road from the tops of the streetlamps, intertwined with tiny bulbs that will, he admits, look pretty nice once the sun has gone down. The street isn't crowded, but there are enough pedestrians to make the town look alive. He suspects that the shops down by the harbor are just as busy. It's times like this when he wishes he had gone into one of those businesses instead of peddling the tourist crap he does. Maybe someday he'd figure out how to sell it to the locals, really add to the pot that's blossoming in the bank.

He belches then, and laughs at himself. He's just had

lunch at the Tide, wants very much to go home and change into something more comfortable, but Mandy has decided to wrap presents today and has ordered him out of the house for at least another hour. Last year she did the wrapping naked, which meant she didn't get a whole hell of a lot done, but this year, for some reason, she's taking the season seriously. He has a bad feeling she expects him to pop the question, which he has no intention of doing. Not this year. Not next. Not ever.

Old man Farelli has gone inside.

Cutler glances at his watch, thinks for a second or two, and decides he's had enough sitting around, waiting around, even though it's only been a few minutes.

It's the deal.

He knows it's the deal.

Time is almost up, his incalculable fortune just about made, and it's making him nervous. Anxious. More so when Stump didn't do the deed the way he was supposed to.

"You didn't say kill him."

"I said take care of him, what do you suppose that means?"

"Didn't think it meant kill him."

Jesus. Working with idiots like that, it's amazing he and Jasper have gotten this far. One more place, though. One more place. And Freck already has his marching orders.

Once that's taken care of, he's pretty sure it won't make any difference whether Chisholm is dead or alive. That end of the island will be all his, and his partner will have nothing to complain about.

It would be nice, of course, if he could find out what the man wanted with all that property. Prime land, but as far as he could tell, no sign of development activity, no matter what Hull claims to have dredged up in Atlanta.

He taps the fingers of his left hand thoughtfully against his chest, considering Hull, thinking maybe, just to keep the old man honest, it wouldn't hurt to have the boys pay him another visit. It wouldn't be, he thinks with a laugh, as if Chisholm would be able to step in again.

Another check of his watch and he gathers his coat closed with one hand, uses the other to push himself off the bench.

Time to go.

Time to see what kind of damage Mandy has done to his bank account—assuming she lets him open the presents early.

He picks up his hat, sets its carefully in place, and walks the straight path to the sidewalk, where he nearly collides with Dermot Alloway.

"Jesus, Dermot," he says, "you ever look where you're going?"

Alloway, his cheeks flushed, his eyes nearly invisible behind a pair of heavy-frame glasses, purses his lips in disapproval. "I could say the same for you, Mr. Cutler." Then everything about him sags, and he looks to Norville like a weary, hunted rabbit. "I have some news."

Cutler eases him away toward the curb, smiling and nodding when several people recognize him and greet him by name. "What news?" Still smiling.

"He knows."

"Who knows?"

"Chisholm. I had a call from a friend on the mainland. Chisholm knows about the medication."

Cutler waves at old man Farelli just leaving his shop. "And so . . ."

"And so what if he tries to do something about it? My God, Norville, I could lose my license."

Cutler buttons his coat, claps the doctor heartily on the shoulder. "Not to worry, Dermot, my friend. Not to worry. Anything comes up, it will be taken care of, you have my word on it. Now you have a great Christmas, you hear? My best to the little woman."

He walks away, head up, back straight. There are those

who studiously ignore him, those whose sideways glances are less than friendly, but he doesn't care. Chisholm knows. So what? Anything he starts, I can finish. In this case, the man's size was too obviously deceptive.

A smile no one can see.

He walks by the sheriff's office, thinks it might do him well to have a word with Deputy Freck, and looks through the glass door just in time to see Freck smash the dispatch radio on the floor.

6

There is a great stillness in the marsh, despite the steady wind that blows overhead. Ronnie stands in a broad-bottom skiff, poling toward the landing where she's left her truck. On the seat that spans the middle are her laptop computer, a thick three-ring binder, and a large canvas sack tied snugly at the top.

She checks the trees she passes under, studies the water and the land that pokes out from the reeds and weeds and the knees of cypress that have been stunted by saltwater seepage. She is afraid that once she sends in this last report of the year, her job will be finished. They'll send someone out to check, they always do when they think she's blown it, and each time it happens, she's able to smile and be gracious as they apologize for the intrusion.

Not this time.

This time they're going to see that she's right, but after the holidays they'll send out an army of researchers and biologists and what-all, and they won't have any need for her. Especially when she tells them she has no idea what's going on, that she has, despite the tests she's run, the quick autopsies she's performed, no idea why the snakes are all dead.

As far as she can tell, every last one of them is dead.

Floating on the surface, caught in the reeds, stretched and tangled on the ground, a few dangling from branches in what was left of the Spanish moss.

It had taken almost all day to realize something else—that none of the bodies had been eaten, even nibbled at. Neither the birds nor the insects had touched a single one.

She probably could have stood that, could have stood seeing all the serpents dead, could have taken it with only a raised eyebrow, a puzzled grunt.

She could have; she knew it.

If it hadn't been for the great silence she couldn't even break by slapping the pole against the water.

7

In the Methodist church, the cross stops swinging, but something creaks just the same.

In the Edward Teach, Pegleg ignores the fruit and nuts Alma has given him, and stares at the door, muttering to himself.

In the sheriff's office, Billy Freck grabs his cap, checks his revolver, and hurries outside, while on the floor, in a hundred pieces, there are whispers. And there is laughter.

On the beach, waves pound the jetties and sawgrass quivers in the wind, seagulls dive for food, a lone cat prowls the dunes.

And Dub Neely sits cross-legged on the head of Daddy whale, every so often taking a sip from his flask. He seems to remember talking the other day with the giant who works for Cutler, but he can't remember what he said, can't remember if the giant answered. He thinks it may be important, but he can't remember why.

It's almost Christmas.

He's alone.

That may be the reason he's crying.

But he can't remember why.

6

1

When Casey opened his eyes, sunlight pushing at the bedroom curtains told him it wasn't the same day he had walked out of the woods. The question was, how long had he been asleep?

Carefully, testing each limb, aware of a lightheadedness that threatened to undermine his equilibrium, he tossed the covers aside and sat up. On the chair in the corner were his shirt and jeans. By the nightstand were his shoes. He stared at them for a long time, as though he wasn't sure what they were, then stood, waited, and headed straight for the bathroom.

Weak or not, there were some things that didn't pay attention to how he felt.

When he checked the mirror and saw the stubble on his cheeks and chin, he figured it had to be Wednesday, good Lord don't let it be Thursday.

It wasn't until he was in the shower that he remembered it all.

As best they could, they had manhandled into the house.

Someone, it might have been him, insisted on lying down in his bed, and they lugged him upstairs, undressed him, covered him up, turned out the light, and . . .

And nothing.

But the fog was gone.

He rinsed and dried quickly, opening the door just a crack so he could listen for voices, for sounds of movement. If they were still here, they would know he was awake. *If* they were still here.

"Oh, sure," he muttered. As if, after traveling all this way, for all this time, they were just going to tuck him in, kiss him goodnight, and leave. Just like that.

As he dressed, he made sure he made a lot of noise. Stomping around the bedroom. Grunting loudly. Glancing at the door now and then to see if anyone was there. When he was finished, and still alone, he walked heavy-heeled down the hall to the stairs and paused, listening.

They were there.

He couldn't hear them, but he knew they were there.

He backed away from the stairs and looked into the guest room. Nodded. Someone had slept in the bed.

In the storeroom the closet door was closed.

Back at the stairs he hesitated. There were going to be a lot of questions, most of which he knew he wouldn't be able to answer to their satisfaction. He could always tell them to leave, though, that he hadn't asked any of them to do this, that they had been fools all this time, chasing after something that no longer existed.

But that wasn't going to happen.

He remembered the looks on their faces when they first saw him that night; he wouldn't be able to stand the looks they'd give him if he threw them out.

So what would he do? What was the best way to handle this mess? The solution didn't take long. He would be friendly, but distant. Interested in their stories, but cool. The most important thing to remember, above all else, was that nothing was going to change.

He took the first step down, and felt the first twinge of panic. The second step added a little sweat to his palms. He nearly missed the third and had to grab the bannister for support. When he was halfway down, Cora stepped out of the living room, a tentative smile, an expectant look.

"Reverend Chisholm," she said, "someone was here to see you before. Some lady."

He stared at her for a long time before he said, "Cora, I am very glad to see you, but don't ever call me that again."

2

Lyman Baylor's office was at the side of the house, with an entrance of its own so he could see parishioners without them having to tramp through the house—Kitra's idea, to preserve at least a little of their privacy. It was a small room made smaller by the bookshelves and texts, the desk and chair, the two armchairs and standing lamp, and a large globe on a carved spiral walnut stand.

In shirtsleeves and stocking feet he sat at the desk and flipped through the Bible his mother had given him. He wanted something new this Christmas, aside from the usual telling of the Story. He wanted something relevant. The problem was the congregation, which, on Christmas morning, didn't want relevance; it wanted joy and remembrance and a promise that the following week wasn't going to bring the end of the world.

It should have been simple, forming a compromise that wouldn't alienate that which he'd worked so hard for so long to create.

He should have been able to do this in his sleep.

But as the news worsened and the local situation became more puzzling, and dangerous to those who bucked the mayor's as yet unknown plans for the island's north end, he couldn't find anything to say but the same old clichés.

Not a bad thing.

Not what he wanted.

So he was pleased when he saw his wife hurrying up the sidewalk. Not only was the impending interruption a blessing of sorts, but it gave him a chance to watch her, to appreciate her beauty, to thank God she had chosen him and not the dozens of other suitors who had pursued her throughout her life.

He grinned shamelessly, then, when she came in without knocking.

"Lyman," she said. "Lyman, my God, you're not going to believe it."

It wasn't difficult to pick up on her distress, and he was immediately on his feet. "What? What happened?"

"Nothing. It's Mr. Chisholm."

His stomach lurched, his temper sparked. "They got him again? Did they—"

"He's a priest, Lyman! That man is a priest!"

3

As soon as Casey saw them waiting in the living room, he knew he couldn't do this in here. There wasn't enough room; he would feel constricted, confined; he needed space. Much more space.

"Get your coats, we're going for a walk."

It was the tone, not the words, that made them move; it was the look on his face that trapped their questions inside.

He waited for them on the porch. Making no plans, no rehearsals, he nodded them out the screen door and down the walk to the street, herded them left and used a wide sweeping gesture when he said, simply, "This is my home."

Bannock and Lisse walked on his right, Cora and Reed on his left.

He flipped up his windbreaker collar, put his hands in

the pockets, and with the sun at their backs, he followed
the long road around the wide bend.

Maple Landing, he began, and sensed Cora and Reed tens-
ing, from the corner of his eye saw them move closer
together and clasp hands.

You weren't there, John. You don't know what all happened, unless the kids told you something. But the short of
it is, Death rode into my village—actually, it was smaller
than that—but Death rode in and tore it apart anyway. She
brought others with her—they'd been riding and killing
across the country for weeks—and almost everyone I
knew, every member of my parish, died in a single night.

I'm told that I fought her, but I don't really remember.

I woke up in the hospital, broken bones everywhere,
more aches than a cranky old man on a rainy November
night. They said I fell from the belfry, was lucky I landed
in some pretty thick bushes. I'm here to tell you, I definitely didn't feel lucky about then, all trussed and casted
up like that, tubes running every which way out of my
body, doped to the gills and still hurting like hell. Funny
thing was, after all that had happened to me, they were too
scared to let me know the least of it—that my hair had
turned white. Every strand of it.

Stupid thing is, that bothered me more than anything
else. Pride, I suppose. No; vanity. Looking way too old
before my time.

What you see here comes from a lot of practice, straight
out of a bottle.

Pride, now, that took a hit somewhere else.

There was a woman. Her name was Helen. I kind of
think we were something like lovers, or at least falling in
love. She stayed with me as long as she could, and then,
one day, she left. It was too much, and she didn't understand what had really happened. I don't blame her. She had
a life to lead, and I sure wasn't it.

Took a while to get better, though faster than they suspected, and I was on my feet again. So I went back to the Landing and saw what had been done.

The only thing left standing in one piece was my church. I had thought, lying there in the hospital, that I'd won. That I'd beaten her. But when I saw what was left—the blackened timbers, the craters, the abandoned houses only barely singed—I knew I had lost.

I lost, John.

Everything I worked for, I lost in one night.

Everything I was, was buried in the ashes of the school and the video store and the luncheonette and the bar; it was as dead as the rotting dock down where this great old man used to rent canoes to the tourists, and Reed here, when he wasn't being too lazy, was one of the guides; dead as the school blown apart by a little kid.

There wasn't a single soul left in Maple Landing. All the survivors had moved away, no forwarding address.

I think it was sometime during those two days I spent wandering those streets that I called you, when I told you you were marked. I don't know how I knew that, I just did. I knew you would end up same as me, somehow. I know I sounded crazy, but I know I was right.

———

He looked over, and John nodded, pushing the hair from his eyes, shoulders slumping.

"My son," he said quietly. "Casey, it was my son."

Casey said nothing.

There was nothing to say.

I had a suitcase, Casey continued, and I threw stuff in it until there was no more room. Then I left, and I haven't been back.

I was foolish enough to think that I could change things. I thought I could make it up to those who had died because

I hadn't won. The place to do that, I figured, was back home, in Tennessee. I had a little money, so I took a bus down, and the first thing I did was visit my mother's grave. I buried her, you know. One of the first things I did after my ordination was bury my mother.

I can remember the day clear as any morning you've ever seen in your life. That day, though, the day I went back, it was drizzly and damp and I had to pull vines from her marker and chase leaves off the grave. I told her what had happened, promised I'd try to keep preaching. But it was hard. Awful hard. 'Cause as it turned out I was doing it for all the wrong reasons.

Like the song, you know? Don't take your guns to town, boy, leave your guns at home? Something like that?

I was mad. Hell, I was so full of rage I was damn near blind and twice as pigheaded. I was determined to let people know what was going on, what was happening right under their noses in their very own towns, even if I had to stomp it into them, but they were so took up with themselves that they used every explanation they could think of for the famines, the sickness, the violence; all but the right one.

And that made me even angrier.

I visited small churches and small tents and living rooms and day rooms and even a bowling alley once. One week, in Knoxville, I took to standing on street corners. But none of it worked. I couldn't do it. I couldn't say the words as if I meant them, because . . . because the anger had long since gone away, and I was just plain tired.

Worse, though. Far worse, was that I couldn't bring myself to believe a blessed word I said.

Can't go after the bad guys if you don't have bullets for your guns.

You have no idea how frightened that made me.

So I figured I had one last chance—I tried to find the priest who had taken me from my cell, promising the moon and God knows what else so I wouldn't have to do my full time. He and his wife took me into his home. Showed me what I was good for. Put me on the road, John, and damn if I didn't end up in Maple Landing.

I should have known he wouldn't be alive after all this time, but when I saw his grave there in North Carolina, it ended.

It all ended.

I took off the collar and I haven't worn it since.

4

"He's *what*?"

Whittaker Hull kicked away from his desk, his chair rolling halfway across the small office, the portable telephone so tight to the side of his head that his ear began to ache.

"A priest," Lyman repeated. "He's a priest."

"I'll be goddamned. Can't be. Impossible. Him? You sure?"

"I checked. Kitra's a magician with a computer, so she did some searching, and there was a priest—an Episcopalian priest, Whittaker—named Casey Chisholm, disappeared about three years ago after a horrible incident at the place he was ministering to, up in New Jersey. Lots of people dead, the town practically burned to the ground."

"New *Jersey*? You've got to be kidding me, Ly. Oh my Lord, you don't suppose—"

"Oh, no, no, Whittaker, he had nothing to do with it, let me assure you. Somehow he ended up in the hospital, but once he was discharged—actually, if I read it right, he walked out—he vanished."

"Son of a bitch."

"Whittaker, please."

"But damnit, Ly, this isn't good, you do realize that, don't you? This isn't any good."

"What do you mean?"

"I thought maybe we'd finally have some muscle on our side. Kind of even up the odds with Cutler and the Teagues. Keep them off our backs, or at least make them think twice before they tried something else. But he's a priest, for crying out loud, Ly, and he's hiding. What the hell kind of ally is that?"

"I hadn't thought of it that way."

"Well, think on it a little, son. Think on it. Senior Raybourn's got the only property left up there that doesn't belong to some blind corporation we both know is owned by Cutler and that weasel Cribbs. Who the hell's gonna protect him? You? Me? Rick? Oh Jesus Christ, Ly, sweet Jesus Christ."

"Whittaker."

"Go away, Lyman. I've got a Christmas editorial to write."

5

"Bullshit!"

They had turned around, late morning sun now in their faces, shadows trailing behind. No one had said anything until Cora, her face red, her hands bunched into quivering fists, took a few running steps, turned, and walked backward, her face twisted in anger.

"That's bullshit, Re—Chisholm. You don't just hang it up just because . . ." She spit dryly to one side. "All this time for nothing? We were . . . all this time for goddamn nothing?" She shook her head violently, faced forward. "No," she yelled at the sky. "No, that's bullshit!"

Reed had drifted away from his side.

John and his lady had done the same.

He didn't know what else to say. He was more sorry than they could imagine that they had come all this way for nothing, to hear his sad story. It was frustrating because they clearly believed there was something he was supposed to do. And whatever that was, they would have a part in it. They couldn't possibly know how often he'd sat on the porch at night, smoking, having a beer, trying to figure out the same thing for himself.

He knew what was happening.

His part in it, however, had ended years ago.

Reed hurried to catch up to Cora, saying something to her, Cora shaking her head vehemently, shaking off the hand he tried to put on her arm.

They were, he thought suddenly, so old. So damned old. The last time he had seen them they had been teenagers, priming themselves for graduation, for letting loose on the world what energy and dreams they had. And now their journey, whatever they had suffered, had stolen all that. Had brought them to him.

And he couldn't heal them.

He couldn't give them back what they had lost.

He should have been angry. He should have demanded an explanation of their expectations so he could . . . what, Casey? Tell them how wrong they've been? Tell them what a waste of time this was?

He slowed. No anger, only a deep wrenching sadness that settled on his shoulders and made his chest and legs heavy. That made him stare at the ground as he walked, because the sun was too damn bright in his eyes.

Lisse moved on to catch up with the kids—he couldn't think of them as anything but that—and John couldn't find anything useful to do with his hands. They burrowed into his pockets, fussed with his hair, rubbed his face, his chest, the back of his neck.

Casey couldn't stand it any longer. "You think it's bullshit, too?"

Bannock shrugged. "I don't know. I don't know because I don't know what's going on, not really."

"Yeah, you do."

A lopsided smile. "Then maybe I still don't want to believe it."

"No one does, John. It's the nature of the beast."

At the top of the bend they watched the others talking in the street. Cora pulling at the ragged cut she'd made of her hair, as if demonstrating a sacrifice she'd made, Reed hanging back as he spoke to Lisse, Lisse herself bowing her head and kicking at invisible pebbles on the tarmac.

As Casey approached, they separated, Cora glaring defiantly at him.

"I am not," she said, "staying in there." She pointed at his house.

Casey nodded his understanding, held up a hand to keep her where she was, and went inside, opened a kitchen drawer, and pulled out two sets of keys. Back on the street he tossed one to her. "These are for that one," he said, indicating with his chin the house directly across from his. The other set he gave to John, told him he could stay in the house next to his.

"The electricity and water are still on. Bedclothes and things are up to you, for however long you plan to stay."

"What about the owner?" Reed asked, his tone anxious to keep things calm.

"He won't care. And if he does, I'll fix it."

Cora immediately went to John's car and stood at the trunk impatiently, until John unlocked it. She grabbed a battered duffel bag from inside and lugged it across the street. "Come on, Reed. Let's see what we've got."

With an apologetic shrug, he grabbed his own bag and followed.

Casey couldn't think of anything to say despite the urge to run after them and shake them both until they at least pretended they understood.

Then, at the foot of the porch steps, Cora turned and yelled, "Hey, Chisholm, I forgot—merry Christmas!" before she disappeared inside.

He didn't move.

He didn't respond.

Without bothering to close the trunk lid, Lisse took the

keys from John and drove the car down to the house they would use. After she parked, she only looked back once before beginning the chore of unpacking her own things, pausing as she did to watch a pair of black-mask gulls soar low over the yard, complaining to themselves.

John poked at the hedge, pulled his hand back with a mild curse. "Sharp," he said.

Casey smiled. "That's what thorns do."

"Yeah. I guess so." He examined a drop of blood gleaming on the heel of his hand, wiped it off on his coat and stepped away, his head darting toward him and away like a bird examining something odd on the ground.

"Think of this, Casey," he said at last. "I had my son, and you had that woman."

Don't, Casey thought.

"We both know which one is riding now. No brain surgery there."

Don't.

"But did you ever wonder if there was somebody else? When you heard about all those people dying in the streets, all those old folks and all those children, did you ever wonder if there was someone marked for the one who spread the disease? Now that you've seen me, are you wondering if that person, whoever it is, if that one survived too?"

Casey finally looked at him, his expression blank, uncaring.

"We're here, Casey. God knows why, but we're here. What are you going to do if that other one shows up? Are you going to tell him that he's wasted his time too?"

"Not my problem anymore," he said flatly. "And it's not yours either."

John walked away, half turned as he did, and said, "Maybe so. Maybe you're right. I'll believe you a lot better, though, if you can tell me with a straight face that you haven't heard the horses."

Part 5

1

1

The car was so dark it seemed to absorb the night.

When it reached the first leg of the Camoret Cause-way, the driver said, "Just a few more minutes, Mr. Stone."

In the backseat a man held a crystal glass half filled with rye. In his more playful moments, he called it rotgut, just to see if anyone knew what he was talking about. He wore a dark suit, a dark cashmere topcoat, on the seat beside him a derby he brushed clean every night. The suit was Saville Row, the shoes Italian, the shirt French, the leather gloves Spanish, the watch one of a kind from a small shop in Montreal.

"Remind me," he said, his voice baritone smooth.

"Cutler," the driver answered. "Norville Cutler. His partner is the mayor, Jasper Cribbs. An obstacle to what they implied was a land development deal. An old man and his retarded son."

"An old black man, right?"

"Yes."

Stone held the glass up, examined its contents. "Are we politically correct these days, Dutch?"

The driver's laugh was a series of high-pitched chokes and wheezes.

"I didn't think so. I assume they have local boys?"

"Yes, sir, they do. Apparently, not as effective as they'd like."

"Obviously." He took a sip, and mock-shuddered. "Is there a timetable?"

"They'd prefer Monday."

"What's the matter with tomorrow?"

"It's Christmas."

"So?"

The driver shrugged.

"And I suppose the next day is out because it's Sunday."

"I suppose so, sir."

"Oh well. They pay the bills, they can call some of the shots." He laughed. "As it were."

The car slid over Hawkins Island and rumbled onto the next leg. Starlight shone off the sea on either side; Camoret's lights shone like stars straight ahead.

"The local law," the man said.

"A sheriff who's on his way to retirement."

"Ah, my favorite kind."

"One deputy on our side, the others too scared to stand one way or the other."

"Ah, my favorite kind."

The driver wheeze-laughed.

"Local opposition?"

"We're not going to be lynched, sir, if that's what you mean. Evidently there's been a lot of noise, the usual kind—people complaining about land being taken off the tax rolls, suspected big money moving to take over the island, a few editorials in a weekly newspaper not big enough to wrap a fish in . . . that's about it."

"This," the man said, "is almost too easy." He took

another sip. "We'd best be careful, Dutch. We don't want to get overconfident or careless."

"No, sir."

"Right. So turn on the radio."

"It'll still be Christmas carols."

"I don't care. I'm in a good mood now. They won't spoil it. In fact, I'm feeling right in the mood."

When they reached St. James Island, the man looked at the Quonset hut stores on either side of the road, his lips pursed in distaste at the hot pink paint and signs. "The same Cutler, Dutch?"

"I think so."

"Call him."

The driver used one hand to dial a number on a cell phone, then handed it over his shoulder. The man in back took it with murmured thanks and held it to his ear, sipping as he waited for the connection to be made.

Then: "Mr. Cutler, Merry Christmas. This is Santa Claus, about to land on your lively little paradise in the sea."

2

Casey stood far from the church, under the wide branches of a tree old enough to be his great-grandfather. There was a sharp-edged moon, there were diamond stars, there was enough chill in the air for it to be no other season than winter. It would have been perfect had there been any snow.

He hadn't planned to be here.

He didn't want to be here now.

Earlier that evening, however, he had been standing in the living room, a sandwich in his hand, and he had seen the kids rush out of the house and across the street. By the time they reached Bannock's car, John and Lisse had joined them, and they all got in and they all drove away.

Not one looked in his direction.

Not one had spoken to him since he'd left them on Wednesday.

He knew, though, that they had been discovering the island. Driving down the harbor to check out the boats, the houses on the Hook's slope, the handful of restaurants down there; walking up and down the main business district, checking the shops, having a late lunch at Betsy's, last night having a drink first at the Tide, then at the Edward Teach. As far as he knew, they had never mentioned his name, except to say they knew him back when and had dropped in to see how he was doing.

Junior told him this.

Early this morning he had ridden up on his scooter, a large bag of warm food in the carrier.

"Mrs. Nazario," he said when Casey met him at the steps. "She says you are supposed to be eating. I think she's mad at you, Mr. Chisholm. I think Mr. Nazario isn't mad at you, but I think she's really mad at you, Mr. Chisholm."

"I'm sorry if she is," he'd said.

Then, his left hand fluttering around his left shoulder, he looked at the houses and said, "There are people around, they say they know you. Do they know you, Mr. Chisholm? Do they really know you from the time when you didn't live here but lived somewhere else?"

He had nodded, said nothing.

Junior told him what his father had told him, what he had heard in the luncheonette. "I know they think I don't hear good, but I do. I think they don't know I know."

Casey smiled. "Yeah, Junior, I know the feeling."

Junior had shaken his head. Flapped his arms. "Lots of new people here, I can't keep sense of them all. Does your friend have a fancy coat and hat?"

"No, I don't think so."

"Boy, one of them does. Funny hat." He tugged at his own, this one with flaps he never tied under his chin, but just as vibrantly red. "Really funny hat. Funny face, too. Holes in it, Mr. Chisholm. Got holes in it all over. His friend has a mustache this big, too." He stretched his arms out as far as they would go. "Funny."

Casey smiled again.

When Junior left, wishing him a merry Christmas and hoping Santa Claus would visit and bring him lots of stuff, he had returned to the house and sat in the living room. The television stayed off; he didn't think he could stand seeing another day of dying.

He tried to read, but somehow the book's language didn't seem to be English.

He tried singing to himself, but somehow he'd forgotten just where all the notes were.

He fixed a leak in the kitchen sink, scrubbed the bathtub and the bathroom sink, swept the floors and vacuumed the rugs, and spent too damn much time standing at the living room window, wondering if maybe he should make the first move.

When they all left, he ate the rest of the sandwich, used the dust pan and a brush to wipe up the crumbs, and decided to make an early night of it. If he turned on the TV, there'd only be church services and five different versions of *A Christmas Carol*, not one of them his favorite, the one with Alistair Sim.

A few minutes before eleven, he put on his coat, grabbed his gloves, and went out.

Fresh night air might help him think, although what he had to think about, he surely didn't know.

Things; that's all, things.

Before he knew it, he had found the tree, and the spot beneath where he could watch and not be seen. Far beyond the reach of the nearest street lamp.

The carillon had played "The First Noel" and "Hark, the Herald Angels Sing," and he had sung along with them, under his breath, watching his breath slip into the night and fade. He noticed how many cars were parked along the street, and wondered how many others had been driven to the mainland and parked on streets similar to this.

How many people were left on Camoret Island?

A stir of annoyance at himself.

So what are you doing, Casey? Standing out here in the cold like a Dickens orphan? You feeling sorry for yourself, boy? You feeling a little lonely? You hoping Cora or Reed will come running out of the church and straight into your arms, beg your forgiveness, and drag you back inside where you'll take your place at the altar while the congregation applauds and weeps and welcomes you home?

What are you looking for, you stupid son of a bitch? You looking for a damn miracle?

Or just a good reason to die.

He waited a while longer—for what, he didn't know—then decided it was time to head back. If he kept well to the side of the road and used the trees wisely, they'd never know he'd been here. No embarrassing questions, no need to lie.

Assuming, of course, they bothered to talk to him.

A last look, a sour smile, and he turned to leave, hadn't left the protection of the tree when he saw a car glide toward him from the north. Its headlights turned the interlocking branches into cage bars, but they didn't touch him as he pressed closer to the trunk.

This late at night, he couldn't help wondering why the vehicle was moving so slowly. Almost as if its occupants needed the time to check things out. Except, since it was halfway to midnight, there wasn't much to see—Christmas lights on the houses, the lights spanning Midway much farther down, and that was about it.

The engine barely made a sound.

As it passed his spot, he tried to see inside, but all the windows were tinted; he couldn't even see the dashboard's glow. And once past the church and the bulk of parked cars, it sped up abruptly and vanished, leaving only a blurred taillight trail behind.

A shrug, a tilt of his head, and he began the trip home. Long strides and swinging arms, not bothering to look behind him because he figured he'd hear any cars first and have plenty of time to get out of the way. Or hide.

He quickened his pace when the carillon sang again, "Joy to the World," sounding distant and small.

Midnight, then.

Merry Christmas.

"Stop it," he whispered harshly. "Stop it, no one's listening, no one cares."

He broke into a trot when he reached his front walk, had the door closed behind him just as John's car pulled up, made a U-turn, and parked. Lisse got out first, the kids climbing out of the back. Their voices were loud, exuberant, and he watched them give over to a round of hugs before separating.

Only John looked his way, and might have come to the door had not Lisse grabbed his hand, laughed, and pulled him away.

When the street was silent again, Casey took off his coat and gloves, tossed them onto the couch, and went upstairs. He made to pass the storeroom, changed his mind, and went in, crossed over to the closet, and stared at the door.

It was open.

Less than an inch, but it was open.

This time he didn't curse it, or kick it, or turn his back to it. He closed it gently with the fingers of one hand, pushing until he heard the latch catch, then reluctantly took his hand away.

It's the season, he told himself as he headed for bed; it's the season, and the sentiment, it's nothing you haven't been through before. Forget it. Ignore it. Sleep in tomorrow, eat, read, and before you know it, Christmas will be gone.

Sure, right, something answered; and then it will be one day closer to the end.

3

Christmas day on Camoret Island:

Junior Raybourn sits cross-legged in front of the Christmas tree, wrapping paper torn and strewn around him, his red hat perched on the back of his head, a bow with an adhesive backing stuck to the back of his hand.

He holds up a red and white cardigan with horn buttons and two pockets. "Is this mine?" he asks.

Senior, from the sofa, nods. "All yours, son."

"Can I wear it to work do you think?"

"I don't know. You'd have to be awfully careful not to get grease on it."

"Oh." He folds it carefully and returns it to its bed of red tissue paper. "I will think about it."

"Good."

"Do you like your present?"

Senior holds up a Sherlock Holmes pipe, with the face of the detective carved into the bowl. There isn't a chance in the world he'll ever smoke it. "Fine, son, very fine."

"Miz Nazario helped me."

"You did a good job."

"I know. Is there football on? I'd like to watch some football now."

"We'll check after breakfast."

Junior turns on his buttocks, raises his knees and hugs them tightly. "I think next time," he says, resting his chin on his knees, "I'm gonna ask Santa Claus to bring me a book."

Jasper Cribbs stands in his driveway, tapping his foot impatiently, checking his watch every ten seconds. The women are, as always, late, and it's getting him mad. They're going to spend the day in Savannah with his in-laws, hardly the way he feels like celebrating the holiday. But it keeps Mary Gwen happy, and it doesn't cost him a dime, so what the hell, bite the bullet, smile like it's an election, and maybe next year they'll both be stone dead.

Now that would be a present he could get his teeth into.

A car honks from the street and he waves without looking, reaches through the driver's window, and pushes his own horn, a long blast that has the front door open and his wife and daughter scurrying out before the sound dies.

"Let's go, let's go," he urges with false joviality, clapping his hands, opening the door for his wife. "Can't get the good stuff if we're not there, you know."

"Oh, you," Mary Gwen says, playfully slapping his arm. "Momma would shoot you if she heard you say that."

Your mother, he thinks sullenly, would shoot me in a heartbeat if she thought she could get away with it.

Mariana, acting as if she were being asked to commit some utterly distasteful sacrifice, opens the back door and gets in on her own. Slams it shut behind her. She lobbied for days to stay home, as she has done every year since she was twelve, and resents the fact that even now, in her twenties, she has to do what Daddy tells her.

He raps a knuckle on her window until she slides it down. "Cheer up," he tells her. "It won't be long, you know that. We'll be back before you know it, and you can still see your friends."

She doesn't answer; she just pouts.

Spare me, he begs the sky as he rounds the back of the car; spare me.

What sustains him today, what has lightened his mood considerably, was the call he'd received late last night from Norville.

"He's here."

"You sure?"

"Just talked to him."

"He knows what to do?"

"Jesus, Jasper, he's a damn professional. Yes, I'm pretty sure he knows what to do."

"Fine. Let me know when it's over."

"Jasper, trust me, I have a feeling you'll know it anyway. Oh, and merry Christmas."

Whittaker Hull looks at his Christmas tie and utters a martyr's sigh, "Darling, next time just give me the money, all right?"

"Dad!" Ronnie protests with a laugh. "You have no idea how long it took me to pick that out."

He sighs again, twice as loudly, and looks sorrowfully at Rick. "She waits till the last minute, then grabs the first thing that sticks to her fingers that won't bite back. Every year, son; she does it every year. I'm telling you now, be careful, or you'll have a steamer trunk full of ties and underwear you wouldn't wear on a bet."

"Dad!" Ronnie's scowling this time. "Rick talk to him."

Rick holds up his hands—*I'm not getting in this, don't even talk to me.*

He has been invited to Christmas dinner, which Ronnie has cooked and which Whittaker has supervised. Their halfhearted arguments last most of the morning and well into the afternoon, but he's jealous anyway, because none of it is very serious. She looks after her father, her father still acts as if she was fifteen years younger. He wishes he had a family of his own to treat him that way.

Whittaker makes a show of unbuckling his belt, pulling apart his bow tie, slapping his hands against his stomach. "Brilliant as always, my dear. Brilliant as always."

Ronnie, still sitting, mimes a curtsy, a finger pushed up under her chin. But she does blush a little.

"Yeah, great," Rick agrees, pleased, and not a little relieved, that he doesn't have to lie.

"She'll have you fat in no time," the old man warns with

a grin. "You'll have to get a bigger boat just to get away from the dock."

"Dad," Ronnie says, "we're not married, you know."

"You will be," he answers confidently. "I just hope you two will figure it out before I am consigned to my grave, listening to your mother complain for the rest of eternity."

"Not nice, Dad," she scolds, rising to fetch the coffee.

"Her mother," he explains to Rick, "was a wonderful woman with but one bad habit—nothing in the universe ever satisfied her. And she was not . . . Lord forgive me, but she was definitely not the type to suffer in silence."

It takes a moment for Rick to understand that it's okay to smile. When he does, the old man nods his approval.

"Now." Whittaker takes his napkin from his lap and folds it to place next to his plate. "So what have you heard about the fish, young Jordan?"

"For crying out loud, Dad," Ronnie complains, bearing a tray of cups and cookies into the room. "I won't have talk like that at the table. It's Christmas, can't you take at least one day off?"

"And you, I suppose, have no desire to know more about your little legless friends?"

"It's not the same thing."

"All the more mysterious, don't you think? Two seemingly unrelated phenomena dealing with mass destruction of unknown cause and origin?"

"I think that's redundant," she mutters.

Whittaker ignores her. "As a matter of fact, since I had a feeling they wouldn't bother to let you know anything, I took it upon myself to contact the state marine biologist who took all those samples. Did you meet him?"

Rick shakes his head. After he'd made his report to Sheriff Oakman, he had gone to the Tower for his volunteer stint and had to watch the whole episode—vans and cars and men he supposed were scientist types—through his binoculars. No one spoke to him, before or after.

"Well, you'll be happy to know that thus far all they can tell me is that the fish are well and truly and still very dead."

"My taxes at work."

"My sentiments exactly."

"Dad, that's enough. Change the subject, okay?"

"Very well, my dear. What about . . ." He taps a finger to his chin and considers the ceiling for a while. "What do you know about the preacher who also happens to be an ex-con?"

Vale Oakman sits at his desk, catching up on reports. Everyone else is off or on standby for the holiday. His decision. It's better than sitting at home all alone.

The last report is a requisition to the mayor's office for a new dispatch radio. He's trying to make it look like a stupid accident instead of Freck going off the deep end.

"Whispering," Billy had said. "It kept whispering at me."

He had kept it up until Vale sent him home.

Verna, of course, was fit to be tied.

And now, in the empty building, he writes the report and tries to ignore the soft whispers he hears in the front room.

In the basement of the Methodist church, where Sunday school and church committee meetings are held, two long tables have been set up, covered with a white cloth and dotted with small white vases of fresh flowers. There are twenty-nine people sitting there this afternoon, all but one very old, all but one having no one at home to cook dinner for them, or to take them away, even for one day.

This was Kitra's idea, first implemented several years ago, and with a decent number of volunteers, and some donations from the local restaurateurs, a fairly good meal has been assembled. Cheerful music plays over the loudspeaker system, Lyman makes the rounds telling jokes and teasing and once in a while whispering a requested prayer for health and good fortune, while Kitra oversees the cooking and serving.

The odd man out is Dub Neely, who sits at the end of the first table, the one nearest the three stairs that lead to the exit door. He has made a noble effort to clean himself, comb his hair, make sure his clothes are if not ironed, at least not smelling as if he'd just crawled out of a sewer.

Few bother to speak to him; even the elderly know his reputation and don't want this day spoiled by having to talk with a drunk. The only ones who show him kindness are the Baylors, and by the time he receives dessert, a large slice of German chocolate cake, he feels practically human again.

"Not bad for a soup kitchen, huh?" Lyman says, dropping into the chair next to him, planting his elbows on the table, chin in his palms. "Makes you feel good and sad at the same time. So how are you, Dub? Taking care of yourself?"

"Best I can, Pastor," Dub answers, brushing crumbs from the corners of his mouth.

"Dub, you call me Pastor one more time, I'm gonna have to start dragging you to services."

Neely grins. A long-standing game between them, one he knows the minister can't win, one in which the minister refuses to accept defeat. "You talk to the other preacher yet?"

Lyman doesn't answer for a while. "No. Not yet."

"No offense, Pastor, but he ain't coming to you, you know."

Lyman nods.

"The way I figure it, he must be really out of it, you know? I mean, he didn't show up last night or this morning, right? Wasn't in church? You're a preacher, whether you preach or not, you got to go to church. So I figure he's out of it."

Lyman waves to an old woman at the far table, who has given him a bright toothless smile of thanks.

Dub finishes his cake, wipes his mouth carefully with a paper napkin, and pushes away from the table. "Got to go, Pastor. Got to take my daily constitutional."

He stands, and Lyman stops him with a hand on his arm. "Dub, I've been meaning to ask you . . ."

Dub looks down at him and knows with a sudden chill exactly what he's going to say. He shakes his head—don't ask, please don't ask.

Lyman's hand drifts to the table where it clasps the other into a double fist. "We, Kitra and I, we thought we were maybe going a little nuts. But it's true, isn't it."

Automatically Dub reaches for his flask, remembers where he is, and wipes his hand nervously on his coat instead.

Lyman doesn't look at him. "So what do you think it means, Dub? Have any thoughts?"

"You're the pastor."

Lyman laughs softly. "Yes . . . I'm the pastor."

For the first time in a long time Dub feels a spike of temper, and lets it out. "I'm a drunk, Pastor, that's all I am. I hear things, I see things, most of the time it's because I'm swimming in an alcoholic haze with no regard for life or limb or the sanctity of human decency." When the minister looks up at him sharply, he grins. "That means I'm a drunk, Pastor, and you shouldn't pay any attention to what I say."

He nods his thanks for the meal and the company, and walks as steadily as he can to the stairs. Only three, but suddenly they seem tripled, and higher, and the door at the top with the small glass window seems a million miles away. There's a small brass railing attached to the cinder block wall, and he grabs it hard when he hears Lyman say, "So how scared are you, Dub? How scared are you, really?"

*   *   *

In the middle of the harbor there's a large raft, and on the raft there's a large Christmas tree which, at night, gives off enough light to make it appear as if it's standing on a tiny island. Gulls stalk the wharves and piers, searching for food. Cats prowl and dogs root and a large blue heron glides overhead, heading for the marsh.

Some of the boats that haven't been placed in dry dock yet are festooned with colored lights from mast to cabin, bow to stern, one or two have artificial trees standing on their prows. The boardwalk that connects them all on the bay's south side is deserted. Everyone is home, or at someone else's home, either celebrating or taking the day off because everyone else is celebrating.

The *Lucky Deuce* rocks and sways with the easy roll of the low waves, occasionally rubbing against the tire bumpers lashed to the dock.

When it explodes, the water burns.

Hector Nazario sits contentedly in front of his television set, stoically enduring yet another commercial interrupting his American football game. Gloria is on the phone to their relatives in Florida, and he half listens with a half smile to her praise of the awful gifts their grandmother has sent them, and to her artful dodging of the monthly question— when are you coming home, Georgia's no place for any respectable Nazario to live, so when are you coming home where you belong?

The commercial ends, there's a brief news report that interrupts the halftime sports report, and for the first time that day he frowns.

"Gloria," he says.

She covers the mouthpiece with one hand. "What?"

He points at the screen. "They say Pakistan has tested another bomb. On a missile, I think. India, too."

"So?"

He shrugs. "I don't know. It's Christmas, it's not right."

"Maybe they blow each other up, we don't have to worry anymore."

Maybe, he thinks; maybe not.

But the second half of the game isn't nearly as much fun.

4

Casey stands at the foot of a jetty, bundled as warmly as he can be with what he has, shoulders up, elbows tight to his sides. He wants to go out there, but the tide is in and the waves are too high. He wouldn't get halfway there before he'd be slammed off and battered.

He had awakened that morning cursing the day he'd ever met those damn kids, or had called that fool Bannock who looks like a young Abraham Lincoln. Had they gotten on with their lives, he would have gotten on with his as he'd reconstructed it, and no one would be hurt. And he wouldn't be feeling the way he did.

That tantrum hadn't lasted very long.

In fact, it had lasted just long enough for him to recognize the absurdity of it and start to laugh. No humor, just a laugh that escaped once in a while as he dressed, and ate breakfast, and read, and ate lunch, and finally decided it was time to hit the beach.

do you ever wonder if there's a third survivor

He glares at the sea, King Canute willing the tide to retreat, then turns north and trudges along the edge of the beach's wet-sand apron.

A wave slips in and teases his shoes and retreats, and he watches for the bubbles that signal a sand crab's burrow; a pair of black-mask gulls land in front of him, squawking softly and skittering away when he doesn't veer around them; the upside-down skeleton of a horseshoe crab in a foam-filled depression; clutches of kelp not yet driven high enough to completely dry out; half a small nautilus shell; shards of other shells bleached of most of their color; a tangle of mussel shells the gulls have emptied and left behind.

do you ever wonder if there's a third survivor

The honest answer, at the time, would have been no. He had survived, and for him that was all that mattered. Survival had destroyed him and everything he'd known; he had been too busy rebuilding to give a damn about anyone else.

Since then, however . . .

He spots the whale family up ahead, and after one last disgusted look at the surf, angles across the sand toward them. He doesn't so much feel the need for communion as for a windbreak, and that somehow makes him feel guilty in a foolish sort of way. When he reaches Daddy, however, he's tempted to climb it, sit on top and play King of the Hill with the gulls and the crows who were scolding him from the trees.

Go south, he orders them silently; get a bird life and go south, you jerks.

He wanders among the boulders, brushing the cold stone with his fingertips, poking a finger into a depression or a crack, brushing away dry sand flung there wet by the wind or someone's racing foot. He blows his nose; he wipes a wind-tear from one eye. He looks up, once and sharply, when he hears the dull smack of a distant explosion. Or what sounds like an explosion but is probably a wave striking a deep recess in one of the jetties. When he hears nothing else, he moves to the front of Daddy's great head and leans back against it.

Stares at the ground.

At his feet, wearing those dumb walking shoes that he knows are nothing more than fat fancy sneakers.

Remembering, suddenly, what it used to be like, what he used to wear, and how comfortable it had all been.

Back when.

In the other life.

In the other life, when he had dared—as some had put it—to speak to the Lord not in archaic, Shakespeare-like language, but in ordinary conversation. How he used to walk into his church first thing each day and say, "Good morning, Lord," and see if there was anything special he had to do.

Blasphemy is how the more ritual-oriented of his parishioners had put it; you don't speak to God as if He were your equal.

They didn't understand that Casey had no such idea in mind. It was just his way. He often thought it had something to do with the fundamental differences between North and South; just as likely, it had something to do with the comfort he felt in the Presence.

God certainly hadn't struck him down for his cheek.

He figured that was a plus.

Idly he digs at the sand with the toe of a shoe, smooths the hole over, and starts another. Looks up once when he thinks he hears a siren, dismisses it as the wind.

You're stalling, he tells himself.

He nods; he knows.

He's gotten real good at that over the years. Pretty much one of the world's experts, he reckons.

And today, like each Christmas since the day he left Maple Landing, would have been pretty much like every other day, if it hadn't been for those damn kids and that damn Bannock and his lady with the stunning auburn hair. All right, maybe not so terribly ordinary, but damnit, certainly not filled with so much pain.

It isn't fair.

It isn't right.

He's out of it.

He had lost.

you're stalling, Chisholm

He digs another hole, and smooths it over; he wriggles his back against Daddy's head to find more comfort; he watches his foot, studies the sand, listens to the gulls and the crows, until he can find no more excuses to keep his head down.

When he looks up, at the sea, at the cloudless sky, at the mist that rises above the jetties each time a wave thunders against them, at the beach that stretches southward as far as he can see, at the birds that ride the wind . . .

When he looks up, he inhales, holds it, lets it out, and finally shakes his head slowly. Says, "Good afternoon, Lord, happy birthday," and it sounds so ridiculous, so phoney, so trite, so unconscionably false, that he wonders if finally he's stepped over the line.

Whether he has or not, though, it doesn't stop him from weeping.

5

He stands in the middle of Midway Road, hands on his hips, staring hard at the house across from his. He has been standing there, virtually unmoving, for almost an hour; whenever the urge to give up makes him shift, he tells himself—patience, boy, patience.

He's aware of movement off to his right and behind him—Bannock and the woman leaving their place and standing in the yard. Neither greets him or calls to him, but he can feel them watching.

Patience, boy. Patience.

When it happens, it happens fast:

Cora slams the porch door open and stomps down the stairs, her head shaking, one hand slashing at the air as if wielding a sword.

"What do you want?" she yells. She wears no coat, only a shirt and jeans and tired sneakers on her feet. "What the hell do you want from me?"

Reed is far behind her, tentative, carrying a sweater in his good hand. Casey sees smudges under his eyes, and his cheeks, once full, are sunken now and pale.

"What do you want?" she shouts, her stride shorter, growing uncertain.

He doesn't move.

He stands there and watches her sternly, the way he used to watch the teenager who had all the ideas that got all her friends in trouble, the one who was sullen and bitter and had only three real friends, Reed the only survivor.

Her head doesn't make it anywhere near his chin, but she plants herself in front of him and takes a swipe at his chest. "What do you want?" she demands, breathing heavily, eyes narrow, lower lip on the verge of trembling.

He glances over her head at Reed, and he winks.

Startled, Reed can't stop himself from grinning.

Cora slaps his chest again, once with each hand, and after the second one he grabs her wrist.

"Let go of me."

But she doesn't struggle.

Softer: "Please, damnit, let go of me."

"Don't swear," he scolds softly.

"Ain't swearing," she says, repeating one of his lessons. "It's cursing. You want swearing, I'll swear you into the goddamn ground."

As soon as she realizes what she's done, she looks up at him, and the lip finally trembles.

"Reverend Chisholm?"

For a long time, he doesn't answer. She expects the truth, because he's never before given her anything else. The problem now is, he's not sure what the truth is.

So he says, with a small smile, "Maybe."

It's honest, and it's enough.

She collapses against him, hugs him as tightly as she can, and he can't see if she's crying, but he wouldn't bet on it. Cora Bowes seldom cried, at least not in front of him. That's a weakness, and she's spent a lifetime trying to purge herself of them all.

"Maybe," he whispers as he puts his arms around her, rests his chin in her hair. "Maybe."

2

1

They spent most of Sunday at Casey's house, sprawled in the living room, a bath towel draped over the TV screen so no one would be tempted. He sat on the couch and listened to their stories, which they seemed determined to make either as harrowing or as comic as they could. They talked over each other, bickered, filled in gaps, contradicted, and once begun, didn't bother to try to hide the pain.

Midway toward sunset, he and John drove down to Betsy's, discovered it closed and moved on to the Tide, a coral-colored stucco building on the left side of the road, a mural of a huge cresting wave stretching from one side of the entrance to the other. The menu was far larger than anything Hector and Gloria delivered, but Casey cautioned him that the food, while decent to not too bad, didn't hold a candle to the Nazarios' Cuban touch. They ordered enough to feed an army, ordered a little more, and dumped it all in the backseat.

When Casey paid and John protested, Casey said, "I've had nothing else to spend it on in a long time. Let it be."

* * *

Let me tell you something, honey, Lisse had said to him during one of John's pauses, you ain't seen nothing until you've seen those crows with those awful blue eyes. Killed one man we know about, the one who got him started writing, can't begin to guess how many others there were. Couldn't really hear their wings, either. There were a whole bunch, a couple dozen or more, but you couldn't hear them flying.

And the horses.

Don't get me started about the horses.

She frowned when Cora said something to her, then shrugged helplessly. I don't know, dear, she said. I don't know what was the worst part. Maybe because it all was, you know what I mean?

Yes, I guess you do.

She shifted in the uncomfortable silence, and raised an eyebrow. No, I take that back. It's his snoring, that's the worst part. The man can wake the long dead and make them wish they were dead again. The trouble is, when he falls asleep he's deaf as a post.

Reed, giggling, wanted to know if they were married.

Not yet.

She nudged John hard, and he blushed.

See? she said, her eyes bright. Softy, the man's a softy. Except when he's asleep and deaf. Then you can poke him all night, it's like kicking a log.

Married? I don't know. Maybe next year.

And Reed had muttered, if there is a next year.

Casey didn't tell her he had already seen the birds.

They hadn't quite reached the church, when John glanced in the rearview mirror and said, "Uh-oh."

Casey checked over his shoulder and groaned.

It was a sheriff's department cruiser, lights twirling, headlamps flashing. John pulled over and rolled his window down.

"What's the procedure here?"

"I don't know. All I own is a bike. I walk the rest of the time." Then he said, "Oh, crap," when he saw Deputy Freck climb out of the car, hitching at his gunbelt, straightening his sunglasses.

John already had his license out, wiggled a finger to get Casey to pull the registration and insurance from the glove box, along with the rental contract.

"Afternoon, gentlemen," Freck said, leaning over, his face filling the window. "Sorry to bother you. Just need to ask a couple of questions."

"Anything you say, Officer," John said politely.

"No kidding." He smiled without parting his lips. "Where were you yesterday afternoon, con?"

Casey didn't answer.

"Hey, con, I'm talking to you. Where were you yesterday afternoon?"

"Ex-con," Casey said, refusing to face him. "And I was at the beach most of the time. Why?"

"You got witnesses?"

"Why?"

Freck leaned an elbow on the door, shook his head as if he were weary of dealing with recalcitrant fools. "You gonna tell me you haven't heard?"

"Don't have a phone and there's no paper, Deputy," he said. "And I'm no psychic, either."

"I'll be damned. Well, Chisholm, seems like somebody blew up the *Lucky Deuce* yesterday. And you wouldn't know anything about it, would you."

Casey did look then. "Rick's boat? Somebody blew up Rick's boat? What the hell for?"

"My, my, don't the man catch on fast. So you were on the beach, that right? No witnesses, that right?"

"A couple of crows."

"All day?"

"No. The rest of the time I was with my friends."

The deputy nodded thoughtfully. "Maybe—"

"Look, Freck," Casey said, his patience gone, "if you want me to make a statement of my whereabouts, say so and we'll go to the office. Otherwise" he jerked a thumb over his shoulder—"we've got our dinner back there, and I don't want it to get cold."

Freck inhaled slowly, deliberately, as he looked up and down the street. Then he said to John, "Mister, you look to me like a reasonable man. Hell"—he took off his sunglasses—"you look like somebody I know. But if this little routine stop here has annoyed you, maybe you'd best think twice about hanging around with ex-cons."

With his sunglasses back on, he touched a finger to the edge of his hat brim in a mock salute, and ambled back to his patrol car. When he left, it was with a squealing U-turn.

John watched him go, in the side mirror. "Something going on here I should know about, Casey?"

"When we get back," he answered. "When we get back."

It wasn't much fun a lot of the time, Reed had said, plucking absently at the sling that bound his arm to his chest. I mean, we saw a lot of things we wouldn't have seen otherwise, I guess, but it wasn't like we were on vacation. Well, sometimes it was. Sometimes we knew Reverend Chisholm wasn't anywhere around, so we used the time to build up our money. It was hard, though. I mean, Cora kept getting fired all the time.

Hey, she said.

Well, you were. She never took anything from anybody, you know? I don't think they want that kind of attitude in a waitress. No offense, Lisse.

None taken, Yank.

He grinned then and started to laugh, sputtered to a halt, apologized, and laughed again.

No, Cora warned.

One time, he said, we were camping out in I forget where it was, in some trees anyway someplace, and the next morning Cora gets up to go ... you know ... you know? ... and I'm getting stuff ready to cook breakfast when she comes screaming back like she's being chased by monsters, pants down around her ankles, and I ... oh, God ... I ...

Turkeys, she said grumpily. It was turkeys, okay? You happy?

But she soon enough began to smile in spite of herself, had to cough away a laugh.

I wasn't looking where I was going, got myself all settled, and there was a whole flock of wild turkeys who I guess kind of took exception to what I was doing.

You know, those damn things are *big*, Reed said. Then he grinned even wider. I bopped one with a frying pan. I learned to cook turkey that night.

My hero, Cora said sarcastically.

Damn right, he said. You're God damn right.

All the food was stored in the kitchen except for what they took back to the living room to eat right away. As they did, Casey told them how he'd been attacked, drugged to keep him in bed, and how he really didn't know exactly why it had all happened.

"All I can figure from some of the old newspapers, and from what I heard while I was in bed—what I remember, that is—is that there's some kind of big land deal thing going on. Everything on this end of the island has been bought up, except for a place owned by a guy named Raybourn. There's a few blind corporations involved, and the speculation is, they're run by the mayor and ... well, my boss."

"I don't get it," John said. "Where do you fit in?"

"I don't, I don't think. I mean, I'm just the handyman. I don't have any interest in any property, the mayor can't be mad at me because I've never met him . . . hell, I just don't know. But people in the way are getting hurt. The story is, an old woman was, essentially, murdered for her house, there's been vandalism against those who talk too loudly about it—"

"But somebody wanted you out of the way, too," Reed said. "Not as in dead, I mean. I mean, like, with all the drugs and stuff."

"Again," Casey began, and stopped. Frowned. "Well, there was one thing."

He told them about the newspaper and the Teagues, but even that didn't make much sense in the long run.

"So I ticked them off and they beat the crap out of me. That doesn't justify getting a doctor involved in keeping me flat on my back. That's serious business. That's, at the least, some form of criminal malpractice."

He spread his arms. "I don't know, guys. I do not know."

He watched Reed struggle with a plate and his sandwich, and couldn't take it any longer.

"Reed," he said, standing, "when did you get hurt, Thanksgiving, right?"

"Yes, sir."

"Get up."

"Huh?"

"Come on, get up, boy. On your feet. Someone go into the kitchen and get me a pair of scissors or a good sharp knife."

Reed looked bewildered, and uneasy, as Cora hurried out of the room, and he flinched a bit when Casey clamped his hands on his shoulders.

"You're milking it, son," he said gently, with a gentle smile.

"I'm . . . no!" Reed protested. "There was . . . muscles got ripped up and they had to put everything back together. They said it would take—"

"Hush," Casey whispered. And squeezed. "Hush."

When Cora returned, he wasted no time cutting away the sling and the broad bandage wrapped around Reed's shoulder. Gently he pulled it away from the skin, grimacing once at the smear of disinfectant that made it seem as if the whole area was one huge bruise.

Then he took Reed's hand. "Straighten your arm."

Reed shook his head. "No, Reverend Chisholm. I can't."

"Sure you can. You can brain a wild tom turkey with a pissant frying pan, you can straighten your arm." His voice deepened, and he stepped back. "Do it, Reed. Slowly. Be careful. But do it."

Reed's face contorted in anticipated pain, but when Casey held out his hand, shaking it impatiently to tell him to grab hold, Reed bit down on his lip, levered the arm away from his chest, an inch at a time, a hiss and a held breath, a grimace when something inside pulled and hurt. But eventually he did it—he grabbed Casey's hand.

"All right!" Cora said, clapping. "Someone else to do the dishes." Reed touched the scar on his upper chest, twisting neck and head so he could look at it. "I'm healed," he said in delighted disbelief. "Wow. I'm healed."

Casey laughed. "No kidding, son. I think you've been healed for a while already."

Reed, rubbing his shoulder gingerly, look around excitedly as Casey headed for the kitchen. "No kidding, really. Look! I'm healed! Reverend Chisholm, you—"

"Stop it," Casey ordered. Looked back, glaring. His voice, while not loud, filled the room. "Stop it, Reed. No more. I didn't do a thing."

* * *

Casey, beer bottle in hand, stood at the back door, looking at the yard, seeing nothing.

From behind him: "What was that all about?"

"I don't want him thinking something's true that isn't. He grabs for things, John. He's been through a lot, but he hasn't changed. He needs explanations and sometimes grabs the first one he finds."

A footstep; the sound of the refrigerator opening.

"Casey, you and I, we don't know each other very well—hell, we've only met twice before—but it seems to me there's more to it than that."

Casey brought the bottle to his lips, lowered it again slowly, without drinking. "No," he said. "No, there isn't."

"Okay."

Footsteps leaving.

Voices in the front room.

No, he thought; no, there isn't.

3

1

Late Monday morning Casey took them down to the harbor, where they stood near the slip where the *Lucky Deuce* had been destroyed. There wasn't much of it left, a portion of the bow was all that remained above water. A handful of nearby boats showed signs of fire, others of the blast itself—one's mast had been snapped in half; on a second the mainmast was gone entirely. Crime scene tape snapped and bent in a slow wind; in one place it had torn, and the ends coiled endlessly on the ground like a headless yellow snake. No one else was there but a few kids poking around, one of the deputies standing on the dock watching them but saying nothing.

In the bay were three rowboats—in one were men taking down the raft tree, in the others men still scouring the surface for clues to the previous day's explosion.

As far as Casey could tell, none of the closest houses had been badly damaged, but a couple of trees showed charred bark. He walked around for a few minutes, but he didn't see Rick.

"What was he?" Reed asked as they headed back for the car. "Some kind of drug dealer or something?"

Casey shook his head. "No, he's one of the people trying to find out what Cutler's up to. I think his girlfriend is the newspaper editor's daughter."

"Damn," said Lisse, "these boys play rough."

John took her arm. "They must think it's worth it."

Cora looked back, shivering. "A good thing he wasn't on it."

"Maybe they thought he was."

Casey hung back. He couldn't help thinking of Jordan, the man's whole livelihood gone in an instant. There was probably some insurance, but he had a feeling, looking at the other, newer and larger boats, that it might not be enough to keep him in competition.

Amazing, he thought; the world's blowing up in every corner, and there are still some men who'll fight over one lousy piece of land on one not so very big island. Amazing.

"Lunch," he announced when they reached the car.

"I'm not hungry," Cora said.

"You'll eat," he told her with a grin. "Or just have a coffee, I don't care. I, however, am starved, and I need to find out a few things."

Her frown quickly became a grin of her own. "Gossip."

"Bingo."

"But you hardly know anyone, you said so yourself."

"I have ears to hear. And a cook who loves to talk."

The lunchroom wasn't full yet, and they took a table at the side wall in Betsy's. Casey introduced the Nazarios as a pair of those who had looked after him after the beating—Gloria seemed embarrassed at his fulsome praise of her help; Hector just beamed and excused himself back into the kitchen.

Not long after they ordered, the other tables and the counter began to fill. Talk was of the explosion, the fires, and the inevitable tales of close calls and heroism. A propane tank theory was scuttled when a fisherman regular insisted Jordan never had one aboard, spontaneous combustion made the rounds, a spark near the fuel tank, clear-sky lightning, kids fooling around to disastrous effect.

No one mentioned Norville Cutler.

Casey never thought they would; he paid more attention to their expressions and tones than their words, and that told him Cutler was at the top of their most wanted list. What bothered him was Stump Teague—the man didn't seem the type to have knowledge of sophisticated explosives, and even if the device turned out to be a crude one, he doubted the little man could use it without blowing himself up.

Personal attention was his style, not destruction from a distance.

By the time the second wave of diners came in, he had heard enough; and besides, the topic had changed to the winter storm that would probably make hash of New Year's Eve. He had one more stop to make, and he didn't want to waste any more time. While John paid at the register, he leaned into the kitchen to say good-bye to Hector and thank him again. Junior, standing at the grill, waved over his shoulder.

"I have a new sweater," he said, pointing proudly at his chest.

"Looks good, Mr. Raybourn," Casey said. "You watch that grease, now."

"Yes. Yes, sir. I can do that. I can watch the grease."

Casey winked at him and turned to go, paused when Hector held up a finger—wait a minute—and finished the platter he had been assembling. As he carried it to a small table near the door for pick-up and rang a small bell, he said, "I heard something this morning, Mr. Chisholm."

"Something good?"

"No, not good at all." He kept quiet until the waitress took her order. "I heard they brought in someone."

Casey frowned. "What do you mean?"

"I mean, they brought in someone. From the mainland. To take care of business, Mr. Chisholm. Like, maybe, what happened to Mr. Jordan." He tapped a light finger against Casey's chest. "And I think I saw him, too. I think he had breakfast here, him and another man, I think maybe he was his partner." He smiled, but it was a poor effort. "I didn't like him, Mr. Chisholm. He was . . ." He smiled again, shrugged, and headed back to his cutting board.

But Casey didn't miss the movement of the man's hand—he had been unable to put a word to his feelings about this stranger; nevertheless, he had crossed himself, kissed the tips of his fingers.

2

They stood at the peacock tail window, Cutler and Cribbs, and watched Midway Road as if it were an experiment whose conclusion they were about to witness.

"He's good, Norville," Cribbs said with an admiring shake of his head. "I got to give him that, he's plenty damn good."

"Gets paid enough, he damn well better be."

"Norville, I sense you're not happy."

"I won't be happy until it's over, Jasper."

"Then I guess you'll be smiling tonight."

Cutler smoothed a sideburn. "No, I'll be happy when I'm off this damn island, that's when I'll be happy."

"Shame," Cribbs said, lowering himself into his chair, propping his heels on the low windowsill. "Going to be a lot more in it for you if you stick around."

"Not a chance." He patted his pockets, searching for a cigarette before he remembered that the mayor didn't allow smoking in the office. He rubbed a finger under his nose. "You heard from our partner?"

"Not a word."

"What? Jesus, Jasper, aren't you worried?"

"About what? The money shows up when he says it will, what's to worry about?"

"Tonight, you fool."

"For heaven's sake, Norville, you're like to drive a saintly man to drink, you know that? I am well convinced that Mr. Stone and Mr. Lauder have matters well in hand. What'll it take to ease your mind?"

Cutler shook his head slowly. "Tell you the truth, Jasper, I'm not exactly sure."

Cribbs chuckled. "You getting bad vibes, son? As we used to say when we were kids?"

"I don't know. Maybe." He massaged the back of his neck, smoothed his hair down. "I'm thinking of adding Chisholm to that list."

"Really. And the reasoning is . . ."

"Dermot says he knows about the drugs."

"And you expect him to cause trouble?" Cribbs laughed loudly. "Him and his gang?" He slapped his thigh and laughed again. "Gang? His gang? Oh, my."

"I expect," Cutler said as he faced the mayor, "I expect him to be royally pissed off is what I expect." He held up a warning finger. "I don't think he's the kind of man who's gonna let this go, Jasper. He's either gonna get himself some damn fancy lawyer, or he's gonna come after us on his own. Either way, I don't want him around to screw things up."

With exaggerated theatrics, Cribbs threw up his hands, sighed, spun his chair around, and folded his hands on the desk. He didn't speak until Cutler came around to the other side, glowering at the show.

"Number one, Norville, he is not going to screw things up. He can't. He sticks his nose in, it gets cut off—at the neck. He stands back, he doesn't get hurt, and he ain't stupid, he damn well knows it.

"Number two, he can raise all the holy hell he wants about the drug thing, but who's going to back him up?

Dermot the Mouse? Like my daughter says in her more perceptive moments, get real. None of his friends are medical folks, they can't testify on what they don't know about. And who's going to take the word of an ex-con anyway? No one, that's who. So who else is there left to give him what he needs, support and evidence and such like? No one, that's who.

"Number three, he comes after us on his own, you'll put Stump back on him, no need to bother Mr. Stone. And make sure that this time the little toad doesn't cut out until the job's done." He sat back, then, and clasped his hands across his belly, considered the ceiling for a few seconds. "Matter of fact, why don't you go ahead and do that very thing? Put a little fear of God in him, make him remember the last time."

Cutler nodded reluctantly. "But what about Oakman? This isn't some simple thrashing we're talking about here, Jasper. Where's he gonna stand on all this?"

Cribbs smiled without mirth, pulled open a side drawer, and pulled out a large, thick manila envelope. "Funny you should mention that, Norville. Seems we're scheduled to have a meeting this very afternoon. Talk about the man's retirement, all the fine service he's given us over the years." He tapped the envelope with his forefinger. "I think it's going to be a fine, successful meeting, I truly do."

Cutler finally smiled. "Jasper, the next time I think you're an idiot, I'll remember this day."

"Good. You do that very thing. Now why don't you get on, talk to whoever you have to talk to. Vale will be trotting in here in a few minutes, and it wouldn't do to have him see you with me so soon before our . . . discussion. The man's got a conscience, Norville. It just needs a little massaging now and then."

Once Cutler was gone, the mayor swiveled around to face the window, watching until the man appeared on the street and headed down toward his office.

"So I'm an idiot, huh?" he whispered.

When the intercom buzzed, he reached back without turning. "What is it, Milli?"

"Mariana's here, Your Honor."

"Send her in, would you? And you might as well take your lunch now, Milli. Then . . . oh, hell, go on home, girl. Won't be nothing going on around here until after the first of the year anyway. Make it half days for the rest of the week."

"Why, thank you, sir, thank you. I'll . . . if you're sure, I'll—"

"Git, Milli," he said with a laugh, and broke the connection.

Shortly afterward his daughter came in, and from the sound of it, she was carrying a ton of shopping bags. "Where," he said as she leaned down to kiss his cheek, "do you find so many things on this island to buy, child?"

"I'm a bargain hunter, Daddy," she said, sitting on the arm of his chair. "Lots of bargains here, you know."

"I'll bet," he said sourly, and she laughed and kissed him again. "So, darlin', what's the story? What do you think?"

"I think Mr. Deputy Freck would walk on water if I asked him."

Cribbs grunted his satisfaction.

Investments paying off left and right, ducks all finally lined up in a row, it made him feel like singing. All he needed now was to get in touch with Mr. Stone, and by the time the sun next rose, why . . . why he just might buy Mary Gwen that pink Caddy she'd been wanting.

3

Casey stood on the sidewalk outside the Camoret Clinic, shading his eyes against the sun with a forearm as he looked up and down the street. The receptionist had been singularly unhelpful, except to say that Dr. Alloway was gone for the day, and no, she had no idea when he would be back.

"Funny way he has of checking up on his patients," he'd said, and took little pleasure in the shock on her face, or the sputtering as she tried to insist that Dr. Alloway had never shortchanged any of his patients.

"So now what?" Reed asked.

"I don't know what else to do," he admitted. "I've still got some of those pills, but . . ." He kicked at a stone. "I'll be damned if I'm going to let it go, though." He draped an arm around the boy's shoulders and led him to the car. "I'll think of something, I guess. I'll let it stew for a while."

"What about the sheriff?" Cora said. "Weren't you supposed to fill out a complaint or something about those men?"

He knew he ought to, just to make good on his threat, but he had a feeling that today wasn't the best time to do it. Not with all the fuss over Jordan's boat. Fill out a form now and it would be conveniently lost among all the other paperwork. He'd give it a day, then see how Sheriff Oakman took care of the people in his trust.

"You know," he said, and interrupted himself with a huge loud yawn.

"Too much," Lisse told him. "Don't care if you are a fast healer, all those days in bed are going to take a while to get over."

"Yeah," he agreed. And yawned again. "Maybe a short nap before supper would be in order."

"What about us?" Cora asked.

Casey, in the middle in the back, looked left at Reed, then right, at her. "I am not your camp counselor, young woman. I'd certainly hope you're old enough to find your own fun for a couple of hours."

She made a face at him, and he puffed his cheeks in feigned insult. But damn, it was good seeing them again.

The summers they had spent together, him being exactly
what he now claimed he wasn't—a counselor, spending
half his days finding things for the Landing's youngsters to
do, because God forbid they should actually use their
imaginations. The rest of the time he spent figuring out
ways to lock them away so they wouldn't give him an
ulcer.

"What are you staring at?" she demanded, her hands
instantly going to her hair. "So it's cut. So it looks like . . .
it looks awful. It'll grow back."

"Wasn't even thinking of it."

"Yeah, he was," Reed said from his other side. "I could
hear it."

Casey's elbow snapped him in the ribs, and he grunted,
bent over, hands on his stomach.

"I don't know, Reverend Chisholm," he managed
between gasps. "I don't think you've changed all that
much."

Oh, my boy, he thought; you have no idea.

They rode in silence the rest of the way, the trees' shadows drawing over them in regular sweeps, a disturbing
strobe effect that had John squinting until Lisse, with a
sigh, pulled down his visor for him.

"See what I mean?" she said to Cora. "Like it says, you
can't live with 'em, and you can't damn shoot 'em."

John grumbled, and made a deliberately sharp turn in
order to park in front of his place. There were protests,
laughter, and Casey, the last one out, was about to ask
someone to wake him up in a couple of hours, when he
saw Lyman Baylor waiting on the porch.

The others hesitated.

"Go ahead," he said quietly. "It's all right. If you feel
like it, why don't you visit the beach for a while. Good
stuff out there if you know where to look. Reed, that's the
trail over there. You can lead."

"I thought you weren't a counselor anymore."

He gave him a look; Reed backed off.

"Okay, okay, but I'm getting a warmer coat."

Casey walked away then, letting them sort it out themselves. Lyman lifted a hand in greeting as Casey came around the hedge, but Casey didn't like the expression on his face.

This, he thought as he forced himself to smile, is not going to be good.

4

The cottage just off Landward Avenue hadn't been occupied for a number of months. It smelled musty, damp, and of the sea, faint echoes of furniture polish and perfume and something Kirkland Stone couldn't quite put his finger on.

Not that it mattered.

He wouldn't be here all that long.

He sat at the kitchen table which had been draped with a lint-free white cloth. His leather gloves had been exchanged for white cotton ones, his suit jacket was off, his sleeves meticulously folded up to the elbows.

Opposite him, Dutch Lauder stared glumly at the pile in the center of the table—springs, grips, barrels, slides, the field-stripped components of two revolvers and two pistols all gathered into a jumble. He had been through this before any number of times, but he still didn't like it. It made him feel as if Stone didn't trust his ability to do what was necessary—either here, or in the field.

"This," he said, pulling on his white gloves, "is an awful lot of stuff for an old black guy with a retard for a kid."

Stone flashed a humorless smile. His long face was severely pocked from cheek to cheek, the edges of each scar smoothed over the years by washing and shaving and a habitual rubbing that often brought people's attention to the condition—which usually led to a chastisement, either from his fists or his guns. His hairline had receded into a prominent widow's peak; there was, somewhat incongruously, a large dimple in his chin.

"Dutch," he said, "that old black guy has a shotgun, and I'm told he's quite good with it. The son is in his late thirties, early forties, and despite his apparent mental disability, I would not discount his ability to assist his father in time of need."

"Yeah, yeah, well, it's still a lot of firepower."

Stone smiled again. "I like the noise."

Lauder shrugged—whatever turns you on.

"Time," Stone said suddenly, and their hands moved to reassemble the weapons.

"So," Stone said conversationally, "what do you think of artificial turf?"

"I think it's a joke. Guys getting hurt more on that than on real grass, the owners don't give a damn, they got insurance, and the fake stuff's easier to keep up."

"Convenience, my friend, is a virtue at times."

"Tell that to the linebacker who keeps spraining his toes, can't get a start on the guy with the ball. Next thing he knows, he's traded because he can't get the job done."

"A fate that comes to us all, Dutch."

"That a threat?"

"I never threaten, you know that. I act."

"Then act this," Lauder said, grinning and pointing a Glock at a point not far from the top of Stone's head. "Win again." Until he looked down and saw a Glock and a Smith & Wesson pointing at his gut.

"Shit." He shook his head in admiration. "Man, you're good."

"Yes, we are, my old friend. Yes, we are." Slowly he took his hands off the weapons and pushed his chair away from the table. As he peeled off his white gloves, he said, "So. Who gets the old man and who gets the son?"

5

Casey stopped at the foot of the porch steps. To go up, to get on the porch would be an implicit invitation he did not want to extend. He did not want to be rude to the young minister, yet neither did he want the man to feel—

"Good afternoon, Father Chisholm."

Casey closed his eyes briefly.

It was out.

"Not 'Father,'" he corrected tonelessly. "You've probably gathered I'm not in the game anymore."

Reverend Baylor gave no indication of either his approval or condemnation. He also seemed to understand what was expected of him, and with a disappointed glance at the door, he left the porch. He did not, however, take all the steps down. He stopped when he was at eye level, and Casey almost smiled.

Not bad, he thought; a position of strength. Or at least equal strength.

"You'll have to admit," the young cleric said, "that you must understand my curiosity."

"Sure."

"But . . ." Baylor smiled ruefully. "But that's all I'm going to get, isn't it."

"No offense, Reverend Baylor, but it's really none of your concern."

"I would argue that, you know. And please, call me Lyman. Or Ly."

Casey did smile then. "Probably. Won't do you any good, though."

Baylor glanced over Casey's shoulder. "It must have been a great tragedy, Maple Landing." His eyes narrowed slightly. "It would be a sore test for any of us."

Casey sniffed, kept the smile. "You live on an island,

Lyman. You should know better than to fish with a harpoon."

Baylor laughed and nodded. "I'm still working on that particular skill."

Casey shifted so that he stood sideways to the man, facing down the road. "From what I've seen, you do very well. They like you here. A lot."

"I hope so."

"Fishing again?"

"No. A little daily prayer."

Casey glanced at him, looked away, tucked a hand into his hip pocket, and cocked a hip to shift his weight. "I'm about to take a nap, Lyman. I've been moving all day, and I'm still not a hundred percent."

"Forgive me." But Baylor didn't move out of the way. "And forgive me again . . . Casey? . . . but I can't just leave without knowing *something*. I've been trying, you know. Ever since I found out, and since your . . . your injuries, I've been trying to understand why someone like you would deliberately turn his back on—"

"Stop," Casey ordered harshly. "Before you say anything we'll both regret, Lyman, please stop." A slow deep breath, a measured exhalation. "All I will tell you, all you're really entitled to know and I'm not so sure about that, is that I have not turned my back. Not on what you think, at least." He turned his head slowly. "There are things, Lyman, you—"

"Actually, I think I do know," Baylor answered, slipping a hand into a pocket, his gaze not leaving Casey's face. "How could I be what I am and not at least suspect? I'm not sure it's true, but I'm not entirely blind." A hint of a smile. "I do have to live in this world as well, Casey. I turn on the TV once in a while. I read the newspapers."

Casey wanted to laugh, knew he would sound too bitter. "At the service," he said, being careful with his words. "At Thanksgiving, I didn't notice you sounding like Paul Revere."

"There are plenty of those folks out there already. No one's listening, or not many anyway, but they're out there. I . . . think it's too late for him anyway. The British have already landed, am I right?"

Casey said nothing.

"If . . . Casey, look, I have my work. You more than anyone know what that means. I have, not to be too mawkish or old-fashioned about it, a duty, an obligation to protect my flock from the . . . from whatever's coming. If I can protect them, that is. Somehow." He paused. "Can I?"

Casey kept silent.

Lyman came off the steps, slowly, head down in defeat. "If I could just know—"

"You can't know," Casey said, almost snarling.

"Of course, I can't know," Lyman retorted loudly, showing temper for the first time. "How can I know? I've been here, not up there in Maple Landing. I've been fighting battles here against men whose pockets are being lined with money and the lives of some very good people. I haven't seen what you've seen, and I can't imagine what you've been through."

"No," Casey agreed, "you can't."

"But I've heard the horses, Casey."

Casey watched as the minister stopped in front of him, eyes narrow with anguish and a shadow of fear. "Kitra has, too. There are others." He studied Casey's face. "Who are you, Casey? Why are you here?"

Impassive, Casey returned the man's gaze until Lyman took a step back, another signal of defeat, and started for the road. At the hedge he paused.

"Tell you something, Casey," he said. "You've had a lot more experience at this pastor thing than I have, I guess. But I think I know something you don't."

"Good afternoon, Reverend Baylor." He took the first step up to the porch. "I'm late for my nap."

"You can stop going to church, and you can put away the clothes, the collar, maybe you can even stop praying."

He reached the porch, reached for the doorknob to let himself in the house.

Lyman spoke louder: "But you can never stop being what you are, Reverend Chisholm. God help you, this is one job from which you can never retire."

Casey stood in the hall and stared into the storeroom, one hand in a tight fist at his side.

As he watched, the closet door opened.

Just a little.

But it opened.

Bed, he ordered silently; forget it, go to bed.

He did, but it took a long time before his eyes stayed closed.

And when they did, he saw a darkness that had nothing to do with the sleeping, a woman not much older than he with hair in easy waves and angel-wing bangs and eyes that looked right at him and knew him and fluttered closed, a spiral of lights spinning on a crimson axis, a church that stood among winking steaming embers, a brown hillside, a brown sky, the darkness again more like the dark in a vast lightless room than the dark where sleep usually held him and rocked him and took him away.

In his sleep he rolled onto his back.

In his sleep the closet door opened wider.

6

Senior stood in his kitchen and looked around, shaking his head with a smile. His son, home from work early, had decided he would make his daddy a late supper, something Senior usually threw together himself. The mess that surrounded him was testament to the effort, a monument to the meal that was never made, because Junior got too frustrated, had a tantrum, and threw things.

Mostly, it was flour.

From the doorway: "It was supposed to be a cake."

Senior laughed. "Hell of a cake now."

Junior took the cue and laughed himself, went to the closet next to the basement stairs and took out a broom. "I can clean now, okay?"

"You know, boy, I think this gonna take both of us all night."

"I'm not tired."

"Well, I am. Lots of folks drinking tonight, they kept me on my toes." With a foot he shoved aside an empty egg carton; at least the eggs were in a bowl, as yet unbroken. "Maybe we just tend to the floor, leave the rest till the morning."

Junior nodded agreeably. "Am I in trouble?"

"A little, I think."

His son's lips pursed in a rebellious pout. "Not my fault."

Senior laughed again. "Then who did this, boy? Some ghost?"

"I did," Junior answered. "It's not my fault you were late. If you came home on time, I wouldn't be in trouble."

"Slower, boy," Senior said as a cloud of flour billowed ahead of the broom. "Don't rush it, nudge it."

He watched his son work the broom more carefully, nodded, and ordered his aching back to wait for a while, until he had picked up the silverware scattered across the floor, a handful of cartons, some napkins he thought he had tossed out months ago. He rolled his eyes at an empty cereal carton, grunted as he held onto the table and reached under for the small tray he used to hold the salt and pepper shakers.

When he straightened, massaging his side with one hand, he glanced at the wall clock and groaned aloud.

"Daddy, you okay?"

"Fine, Junior, keep working. Just later than I figured."

Almost midnight. Probably some after, the way that old clock ran. This was one of those times when he was glad he didn't have a job that required him to get up bright and early. He was already dog-tired; by the time this mess was gone, he'd be ready for an early grave.

From the living room he heard music, a radio station he picked up once in a while that played real music, not that hip-hop rock 'n' rock, talking-without-singing crap supposed to pass for black music. This was real music. The Duke. The Count. Bessie and Billie. Billie singing now, and it amused him to notice Junior sweeping in time with the song.

He almost didn't hear the knock on the door.

Reed stood shivering on the porch. "He's gonna be ticked."

Cora peered through the living room window. "I don't see him."

"He was only supposed to sleep for a couple of hours."

"I heard you the first time, an hour ago, Reed." She opened the door, stepped quietly in. "Don't sweat it, okay?"

Reed nodded, but he didn't look very convinced.

John sat in the living room, television on, sound low, only a single lamp burning on the end table beside him. He heard Lisse before he saw her.

"Couldn't sleep," he said as she wandered sleepily into the room.

She squinted at the screen. "So you'd rather watch people blowing each other up than lie in bed with me?"

He would have said no, but she would have asked if he didn't then care about what was happening in the world, and he would have had to look a long way up from the bottom of the ditch he hadn't known he was digging.

"Sorry." He pointed. "Seems some hotheads launched a couple of missiles into India."

"Oh, God."

"No response yet."

"Thank God."

"Yeah. Maybe."

Senior moved to the kitchen door, frowning, trying to listen over Billie's lament, another bad man snaking into her life. Maybe he was mistaken. Might have been the wind, except, he thought, there was no wind. Least none that mattered.

The radio switched Billie off, put Marty Robbins on, and Senior glared at it, shook his head in disgust. Singing about Texas when poor Billie's got the blues. Some kind of sacrilege, that's what it was; some kind of goddamn cowboy sacrilege.

"Almost done, Daddy."

"That's good, boy. That's good."

This time he heard it, and he checked the clock again.

Vale Oakman lay on his bed. Fully dressed in his uniform, gunbelt draped over the footboard. His hands were cupped behind his head, his legs crossed at the ankles. He stared at the ceiling, waiting for the call, wondering if this was the time not to answer.

Although the lamp was off, a bright December moon gave him enough light to see the fat manila envelope sitting on the dresser, right next to the mother-of-pearl-backed brush set that used to be his granddaddy's, a lawman himself over in Missouri. He hadn't counted the money inside. He didn't want to touch it.

A cramp in the arch of his left foot.

He let it run its course, bearing the pain.

That was the least he could do, considering what he might have to do later.

When the overhead light in the kitchen blared on, Cora slapped a hand to her chest and yelled, "Jesus!"

Reed fell back against the door. He couldn't yell; he had no breath left in his lungs.

"Two hours," Casey's voice boomed out of the kitchen. "You were supposed to wake me in two hours." He stood in the doorway then, a dark figure with hands on his hips. "Can't I trust you kids to do anything right?"

Cora had any number of answers—none of them polite—ready to give him, but she had never seen him in a T-shirt before, and she couldn't help noticing, even without his usual loose shirt or windbreaker, how big he was.

"You hungry?"

Reed tried to say yes, but it came out as a bleat.

Casey laughed. "You know, you two never change, do you?"

"What's that supposed to mean?" Cora asked when she finally found her voice.

"Oh, just get in here," he said. "I'm making a sandwich. You're welcome to join me if you don't have anything better to do."

Mayor Jasper Cribbs rolled slowly off his wife, who smiled at him and said, "You are always the best, dear. Always the best."

He passed a hand over her breast, propped himself up on one elbow, and kissed her. Hard.

Her eyes closed, and she moaned.

His eyes shifted so he could see the green numerals of the bedstand clock.

Good, he thought; call coming soon.

Senior, after making sure his son was still working, walked slowly toward the door. As he passed the wall rack in the short hallway, he reached up and took down the Remington, checked to be sure there was a chambered shell, and let it hang loosely at his side.

No one calls this late at night without something going on.

No one on this island calls on a black man this late at night without something bad going on.

Standing beside the door, shoulder to the wall, he wished for the hundredth time he'd taken a few minutes to put in one of them peephole things, or a little window.

"Who is it?" he called.

"Need to use your phone, sir, if that's all right."

"Too late."

"Sir, I have an awfully sick man in the car. I don't know where I am, I don't know how to get a doctor. Just want to call nine-one-one."

Senior didn't believe it for a minute. The street runs north and south; all the fool has to do is turn around, he'll run into someone soon enough.

Someone with neighbors.

"Ain't letting no one in this late. Go away."

"Sir, I think perhaps he's dying."

Senior moved away from the door, brought the shotgun up to his hip. "Go away."

"Daddy?"

"Junior," he snapped, "you finished yet? You finish, I'll take care of this." He raised his voice. "Go away."

His hands shook; his vision fogged over for a second; his stomach tightened.

He knew what it was—they were finally coming to get him. Wouldn't sell, couldn't drive him off with those sorry-ass Teagues, so they coming themselves, the sons of bitches; they coming themselves.

He bared his teeth.

Too bad they didn't listen last time they came.

"Cutler, that you? You trying—"

It happened too fast:

What sounded like an explosion at the front door, the door slamming inward, splitting in half, showering the hall and the old man with splinters from the frame and the door itself; a handheld steel battering ram dropping to the threshold as a man in a topcoat and derby stepped calming into the opening, a gun in each hand.

What sounded like an explosion at the back door, the door slamming inward, its window pane shattering, a man in a football jacket and baseball cap standing in the opening, a gun in each hand.

When the firing began, Junior shrieked and ran for the cellar, throwing the broom at the intruder, left hand waving wildly at his shoulder.

When the firing began, Senior Raybourn yelled for a divine army to stand at his back, and spun into the kitchen, pulling the trigger.

When the firing began, it was just after midnight.

7

As soon as Casey heard the shots, he knew what they were. He yelled for the kids to go for the cops, grabbed his coat from the chair, and ran out. Hesitated only a second to get his bearings, until he saw pops of light off to his left and leaped off the stoop, landed running at full speed. Plowed through the hedge in back, thinking it a miracle this side didn't have the thorns, and angled left toward Raybourn's house.

No shooting now, and in the moonlight he spotted a man trotting alongside the house from the back, heading for a car parked at the curb, headlamps on. A second man walked calmly down the porch steps through drifting, horizontal layers of smoke.

Suddenly the first man stopped and said something to his partner, and they both turned toward him.

He froze, crouched, not sure they had seen him until the shorter man raised his weapons and began firing into the night. Casey instantly flattened himself on the ground, cursing his size and the moon because the combination pure and simple painted a target on his heart.

The gunshots were deafening, grass erupted not five feet from where he lay, the eruptions moving closer, and he looked frantically, desperately for something to hide behind, it didn't matter how large as long as it gave him cover.

Nothing; there was nothing, not even a decent tree.

Dirt, grass, and pebbles stung his cheek and scalp as he tried to wriggle backward, his only hope the hedge because Mrs. Essman's empty house was too far away. That he was going to die only entered his mind when he heard one of the gunmen laugh, a mocking, sporting laugh echoed by another round of gunfire that gouged the lawn not a foot from his left shoulder.

Time to pray, Case, he thought; time to pray.

But he hadn't even begun, when the gunfire abruptly intensified. Against all reason he raised his head, and saw the two men backing away at speed toward the parked car. A moment before he realized some of the shooting was at his back. He dared a look behind, and saw two figures kneeling by the hedge, and in the flare of one muzzle-flash he thought he saw John Bannock's face.

The first gunman, his weapons out of sight, slid quickly behind the wheel; the second opened the back door, looked over the roof toward Casey, then took off what looked like a derby, and climbed in. By the time Casey was on his feet, the car was already on the move.

Taking its time; slipping out of the moonlight.

Oh, Lord, he thought, swallowing hard, desperate for a breath; oh, Lord.

"Casey, you all right?"

It was John, and Casey grinned even though he knew the man couldn't see him clearly. A grateful wave, and he was off again, running as fast as his shaky legs would take him.

He took the Raybourn porch at a leap, calling Senior's

name, stepping over a thick battering ram and barging through the wreck of the front door without thinking. Swinging up his hands when Senior, sitting against the hallway wall, brought a shotgun to bear on his chest.

"It's me, Chisholm," he said loudly. "Raybourn, it's me, Casey Chisholm. You all right?"

Holes and gouges and smoke and stench everywhere.

From the living room, a radio playing "El Paso."

From somewhere deeper in the house, the sound of glass falling and breaking.

He swept the shotgun's barrel aside easily as he knelt beside the old man, searching him for signs of injury, inhaling sharply when he saw blood on the man's arm, his shoulders, his temple, his shirt covered with it.

Senior had a difficult time holding his head up. "Preacher? You the preacher?"

"Chisholm," Casey answered. "Hang on, I'll get some—" He stopped, looked around. "Where's your son, Mr. Raybourn. Where's Junior?"

Senior jerked violently at his boy's name, tried to stand, but Casey pushed him back down. "Stay here. I'll find him."

"Find him, Preacher," Senior begged. He brushed a hand over his chest, and moaned at all the blood gleaming on his palm. "Get him, Preacher, find my boy."

Casey stepped over the debris into the kitchen, batted away smoke and dust. The back door had been busted in, glass all over, and white powder drifting in the air, rising and falling lazily as the night wind slipped in. A moment later he realized it was, of all things, flour.

"Find him, Preacher, find him."

He didn't see the younger Raybourn until he looked hard to his right. Junior lay facedown in front of an open door with stairs on the other side. Blood seeped through his shirt, mixed briefly into pink by the flour that settled there.

"Preacher, you find him?"

Casey dropped to his knees, rocking, feeling a chill in his stomach turn swiftly to cold. He leaned closer, not wanting to move the man, not wanting to take the chance of hurting him further.

"Preacher."

Excited voices outside, and a high distant siren. A quick prayer of thanks to the kids for whatever they'd done, and he laid a hand on the side of Junior's neck, pressing lightly, searching for a pulse.

"Preacher?"

Son of a bitch, he thought, and glared helplessly around the room, rocking faster, left hand in a fist thumping his leg; son of a bitch, son of a bitch.

Sooner, and he might have helped.

Sooner, something answered, and you'd be dead too. They weren't just shooting at you to scare you away.

He tried again to find the pulse, while the cold in his stomach deepened, and he began to tremble at it, tightened his jaw so his teeth wouldn't chatter.

"Preacher."

Aw, Junior, damnit, he thought as he bit down on his lower lip and slid a hand under the man's chest. No dampness there; the bullets hadn't gone through.

A wail: "Oh my God!"

Voices in the hall, and for a moment there was confusion, until he whipped his head around and demanded someone, he didn't care who, take the old man out, put him in the living room and do something about his wounds until the ambulance arrived.

He heard Lisse gasp.

He saw again the two men leaving the house. Not hurrying. Casual visitors on their way home.

He heard Senior protesting but unable to stop them from taking him away. "Preacher," he called, and then he sobbed loudly.

Casey looked at his hands as the cold strengthened and made his spine rigid, his neck muscles bulge. He flexed his fingers. He thought: I don't dare, this isn't right, I don't dare. Flexed his fingers again.

The siren grew louder, more than one now.

He braced himself, fighting the cold, fighting the memories, fighting the helpless anger; braced himself until he couldn't restrain it any longer, couldn't hold back the cold that began to turn to fierce heat that broke sweat across his face, that made his throat and eyes dry.

He sagged abruptly, bowed his head and shook it, then placed a palm over Junior Raybourn's back, spreading his fingers as if to cover all the holes. The voices he heard became unintelligible, a buzzing, nothing more; the man below him became a figure in a thick grey-black fog. His lips moved in a prayer he hadn't uttered for years, but he hadn't forgotten the words, and he whispered them again.

Someone knelt beside him.

He didn't look; he pressed harder.

A hand on his shoulder; he didn't look; he pressed harder, prayed again.

A woman's voice, through the buzzing: "I think he's dead."

And he said, "No."

Not rocking anymore; still now, moving his fingers without moving the palm.

Sirens, and more voices, commands and demands, protests and more demands.

"Please," the woman said.

Another voice: "You'll have to move away, sir, we'll take care of him now."

His lips moved, his fingers moved.

"Sir?"

The woman said, "Please."

A strong hand tried to tug him away, but he shrugged it off easily and said, "Wait. Wait a second."

"Come on, sir, you can't do anything, you're not a doctor, right? Come on, sir, please move."

The woman said, "Please."

A shudder that made Casey snatch his hand away, and Junior Raybourn moaned, shuddered again, kicked a leg that hit a wall, and was still.

"That's it, get the hell out of the way before you do any more damage."

"Please," the woman said, and he allowed her to pull at him gently, back to his heels, up to his feet. Immediately, the paramedics roughly shoved him farther away and swarmed around Junior, snapping soft orders to each other as they assembled their equipment.

The cold was gone; the heat was gone.

Numbed and bone-tired, he stumbled to the back door and through it, to the stoop. Took in huge gulps of the night's air. Put the heel of one hand to his forehead and moved it around in circles. For one terrifying moment he thought he was going to throw up; for one terrifying moment he thought he was going to pass out.

"Are you all right?"

It was the woman.

He nodded. "Yes. Yeah, I think so." He looked over as he said, "I guess I should thank—" And he stopped.

She stood under the shattered porchlight, her hair in easy waves and angel-wing bangs. She was, at that moment, the most beautiful thing he had ever seen.

"Casey Chisholm," he said weakly.

She smiled. "Yes. I know. I'm Beatrice Harp, and I think I've been searching this whole bloody country for you."

4

1

The night was endless:

Casey sat in the living room, jacket draped over his shoulders. Chills regularly walked his spine, and his head felt as if someone had jammed it full of damp cotton.

Freck had been the first to arrive, came into the house with gun drawn, followed immediately by the ambulance crew. Now the ambulance was long gone. As soon as the paramedics had uncovered the extent of the victims' injuries, they had radioed for a medevac, then took the Raybourns to the beach to meet the helicopter that would take them to Savannah. Casey heard one of them doubt that Senior would last the night, and Junior's chances weren't much better.

"Let me get this straight," Sheriff Oakman said, notepad in hand, pure skepticism in his tone. "You saw two men come out of Raybourn's house. They spotted you, they fired at you, they didn't hit you, and they ran away."

"Close enough."

From the doorway, Freck folded his arms and snorted outright disbelief.

The sheriff ignored him. "Four guns by your count, and they didn't hit you."

"It was dark. Mostly dark, there was some moonlight. I dropped to the ground and"—he gestured wearily at John and Lisse—"they fired back. The two men ran, got in their car and drove off."

"You had no weapon of your own."

"No."

"You heard shots and you ran over here with no weapon of your own."

"No. I mean, right. And anyway, I'm an ex-con, as you keep reminding me. Where would I get a gun?"

"Ex-cons have ways," Freck said, slipping a toothpick between his lips.

"I didn't have one."

Oakman said, "So unarmed, you ran straight into a gun battle."

"By the time I reached the yard, it was over."

"Until they started shooting at you."

"Yes."

"You didn't know them."

"Nope."

"Never saw them before in your life."

"No, I haven't."

"So what you're saying is, two men, who were probably professionals by the sound of it, came fully armed to the house of an old man and his retarded son, shot them and the place up, you were on the scene in seconds, and you have no idea what was going down here."

"Pretty much, yes."

"Don't go away, I'll be back."

*   *   *

Sometime during the interminable interrogations, the murmur of deputies photographing the rooms and taking measurements, Casey looked up and saw Reed and Cora on the porch. He walked over to the open living room window and said, "Thanks, guys. That was quick."

"For what?" Reed said.

"For getting the sheriff."

"We never called anyone."

"What?"

Reed looked to Cora. "John was already out of his house, we didn't have the car keys." He shrugged. "Someone else must have done it when they heard all the shooting."

He turned to Beatrice and said, "Who are you?"

"Later," she said, smoothing the jacket over his shoulders. "I think you're a little busy right now."

Lisse knelt in front of him, lowered her head, lowered her voice. "I thought he was going to shoot you," she said, a quick glance indicating Freck.

"I didn't see him."

"Casey, I saw him go in the house, and if those men hadn't been here, I swear he would have killed you."

John, already questioned by Oakman but told to stick around, hunkered down in front of him, put a hand on his knee. "You okay?"

"I don't know. I think so. And what the hell are you doing with guns?"

"We've been on the road a long time, Casey. You don't travel like that, through places we've been, without protection, believe me."

"Well . . . thanks."

"My pleasure."

"This'll sound awful, but I wish you'd gotten one. For the sheriff, anyway."

John grinned. "I carry the gun, Case. That doesn't mean I can use it."

Oakman flipped his notepad open again. "They said you obstructed the medics' attempts to revive Junior."

"I was trying to help."

"They said you weren't doing anything."

"I was . . . I was praying."

Freck shifted the toothpick from one corner of his mouth to the other. "Oh, that's right. They say you're a preacher. What were you trying to do, do one of them TV evangelist things? Bring him back from the dead or something?"

"I was praying," he repeated flatly.

"Man, can you beat it?" Freck laughed snidely. "Ex-con and preacher, a hell of a combination. What did you do in prison, Chisholm, pray for their souls while they lined up in the shower and bent you over and—"

Casey half rose, and the deputy's hand went immediately to his gun. Beatrice grabbed his arm; the sheriff didn't move.

"You got here awfully fast," Casey said to Oakman.

"We pride ourselves on quick responses around here," the sheriff told him. "Now let's go over this again."

"I've already told you four or five times."

"Then tell me a sixth. Make me happy, Chisholm. Tell me again how you managed not to get shot when two guys, who were professionals, were firing four guns right at you."

* * *

"You got a license for those weapons?" Freck asked Bannock.

John nodded.

"Let's see it."

John opened his wallet and pulled out two pieces of tightly folded paper, handed them over, and watched as Freck took them to the nearest lamp and studied them carefully.

"These are Illinois. I don't think they're good in Georgia."

"Trust me, Deputy, they're good anywhere."

"You're a friend of his," Freck answered disdainfully. "I don't trust you at all."

"He thinks I'm involved," Casey said in stunned disbelief.

"Yes, it does sound like that, doesn't it," Beatrice answered.

"I'm not."

"I know."

"Who are you?"

The sheriff flipped his notepad shut and tucked it into his breast pocket. "Go home, Chisholm. Stay there. Have your friend bring you to the office first thing in the morning. I want your statement, a description of the men and the car, and a damn good reason why I shouldn't hold you."

Casey nodded, looked up. "You know, you guys came so fast, I'm surprised you didn't see that car yourself."

Oakman adjusted his hat. "Lots of side streets between here and there. Get up, get out of here, we have work to do."

A pause before Casey rose. The jacket slipped off his shoulders and he caught it in one hand before it hit the floor. He looked around at what was left of Senior's house and, as he passed Oakman, he leaned over and said quietly,

"I hope this was worth it, Sheriff. I really hope this was worth it."

Oakman said nothing, but Casey saw the look in his eyes, the abrupt intake of air.

He brushed by Freck, whose hand went instinctively for his weapon again.

Casey stopped. Stared out the front door. Didn't turn his head when he said, "That's three times, Deputy. How many chances did they give you before they get someone else to do it right?"

He did look then. Not a smile. Not a blink.

Freck, sneer still in place, tried to stare him down, couldn't and looked away.

Once outside, Beatrice said, "It seems, Reverend Chisholm, you can be a very scary person."

His smile was brief. "So I'm told, Miz Harp. So I'm told." Then he looked down at her and said, "Who are you?"

2

Stone sat at the kitchen table, his shirt off, a bandage wrapped tightly around his upper left arm. "What do you think, Mr. Lauder?"

Lauder, rinsing blood off his hands at the sink, shrugged. "I think we got 'em. Not the other guy, though."

"That's what I'm thinking." He rubbed absently below the bandage. "I'm also thinking I am not happy. Messy. It was very messy."

"Not our best," Lauder agreed.

"Far from it."

"We didn't count on the effing cavalry."

"No one does, Dutch. No one does."

Lauder turned off the water, dried his hands on a small towel.

Stone lit a cigarette, blew smoke at the ceiling. "I don't like loose ends."

"Me neither."

"Storm coming, you know."

"I heard. One of those winter jobs."

"Yes. So, I'm thinking then that perhaps we ought not to leave as planned."

Lauder smiled, stroked his mustache.

"I'm wondering if our employers would mind if we took care of those loose ends."

"Screw 'em," Lauder said.

Stone smiled. "Thank you, Dutch. My thoughts exactly."

3

Mayor Cribbs stared at the ceiling, trying to keep his mind from running off the rails. Beside him, Mary Gwen slept contentedly, snoring lightly, her right hand lying on his thigh. He wanted to go down to the small office he kept in the house, but if he did, she'd wake up, and Lord, that woman was insatiable. Better he remain where he was, figure things out, deal with them in the morning.

The Raybourns were as good as dead; Chisholm was still alive.

Cutler's call had been quick and furious, and with Mary Gwen lying right there, Cribbs had no opportunity to calm him down, get him to see the good sides.

And that was his problem as he stared at the ceiling—trying to find the good sides.

Of which, he suddenly decided, there were quite a few.

He smiled.

After all, they still had until Friday, and it was only some godawful hour Tuesday morning. A lot could happen in four days. Long as everyone kept cool, a whole lot could happen.

4

Casey paused at the foot of the stairs.

There were people in the front room who had saved his life tonight, people in the front room he had never seen before. For nearly an hour after they'd returned, there had been excited chatter amid cautious introductions, but when the inevitable lull arrived, he could think of nothing he wanted better than to sleep, wake up, and find himself alone and life returned to what he had redefined as normal.

He wondered who the woman with the British accent was, the woman who wore the veil, the two children; he couldn't stop thinking about tonight, all the blood and the smell of gunpowder and Senior begging him to help his son and Freck and the sheriff and . . . Junior.

"In the morning," he said, and climbed the stairs, went straight to his room, and fell onto the bed. A few minutes later, without sitting up, he undressed, grunting, swearing, finally pulling the covers up to his chest.

Staring at the ceiling.

Blinking once, and it was daylight, and Lisse was in the doorway. "Time to go."

If he slept, he didn't feel like it; if his brain was in reasonable working order, it didn't feel like it.

It was difficult to concentrate on the task at hand, a chore to move, and impossible to sort through all the images and voices that clamored for attention in his mind, every one of them demanding a decision of some kind, but he didn't know what it was and didn't want to know.

What he knew was, he ate something that might have been a quick breakfast, allowed Bannock and Lisse to take him to the sheriff's department, where he was questioned again in the presence of a uniformed woman who took his statement down, typed it up, and waited for him to sign it.

There were no further accusations of complicity, or, if there were, he didn't catch them; evidently the gunmen had not yet been found and were assumed to have left the island.

What he knew was, Billy Freck was nowhere around, and Vale Oakman refused to look him in the eye.

What he knew was, Whittaker Hull tried to interview him on the street, and he had been curt, almost rude, giving gruff one-word answers that left the editor frustrated and disappointed, unable to think of ways to change Casey's mind.

What he knew was, something had changed.

5

When he returned home and climbed stiffly out of the car, he saw two girls on the porch. They watched him for a moment, then ran inside. He put a hand to his eyes as if shading them. He propped his forearms on the roof of the car, hands clasped, and told John and Lisse to go ahead, he'd only be a minute. When they were gone, he studied the simple house and saw nothing special there, checked the sky and saw nothing of the storm that was on its way; he spread his hands on the roof and felt the cool metal, lowered his shoulders and felt the cool breeze tuck in under his collar; he stared blindly at the thorned hedge and with an effort shunted aside all the voices and the questions.

A pale face in the window, made more so through the porch screen.

When it vanished, he leaned back, let his arms fall to his side, let his legs carry him up the walk to the front door.

Easy, isn't it, Chisholm, he thought as he went in; once you figure it out, everything else is easy.

What he had figured out was what had changed, but there was nothing easy about it at all.

* * *

He paused at the foot of the stairs and said, "I have to do something. Come or not, I don't care," before taking the steps two at a time and hurrying into the bedroom. He didn't permit himself to think—he took a sweater from the dresser and pulled it on, returned downstairs to grab an old denim jacket from the hall closet.

And left without saying a word.

Halfway to the beach he heard them following, not voices but footsteps crushing dead leaves, scuffling sand, kicking pebbles. He didn't look back; it wouldn't have mattered if he had. He kept his gaze straight ahead, kept his mind as blank as he possibly could, and when he left the trees behind, he headed straight for the jetty.

A cold wind slapped his face, forced him to tighten his jaw to keep his teeth from chattering. With arms out for balance, he climbed awkwardly over the rocks, slipping only a few times, going down once on his knees and hissing at the pain. By the time he reached the end, one hundred yards from the beach, the jacket was speckled damp, droplets of seawater shone in his hair.

He pulled his collar up, and stood on the last boulder, legs apart, braced against the thunder that trembled beneath him.

"All right," he whispered. "All right."

no sign, case

Rhythmic explosions from twenty feet below as the cold December sea tore itself apart against the uneven boulders. His hands burrowed into his pockets, only once in a long while slipping away to clear the cold spray that dripped from his face. With no hat for protection his hair ducked and twisted in the wind.

no sign, case; there won't be a sign and you know it

He faced the horizon and looked at the water and saw nothing but waves rolling steadily toward him. Rising as if taking his measure, falling as if needing less distance before they could rise again, and crest, and drive him at last into the slick and jagged brown-black stone.

No clouds.

Distant sun.

No gulls on the currents, scolding him, warning.

He stood for an hour, waiting.

He stood for two hours, waiting.

Only the sea, and the sky, and the thunder of the waves, the explosions, the mist, and the ragged hasp of his own breathing.

Finally there was a long deep breath, a long and slow and shuddering exhalation while his eyes closed and his shoulders slumped and his lips moved in a silent prayer he feared wouldn't be answered.

no sign, case; no sign.

it's just you, and now you know it

He raised his head slowly to face the horizon again, and for a brief moment, a flicker of an eyelid, the waves rolled instead of crested, the thunder died, and he was alone despite the people who were on the beach behind him.

"All right," he said aloud, and nodded. And sighed. "All right."

A brush of his hands over his jacket, and he made his way back to the beach. The others had already left, he could hear them ahead on the path, whispers now and muted speculation. He reached for a pine branch and missed it, reached for another and closed his fingers around it, pulling the needles off, scattering them on the ground.

Midway was empty when he reached it.

The cold wind had softened, blocked by the woodland, warmed by the sun.

He shrugged off his jacket as he entered the house, dropped it over the newel post before walking into the living room. He stood in front of the window, hands behind his back. Lisse, John, and the British woman were on the couch; the woman with the veil sat in the armchair, the two girls flanking her. Cora sat on the floor at John's feet. Reed looked around, hurried into the kitchen, and brought back a towel, and a chair which he set in front of Casey.

"You're scaring the kids," he whispered. "It'd be better if you sat, you know?"

Casey stared at him, finally understood, and nodded. Once he was seated, passing the towel over his hair and face, and Reed was on the floor beside Cora, he looked at Beatrice Harp and said, gently, "Tell me."

And she did, saying, "His name was Trey Falkirk, and unlike you, he didn't make it."

When the telling was over, he leaned forward, resting his arms on his legs, hands loosely clasped between his knees. He stared at the floor for a while, glanced up only when Cora got to her feet and left the room, trying to be as quiet as she could. Then he turned his attention to Jude Levin and her daughters.

He kept his voice soft, but the girls flinched anyway: "I'll bet you've asked yourself more times than you can count why this has had to happen to you."

Those big dark eyes over the veil filled instantly with tears as Jude nodded.

"John's asked himself the same thing, I know," he told her. "So have I." He looked at the floor again. "I wish I could—"

"Wait."

It was Cora.

She stood under the entrance arch, hands behind her back. He frowned puzzlement—she seemed unaccountably nervous, didn't settle down even when Reed scrambled over to join her. He, however, had a smile on his face.

He would have scolded them for interrupting, but he knew they had something important to say, and it was equally clear they'd been rehearsing it while he'd been gone.

So he gave them a one-sided smile and said, "Cora, I have never, ever known you to be without words." A mock glare. "This had better be good."

Cora brought her hands around to the front.

He sat up sharply, lips working but no sound.

In her hands were a pair of black western boots, as clean and polished as the day he'd first brought them home, over fifteen years ago.

She swallowed. "Reverend Chisholm . . ." She swallowed again. "Reverend Chisholm, if you're . . . oh, hell . . . if—"

"I'll say it," Reed told her softly.

"No!" An apologetic smile. "No." She licked her lips and swallowed again. "If you're going to . . . to tell us things we don't want to hear . . . if we're . . ."

He saw the tears and rose slowly to his full height, from the corner of his vision seeing the girls edge closer to their mother, seeing Lisse fumble for and take John's hand and squeeze it tightly. He stepped over to Cora and took the boots from her, inhaled the scent of fresh polish and old leather, and smiled wondering if it was possible he could love two people more than these two, right now.

"It's got to be right," she said in a small voice, not Cora's voice at all. "You know what I mean. It's got to be right."

He saw the two Coras in her face then, the ones he used to know—the one who was raised on abuse and disdain, cowering a little, terrified of being wrong . . . and the one who tried not to give a damn about anything, especially herself.

He laid a finger on her cheek, brushed away a tear, put a hand on Reed's shoulder, and squeezed it, once.

It was difficult to say the words they wanted to hear, more difficult because he never believed he'd ever hear himself say them again: "You two are right. I think . . . I think I'd better go upstairs and change."

Cora put a hand to her mouth and said, "Oh . . ." and couldn't say any more.

He smiled gently and winked at them, pushed between them, and said, "Cora, while I'm gone, why don't you have a talk with Starshine there. Maybe you two can exchange the names of the butchers who attacked your hair."

He didn't look back as he climbed the stairs, but he heard Cora laughing, and Lisse sighing, and the girl named Starshine demanding to know what he was talking about, what's the matter with her hair?

At the top of the stairs he turned automatically toward the bedroom, took a step, and stopped.

Do it right, he told himself; if you're going to do it, you pig-headed oaf, then you'd damn well better do it right.

6

Cribbs paced his office, alternating between fear and righteous anger. "What the hell do you mean, they aren't gone yet?" he yelled at the speakerphone on his desk.

"I mean, they ain't left yet," Cutler said, his voice sounding well-hollow.

"You talk to them?"

"No, I ain't talked to them. How can I talk to them? You want me to drive right over, let half the world know I know where they are and who they are?"

Cribbs waved his arms. "Goddamnit, Norville, you're the damn owner of that place. All you want to do is see who's squatting there, you idiot."

"Idiot? Me? Who's the one come up with these jokers in the first place?"

Cribbs took in a breath, puffed his cheeks, and let the air out slowly. He took a position at the window and looked down at Midway, the cars and the people. On the horizon he could see smears of clouds as that storm made its way closer.

"All right," he said. "All right, Norville, no sense us going at each other's throats here. The thing we need to know is, why haven't they left?"

"You ask them. I'm not going anywhere near them."

The mayor shook his head. "We got to know, Norville. Even I can't stop Oakman from doing something dumb if he knows they're still around." He slammed a fist onto the desk. "Damn! Good Lord, why the hell can't anything go like we want it to? Why the hell does this have to happen now, of all times."

"You want me to answer that, Jasper?"

"Oh, shut up, Norville, that was a rhetorical question." He shook his head again. "Tell you the truth, in a perfect world, I'd sic those bastards on Freck, the son of a bitch can't even shoot a man in the back, for God's sake."

"Freck's an idiot."

"Now that I can agree on. And I own up, it's my fault, I thought I could count on him. I—" He stopped, looked at the street again, and grinned. "Norville, you thinking what I'm thinking?"

"It'll cost us extra."

"Who cares? What's another million here or there, what with what we've already got?"

"So who's gonna talk to them. Not me. I've already talked to them once, on the phone, and I heard what they done. I ain't going anywhere near them, and that's something else you can take to the bank."

"Don't worry," Cribbs said. "I got an idea, kill a couple of birds with a couple stones. Talk to you later."

He broke the connection and couldn't stop smiling, couldn't stop chuckling.

Jesus, Jasper, he thought; why the hell aren't you ruling the world yet?

Ronnie Hull stood at the counter in the *Camoret Weekly*'s office and swore as she punched a number into her cell phone. It would be the fifth attempt, and she hoped this time she'd gotten it right. The buttons were so small she kept hitting the wrong ones, the last time getting some music store in Hilton Head, for God's sake.

Daddy was going to hit the ceiling when he saw the next bill.

"Rick," she said in relief when the connection was made, "it's me, Ronnie."

"Hey, Ron, what's up? You coming up, keep me company?"

"Very funny. Look, I can't talk long. Can you see all the streets from up there? With those binoculars?"

"Most of them, yeah. Trees get in the way, but yeah, most of them."

A distant sound of wind; she hoped he was all right up there.

"Would you please look for Daddy's car if you can?"

"What's the matter?"

"I'm not sure. He's been pissy all day, and stormed out of here a little while ago, saying if no one's going to help him with his story, then he'd get it himself."

"Sorry, I don't get it."

"Rick, he doesn't think those guys from last night have left the island. He thinks they're still here, and he's going to try to find them."

Ben Pellier hung up the bar's wall phone and rested his forehead against it, tapping the floor with one heel.

Alma bustled out of the kitchen, wiping her hands on her apron. "Ben, I can't find the—what's wrong?"

He closed his eyes, pressed a fist to the wall.

"That was Hector. It's . . . it's Senior."

"Oh, dear Lord, no."

"About twenty minutes ago."

"What about Junior?"

"Gonna be all right so far. Touch and go."

He could hear her weeping, could hear Pegleg scratching at something at the bottom of his cage, could hear the front door open and Billy Freck say, "Come on, Pellier, give it over, I ain't got all day."

Verna wrinkled her nose, looked to her left at the sheriff's closed door. Trying to hold her breath without seeming to, she hit the intercom button.

"Sheriff?"

"I told you not to bother me."

"It's Neely, Sheriff. He's here at my desk, and he says he knows where those men are, the ones who shot the Raybourns."

"He what?" Cribbs yelled.

Oakman winced and pulled the receiver away from his ear for a second. "He says he knows where those killers are staying. Thought you ought to know, you being the mayor and all."

"He's a drunk, throw him in a cell."

"Can't do that, sir."

"What, you're not making enough money already?"

"Deputy Dewitt's already taken his statement."

"She what? Are you crazy?"

"Just doing my job, sir."

"Goddamnit, Vale, you'd better be packed, because if this goes bad, I swear I'll run you out of town on a rail."

"Yes, sir," he said, nodding to Verna. "Yes, sir, I understand."

He hung up, rubbed his ear, and with his left foot nudged the suitcase resting in the well of his desk. "Dub, I'm telling you again, if you're wrong about this, I'm gonna look like ten kinds of a jackass, the mayor's gonna want your scalp, and I'm gonna be standing right behind him, sharpening the damn knife."

Neely pushed out of his chair, clapped his hands once. "Then let's go, Sheriff. Saddle up, and let's get them there bad guys."

"In a minute, Dub, in a minute. For this kind of thing, I'm going to need reinforcements."

When the telephone rang, Stone exchanged a questioning glance with Lauder, then shrugged, and answered.

"Stone?"

"Indeed."

"This is Cutler."

"I know, sir, I know."

"Good, then get your ass outta there. The sheriff'll be on his way in a few minutes, and he's bringing a posse."

Stone thanked him, hung up, and said, "Well, Dutch, it seems our luck isn't so good today. Pack up, we have five minutes."

"Where'll we go?"

"Seeing as how he's paying the bills, I suggest we drop in on the mayor."

7

Casey stood in front of the storeroom closet.

The door was closed, and his hand on the knob, but he couldn't yet bring himself to turn it.

His arm trembled; his throat was dry.

He glanced at the boots on the floor beside him and remembered an evening not so many years ago when he had walked up the main street of Maple Landing, moon casting his shadow ahead of him, boot heels hard on the ground, and he'd imagined himself the local hero, the gunfighter who was out to protect the people of his town. He had laughed at the conceit then, knew it to be a vivid by-product of his pride.

He wasn't laughing now.

If you do this, Case, you may not be around when it's over, you know.

They used to tease him, his friends, when he cursed now and then, and he never tired of reminding them that just because he was a priest didn't mean he wasn't a man. Not perfect, was how he put it; doing my best, but not perfect.

If you do this, the others may not be around, either.

He tightened his grip on the doorknob.

"Lord," he whispered, "no offense, but if this is wrong, I'd sure appreciate a lightning bolt about now."

He grinned.

He laughed.

He opened the door.

He showered in the hottest water he could stand, scrubbed himself as hard as he could without drawing blood. When the water began to chill, he turned it off, climbed out of the tub, and stood in front of the mirror, and sighed. Only once.

The coloring had left his hair; it was white again, pure white.

In the bedroom he put on the black jeans he hadn't worn since he'd thrown in the towel; the black collarless shirt that suggested he'd put on a few pounds; black socks over which he pulled the boots, wondering why he'd ever given them up. Lots of folks had laughed at them, mockingly called him an urban preacher cowboy, but he'd never found a pair of shoes that had been halfway as comfortable. And even if he hadn't become a priest, he would have worn black anyway, because he hated trying to figure out which color matched which. That, too, had been a great source of good-natured amusement among his friends.

Friends long gone.

Friends too long unavenged.

On the dresser he placed a small box lined with velvet, a gift from his momma. He opened it carefully, hesitated, fingers trembling, before he took out a simple gold cross on a simple gold chain, and hung it around his neck.

He opened a second box, a longer, wider one, velvet-lined, with narrow compartments, and again he hesitated. This was the last step. This was the final move. He could stop now, and nothing would change; he could stop now, still retreat. Dishonored perhaps, but still alive.

don't take your guns to town, son
leave your guns at home

The boy in the song hadn't left them, and he'd died.

A wry smile: you're stalling, Case, get moving.

He reached into the box and pulled out a white starched collar, used one hand to put it around his neck, used the other to close it in back with an amber tab. Quickly. Without thinking.

Then he turned around to face the bed. On it lay a black suit jacket and a black denim jacket. Except when his duties took him to the hospital or a meeting out of town, they were virtually interchangeable as far as he was concerned.

"Move it," he ordered quietly. "Move it, they're waiting."

He grabbed the denim, draped it over his arm, and hurried down the stairs, aware of how he sounded, too aware of the cold wings batting in his stomach, the faint buzzing in his head, the weakness in his legs.

"All right, ready or not," he called before he reached the bottom, trying to sound light and casual, wincing when he realized he had instinctively used what Reed called "the voice," the one that filled his church, the one that filled the valley that lay below his mother's grave.

To his embarrassment they all stood when he walked into the front room, but of all the reactions he might have guessed he'd witness, he never would have guessed he'd see John Bannock, weeping.

He motioned the others to sit, stepped over to John, and grasped his shoulders.

"My . . . son," John said, biting his lips.

Casey shook his head. "No, John, he isn't. You know that. He isn't your son, and he never was your son. He's one of them, John, and now they're all riding." He looked at the others. "And they know you're with me."

5

1

He felt like the conductor of an orchestra that preferred its own rhythm. Standing in the kitchen, he waved his arms to direct food onto the table, sandwiches to be made, food to be microwaved, sandwiches on plates to be taken elsewhere, kids who didn't want to go elsewhere, Lisse who had reverted to waitress mode and spent twenty minutes giggling with the girls as she showed them carrying tricks . . . he sang nonsense songs that had the Levin girls giggling in spite of their still obvious distrust of him, old cowboy songs that John sometimes joined in on with mostly the wrong words, a few hand-clapping, foot-stomping, raise the roof and the hell with the neighbors Gospel pieces, and anything else he could think of so no one had time to ask questions.

The sun was nearly down when the house quieted, and he leaned against the sink, head down, looking for a decent breath.

"You're quite good, you know."

Moving only his eyes, he saw Beatrice standing in the

doorway. "When you have to keep a bunch of teenagers from killing each other on a camping trip, you catch on pretty fast."

She sat at the table, blew an angel-wing out of her eye. "Do you have a plan? Or is that too presumptuous at this point?"

"Lady Harp, I—"

"Beatrice, please," she said quickly. "We're a little too involved for such formalities."

"Sure. And no, Beatrice, I don't have a plan. I feel like a general who's fighting a war on two fronts, and I'm making myself plenty dizzy just trying to keep them straight."

She picked up a spoon, tapped the bowl against her palm. "I should think one at a time would be best, don't you?"

"Pick one, then."

"Your problems on the island, I should think," she answered without hesitation. "The other will . . . today's Wednesday, New Year's Eve isn't until Friday."

"And what do you propose I do?"

She smiled. "Ah, there's where the general is supposed to make the decisions." She watched the spoon as though it were moving on its own. "But have you considered the possibility that the two are connected?"

He pushed away from the sink, dropped into the chair opposite her. From the living room he heard Cora laughing and one of the Levin girls protesting, and laughing.

"Beatrice, I'm not a general. And it's only been a few hours since I decided I was going to do something at all. I haven't had time to think, hardly time to take a breath."

"So you don't know why these people are after you."

He shook his head.

"Perhaps it's because someone else doesn't want you around."

He opened his mouth to tell her that was awfully farfetched, closed it when he realized it wasn't that farfetched at all. Two of the three people who had faced the first three Riders were here on Camoret Island. And he had a strong feeling Lady Harp had more to do with matters in Las Vegas than she'd admitted.

Impulsively he reached over and covered her hands, trapping the spoon into silence. "Beatrice, the Riders, they can't be killed, you know. They—" He closed his eyes for a second, then looked helplessly at her. "I don't know what's expected of me. Of us. I'm not Joan of Arc, I don't hear voices." A glance toward the living room, and he lowered his voice. "They forget that I lost, Beatrice. She's still out there, riding."

He watched her eyes move as she studied his face, and he could almost feel their touch. Wanted, for some reason, to feel their touch. Started but didn't retreat when she pulled her hands gently from under his, put them in her lap.

"By that definition," she said tightly, "we all did, didn't we? Are you telling me, then, it was all for nothing?"

He could almost feel the cold anger he saw in her eyes, in the set of her lips, and he pushed away from the table, walked over to the back door, and looked out at the yard. No demons lurking there, no gouts of hellfire, no monsters—pale fading sunlight, and grass settling in for the winter, and a hedge with a ragged gap where he'd crashed through last night; fragments of blue sky, subtle movement to suggest a breeze.

He almost said it again: I don't hear voices, I'm not told what to do.

Instead, without apology: "They're riding together this time, and they have help."

"They've had help before."

"They've never ridden together before."

"Well, I'm not a tactician, Casey, but I'm fairly sure that a good principle in this case then would be to even the odds."

He turned with a rueful smile. "And what—"

He stopped when Lisse came to the door, held his breath when he saw the look on her face.

"What?" he said grimly.

"There's someone here, Casey. He says—"

He saw Hector Nazario over her shoulder, waiting by the front door, and he knew.

As Beatrice rose from her chair, he strode from the kitchen, eyes narrowed, a sudden hollow feeling in his chest. Lisse backed away hastily, pressed against the wall as he passed. Hector's eyes widened when he saw the black, and the collar, and the size of the man who marched toward him down the hall.

"Hector," Casey said, so quietly that Hector took a step back.

He stammered, staring at the people gathered in the living room, staring at Casey.

"Who?" Casey asked.

Hector shook his head. "It . . . Senior. Gloria, she thought you should know."

Casey put a hand on his shoulder and turned him around, led him onto the porch and down the walk. Junior's motor scooter was parked at the curb. An angry sorrow kept him silent until Hector said, "Casey, you're—" A gesture at the clothes.

"Yes."

"I didn't know."

"No matter. How is Junior?"

"Not good. They don't know yet. Gloria is there, no one else would go." He rubbed his hands nervously, against his coat, against each other. "Father, I'm sorry, I didn't know you—"

Casey stopped him with a raised hand. "Are you working today?"

"Yes."

"Alone?"

"No, Father, Miss Hull, she helps me out."

With a nod Casey urged him onto the scooter. "Have you seen the mayor or Cutler today?"

Hector frowned. "Yes." He nodded quickly. "Yes, just before I came here. He, Mayor Cribbs, I saw him going into the town hall." He looked up; a revelation. "With two men, Father. He was with two men, the ones I told you about."

Casey stared down Midway Road, seeing nothing but a dance of dark motes over the blacktop, motes that coalesced and vanished, became a centered heat in his chest.

"Go on back, Hector. See if you can get hold of Rick, and anyone else who gives a damn. I'll be there in a few minutes."

"What are you going to do, Father?"

For an answer Casey slapped him on the back to send him on his way. He watched the scooter move faster than Junior ever drove it, for a second saw the bright red hat, and shook his head quickly to clear it. A glance to the sky, and he hurried back inside.

"Jude," he said, "I'd like to see you and your girls in the kitchen, please." He started down the hall without waiting for an answer, called over his shoulder, "John, get the car warmed up, and fetch those peashooters of yours."

He heard them scrambling, heard Cora wanting to know what she should do, and stopped at the table. When Jude came in, the girls close behind her, he nodded at the chairs. Jude sat; the girls ignored him and stood behind her.

Remembering what Reed had told him, and seeing the looks on Starshine's and Moonbow's faces, he took a chair himself, and a moment to calm himself down. While he wondered how bad it really was behind that veil.

"We haven't had a chance to talk," he began, smiling regretfully. "And I'm afraid there's not going to be much chance now."

"That's all right," she said with a slight bow of her head. Her voice was soft, and rough. The veil shifted. Her long hair caught the sunlight and returned it. He wondered if her chin had the same dimples as her daughters', wondered if they were as strong as she. "I dreamed about you, you know."

"So I heard." He scratched his forehead slowly. "I'm sorry about Mr. Falkirk. I—"

"He was gonna buy us a castle," Moonbow blurted.

"Shhh," her sister scolded, and jabbed her with an elbow.

"I wouldn't doubt it," Casey said. "He was a special man."

Jude's eyes closed; Starshine put a hand on her shoulder.

"Are you gonna fight Eula?" Moonbow asked.

He blew out a quick breath, rubbed one hand over the back of the other.

"It's the end of the world, you know," she said, nodding. "That's what Trey said. Eula made people sick. She sang all over the world, and she made people sick." She glared then. "So are you gonna fight her?"

"Are you really a priest?" Starshine asked.

He blinked rapidly several times.

"They gang up on you if you're not careful," Jude said, clear pride in her voice. She lifted her hands, patted Star's with one, took one of Moonbow's with the other and pressed it to her arm. "They take care of me."

"I'll bet."

"Reverend Chisholm," Reed called from the front door, "John's ready."

He lifted a hand—in a minute—and sat up, and lost his smile.

"I want you to go over to where Cora and Reed are staying. While I'm gone, it's not safe for you here. Don't be fooled by them. They can take care of you."

"We can take care of ourselves," Starshine said defiantly.

"Yes, and now you'll have help," he told her. "Jude, I'm being honest when I tell you I don't know what's going to happen. And I don't know what part you'll be playing in any of this." He reached out a hand, and after a slight hesitation, she took it, and he curled his fingers over hers. "But I'm glad you're here. And I'll repay you somehow, you have my word on it."

He saw her eyes move as Beatrice's had, studying him intently. "I'd offer to go," she said at last, "but I'm afraid the sheriff . . . he might know who . . ." She lifted her head, indicating the veil, and what lay beneath it. "I'm not exactly hard to spot."

"That will be *our* problem now," he answered. And winked.

Another call from the front put him on his feet. He grabbed the black jacket from the back of the chair and, as he put it on, he said, "Who is Lady Harp, anyway?"

Jude said nothing.

Then Moonbow said, "She's an angel."

2

Trees and tall shrubs sent sharp-edged fencepost shadows across the road. The onshore breeze had turned into a wind that lifted dust devils in the gutters, that pushed at the traffic light hanging over the Midway-Landward intersection. Shop signs were lit. Cars began to arrive with those who worked on the mainland. The temperature began a slow slide. A wave of children walked and pedaled home from the playground, their voices filling the air briefly like the cries of small birds.

In the Edward Teach, Ben checked the barometer that hung on the wall near the telephone, tapping it with one finger. Scowling. Turning to tell Senior that the damn storm was on its way, and grabbing onto the lip of the bar when he remembered.

In the Tower on Hook Ridge, Rick Jordan packed up and jammed his arms into his coat, ready to leave, cutting his tour short by half an hour. He wasn't sure he'd make it to Betsy's in time, but he was damn sure going to try. One more day of this crap and his volunteer tour was over for the year, the best present he'd gotten this season. Staying up here, watching clouds smear the horizon, shivering in the wind . . . it gave him too much time to think about the *Deuce*, to think about what options he had for the coming season. Options which pretty much amounted to zero.

In the *Camoret Weekly* office, Whittaker sat at his computer and wrote the last story for next week's edition. He had no notes; he took it all from his head. It contained everything he knew, everything he thought he knew, and enough speculation to put him in jail for the rest of his life when the mayor and Cutler came after him for libel. He didn't care. The front page story was shared with Senior Raybourn's obituary, and Whittaker just didn't care what happened to him now.

In the sheriff's department's main room, Deputy Freck sat at his desk, bouncing a little, wondering if maybe he'd finally gone too far. If maybe he ought to cut out while the cutting was good. When Verna spun around and told him to for God's sake sit still, he gave her the finger—with both hands.

In Vale Oakman's private office, the sheriff looked at the report he'd just finished, sniffing, blowing his nose, pulling at an earlobe, his right hand hovering over the signature line, not yet ready to sign. He had gone to the cottage Dub Neely had identified, had gone in, and had found nothing. Not at first. Freck had been so mad, he'd lashed out with his gun, accidentally catching Dub across the temple, and was so instantly contrite he had taken the unconscious drunk to the clinic himself. Shortly afterward, Vale discovered a small wad of cotton wedged behind the unplugged refrigerator. He sniffed it, and the smell was enough to tell him someone had been cleaning a weapon in here. Dub had been right. And *was it worth it?* Chisholm had asked him. He looked at the report for the hundredth time, didn't sign, didn't put the pen down; *was it worth it?*

In the third floor outer office, Millicent Grummond did her level best not to listen to the voices in the mayor's office. They weren't yelling exactly, but they weren't engaged in polite conversation, either. When she couldn't take it any longer, when she grew afraid of the intensity she could hear beyond the door, she started gathering her things together, ready to go home. She wouldn't ask Mayor Cribbs's permission; she somehow knew it would be all right.

Cora stormed through the house. "Why can't we go?" she demanded of no one in particular.

"Because we're just women," Starshine answered bitterly, standing at the front door, looking out at the empty darkening street.

Jude and Beatrice laughed.

"That's not funny," Cora said. "It's true. He doesn't trust us because we're women."

"Of course he trusts you," said Lady Harp sharply. "He doesn't want us with him because he doesn't need an army. And Lisse isn't exactly a man, you know. I expect she's a better shot than any of us." She looked at them one by one. "We'll have plenty to do on Friday."

Lyman Baylor hurried out of his office when he saw the car stop in front of the house. When the giant in black stepped out, he froze, knowing he looked stupid with his mouth open, his hands twitching, but he couldn't help it.

When Casey beckoned with a friendly smile, he couldn't move, not at first. It was one thing to know, it was another to *know*. And this wasn't anything like he expected.

"Is it open, Ly?" Casey asked, tilting his head at the church.

Lyman nodded mutely.

"May I?"

Lyman nodded again, and again couldn't speak.

Casey thanked him with a gesture and started up the walk, pausing only to wave toward the house. Lyman turned and saw Kitra on the steps, staring, then looking at him for an explanation, and he could only shrug. When she frowned and jerked her head, he realized she wanted him to follow. And why not? he thought as he did; it's my church, I have a right to know.

He walked as fast as he could without running, reached the doors just in time to hear Casey say, "Afternoon, Lord, looks like I'm in some trouble here. You have any ideas?"

Hector turned the OPEN sign around to CLOSED, and took off his apron. Rick wasn't here yet, but as far as he could tell, neither was Father Chisholm.

He blinked.

Father Chisholm. All this time, and not even a hint.

"Done, Hector," Ronnie called from the kitchen. She came out wiping her hands on a towel, moving toward the rifle lying on the counter. "Now what do we do?"

He lifted a shoulder. "Wait, I guess. Nothing else to do, he just said he was coming."

She joined him at the door, looked right, and said, "Come on, Rick, move it. You're gonna miss all the fun."

The telephone call had been short and blunt: "Get your ass to town, there's gonna be trouble and I don't trust those guys to stick around when it starts."

"Count on me," Stump said, grinning at his brothers, giving them a thumbs-up.

"Oh, I am, Teague, I am."

"Who are the bad guys?"

"Anyone but us," said Norville Cutler. "And I mean, anyone."

3

Casey told John to drive past the Landward intersection, make a U-turn, and park on the wrong side in front of the tobacco shop, facing north. When Bannock looked a question at him, he said, "The mayor can't see us from his office this way."

Once parked, he put his hand on the door handle and watched the street, both ahead and in the side mirror. Reed shifted impatiently in back; Lisse whispered, and the shifting stopped. A van swung around the corner and headed south, an angry touch to the horn for the car being on the wrong side of the road. John backed up a few feet, turned the engine off.

Casey nodded, opened the door, and slid out, making his way around the trunk to the sidewalk. He had little specific idea what he was going to do, but he didn't dare stop to think things through. Not now. His anger propelled him, and fed him, and the cross bouncing against his chest reminded him of the boundaries.

A pause at the corner, no cars in any direction, and he crossed over, feeling the heat gathering in his cheeks again. His initial plan had been to confront the mayor directly, but Reed and John had calmed him enough to extract a promise that he'd take the step most others would first.

He swung into the sheriff's department, shoving the glass door open with a smack of his palm. Deputy Freck took one look at him and yelled, "Jesus Christ!" He leaped to his feet, got tangled in his chair, and stumbled backward, grabbing frantically for something to keep him from falling. Verna had turned to snap at him, but when she saw Casey her voice became a short-lived squeak.

"Is he in?" Casey asked, grateful for the chance to smile for a change.

"He's . . ." She waved vaguely. "Busy."

"No, he's not. But thanks anyway." A grin as he pushed through the gate and headed for Oakman's office.

"Stop, please," Verna called after him.

A clatter and curse told him Freck had met his match in a wastebasket and had finally landed on the floor.

The smile was still there when he opened the door and stepped over the threshold, put up a cautionary hand to keep the startled sheriff in his seat, and stopped only when the desk got in his way.

"Two men," he said. "The two men who killed Senior were seen going into the Town Hall. As far as I know, they're still there. Get up, get over there, and put them in jail."

"Now wait a minute," Oakman said, shaking his head, his own hand up to hold off the giant who loomed over his desk. "I can't just go into—"

"You can," Casey said. "You will."

"Sheriff?" Verna called from the other room. "Are you all right?"

"He's fine," Casey answered without turning around. "You *are* fine, aren't you, Sheriff?"

The instant the man paled, Casey knew it was a lost cause. Oakman, however it was done, was too compromised to act. His voice softened, but his eyes didn't. "It would be nice to have you with me when I pay my next call," he said. "And just so you know," he added, tapping the white collar with his finger, "this came after prison, not before. Sometimes, Sheriff, it works out that way."

He left, saddened when he didn't hear the man leave his chair, angered when he saw Freck back on his feet, hand on his holster. He glared, and Freck unsnapped the flap, but his hand shook so badly he couldn't get it out of the way.

As he pushed back through the gate, he said, "Sorry, ma'am," to Verna, who smiled automatically before she realized what she'd done and snapped the smile off.

Are you going to shoot? he thought as he headed for the

door without pausing; come on, Deputy, are you going to shoot a priest in the back?

On the sidewalk, he took a deep gulp of refreshing cold air, slapped his hand against his thigh, and turned left, toward the Town Hall. Footsteps ran up behind him, and flanked him, and he said as he went in, "Keep them under your coats. I don't want any shooting unless they shoot first."

"Are you sure you're a priest?" Lisse asked softly.

He laughed, a single explosion that filled the marble-floor lobby.

A single elevator at the far end, and an open staircase that spiraled gently all the way up; he took the stairs.

He reached the top long before the others, stepping into a wide, carpeted reception area. A bosomy woman in her fifties stood at a long narrow desk, a large purse in one hand.

"I'm sorry, Father," she said, "but the mayor's in conference right now and can't be disturbed."

Casey glanced at the only door. "In there?"

"Yes, Father, but I told you, he's busy." Her eyes shifted from him to the others as they filed up the stairs behind him. "Now look, this is awfully irregular. You people—"

He leaned over her desk and, with a smile, pointed at the intercom. Flustered, she dropped the purse, bent over to pick it up, changed her mind, and dropped into her seat. "This is most irregular. I could get in trouble, you know, I really could."

"Please," he said.

A trembling finger pressed a button, lit a white bulb. "Mayor Cribbs?"

"God!" a tinny voice yelled. "Damnit, Milli, I told you I was busy."

"I'm sorry," she said, glancing fearfully at Casey, "but there's a gentleman out here to see you. Three gentlemen, actually, and a . . . a lady."

"She had to think about it?" Lisse muttered indignantly.

"I don't care if the damn President is out there, Milli, tell him to get the hell—"

Casey reached out and gently pulled Mrs. Grummond's hand away from the intercom. Then he picked up her purse and stepped away from the desk, holding the purse out—a clear suggestion that this would be a good time to leave for the day. She fussed and fluttered, but she didn't refuse him, and he wished he could think of a way to take the terror from her eyes when Reed escorted her to the elevator and pushed the button for her.

"Milli!" the intercom voice snapped.

The elevator door opened.

"Milli, damnit, did you get rid of them?"

The elevator door closed, and Casey pushed the white light button: "No."

He imagined the confusion in there as he crossed the room and took hold of the doorknob; he imagined as he tried to turn the knob that just about now would be the first stirring of concern. But with the door locked, he did the only thing he knew might work—he reared back and kicked the door just above the lock as he bellowed wordlessly.

The door splintered as it flew in, and one of the hinges snapped.

"Who the damn hell," the mayor shouted from behind his desk, "do you think you are?"

Casey marched across the carpet, seeing Cutler off to the left, two men to his right. One wore a derby, the other a balmoral, and both wore long open topcoats that brushed across the tops of their shoes. Both reached into their coats as Casey swerved instantly toward them, ignoring the red-faced mayor, who had taken to pounding a fist on his desk as he demanded explanations at the top of his voice.

"Don't," Casey said to Stone and Lauder, who continued to draw their guns.

Too late.

His hands grabbed their throats and, still walking,

shoved them into the bookcase. Lauder dropped his weapon immediately when his elbow struck the edge of a shelf; Stone, mouth twisted as he fought for a breath, grabbed Casey's wrist with one hand while the other brought the gun up between them.

Too late.

Casey released the shorter man and grabbed Stone's gun, twisting it so violently to the side that Stone's knees buckled, and his yell had no force behind it—it came out a wheeze.

"Don't," Casey heard John warn from the doorway.

"Guns?" the mayor sputtered indignantly. "You've brought guns into this office? How—"

Casey backed up, and Stone had no choice but to follow, sagging to his knees, both hands now trying to remove the grip on his throat. Reed had already picked up Lauder's gun; John remained in the doorway with Lisse just behind, hands in their pockets, no guns visible but the implication was clear.

"This is intolerable," Cribbs said weakly. "Intolerable."

"Sit," Casey ordered.

The mayor looked to Cutler, and sat.

Casey opened his hand, and Stone fell to the floor, unconscious. Then he pressed his palms on the desk and felt no compunctions at all about using every trick in his book, from the voice to his face, to his size.

"These men killed Senior Raybourn." A light slap on the desk that made the mayor flinch. "They nearly killed Junior." Another slap, another flinch. "They tried to kill me." He lifted his hand, and the mayor flinched. "They work for you."

No sound but Lauder's faint choking, gasping.

Casey watched, then, as Cribbs's expression changed in small stages, from terror and outrage to a man freed from persecution, his deliverer before him. His eyes actually glittered from a tear that formed in each.

"These men," he said, glaring at Lauder, "these men do

not work for me, although I can certainly see why you would think that." A twitch of a smile, testing. "That bluster and thunder earlier? Upon your arrival? For them, sir, for them, so they wouldn't kill us out of hand. Isn't that right, Mr. Cutler? Isn't that right?"

Cutler, who had positioned himself midway along the wall, nodded. "Damn right. Came in here waving guns and demanding who the hell knows what." Courage regained, he stepped away from the wall. "And who the hell are all those people in my houses, Chisholm? You think you can run some kind of commune or something out there without my knowing about it?"

Casey ignored him. "A victim, Mr. Mayor?"

"Absolutely," Cribbs said, nodding solemnly. "Mr. Cutler and I were preparing for the annual New Year's Eve celebration, which he so generously funds each year, and—"

"You're fired, Chisholm. You and your people get the hell off my property."

Cribbs shook at finger at him. "Now, Norville, let's not be too hasty here. The reverend has saved us from a terrible situation, and perhaps we should show him some charity, don't you think?"

"Jesus, Jasper, what the hell—" And he jumped when Casey slapped the desk again and straightened, looked over to be sure Reed still had Lauder covered, then walked around toward the mayor.

Cribbs scrambled out of his chair, hands up in front of him. "Now listen, there's no call—"

Casey grabbed him by the shirt, kicked his chair around, and shoved him into it. Then he waved a hand at the peacock-feather window. "Do you feel like God up here, Mr. Mayor?"

"Now really, that's—"

Casey swung his head around. "Do you feel like the puppet master? The man who pulls the strings and makes people jump? Makes people . . . die? Is that what you do up here, Mr. Mayor? Do you decide who lives and dies?"

Panic, and fear, as the mayor looked futilely to Cutler for help, looked back to the window, unable to meet Casey's glare.

Casey shifted to stand behind him, hands gripping the top of the chair. Swinging it slowly, very slowly, side to side.

"A friend of mine," he said, sounding a bit puzzled, "suggested that maybe you're not in this alone, Mr. Mayor. Nor you, either, Cutler." He leaned forward slightly, stretching his neck as if searching for something down on the street. "She suggested there's someone else, someone who doesn't live on Camoret, someone who . . . I don't know quite how to put it." He chuckled. "Made you an offer you can't refuse?"

Cribbs's hands fought with each other in his lap, but he kept his silence.

"The theory goes, Mr. Mayor, that—Reed, if Mr. Lauder moves again, be a gentleman and put a bullet in his brain?"

"Yes, sir, Reverend Chisholm," Reed said.

Casey glanced over and smiled as Lauder, who had been carefully moving to sit on his heels, dropped back to the floor with a you-got-me smile. Stone groaned, but didn't move.

"The theory goes, Mr. Mayor, that you and Cutler aren't planning anything at all up at the north end. You're just clearing the land, so to speak. Making a few bucks, socking some away, using the rest to invite people like these two to help you when somebody else gets too nosy." He leaned over quickly, tilting the chair back so that Cribbs was forced to stare at him upside down. "Am I close, Jasper? Am I really close?"

"Son of a bitch, how did you know?" Cutler whispered. "How the goddamn hell did you know?"

Casey released the chair so it snapped forward and nearly dumped the mayor into the window. "Because, believe it or not," he said, "they don't care about you. Your friend and *his* partners. They don't care about the island.

They don't care about the money." He looked over his shoulder. "They're after me, Cutler. And if they get me, nothing in this world is going to save you."

4

The tail end of twilight, the beginning of dusk, when streetlamps and headlamps glared, not glowed; when shadows had razor edges; when nothing was ever as close as it seemed.

The wind skated a leaf across the peacock window, and Cribbs darted from his chair as if scorched, stood panting at the desk corner as a hand and his lips tried to find a way to explain.

Casey wanted an explanation, but movement outside distracted him. A car pulled up in front of the *Weekly* building, the man behind the wheel keeping the engine running as two others left the vehicle in a hurry and ran into the office. Casey squinted, almost lifting a hand as if it could wipe away the dusk to let him see the car more clearly.

"Now listen," Cribbs said, composure under control, "I think perhaps this can be—"

The *Weekly* door opened, and Casey nearly rose off the floor.

"Damn!" he yelled as he saw Stump Teague and Billy Ray dragging Whittaker between them, each with a shotgun in one hand. "Damn!" he yelled again as he whirled to face Cutler. "You!" and he pointed. "This is your doing, isn't it?"

Cutler could have done anything, could have reacted in any one of a hundred ways, but it was obvious he knew what Casey meant, and at the same time as his hands came up in a posture that claimed he knew nothing about anything . . . he smirked.

Casey's temper broke.

"John, get downstairs, they're after Whittaker," he ordered, and said to Cutler, pointing, "Don't you dare move, little man, or I'll crush you where you stand."

Cribbs had moved over to the window, watching as the old man struggled with the Teagues. "My God," he whispered. "My God." And then, "Oh, no."

Casey looked down.

Sheriff Oakman was at the curb in a half-crouch, his gun drawn. Casey couldn't hear what he said, but from behind the wheel Cord pulled a weapon of his own and fired, dropping Oakman to his knees, firing back wildly. Almost at the same instant, a pickup roared up the street, Ronnie Hull standing in back with a rifle in her hand. She fired, and Billy Ray spun to one side, leaving Stump to handle the old man alone.

A car tire blew.

Stump clubbed Whittaker with the shotgun's butt, spun it into his hands and fired at the onrushing vehicle just as Billy Ray, leaning against the window, brought his gun up and fired as well.

The windshield became spider-glass, and Ronnie snapped forward, tumbled backward, when the pickup slammed into the back of the parked car, lifting it off its rear wheels. When they came down, the truck's hood was on the car's trunk.

Someone fired from the pickup and Billy Ray went through the plate glass window.

A second car tire blew, and the rear window shattered.

Standing over Whittaker's body, Stump pumped and fired again, pumped and fired, and Oakman fell back over his heels and lay still, arms outstretched, staring at the sky through a dark mask of blood.

Gunshots in swift succession sent Stump diving behind the car, Cord scrambling over the passenger to climb through the window and drop beside his brother.

John, Casey thought.

And Reed cried, "Reverend Chisholm!"

* * *

He turned to see Lauder bring up a second gun and slam it against the boy's wrist; the crack of the bone couldn't have been any louder.

When Casey charged around the desk, Cutler was already at the door, had a hand out to shove Lisse aside, when he was shoved aside himself by Billy Freck, who charged in with weapon drawn.

"Down," he screamed at Casey. "Get down, you son of a bitch."

Casey didn't stop.

Freck pulled the trigger as he moved, but the shot went over Casey's shoulder and punched a small hole in the window. Before he could fire again, Casey grabbed his arm in both hands and spun him around with a roar.

Let him go as he staggered backward and lost his footing.

Watched the deputy fly over the desk as he landed on the floor.

Watched him hit the window with his back. Arms out to either side. Mouth open in a silent scream as the window cracked. And he went through.

The scream wasn't silent now, and it didn't last very long.

He couldn't move.

He sat on the carpet and he couldn't move as the wind stormed into the office, lifting papers and twisting them, spinning them, mixing them with dead leaves that dropped the mayor to the floor, cowering and whimpering.

Lauder went to his partner and helped him up by an elbow, his gun darting between Reed kneeling and holding his wrist, and Casey.

Who couldn't move.

When they reached him, Stone made Lauder stop, looked down, and said hoarsely, bewildered, not a little afraid, "What kind of priest *are* you?" He shook his head.

"Doesn't matter. You're going to die anyway." And nodded for Lauder to take him away.

Casey heard the gunfire brought in by the wind, watched as Reed half crawled to his side, saw the blood seeping between the boy's fingers.

"He could have killed me," Reed said, not understanding, glancing back at the office door. "He could have killed me, but he didn't." He stared at what was left of the peacock window. "Aw, shit, my hand hurts. Are you okay? Reverend Chisholm, are you okay? Say something."

There was nothing to say.

Not until he stopped listening to the scream.

6

The wind stopped.

An arm around Reed's waist, Casey made his way down the stairs to the lobby. He wasn't hurt, but his legs had a hard time keeping him up, and his lungs refused to fill, keeping his mouth open to gulp for air. Neither had said a word since leaving the mayor's office, and the last they'd seen of Cribbs, he'd been trying to pull himself into his leather swivel chair.

The wind stopped.

At first Casey thought he'd been struck deaf; he couldn't even hear his own heartbeat, his own footsteps. But as they approached the door, a shoe kicked a piece of glass and it skittered across the marble floor. Scraping like a file drawn across a blackboard.

The crackle, then, of flames; a woman's enraged wailing; a stuck car horn; glass falling somewhere down the street; a man groaning nearby; a fast-approaching siren; voices, lots of voices.

They stood in the doorway, and Reed said, "God."

The Teague's car spat flame from the backseat, acrid smoke fanning upward, almost masking the fire that curled up and around the pickup's crumpled hood.

With a look to be sure Reed was all right, Casey stepped outside, swaying until he forced his equilibrium back in line. He went directly to the sheriff, just as Verna left the department building. With only a glance at each other, they straightened the man's legs, and she laid a jacket over what was left of his face. Casey laid a hand on the jacket lightly and whispered a prayer, stood slowly, stiffly, and headed across the street.

Billy Ray Teague still lay half in and out of the *Weekly*'s shattered window, blood slithering down the wall to gather beneath his legs. The first coils of smoke drifted through the ragged gap.

Stump and Cord were gone, Ronnie left to sit on the sidewalk, her father's bloodied head in her lap. A red smear across her brow, a sleeve torn and gone from an elbow, she looked up at his approach, tears drowning her cheeks, dripping from her chin.

He crouched beside her, brushed a leaf from the old man's unmoving chest.

"He hardly ever went to church," she said.

"Doesn't matter," he told her, and closed his eyes for a moment, left hand lightly holding the gold cross.

The car horn was cut off.

He rose and looked down Landward, and saw two automobiles buckled against the side of the sheriff's department building, commuters who had apparently tried to avoid the battle at the intersection and couldn't turn sharply enough. A man sat dazed at the curb, another beside him, gripping his shoulder, looking angry.

A patrol car, lights blaring, screamed up the road, followed by a fire engine and another cruiser.

He watched as Verna took immediate charge, stepping into the street, waving them down, calling out instructions as she pointed, waved her arms. People ran up both streets, some wearing coats, others in shirtsleeves. Most of them stopped half a block away, unable to understand what they saw; the others moved forward cautiously, listening to Verna, and Deputy Salter, who had taken it upon himself to create a makeshift police line, grabbing a few people he knew to help keep the others back.

Casey turned away and walked up the street. Stepped off the curb. Put his hands in his pockets and stood in the middle of the road, looking down at Billy Freck, who had landed with his head against the opposite curb, glass spread around him catching the last light, glowing in the neon of the barbershop window. Incredibly, he still had his gun in his hand; incredibly, there was no visible blood.

God forgive me, I killed you, Casey thought.

Verna puffed up beside him. "Damn," she said, "who's the lucky son of a bitch who did this?"

Casey stared at her.

"Sorry," she said, not sounding apologetic at all. "But it happens, Reverend, you know? Sometimes you just don't care." She called for a paramedic or a doctor, stared as if committing the dead man's image to memory, and strode away. There was fire to attend to, some injured and wounded; the dead, right now, was the last thing on her mind.

Suddenly he spun around in near panic, unable to believe he'd forgotten Bannock and Lisse. A step toward Reed, who was sitting on the Town Hall steps, and he spotted John in the small park, back to him, kneeling beside a fallen woman.

Casey stumbled into a run, brusquely waving off Reed's call, calling himself until John looked back, his face grim as he swayed to his feet.

"She ran right out," he said as Casey slowed, and stopped. "I tried to grab her, but she ran right out."

Milli Grummond lay on her stomach, skirt pulled to her knees, purse lying beside her, its contents spilled on the ground. A large stain in the middle of her back.

"Casey, I swear I tried to stop her." He looked around, head shaking, before he said, "It was that deputy. Freck. She ran out and got in his way and, Jesus Christ, Casey, he just shot her. He just shot her. I was so . . . I couldn't do anything. Those guys were . . . the shotguns . . . I couldn't do anything, and he ran right past me and, damn, but why didn't he shoot me too?" He stepped over Milli's body and sat hard on the bench, hands helpless in his lap. "He just shot her, Casey. The son of a bitch just shot her."

He wandered back to the sidewalk, into the stench of smoke and burning metal and blood and fire; into a slow-growing chaos as Verna and Salter did their best to organize and contain with what little they had at hand.

He looked back. "Where's Lisse, John?"

Bannock stared at him, rubbed his eyes. "In the sheriff's office. She's okay. She wanted . . . she's making calls for that deputy. More cops, doctors, I guess."

Casey nodded absently, jerked to his left when he heard Reed cry out in pain, saw him sprawled on the ground, scrabbling for Norville Cutler's ankles as the man tried to run. Cutler kicked him in the face, Reed cried out again and rolled over, and Cutler took off.

"No," Casey whispered, and ran.

Half a block later he raised a fist and clubbed the man

between the shoulders, grabbed him before he fell, spun him around and lifted him off the ground by the lapels of his coat. Cutler almost screamed at the look on his face, struggled feebly as Casey carried him that way back to the station. Glaring. Daring him to try something without saying a word. He sensed people staring, and didn't care; saw Verna hustle over, uncertain until he said, "He's part of it, Deputy, the Teagues were following his orders."

Amazingly, she grinned. "Follow me, I'll show you where to dump him."

Into the station, through a door on the left and down a short flight of stairs.

Cutler's struggles increased, and Casey snarled and shook him, and when Verna opened the middle of three cells, carried him in and threw him down on the cot. Stood over him, breathing heavily, hands still in tight fists.

"Get him out of here," Cutler begged, frantically pushing himself back until he was blocked by the cinder block wall. "For God's sake, get him outta here."

In the relative quiet of the main office, Verna slumped against her desk, took off her glasses, and pushed hair out of her eyes. Lisse came out of Oakman's office, grinned when she saw him, and sobered instantly when she saw his face.

"I think I got everybody," she told Verna.

Verna nodded. "Thanks. Appreciate it." With a sigh she pushed back to her feet. "Got to get back out there," she said to Casey with a wan smile. "If I stay here, I think I'll just . . . you know, Father?"

He nodded.

She shook herself, rubbed a thumb under her nose. "All those people," she said as she headed for the door. "Damn, all those people." She paused then. "Maybe you'd like to know, Father, but they found Cord, Cord Teague? in the alley behind the *Weekly*. Took a bullet in the hip. Can't find Stump nowhere." And she left, letting the door swing slowly shut behind her.

Casey held out his hand, left it there until Lisse took it and squeezed it. "You're not doing so hot, are you?"

"No, can't say that I am."

She pressed her head briefly against his arm. "Is John all right?"

"He's in the park. He's not so hot, either. I think he could use you right about now."

"What about you?"

He looked down at her and smiled. "I get along."

She hesitated, skeptical, then left, and he exhaled sharply, stepped back until he felt the railing against his legs, and sat on it gingerly, testing its ability to hold his weight. Through the glass door he watched her disappear into the smoke that diffused the moving lights, the steady lights, and the flickering light of the several fires that couldn't quite keep the dusk from turning into full dark.

Lyman Baylor rushed past without a sideways glance.

An ambulance whooped and left, leaving Ronnie Hull standing alone in the street until Rick Jordan came up behind her, put his arm around her shoulders, and led her away. There was a bandage around his head, his left leg was stiff.

Ghosts moved through the thickening smoke, some running, some wandering.

One of them stopped and looked his way, waving at the haze in front of its eyes, then pushed at the door, scowled, and pulled it open.

"Are you responsible for all that?" Beatrice said, gesturing awkwardly behind her.

A weary shrug. "Some."

"My." She perched beside him. "I don't suppose your middle name is Michael, is it?"

He took a long time before he turned his head. "Are you an angel?" he asked in return.

Her smile made him think for no reason of a summer's soft moon. "I'll tell you when it's over."

He nodded. "All right. Me, too."

The wind returned, and brought the clouds with it.

The State Police arrived in force within the hour, taking over most of the operations without, Casey noted, being officious about it.

Within two hours, the mayor had appointed Verna Dewitt Acting Sheriff. Five minutes after that, she threw him in the cell next to Cutler.

A grim-faced sergeant took Casey's statement; it took over two hours, and not once did the man react to any of his mild jokes or other attempts to lighten the mood. The trooper asked questions, wrote the answers down, checked the tape recorder on the desk to be sure the batteries were still working, and once in a while conferred with his colleagues or a superior to cross-check a response against another witness's declaration.

For several hours Casey could hear the distinctive sound of helicopters flying low over town.

He overheard one trooper tell another that his mother-in-law was moving in that night because the approaching storm was going to be a beaut, and why the hell didn't she live in Florida, for crying out loud, the woman was the kind who gave witches and bitches a bad name.

Someone wanted to know, loudly, what Oakman had been doing with a packed suitcase in his office.

Casey said nothing; he couldn't read a dead man's mind.

When at last they were through with him, it was nearly midnight, and Sheriff Dewitt told him he could go.

"Are you sure?" he asked, trying vainly to rub some of the weariness from his eyes.

She looked him up and down frankly. "Well, isn't like you're gonna be able to hide all that well, Father."

He grinned and shook her hand, stretched his back, massaged his sides as he picked up his coat and left the building. The wind nearly toppled him, not for its strength but because he was so tired. Hoses crisscrossed the street; puddles lay everywhere, reflecting flame and light. He put his back to it all and walked away, not wanting to watch the firefighters still working, not wanting to see the sparks dancing on the wind's back. Beyond the police line he saw John waiting by the car, blowing on his hands, stamping his feet to get warm.

"Why didn't you sit inside?" he said, opening the passenger door.

"Too warm, Case. I'd be asleep in less than a minute, and you'd never get me up again, not for a week."

On the way home, John said, "Casey, is this their doing? I mean, is this the start?"

"To the first," he said, "I think yes. I don't know about the other."

"Casey, what are we going to do? We're exhausted, we're beat up . . . what are we going to do?"

"You want a sermon or do you want an answer?"

"An answer. No offense, but I'll sleep during the sermon."

Casey laughed, leaned back, closed his eyes. "I have no idea, John. I have absolutely no idea."

Although he couldn't see them when he walked through the door, he knew they were all here, scattered throughout the house. The kids were in the living room, watching television, Cora on the couch next to Reed, who sported a cast from wrist to elbow and a new sling; someone was upstairs taking a shower, someone else paced the hallway impatiently.

Beatrice was in the kitchen, pouring coffee into cups she had lined up on the counter.

"I'm sorry," she said. A wave toward the front. "No one wanted to be alone tonight."

I did, he answered silently, and went to the back door. There was nothing out there but the night, and the feel of the wind as it careened around the houses.

"Casey," she began, and he waggled a hand to hush her.

"John already asked me, and I don't know."

"Why here, then? So many places, why here?"

He laid his palm against the pane, felt the cold, the tremor of the wind.

"Ask God."

"I did. He's not answering, so I'm asking you."

He smiled, and saw his reflection smile back.

"Bea, this is no time for philosophy, for dancing with angels on the heads of bloody pins. It's here because it's here. And if I had an explanation, it wouldn't satisfy you anyway. It's here because it's here."

"And we are . . . what, then? The last bastion of hope against Armageddon?" He heard the coffeepot rattle as she placed it on its stand. He almost didn't hear her ask, "Am I going to die, Casey? Is this my last night?"

The door shook in its frame when the wind punched it.

He put his other hand on the glass and lowered his head.

"Listen to me," he said.

A very long time ago, a very good man, who happened to be my bishop, told me I had a great violence inside. One of the reasons he sent me to Maple Landing, in fact. One of the reasons I accepted the assignment without arguing.

Momma, she tried to control me, and God bless her, she did her best, but she couldn't.

The bishop was no better at that than she was.

I killed a man tonight, Bea, and damn near throttled another. I lost my temper . . . I lost control . . . and a man is dead because of it. The odd thing is, no one mourns him but me.

Maybe Whittaker's death is my fault too, and the Teagues, maybe others I don't even know about yet.

But forgive me, Bea, if I sound cold and uncaring, but I can't worry about that now. I just can't. I've been given something to do, and I've tried like hell to give it back, and it turns out I can't. I thought I could do it—give it back, go away—I thought I had done it, yet . . . here it is. Bad penny keeps turning up no matter how far I fling it.

Damn thing just keeps turning up.

He raised his head and looked through the pane at the blackness outside. Lowered his arms. Turned around and saw the others in the kitchen. Watching him. Listening.

He touched his collar, touched his cross.

These . . . do not make me special. I am not special. I am no more special than any of you, and you can't think of me that way if we're to do what we have to do.

But we are different, somehow we're different and that's why we're here.

Don't ask me if you'll live, because I don't know. Don't ask me if you're going to die, because I don't know that either. Don't ask me for miracles, because miracles are reserved for the special, not the different. Don't ask me to bless you, because . . . I killed a man tonight.

But if you're wondering now, right now, after all this, how we can take on those Riders, how we can possibly win, then I'll remind you that I and my friends once stopped a woman in a great white car, and John there once stopped a boy on a great and dark palomino, and Trey

Falkirk, bless his soul and rest it, did the same in the desert.

I . . .

He couldn't speak.

I . . .

He couldn't smile.

Go to bed, he finally told them. All of you, go to bed. Try to get some rest, I know you won't get any sleep. If you're going to stay here, there's my bed too, someone take it. I have some hard thinking to do, and I doubt I'll get to use it. Go on now, scoot. Don't worry about me sneaking off. For all your miserable sins, I'll still be here come daybreak.

They crowded through the door, not looking at him, not speaking to him, not speaking to each other. When he was alone, he grabbed the nearest chair and fell into it, limp, exhausted, not entirely sure he'd be able to get up again.

He listened to the wind.

He listened as the house, bit by bit, fell silent.

And then he listened to the silence.

7

1

He stands at the end of a long rough jetty, nearly one hundred yards from the safety of the shore. Rhythmic explosions from twenty feet below as the cold December sea tears itself apart against the uneven boulders. His hands are in his pockets, only once in a long while slipping away to clear the cold spray that drips from his face. He wears a black denim jacket over a thick dark sweater; faded jeans, worn sneakers. With no hat for protection his hair ducks and twists in the wind.

He faces the horizon and looks at the water and sees nothing but waves rolling steadily toward him. Rising as if taking his measure, falling as if needing less distance before they can rise again, and crest, and drive him at last into the slick and jagged brown-black stone.

Clouds low and heavy.

Feathers of rain in the distance.

Every few minutes, a flare of lightning, and thunder warns.

He has been here for hours, since the winter sun first

rose, and finally there's a long deep breath, a long and slow exhalation while his eyes close and his shoulders slump and his lips move in a silent prayer he fears won't be answered.

Far behind him, on the beach, people wait, huddled and shivering. Watching. Afraid that he won't turn around, that he'll forget they are there, that he will instead take that next step. Into the sea. That after all this time and after all he has told them he will be lost to them, and they'll be lost.

Yet none move to join him, and none move to speak to him, and none move to help him because there is nothing they can do. They can only stand there. Waiting. And watching. While the cold stiffens their limbs and discolors their faces and takes their breath and turns it into ghosts the wind blows back into their dark and fearful eyes.

Every few minutes someone will look at someone else, a raised eyebrow, a pulled-in lip, a tilt of a head, a confused shrug. With nothing to say to the man on the jetty, they have nothing to say to each other as well. Not anymore. It's all been said and it's all been done, and there's no sense in doing anything else.

Just wait.

Ignore the bloodstains, ignore the cuts and bruises, pay no attention to the rough bandages and heavy cast and deeply aching muscles and sharp aching bones and the sure and certain knowledge that what they've been through so far can't possibly shine a light on what they know is to come.

A tall man, lank and bowed, turns to stare at the trees that line the miles of sand that face the ocean. Nothing moves there but the branches, needled or bare. Nothing moves but clumps of violently trembling sawgrass that tops the few dunes he can see from where he stands. Nothing moves, and he turns back, expecting nothing more, a quick smile and a soft grunt when the woman beside him slips her arm around his waist.

Two children, young girls, flank a woman who wears a weighted veil over her face, only her eyes exposed. The three hold hands and dare the wind to knock them down.

A young man and a young woman stand close without touching.

There are others. Not many.

And apart from them all is a woman who holds the neck of her thin coat closed at her throat. A scarf over her hair flutters as if trying to break loose and fly. Of them all she is the only one whose eyes are red and puffed from weeping. Yet her back is straight and her chin is up, and alone among all the others she has no trouble with a smile.

Alone among all the others, she seems to know, and she is ready.

2

scarlet fire
emerald sparks

Acting Sheriff Verna Dewitt sits at her old desk—she can't bear to use Vale's office—and listens as the state cop tells her for at least the zillionth time that for such a small island, the son of a bitch is pretty damn big, but not to worry, they'll leave a presence on the mainland end of the causeway, no way those guys are fool enough to try to leave by boat in this weather. If they try to get off, they'll be caught.

They shake hands and she walks him to the door, says, "Wait, I forgot."

The captain seems impatient, but he's too polite to walk away.

"The waves," she tells him. "They'll be plenty damn big now, so watch it crossing. The trick," she continues before he can interrupt, "is to wait for the second one."

He frowns. "What?"

"The second one. Don't ask me why, it's some kind of thing to do with the bottom, but in a storm like this, there'll be one huge wave washing over the road, and some people figure it's okay, and they gun it. Don't. There's always a second big one, sometimes bigger than the first. That one'll knock you clear to Carolina. When *that* one's gone, then you gun it." She smiles sweetly. "Got it?"

He tips his cap. "Thanks, Sheriff. Appreciate the tip."

"No problem," she answers. And when he's gone, she turns to Salter and says, "Stupid son of a bitch didn't believe a word I said. That man's going to drown, Dwight, I swear to God."

"He's the last one, huh?"

"Yes. You and me, Dwight. Let's hope the Indians don't attack, or we're up poop creek."

Salter laughs and shakes his head. "That's not the way I heard it, Verna."

"Yeah? Well, you heard it that way now." She reaches for her slicker and floppy rain hat. "I'm going to ride around a little. Maybe I'll get lucky and run Stump over." She grins as she jams the hat on. "By accident, of course. Purely by accident."

"What about the prisoners? They're complaining about not getting any lunch."

"Lunch?" She pauses at the door. "Damn. Give 'em an hour, then give Hector a call, have him make something up. Christ," she mutters as she pushes the door open, grunting against the wind that tries to break into the room, "you'd think he was still the goddamn mayor."

The storm clouds bulge and contract, black patches and grey, as they speed over the island on their way north. Far off the coast a waterspout bounces over the surface, bending, swaying, finally collapsing in silver sparks. A few minutes before noon, a rain shower slaps the streets and windows, and ends as suddenly as it began. A few minutes later parts of the cloud-sky turn a vivid ugly green, sign of a tornado that doesn't appear.

Whitecaps on the bay spit foam and spray.

The sea rises, and the waves rise with it.

Although Hector is at Betsy's, he hasn't bothered to open. No one's going to be out today unless they absolutely have to be, and he might as well keep his promise to Gloria and get himself off the island before the tide and high seas cut him off.

Resolved as he may be, however, he can't stay away from the window. He can't stop watching the clouds, listening to the wind. Gloria will think he's loco, that's for sure, but there's something odd about this one and he doesn't want to leave until he figures it out.

Besides, if the causeway's flooded, that means wrestling with the car, and his shoulder still aches from the kick it received when he shot Ronnie Hull's extra rifle at that scum of the earth, one of the Teagues. There's a bruise—it looks like he's collided with an anvil—and he can barely lift the arm. Steering that old car . . . he shakes his head, and sighs.

He's stuck, and thinks, Gloria's going to kill me.

Despite warnings from the cops, the firemen, and just about everyone else who had an opinion, Ronnie has spent the whole morning sifting through her father's office, and their apartment, looking for things to salvage.

The fire, started with a few gallons of gasoline and a match, has left little for her to use. She knows that, after the first of the year, the whole building will have to come down; she knows that the storm will drown anything left behind.

She's not looking for anything special. A keepsake, a

utensil, a photograph, a ballpoint pen . . . she doesn't care; as long as it was hers or Daddy's, she doesn't care.

Every hour or so she takes a break, pulls off her work gloves and climbs over the debris into the front room, where she stares through the shattered window at the spot where her father died. Remembering how Stump looked when he saw her riding down on him, how her father looked as he was cast aside like an old rag; remembering the voice of the preacher, the one they all thought was nothing more than a thick-neck handyman, and the look on his face, such sorrow; remembering what she had said, and that he'd prayed for Daddy anyway.

She looks, and she remembers, and then she returns to the ash and char and sodden paper and crumbling walls, and looks again for something she can bring out, so she can remember.

Kirkland Stone sits on the loveseat, his feet propped on the chipped coffee table. In the corner is his bloodstained shirt, thrown there after Lauder cut it off him. He inhales deeply as one finger brushes over a vicious bruise across the front of his neck. Then he smiles around the room before suggesting to Stump Teague that the next time he wants a battle, he use something less primitive than a shotgun, so he can be sure he'll win.

"Did the job," Stump says, not in the least impressed with either the man or his speech.

"Yes, perhaps, but a good machine pistol might have saved the lives of your brothers."

Teague starts from his armchair, then shrugs and slumps again. "Lucky shots."

"If you say so."

"Whether or not," Lauder calls from the kitchen where he is trying to put together a decent lunch from the larder discovered in this empty house's pantry. "Remember, we still have work to do, Mr. Stone."

"I realize that, Dutch, I realize that. The question is, exactly what are our priorities, and how do we go about achieving their completion?"

"The faggot preacher," Stump says without hesitation. "I don't care what you guys do, but I'm getting that preacher."

"Well, so are we, Mr. Teague, so are we." Stone crosses his legs at the ankles, splayed fingers across his chest. "But how?" He nods to the window, to the early darkness outside. "It isn't going to be easy moving around in this weather. We don't have transportation now that our . . . benefactor has been eliminated from the operating equation."

Stump squints at him. "What?"

"We need a car, you jackass," Lauder calls angrily.

"Why the hell didn't you say so? I got a car."

"Really," says Stone.

"Really," Stump answers, sneering. "When do you want it?"

"As soon as we eat, if that would be convenient."

"You got it, Stone."

"And after we get your preacher man, Mr. Teague, may I assume you will assist us with our own little endeavor?"

"Which is?"

Lauder walks into the room with a tray loaded with sandwiches and bottles of imported beer. "I," he says, setting the tray on the coffee table, "want to shove a stick of dynamite up that porky mayor's ass."

"Mr. Lauder," Stone scolds with a coy smile.

Stump shrugs. "Sounds good to me. What about the money?"

"Finders keepers, Mr. Teague. Share and share."

"Better and better. Then, what? We come back here for the night?"

"Heavens no. My friend and I are leaving the island as soon as we're finished."

Stump looks from Lauder to Stone and back again. "He's kidding, right?"

"He seldom kids," Lauder informs him.

"Whatever." Stump grabs a sandwich, takes such a huge bite it makes Stone wince. "But I sure as hell hope you guys can swim good, 'cause it's the only way you're gonna get off this piece of shit today."

The vanguard of the storm system has nearly completed its run, and Rick has decided that he isn't going to stay in the Tower one second more. The structure, solid enough to last through any number of hurricanes and other winter storms, sways with each gust, enough that he's beginning to learn what it's like to feel seasick. Not to mention the incessant throbbing behind the lump in the middle of his forehead, where his skull met the steering wheel when he crashed into Teague's car. Not to mention the slight sprain his left wrist suffered.

Trifles, he figures, compared to what will happen to him if he stays here.

He can see the rain on its way, a dark grey curtain that stretches from cloud to ocean; he can feel the subtle change in the wind's direction; he blinks each time lightning snakes through the clouds; the thunder is still too far away to be more than a grumbling.

That much he supposes he could stand if he had to stay.

It's the ocean itself that bothers him.

He's been watching the waves as they roll toward shore, and it took him a while to realize exactly what he was seeing—the presage of a storm surge.

He has already called as many people as he can, asking them to spread the word. Within the last hour his binoculars have tracked at least two dozen vehicles speeding up Midway toward Landward and the causeway. Islanders know the drill—pack and run before the causeway's flooded. Money and clothes, people and pets, the hell with everything else.

A normal surge might bring water all the way through to

Midway, flood a few cellars, knock down a few old trees, raise the level of the harbor and damage a few boats, unpin a pier or two—nothing that hasn't happened a dozen times before.

But from the looks of it, the feel of it, he's convinced this one is going to be a monster, and has no compunction about telling folks this. If he's wrong, the worst that will happen is that he'll look like an idiot, and Ben Pellier will buy him drinks for a week just so he can poke a little fun.

If he's right . . .

The Tower sways sharply, nearly knocking him off his feet.

"That's it. I'm outta here."

He grabs the binoculars and the cell phone, opens the trap door, and double-checks to make sure he's left nothing important behind. Then he starts down the ladder, favoring his left hand, looking around at the dipping treetops, gaping once when he thinks he sees scarlet lightning over the water.

Then the trees are around him, the wind's power has lessened, and he's thinking about sliding the rest of the way down when an explosion overhead throws him off the ladder.

Damn lightning, he thinks, just before he hits the ground and the tower buckles around him.

Lyman Baylor stands at the living room window, hands twisting at his side. "Kitra, have you seen this?"

"I've seen storms before, Ly. Come help me find the candles. We never have them ready when the power goes off."

"Kitra, please, just look."

"Ly, I just told you I haven't got—Lyman Baylor, where are you going?"

He has grabbed his raincoat from the coatrack in the hall and is hurrying to the door.

"Lyman!"

"Reverend Chisholm," he calls over his shoulder. "I have to see Reverend Chisholm."

He's gone before she can protest or stop him, but he hopes she takes the time to look at the sky.

At the red lightning.

At the green fire that dances within the clouds.

It's happening; he knows it's happening, and Chisholm, he's positive, has something to do with it. By the time he's opened the garage door, he's praying harder than he's ever prayed in his life.

Hector watches the increasing play of red and green in the sky and crosses himself, backs away from the window when it shimmers in the wind.

Gloria, he thinks, is definitely going to kill me.

"What is it?" Ben asks softly, standing at the Teach's small front window. "What is it, Peg?"

Pegleg is on the bar, out of his cage, bobbing his head. Muttering to himself.

"What's going on out there, Peg? What's going on?"

3

Casey can't keep away from the porch, despite the wind, despite the cold.

After he'd climbed off the jetty, almost falling in several times, he was positive he knew where the battleground would be. Just before he left, he had seen, behind closed eyes, what looked like a dark wall where the clouds met the sea. But the wall moved, and it grew, and when he narrowed his eyes and looked harder, he realized it was a huge wave rising slowly, blackly, out of the water toward the clouds. Scarlet fire laced and twined inside it, and emerald sparks flared and popped where the crest should have been.

And on the top, amid the fire and sparks, were the Riders, their mounts cantering easily over the surface, manes and tails flying in the direction of the wind. Smoke from their nostrils, flame from their hooves.

He recognized Susan, and his stomach contracted; the little one must be Joey, and the old woman, Eula.

The one slightly ahead of the others he could barely see at all, but he knew this too—that this was the Rider who would bring the world down.

hello, casey, he'd said, across the miles, across the sea; *heard you killed a man today.*

Now he stands on the porch, tapping a nervous heel, trying to think. The other had accepted the vision without question, almost hopeful now that they had something concrete to work with. But it was clear they hadn't thought about it very long. How can he—they—fight something like that? The wave would sweep them away before they even met the Riders.

Was the vision wrong?

Was there some interpretation he was missing? Had he seen it all wrong?

"Casey."

He shakes his head angrily. Not now. Not now.

He shuts his eyes, tries to bring the scene back, but there is only darkness, and tiny points of light.

"Casey."

He turns sharply, with a scowl, but says nothing when he sees the look on Beatrice's face, how her hands are clasped at her stomach as if trying to hold it in.

"Pakistan," she says. Stops. Takes a breath. "Pakistan has launched another missile into India. They claim it's an accident, like the others, but no one thinks India's listening." Her eyes close, open. "And China has declared war on Australia, Casey. Britain and the Commonwealth are mobilizing. It's . . ." She can't find the words, or doesn't want to use the ones she's thinking, and she closes the door, cuts him off.

With a low moan of frustration, he braces his hands against the posts that hold up the roof on either side of the screen door, and for a moment he sees himself as Samson about to bring the Temple down around his ears.

"Fat chance," he mutters, but just for the heck of it, he pushes anyway, not very hard and only for a few seconds. Then his arms drop, his head bows and shakes, and he thinks maybe it's time to let the others figure it out, because it's too much for him, and there's no time to play the lone hero. There's no time . . . to be . . .

He blinks slowly.

The lone gunman.

He blinks again.

Cautions himself not to smile as he presses a calming hand against his chest.

Too soon; you could be wrong.

A lungful of cold air, another, and he returns inside and stands under the arch.

He points at the television. "Turn that off."

"But Reverend Chisholm," Reed protests.

"Now."

Cora scrambles to obey, and the children leave their places on the floor and gather around their mother, in her chair beside the couch.

"It's coming," he says. "You know it is. You've seen the sky. John, was there anything . . . I don't know how to put it. Not magical, exactly. Not . . ." He taps the heel of his hand against his brow. "Like what I think I saw, I mean. You understand?"

"Sure," John answers. "And no, not really. It wasn't ordinary, not by anyone's definition, but it certainly wasn't anything like a monster tidal wave."

"Jude." He looks to her and the kids, and spreads his hands.

Moonbow wrinkles her brow, looks to her sister, and

says, "She—Eula, I mean—she made some people better. So they could—"

"—fight us," Starshine finishes. "And ride horses and shoot guns." She shrugs. "Like that."

"Nothing like the wave?"

Moonbow makes a face. "In the desert? Don't be silly."

Casey cocks an eyebrow at her and, before anyone can move, crosses the room and picks her up by the waist. Holds her at arm's length while she kicks her legs, then pulls her close and plants a big and loud kiss on her brow.

"You," he declares, "are a certified genius, my girl."

Moonbow ducks her head and blushes, and sneers at her giggling sister. When he puts her down, she stands beside him and holds his hand shyly; he doesn't try to pull away.

"Silly, she says," Casey tells them. "Don't be silly, it's the desert. Well, this is an island. This"—he stamps on the floor—"is an island! This is *the* island. Lady Harp asked me why this place, and I told her I didn't rightly know. I still don't, except that this is the place where we have to be, and if the past is a teacher, there won't be a tidal wave to get in our way."

Cora's face is twisted in confusion. "I don't get it. They're coming on . . . what, a boat?"

"With horses?" Reed says.

"Right." Casey watches them, willing them, demanding they put aside what their imaginations are feeding.

Starshine yells, "The causeway!"

And Casey says, "You're right. Now get your coats. It's time."

4

Casey watches them on the porch. Excited. Afraid. Watching the emerald sparks and scarlet fire light the clouds, and make them darker.

Lord, he thinks, there's one more thing, if You don't mind. Something special. For those kids.

He opens the door and grabs Jude's arm, pulls her inside before she can stop him.

"Just be a minute," he tells her daughters, and takes her into the kitchen, eases her away from the door.

"I don't understand," she says, trembling so hard the veil ripples and sways.

"You don't have to," he tells her softly.

And before she can stop him, he cups her cheeks in his hands, and feels the cold and feels the heat and feels the bone beneath his fingers and the flesh beneath his palms and the blood in her veins and the breath in her lungs and he whispers, "For your girls," and yanks his hands away.

Jude grabs his arm to keep her balance, blinking rapidly, breathing hard.

"Okay," he says, breathing a little heavily himself. "Okay, Jude, let's go, they're waiting." But when she reaches for the veil, he takes her wrist gently and shakes his head. "For later," he tells her. "Maybe nothing, but it's for later."

On the porch they waste a few minutes arguing about how they're all going to fit in one car, and raise a ragged cheer when Lyman Baylor pulls up.

"Commandeer him," Casey tells John. "I don't think you'll have to explain."

They rush out into the wind, into the first icy pellets of rain, shrieking at the cold while scarlet and emerald flash above them.

"Casey?"

It's Beatrice, and he shakes his head.

"I told you, I don't know."

"In that case," and she tugs at his arm until he bends over, and she kisses him on the cheek. A feather kiss. An angel's kiss. "Just in case," she says, pulling her scarf over her head.

"Maybe not," he says as he opens the screen door for her, and when she looks up at him before leaving, he knows what she's thinking, and he knows she's probably right—miracles are for special people, and we . . . we're only different.

8

1

Scarlet fire in the clouds becomes serpentine lightning reaching for the ground; emerald sparks become the rain.

The wind throws whitecaps far up the Savannah River, rips old branches from old trees and spins them into cars and houses and a storefront church whose blue and red neon cross explodes into blue and red sparks; the rain is at first a few stinging droplets that soon become a shower that soon becomes a downpour that raises rivers in gutters and smears dirt across windows and turns side streets into creeks quickly filling the drains; lightning scorches power lines and creates pockets of night before real night arrives, strikes the wing on an airliner that almost makes it to Atlanta; thunder prowls.

Celebrations are canceled, no one can move in the storm; churches fill, and churches empty; a comedian jokes about the end of the world; a riverboat flounders, a bridge sags and moans; a weatherman tells his radio audience that as fierce as the storm is it's too fierce to last long.

Waves swell and rise and pound the jetties and shift the

boulders; the traffic light over Midway and Landward jerks and tugs on its wires; lights go out; lights come on; there's a rumbling underground as if the island's going to shift.

Scarlet fire.

Emerald sparks.

They sit in the white Continental in the parking lot of the Lobster Hut. No one has spoken for quite some time, but there's nothing much left to say.

Eula, in the backseat, hums a tune to herself, snapping the fingers of one white-gloved hand, tapping a foot against the floorboard, her head swaying side to side. A knowing smile on her lips.

Joey bounces with impatience. He keeps wiping his window with a palm, frowning at the rain. He tries playing with his six-guns, but they're no fun anymore. He puts his hat on, he takes it off, he finally drops it on the seat and wipes the window again.

Susan has her hands still on the steering wheel, and every so often she turns it, just a little, as if she's still driving. When lightning strikes the ground a few yards down the road, she can smell burning tar.

The engine is off.

The only sound is Eula's humming, and the thunder. Always the thunder.

Norville Cutler cowers in his cell, curled into the corner, and watches the rain on the window a few feet above his head.

"Damnit, Norville," Cribbs says from the adjoining cell, "you stop acting like a baby, for Christ's sake? It's only a little rain, for crying out loud."

"It's gonna be bad," Cutler says, knees drawn to his chest. "Ain't ever seen it this bad."

"Oh, you have to. God almighty, back in, when was it?

Seventy-six? Seventy-four? Water up to our asses, some-body's damn boat floating down the street? God almighty, now *that* was a storm. Compared to that, this is just pissing."

Cutler tries to push harder against the wall. "But that didn't have those colored lights and all."

Cribbs rolls his eyes. "More pollution, you idiot. You got more pollution, you got more colors. That's why you see so many beautiful sunsets. More crap in the air, that's all. Just more crap in the air."

Thunder makes the building vibrate.

Cutler yells and ducks his head.

Jasper grabs a couple of bars and bellows for a deputy. He's been doing that for over an hour; no one's come yet to see him.

"Jesus, Casey," John complains, reaching over the steering wheel to give a swipe at the windshield, try to clear some of the condensation away. "We're going to drown before we even get there. Jesus."

"Watch it, son," Casey tells him.

John looks at him and curls his lip.

Casey grins.

Kitra stands in her living room, ordering herself to remain calm. It's only a winter storm, she's seen enough of them before, all she has to do is make sure all the candles are ready for the inevitable, and what's in the freezer is ready to be transferred to the picnic cooler where she's already laid in some ice.

Lightning makes her jump; it fills the room with glaring white.

Thunder makes her whimper; it's too close, too damn close.

If she weren't so angry, she'd be petrified.

Lyman has left her, and that's about all she can concentrate on. He's left her alone to take care of things for his return. She wished she were a swearing woman, because the right, the proper words were hard to come by just now.

And to make it worse, she saw him drive by only a few minutes ago, trailing behind the car that belongs to one of Chisholm's friends. Not a honk. Not a quick stop to explain what he was doing. If she hadn't been checking the window seals just then, she would have never known it, never seen him go by.

She would have, in time, thought he'd been killed by a falling branch, or lightning, or some other horrid thing.

Not a honk.

Not a quick stop.

That man was going to pay.

Lightning-and-thunder, and she held her breath until she could hear the rain once again.

That was all.

She frowned.

Something was missing.

"All right," she said aloud to give herself some company. "All right, think it through, Kit, think it through."

She cocked her head, listened hard.

Then she said, "Oh, dear Lord."

The furnace had stopped.

The only good thing about the clinic is that the beds are soft, and no one bothers him.

Dub Neely rolls over and pulls the thin thermal blanket up to his shoulders. He's pretty sure he's alone now, that the snotty receptionist and that grumpy nurse who stitched him up have gone. They didn't even bother to stick a head in, see how he was doing.

Yet that isn't the worst part.

What he's doing is sobering up.

He isn't sure exactly what had happened after the fiasco at the cottage, only that the next thing he knew after he saw Freck coming at him was the bright light in the ceiling, and a nurse saying, "Are you sure?"

"Yeah, yeah," Freck had said, his voice uncharacteristically soft. "You should have seen it, man, it was incredible, all that fighting and stuff. We were lucky to get out alive. This guy was clobbered with something, I don't know what, and the sheriff wants you to fix him, treat him right, put it all on the town's bill."

"Are you sure?" the woman asked again.

"Just do it, okay? Jesus H, lady, don't argue, just do it."

And she had.

And then she'd left him, and Dub hasn't seen her since. Which, for the most part, is all right with him. He doesn't want to figure out why Freck had done it, the hitting and the lying; he really doesn't care. The bed is soft, the building is warm, and if he could only find his damn flask, he'd be in Dub Neely heaven.

"Then get outta bed, you dumb jackass, and go find it."

Torn; he's torn.

Fearful that this is, somehow, a function of his injury, he doesn't want to leave the bed because it might not be here when he returned; he might not even be in the clinic, but in someone's empty house, waking up to the aftermath of a binge.

But he's sobering up, and while that might be a good thing considering the weather outside, there would also be the inevitable shakes and hallucinations, the pain and self-recrimination.

Torn; he's torn.

And then: "Oh, what the hell," and he tosses the covers aside, swings to a sitting position, and yells and grabs his head when the pain lashes through his system.

No question about it now; he has got to find that flask.

* * *

Verna Dewitt drives slowly, using the powerful spotlight
on the cruiser's roof to help her see through the gloom and
the rain. Nothing terrible so far, and for such small things
she's grateful. A few branches down. A broken window
here and there. A couple of chairs wind-transferred from
porches to lawn. Nothing terrible so far.

The power is still on, and that's a plus, although she
knows that particular blessing won't last very long. A
number of the houses she's checked seemed to be empty,
either people stuck on the mainland, or people who left
after Jordan sounded the alarm.

She hopes he's okay.

She's done her bit in the Tower, and doesn't envy him
there tonight. Today. Whatever it was now. But she's still
going to ream him a new one once this is over. There
wasn't a panic, but he'd forgotten to call her first, so she
could assist in coordinating the leaving, if leaving is what
people wanted. That's the procedure, and he hadn't followed it.

Not that she doubts him.

He knows the sea far better than she does, and if he says
there's a surge coming, then there's a damn surge coming.

She just wishes he hadn't called it a monster.

The patrol car shimmies when the wind catches it
broadside. She's past the bay shops and houses now, into a
short stretch of woodland; no light but the lightning, and
the spotlight on the roof. A few seconds later, the white
beam picks up what looks to be a body, a sight that stops
her heart until, closer, she sees it's just a dark plastic
garbage bag.

"That's it," she tells the dashboard. She's been out here
too long; she's seeing things now, so it's time to get back
to the office and let Dwight drive for a while. But she
doesn't speed up, because she still has a job to do.

It does not, however, include checking that garbage bag

over there, the one poking out of that ditch practically filled with water.

"Damn people can't even use their garbage cans," she says angrily. "God, you'd think—"

She hits the brakes and stares.

"Oh . . . shit."

It's not garbage; it's a body.

"Don't you think we should hurry?" Lisse asks from the backseat.

Reverend Baylor shrugs. "I can only go as fast as Mr. Bannock, ma'am. And he doesn't seem to be in a hurry."

Once again she's amazed at how calm he sounds. In the past few minutes he's been grabbed by a horde of what he must have thought were jabbering fools, convinced to take part in part of the end of the world, and found himself driving through the worst winter storm he can remember.

Calm, or scared to death.

The wind slaps them.

The rain tries to drown them.

She clasps her hands in her lap and hopes John is all right.

She does not, resolutely does not think about what's going to happen, because then she'd start to scream. Cry. And damn Casey Chisholm for getting her into this mess.

Beside her, Cora shifts impatiently, murmuring tonelessly, but Lisse knows it's not praying.

She wants it over with, and over with now.

Lisse does too, but she can wait. She can wait.

Rick Jordan blinks his eyes free of the rain, takes stock, and decides that if he doesn't drown first, he'll probably be all right. The ladder has shattered and crumpled, and most of it lies across his legs. The Tower fell away from him, and as far as he can see in too frequent flares of lightning, the only damage it's done is take out some trees.

What he needs to do now is decide whether to find shelter in the Tower's ruins, or try to make his way down the Hook to a road and someone's house.

Danger in either choice.

Pushing with elbows and hands in slippery mud gets him to a sitting position. Squinting against the rain, he tries to figure out which way is the right way down. He can't see any lights, so he figures the power's gone out.

Until lightning flares again, and he realizes he's facing south, toward the ocean.

A bit of luck, he thinks, until another bolt shows him the ocean again. It's moving.

Susan doesn't move when someone raps on her window.

"All right," she tells the others. "All right, he's here."

Three doors open simultaneously; no one flinches at the cold, no one complains about the wind and rain.

The great black steams and smokes, skittish, tossing its head, while Red holds the reins tightly and looks down at them with a smile. Quick, and done.

"There," he says, and nods toward the deserted restaurant.

"Well, well," Eula says with a white-tooth grin, and hurries across the slippery ground to a smaller black horse, who whickers at the sight of her and nuzzles her chest when she gets close enough. She strokes its neck, whispers something in its ear, and with the ease of a woman half her age, swings up into the saddle.

Joey whoops with joy and runs and slips to a palomino almost as big as the great black. "Hello, boy, hello," he says a dozen times as he dances around it, patting it, checking it, before clambering into the saddle and grabbing the horn. "Hello, boy, hello, I missed you."

Susan looks a question up at Red, who says, simply, "Your choice."

She smiles. "Not really."

Red laughs. "You're right."

A lift of her shoulders in a sigh, an impatient wipe of a hand across her face to clear her eyes, and she walks to the hood and looks down the length of the Continental. Shakes her head sadly. Then puts a hand on the head of the silver hood ornament and strokes it down to the tip of its tail.

"It rode nice," she says to no one in particular. "Like driving a cloud."

Another sigh, and her hand reaches up to stroke the neck of a white stallion that turns silver the next time lightning fills the clouds. Its mane and tail are black. When lightning streaks again, the black almost looks bright blue.

Red looks at them all—a smile, here and gone—and he touches his hat brim with the tip of a finger.

By the time he reaches the road, they're riding four abreast.

The marsh has risen and spills over Landward Avenue, ripples across its surface, waves in the making. The sodden body of a blue heron floats to the other side.

Kitra can't move.

The house has grown cold, but she can't move; she just can't.

The lightning is worse, the thunder louder, but she can't move because she's heard something else.

"Lyman," she whispers. "Dear Lord, Lyman, where are you?"

Deputy Dwight Salter frowns as he moves from the desk to the door. There's not much to see out there, just the rain and a few lights, and he doesn't want to open the door, not even a crack. Verna would kill him if any of the storm got inside, but he can't help it. He has to know. Because what he's just heard, he can't believe.

"What the hell was that?" Cutler says, pushing out of his corner and off the cot. "Did you hear that?"

"Hush, Norville," Cribbs says, with a slash of his hand. "Hush, I want to listen."

Hector Nazario throws up his hands and says to the ceiling, "I tried, Gloria, I tried, but the phones are still out."

She's gonna kill me, he thinks; she's gonna kill me.

So preoccupied is he that he barely reacts when Ronnie Hull slams through the door at a run, drenched through and puffing, using the end of the counter to stop her before she falls. "Hector, did you hear that?"

"Hear what?"

Verna, on one knee beside the body, looks up sharply, instantly regrets it when the rain hits her glasses and blinds her. Angrily she yanks them off, lets them dangle against her chest on today's yellow cord, and turns her ear to the north. Trying to concentrate. Trying to hear.

"Stop the car," Casey says, and before it's fully stopped, he's out and in the road. The edge of the flooding laps at the front tires. Except for the vehicle behind, he can see little else.

"What, Casey?" John asks, leaning over the seat. "What's going on?"

He hushes him with a hand.

And he hears it again.

* * *

The deep hollow resonance of a large church bell, tolling.

2

Impossible, thinks Verna, but she hasn't got time to ponder. She has to drag Dermot Alloway's body back to the car and get it in the trunk. Dwight, she thinks, is gonna shit when he sees this.

Impossible, Kitra thinks as she sinks to the floor and hugs herself and trembles; there's only a carillon, there's no bell.

But it's loud enough to shake the house when the church bell tolls again.

"Impossible," snaps Cribbs. "Preposterous. It must be the storm."

"You ever hear a storm make a noise like that?"

"I've heard them make lots of noises, Norville. Now shut up while I try and get that sorry-ass deputy down here."

Impossible, thinks Dub as he empties the flask and wipes a spill from his chin, then licks the finger to get every drop. He's drunk it all, and already he's having the stupid hallucinations. Still, he figures as he begins a room by room search of the building for something to complement the liquor, it's a lot better than pink elephants. Or skeleton birds who want to kill him.

"Can't be," Hector protests, standing at the luncheonette's window. "We don't got anything like that on the island."

"Good," Ronnie says, toweling herself off. "Then you tell me what it is, okay? You tell me what that is."

Dwight mutters, "Impossible," because there's only one church on the island, and it has one of those electric bell things, not something that sounds like it belongs in some cathedral.

He snorts and turns away, hears something else, and turns back to the door.

Reaches for his gun.

But Stump Teague has already pulled his shotgun's trigger.

Impossible, Rick thinks as lightning shows him again the height of the surge; damn, that's impossible—unless it's not a surge at all. He gasps, and scrambles to find the cell phone, praying that somehow, with all this lightning, it still works.

3

The two cars move slowly through the water, not much faster than a crawl. When the hubcaps are half submerged, it stops rising, begins to fall, and Casey closes his eyes in relief. Once on the other side, he tells John to stop again, and gets out, walks back to the second car and mimes rolling down the window for Lyman Baylor.

"Well, we're here," he says, pointing without looking at the end of the causeway. When Lyman moves to open his door, Casey shakes his head. "No. Not you."

As the others leave, Baylor frowns. "But why not?"

"It's not your fight, Lyman."

"What? You can't mean that. Of course it's my fight."

Casey nods. "Sorry, yes, you're right. But your fight isn't here, it's back there."

Baylor looks as if he's going to cry. "Reverend Chisholm, I don't think—"

"Your wife," Casey says. Rain drips from his brow. "Right now, you belong with your wife. And your church."

Baylor's fingers grip and release the steering wheel. Grip and release. Grip and release. He shakes his head, and Casey grabs his arm. He doesn't speak, but his look says it all, and Baylor slumps for a moment before, finally, reluctantly, nodding.

He stares straight ahead. "I'm not dreaming."

"No."

"I never thought . . . I never believed . . ."

"No. No one does, when it happens. But it happens just the same."

Lyman covers Casey's hand with his own. "God bless you, Casey. I . . . God bless you."

Casey squeezes the arm in thanks, and steps away, moves to the middle of the road to watch the car back up. A gesture to move it to the right just a little, another to move it back to the left.

When Lyman reaches the other side, the headlights snap to high. To low. To high again, and Casey raises a hand in farewell and puts his back to the light.

"Okay," he says. "Okay, let's go."

He stands at causeway's end, arms away from his sides, fingers open, and he waits . . . until Moonbow takes his right hand, Starshine takes his left. He looks down at them and smiles, looks around to the others and smiles at them.

"No sermons, John. I want you awake."

Bannock shudders a deep breath.

Casey begins to walk, the girls beside him, the others behind. Feeling the roadway vibrate beneath his boots as the waves attack and pull back, attack and spill over the

tarmac with a rush that sounds less like hissing than wild-
fire. The wind snatches at him, pokes him, tries to push
him back; the rain has slackened somewhat, but it still tries
to blind him.

scarlet fire overhead
  emerald sparks over the water
  and the church bell tolls

4

Verna pulls up in front of the office, not caring she's facing
the wrong way. No way is she going to get any wetter than
she has to. She checks to be sure she has everything, then
opens the door and makes a dash for the recess. Slips to a
halt and bangs her shoulder against the wall when she sees
Dwight's body spread-eagled on the floor.

She draws her gun; she swallows.

She eases her way to the door, gaze checking everything
inside, and checking it again. Only when she's reasonably
sure she has a chance does she open the door and move in
as fast as her wet soles will allow.

The office is empty; it feels empty.

Voices, then, to her right, and she can't believe what
she's thinking—that in this lousy miserable stinking
weather, somebody has come to visit the damn mayor.

Or, she thinks, to get him out.

One step, and her shoe squeaks. A soft curse under her
breath, and she leans down, gun aimed at the door that
leads to the cells below, and unties one shoe, then the
other. Kicks them off. Moves to the door, and listens.

"Did you have to kill him?" Cutler sounds hysterical.
"Jesus, Stump, did you have to kill him?"

"Mr. Cutler, calm down," Kirkland Stone suggests sternly. "That sort of attitude will get you nowhere. Just be calm, relax, we'll get you out—unlock the door, will you, please, Dutch—and we'll all be on our way."

"You're a miracle, Mr. Stone," Cribbs says. "Nothing to it but a flat-out, genuine miracle."

"You're too kind, Mr. Mayor."

"A bonus is in order, I think."

"Much too kind. But I won't say no."

The two men laugh.

"Come on, Lauder," Cutler says impatiently. "Jesus Christ, can't you even work a goddamn key?"

Lauder stares at him, looks over at Stone and the mayor, who pay him no heed, and takes one of his guns from its holster.

"Aw, Jesus," Cutler says, backing away from the door, palms out. "Come on, Lauder, no call for that."

"Mr. Lauder," Stone says wearily, "one or the other, we're running out of time."

Lauder pulls the trigger.

Four times.

Cribbs barely blinks. "You men just do not fool around, do you?"

"Only when we're off-duty, Mr. Mayor. Only when we're off-duty."

and the church bell tolls

Verna's initial reaction at the gunfire is to leap down the steps, gun blazing, take out whoever is down there, and ask questions later. Her second reaction, the one she knows is more likely to keep her alive, is to close the upper door as quietly as she can, and lock it. Unless they have a blowtorch down there, no one, she thinks, is getting out real soon.

What she needs to do now is find help. If there's going to be more trouble—and that door, even if it is metal, won't keep them down there forever—she knows she won't be able to handle it alone. Luckily, there was a light on at Betsy's, and she's fairly sure she'd seen someone there when she'd passed a while ago.

If she's wrong, she figures the storm is going to be the least of her problems.

Rick crouches under one of the Tower's thick legs, feeble protection from the wind and rain, but better than being out in the open. The phone didn't work, and after one near disastrous attempt, he knows he won't be able to get off the Hook until the storm's passed. He's stuck. Really stuck. But not, he supposes, as stuck as the people who've stayed behind down below.

He reckons the surge will do a good bit of flooding. The Hook will block much of it from the bay, but he is glad he won't have to see the *Deuce* in the morning, lying bashed and splintered in someone's front yard. He doesn't think the jetties will do a damn bit of good now, and prays that Ronnie has somehow gotten off the island.

Lightning makes him cringe.

Thunder shakes the ground.

He can't see it, but he can feel it—the surge is climbing toward Camoret.

Any minute now; any minute.

5

Casey is surprised at how quickly they were able to cross over to St. James Island. Although the sea threw itself at them, the barriers held, the road held, and despite water once riling around their knees, they all held.

But this, he decides, is as far as they'll go.

They're coming.

They're out there, in the dark; he can't see them, but he can feel them, and they're coming.

"John, the first thing we have to do is get some shelter for the girls. If that door's locked, smash it in."

John grins. "Isn't that a sin or something?"

"Just bash the damn thing in, John, we'll worry about the sins later."

The door is locked, and Reed doesn't think twice—he uses his cast to smash the glass, reach in, and turn the bolt. Casey can see the pain in the boy's face, but he says nothing. But he nods Cora over to take care of him until it's time.

The girls leave him reluctantly, and he's reluctant to let go of them—their hands, so small, so warm, were more comfort than they would ever be able to understand. He just wishes that touch had brought him a brilliant plan.

Right now, all he can do is stand in the middle of the road and look east. The two streetlights at each end of the island do nothing but turn the air behind them black, casting a pale white haze like a pale white wall across the road front and back. Camoret is invisible; the mainland is invisible. The sea, for all it climbs and roars and slams and batters, is invisible.

Scarlet lightning overhead.

Movement beside him.

"We've evened the odds. Now what?"

"I thought you were the general," Beatrice answers, standing close but not touching, arms folded, shoulders up. Her voice is raised to be heard above the wind, the sea, the clatter of the rain on the Quonset huts.

"I thought I told you I wasn't a general."

"Well . . ." She shrugs, and tilts her head toward the Last Stop. Breaking glass, shouts, and cracking wood. "John is trying to find something to use as weapons. I wonder if it will do any good."

He doesn't know. He doesn't know anything, except what's about to happen, and even then he doesn't know what he's supposed to do when it does. His lips press tightly together, his left foot taps a heel against the ground. He takes a step forward, turns, and steps back; forward again, and back. Scowling. Lifting a hand in exasperation. Another in resignation. He doesn't feel the rain anymore, the cold; he hears nothing but a sustained roar, a blend of sea and wind.

He stares at the dark over the store. "Lord," he says, trying not to sound too frustrated, "we don't have any time left. I don't know if You . . ." A helpless look at Cora, standing in the doorway, face in shadow. "I don't know what You're after here. It's time and this is the place." A wave behind him. "The island's the place, I mean. But what . . ."

His head snaps to his left, and he stares toward Camoret.

"What . . ."

His head snaps to the right, and he stares toward the pale white wall of light, and the mainland beyond.

"Casey?"

"Time," he says, barks a laugh, swallows, and says again, "time." He strides back to Beatrice and says, louder, "Time," and grabs her around the waist, lifts her as he had Moonbow, and plants a large and loud kiss in the middle of her forehead.

"Casey!"

But she grins.

Quickly he puts her down, steps back, waves excitedly at the others to get out here, now.

"Time." He laughs, and sobers. "Bea, what time is it?"

"I beg your pardon," she answers, sounding insulted.

Casey groans. "Bea, Beatrice, Lady Bea, Lady Harp, for God's sake, what time is it?"

Four answers come at him from four different people at the same time: ten minutes to the new year.

He nods; he grins; he fakes reaching for Beatrice again, and laughs when she backs away hastily.

Then Lisse gasps and says, "Oh my God, Casey, look."

6

The jetties disappear under the surge as it rises out of the dark, so much of it that it appears to be barely moving at all.

The whale family vanishes.

The dunes vanish.

Trees bend, some snap; bushes pull away by the roots to become part of the wall, spinning slowly inside, tangling with each other, becoming walls themselves.

The houses have high foundations built for just such a time; most of them hold, some of them don't, and the cry of tortured wood and stone rises and falls with the water.

Casey's left hand automatically goes to his chest, pressing the small cross into his palm.

Four shadows moving through the white wall; four shadows on horseback. Pale, almost transparent.

He can hear the wind now, and the sea, and he can hear the hooves on the road, like iron on hollow wood. Moving slowly. Shedding sparks. Steam curling from the horses' nostrils, steam rising from their flanks untouched by the wind.

Pale.

Growing darker.

"I'll shoot the lock, okay, Mr. Stone?"

"Be my guest, Dutch. It's getting stuffy down here."

Hector grabs Verna's arm and pulls her away from the door. "You aren't going anywhere," he says.

"I have to get back," she insists.

"No," he tells her, and points at the surge welling out of the alleys.

Kitra screams when the front door bangs open, jumps to her feet when Lyman races in, casting aside his coat, opening his arms. Weeping.

The rear windows of the clinic explode inward, and the water pours in waterfall hard. Dub hears it before he sees it, and he streaks for the exit, flinging aside a bottle he'd found in Alloway's office.

If I can make it outside, he thinks; if I can just make it outside.

while the church bell tolls

The surge, already broken and fading, crosses Midway Road. It shatters windows, topples light poles, cleanses the lot where the *Camoret Weekly* once stood; it swirls around Town Hall and sweeps the tiny park clear; it pushes at the sheriff's department building, curves around it and pushes at the windows behind.

When they break, the water follows.

When they break, Jasper Cribbs begins to scream.

When they break, Kirkland Stone climbs to the unopen door and looks through the small window to the empty office behind.

When the mayor stops screaming, he looks down to see the water surging after him, somebody's shoe spinning on the surface.

"Open it," he says desperately, grabbing Lauder's arm. "Open it!"

Lauder knocks the hand away. "I can't."

"Then break the glass. Shoot it out. The water will—"

The water grabs him and he falls, and Dutch Lauder pulls his trigger.

while the church bell tolls

7

Pale riders, growing darker.

John slaps at Casey's arm to force his attention, then hands him a gleaming and long piece of polished wood. Casey is puzzled until he recognizes it as a mount for a stuffed game fish, and he almost laughs aloud.

"Best I could do," John says without apology.

"Time," Casey answers.

"You've said that a dozen times already."

"Midnight. The New Year." He points at Camoret. "The place, John. The place. Don't let them reach the place." He walks away quickly, telling the others, praying that he's right because if he's not, he's lost again. Then he takes Jude by the shoulder and says, "Take the girls inside. Pray if you want to, scream if you have to, but keep them away."

"Reverend Chisholm, I can't leave—"

"No," he says fiercely. "What you can't leave are your girls." He glances at the Riders, looks back at her. "Do it. Please. If you have to help, find things to throw. Spook the horses. I don't know. Just go, Jude, just go."

He doesn't move until she does, then returns to the road and stakes his place out in the center. John is to his far right, Lisse beside him, Cora beside her. Reed to his far left, Beatrice between them.

Dark Riders, growing darker.

Iron on hollow wood.

A wave slams against the store beyond the eastbound

lane, and the Quonset hut shudders, the roof sign screeching as it topples and breaks apart before it reaches the ground.

A huge wave sweeps out of the storm just ahead of the Riders, washing across the road, spray adding to the rain, foam bobbing on the surface.

Casey braces himself.

A second wave, larger, suddenly looms out of the dark, follows behind the first and takes part of the roadway with it.

It's breaking up, Casey thinks; the causeway's breaking up.

The Riders, moving faster, dark ghosts against the wall of pale light.

scarlet fire and emerald sparks

John looks left and gives Lisse a smile to display a bravery he doesn't feel; when she returns with one of her own, he wants desperately to tell her he loves her, but it's too late; it's much too late.

"Daddy," Joey calls, waving his hat, spurring his mount. "Daddy, hi, it's me!"

The Riders, moving faster.

Beatrice sees a shadow standing by the Last Stop door, lifts a hand in a tremulous wave, tries a smile, and fails.

Good-bye, my dear, Sir John says. Take care of him for me.

"John," she whispers. "John, we're going to die."

Good-bye, my dear. Stop fussing. I'm sure you'll do just fine.

The shadow fades; the shadow's gone; Beatrice holds a shieldlike piece of wood in her hands, hefts it once, and shakes her head.

We're going to die, she thinks, and I'll never get to answer his question.

The Riders . . . charging.

From each corner of his vision, Casey can see the others bracing themselves. Turning sideways or spreading legs or bouncing on their toes.

One chance.

All they'll get is one chance.

He knows which one is his.

Riding the great black, stubbled cheeks, stubbled chin, Indian-bead vest blown open by his wind; long hair in braids that bounce against his chest; flat green eyes.

He rubs a thumb across the cross and takes a backward step. Turning his left shoulder to the horsemen. Gauging speed and distance, holding his weapon like a club.

"Hi, Daddy!"

Scarlet lightning strikes the Last Stop on his right, and it mushrooms into flames that hiss and steam in the rain, cast shadows of their own as well as shadows of the Riders; add color to the air, and most of it is red.

Heat and cold in equal measure, despite the storm, despite the sea.

He wants to see everything at once, to help if he can, to guide, but as the Riders fan out side to side, he can only see the great black, bearing down on him, hooves kicking emerald sparks.

He swallows and takes a breath.

Beatrice calls, "Two minutes."

He nods and takes a breath.

And for that moment between the ticks of a clock, he sees as if he were looking at the fragments of a broken mirror:

Jude and the girls racing screaming from the store, hands filled with shining things that glow in the firelight, that glitter and dazzle in the firelight as they're thrown at the Riders in a hail-and-shower of glass and stone;

Cora racing behind him, and up to join Reed, who is looking straight at Susan and daring her to come on, come on, it's me, you remember? It's me, come on, come on;

Beatrice running toward the girls, waving her club, screaming something at the Rider dressed in green, who looks down from her mount and laughs;

John and Lisse, side by side, Joey taking out his six-guns;

a wave tumbling over the road, leaving bedrock behind;

scarlet lightning;

a white horse slipping on the slick tarmac, legs frantic to find purchase;

emerald sparks;

a horse bucking and rearing at the glass and stone that bounce off its head and face;

and the fire taken and bloated by the storm, reaching toward them, roaring.

while the church bell tolls

Casey blinks and shakes his head, deafens himself to the shouts and screams of men and horses and children, concentrating on the Rider who ignores them as well. Smiling at him. Grinning at him. Quickly; here and gone.

Hello, Reverend Chisholm, hear you killed a man the other night.

He waits.

The other rides.

He waits, and holds his breath, and when the black storms up to take him and trample him to the ground, he yells and swings and jumps backward, lands a blow on the Rider's leg that makes the Rider groan aloud, and yank the reins, and turn around.

Not a ghost, Casey thinks; at least he's not a ghost.

The black charges again, and again Casey swings and steps away, missing this time, and slipping to one knee. Paying no attention to the pain when the Rider turns again.

Grinning.

Here and gone.

The crackling sound of gunfire.

Someone screaming; someone singing.

A quick desperate look—

Reed and Cora clubbing white horse and Rider, Moon-bow and Starshine dodging the hooves of the green Rider's horse, Beatrice swinging her club, and it's all gone again as—

Casey winces at the fire-pain he feels growing in his knee, sees the great black upon him and swings wildly, desperately, catching it across the chest with the flat of his makeshift club. The black stumbles and nearly throws the Rider, rear legs slipping, spreading, casting fire, casting sparks, until it settles and prances in agitated place, and the Rider looks at him, and at the sky, leans over, and says, "Too late," and smiles and rides away.

Here.

And gone.

Casey starts to run; it's the only thing he can think to do. Tossing the club aside, he prays for speed and sprints. Watching the Rider, watching the horse, slow and arrogant in their leaving. Tail snapping, mane bouncing, steam and sparks, flat green eyes.

When the Rider turns and sees him, he lifts his head and laughs, turns away and lifts his hat, a scornful mocking good-bye.

Casey runs; it's the only thing he can do.

And when the wave curls out of the darkness, the great black shies and turns aside, turns in a nervous circle while the water crashes on the road, turns spray to rain, and shakes the roadway.

Casey runs, and reaches out, grabs the Rider's leg and, startled, the Rider kicks out and kicks him aside. Glares and snaps, and puts his spurs to the great black's sides.

The horse leaps and gallops.

Casey leaps and snares the stirrup, runs helplessly a few feet before he reaches up and grabs the Rider's waist. And as soon as he realizes he won't be able to drag him off, he uses the horseman as counterweight, and swings up behind him on the saddle.

The Rider laughs, and gallops on.

scarlet fire

Casey looks up.

emerald sparks

The second wave is high, much higher than the first, and he thinks, I have to jump, until the Rider laughs again, and Casey wraps both arms around him, checks the wave, and holds him close until it falls.

8

Beatrice on the ground, blood in her eye, right arm broken, sees the wave and the Rider and Casey on the great black's back.

"No," she says softly, and, "No," again when the road is clear, the water ebbs . . . and Casey's gone.

For what? she thinks as she struggles to her hands and knees, cries out and holds her injured arm against her chest; dear Lord, for what?

"You okay, Lady Beatrice?" Moonbow asks as she kneels beside her. "Hey, you're hurt. Momma, she's hurt, Lady Beatrice's hurt real bad."

Beatrice brushes away the offer of a helping hand. Her head's too heavy and she lets it hang; her arm throbs and stabs, her legs can barely hold her.

She feels Moonbow poking at her good wrist, can't slap the hand away without falling on her face, and leans back, sits back, lifts her head to the wind and rain, and allows the child to take her hand.

And then she knows.

She looks, and Moonbow nods. And grins. And says, "I think we won."

Beatrice smiles, weak and pained, but when Moonbow leaves to fetch her mother, she sags, and says, "For what?"

"For him," Lisse tells her, kneeling down, taking her hand.

Beatrice shakes her head, and Lisse smiles and holds out a fist, gestures until Beatrice turns her hand around. Then Lisse covers the hand with hers, and when she pulls it away, Casey's small cross and chain lies in Beatrice's palm.

"Oh, dear," is all she can say, and gasps a little pain when Lisse helps her to her feet.

"You know," she says, "this is the time when the sun's supposed to shine. Battle over, victory ours. I want the sun, Miss Montgomery. I'm sick of all this rain, I truly want the sun."

Lisse doesn't answer, and after a moment she knows why.

The fire has died down, but it hasn't died, and in the light of its flames she can see Reed sitting in the parking lot, Cora's head in his lap as she squirms and twists, lifts a leg, and drops it; she can see John Bannock lying face-down on the road across the way, a toy gun lying beside him; she can see the way Lisse limps away, a hand pressed against her hip, that lovely auburn hair dark and hanging in the rain; she can see Jude and the children huddled in the store's doorway; and in the middle of the road, near the fall of pale white light, a long and old white Continental, its tires flat, no ornament at all.

Dear God, she thinks; dear Lord.

Thunder, and white lightning.

She can't stand; she starts to fall.

An arm slips around her waist to catch her, and a deep voice says, "It's Casper. My middle name is Casper."